THE SEAS OF GOD

Have we not stood here like trees in the ground long enough?
Have we not groveled here long enough, eating and drinking,
    like mere brutes?
Have we not darkened and dazed ourselves with books
    long enough?
Sail forth—steer for the deep waters only.
Reckless, O soul, exploring, I with thee, and thou with me,
For we are bound where mariner has not yet dared to go,
And we will risk the ship, ourselves and all.

O my brave soul!
O farther, farther sail!
O daring joy, but safe! are they not all the seas of God?
O farther, farther, farther sail!

WALT WHITMAN

Passage to India

Nec fasces, nec opes, solum artis sceptra perennant.

THE DEVICE OF TYCHO BRAHE

16th Century Astronomer

The Seas of God

GREAT STORIES OF THE HUMAN SPIRIT

Edited by Whit Burnett

J. B. Lippincott Company
Philadelphia, New York

Contents

I

God's Lonely Man

II

The Vineyard

III

Shadows of Childhood

IV

Through a Glass, Darkly

V

The Inward Vision

VI

City of God

VII

The Green Bough

VIII

Testament

Acknowledgments

In addition to the numerous individuals and organizations to whom more formal acknowledgment of their splendid cooperation is accorded elsewhere, the editor wishes here to record his debt of gratitude to Dorothy Canfield Fisher with whom the idea of this book was often discussed; to Dr. George Shuster of Hunter College (for his many valuable suggestions of material) ; to Dr. Vernon Loggins of Columbia University for similar valuable assistance; to James Gillis, of *The Catholic World* and to Henry Hurwitz of The *Menorah Journal* for specific aid in the selection of stories for this book; and to the cooperation of the editorial staffs of *The Commonweal, The Christian Herald, The Christian Century, The Protestant, The Jewish Publications Society of America;* the *Zion Herald, The Churchman, The Christian Leader* and *Common Ground*. The editor particularly wishes to acknowledge the help given by many distinguished men of letters, some of whom not only contributed their own stories to this collection but nominated those of others. Dr. Thomas Mann, Aldous Huxley, Manual Komroff and Mary O'Hara were especially generous. For similar advice the editor gratefully appreciates the assistance of the Right Rev. Bishop Nelson Spencer of the Diocese of West Missouri, the Rev. Thomas C. Cannon, Minister of the Cranston Memorial Presbyterian Church of New Richmond, Ohio; Col. William D. Cleary, Chaplain, Commandant of the Headquarters Chaplain School, Harvard University; Dr. Thomas F. Opie of Great Barrington, Mass.; the Rev. Samuel M. Shoemaker, Calvary Rectory, New York City; the Rev. Joseph Fort Newton, Church of St. Luke and the Epiphany, Philadelphia. The editor is grateful for the ready response of the many publishers whose authors are here represented. And, finally, a special word of gratitude is due to Miss Tay Hohoff for her rare qualities of perception and sympathy, and for extended and invaluable assistance editorially.

Foreword

—It is not wisdom to be only wise,
And on the inward vision close the eyes,
But it is wisdom to believe the heart.
GEORGE SANTAYANA

This is a book which, in its essential characteristics, might have been assembled at any time in the last fifty years. And yet it was not. And since today is a time of wars, when every reference must deal in some way or another with urgent and most topical matters, it may be fitting to attempt a word of explanation.

This is not a book about the war. Nor about the peace to come. Or any wars to follow. It is about a war that has been going on for as long as man has thought about his place in nature. The wars in its pages are the wars inside the human heart. It is a book about the human spirit. It is a book of stories—and above all else these *are* stories—about the spirit of man which, from time to time flashes him into an existence beyond his ordinary self and moves him through his days further, at times faster, always more deeply, than he would move had he nothing that he could call his spirit.

It is a book of many aspects. And while in these pages there is fighting will, and man in his sacrificial role of surrender, his heroism and endurance, there are moments of affection and tranquillity, too. And here perhaps is where it may be most rewarding. In a time of deaths and dying and shriekings of change, it may be good in all this noise to come upon the wonder of a still moment, to catch the glimpse of an occasional pool reflecting an eternal sky, and give one's self over for a time to poets, thinkers and lovers who in the midst of death still listen for the voice of life.

The plan of this book was a very simple one. It was hoped to bring together (for the first time, it seems now) some of the deepest stories of the human spirit by some of the greatest authors of our times. There are half a hundred writers here, all distinguished, many famous around the world. Each story, in its way and in its writing, was an act of faith. Some stories were written many years ago and their authors have passed into literary immortality. Some stories are by our neighbors in America, Sweden, France, or England, still alive and wondering as they write. All are, in the literary sense, "modern." Five of the authors have received the Nobel Prize for Literature. Others are here with their first or second, or their last, or best story—less famous folk, but all honest and sincere. From all these have come a gleaning of creative moods, stories which, in the last analysis, for their depth of insight, their inwardness of vision, their intensity and their faith in man, can only be described—however anyone may be embarrassed by a word so large—by the broad term "spiritual."

It is a book which, when paper is so scarce and values hardly less so, must be offered with a sense of humbleness, and without self-consciousness. No author here has written with tongue in cheek. No author has written shallowly or cheaply. Devout, agnostic, or sceptic, every author has at some still time questioned his values, and produced, in the terms of human beings moving through a situation, a story of finalities. These writers are not of any single creed; many are not members of any orthodox assemblage. There are Catholics, Protestants and Jews. But, for a reader, they are primarily writers. A writer is a man with a gift, and a gift, as Thomas Mann has said, "is a compulsion . . . not a thing to play with . . . but a critical knowledge of the ideal, a permanent dissatisfaction which rises only through suffering to the height of its power." Writers, in the way of all artists, tend to go away from the forms and conventions, and here they have struck inward where the individual man and woman has tried to find his own answer, as William James has said, "without the essential need of doctrinal apparatus or propitiatory machinery." For modern man has long been in search of a soul, perhaps as intensely in the laboratories of science as in the rectories.

The people who move through these stories have been understood more deeply by their authors than is common in the run of stories written for casual publication. Here is the lonely spirit of Thomas Wolfe, a spirit which despaired of its loneliness; and the hermit soul of a Thoreau, who in the lavish spring of green New England, welcomed his loneliness and fashioned it into poetry. There is the spirit of the brotherhood of man in the workers' vineyard; the spirit of the child, frightened of the bogies of its elders, candid with the beauties of the world, and hopeful; the doubting spirit, filled with knowledge and with torment; the spirit of reflection, nostalgia for another time and place and a life of the ideal; the spirit of the dream and re-formation of the world, of re-birth and revival; and the spirit of conscience and of testament.

It would be presumptuous to think that these are the greatest stories of the human spirit that the literatures of the world have produced. These are stories, in the main, of our times—although the times go back to Tolstoy and the freedom of the serfs. And the problems and the points of view are of our age. There are priests and nuns and non-believers. There are few saints and fewer devils. And the language is, in the main, our language, of our day.

Understandably, these stories are of such a nature that their authors must have felt they had to write them. One senses that this was so quite generally, whether the story was by a suffering Tolstoy, a reminiscing Rilke, a questioning Wolfe, or a believing Undset. Many a time the flesh was weak, but the spirit was strong. And it is not a little interesting to note how in the lives of so many authors in this book creation wrested with more than its usual difficulties: how with Kafka, his writings had to combat poverty and disease and post-war Austrian starvation; how Olive Schreiner fought for publication, after weary years of isolation and despair; how Chekhov battled poverty and illness, and with Lagerlöf and Clarence Day how each pursued their way through a lifetime each of crippled limbs and how Pirandello dwelt for fourteen years in the companionship of an insane wife whom he would not put away.

Man's spirit is more than the morality of keeping a good conscience, Mann's Schiller says in his weary hour: "It is the struggle and compulsion, the passion and the pain."

More, it is more too than one man's struggle, it is every man's struggle. "The wound is mortal and is mine." . . . In war-time there is a heightened awareness of the brevity of life. And a hunger for values that cannot be wiped out with a bullet. The literature of the human spirit is very vast. Literature is a reservoir of values, the common pool for all, filled by those bearers of their special gift. This is one book in a world of books. But it has, in spite of its many aspects, a singleness of faith. The spirit of man is no mean thing; its manifestations are tremendous. Man's spirit has lived thus far; it cannot now, by an act of consciousness, be ignored, denied, or destroyed.

WHIT BURNETT

I

God's Lonely Man

DOROTHY CANFIELD FISHER

In Memory of L. H. W.

As a Vermonter I was born and bred in the intense Vermont dislike for platform personalities, for people who "show off," for men and women who reveal by their manner that they know they are being looked at. "To act natural" is, in the Vermont code, the only self-respecting way to act. The canonized saints, with whom I was very familiar from part of my up-bringing, never made a very warm appeal to my affections because, as they were described in pious "Lives" surrounded by adoring followers watching their every action, and as they were shown, posturing on stained-glass windows in what might be called professional saintly garb, it was quite evident to a child's fresh eyes, that they must have been entirely conscious that people were looking at them. It was hard to imagine one of these diplomaed saints acting natural with the quiet unself-consciousness which is the Vermont norm of civilized behavior. I could quite understand my great-uncle's laughing, contemptuous distaste for them.

But after I learned—when? how?—that the Church itself, with all its sonorous, colorful, ecclesiastical ritual, honors on the feast of All Saints, holy men and women who are now and always were unknown as saints to others, who presumably, themselves, never dreamed that they were saints—the spiritual horizon widened for me far beyond the amused mockery of the old sceptic, far beyond the fixed theological rules-of-thumb in which my dear father took such comfort.

From that day, whenever it was, in the long-ago dimness of my little-girl-hood, my heart opened my eyes as I looked at the everyday men and women around me. And presently, in a rather dirty, not very bright, old farmer, with an impediment in his speech, whose whole life I knew from long before I was born, as children in unchanging old rural communities do know people, I saw that one of our fellow-townsmen was a saint.

So when I grew up and wrote stories, I set down his.

DOROTHY CANFIELD FISHER

HE BEGAN life characteristically, depreciated and disparaged. When he was a white, thin, big-headed baby, his mother, stripping the suds from her lean arms, used to inveigh to her neighbors against his existence. "Wa'n't it just like that *do*-less Lem Warren, not even to leave me foot-free when he died, but a baby coming!"

15

"*Do*-less," in the language of our valley, means a combination of shiftless and impractical, particularly to be scorned.

Later, as he began to have some resemblance to the appearance he was to wear throughout life, her resentment at her marriage, which she considered the one mistake of her life, kept pace with his growth. "Look at him!" she cried to anyone who would listen. "Ain't that Warren, all over? Did any of *my* folks ever look so like a born fool? Shut your mouth, for the Lord's sake, Lem, and maybe you won't scare folks quite so much."

Lem had a foolish, apologetic grin with which he always used to respond to these personalities, hanging his head to one side and opening and shutting his big hands nervously.

The tumble-down, two-roomed house in which the Warrens lived was across the road from the schoolhouse, and Mrs. Warren's voice was penetrating. Lem was accepted throughout his school-life at the home estimate. The ugly, overgrown boy, clad in cast-off, misfit clothing, was allowed to play with the other children only on condition that he perform all the hard, uninteresting parts of any game. Inside the schoolroom it was the same. He never learned to shut his mouth, and his speech was always halting and indistinct, so that he not only did not recite well in class, but was never in one of the school entertainments. He chopped the wood and brought it in, swept the floor and made the fires, and then listened in grinning, silent admiration while the others, arrayed in their best, spoke pieces and sang songs.

He was not "smart at his books" and indeed did not learn even to read very fluently. This may have been partly because the only books he ever saw were old schoolbooks, the use of which was given him free on account of his mother's poverty. He was not allowed, of course, to take them from the schoolroom. But if he was not good at book-learning he was not without accomplishments. He early grew large for his age, and strong from much chopping of wood and drawing of water for his mother's washings, and he was the best swimmer of all those who bathed in the cold, swift mountain stream which rushes near the schoolhouse. The chief consequence of this expertness was that in the summer he was forced to teach each succeeding generation of little boys to swim and dive. They tyrannized over him unmercifully—as, in fact, everyone did.

Nothing made his mother more furious than such an exhibition of what she called "Lem's meachin'ness." "Ain't you got no stand-up *in* ye?" she was wont to exhort him angrily. "If you don't look out for your-self in this world, you needn't think anybody else is gunto!"

The instructions in ethics he received at her hands were the only ones he ever knew, for, up to his fourteenth year, he never had clothes respecta-ble enough to wear to church, and after that he had other things to think of. Fourteen years is what we call in our State "over school age." It was a date to which Mrs. Warren had looked forward with eagerness. After that, the long, unprofitable months of enforced schooling would be over, Lem would be earning steady wages, and she could sit back and "live" . decent."

It seemed to her more than she could bear, that, almost upon her son's birthday, she was stricken down with paralysis. It was the first calamity for which she could not hold her marriage responsible, and her bitterness thereupon extended itself to fate in general. She cannot have been a cheerful house-mate during the next ten years, when Lem was growing silently to manhood.

He was in demand as "help" on the farms about him, on account of his great strength and faithfulness, although the farmers found him ex-asperatingly slow and, when it was a question of animals, not always sure to obey orders. He could be trusted to be kind to horses, unlike most hired men we get nowadays, but he never learned "how to get the work out of their hide." It was his way, on a steep hill with a heavy load, to lay down the whip, get out, and put his own powerful shoulder to the wheel. If this failed, he unloaded part of the logs and made two trips of it. The uncertainty of his progress can be imagined. The busy and impatient farmer and sawyer at the opposite ends of his route were driven to exhaust their entire vocabulary of objurgation on him. He was, they used to inform him in conclusion, "the most *do*-less critter the Lord ever made!"

He was better with cows and sheep—"feller-feelin'," his mother said scornfully, watching him feed a sick ewe—and he had here, even in comparison with his fellow-men, a fair degree of success. It was indeed the foundation of what material prosperity he ever enjoyed. A farmer, short of cash, paid him one year with three or four ewes and a ram. He worked for another farmer to pay for the rent of a pasture and had, that first year, as everybody admitted, almighty good luck with them. There were several twin lambs born that spring and everyone lived. Lem used to make frequent night visits during lambing-time to the pasture to make sure that all was well.

I remember as a little girl starting back from some village festivity late one spring night and seeing a lantern twinkle far up on the mountainside. "Lem Warren out fussin' with his sheep," some one of my elders remarked. Later, as we were almost home, we saw the lantern on the road ahead of us and stopped the horses, country-fashion, for an interchange of salutation. Looking out from under the shawl in which I was wrapped, I saw his tall figure stooping over something held under his coat. The lantern lighted his weather-beaten face and the expression of his eyes as he looked down at the little white head against his breast.

"You're foolish, Lem," said my uncle. "The ewe won't own it if you take it away so long the first night."

"I—I—know," stuttered Lem, bringing out the words with his usual difficulty; "but it's mortal cold up on the mounting for little fellers! I'll bring him up as a cosset."

The incident reminded me vaguely of something I had read about, and it has remained in my memory.

After we drove on I remember that there were laughing speculations about what language old Ma'am Warren would use at having another cosset brought to the house. Not that it could make any more work for her, since Lem did all that was done about the housekeeping. Chained to her chair by her paralyzed legs, as she was, she could accomplish nothing more than to sit and cavil at the management of the universe all day, until Lem came home, gave her her supper, and put her to bed.

Badly run as she thought the world, for a time it was more favorable to her material prosperity than she had ever known it. Lem's flock of sheep grew and thrived. For years nobody in our valley has tried to do much with sheep because of dogs, and all Lem's neighbors told him that some fine morning he would find his flock torn and dismembered. They even pointed out the particular big collie dog who would most likely go "sheep-mad." Lem's heavy face drew into anxious, grotesque wrinkles at this kind of talk, and he visited the uplying pasture more and more frequently.

One morning, just before dawn, he came, pale and shamefaced, to the house of the owner of the collie. The family, roused from bed by his knocking, made out from his speech, more incoherent than usual, that he was begging their pardon for having killed their dog. "I saw wh-where he'd bit th-the throats out of two ewes that w-was due to lamb in a few days and I guess I—I—I must ha' gone kind o' crazy. They was ones I liked special. I'd brought 'em up myself. They—they was all over blood, you know."

They peered at him in the gray light, half-afraid of the tall apparition. "How *could* you kill a great big dog like Jack?" They asked wonderingly.

In answer he held out his great hands and his huge corded arms, red with blood up to the elbow. "I heard him worrying another sheep and I—I just—killed him."

One of the children now cried out: "But I shut Jackie up in the wood-shed last night!"

Someone ran to open the door and the collie bounded out. Lem turned white in thankfulness. "I'm *mortal* glad," he stammered. "I felt awful bad—afterward. I knew your young ones thought a sight of Jack."

"But what dog did you kill?" they asked.

Some of the men went back up on the mountain with him and found, torn in pieces and scattered wide in bloody fragments, as if destroyed by some great revenging beast of prey, the body of a big gray wolf. Once in a while one wanders over the line from the Canada forests and comes down into our woods, following the deer.

The hard-headed farmers who looked on that savage scene drew back from the shambling man beside them in the only impulse of respect they ever felt for him. It was the one act of his life to secure the admiration of his fellow-men; it was an action of which he himself always spoke in horror and shame.

Certainly his marriage aroused no admiration. It was universally regarded as a most addlepated, imbecile affair from beginning to end. One of the girls who worked at the hotel in the village "got into trouble," as our vernacular runs, and as she came originally from our district and had gone to school there, everyone knew her and was talking about the scandal. Old Ma'am Warren was of the opinion, spiritedly expressed, that "Lottie was a fool not to make that drummer marry her. She could have, if she'd gone the right way to work." But the drummer remained persistently absent.

One evening Lem, starting for his sheep-pasture for his last look for the night, heard someone crying down by the river and then, as he paused to listen, heard it no more. He jumped from the bridge without stopping to set down his lantern, knowing well the swiftness of the water, and caught the poor cowardly thing as she came, struggling and gasping, down with the current. He took her home and gave her dry clothes of his mother's. Then leaving the scared and repentant child by his hearth, he set out on foot for the minister's house and dragged him back over the rough country roads.

When Ma'am Warren awoke the next morning, Lem did not instantly answer her imperious call, as he had done for so many years. Instead, a red-eyed girl in one of Mrs. Warren's own nightgowns came to the door and said shrinkingly: "Lem slept in the barn last night. He give his bed to me; but he'll be in soon. I see him fussin' around with the cow."

Ma'am Warren stared, transfixed with a premonition of irremediable evil. "What you doin' here?" she demanded, her voice devoid of expression through stupefaction.

The girl held down her head. "Lem and I were married last night," she said.

Then Mrs. Warren found her voice.

When Lem came in it was to a scene of the furious wrangling which was henceforth to fill his house.

". . . to saddle himself with such trash as you!" his mother was saying ragingly.

His wife answered in kind, her vanity stung beyond endurance. "Well, you can be sure he'd never have got him a wife any other way! Nobody but a girl hard put to it would take up with a drivel-headed fool like Lem Warren!"

And then the bridegroom appeared at the door and both women turned their attention to him.

When the baby was born, Lottie was very sick. Lem took care of his mother, his wife, and the new baby for weeks and weeks. It was at lambing-time, and his flock suffered from lack of attention, although as much as he dared he left his sick women and tended his ewes. He ran in debt, too, to the grocery-stores, for he could work very little and earned almost nothing. Of course the neighbors helped out, but it was no cheerful morning's work to care for the vitriolic old woman, and Lottie was too sick for anyone but Lem to handle. We did pass the baby around from house to house during the worst of his siege, to keep her off Lem's hands;

but when Lottie began to get better it was haying-time; everybody was more than busy, and the baby was sent back.

Lottie lingered in semi-invalidism for about a year and then died, Lem holding her hand in his. She tried to say something to him that last night, so the neighbors who were there reported, but her breath failed her and she could only lie staring at him from eyes that seemed already to look from the other side of the grave.

He was heavily in debt when he was thus left with a year-old child not his own, but he gave Lottie a decent funeral and put up over her grave a stone stating that she was "Charlotte, loved wife of Lemuel Warren," and that she died in the eighteenth year of her life. He used to take the little girl and put flowers on the grave, I remember.

Then he went to work again. His sandy hair was already streaked with gray, though he was but thirty. The doctor said the reason for this phenomenon was the great strain of his year of nursing; and indeed throughout that period of his life no one knew when he slept, if ever. He was always up and dressed when anyone else was, and late at night we could look across and see his light still burning and know that he was rubbing Lottie's back or feeding little Susie.

All that was changed now, of course. Susie was a strong, healthy child who slept all through the night in her little crib by her stepfather's corded bed, and in the daytime went everywhere he did. Whenever he "worked out" he used to give her her nap wrapped in a horse blanket on the hay in the barn; and he carried her in a sling of his own contrivance up to his sheep-pasture. Old Ma'am Warren disliked the pretty, laughing child so bitterly that he was loath to leave her at home; but when he was there with her, for the first time he asserted himself against his mother, bidding her, when she began to berate the child's parentage, to "be still!" with so strange and unexpected an accent of authority that she was quite frightened.

Susie was very fond of her stepfather at first, but when she came of school age, mixed more with the other children, and heard laughing, contemptuous remarks about him, the frank and devouring egotism of childhood made her ashamed of her affection, ashamed of him with his uncouth gait, his mouth always sagging open, his stammering, ignorant speech, which the other children amused themselves by mocking. Though he was prospering again with his sheep, owned the pasture and his house now, and had even built on another room as well as repairing the older part, he spent little on his own adornment. It all went for pretty clothes for Susie, for better food, for books and pictures, for tickets for Susie to go to the circus and the county fair. Susie knew this and loved him by stealth for it, but the intolerably sensitive vanity of her twelve years made her wretched to be seen in public with him.

Divining this, he ceased going with her to school-picnics and Sunday-school parties, where he had been a most useful pack-animal, and, dressing her in her best with his big calloused hands, watched her from the window join a group of the other children. His mother predicted savagely that his "spoilin' on that bad-blooded young one would bring her to no good end," and when, at fifteen, Susie began to grow very pretty and saucy and willful and to have beaux come to see her, the old woman exulted openly over Lem's helpless anxiety.

He was quite gray now, although not yet forty-five, and so stooped that he passed for an old man. He owned a little farm, his flock of sheep was the largest in the township, and Susie was expected to make a good marriage in spite of her antecedents.

And then Frank Gridley's oldest son, Ed, came back from business college with store clothes and city hats and polished tan shoes, and began idling about, calling on the girls. From the first, he and Susie ran together like two drops of water. Bronson Perkins, a cousin of mine, a big, silent, ruminative lad who had long hung about Susie, stood no show at all. One night in county-fair week, Susie, who had gone to the fair with a crowd of girl friends, was not at home at ten o'clock. Lem, sitting in his doorway and watching the clock, heard the approach of the laughing, singing straw-ride in which she had gone, with a long breath of relief; but the big hay-wagon did not stop at his gate.

He called after it in a harsh voice and was told that "Ed Gridley and she went off to the hotel to get supper. He said he'd bring her home later."

Lem went out to the barn, hitched up the faster of his two heavy plow-horses and drove from his house to Woodville, eight miles and up-hill, in forty-five minutes. When he went into the hotel, the clerk told him that the two he sought had had supper served in a private room. Lem ascertained which room and broke the door in with one heave of his shoulders. Susie sprang up from the disordered supper-table and ran

to him like a frightened child, clinging to him desperately and crying out
that Ed scared her so!

"It's all right now, Susie," he said gently, not looking at the man.
"Poppa's come to take you home."

The man felt his dignity wounded. He began to protest boisterously
and to declare that he was ready to marry the girl—"*now,* this instant,
if you choose!"

Lem put one arm about Susie. "I didn't come to make you marry her.
I come to keep you from doin' it," he said, speaking clearly for once in
his life. "Susie shan't marry a hound that'd do this." And as the other
advanced threateningly on him, he struck him a great blow across the
mouth that knocked him down unconscious.

Then Lem went out, paid for the broken lock, and drove home with
Susie behind the foundered plow-horse.

The next spring her engagement to Bronson Perkins was announced,
though everybody said they didn't see what use it was for folks to get
engaged that couldn't ever get married. Mr. Perkins, Bronson's father,
was daft, not enough to send him to the asylum, but so that he had to
be watched all the time to keep him from doing himself a hurt. He had
a horrid way, I remember, of lighting matches and holding them up to
his bared arm until the smell of burning flesh went sickeningly through
the house and sent someone in a rush to him. Of course it was out of the
question to bring a young bride to such a home. Apparently there were
years of waiting before them, and Susie was made of no stuff to endure
a long engagement.

As a matter of fact, they were married that fall, as soon as Susie could
get her things ready. Lem took old Mr. Perkins into the room Susie left
vacant. " 'Twon't be much more trouble taking care of two old people
than one," he explained briefly.

Ma'am Warren's comments on this action have been embalmed forever
in the delighted memories of our people. We have a taste for picturesque
and forceful speech.

From that time we always saw the lunatic and the bent shepherd together. The older man grew quieter under Lem's care than he had been
for years, and if he felt one of his insane impulses overtaking him, ran
totteringly to grasp his protector's arm until, quaking and shivering, he
was himself again. Lem used to take him up to the sheep-pasture for the

day sometimes. He liked it up there himself, he said, and maybe 'twould be good for Uncle Hi. He often reported with pride that the old man talked as sensible as anybody, "get him off where it's quiet." Indeed, when Mr. Perkins died, six years later, we had forgotten that he was anything but a little queer, and he had known many happy, lucid hours with his grandchildren.

Susie and Bronson had two boys—sturdy, hearty children, in whom Lem took the deepest, shyest pride. He loved to take them off into the woods with him and exulted in their quick intelligence and strong little bodies. Susie got into the way of letting him take a good deal of the care of them.

It was Lem who first took alarm about the fall that little Frank had, down the cellar stairs. He hurt his spine somehow—our local doctor could not tell exactly how—and as the injury only made him limp a little, nobody thought much about it, until he began to have difficulty in walking. Then Lem sent for a doctor from Rutland who, as soon as he examined the child, stuck out his lower lip and rubbed his chin ominously. He pronounced the trouble something with a long name which none of us had ever heard, and said that Frank would be a hopeless cripple if it were not cured soon. There was, he said, a celebrated doctor from Europe now traveling in this country who had a wonderful new treatment for this condition. But under the circumstances—he looked about the plain farm sitting-room—he supposed that was out of the question.

"What did the doctor from foreign parts ask?" queried Bronson, and, being informed of some of the customary prices for major operations, fell back hopeless. Susie, her pretty, childish face drawn and blanched into a wan beauty, put her arms about her sick little son and looked at her stepfather. He had never failed her.

He did not fail her now. He sold the land he had accumulated field by field; he sold the great flock of sheep, every one of which he could call by name; he mortgaged the house over the protesting head of his now bedridden mother; he sold the horse and cow, and the very sticks of furniture from the room where Susie had grown up and where the crazy grandfather of Susie's children had known a peaceful old age and death. Little Frank was taken to New York to the hospital to have the great surgeon operate on him—he is there yet, almost completely recovered and nearly ready to come home.

Back in Hillsboro, Lem now began life all over again, hiring out humbly to his neighbors and only stipulating that he should have enough free time to take care of his mother. Three weeks ago she had her last stroke of paralysis and, after lying speechless for a few days, passed away, grim to the last, by the expression in her fierce old eyes.

The day after her funeral Lem did not come to work as he was expected. We went over to his house and found, to our consternation, that he was not out of bed.

"Be ye sick, Lem?" asked my uncle.

He looked at us over the bedclothes with his old foolish, apologetic smile. "Kind o' lazy, I guess," he whispered, closing his eyes.

The doctor was put out by the irregularity of the case. "I can't make out anything *really* the trouble!" he said. "Only the wheels don't go round as fast as they ought. Call it failing heart action if you want a label."

The wheels ran more and more slowly until it was apparent to all of us that before long they would stop altogether. Susie and Bronson were in New York with little Frank, so that Lem's care during his last days devolved on the haphazard services of the neighbors. He was out of his head most of the time, though never violent, and all through the long nights lay flat on his back, looking at the ceiling with bright, blank eyes, driving his ox-team, skidding logs, plowing in stony ground and remembering to favor the off-horse whose wind wasn't good, planting, hoeing, tending his sheep, and teaching obstinate lambs to drink. He used quaint, coaxing names for these, such as a mother uses for her baby. He was up in the mountain-pasture a good deal, we gathered, and at night, from his constant mention of how bright the stars shone. And sometimes, when he was in evident pain, his delusion took the form that Susie, or the little boys, had gone up with him, and got lost in the woods.

I was on duty the night he died. We thought a change was near, because he had lain silent all day, and we hoped he would come to himself when he awoke from this stupor. Near midnight he began to talk again, and I could not make out at first whether he was still wandering or not. "Hold on hard, Uncle Hi," I heard him whisper.

A spoon fell out of my hand and clattered against a plate. He gave a great start and tried to sit up. "Yes, mother—coming!" he called hoarsely, and then looked at me with his own eyes. "I must ha' forgot about mother's bein' gone," he apologized sheepishly.

I took advantage of this lucid interval to try to give him some medicine the doctor had left. "Take a swallow of this," I said, holding the
glass to his lips.

"What's it for?" he asked.

"It's a heart stimulant," I explained. "The doctor said if we could get
you through to-night you have a good chance."

His face drew together in grotesque lines of anxiety. "Little Frank
worse?"

"Oh, no, he's doing finely."

"Susie all right?"

"Why, yes," I said wonderingly.

"Nothing the matter with her other boy?"

"Why, no, no," I told him. "Everybody's all right. Here, just take this
down."

He turned away his head on the pillow and murmured something I
did not catch. When I asked him what he said, he smiled feebly as in
deprecation of his well-known ridiculous ways. "I'm just as much obliged
to you," he said, "but if everybody's all right, I guess I won't have any
medicine." He looked at me earnestly. "I'm—I'm real tired," he said.

It came out in one great breath—apparently his last, for he did not
move after that, and his ugly, slack-mouthed face was at once quite still.
Its expression made me think of the time I had seen it as a child, by
lantern-light, as he looked down at the new-born lamb on his breast.

SELMA LAGERLÖF

A Fallen King

The first woman to win the Nobel Prize for literature and known in America primarily for her long saga-like novels, Selma Ottiliana Lovisa Lagerlöf, the Swedish novelist who died in 1940, has written many beautiful short stories. "A Fallen King" is one of her most unusual, and its meanings run deep.

> *"Mine of old was Fancy's Kingdom,*
> *Now I am a fallen king."*—Snoilsky

CLATTERING on the cobblestones; the agitated tramp of clogs. The street urchins hurried past, clamouring, whistling; all at full speed. The houses shook, and the echo rushed forth from the side-streets like a watch-dog from its kennel.

Faces appeared behind the window panes. Had anything happened? Was anything amiss? The din drifted away into the suburb, and thither hurried the servant-girls in the wake of the street-boys. They clasped their hands together and shrieked:

"Lord a Mercy! Lord a Mercy! Is it a murder—or a fire?"

No answer; only the clogs clattering in the distance.

Behind the girls came hastening the wise matrons of the town. They asked:

"What is the matter? What is disturbing our morning's peace? Is it a wedding? Or a funeral? Or a fire? What is the watchman doing? Is the town to be burned down before he even begins to ring the bell?"

The whole crowd came to a halt in front of the shoemaker's little house in a remote part of the suburb—the little house with the vine round the doors and windows, and down below, between house and street, an ell-wide garden. A summer-house of straw, cover for a rat, foot-paths for a kitten! Everything in perfect order. Peas and beans, roses and lavender, a mouthful of grass, three gooseberry bushes and an apple tree.

The boys stood in front, spying and discussing. The dark polished window panes prevented them seeing further than the white lace curtains. One of the boys clambered up the vine and pressed his face against the window.

"What can he see?" whispered the others. "What can he see?"

The shoemaker's workshop and bench, grease pots and bundles of leather, lasts and pegs, rings and straps. "Can't he see any human being?" He can see the journeyman, heeling a shoe. "Nobody else? Nobody else?" Great black flies are running over the window pane and he can't see clearly. "Can't he see any one besides the journeyman?" Nobody else; the master's stool is empty. He looked again—twice, three times: the master's stool was empty.

The crowd stood still, guessing and wondering. Then it must be true— the old shoemaker had gone off. No one would believe it; they stood and waited for signs. The cat came out on the steep roof, spread its claws and glided down towards the gutter. Yes, the master of the house was away, so the cat was free to go hunting. The sparrows fluttered and shrieked helplessly.

A white chicken peeped round the corner of the house. It was nearly full-grown, with a comb that shone red as a vine-leaf. It spied and pried, crowed and called. The hens came running, a string of white hens, waddling along with flapping wings and yellow legs like drumsticks, hopping between the rows of stuck peas. Jealousy developed into a battle royal. One hen ran off with a full pod and two cocks grabbed her by the neck. The cat left his sparrows' nests to look on. Down he fell with a thud, right in the middle of the lot! The hens fled in a long waddling line, and the people thought: "It's true enough; the shoemaker has cleared out; one can tell by the cat and the hens that the master of the house is away."

The rutty suburban road, sloshy with rain, resounded with talk. Doors stood open, windows swung. Head leant towards head in astonished whispers. "He's gone!" People whispered, sparrows shrieked, clogs clattered: "He's gone! The old shoemaker's gone. The little house's owner, the young wife's husband, the pretty child's father—he's gone. Would you believe it? Would you believe it?"

There is a song that runs like this: "*An old man in the homestead; a young lover in the wood; a wife who runs away; a child who weeps; a home without a mistress.*" That song is old; it is often sung, and everybody understands it.

This was a new song; it was the old man that had gone. On his work-table lay his declaration—that he intended never to return. A letter had lain beside it; his wife had read it—no one else.

The young wife was in the kitchen, doing nothing. The woman from next door went about busily arranging things, setting out cups, putting on firewood, cutting up clearing-skin for the coffee, weeping a little and drying her tears on the dishcloth.

The wise women of the neighbourhood sat stiffly along the walls. They knew what was fitting in a house of mourning. They observed strict silence and all the signs of mourning. They took a holiday in order to support the deserted wife in her sorrow. Coarse hands lay quietly in laps, weather-beaten skin was furrowed in deep wrinkles, thin lips pinched together over toothless jaws.

The wife sat among the bronze-hued women, fair and gentle, with a lovely dove-like face. She did not weep, but she was trembling. She was so frightened that she almost died of fear. She clenched her teeth so that no one should hear them chattering. When steps were heard, or knocks came or she was spoken to, she started.

She was sitting with her husband's letter in her pocket, remembering first one line and then another. There was this: *"I cannot endure any longer the sight of you two together."* And again: *"I now know for certain that you and Eriksson intend to elope."* And then: *"You shan't do that; evil tongues would make you unhappy. I will run away; then you can get a divorce and be properly married. Eriksson is a good worker and should be able to provide for you."* And then lower down: *"Let people say what they like about me! I am content, if only they believe no evil of you; for that you could not bear."*

She couldn't understand it; she had never meant to betray him. Even if she had liked talking to the young journeyman, how did that hurt her husband? Love is a sickness, but not unto death. She had intended to endure it patiently all her life; how had her husband divined her most secret thoughts?

She was tortured at the thought of him, of all that anxiety and watchfulness! He had wept at the thought of his age, raved at the strength and courage of the young. He had trembled at the sight of smiles, of whispers, of handclasps. His burning madness, his grinding jealousy had made what as yet was nothing into a complete elopement case.

She considered how old he must have been last night when he left her. His back was bent, his hands shaky; the long night's torture had made him like that. He had gone away to escape that life of irritating doubt.

She remembered some other lines in the letter: *"It is not my wish to bring you to shame. I have always been too old for you."* And then another: *"You shall always be respected and honoured. Only keep silence yourself and all the shame will fall on me!"*

Her anguish increased; was it possible that people could be deceived like that? And was it really right thus to lie unto God also? Why was she sitting in her cottage, sympathized with like a mourning mother, honoured like a bride on her wedding-day? Why was it not she that was homeless, friendless, despised? How can such things be? How can God let Himself be deceived thus?

A little bookshelf hung above the big chiffonier. At the top of the shelf was a large book with brass clasps. Concealed by the clasps was the story of a man and a woman who lied unto God and unto men. *"Woman, who moved thee to act thus? Behold, the young men are at the door, to carry thee out!"*

The woman stared at the book, listening for the young men's feet. She trembled at every knock, shuddered at every footstep. She was ready to stand up and confess, ready to fall down and die.

Coffee was ready; the women glided sedately towards the table. They filled their cups, put some sugar in their mouths and began to lap up the boiling-hot coffee, silently and demurely, the artisans' wives first, the charwomen last. But the wife noticed nothing; she was beside herself with anguish. She had a vision. In the middle of the night she was sitting out of doors in a newly-ploughed field. All around her were great birds with strong wings and sharp beaks. They were grey, hardly noticeable against the grey ground, but they kept watch over her; they sat in judgment on her. Suddenly they flew up and began to swoop down above her head. She could see their sharp claws, their pointed beaks, as their thrashing wings came nearer. It was like a death-dealing rain of steel. She bowed her head and felt that her hour was come. But when they came near, quite close to her, she had to look up. Then she perceived that the grey birds were all these old women.

One of them began to speak; she knew what was decent, what was suitable for a house of mourning: the silence had lasted long enough. But the wife sprang up as though she had been struck by a whip. What did the woman intend to say?

"Anna Wik, wife of Matts Wik, confess! You have lied long enough to God and to us. We are your judges; we shall condemn you and tear you to pieces."

No, the woman was merely beginning to talk about men, and the others joined in as the occasion demanded. They did not sing their praises. All the ill that they had done was dragged into the light of day. It was their consolation for a deserted wife.

Wrong was piled upon wrong. Strange creatures, these men! They beat us, they drink up our money, they pawn our household goods. Why on earth had our Lord created such beings?

The tongues became like dragon-stings, spewing out poison, squirting fire. Each made her contribution: tale was heaped upon tale. Wives fleeing from their homes in fear of drunken husbands: wives slaving for worthless men: wives deserted for other women. The tongues whistled like whip-lashes. The miseries of the home were laid bare. Long litanies were recited: "From the tyranny of man, Good Lord, deliver us!"

Sickness and poverty, the deaths of children, winter's cold, trouble with the aged—all these come from man. The slaves hissed at their masters; they turned the dagger point against him at whose feet they crept.

The ears of the abandoned wife felt pierced and lacerated. She dared to defend the incorrigible:

"My husband," she said, "is a good man."

The women sprang up, snarling and sniffing:

"He has run away; he's no better than the others. He, an old man, ought to have known better than to run away from wife and children. Can you believe that he is better than the rest?"

The wife trembled; she felt as though she were being dragged through spiky thorn bushes. Her husband counted among the sinners! She blushed with shame, tried to speak, but was silent. She was afraid; she could not do it. But why did not God speak? Why did God let such things happen?

Suppose she took out the letter and read it aloud? That would change the course of the poisonous stream; the venom would drip on herself. The horrors of death were upon her; she did not dare. She half wished that some impudent hand had been thrust into her pocket and taken out the letter. She could not give herself away of her own accord. From the workshop came the sound of a shoemaker's hammer. Could not one hear the triumphant ring of that tapping? She had heard it and resented it the whole day; but none of the women understood it. "O God, that knowest all things, hast Thou no servant who can pierce the secrets of the heart?" Gladly would she receive her sentence, if only she need not confess. Gladly would she hear some one say: "Who moved thee to lie unto God?" She listened for the sound of the young men's feet, to fall down dead.

Some years later a divorced woman was married to a shoemaker who had been journeyman to her former husband. She had not wished for this but had been dragged into it, just as a pike is dragged over the gunwale after it has been hooked. The fisherman plays it; he lets it dart hither and thither; he lets it think it is free. But when it is tired out, when it can do no more, then he pulls it with an easy jerk towards the boat, hauls it in, and heaves it to the bottom of the boat before it knows what it is all about.

The wife of the shoemaker who had left her had dismissed her journeyman and wanted to live alone. She had wanted to show her husband that she was innocent. But where was her husband? Didn't he trouble himself about her faithfulness? She was badly off; her child went about in rags. How long did Matts Wik think she could wait? She was unhappy, with no one to attach herself to.

Eriksson was getting on well; the journeyman now had a shop in the town. His shoes were exhibited on glass shelves behind wide windows. He enlarged his workshop, hired a flat and furnished the parlour in plush. Everything was waiting for her, and when she was quite tired of poverty, she went.

At first she was very much afraid. But no misfortunes befell her and she felt more secure every day and more and more happy. People respected her and she knew that she did not deserve it. This kept her conscience awake, so that she became a good woman.

After some years her first husband came back to the house in the suburb. This was his own property and he settled down there again and tried to start work. But he couldn't get any work, nor would decent people associate with him. He was despised, while his wife was held in the highest esteem. Yet it was he who had acted rightly, while she had done wrong.

The man kept his secret, though it came near choking him. He felt degraded because everybody thought him bad. No one relied on him, no one would entrust any work to him. He accepted such society as he could get, and acquired the habit of drinking.

While he was in this plight the Salvation Army visited the town. They hired a large hall and began their activities. From the very first evening all the rabble came to the meetings to make a disturbance. When this had been going on for about a week Matts Wik came to take part in the fun.

The street was thronged, the doorway blocked. Here were sharp elbows and bitter tongues; street-boys and soldiers, maidservants and charwomen, peaceful police and an uproarious mob. The "Army" was a novelty. Balls lost their bloom, taverns their taste. Leaders of fashion and toughs from the docks—all went to see the Salvation Army.

The inside of the hall was low in the roof. At the extreme end was an empty platform. Unvarnished benches, borrowed chairs. A splintered floor, damp-stains on the ceiling, lamps that smoked. The iron stove in the middle of the floor gave out warmth and fumes. All the seats were filled at once. Next to the platform women were sitting, demure as though they were in church, solemn as a bride in her chair; and behind them longshoremen and sempstresses. Furthest away sat the boys, urchin on urchin's knee. In the doorway a fight was going on among those who could not get in.

The platform was empty; the clock had not yet struck, the performance not yet begun. There was whistling and laughter; benches were kicked to pieces. The *War Cry* flew from group to group like a kite. The public was enjoying itself.

The side door was opened, and cold air streamed into the room. The stove blazed up. There was silence; an air of watchful expectancy breathed through the hall. At last they arrived—three young women carrying guitars, their faces almost hidden under broad-brimmed hats. The moment they had mounted the steps to the platform they fell upon their knees.

One of them prayed aloud, lifting her head but with closed eyes. Her voice cut like a knife. There was silence during the prayer; the street-boys and harbour roughs had not yet got into their stride. They were waiting for the confessions and the exciting tunes.

The women warmed to their work; they sang and prayed, sang and preached, smiling and talking of their own happiness. In front of them were some rows of harbour roughs, who began to get up and stand on the benches. A menacing clamour rose from the throng; the women on the platform had glimpses of horrible faces through the smoky air. The men wore dirty, wet, ill-smelling clothes; they spat out tobacco juice every second, they swore at every word. These women who were to fight with them talked about their happiness!

What a brave little army! Ah, how lovely to be brave! Is it not something to be proud of—to have God on one's side? It would not pay to laugh at them in their big hats. As likely as not they would win the fight against the horny hands, the cruel faces, the blaspheming lips.

"Sing with us!" called the Salvation Army, "Sing with us! It is a good thing to sing." They struck up a well-known tune, plucking their guitars and repeating the same verse over and over again. They managed to get one or two of the nearest to them to join in the song. But now came thundering back from the door a frivolous street-song. Note fought with note, word with word, guitar with whistle. The strong trained voices of the women strove against the hoarse breaking notes of the boys, the booming basses of the men. When the street song was on the point of giving in, stamping and whistling began down by the door. The Army song sank like a wounded warrior. The noise was terrible; the women fell upon their knees.

They knelt there powerless, their eyes closed, their bodies rocking in silent pain. The clamour died down. The Army Captain began at once:

"Lord, all these shalt Thou make Thine own. I thank Thee, Lord, for bringing them all into Thine Army! I thank Thee, Lord, for allowing us to lead them to Thee!"

The crowd clamoured, whistled, and yelled. It seemed as if all these throats had been tickled by a sharp knife; as if they feared to be defeated; as if they had forgotten that they had come of their own accord.

But the woman continued, and it was her sharp, piercing voice that won the victory. They had to listen.

"Ye shriek and yell. The old serpent within you writhes and raves. But that is just the sign. Blessings on the old serpent's roar. It shows that he is in torment, that he is afraid. Yes, laugh at us! Smash in our windows! Hunt us from the platform! To-morrow ye will hearken to us. We shall

possess the earth. How would you withstand us? How would ye withstand God?"

Immediately after this the Captain ordered one of her comrades to step
forward and make a confession. She came forward smiling. Bold and
unafraid she stood, flinging out to the mockers the story of her sin and
her conversion. Who taught that kitchen-maid to stand smiling beneath
all that mockery? Some who had come to jest grew pale. Whence took
these women their courage and their power? There was some one at the
back of them.

The third soldier stepped forward, a most beautiful girl, the daughter
of wealthy parents, with a clear, merry singing voice. She said nothing
about herself; her testimony was one of the usual hymns.

It was the shadow of a victory to come. The meeting forgot itself and
listened. The girl was pretty to look at, lovely to hear. But when she
ceased the noise became more frightful than ever. Down by the door
they built a platform of benches, climbed up on it and confessed.

The hall became more uncomfortable than ever. The iron stove grew
red-hot, exhausted the air and panted forth heat. The respectable women
on the front benches looked about for a way of escape, but saw no possibility of getting out. The soldiers on the platform sweated and faltered,
cried aloud and prayed for strength. Suddenly a blast ran through the
atmosphere, a whispering reached their ears; whence, they knew not, but
they perceived a change. God was with them, was fighting for them.

"To battle again!" The Captain stepped forward, holding the Bible
above her head.

"No more! no more! We perceive that God is working in our midst. A
conversion is at hand. Help us to pray! God means to give us a soul."

They fell on their knees in silent prayer, and some of those in the hall
joined in the prayer. Tense expectation pervaded them all. Was it true?
Was some great change in the soul of a fellow creature taking place, here
in their very midst? Would they be able to see it? Could these women
accomplish anything?

For a time the crowd was vanquished; they were as eager for a miracle
as they had been for blasphemy. None dared to stir; all panted in expectation, but nothing happened.

"O God, thou desertest us! Thou desertest us, O God!"

The pretty Army lass began to sing; she chose that gentlest of tunes, longing's tenderest child: "Far from the green-growing valleys he lingers."

The words were only slightly altered; the Finnish cow-girl's song was easily adapted to the longing of Jesus for a soul. "O my beloved, comest thou not soon?"

Gently persuasive as a beseeching child, the song found its way to their hearts, like a caress, like a blessing.

The meeting was silent, lost in those sounds. "Mountains and woods are longing, heaven and earth live in yearning. O man, everything in the world is athirst for thee to lay bare thy soul to the light. Then will glory be spread over the world, then will the beasts arise from their degradation. The groaning of creation will be at an end."

"O my beloved, comest thou not soon?"

True thou hast not "tarried too long in the high kingly halls." Low taverns, miserable hovels are thy dwelling-place. And yet thou wilt not come; my shining heaven allures thee not.

"O my beloved, comest thou not soon?"

Down in the hall still more people joined in the refrain; voice after voice chimed in. They did not really know what words they were singing; the tune was enough. All longing could sing itself away in those notes. Even down by the door they sang. It burst the heart, it subdued the will. The sound was no longer a pitiful complaint, but strong, compelling, commanding.

"O my beloved, comest thou not soon?"

Down by the door, in the worst part of the crowd, stood Matts Wik. He looked very besotted, but that evening he was not drunk. He stood still, thinking, "If only I might speak, if only I might speak!"

This was the most marvellous place he had seen, the most marvellous opportunity. A voice came to him: "This is the reed you shall whisper to, the waves that shall carry your voice."

The singers started; it was as if they had heard a lion roaring in their ears. A strong, terrible voice was uttering terrible words.

It mocked at God.

"Why did mankind worship God? He deserted all who worshipped Him; He betrayed His Son. God helped no one."

Every minute the voice became more powerful, more deafening in its roar. Who could have thought such power could dwell in human lungs?

None had ever heard such madness burst forth from a trampled heart. They bowed their heads like travellers in the wilderness when the storm breaks over them.

Mighty, mighty words; like thundering hammer-strokes against the throne of God; against Him who tormented Job, who allowed the martyrs to suffer, and those who confessed Him to be burnt at the stake. When will He establish His kingdom, that God the Impotent? When will He cease to lead evil on to victory?

At first some tried to laugh it off; some of them thought it was a joke. Now they saw, trembling, that it was deadly earnest. Already some had got up to escape to the platform. They wanted the Army's protection from him who was bringing upon them the wrath of God.

In hissing accents the voice asked them what reward they expected for their pains in serving God. They needn't expect Heaven; God was stingy about His Heaven. A man, he said, had done more good than was necessary to obtain salvation. He had made greater sacrifices than God demanded. Then he was enticed into sin. Life is long. He had already spent in this life the grace that he had earned. He would go the way of the damned.

His speech was the terrifying northern gale that drives the vessel into port. Women rushed up on to the platform during the mocker's speech. The hands of the Army soldiers were grasped and kissed. Conversion followed conversion; the soldiers could scarcely receive them all. Boys and old men praised God.

The speaker continued; words intoxicated him. He said to himself: "I am speaking, I am speaking, at last I am speaking! I am telling them my secret, and yet I am not telling them." For the first time since his great sacrifice he was free from grief.

It was a Sunday afternoon at the height of summer. The town looked like a wilderness of stone, a landscape in the moon. Not a cat, not a sparrow was to be seen; scarcely even a fly on a sunny wall. Not a chimney was smoking; not a breath of air in the stifling streets. Everything was just a field sown with stones, from which walls of stone were growing.

What had become of dogs and men? Of the young ladies in narrow skirts and wide sleeves, long gloves and red parasols? Where were the soldiers and dandies, the Salvation Army and the street-boys?

Whither were they bound on that dewy-fresh morning, all these gaily dressed troops of pleasure-seekers, all the baskets and concertinas and bottles which the steamer put ashore? And what had become of the procession of good-templars? Flags were waving, drums thundering, streetboys swarming, stamping, hurrahing. And what had become of the blue hoods beneath which the little ones slept while father and mother pushed them devoutly along the road?

They were all on their way to the forest. They complained of the length of the streets; they felt as if the stone houses were pursuing them. At last, at last a glimpse of green! And there, just outside the town, where the road wound over flat, damp fields, where the song of larks was at its height and the scent of clover honey-sweet—there lay the first stragglers. Caps on neck, noses in the grass; bodies bathed in sunshine and the scent of flowers; souls refreshed by idleness and peace.

Along the road to the forest toiled the basket-carriers and cyclists. Boys came along with spades and shining knapsacks; girls danced in clouds of dust. Crowds and flags: children and trumpets. Artisans with their wives and families. Horses reared, flourishing their forelegs over the crowds. A journeyman, mad with drink, jumped up on the wheel; some women promptly pulled him down and he lay sprawling on his back in the road gravel below.

Inside the woods fluted and warbled a nightingale. The birches were faring badly, blackened round the stems. The beeches built high temples, story on story of cross-striped green. The frog sat taking aim with his tongue, snapping up a fly with every shot. The hedgehog trudged about among the crackling old beech leaves. Dragon-flies darted across the bogs with glittering wings. Men and women sat down round their food baskets. Gold-beetles crept about them in the grass. Crickets chirped and jumped, trying to cheer their Sunday for them.

Suddenly the hedgehog vanished, withdrawing in fright into his prickles. The crickets, reduced to silence, dived down into the grass. The nightingale's song became almost frenzied. It was the guitars, the guitars. The Salvation Army was appearing under the beeches. All sprang up from their idle rest beneath the trees. The dancing place and croquetground emptied; swings and roundabouts got an hour's rest. Everybody moved towards the Army's camp; the benches were filled and listeners sat on every hillock.

By this time the Army had grown strong and powerful. The "Salvation" hat was bent down over many a fair cheek, many strong men wore the red jacket. Peace and order reigned in the crowd; not a jeer dared pass their lips; oaths were checked in harmlessness behind closed teeth. And Matts Wik the shoemaker, that mighty slanderer of God, now stood beneath the platform as standard-bearer. He too was among the faithful, and the folds of the red flag caressed lovingly his grey head.

The Army had not forgotten the old man; it was he they had to thank for their first victory. They had come to him in his loneliness, scrubbed his floor and mended his clothes. They were not ashamed to be seen with him, and they allowed him to speak at their meetings.

Ever since he had broken his silence he had been happy. He stood forth no longer as an enemy of God. He felt a rushing force within him, and was happy when he could give it air. He was happy when the halls shook beneath his lion's voice.

He spoke always about himself, told always his own story. He sketched the fate of the misunderstood, spoke of bleeding sacrifices, without recompense, without recognition. He disguised his narrative: told his secret, and yet did not tell it.

He became an artist in words, with power to win hearts. Crowds assembled before the Army's platform to hear him, drawn thither by the lovely fantastic images that filled his sick brain; captivated by the words of thrilling pathos which he had learnt in the agony of his soul.

Is it possible that his spirit had once before visited this world of death and change? That he had then been some mighty bard, skilled at playing on the heart-strings? Doomed for some grievous crime to begin anew his life on earth, to live by the work of his hands, in ignorance of his spiritual power. But now grief had burst his spirit's prison; his soul was a captive just set free. Confused and shunning the light, yet rejoicing in his freedom, it passed again over the old-time battlefields.

That wild artless singer, the blackbird, nurtured among starlings, listened mistrustfully to the words that came to his lips. Whence did he derive the power to compel the crowd to listen entranced to his speeches? Whence did he derive the power that forced proud men to their knees, wringing their hands? He trembled before he began to speak, but soon a feeling of quiet confidence came over him. From the depths of his unmeasured suffering rose ceaseless clouds of agonizing words.

Those speeches never got into print. They were hunting cries, blaring horn-blasts, inspiriting, animating, terrifying, harrying. Nothing to take hold of, nothing to reproduce. Lightning flashes and rolling thunder, making the heart quake with gloomy terror. But they were transient, never to be recaptured. One can measure the waterfall to the last drop, one can paint the eddying play of the sea foam, but not the wild, mocking, ever-increasing power of the stream of those speeches.

In the woods that day he asked those assembled if they knew how to serve God.

"As Uriah served his King."

And at once he, the man in the pulpit, became Uriah. He was riding through the wilderness with the King's letter. He was alone there; the desolation terrified him; his thoughts were gloomy. But he smiled as he thought of his life; the wilderness became a flowering field when he remembered her; springs rose out of the earth at the thought of her.

His camel fell down dead. His heart was filled with forebodings of evil. Misfortune, thought he, is a vulture that loves the desert. But he did not turn back; he went on, bearing the King's letter. He trod on thorns, walked among adders and scorpions. He was hungry and thirsty. He could see the dark outlines of caravans passing along the desert sands. He did not try to find them; he dared not visit strangers. The bearer of the King's letter must travel alone. In the evenings he could see the herdsmen's white tents, alluring as the sight of his wife's smiling abode. In fancy he saw white veils waving to him. He turned away from the tents into the solitude. Woe to him if they stole his King's letter!

Stumbling he walks, and suddenly he sees that the spying thieves are pursuing him. He remembers the King's letter, reads it in order to be able to destroy it. The reading renews his courage. "Stand up, thou warrior of Judah!" He does not destroy the letter; he does not give himself up to the robbers. He fights and wins; and then on, on! Through a thousand perils he carried with him his own sentence of death. . . .

It is thus that God's will is to be obeyed, unto blood, unto death. . . .

While Wik was speaking his divorced wife stood listening to him. She had gone out to the forest in the morning, beaming and happy as she leaned on her husband's arm; the perfect matron, respectable in every detail. Her daughter and the journeyman carried the picnic basket; the servant girl followed with the youngest child. All had been contentment, happiness, peace.

Afterwards they had gone off to lie in a thicket, where they ate and drank, handed things to one another, played games and laughed. Never a thought of the past! Conscience slept like an infant that has been fed. Formerly, when her first husband had slunk past her window half-drunk, she had felt thorns piercing her soul.

Later she heard how he had become the idol of the Salvation Army, and the news set her mind completely at rest. Now she had come to hear him. And she understood him too; he was not talking about Uriah, he was telling the story of himself. He was tormenting himself at the thought of his own sacrifice, tearing his own heart to pieces and casting them out among the people. She knew this rider in the wilderness, this conqueror of thieves. And this unabated torture stared at her like an open grave.

Night came on; the woods were free of their human visitors. Farewell, green trees and flowers! Wide heaven, a long farewell! Snakes began to glide about the tufts, toads crept out on the roads. The forest became ugly; all longed to get home, to their stony wilderness, their landscape of the moon. There is the place where it is good for men to be. There perhaps the sorrowing heart might swiftly suffer a change to stone.

Anna Eriksson was giving a party to her old friends. The artisans' wives in the suburb and the poor charwomen came to her house for morning coffee. They were the same that had been with her on the day of her desertion. One was new, Maria Andersson, the Salvation Army Captain.

Anna Eriksson had visited the Salvation Army many times. She had heard her husband—always talking about himself. He disguised his story; she always recognized it. He was Abraham; he was Job; he was Jeremiah, whom the people cast into a well. He was Elisha, whom the children mocked on his way.

That pain seemed to her unfathomable; that grief seemed to borrow all voices, to fashion masks out of all that it met. She did not realize that her husband was talking himself into sanity, that within him played and smiled the joy of his creative power.

She had dragged her daughter with her to the Army. Her daughter had not wanted to go. She was strict, demure and dutiful. Youth had no play in her blood; she was born old.

She had grown up ashamed of her father. She walked upright, stiffly, as though she were saying:

"Behold the daughter of an outcast! See if there is any dust on my dress, any flaw in my behaviour!" Her mother was proud of her; yet sometimes she sighed: "Ah, if my daughter's hands were less white, perhaps her caresses would be warmer!"

The daughter sat among the Army, smiling disdainfully. She despised theatrical performances, and when her father got up to speak, she wanted to go. Anna Eriksson seized her hand in a grip like a vise, and the girl sat still. The stream of words began to rush over her, but that which spoke to her was not so much his words as her mother's hand.

That hand was suffering agonies from cramp; it lay in hers limply, as if it were dead; it clenched itself wildly, hot with fever. Her mother's face betrayed nothing; only her hand suffered and fought.

The old speaker was describing the martyrdom of silence. A friend of Jesus lay sick and his sisters sent word to Him. But His hour was not yet come; for the sake of God's Kingdom Lazarus had to die.

He suffered now all the doubts, all the calumnies in the world, to come murmuring down upon Christ. He described His agony—tortured by His own sympathy. He passed through the valley of death, He too, like Lazarus. And yet He had to keep silent.

He had only to say one word to win back his friends' respect. He remained silent. He had to listen to the sisters' complaints. He told them the truth in words which they did not understand. His enemies mocked Him.

And so on: more and more soul-stirring.

Anna Eriksson's hand still lay in her daughter's. It made confession and acknowledged:

"That man there has himself endured the martyrdom of silence. He is accused unjustly. With a single word he could have set himself free."

The daughter went home with her mother. They walked in silence. The young girl's face was like stone. She was thinking, trying to recover all that memory could tell her. Her mother watched her anxiously: What did she know?

On the following day Anna Eriksson had her coffee party. The talk

touched merrily on the day's market, on the price of clogs, on the pil-
fering of servants. The women chattered and laughed. They poured their
coffee into the saucers. They were peaceful and light-hearted. Anna
Eriksson could not understand how it was that she used to fear them,
that she had always believed that these women would condemn her.

As soon as they had got their second cups and were sitting contentedly
with the coffee trembling on the brims, and plates were piled with white
bread, Anna began to address them. Her speech was a trifle ceremonious,
but her voice was calm.

"Youth is improvident. A girl who marries without due consideration
of what awaits her may get into great trouble. Who fared worse than I?"

They all knew that; they had been with her and mourned with her.

"Youth is irrational. It is ashamed to say what should be said; it dare
not speak out for fear of what people may say. She who does not speak
out at the proper time may repent it for the rest of her life."

All agreed on the truth of this.

She had heard Wik yesterday, as often before. Now she must tell them
all something about him. A painful agitation came over her as she thought
of what he had suffered for her sake. Yet it seemed to her that he, who
was old, ought to have known better than to take her, a young girl, as
his wife.

"I did not dare say this when I was young, but he left out of kindness,
believing that I wanted Eriksson. I have his letter about it."

She read them the letter, while a becoming tear came gliding down
her cheek.

"He had been blinded by his jealousy—that was all. There was nothing
between Eriksson and me at that time; it was four years before we were
married. But I must tell you now, for Wik is too kind to be misunderstood; he did not desert his wife and child from wantonness, but with
the best intentions. I wish this to be known everywhere. Perhaps Captain
Andersson will read out the letter at the Army meeting. I want him to be
exonerated. Oh, I know I have kept silent too long, but it is not easy to
sacrifice oneself for a drunkard. Now it is another matter."

The women sat still, almost petrified. Anna Eriksson faltered in her
speech and said with a faint smile:

"And now I suppose you ladies will never come to see me again?"

"Oh, of course we shall! Why, you were so young! There was nothing you could possibly help. It was his fault for imagining things."

She smiled slightly. These then were the cruel beaks that would have torn her to pieces! The truth was no more dangerous than lying. The young men's feet were not waiting outside her door.

Did she, or did she not know that her eldest daughter, that very morning, had left her home and gone to live with her father?

The sacrifice that Matts Wik had made to save his wife's good name became known. He was admired: he was laughed at. His letter was read out before the Army; there were some that wept with emotion. People came and pressed his hand in the street. His daughter moved into his house.

On the following evenings he did not speak at the meetings; he was conscious of no call. On one occasion they invited him to speak. He went up on the platform, folded his hands and began.

After saying a few words he stopped in amazement. He could not recognize his voice. Where was the lion's tone, the rushing northern gale, the stream of words? He could not understand it, he could not understand it.

He tottered backwards.

"I can't do it," he said. "God is not yet giving me the power to speak." He sat down on the bench and bowed his head in his hands. He concentrated all his thinking-power on finding out first what he wanted to talk about. But used he to ponder in the old days? Was he able to ponder now? His thoughts seemed to swim round with him.

Perhaps it would be all right if he got up again, took his usual place and began with his customary prayer? He tried it. His face became an ashen grey; people watched him; cold sweat dripped from his forehead. Not a word came to his lips.

He sat down in his place and wept, groaning heavily. His gift had been taken from him. He tried to speak, tried it inaudibly, to himself. What was there to speak about? His sorrow had been taken from him. He had nothing to say to people that he was not allowed to say to them. He had no secret to disguise. He had no necessity to invent, so his invention had deserted him.

That was the agony of death, a struggle for life. He wanted to keep what was already gone. He wanted to have his sorrow back so that he might be able to speak again. His sorrow was gone; he could not get it back.

Like a drunken man he reeled forward to the platform, again and again. He stammered out some meaningless words; he recited, like a lesson learned by heart, what he had heard others say. He tried to imitate himself. He searched for devotional glances, sudden gasps and trembling silences. He could find nothing; he had been robbed of the source of his happiness.

He sank back into the darkness, cursing the thought that his speeches had converted his wife and daughter. He had owned the most priceless of treasures, and lost it. His pain was terrible, but it is not to such sorrow that genius owes its life.

He was a painter without hands, a singer who had lost his voice. All his speeches had been about his own sorrow; what should he speak about now?

He prayed.

"O God, since honour is dumb and misunderstanding eloquent, give me back misunderstanding! Since happiness is dumb and grief eloquent, give me back my grief!"

But his crown had been taken from him. He sat there, more wretched than the most wretched, for he had tumbled down from the heights of life. He was a fallen king.

—Translated from the Swedish by C. D. LOCOCK

THOMAS MANN

A Weary Hour

Sometimes not the worst among our works comes into being as the result of an incitement from the outside, as the execution of an order. The following short story I wrote in 1905 on the occasion of the hundredth anniversary of Friedrich Schiller's death, and on the order of a periodical. Strangely enough, it was the satirical weekly *Simplicissimus*. There this little work was published first and created an impression unexpectedly favorable for its author. Since then it has been reprinted frequently and has been translated into many languages. Its hero is the great German poet who is represented here working at Jena, deep in the night, on his tragedy "Wallenstein." The man to whom his thoughts wander repeatedly in loving jealousy, is Goethe.

THOMAS MANN

HE GOT up from the table, his little, fragile writing-desk; got up as though desperate, and with hanging head crossed the room to the tall, thin, pillar-like stove in the opposite corner. He put his hands to it; but the hour was long past midnight and the tiles were nearly stone cold. Not getting even this little comfort that he sought, he leaned his back against them and, coughing, drew together the folds of his dressing-gown, between which a draggled lace shirt-frill stuck out; he snuffed hard through his nostrils to get a little air, for as usual he had a cold.

It was a particular, a sinister cold, which scarcely ever quite disappeared. It inflamed his eyelids and made the flanges of his nose all raw; in his head and limbs it lay like a heavy, sombre intoxication. Or was this cursed confinement to his room, to which the doctor had weeks ago condemned him, to blame for all his languor and flabbiness? God knew if it was the right thing—perhaps so, on account of his chronic catarrh and the spasms in his chest and belly. And for weeks on end now, yes, weeks, bad weather had reigned in Jena—hateful, horrible weather, which he felt in every nerve of his body—cold, wild, gloomy. The December wind roared in the stove-pipe with a desolate god-forsaken sound—he might have been wandering on a heath, by night and storm, his soul full

46

of unappeasable grief. Yet this close confinement—that was not good either; not good for thought, nor for the rhythm of the blood, where thought was engendered.

The six-sided room was bare and colourless and devoid of cheer: a whitewashed ceiling wreathed in tobacco smoke, walls covered with trellis-patterned paper and hung with silhouettes in oval frames, half a dozen slender-legged pieces of furniture; the whole lighted by two candles burning at the head of the manuscript on the writing-table. Red curtains draped the upper part of the window-frames; mere festooned wisps of cotton they were, but red, a warm, sonorous red, and he loved them and would not have parted from them; they gave a little air of ease and charm to the bald unlovely poverty of his surroundings. He stood by the stove and blinked repeatedly, straining his eyes across at the work from which he had just fled: that load, that weight, that gnawing conscience, that sea which to drink up, that frightful task which to perform, was all his pride and all his misery, at once his heaven and his hell. It dragged, it stuck, it would not budge—and now again. . . ! It must be the weather; or his catarrh, or his fatigue. Or was it the work? Was the thing itself an unfortunate conception, doomed from its beginning to despair?

He had risen in order to put a little space between him and his task, for physical distance would often result in improved perspective, a wider view of his material and a better chance of conspectus. Yes, the mere feeling of relief on turning away from the battlefield had been known to work like an inspiration. And a more innocent one than that purveyed by alcohol or strong, black coffee.

The little cup stood on the side-table. Perhaps it would help him out of the impasse? No, no, not again! Not the doctor only, but somebody else too, a more important somebody, had cautioned him against that sort of thing—another person, who lived over in Weimar and for whom he felt a love which was a mixture of hostility and yearning. That was a wise man. He knew how to live and create; did not abuse himself; was full of self-regard.

Quiet reigned in the house. There was only the wind, driving down the Schlossgasse and dashing the rain in gusts against the panes. They were all asleep—the landlord and his family, Lotte and the children. And here he stood by the cold stove, awake, alone, tormented; blinking across at the work in which his morbid self-dissatisfaction would not let him believe.

His neck rose long and white out of his stock and his knock-kneed legs showed between the skirts of his dressing-gown. The red hair was smoothed back from a thin, high forehead; it retreated in bays from his veined white temples and hung down in thin locks over the ears. His nose was aquiline, with an abrupt whitish tip; above it the well-marked line of the brows almost met. They were darker than his hair and gave the deep-set, inflamed eyes a tragic, staring look. He could not breathe through his nose; so he opened his thin lips and made the freckled, sickly cheeks look even more sunken thereby.

No, it was a failure, it was all hopelessly wrong. The army ought to have been brought in! The army was the root of the whole thing. But it was impossible to present it before the eyes of the audience—and was art powerful enough thus to enforce the imagination? Besides, his hero was no hero; he was contemptible, he was frigid. The situation was wrong, the language was wrong; it was a dry pedestrian lecture, good for a history class, but as drama absolutely hopeless!

Very good, then, it was over. A defeat. A failure. Bankruptcy. He would write to Körner, the good Körner, who believed in him, who clung with childlike faith to his genius. He would scoff, scold, beseech —this friend of his; would remind him of the *Carlos,* which likewise had issued out of doubts and pains and rewritings and after all the anguish turned out to be something really fine, a genuine masterpiece. But times were changed. Then he had been a man still capable of taking a strong, confident grip on a thing and giving it triumphant shape. Doubts and struggles? Yes. And ill he had been, perhaps more ill than now; a fugitive, oppressed and hungry, at odds with the world; humanly speaking, a beggar. But young, still young! Each time, however low he had sunk, his resilient spirit had leaped up anew; upon the hour of affliction had followed the feeling of triumphant self-confidence. That came no more, or hardly ever, now. There might be one night of glowing exaltation—when the fires of his genius lighted up an impassioned vision of all that he might do if only they burned on; but it had always to be paid for with a week of enervation and gloom. Faith in the future, his guiding star in times of stress, was dead. Here was the despairing truth: the years of need and nothingness, which he had thought of as the painful testing-

time, turned out to have been the rich and fruitful ones; and now that
a little happiness had fallen to his lot, now that he had ceased to be an
intellectual freebooter and occupied a position of civic dignity, with office
and honours, wife and children—now he was exhausted, worn out. To
give up, to own himself beaten—that was all there was left to do. He
groaned; he pressed his hands to his eyes and dashed up and down the
room like one possessed. What he had just thought was so frightful that
he could not stand still on the spot where he had thought it. He sat down
on a chair by the further wall and stared gloomily at the floor, his clasped
hands hanging down between his knees.

His conscience . . . how loudly his conscience cried out! He had
sinned, sinned against himself all these years, against the delicate instrument that was his body. Those youthful excesses, the nights without sleep,
the days spent in close, smoke-laden air, straining his mind and heedless
of his body; the narcotics with which he had spurred himself on—all that
was now taking its revenge.

And if it did—then he would defy the gods, who decreed the guilt and
then imposed the penalties. He had lived as he had to live, he had not
had time to be wise, not time to be careful. Here in this place in his chest,
when he breathed, coughed, yawned, always in the same spot came this
pain, this piercing, stabbing, diabolical little warning; it never left him,
since that time in Erfurt five years ago when he had catarrhal fever and
inflammation of the lungs. What was it warning him of? Ah, he knew
only too well what it meant—no matter how the doctor chose to put him
off. He had no time to be wise and spare himself, no time to save his
strength by submission to moral laws. What he wanted to do he must do
soon, do quickly, do today.

And the moral laws? . . . Why was it that precisely sin, surrender
to the harmful and the consuming, actually seemed to him more moral
than any amount of wisdom and frigid self-discipline? Not that constituted morality: not the contemptible knack of keeping a good conscience
—rather the struggle and compulsion, the passion and pain.

Pain . . . how his breast swelled at the word! He drew himself up
and folded his arms; his gaze, beneath the close-set auburn brows, was
kindled by the nobility of his suffering. No man was utterly wretched so
long as he could still speak of his misery in high-sounding and noble
words. One thing only was indispensable; the courage to call his life by

large and fine names. Not to ascribe his sufferings to bad air and consti-
pation; to be well enough to cherish emotions, to scorn and ignore the
material. Just on this one point to be naïve, though in all else sophisticated. To believe, to have strength to believe, in suffering. . . . But he
did believe in it; so profoundly, so ardently, that nothing which came
to pass with suffering could seem to him either useless or evil. His glance
sought the manuscript, and his arms tightened across his chest. Talent
itself—was that not suffering? And if the manuscript over there, his
unhappy effort, made him suffer, was not that quite as it should be—a
good sign, so to speak? His talents had never been of the copious, ebullient
sort; were they to become so he would feel mistrustful. That only happened with beginners and bunglers, with the ignorant and easily satisfied,
whose life was not shaped and disciplined by the possession of a gift.
For a gift, my friends down there in the audience, a gift is not anything
simple, not anything to play with; it is not mere ability. At bottom it is
a compulsion; a critical knowledge of the ideal, a permanent dissatisfaction, which rises only through suffering to the height of its powers. And
it is to the greatest, the most unsatisfied, that their gift is the sharpest
scourge. Not to complain, not to boast; to think modestly, patiently of
one's pain; and if not a day in the week, not even an hour, be free from
it—what then? To make light and little of it all, of suffering and achievement alike—that was what made a man great.

He stood up, pulled out his snuff-box and sniffed eagerly, then suddenly
clasped his hands behind his back and strode so briskly through the room
that the flames of the candles flickered in the draught. Greatness, distinction, world conquest and an imperishable name! To be happy and
unknown, what was that by comparison? To be known—known and
loved by all the world—ah, they might call that egotism, those who knew
naught of the urge, naught of the sweetness of this dream! Everything
out of the ordinary is egotistic, in proportion to its suffering. "Speak for
yourselves," it says, "ye without mission on this earth, ye whose life is
so much easier than mine!" And Ambition says: "Shall my sufferings be
vain? No, they must make me great!"

The nostrils of his great nose dilated, his gaze darted fiercely about
the room. His right hand was thrust hard and far into the opening of his
dressing-gown, his left arm hung down, the fist clenched. A fugitive
red played in the gaunt cheeks—a glow thrown up from the fire of his

artistic egoism: that passion for his own ego, which burnt unquenchably
in his being's depths. Well he knew it, the secret intoxication of this love!
Sometimes he needed only to contemplate his own hand, to be filled with
the liveliest tenderness towards himself, in whose service he was bent
on spending all the talent, all the art that he owned. And he was right so
to do, there was nothing base about it. For deeper still than his egoism
lay the knowledge that he was freely consuming and sacrificing himself
in the service of a high ideal, not as a virtue, of course, but rather out of
sheer necessity. And this was his ambition: that no one should be greater
than he who had not also suffered more for the sake of the high ideal.
No one. He stood still, his hand over his eyes, his body turned aside in
a posture of shrinking and avoidance. For already the inevitable thought
had stabbed him: the thought of that other man, that radiant being, so
sense-endowed, so divinely unconscious, that man over there in Weimar,
whom he loved and hated. And once more, as always, in deep disquiet,
in feverish haste, there began working within him the inevitable sequence
of his thoughts: he must assert and define his own nature, his own art,
against that other's. Was that other greater? Wherein, then, and why?
If he won, would he have sweated blood to do so? If he lost, would his
downfall be a tragic sight? He was no hero, no; a god, perhaps. But it
was easier to be a god than a hero. Yes, things were easier for him. He
was wise, he was deft, he knew how to distinguish between knowing and
creating; perhaps that was why he was so blithe and carefree, such an
effortless and gushing spring! But if creation was divine, knowledge was
heroic, and he who created in knowledge was hero as well as god.

The will to face difficulties. . . . Did anyone realize what discipline
and self-control it cost him to shape a sentence or follow out a hard train
of thought? For after all he was ignorant, undisciplined, a slow, dreamy
enthusiast. One of Cæsar's letters was harder to write than the most ef-
fective scene—and was it not almost for that very reason higher? From
the first rhythmical urge of the inward creative force towards matter,
towards the material, towards casting in shape and form—from that to
the thought, the image, the word, the line—what a struggle, what a
Gethsemane! Everything that he wrote was a marvel of yearning after
form, shape, line, body; of yearning after the sunlit world of that other
man who had only to open his godlike lips and straightway call the bright
unshadowed things he saw by name!

And yet—and despite that other man. Where was there an artist, a poet, like himself? Who like him created out of nothing, out of his own breast? A poem was born as music in his soul, as pure, primitive essence, long before it put on a garment of metaphor from the visible world. History, philosophy, passion were no more than pretexts and vehicles for something which had little to do with them, but was at home in orphic depths. Words and conceptions were keys upon which his art played and made vibrate the hidden strings. No one realized. The good souls praised him, indeed, for the power of feeling with which he struck one note or another. And his favourite note, his final emotional appeal, the great bell upon which he sounded his summons to the highest feasts of the soul— many there were who responded to its sound. Freedom! But in all their exaltation, certainly he meant by the word both more and less than they did. Freedom—what was it? A self-respecting middle-class attitude to- wards thrones and princes? Surely not that. When one thinks of all that the spirit of man has dared to put into the word! Freedom from what? After all, from what? Perhaps, indeed, even from happiness, from hu- man happiness, that silken bond, that tender, sacred tie. . . .

From happiness. His lips quivered. It was as though his glance turned inward upon himself; slowly his face sank into his hands. . . . He stood by the bed in the next room, where the flowered curtains hung in mo- tionless folds across the window, and the lamp shed a bluish light. He bent over the sweet head on the pillow . . . a ringlet of dark hair lay across her cheek, that had the paleness of pearl; the childlike lips were open in slumber. "My wife! Beloved, didst thou yield to my yearning and come to me to be my joy? And that thou art. . . . Lie still and sleep; nay, lift not those sweet shadowy lashes and gaze up at me, as sometimes with thy great, dark, questioning, searching eyes. I love thee so! By God I swear it. It is only that sometimes I am tired out, struggling at my self- imposed task, and my feelings will not respond. And I must not be too utterly thine, never utterly happy in thee, for the sake of my mission."

He kissed her, drew away from her pleasant, slumbrous warmth, looked about him, turned back to the outer room. The clock struck; it warned him that the night was already far spent; but likewise it seemed to be mildly marking the end of a weary hour. He drew a deep breath, his lips closed firmly; he went back and took up his pen. No, he must not brood, he was too far down for that. He must not descend into chaos; or at least he must not stop there. Rather out of chaos, which is fullness, he must draw up to the light whatever he found there fit and ripe for form. No brooding! Work! Define, eliminate, fashion, complete!

And complete it he did, that effort of a labouring hour. He brought it to an end, perhaps not to a good end, but in any case to an end. And being once finished, lo, it was also good. And from his soul, from music and idea, new works struggled upward to birth and, taking shape, gave out light and sound, ringing and shimmering, and giving hint of their infinite origin—as in a shell we hear the sighing of the sea whence it came.

—Translated from the German by H. T. LOWE-PORTER

LLOYD DOUGLAS

The Road to Jerusalem

Among the many story units in Mr. Douglas's widely distributed novel of the garment of Christ, THE ROBE, this section (which occurs near the beginning of the book) has been often mentioned for republication.

EARLY in the morning, the militia from Minoa broke camp and prepared to complete the journey into the city. Demetrius had been glad to see the sunrise. It was the first night, since he had been the slave of Marcellus, that he had slept beyond the sound of his master's call. After the encampment had been made, late yesterday afternoon, the Legate and four of the senior staff officers had decided to ride on into Jerusalem. None of the slaves, except the Syrian camel-boys, had been taken along. Demetrius, left to guard Marcellus' effects, had slept in the ornate tent alone.

Rousing at dawn, he had drawn the curtains aside, and was amazed at the tide of traffic already on the highway; processions of heavily laden camels, rhythmically lifting their haughty noses at every step; long trains of pack-asses, weighted with clumsy burdens; men, women, children, slaves—all carrying bundles and baskets and boxes of every shape and size. The pestilential dust rolled high.

With the speed and skill of long experience, the contingent from Minoa leveled their camp, rolled up the tents, packed the stores, and took to the road. Proudly the uniformed company marched down the highway, the pilgrims scurrying to the stone fences at the trumpet's strident command. But the pack-train did not fare so well. The laden asses from Minoa, not carrying banners or blowing trumpets or wearing the Roman uniform, were considered by the travelers as of no more importance than a similar number of pack-asses from anywhere else.

Melas, ever anxious to display large knowledge to the newcomer, seemed by Demetrius' efforts to keep his string of donkeys in hand. It was quite apparent that the unkempt Thracian was enjoying the Co-

54

rinthian's dilemma. At a disadvantage in Demetrius' company, the odds were all in his favor now. He wasn't as cultured as the Legate's slave, but when it came to managing pack-asses in a dense crowd of uncivil travelers, Melas was in a position to offer counsel. He looked back and grinned patronizingly.

It was a peculiar crowd! In Rome, on a feast-day, there was plenty of rough jostling and all manner of rudeness. Arrogant charioteers thought nothing of driving their broad iron wheels over the bare feet of little children. People on foot treated one another with almost incredible discourtesy. One favorite method of making one's way through a crowd was to dive in with both hands full of mud and filth scooped up from the street. Few cared to debate the right of way with persons thus armed. No—Rome had won no prizes for the politeness of her gala-day multitudes. But, in spite of her forthright brutality, Rome—on such occasions —was hilarious. Her crowds sang, cheered, laughed! They were mischievous, merciless, vulgar—but they were merry!

There was no laughter in this pilgrim throng that crowded the widening avenue today. This was a tense, impassioned, fanatical multitude; its voice a guttural murmur as if each man canted his own distresses, indifferent to the mumbled yearnings of his neighbors. On these strained faces was an expression of an almost terrifying earnestness and a quality of pietistic zeal that seemed ready to burst forth into wild hysteria; faces that fascinated Demetrius by the very ugliness of their unabashed contortions. Not for all the wealth of the world would he have so bared his private griefs and longings to the cool stare of the public. But apparently the Jews didn't care who read their minds. All this, thought the Corinthian was what the sight of their holy city had done to their emotions.

Suddenly, for no reason at all that Demetrius could observe, there was a wave of excitement. It swept down over the sluggish swollen stream of zealots like a sharp breeze. Men all about him were breaking loose from their families, tossing their packs into the arms of their overburdened children, and racing forward toward some urgent attraction. Far up ahead the shouts were increasing in volume, spontaneously organizing into a concerted reiterated cry; a single, magic word that drove the multitude into a frenzy.

Unable to keep his footing in this onrushing tide, Demetrius dragged and pushed his stubborn charges to the roadside where Melas stood savagely battering his tangled donkeys over their heads with his heavy cudgel.

"Crack them on the nose!" yelled Melas.

"I have no club," shouted Demetrius. "You take them!"

Melas, pleased to have his competency appealed to, grasped the lead-strap to the other string of donkeys and began laying on the discipline with a practiced hand. While he was thus engaged, Demetrius set off after the hurrying crowd, forcing his way with the others until the congestion was too dense for further progress. Wedged tight against his arm and grinning up into his face, was another Greek, older but smaller than himself; a slave, easily recognizable by the slit in his ear-lobe. Impudently, the ill-scented little fellow bent about for a glimpse of Demetrius' ear, and, having assured himself of their social equality, laughed fraternally.

"Athens!" he announced, by way of introduction.

"Corinth!" returned Demetrius crisply. "Do you know what is going on?"

"They're yelling something about a king. That's all I can make of it."

"Understand their language?"

"A little. Just what I've picked up on these trips. We come up every year with a load of spices."

"You think they've got somebody up front who wants to be their king? Is that it?"

"Looks like it. They keep howling another word that I don't know—Messiah: The man's name, maybe."

Demetrius impulsively turned about, thrust a shoulder into the steaming mass, and began pushing through to the side of the road, followed closely—to his distaste—by his diminutive countryman. All along the way, men were recklessly tearing branches from the palms that bordered the residential thoroughfare, indifferent to the violent protests of the property-owners. Running swiftly among the half-crazed vandals, the Greeks arrived at the front of the procession and jammed their way into it.

Standing on tiptoe for an instant in the swaying crowd, Demetrius caught a fleeting glimpse of the obvious center of interest, a brown-haired, bareheaded, well-favored Jew. A tight little circle had been left open for the slow advance of the shaggy white donkey on which he rode. It instantly occurred to Demetrius that this coronation project was an impromptu affair for which no preparation had been made. Certainly there had been no effort to bedeck the pretender with any royal regalia. He was clad in a simple brown mantle with no decorations of any kind, and the handful of men who tried to shield him from the pressure of the throng, wore the commonest sort of country garb.

The huzzas of the crowd were deafening. It was evident that these passionate zealots had all gone stark-raving mad! Paulus had drawn a very clear picture of the Jew's mood on these occasions of the holy festival commemorative of an ancient flight from bondage.

Again Demetrius, regaining his lost balance, stretched to full height for another look at the man who had somehow evoked all this wild adulation. It was difficult to believe that this was the sort of person who could be expected to inflame a mob into some audacious action. Instead of receiving the applause with an air of triumph, or even of satisfaction, the unresponsive man on the white donkey seemed sad about the whole affair. He looked as if he would gladly have had none of it.

"Can you see him?" called the little Athenian, who had stuck fast in the sticky-hot pack an arm's length away.

Demetrius nodded, without turning his head.

"Old man?"

"No—not very," answered Demetrius, candidly remote.

"What does he look like?" shouted the Athenian impatiently.

Demetrius shook his head—and his hand too—signaling that he couldn't be bothered now, especially with questions as hard to answer as this one.

"Look like a king?" yelled the little Greek, guffawing boisterously.

Demetrius did not reply. Tugging at his impounded garments, he crushed his way forward. The surging mass, pushing hard from the rear, now carried him on until he was borne almost into the very hub of the procession that edged along, step by step, keeping pace with the plodding donkey.

Conspicuous in the inner circle, as if they constituted the mysterious man's retinue, were the dozen or more who seemed stunned by the event that obviously had taken them by surprise. They too were shouting, erratically, but they wore puzzled faces and appeared anxious that their honored friend would measure up a little more heroically to the demands of this great occasion.

It was quite clear now to Demetrius that the incident was accidental. It was quite understandable, in the light of Paulus' irreverent comments on the Passover celebration. All these proud, poverty-cursed, subjugated pilgrims, pressing toward their ancient shrine, would be on the alert for any movement that savored of revolt against their rapacious foe. It needed only the shout—"Messiah!"—and they would spring into action without pausing to ask questions. That explained it, believed Demetrius. In any case, whoever had started this wild pandemonium, it was apparent that it lacked the hero's approbation.

The face of the enigmatic Jew seemed weighted with an almost insupportable burden of anxiety. The eyes, narrowed as if in resigned acceptance of some inevitable catastrophe, stared straight ahead toward Jerusalem. Perhaps the man, intent upon larger responsibilities far removed from this pitiful little coronation farce, wasn't really hearing the racket at all.

So deeply absorbed had Demetrius become in his wide-eyed study of the young Jew's face, that he too was beginning to be unmindful of the general clamor and confusion. He moved along with inching steps, slanting his body against the weight of the pressing crowd, so close now to the preoccupied rider that with one stride he could have touched him.

Now there was a temporary blocking of the way and the noisy procession came to a complete stop. The man on the white donkey straightened, as if roused from a reverie, drew a deep sigh and slowly turned his head. Demetrius watched, with parted lips and a pounding heart.

The meditative eyes, drifting about over the excited multitude, seemed to carry a sort of wistful compassion for these helpless victims of an aggression for which they thought he had a remedy. Everyone was shouting, shouting—all but the Corinthian slave, whose throat was so dry he couldn't have shouted, who had no inclination to shout, who wished they would all be quiet, quiet! It wasn't the time or place for shouting. Quiet! This man wasn't the sort of person one shouted at or shouted for. Quiet! That was what this moment called for—Quiet!

Gradually the brooding eyes moved over the crowd until they came to rest on the strained, bewildered face of Demetrius. Perhaps, he wondered, the man's gaze halted there because he alone—in all this welter of hysteria—refrained from shouting. His silence singled him out. The eyes calmly appraised Demetrius. They neither widened nor smiled; but, in some indefinable manner, they held Demetrius in a grip so firm it was almost a physical compulsion. The message they communicated was something other than sympathy, something more vital than friendly concern; a sort of stabilizing power that swept away all such negations as slavery, poverty, or any other afflicting circumstance. Demetrius was suffused with the glow of this curious kinship. Blind with sudden tears, he elbowed through the throng and reached the roadside. The uncouth Athenian, bursting with curiosity, inopportunely accosted him.

"See him—close up?" he asked.

Demetrius nodded; and, turning away, began to retrace his steps toward his abandoned duty.

"Crazy?" persisted the Athenian, trudging alongside.

"No."

"King?"

"No," muttered Demetrius soberly, "not a king."

"What is he, then?" demanded the Athenian, piqued by the Corinthian's aloofness.

"I don't know," mumbled Demetrius, in a puzzled voice, "but—he is something more important than a king."

THOMAS WOLFE

God's Lonely Man

The first draft of "God's Lonely Man" was written probably as early as 1930 and was entitled "On Loneliness at Twenty-Three." Later versions dropped that title, no doubt because Tom realized by then that loneliness was not a phenomenon confined to youth. The piece does not belong to any one period of his career or writing, but rather to his whole life. Written in the first person, it is straight autobiography. It is a very beautiful and tragic work, and proves, I think, if further proof is needed beyond his books themselves, that Tom was a deeply religious man in the unconventional and truest sense of the word. Of his profound loneliness, none who knew him well can be in any doubt. But it was at the end a wise and friendly sort of loneliness, a self-contained loneliness, a loneliness that had long since accepted loneliness as the inescapable condition of life.

During the final period preceding his death these qualities in him were unmistakable. He was working very hard that last year, harder probably than he had ever worked before, harder certainly than I had ever seen anyone else work. In a way I think his work had become a refuge from his loneliness. He rarely went out to see people any more. I doubt if there were more than half a dozen whom he saw with any frequency during that entire year. He saw me once or twice each week because we were working together. He saw regularly Miss Elizabeth Nowell, his agent, for the same reason, and because they were old friends. Beyond that, three or four people now and then—no more except for casual encounters. He had his work to do, and his time was running out.

EDWARD ASWELL*

MY LIFE, more than that of anyone I know, has been spent in solitude and wandering. Why this is true, or how it happened, I cannot say; yet it is so. From my fifteenth year—save for a single interval—I have lived about as solitary a life as a modern man can have. I mean by this that the number of hours, days, months, and years that I have spent alone

---

* Mr. Aswell, editor of Harper & Bros., was a close friend of Thomas Wolfe and the literary editor of his late book. He included "God's Lonely Man" in the posthumous collection THE HILLS BEYOND, published by Harper & Bros. in 1941.

has been immense and extraordinary. I propose, therefore, to describe the experience of human loneliness exactly as I have known it.

The reason that impels me to do this is not that I think my knowledge of loneliness different in kind from that of other men. Quite the contrary. The whole conviction of my life now rests upon the belief that loneliness, far from being a rare and curious phenomenon, peculiar to myself and to a few other solitary men, is the central and inevitable fact of human existence. When we examine the moments, acts, and statements of all kinds of people—not only the grief and ecstasy of the greatest poets, but also the huge unhappiness of the average soul, as evidenced by the innumerable strident words of abuse, hatred, contempt, mistrust, and scorn that forever grate upon our ears as the manswarm passes us in the streets—we find, I think, that they are all suffering from the same thing. The final cause of their complaint is loneliness.

But if my experience of loneliness has not been different in kind from that of other men, I suspect it has been sharper in intensity. This gives me the best authority in the world to write of this, our general complaint, for I believe I know more about it than anyone of my generation. In saying this, I am merely stating a fact as I see it, though I realize that it may sound like arrogance or vanity. But before anyone jumps to that conclusion, let him consider how strange it would be to meet with arrogance in one who has lived alone as much as I. The surest cure for vanity is loneliness. For, more than other men, we who dwell in the heart of solitude are always the victims of self-doubt. Forever and forever in our loneliness, shameful feelings of inferiority will rise up suddenly to overwhelm us in a poisonous flood of horror, disbelief, and desolation, to sicken and corrupt our health and confidence, to spread pollution at the very root of strong, exultant joy. And the eternal paradox of it is that if a man is to know the triumphant labor of creation, he must for long periods resign himself to loneliness, and suffer loneliness to rob him of the health, the confidence, the belief and joy which are essential to creative work.

To live alone as I have lived, a man should have the confidence of God, the tranquil faith of a monastic saint, the stern impregnability of Gibraltar. Lacking these, there are times when anything, everything, all or nothing, the most trivial incidents, the most casual words, can in an instant strip me of my armor, palsy my hand, constrict my heart with frozen horror, and fill my bowels with the gray substance of shuddering impotence. Sometimes it is nothing but a shadow passing on the sun; sometimes nothing but the torrid milky light of August, or the naked, sprawling ugliness and squalid decencies of streets in Brooklyn fading in the weary vistas of that milky light and evoking the intolerable misery of countless drab and nameless lives. Sometimes it is just the barren horror of raw concrete, or the heat blazing on a million beetles of machinery darting through the torrid streets, or the cindered weariness of parking spaces, or the slamming smash and racket of the El, or the driven manswarm of the earth, thrusting on forever in exacerbated fury, going nowhere in a hurry.

Again, it may be just a phrase, a look, a gesture. It may be the cold, disdainful inclination of the head with which a precious, kept, exquisite princeling of Park Avenue acknowledges an introduction, as if to say: "You are nothing." Or it may be a sneering reference and dismissal by a critic in a high-class weekly magazine. Or a letter from a woman saying I am lost and ruined, my talent vanished, all my efforts false and worthless—since I have forsaken the truth, vision, and reality which are so beautifully her own.

And sometimes it is less than these—nothing I can touch or see or hear or definitely remember. It may be so vague as to be a kind of hideous weather of the soul, subtly compounded of all the hunger, fury, and impossible desire my life has ever known. Or, again, it may be a half-forgotten memory of the cold wintry red of waning Sunday afternoons in Cambridge, and of a pallid, sensitive, æsthetic face that held me once in earnest discourse on such a Sunday afternoon in Cambridge, telling me that all my youthful hopes were pitiful delusions and that all my life would come to naught, and the red and waning light of March was reflected on the pallid face with a desolate impotence that instantly quenched all the young ardors of my blood.

Beneath the evocations of these lights and weathers, and the cold, disdainful words of precious, sneering, and contemptuous people, all of the joy and singing of the day goes out like an extinguished candle, hope seems lost to me forever, and every truth that I have ever found and known seems false. At such a time the lonely man will feel that all the evidence of his own senses has betrayed him, and that nothing really lives and moves on earth but creatures of the death-in-life—those of the cold, constricted heart and the sterile loins, who exist forever in the red waning light of March and Sunday afternoon.

All this hideous doubt, despair, and dark confusion of the soul a lonely man must know, for he is united to no image save that which he creates himself, he is bolstered by no other knowledge save that which he can gather for himself with the vision of his own eyes and brain. He is sustained and cheered and aided by no party, he is given comfort by no creed, he has no faith in him except his own. And often that faith deserts him, leaving him shaken and filled with impotence. And then it seems to him that his life has come to nothing, that he is ruined, lost, and broken past redemption, and that morning—bright, shining morning, with its promise of new beginnings—will never come upon the earth again as it did once.

He knows that dark time is flowing by him like a river. The huge, dark wall of loneliness is around him now. It encloses and presses in upon him, and he cannot escape. And the cancerous plant of memory is feeding at his entrails, recalling hundreds of forgotten faces and ten thousand vanished days, until all life seems as strange and insubstantial as a dream. Time flows by him like a river, and he waits in his little room like a creature held captive by an evil spell. And he will hear, far off, the murmurous drone of the great earth, and feel that he has been forgotten, that his powers are wasting from him while the river flows, and that all his life has come to nothing. He feels that his strength is gone, his power withered, while he sits there drugged and fettered in the prison of his loneliness.

Then suddenly, one day, for no apparent reason, his faith and his belief in life will come back to him in a tidal flood. It will rise up in him with a jubilant and invincible power, bursting a window in the world's great wall and restoring everything to shapes of deathless brightness. Made miraculously whole and secure in himself, he will plunge once more into the triumphant labor of creation. All his old strength is his again: he knows what he knows, he is what he is, he has found what he has found. And he will say the truth that is in him, speak it even though the whole world deny it, affirm it though a million men cry out that it is false.

At such a moment of triumphant confidence, with this feeling in me, I dare now assert that I have known Loneliness as well as any man, and will now write of him as if he were my very brother, which he is. I will paint him for you with such fidelity to his true figure that no man who reads will ever doubt his visage when Loneliness comes to him hereafter.

The most tragic, sublime, and beautiful expression of human loneliness which I have ever read is the Book of Job; the grandest and most philosophical, Ecclesiastes. Here I must point out a fact which is so much at variance with everything I was told as a child concerning loneliness and the tragic underweft of life that, when I first discovered it, I was astounded and incredulous, doubting the overwhelming weight of evidence that had revealed it to me. But there it was, as solid as a rock, not to be shaken or denied; and as the years passed, the truth of this discovery became part of the structure of my life.

The fact is this: the lonely man, who is also the tragic man, is invariably the man who loves life dearly—which is to say, the joyful man. In these statements there is no paradox whatever. The one condition implies the other, and makes it necessary. The essence of human tragedy is in loneliness, not in conflict, no matter what the arguments of the theater may assert. And just as the great tragic writer (I say, "the tragic writer" as distinguished from "the writer of tragedies," for certain nations, the Roman and French among them, have had no great tragic writers, for Vergil and Racine were none, but rather great writers of tragedy): just as the great tragic writer—Job, Sophocles, Dante, Milton, Swift, Dostoevski—has always been the lonely man, so has he also been the man who loved life best and had the deepest sense of joy. The real quality and substance of human joy is to be found in the works of these great tragic writers as nowhere else in all the records of man's life upon the earth. In proof of this, I can give here one conclusive illustration:

In my childhood, any mention of the Book of Job evoked instantly in my mind a long train of gloomy, gray, and unbrokenly dismal associations. This has been true, I suspect, with most of us. Such phrases as "Job's comforter," and "the patience of Job," and "the afflictions of Job," have become part of our common idiom and are used to refer to people whose woes seem uncountable and unceasing, who have suffered long and silently, and whose gloom has never been interrupted by a ray of hope or joy. All these associations had united to make for me a picture of the Book of Job that was grim, bleak, and constant in its misery. When I first read it as a child, it seemed to me that the record of Job's tribulations was relieved only by a kind of gloomy and unwilling humor—a humor not intended by the author, but supplied by my own exasperation, for my childish sense of proportion and justice was at length so put upon by this dreary tidal flood of calamities that I had to laugh in protest.

But any reader of intelligence and experience who has read that great book in his mature years will realize how false such a picture is. For the Book of Job, far from being dreary, gray, and dismal, is woven entire, more than any single piece of writing I can recall, from the sensuous, flashing, infinitely various, and gloriously palpable material of great poetry; and it wears at the heart of its tremendous chant of everlasting sorrow the exulting song of everlasting joy.

In this there is nothing strange or curious, but only what is inevitable and right. For the tragic writer knows that joy is rooted at the heart of sorrow, that ecstasy is shot through with the sudden crimson thread of pain, that the knife-thrust of intolerable desire and the wild, brief glory of possession are pierced most bitterly, at the very instant of man's greatest victory, by the premonitory sense of loss and death. So seen and so felt, the best and worst that the human heart can know are merely different aspects of the same thing, and are interwoven, both together, into the tragic web of life.

It is the sense of death and loneliness, the knowledge of the brevity of his days, and the huge impending burden of his sorrow, growing always, never lessening, that makes joy glorious, tragic, and unutterably precious to a man like Job. Beauty comes and passes, is lost the moment that we touch it, can no more be stayed or held than one can stay the flowing of a river. Out of this pain of loss, this bitter ecstasy of brief having, this fatal glory of the single moment, the tragic writer will therefore make a song for joy. That, at least, he may keep and treasure always. And his song is full of grief, because he knows that joy is fleeting, gone the instant that we have it, and that is why it is so precious, gaining its full glory from the very things that limit and destroy it.

He knows that joy gains its glory out of sorrow, bitter sorrow, and man's loneliness, and that it is haunted always with the certainty of death, dark death, which stops our tongues, our eyes, our living breath, with the twin oblivions of dust and nothingness. Therefore a man like Job will make a chant for sorrow, too, but it will still be a song for joy as well, and one more strange and beautiful than any other that man has ever sung:

Hast thou given the horse strength? hast thou clothed his neck with thunder?
Canst thou make him afraid as a grasshopper? the glory of his nostrils is
terrible.

He paweth in the valley, and rejoiceth in his strength: he goeth on to meet
the armed men.

He mocketh at fear, and is not affrighted; neither turneth he back from the
sword.

The quiver rattleth against him, the glittering spear and the shield.

He swalloweth the ground with fierceness and rage; neither believeth he
that it is the sound of the trumpet.

He saith among the trumpets, Ha, ha; and he smelleth the battle afar off,
the thunder of the captains, and the shouting.

That is joy—joy solemn and triumphant; stern, lonely, everlasting joy,
which has in it the full depth and humility of man's wonder, his sense
of glory, and his feeling of awe before the mystery of the universe. An
exultant cry is torn from our lips as we read the lines about that glorious
horse, and the joy we feel is wild and strange, lonely and dark like death,
and grander than the delicate and lovely joy that men like Herrick and
Theocritus described, great poets though they were.

Just as the Book of Job and the sermon of Ecclesiastes are, each in its
own way, supreme histories of man's loneliness, so do all the books of
the Old Testament, in their entirety, provide the most final and profound literature of human loneliness that the world has known. It is
astonishing with what a coherent unity of spirit and belief the life of
loneliness is recorded in those many books—how it finds its full expression in the chants, songs, prophecies, and chronicles of so many men, all
so various, and each so individual, each revealing some new image of
man's secret and most lonely heart, and all combining to produce a single
image of his loneliness that is matchless in its grandeur and magnificence.

Thus, in a dozen books of the Old Testament—in Job, Ecclesiastes,
and the Song of Solomon; in Psalms, Proverbs, and Isaiah; in words of
praise and words of lamentation; in songs of triumph and in chants of
sorrow, bondage, and despair; in boasts of pride and arrogant assertion,
and in stricken confessions of humility and fear; in warning, promise,
and in prophecy; in love, hate, grief, death, loss, revenge, and resignation;
in wild, singing jubilation and in bitter sorrow—the lonely man has

wrought out in a swelling and tremendous chorus the final vision of his life.

The total, all-contributary unity of this conception of man's loneliness in the books of the Old Testament becomes even more astonishing when we begin to read the New. For, just as the Old Testament becomes the chronicle of the life of loneliness, the gospels of the New Testament, with the same miraculous and unswerving unity, become the chronicle of the life of love. What Christ is saying always, what he never swerves from saying, what he says a thousand times and in a thousand different ways, but always with a central unity of belief, is this: "I am my Father's son, and you are my brothers." And the unity that binds us all together, that makes this earth a family, and all men brothers and the sons of God, is love.

The central purpose of Christ's life, therefore, is to destroy the life of loneliness and to establish here on earth the life of love. The evidence to support this is clear and overwhelming. It should be obvious to everyone that when Christ says: "Blessed are the poor in spirit: for theirs is the kingdom of heaven," "Blessed are they that mourn: for they shall be comforted," "Blessed are the meek: for they shall inherit the earth," "Blessed are they which do hunger and thirst after righteousness: for they shall be filled," "Blessed are the merciful: for they shall obtain mercy," and "Blessed are the pure in heart: for they shall see God"— Christ is not here extolling the qualities of humility, sorrow, meekness, righteousness, mercy, and purity as virtues sufficient in themselves, but he promises to men who have these virtues the richest reward that men were ever offered.

And what is that reward? It is a reward that promises not only the inheritance of the earth, but the kingdom of heaven as well. It tells men that they shall not live and die in loneliness, that their sorrow will not go unassuaged, their prayers unheard, their hunger and thirst unfed, their love unrequited: but that, through love, they shall destroy the walls of loneliness forever; and even if the evil and unrighteous of this earth shall grind them down into the dust, yet if they bear all things meekly and with love, they will enter into a fellowship of joy, a brotherhood of love, such as no man on earth ever knew before.

Such was the final intention of Christ's life, the purpose of his teaching. And its total import was that the life of loneliness could be destroyed forever by the life of love. Or such, at least, has been the meaning which

I read into his life. For in these recent years when I have lived alone so much, and known loneliness so well, I have gone back many times and read the story of this man's words and life to see if I could find in them a meaning for myself, a way of life that would be better than the one I had. I read what he had said, not in a mood of piety or holiness, not from a sense of sin, a feeling of contrition, or because his promise of a heavenly reward meant very much to me. But I tried to read his bare words nakedly and simply, as it seems to me he must have uttered them, and as I have read the words of other men—of Homer, Donne, and Whitman, and the writer of Ecclesiastes—and if the meaning I have put upon his words seems foolish or extravagant, childishly simple or banal, mine alone are not different from what ten million other men have thought, I have only set it down here as I saw it, felt it, found it for myself, and have tried to add, subtract, and alter nothing.

And now I know that though the way and meaning of Christ's life is a far, far better way and meaning than my own, yet I can never make it mine; and I think that this is true of all the other lonely men that I have seen or known about—the nameless, voiceless, faceless atoms of this earth as well as Job and Everyman and Swift. And Christ himself, who preached the life of love, was yet as lonely as any man that ever lived. Yet I could not say that he was mistaken because he preached the life of love and fellowship, and lived and died in loneliness; nor would I dare assert his way was wrong because a billion men have since professed his way and never followed it.

I can only say that I could not make his way my own. For I have found the constant, everlasting weather of man's life to be, not love, but loneliness. Love itself is not the weather of our lives. It is the rare, the precious flower. Sometimes it is the flower that gives us life, that breaches the dark walls of all our loneliness and restores us to the fellowship of life, the family of the earth, the brotherhood of man. But sometimes love is the flower that brings us death; and from it we get pain and darkness; and the mutilations of the soul, the maddening of the brain, may be in it.

How or why or in what way the flower of love will come to us, whether with life or death, triumph or defeat, joy or madness, no man on this earth can say. But I know that at the end, forever at the end for us—the houseless, homeless, doorless, driven wanderers of life, the lonely men—there waits forever the dark visage of our comrade, Loneliness.

But the old refusals drop away, the old avowals stand—and we who were dead have risen, we who were lost are found again, and we who sold the talent, the passion, and belief of youth into the keeping of the fleshless dead, until our hearts were corrupted, our talent wasted, and our hope gone, have won our lives back bloodily, in solitude and darkness; and we know that things will be for us as they have been, and we see again, as we saw once, the image of the shining city. Far flung, and blazing into tiers of jeweled light, it burns forever in our vision as we walk the Bridge, and strong tides are bound round it, and the great ships call. And we walk the Bridge, always we walk the Bridge alone with you, stern friend, the one to whom we speak, who never failed us. Hear:

"Loneliness forever and the earth again! Dark brother and stern friend, immortal face of darkness and of night, with whom the half part of my life was spent, and with whom I shall abide now till my death forever—what is there for me to fear as long as you are with me? Heroic friend, blood-brother of my life, dark face—have we not gone together down a million ways, have we not coursed together the great and furious avenues of night, have we not crossed the stormy seas alone, and known strange lands, and come again to walk the continent of night and listen to the silence of the earth? Have we not been brave and glorious when we were together, friend? Have we not known triumph, joy, and glory on this earth—and will it not be again with me as it was then, if you come back to me? Come to me, brother, in the watches of the night. Come to me in the secret and most silent heart of darkness. Come to me as you always came, bringing to me again the old invincible strength, the deathless hope, the triumphant joy and confidence that will storm the earth again."

LEO TOLSTOY

Where Love Is

A maker of parables and a teller of tales, whose force of simple and universal utterance came from the heart, Count Leo Tolstoy left a large body of short stories of which it has been said they represent "the natural secretion of a life carried out to its moral ultimate." "Where Love Is, There God Is Also" appeared in its first English translation in 1885.

IN A certain town there lived a shoemaker named Martin Avdeitch. He lived in a basement room which possessed but one window. This window looked onto the street, and through it a glimpse could be caught of the passers-by. It is true that only their legs could be seen, but that did not matter, as Martin could recognize people by their boots alone. He had lived here for a long time, and so had many acquaintances. There were very few pairs of boots in the neighbourhood which had not passed through his hands at least once, if not twice. Some he had resoled, others he had fitted with side-pieces, others, again, he had resewn where they were split, or provided with new toe-caps. Yes, he often saw his handiwork through that window. He was given plenty of custom, for his work lasted well, his materials were good, his prices moderate, and his word to be depended on. If he could do a job by a given time it should be done; but if not, he would warn you beforehand rather than disappoint you. Everyone knew Avdeitch, and no one ever transferred his custom from him. He had always been an upright man, but with the approach of old age he had begun more than ever to think of his soul, and to draw nearer to God.

His wife had died while he was still an apprentice, leaving behind her a little boy of three. This was their only child, indeed, for the two elder ones had died previously. At first Martin thought of placing the little fellow with a sister of his in the country, but changed his mind, thinking: "My Kapitoshka would not like grow up in a strange family, so I will keep him by me." Then Avdeitch finished his apprenticeship, and went to live in lodgings with his little boy. But God had not seen fit to give Avdeitch happiness in his children. The little boy was just growing up and beginning to help his father and to be a pleasure to him, when he fell ill, was put to bed, and died after a week's fever.

Martin buried the little fellow and was inconsolable. Indeed, he was so inconsolable that he began to murmur against God. His life seemed so empty that more than once he prayed for death and reproached the Almighty for taking away his only beloved son instead of himself, the old man. At last he ceased altogether to go to church.

Then one day there came to see him an ancient peasant-pilgrim—one who was now in the eighth year of his pilgrimage. To him Avdeitch talked, and then went on to complain of his great sorrow.

"I no longer wish to be a God-fearing man," he said. "I only wish to die. That is all I ask of God. I am a lonely, hopeless man."

"You should not speak like that, Martin," replied the old pilgrim. "It is not for us to judge the acts of God. We must rely, not upon our own understanding, but upon the Divine wisdom. God saw fit that your son should die and that you should live. Therefore it must be better so. If you despair, it is because you have wished to live too much for your own pleasure."

"For what, then, should I live?" asked Martin.

"For God alone," replied the old man. "It is He who gave you life, and therefore it is He for whom you should live. When you come to live for Him you will cease to grieve, and your trials will become easy to bear."

Martin was silent. Then he spoke again.

"But how am I to live for God?" he asked.

"Christ has shown us the way," answered the old man. "Can you read? If so, buy a Testament and study it. You will learn there how to live for God. Yes, it is all shown you there."

These words sank into Avdeitch's soul. He went out the same day, bought a large-print copy of the New Testament, and set himself to read it.

At the beginning Avdeitch had meant only to read on festival days, but when he once began his reading he found it so comforting to the soul that he came never to let a day pass without doing so. On the second occasion he became so engrossed that all the kerosene was burnt away in the lamp before he could tear himself away from the book.

Thus he came to read it every evening, and, the more he read, the more clearly did he understand what God required of him, and in what way he could live for God; so that his heart grew ever lighter and lighter. Once upon a time, whenever he had lain down to sleep, he had been used to moan and sigh as he thought of his little Kapitoshka; but now he only said—"Glory to Thee, O Lord! Glory to Thee! Thy will be done!"

From that time onwards Avdeitch's life became completely changed. Once he had been used to go out on festival days and drink tea in a tavern, and had not denied himself even an occasional glass of *vodka*. This he had done in the company of a boon companion, and, although no drunkard, would frequently leave the tavern in an excited state and talk much nonsense as he shouted and disputed with this friend of his. But now he had turned his back on all this, and his life had become quiet and joyous. Early in the morning he would sit down to his work, and labour through his appointed hours. Then he would take the lamp down from a shelf, light it, and sit down to read. And the more he read, the more he understood, and the clearer and happier he grew at heart.

It happened once that Martin had been reading late. He had been reading those verses in the sixth chapter of the Gospel of St. Luke which run:

"And unto him that smiteth thee on the one cheek offer also the other; and him that taketh away thy cloak forbid not to take thy coat also. Give to every man that asketh of thee; and of him that taketh away thy goods ask them not again. And as ye would that men should do to you, do ye also to them likewise."

Then, further on, he had read those verses where the Lord says:

"And why call ye Me, Lord, Lord, and do not the things which I say? Whosoever cometh to Me and heareth my sayings, and doeth them, I will show you to whom he is like: He is like a man which built an house, and digged deep, and laid the foundation on a rock: and when the flood arose, the storm beat vehemently upon that house, and could not shake it: for it was founded upon a rock. But he that heareth and doeth not, is like a man that without a foundation built an house upon the earth; against which the stream did beat vehemently, and immediately it fell; and the ruin of that house was great."

Avdeitch read these words, and felt greatly cheered in soul. He took off his spectacles, laid them on the book, leaned his elbows upon the table, and gave himself up to meditation. He set himself to measure his own life by those words, and thought to himself:

"Is my house founded upon a rock or upon sand? It is well if it be upon a rock. Yet it seems so easy to me as I sit here alone. I may so easily come to think that I have done all that the Lord has commanded me, and grow careless and—sin again. Yet I will keep on striving, for it is goodly so to do. Help Thou me, O Lord."

Thus he kept on meditating, though conscious that it was time for bed; yet he was loathe to tear himself away from the book. He began to read the seventh chapter of St. Luke, and read on about the centurion, the widow's son, and the answer given to John's disciples; until in time he came to the passage where the rich Pharisee invited Jesus to his house, and the woman washed the Lord's feet with her tears and He justified her. So he came to the forty-fourth verse and read:

"And He turned to the woman, and said unto Simon, Seest thou this woman? I entered into thine house, and thou gavest Me no water for My feet: but she hath washed My feet with tears, and wiped them with the hairs of her head. Thou gavest Me no kiss: but this woman since the time I came in hath not ceased to kiss My feet. My head with oil thou didst not anoint: but this woman hath anointed My feet with ointment."

He read these verses and thought:

" 'Thou gavest Me no water for My feet' . . . 'Thou gavest Me no kiss' . . . 'My head with oil thou didst not anoint' . . ."—and once again he took off his spectacles, laid them on the book, and became lost in meditation.

"I am even as that Pharisee," he thought to himself. "I drink tea and think only of my own needs. Yes, I think only of having plenty to eat and drink, of being warm and clean—but never of entertaining a guest. And Simon too was mindful only of himself, although the guest who had come to visit him was—who? Why, even the Lord Himself! If, then, He should come to visit me, should I receive Him any better?"—and, leaning forward upon his elbows, he was asleep almost before he was aware of it.

"Martin!" someone seemed to breathe in his ear.

He started from his sleep.

"Who is there?" he said. He turned and looked toward the door, but could see no one. Again he bent forward over the table. Then suddenly he heard the words:

"Martin, Martin! Look thou into the street to-morrow, for I am coming to visit thee."

Martin roused himself, got up from the chair, and rubbed his eyes. He did not know whether it was dreaming or awake that he had heard these words, but he turned out the lamp and went to bed.

The next morning Avdeitch rose before daylight and said his prayers. Then he made up the stove, got ready some cabbage soup and porridge, lighted the samovar, slung his leather apron about him, and sat down to his work in the window. He sat and worked hard, yet all the time his thoughts were centred upon the night before. He was of two minds about the vision. At one moment he would think that it must have been his fancy, while the next moment he would find himself convinced that he had really heard the voice. "Yes, it must have been so," he concluded.

As Martin sat thus by the window he kept looking out of it as much as working. Whenever a pair of boots passed with which he was acquainted he would bend down to glance upwards through the window and see their owner's face as well. The doorkeeper passed in new felt boots, and then a water-carrier. Next, an old soldier, a veteran of Nicholas' army, in old, patched boots, and carrying a shovel in his hands, halted close by the window. Avdeitch knew him by his boots. His name was Stepanitch, and he was kept by a neighbouring tradesman out of charity, his duties being to help the doorkeeper. He began to clear away the snow from in front of Avdeitch's window, while the shoemaker looked at him and then resumed his work.

"I think I must be getting into my dotage," thought Avdeitch with a smile. "Just because Stepanitch begins clearing away the snow I at once jump to the conclusion that Christ is about to visit me. Yes, I am growing foolish now, old greybeard that I am."

Yet he had hardly made a dozen stitches before he was craning his neck again to look out of the window. He could see that Stepanitch had placed his shovel against the wall, and was resting and trying to warm himself a little.

"He is evidently an old man now and broken," thought Avdeitch to himself. "He is not strong enough to clear away snow. Would he like some tea, I wonder? That reminds me that the samovar must be ready now."

He made fast his awl in his work and got up. Placing the samovar on the table, he brewed the tea, and then tapped with his finger on the window-pane. Stepanitch turned round and approached. Avdeitch beckoned to him, and then went to open the door.

"Come in and warm yourself," he said. "You must be frozen."

"Christ requite you!" answered Stepanitch. "Yes, my bones are almost cracking."

He came in, shook the snow off himself, and, though tottering on his feet, took pains to wipe them carefully, that he might not dirty the floor.

"Nay, do not trouble about that," said Avdeitch. "I will wipe your boots myself. It is part of my business in this trade. Come you here and sit down, and we will empty this tea-pot together."

He poured out two tumblerfuls, and offered one to his guest; after which he emptied his own into the saucer, and blew upon it to cool it. Stepanitch drank his tumblerful, turned the glass upside down, placed his crust upon it, and thanked his host kindly. But it was plain that he wanted another one.

"You must drink some more," said Avdeitch, and refilled his guest's tumbler and his own. Yet, in spite of himself, he had no sooner drunk his tea than he found himself looking out into the street again.

"Are you expecting anyone?" asked his guest.

"Am—am I expecting anyone? Well, to tell the truth, yes. That is to say, I am, and I am not. The fact is that some words have got fixed in my memory. Whether it was a vision or not I cannot tell, but at all events, my old friend, I was reading in the Gospels last night about Our Little Father Christ, and how He walked this earth and suffered. You have heard of Him, have you not?"

"Yes, yes, I have heard of Him," answered Stepanitch; "but we are ignorant folk and do not know our letters."

"Well, I was reading of how He walked this earth, and how He went to visit a Pharisee, and yet received no welcome from him at the door. All this I read last night, my friend, and then fell to thinking about it—to thinking how some day I too might fail to pay Our Little Father Christ due honour. 'Suppose,' I thought to myself, 'He came to me or to anyone like me? Should we, like the great lord Simon, not know how to receive Him and not go out to meet Him?' Thus I thought, and fell asleep where

I sat. Then as I sat sleeping there I heard someone call my name; and as I raised myself the voice went on (as though it were the voice of someone whispering in my ear): 'Watch thou for me to-morrow, for I am coming to visit thee.' It said that twice. And so those words have got into my head, and, foolish though I know it to be, I keep expecting *Him*— the Little Father—every moment."

Stepanitch nodded and said nothing, but emptied his glass and laid it aside. Nevertheless Avdeitch took and refilled it.

"Drink it up; it will do you good," he said. "Do you know," he went on, "I often call to mind how, when Our Little Father walked this earth, there was never a man, however humble, whom He despised, and how it was chiefly among the common people that He dwelt. It was always with *them* that He walked; it was from among *them*—from among such men as you and I—from among sinners and working folk—that He chose His disciples. 'Whosoever,' He said, 'shall exalt himself, the same shall be abased; and whosoever shall abase himself, the same shall be exalted.' 'You,' He said again, 'call me Lord; yet will I wash your feet.' 'Whosoever,' He said, 'would be chief among you, let him be the servant of all. Because,' He said, 'blessed are the lowly, the peacemakers, the merciful, and the charitable.' "

Stepanitch had forgotten all about his tea. He was an old man, and his tears came easily. He sat and listened, with the tears rolling down his cheeks.

"Oh, but you must drink your tea," said Avdeitch; yet Stepanitch only crossed himself and said the thanksgiving, after which he pushed his glass away and rose.

"I thank you, Martin Avdeitch," he said. "You have taken me in, and fed both soul and body."

"Nay, but I beg of you to come again," replied Avdeitch. "I am only too glad of a guest."

So Stepanitch departed, while Martin poured out the last of the tea and drank it. Then he cleaned the crockery, and sat down again to his work by the window—to the stitching of a back-piece. He stitched away, yet kept on looking through the window—looking for Christ, as it were —and ever thinking of Christ and His works. Indeed, Christ's many sayings were never absent from Avdeitch's mind.

Two soldiers passed the window, the one in military boots, and the other in civilian. Next, there came a neighbouring householder, in polished goloshes; then a baker with a basket. All of them passed on. Presently a woman in woollen stockings and rough country shoes approached the window, and halted near the buttress outside it. Avdeitch peered up at her from under the lintel of his window, and could see that she was a plain-looking, poorly-dressed woman and had a child in her arms. It was in order to muffle the child up more closely—little though she had to do it with!—that she had stopped near the buttress and was now standing there with her back to the wind. Her clothing was ragged and fit only for summer, and even from behind his window-panes Avdeitch could hear the child crying miserably and its mother vainly trying to soothe it. Avdeitch rose, went to the door, climbed the steps, and cried out: "My good woman, my good woman!"

She heard him and turned round.

"Why need you stand there in the cold with your baby?" he went on. "Come into my room, where it is warm, and where you will be able to wrap the baby up more comfortably than you can do here. Yes, come in with you."

The woman was surprised to see an old man in a leather apron and with spectacles upon his nose calling out to her, yet she followed him down the steps, and they entered his room. The old man led her to the bedstead.

"Sit you down here, my good woman," he said. "You will be near the stove, and can warm yourself and feed your baby."

"Ah, but I have no milk left in my breast," she replied. "I have had nothing to eat this morning." Nevertheless she put the child to suck.

Avdeitch nodded his head approvingly, went to the table for some bread and a basin, and opened the stove door. From the stove he took and poured some soup into the basin, and drew out also a bowl of porridge. The latter, however, was not yet boiling, so he set out only the soup, after first laying the table with a cloth.

"Sit down and eat, my good woman," he said, "while I hold your baby. I have had little ones of my own, and know how to nurse them."

The woman crossed herself and sat down, while Avdeitch seated himself upon the bedstead with the baby. He smacked his lips at it once or twice, but made a poor show of it, for he had no teeth left. Consequently the baby went on crying. Then he bethought him of his finger, which he wriggled to and fro towards the baby's mouth and back again—without, however, actually touching the little one's lips, since the finger was blackened with work and sticky with shoemaker's wax. The baby contemplated the finger and grew quiet—then actually smiled. Avdeitch was delighted. Meanwhile the woman had been eating her meal, and now she told him, unasked, who she was and whither she was going.

"I am a soldier's wife," she said, "but my husband was sent to a distant station eight months ago, and I have heard nothing of him since. At first I got a place as cook, but when the baby came they said they could not do with it and dismissed me. That was three months ago, and I have got nothing since, and have spent all my savings. I tried to get taken as a wet nurse, but no one would·have me, for they said I was too thin. I have just been to see a tradesman's wife where our grandmother is in service. She had promised to take me on, and I quite thought that she would, but when I arrived to-day she told me to come again next week. She lives a long way from here, and I am quite worn out and have tired my baby for nothing. Thank Heaven, however, my landlady is good to me, and gives me shelter for Christ's sake. Otherwise I should not have known how to bear it all."

Avdeitch sighed and said: "But have you nothing warm to wear?"

"Ah, sir," replied the woman, "although it is the time for warm clothes I had to pawn my last shawl yesterday for two *grivenki*."

Then the woman returned to the bedstead to take her baby, while Avdeitch rose and went to a cupboard. There he rummaged about, and presently returned with an old jacket.

"Here," he said. "It is a poor old thing, but it will serve to cover you."

The woman looked at the jacket, and then at the old man. Then she took the jacket and burst into tears. Avdeitch turned away, and went creeping under the bedstead, whence he extracted a box and pretended to rummage about in it for a few moments; after which he sat down again before the woman.

Then the woman said to him: "I thank you in Christ's name, good grandfather. Surely it was He Himself who sent me to your window. Otherwise I should have seen my baby perish with the cold. When I first came out the day was warm, but now it has begun to freeze. But He, Our Little Father, had placed you in your window, that you might see me in my bitter plight and have compassion upon me."

Avdeitch smiled and said: "He did indeed place me there: yet, my poor woman, it was for a special purpose that I was looking out."

Then he told his guest, the soldier's wife, of his vision, and how he had heard a voice foretelling that to-day the Lord Himself would come to visit him.

"That may very well be," said the woman as she rose, took the jacket, and wrapped her baby in it. Then she saluted him once more and thanked him.

"Also, take this in Christ's name," said Avdeitch, and gave her a two-*grivenka* piece with which to buy herself a shawl. The woman crossed herself, and he likewise. Then he led her to the door and dismissed her.

When she had gone Avdeitch ate a little soup, washed up the crockery again, and resumed his work. All the time, though, he kept his eye upon the window, and as soon as ever a shadow fell across it he would look up to see who was passing. Acquaintances of his came past, and people whom he did not know, yet never anyone very particular.

Then suddenly he saw something. Opposite his window there had stopped an old pedlar-woman, with a basket of apples. Only a few of the apples, however, remained, so that it was clear that she was almost sold out. Over her shoulder was slung a sack of shavings, which she must have gathered near some new building as she was going home. Apparently, her shoulder had begun to ache under their weight, and she therefore wished to shift them to the other one. To do this, she balanced her basket of apples on the top of a post, lowered the sack to the pavement, and began shaking up its contents. As she was doing this, a boy in a ragged cap appeared from somewhere, seized an apple from the basket, and tried to make off. But the old woman, who had been on her guard, managed to turn and seize the boy by the sleeve, and although he struggled and tried to break away, she clung to him with both hands, snatched his cap off, and finally grasped him by the hair. Thereupon the youngster began to shout and abuse his captor. Avdeitch did not stop to make fast his awl, but threw his work down upon the floor, ran to the door, and went stumbling up the steps—losing his spectacles as he did so. Out into the street he ran, where the old woman was still clutching the boy by the hair and threatening to take him to the police, while the boy, for his part, was struggling in the endeavour to free himself.

"I never took it," he was saying. "What are you beating me for? Let me go."

Avdeitch tried to part them as he took the boy by the hand and said:

"Let him go, my good woman. Pardon him for Christ's sake."

"Yes, I will pardon him," she retorted, "but not until he has tasted a new birch-rod. I mean to take the young rascal to the police."

But Avdeitch still interceded for him.

"Let him go, my good woman," he said. "He will never do it again. Let him go for Christ's sake."

The old woman released the boy, who was for making off at once had not Avdeitch stopped him.

"You must beg the old woman's pardon," he said, "and never do such a thing again. I saw you take the apple."

The boy burst out crying, and begged the old woman's pardon as Avdeitch commanded.

"There, there," said Avdeitch. "Now I will give you one. Here you are,"—and he took an apple from the basket and handed it to the boy. "I will pay you for it, my good woman," he added.

"Yes, but you spoil the young rascal by doing that," she objected. "He ought to have received a reward that would have made him glad to stand for a week."

"Ah, my good dame, my good dame," exclaimed Avdeitch. "That may be *our* way of rewarding, but it is not God's. If this boy ought to have been whipped for taking the apple, ought not we also to receive something for our sins?"

The old woman was silent. Then Avdeitch related to her the parable of the master who absolved his servant from the great debt which he owed him, whereupon the servant departed and took his own debtor by the throat. The old woman listened, and also the boy.

"God has commanded us to pardon one another," went on Avdeitch, "or *He* will not pardon us. We ought to pardon all men, and especially the thoughtless."

The old woman shook her head and sighed.

"Yes, that may be so," she said, "but these young rascals are so spoilt already!"

"Then it is for us, their elders, to teach them better," he replied.

"That is what I say myself at times," rejoined the old woman. "I had seven of them once at home, but have only one daughter now." And she went on to tell Avdeitch where she and her daughter lived, and how they lived, and how many grandchildren she had.

"I have only such strength as you see," she said, "yet I work hard, for my heart goes out to my grandchildren—the bonny little things that they are! No children could run to meet me as they do. Aksintka, for instance, will go to no one else. 'Grandmother,' she cries, 'dear grandmother, you are tired' "—and the old woman became thoroughly softened. "Everyone knows what boys are," she added presently, referring to the culprit. "May God go with him!"

She was raising the sack to her shoulders again when the boy darted forward and said:

"Nay, let me carry it, grandmother. It will be all on my way home."

The old woman nodded assent, gave up the sack to the boy, and went away with him down the street. She had quite forgotten to ask Avdeitch for the money for the apple. He stood looking after them, and observing how they were talking together as they went.

Having seen them go, he returned to his room, finding his spectacles— unbroken—on the steps as he descended them. Once more he took up his awl and fell to work, but had done little before he found it difficult to distinguish the stitches, and the lamplighter had passed on his rounds. "I too must light up," he thought to himself. So he trimmed the lamp, hung it up, and resumed his work. He finished one boot completely, and then turned it over to look at it. It was all good work. Then he laid aside his tools, swept up the cuttings, rounded off the stitches and loose ends, and cleaned his awl. Next he lifted the lamp down, placed it on the table, and took his Testament from the shelf. He had intended opening the book at the place which he had marked last night with a strip of leather, but it opened itself at another instead. The instant it did so, his vision of last night came back to his memory, and, as instantly, he thought he heard a movement behind him as of someone moving towards him. He looked round and saw in the shadow of a dark corner what appeared to be figures—figures of persons standing there, yet could not distinguish them clearly. Then the voice whispered in his ear:

"Martin, Martin, dost thou not know Me?"

"Who art Thou?" said Avdeitch.

"Even I!" whispered the voice again. "Lo, it is I!"—and there stepped from the dark corner Stepanitch. He smiled, and then, like the fading of a little cloud, was gone.

"It is I!" whispered the voice again—and there stepped from the same corner the woman with her baby. She smiled, and the baby smiled, and they were gone.

"And it is I!" whispered the voice again—and there stepped forth the old woman and the boy with the apple. They smiled, and were gone.

Joy filled the soul of Martin Avdeitch as he crossed himself, put on his spectacles, and set himself to read the Testament at the place where it had opened. At the top of the page he read:

"For I was an hungred, and ye gave Me meat: I was thirsty, and ye gave Me drink: I was a stranger, and ye took Me in."

And further down the page he read:

"Inasmuch as ye have done it unto one of the least of these my brethren ye have done it unto Me."

Then Avdeitch understood that the vision had come true, and that his Saviour had in very truth visited him that day, and that he had received Him.

HENRY DAVID THOREAU

Solitude

THIS is a delicious evening, when the whole body is one sense, and imbibes delight through every pore. I go and come with a strange liberty in Nature, a part of herself. As I walk along the stony shore of the pond in my shirt-sleeves, though it is cool as well as cloudy and windy, and I see nothing special to attract me, all the elements are unusually congenial to me. The bullfrogs trump to usher in the night, and the note of the whip-poor-will is borne on the rippling wind from over the water. Sympathy with the fluttering alder and poplar leaves almost takes away my breath; yet, like the lake, my serenity is rippled but not ruffled. These small waves raised by the evening wind are as remote from storm as the smooth reflecting surface. Though it is now dark, the wind still blows and roars in the wood, the waves still dash, and some creatures lull the rest with their notes. The repose is never complete. The wildest animals do not repose, but seek their prey now; the fox, and skunk, and rabbit, now roam the fields and woods without fear. They are Nature's watchmen,—links which connect the days of animated life.

When I return to my house I find that visitors have been there and left their cards, either a bunch of flowers, or a wreath of evergreen, or a name in pencil on a yellow walnut leaf or a chip. They who come rarely to the woods take some little piece of the forest into their hands to play with by the way, which they leave, either intentionally or accidentally. One has peeled a willow wand, woven it into a ring, and dropped it on my table. I could always tell if visitors had called in my absence, either by the bended twigs or grass, or the print of their shoes, and generally of what sex or age or quality they were by some slight trace left, as a flower dropped, or a bunch of grass plucked and thrown away, even as far off as the railroad, half a mile distant, or by the lingering odor of a cigar or pipe. Nay, I was frequently notified of the passage of a traveller along the highway sixty rods off by the scent of his pipe.

There is commonly sufficient space about us. Our horizon is never quite at our elbows. The thick woods is not just at our door, nor the pond, but somewhat is always clearing, familiar and worn by us, appropriated and fenced in some way, and reclaimed from Nature. For what reason have I this vast range and circuit, some square miles of unfrequented forest, for my privacy, abandoned to me by men? My nearest neighbor is a mile distant, and no house is visible from any place but the hill-tops within half a mile of my own. I have my horizon bounded by woods all to myself; a distant view of the railroad where it touches the pond on the one hand, and of the fence which skirts the woodland road on the other. But for the most part it is as solitary where I live as on the prairies. It is as much Asia or Africa as New England. I have, as it were, my own sun and moon and stars, and a little world all to myself. At night there was never a traveller passed my house, or knocked at my door, more than if I were the first or last man; unless it were in the spring, when at long intervals some came from the village to fish for pouts,—they plainly fished much more in the Walden Pond of their own natures, and baited their hooks with darkness,—but they soon retreated, usually with light baskets, and left "the world to darkness and to me," and the black kernel of the night was never profaned by any human neighborhood. I believe that men are generally still a little afraid of the dark, though the witches are all hung, and Christianity and candles have been introduced.

Yet I experienced sometimes that the most sweet and tender, the most innocent and encouraging society may be found in any natural object, even for the poor misanthrope and most melancholy man. There can be no very black melancholy to him who lives in the midst of Nature and has his senses still. There was never yet such a storm but it was Æolian music to a healthy and innocent ear. Nothing can rightly compel a simple and brave man to a vulgar sadness. While I enjoy the friendship of the seasons I trust that nothing can make life a burden to me. The gentle

rain which waters my beans and keeps me in the house to-day is not
drear and melancholy, but good for me too. Though it prevents my
hoeing them, it is of far more worth than my hoeing. If it should continue so long as to cause the seeds to rot in the ground and destroy the
potatoes in the low lands, it would still be good for the grass on the
uplands, and, being good for the grass, it would be good for me. Sometimes, when I compare myself with other men, it seems as if I were more
favored by the gods than they, beyond any deserts that I am conscious
of; as if I had a warrant and surety at their hands which my fellows have
not, and were especially guided and guarded. I do not flatter myself, but
if it be possible they flatter me. I have never felt lonesome, or in the
least oppressed by a sense of solitude, but once, and that was a few weeks
after I came to the woods, when, for an hour, I doubted if the near neighborhood of man was not essential to a serene and healthy life. To be
alone was something unpleasant. But I was at the same time conscious
of a slight insanity in my mood, and seemed to foresee my recovery. In
the midst of a gentle rain while these thoughts prevailed, I was suddenly
sensible of such sweet and beneficent society in Nature, in the very pat-
tering of the drops, and in every sound and sight around my house, an
infinite and unaccountable friendliness all at once like an atmosphere
sustaining me, as made the fancied advantages of human neighborhood
insignificant, and I have never thought of them since. Every little pine
needle expanded and swelled with sympathy and befriended me. I was
so distinctly made aware of the presence of something kindred to me,
even in scenes which we are accustomed to call wild and dreary, and
also that the nearest of blood to me and humanest was not a person nor
a villager, that I thought no place could ever be strange to me again.—

> "Mourning untimely consumes the sad;
> Few are their days in the land of the living,
> Beautiful daughter of Toscar."

Some of my pleasantest hours were during the long rainstorms in the
spring or fall, which confined me to the house for the afternoon as well
as the forenoon, soothed by their ceaseless roar and pelting; when an
early twilight ushered in a long evening in which many thoughts had
time to take root and unfold themselves. In those driving northeast rains

which tried the village houses so, when the maids stood ready with mop and pail in front entries to keep the deluge out, I sat behind my door in my little house, which was all entry, and thoroughly enjoyed its protection. In one heavy thunder-shower the lightning struck a large pitch pine across the pond, making a very conspicuous and perfectly regular spiral groove from top to bottom, an inch or more deep, and four or five inches wide, as you would groove a walking-stick. I passed it again the other day, and was struck with awe on looking up and beholding that mark, now more distinct than ever, where a terrific and resistless bolt came down out of the harmless sky eight years ago. Men frequently say to me, "I should think you would feel lonesome down there, and want to be nearer to folks, rainy and snowy days and nights especially." I am tempted to reply too such,—This whole earth which we inhabit is but a point in space. How far apart, think you, dwell the two most distant inhabitants of yonder star, the breadth of whose disk cannot be appreciated by our instruments? Why should I feel lonely? is not our planet in the Milky Way? This which you put seems to me not to be the most important question. What sort of space is that which separates a man from his fellows and makes him solitary? I have found that no exertion of the legs can bring two minds much nearer to one another. What do we want most to dwell near to? Not to many men surely, the depot, the post-office, the bar-room, the meeting-house, the school-house, the grocery, Beacon Hill, or the Five Points, where men most congregate, but to the perennial source of our life, whence in all our experience we have found that to issue, as the willow stands near the water and sends out its roots in that direction. This will vary with different natures, but this is the place where a wise man will dig his cellar. . . . I one evening overtook one of my townsmen, who has accumulated what is called "a handsome property,"—though I never got a *fair* view of it,—on the Walden road, driving a pair of cattle to market, who inquired of me how I could bring my mind to give up so many of the comforts of life. I answered that I was very sure I liked it passably well; I was not joking. And so I went home to my bed, and left him to pick his way through the darkness and the mud to Brighton,—or Bright-town,—which place he would reach some time in the morning.

Any prospect of awakening or coming to life to a dead man makes indifferent all times and places. The place where that may occur is always the same, and indescribably pleasant to all our senses. For the most part we allow only outlying and transient circumstances to make our occasions. They are, in fact, the cause of our distraction. Nearest to all things is that power which fashions their being. *Next* to us the grandest laws are continually being executed. *Next* to us is not the workman whom we have hired, with whom we love so well to talk, but the workman whose work we are.

"How vast and profound is the influence of the subtile powers of Heaven and of Earth!"

"We seek to perceive them, and we do not see them; we seek to hear them, and we do not hear them; identified with the substance of things, they cannot be separated from them."

"They cause that in all the universe men purify and sanctify their hearts, and clothe themselves in their holiday garments to offer sacrifices and oblations to their ancestors. It is an ocean of subtile intelligences. They are everywhere, above us, on our left, on our right; they environ us on all sides."

We are the subjects of an experiment which is not a little interesting to me. Can we not do without the society of our gossips a little while under these circumstances,—have our own thoughts to cheer us? Confucius says truly, "Virtue does not remain as an abandoned orphan; it must of necessity have neighbors."

With thinking we may be beside ourselves in a sane sense. By a conscious effort of the mind we can stand aloof from actions and their consequences; and all things, good and bad, go by us like a torrent. We are not wholly involved in Nature. I may be either the driftwood in the stream, or Indra in the sky looking down on it. I *may* be affected by a theatrical exhibition; on the other hand, I *may not* be affected by an actual event which appears to concern me much more. I only know myself as a human entity; the scene, so to speak, of thoughts and affections; and am sensible of a certain doubleness by which I can stand as remote from myself as from another. However intense my experience, I am conscious of the presence and criticism of a part of me, which, as it were, is not a part of me, but a spectator, sharing no experience, but taking note of it, and that is more I than it is you. When the play, it may be the tragedy, of life is over, the spectator goes his way. It was a kind of fiction, a work of the imagination only, so far as he was concerned. This doubleness may easily make us poor neighbors and friends sometimes.

I find it wholesome to be alone the greater part of the time. To be in company, even the best, is soon wearisome and dissipating. I love to be alone. I never found the companion that was so companionable as solitude.

II

The Vineyard

JOHN COURNOS

The Story of the Stranger

I played with the idea of this story for years before actually writing it, and I dare say that the story grew up subconsciously in me. I should add that the end of the story came only in the writing of it.

JOHN COURNOS

"I HAD been living in Russia for some years—mostly in St. Petersburg and Moscow, and when I had mastered the outlandish tongue sufficiently, it occurred to me that I'd like to see more of the country, particularly the small provincial towns and villages, and the people Tolstoy and Chekhov wrote so much about. I followed Chekhov's advice of travelling in third-class carriages, for that's where one's likely to get to know the simple people of a country. As you know, first-class passengers are generally too haughty to enter into conversation with a stranger, and there's nothing to be learned by travelling in first-class carriages in this country or any other.

"It was while on the way from Moscow to Nijni-Novgorod that a prosperous peasant got into my compartment. He was well about forty, tall and healthy, with a long dark beard, and he was well dressed in peasant fashion. Russians do not stand on ceremony. We plunged at once into conversation, and it wasn't long before he called me 'Brother'!

"When lunch time came he opened a parcel and, spreading its contents on a newspaper, begged me to join him in a repast. Being an Englishman and a stranger, I politely refused, but on his repeated insistence I yielded, rather gladly I must admit, for I was getting hungry, and the things spread out before me looked appetizing. 'There's plenty for us both,' he said. 'I always take enough for two, so that if I meet a stranger on the way he can share with me. It is not good to live alone and to eat alone. I've done a good piece of business in lumber hereabouts, and am on my way home to wife and little ones, and I've brought a little present for each!' He pointed to a large clean sack he had fetched into the compartment with him . . . 'And what brings you this way, brother?'

"I had already explained to him that I was an Englishman, and, in answer to his questions, told him a great deal about my country which astonished him, sometimes pleasantly, more often unpleasantly. 'That's not good, brother,' he would say, as when for example I told him about the huge factories and the immense slums and all that sort of thing. 'People are not meant to live like that. God has meant people to live by their hands, by the sweat of their brows, as the Book says. It's the work of Antichrist! . . . And are the people happy?' he asked. 'I don't think they're either happy or unhappy,' I said. 'They work hard and some of them have their small pleasures. As for happiness, that's a different thing!' 'So that's it!' he went on saying, scratching his head as Russians do when they're perplexed. 'Happiness lies in faith. Do your people have faith?' 'They have many beautiful churches,' I said, 'and men go to them, but mostly out of habit, I should say.' 'So that's it,' he went on saying, 'so that's it!' 'And do you have pilgrims as we do who forsake home and family and all they possess and wander to holy places for Christ's sake?' 'No. We had them about five hundred years ago,' said I, and I told him all about Canterbury, and about the wonderful cathedral there, and how the feet of pilgrims had worn away the paving-stones of the place. 'They must have been happy men,' he said, 'though even among us there are unbelievers who say that such men are out of their wits! Well, maybe they are, but I see it's not they who fleece the poor brother, but the clever ones! But what good is their cleverness, I ask myself, if it stands in the way of their entering the kingdom of God? The only judgment is the Last Judgment. Isn't that so, brother? The miserable sinners will be put into one place, where they can fleece one another to their hearts' content, eh?' 'That will provide an excellent test for their cleverness,' said I, laughing. 'So it will,' he agreed, and also laughed. 'But they will have Satan to deal with, and they will be hard put to fleece *him!* That will be a just punishment. Ha ha ha!' It was then he offered me lunch, and sprang the question at me. 'And what brings you this way, brother?'

"I said, 'I like what I've seen of your people, and I am taking this journey to see how the simple folk live.'

" 'That's fine! What do you say, brother, to getting off with me? It's the next stop. We're a large family—there are seven of us—but there's always room for a stranger. You can stop as long as you like, and I promise you won't go cold or hungry!'

"I was, of course, overjoyed at the opportunity to see peasant life at first-hand, and only too readily agreed. He was hugely delighted, and said: 'We stop at Podevka. There a team will be waiting to take us to Yarkoe, my village, a matter of ten versts or so.'

"Well, at last we got out, and, true to his word, a handsome troika awaited us. I shall never forget that wonderful sleigh ride. The fields were deep with snow drifts, and we passed through forests of pines and firs adorned with snow and ice shining like crystal in the sun. The air was sharp with frost, and crisp. You can have no idea of the exhilaration of a Russian troika going at full speed. An incomprehensible gaiety gets into your blood, and the crack of the whip in the crisp air and the jingle of the bells are a part of that enhantment.

"We passed a smallish town on the way. Here was a white many-domed church, its tiny golden minarets glinting in the sun; a little farther on, a little roadside chapel all lighted up with candles. . . . In some places these roadside chapels are almost as frequent as gasolene stations here. . . . We scarcely emerged from the town than on the very out-skirts we passed between rows of thatched-roofed cottages, and just beyond them on the very edge of this semi-civilized oasis there stood side by side two largish buildings with barred windows. The first was pointed out to me as the county jail; the second, said my host, served as the 'House for Cracked Wits.'

" 'Ah, even here—' I murmured.

" 'Yes,' my host agreed, 'even here. But,' he added, significantly, 'there are always more out than in. And that is as true of the jail, brother. We are miserable sinners, a dark people . . . !'

"We went another five versts or so before the troika slowed down. We turned into a road running between two rows of gigantic firs: straight ahead of us was a hospitable-looking, rambling, well-cared-for, thatched-roofed house, and on both sides were huddled the barns and the threshing-floors and high piles of fire-logs. It was altogether a prosperous-looking place. We drove into the yard and stopped before the door of the house.

"All at once, the place became animated. The driver jumped from his seat, and opened the sleigh-door for us. A young man, one of the farm hands, came sauntering from the barn and greeted his master. The door of the house opened, and a comely, buxom woman of about thirty-five, with a red shawl around her head, appeared, followed by three or four children of various ages between six and twelve.

" 'Well, Marusya, how have things been going?' my host asked.

" 'Not so bad,' replied his wife. 'Only poor Vaska hasn't been himself. He's got the fever or something. He's been crying all day!'

" 'So. . . . I've brought a guest, Marusya!'—She and the children had been studying me with some curiosity. 'He comes from a far country—he's an Englishman—and he's come to see how we Russians live. Give him the large room with the soft bed, that he may see that we are hospitable, God-fearing people. . . . *Bozhe moi*—My God!' he said, turning to me, 'and I don't even know your name!'

" 'Richard Henryovitch, I suppose you'd call me.' The Russians, as you doubtless know, use the patronymic.

" 'And I am Anton Antonovitch,' he said. 'This is my wife, Marusya— and this is my eldest boy, Vladya—and this Artemy—and this is Marta— and this Nactasya. Vaska—he's the baby—is in bed. You can hear him crying. . . . Have you given him anything?' he asked his wife.

" 'Yes, I've soaked some herbs in hot water, and I've given it to him to drink, but he won't stop crying. I've sent for the doctor.'

" 'We're forgetting our guest, Marusya. Get a samovar ready, and a snack to eat.'

"And soon such a hospitable table was spread before me. . . . Well, I won't go into that. . . . The interesting thing I started telling you about happened in the evening. . . .

"It was the eve of some saint's day and there were the blazing logs and lots of candles. And Marusya had prepared quite a feast. It was a place of good cheer. Only that child went on crying. . . . The district doctor— an oldish man who had learned all he knew forty years before and hadn't looked at a medical book or journal since—had been there in the afternoon and given him quinine and a sedative, but both had worked off, and just as we sat down to enjoy our dinner the little fellow started bawling harder than ever. . . . Now Anton Antonovitch, now Marusya, left the table to minister to his wants—without much success. Vaska went on crying. We were all beginning to feel uncomfortable.

"We already had had some *zakuski*—the Russian *hors-d'œuvre*—and a drop of vodka—and were starting on *stchi*—a kind of cabbage soup— when there was a loud knock on the door. Anton Antonovitch went to

open it. A stranger appeared in the doorway. He was tall, and as yet only
the folds of his monk's cassock falling to the ground were visible in the
shadow. But we heard his voice, a deep, melodious bass:—

" 'Do let me in—*radi Khrista*—for Christ's sake!'

" 'Enter, father. Food and shelter await thee.'

"The stranger, emerging from the darkness, paused on the threshold,
surveying the faces of the household. It was the strangest face I'd ever
seen, and as near like a holy man's as I ever expect to see in this life. He
was about forty, he had a handsome long face and a magnificent flowing
beard. His pointed hood fell to his shoulders, and newly-fallen snow,
turned to ice and sparkling like diamonds, clung about his flowing hair,
giving the impression of a halo. And ice crystals formed on his tufted
eyebrows. The strangest thing of all were his eyes. They were genial and
kind, yet burned like two glowing coals with a kind of inner ecstasy.

"Inevitably—as it were, helpless before the stranger—Anton Antonovitch made way for him and bade him sit down in the vacant chair at one
end of the long table. Anton Antonovitch had previously told me that
this vacant chair was always there for the chance wanderer.

"The remarkable stranger was about to sit down when it became apparent that he was listening to the crying of the child.

" 'Is the little boy ill?' he asked. 'He is crying as if he were ill.' How did
he know it was a boy, I asked myself.

" 'Yes,' said my host. 'Poor Vaska has been crying all day long. The
doctor's been here and quieted him down for a bit. And now he's crying
again.'

" 'The doctor is for the unbeliever,' said the stranger, with a contemptuous shrug. 'But the Orthodox should heal with faith and the laying on
of hands. . . . Let me see the little one,' he added in a commanding
voice. 'Is he in there?' he asked, pointing to the closed door whence the
cries came.

"While we all watched with baited breaths, Anton Antonovitch—as
it were, submitting—went before the stranger, opening the door for him
and standing aside to let him pass. The room into which the door opened
was dark. 'Would you like a candle?' the host asked. 'No,' replied the
other. 'Haven't you heard it said, "I am the Light . . ." and again, "The
light shineth in the darkness, but the darkness comprehendeth it
not . . ." ?'

" 'A healer,' whispered Marusya to me. 'May God grant that he puts Vaska right!'

"We were all, including the children, awed by the stranger's presence, and waited for what would happen. No one dared follow him into the dark room. We heard murmurs as of a holy chant or a prayer. . . . Barely a minute elapsed when the shrill cries of Vaska suddenly ceased. The stranger, smiling benignly, re-emerged quietly, closing the door behind him.

" 'A miracle!' we all thought to ourselves.

" 'He's asleep,' said the stranger. 'Let him sleep. . . . And you, good woman, don't worry about the little fellow,' he said, turning to Marusya, who had a worried look on her face. 'Your little son is quite all right now, the pain and fever have left him. They shall not come back again . . . I promise you. . . . Blessed be He in whose Name we exorcise the griefs and aches of the living and help bring to pass the Kingdom of Heaven on earth! . . . And now let us break bread and drink wine—for there is wisdom in bread and wine not understood by unbelievers. But we Orthodox men shall live in Jesus Christ and He in us through atonement and sacrifice. Amen!'

" 'Amen!' repeated after him Anton Antonovitch, his wife, and the eldest of the children.

"And the stranger drank a small glass of wine. . . . Then he broke some bread and dipped his spoon into the *stchi.*

"For a while we ate in silence. I was intensely fascinated, as you may suppose; feeling rather uncomfortable too—rather out of place, I should say. The stranger glanced at me once or twice—not exactly unkindly, but with curiosity—as if he detected the fact that I didn't belong there, in spite of my disguise in the shape of a Russian embroidered shirt buttoned askew across the chest. . . .

" 'Who's this?' He suddenly turned to the host, indicating me.

" 'He's a stranger, father, and he's come a long way, across land and water, to see how we Orthodox men live.'

" 'Well, he's come to the right place,' said the stranger, dryly. 'The world is full of unbelievers, and Christ with bleeding feet is walking across the travailing Russian earth. . . . The young man will learn a great deal here.'

" 'I trust so, father,' said I, scarcely knowing what else to say.

"He suddenly laughed—for the first time, and his strange eyes lighted up as at some recollection. 'I've lived as a novice in a lonely monastery in the far North—Archangel-way. And there is a marvellous old picture there painted by some ancient monk whose name has been forgotten. The picture is called "The Last Judgment." Upon a golden throne in golden sunlit clouds the Russian Christ sits surrounded by winged angels. And below Him on the earth are those on whom He sits in judgment divided in two camps. . . . A marvellous picture. . . . On one side are the saints and the good men judged worthy of the Kingdom of God, on the other are the sinners condemned to eternal perdition. . . . All the saints and good men are Orthodox Russians. . . . All the sinners are foreigners. . . . Englishmen, I think. Ha ha ha!' He laughed immoderately. I laughed too, even though the joke was at my expense. Still, I was pleased. Our saint was human. . . . His humour was 'That touch of nature' that Shakespeare speaks of. It restored my confidence in myself, I was beginning to feel more at home.

" 'They say that in your land,' the stranger said, 'men no longer walk on bare feet and that men are beginning to ride in carriages that go by themselves without horses; and that there are even men who are learning to fly in the air in iron machines built to look like great birds; and that you have boxes in which you shut a man's voice, so that when the man's not there you can hear him sing or speak as if he were there! Is that the truth?'

" 'Yes, father, that's the truth!'

" 'That's bad! Bad! It's Antichrist at work!' he said, with a fierce gusto. 'Black magic. Yes, black magic. Men are turning to Antichrist. . . . Let me tell you what I saw at the Fair at Nijni-Novgorod. . . . I saw a magician standing up on a box. . . . He was a German, I think, or a Swede, though he jabbered our tongue almost as well as an Orthodox Russian. There was a big crowd round him and he was showing them tricks—such tricks! Black magic, I call it. . . . He called upon men in the crowd to give him their watches. A dozen or so were handed up to him. And what do you think he did? He put all these watches in one little heap on a stone block and, with a hammer, smashed them all into bits right before their eyes. Then he put the kerchief on the block, untied it, and called upon all who gave their watches to come and claim their property.

And just imagine it—there were all the watches just as before—the works going and keeping time up to the minute. . . .

"There was a priest there in the crowd, a tall meagre fellow as thin as a tallow-candle and the light of God in his eyes, and he in a fury about it all. He started to exhort the crowd about black magic, and called the man a blasphemer, and challenged him to show that he wasn't a servant of Antichrist. The magician laughed, and said if the priest could show any better tricks than he, why didn't he show them? 'Yes,' shouted the crowd. 'Show us a better trick, if you can!' The priest, a fine honest fellow, took him up. He called for the watches, and the same fools came forward to give them up. The priest piled them up all in one heap as the other chap had done, and took the same hammer and with a single blow smashed them into smithereens. Then, with the bits before him, he began to talk to the crowd in this wise:—

" 'What do you folks want watches for? To keep time, you will say. What's the good of keeping time? What's a minute, an hour, a day, or even a year in eternity? You have daylight—the sun—to tell you when it's time to labour; you have night, darkness, the stars and the moon, to tell you that it's time to sup, to pray, and to go to bed. Time was given man to prepare for death—for eternal life. Time was given you that ye might bethink yourselves and repent ere it is too late. What are you doing to prepare for the life to come? When God's hammer has descended on your heads, and ye are as these smashed watches, ye—' 'What about our watches?' some one shouted at the priest. 'What about them?' the priest asked. 'When are we going to have them back?' 'Here they are! Come and take them!' 'But they are all in bits!' Came up one hefty fellow, threatening. 'So they are! So they are!' answered the priest. 'Why don't you get this clever fellow to put them together for you?' 'Yes, yes,' shouted some one. 'He's put them together before. See if he can do it now?'

"Well, there was a great hullabaloo, let me tell you, before the thing was over, and the priest nearly lost his life. . . . The police got there in time to save him. . . . As for the magician, he got some rough handling, too, for not being able to do again what he seemed to be able to do so easily before. . . .

" 'Who was right in this affair?' Anton Antonovitch, very much perplexed, ventured to ask his visitor.

" 'The priest, of course!' said the stranger, with no indecision in his voice. 'The man of God spoke for God. The little watch ticks off the minutes, but God ticks off the millenniums. Isn't that so?' The minutes of a man's life tick off as the sands ebb in the sand-glass. . . .'

" 'There's something in what you say, father!'

" 'As for that, look at the children! And didn't the Lord bid us to become as little children? Do little children ever think of time? They don't bother about anything. . . . I cherish the little ones as the source and goal of human being. . . .' And as if to demonstrate his faith in this, he began after dinner to entertain the children by telling the most marvellous tales, and he knew how to tell them, too. . . . The most illiterate peasants often have a natural eloquence rare in more civilized society. . . . The children were in the seventh heaven and clung round him. . . .

"He was in the midst of a particularly fascinating tale, to which the elders as well as the children intently listened, when there came a violent knock on the door, impetuously repeated.

"Anton Antonovitch went to the door and, opening it, peered out. We heard voices out of the darkness. One voice said:—

" 'We are from Brodnoe—from the Insane Asylum. An inmate has escaped this afternoon. And as it's a cold night, we thought he might be asking for shelter hereabouts. Has any one passed this way? . . .'

" 'No one but a holy stranger . . .' answered Anton Antonovitch.

" 'In a monk's clothes?'' asked the second voice.

" 'Yes. . . .'

"Suddenly, two pairs of eyes, in heads leaning forward, peered in. . . .

"Before we knew what had happened two big men ran in and pounced on the stranger. . . . There was a brief scuffle. . . . He was terribly strong. . . . So were they. . . . Presently, his arms tied, they led him out to the waiting sleigh. We were all very much frightened. It was as if we had seen a ghost. . . .

"That wasn't the end of our excitement—for, suddenly, Marusya rose from her chair and, snatching a candle, rushed to the bedroom where Vaska lay in his crib. . . . We all followed, sure that the stranger had strangled him. . . . 'Poor Vaska! My poor Vaska!' cried Marusya. Holding a candle in one hand, she bent over the crib. We all looked. There was Vaska asleep with the most beatific smile on his face. On Marusya shaking him, he opened his eyes and surveyed us with a grave calm. . . . He was a handsome youngster of three. . . . He asked in a sleepy, lisping voice:—

"'Mamma, was there any one here? . . . Such good hands touched me. . . . Who chased him away? . . .'

"'I leave it to you—was the man mad? Or was it we who had gone out of our wits?'

"'He must have escaped from the House of Cracked Wits I pointed out to you!' said Anton Antonovitch, and crossed himself."

PEARL BUCK

Father Andrea

"Father Andrea" was one of the first stories which I ever wrote. Living far inland in China and traveling still farther to places where few white people went, I often came across a lonely priest, serving his flock by day and at night studying the stars for his comfort. I used to wonder why so often they turned to the stars—I suppose because living in a world of poor and troubled people they needed to be reassured of the existence of God. Father Andrea was one of those priests and I saw him die and that is what the story is about.

PEARL BUCK

FATHER ANDREA lived all day for the hours at night when he might study the stars. The days in his parish in the Chinese city were long and crowded, filled with people and voices crying and complaining and demanding, and the nights were short and radiant with the silent, peaceful stars, shining like torches out of the dark purple sky. He could never get enough of them. The hours with his telescope went so quickly that many times he remembered to sleep only when the dawn came up out of the east with such ruddy splendor that the stars faded. But he did not need sleep. He could return to the day refreshed and braced by those hours of study and observation of the golden stars, when the voices that clamored after him all day were asleep for a brief while. "Bless sleep!" he would say to himself, chuckling as he climbed the steps to the tiny observatory he had built on top of the schoolhouse.

He was a small, stout, smiling man, whose exterior revealed nothing of his soft, mystic soul. If one saw only his apple cheeks and dark beard and red, smiling mouth, one would say that he was a lover of visible life. One needed to see his eyes to discover that he was a lover of things unseen. His lips went on smiling even when a leper came twisting and beseeching about his feet, or a wretched slave-girl ran in, cowering and crying, through the gates of the mission. But his eyes, deep set and dark, were often full of tears.

During the day he lifted up the lepers with his hands and washed them and fed them and soothed them and smeared oil upon their wounds. He stood between the slave-girl and her angry, cursing mistress, smiling, waiting, talking in that quiet, ceaseless, murmuring way he had. The woman's angry voice rose above it like a storm above a brook, but sooner or later his gentle, insistent speech won, and she would sit sulking, in answer to his invitation, in the seat of honor at the right of the square table in his little guest-hall, and sip the tea he had asked the servant to bring. And then, with his small, dark, tragic eyes grave above his smiling mouth, he would talk on, praising, suggesting, regretting, hinting gently of the necessity of better things, until in the end the slave went away with the mistress. He would never help people to break away from what held them fast. His great concern always was to help them bear more easily the inevitable yoke that life had placed upon each of them. That was the one thing he was sure of—that there was no getting away from the oppression that life itself brought.

Talking in the morning to the boys in his school, he said one day more earnestly than he had ever before said anything:

"My sons, I will tell you a thing. You think, when you are children, that you will break away from the bondage of your parents and that when you go to school you will be free of them. In school you dream of manhood, when there will be no more teachers for you to obey. But you can never be free! When your immortal souls took on flesh, they became even as the Son of Man was—bound. No man is free—we are not free of one another—we can never be free of God.

"The thing is, not to cry futilely after freedom, but to discover cheerfully how to bear the burden of bondage upon us. Even the stars in heaven are not free. They too must obey the paths of order in law, lest by their wantonness they wreck the universe. You have seen the shooting stars in the sky in summer. They seem beautiful in freedom, a burst of light and splendor against the clouds. But their end is destruction and darkness. It is the stars marching steadily on in their appointed ways which endure to the end."

The little blue-coated Chinese boys stared at him, wondering at the passion in his quiet voice and at the unwonted somberness of his round, smiling face. They did not understand him at all.

All day long he trotted hither and thither about his duty, beginning at dawn by saying mass for a few faithful old women who came decently garbed in their cotton coats and trousers, with black kerchiefs folded about their heads. It troubled him sometimes that they did not grasp much of what he said; his Chinese had never been perfect and it was spoken with a soft Italian elision that could never seize the gutturals firmly. But at last, seeing their patient faces as they fixed their eyes on the Virgin and her Son, he decided that it did not matter what he said so long as they looked at the sacred picture and struggled to think of its meaning.

Before noon he tried to teach a little in the boys' school, but it was a harried business, because at any moment he would be called without to settle some affair of the poor.

"Father, I sold this man tenpence of rice last night and trusted him until this morning for the money, and now, having eaten the rice, he tells me he has nothing."

Two men in coolie trousers, their backs bare and blackened with the sun, stood before him, one angry, one defiant.

"Now, then, was not my stomach empty? Am I to starve when you have food? The revolutionists are coming, and, when they come, all men like you who have rice must give to us who have not, and no talk of money, either!"

The two glared at each other as angry cocks will glare before attacking, and Father Andrea put a hand on each man's arm. His hands told the story begun by his eyes, small, brown, perfectly shaped hands that were broken and wrinkled with the washings and scrubbings he gave them. It was one of the agonies of his life that he could not subdue his flesh to the point of touching dark, unwashed bodies without some shrinking of his spirit. It was an obsession with him to wash his hands again and again, so that they were always scented faintly with carbolic soap. One of his private penances was to go without washing his hands, making himself endure the shuddering when he put them upon a child's head, crusted with the scald of disease. He had schooled himself to touch everything that made him recoil and, seeing his freely moving, kindly, expressive hands, no one dreamed of the inner withdrawal.

So now, one of his hands warm and persuasive upon the arm of each man, he said to the defiant one: "My friend, I know nothing of the revolutionists. But this I do know. My garden needs weeding today, and, if you will weed it, I will gladly pay you wages and, out of the wages, I who know your good heart am sure you will not withhold the tenpence to your neighbor. He is a poor man with children, and you have eaten his rice. It is written, 'If any would not work, neither should he eat.' It is one of the laws of life, which even the revolution cannot rightly change."

Instantly the tension on the two faces faded away, and the two men laughed and showed their white teeth, and Father Andrea laughed, wrinkling his round, rosy face, and went back to his boys. At the end of the day he paid the man double wages. "Take it," he said when the man made a feint of refusal. "Some day I will ask you to work for me again, and on that day I may not have the money by me."

In the afternoon, after his dish of rice and beans and macaroni, he put on his flat black hat and went out and visited the people and drank tea with them and ate the hard-boiled eggs the housewives would cook for him, although his soul loathed them, and listened, smiling, to all that was said. He knew no rich people. These scorned him as a Catholic priest and a foreigner, and he would not have forced his presence upon them even if he could. He went into the low, thatched houses of the poor and into the mat sheds of beggars, and he gave them his money as fast as it came into his hands. Of the great storm gathering without, the storm of the revolution, these people knew nothing, and no more did Father Andrea know. He had read no newspapers for years, and he had no idea of anything that was happening beyond this round of days and splendid nights.

Once a week he allowed himself to remember his own country. On the evening of the seventh day he washed himself and trimmed his dark beard and put a little scent upon his hands, and then he went up into the tiny observatory and sat in an old easy chair he had there. On the other nights he sat upon a stool by the table and took out his pens and papers and his measuring instruments and in his small, accurate handwriting he made notes which he sent to his Superior in Siccawei. Through all these years of evenings he had gradually become one of the chief of a group of astronomers in the Far East, although he did not know it. To him his study of the heavens was the relaxation and exhilaration of a brain formed for meticulous observation and keen, hard thinking.

But on this seventh day he took no paper and pens. He sat down and opened the windows and fixed his eyes upon the stars and allowed his

thoughts to take him back to Italy, his country, to which he had not returned for twenty-seven years and which he would never behold again.
He had been a young man when he left, scarcely thirty, but even after all
these years he remembered with passionate sharpness the agony of that
parting. Even yet he could see the bay, rounding into a circle smaller and
smaller as the ship drew out from the land. Every week he thought gravely
and with a sense of guilt that above his sense of mission still was the
memory of that parting, and that sharper than the parting of his body
from his motherland, from his home and parents and his sister and his
brother, was the parting of his spirit from his beloved, his Vitellia, who
had loved his brother more than him.

He had done penance all these years for this sin, that he had come
into the Church, not for devotion to God and Mary, but because Vitellia
did not love him. Not that she or anyone else knew it. His brother was
tall and handsome and grave, with beautiful, languishing brown eyes,
and Vitellia was tall and pale and exquisite as an olive-tree in new leafage,
her colors all soft and subdued and mistlike. She was head and shoulders
above the little rosy man he always was. No one thought of him seriously.
He was always laughing and joking and merry, his small, deep-set, black
eyes crackling with humor.

Even after his brother's marriage he did not stop his joking. But he
waited to see whether or not his brother was good to Vitellia. There was
nothing to complain of there. His brother was a good man, although a
little dull inside his beauty of body, and, when he found himself married
and soon with a child coming, he settled down into his father's wine
business and they were very happy. No, there was nothing to complain
of there.

Then it was that Andrea became frightened at the power of his passion. He saw that nothing would keep him from revealing himself except
entire submission to his fate. That took a year of fever and agony, and
it was not complete until he saw that for him there was no renunciation
wholly efficacious except priesthood in some far country. Then he fled to
the fathers in his village.

His family had laughed at him—everyone laughed at him—and Vitellia
had nearly ruined him by clinging to his hand and saying in that voice
of hers that was more to him than music, "But brother mine, my Andrea,
who will play with my children and be always in my house?" He had

shaken his head, smiling and speechless, and she had looked at him in surprise and seen that his eyes were full of tears. "Must you, if you mind so much, Andrea?" And he had nodded.

Ah, well, it was all done, long, long ago. For many years he had not not allowed himself to think of her because she was another man's wife, and he had come to the stars night after night and prayed passionately for peace. It seemed to him that he could never do penance enough for loving Vitellia more than anyone else always to the very end. That made him deny himself fiercely and force himself to every distasteful touch and duty. Once, when his flesh had burned after her, he had gone wildly out into the streets and had brought in a beggar from the winter's night, a poor, shivering wretch, and had laid him in his bed and covered him with his blankets and had stretched himself out beside the creature all night long, his teeth clenched and his stomach sick. But in the morning he whispered triumphantly to his body, "Now will you be quiet and cease troubling me!" All this explained the smiling tragedy in his eyes and his constant preaching of bearing one's yoke.

When one day a black-bordered letter came, the first letter in many years, he opened it, and within was the news of Vitellia's death. Then it seemed that peace of a sort came upon him, and after a while he allowed himself this relaxation on the evening of seventh days and even at last permitted himself to think a little of her. Now that she was dead, he could imagine her up yonder, moving in that free, light way she had, among the stars. She was no one's wife now—she belonged to no one. She was a part of heaven, and he could think of her as of a star and be without sin.

He began to preach less vehemently and more patiently about bearing the yoke. When one of his schoolboys ran away to join the revolutionists, he went out with a sigh and sought him and talked with him gently, begging him to come back to his weeping mother.

"The good God puts us into life with a duty to perform," he said tenderly, smiling a little, with his arm about the boy's shoulders.

But the boy shook himself free and moved away. "In the revolution there is no God and there is no duty," he said imperiously. "We are all free, and we preach a gospel of freedom for everyone."

"Ah?" said Father Andrea softly.

For the first time a premonition fell upon him. He had up to this time paid no attention to the talk of revolution. His paths had not led him a mile from the congested quarter where he lived. It occurred to him that now he must look into such talk, especially if his boys were going off like this. He began to speak then of other things, but the boy was wary and obviously eager to have him gone. There were other lads about and an officer or two. The boy's answers grew shorter and shorter. He cast angry looks at his fellows. At last Father Andrea said kindly: "I see that you have other things on your mind. I will leave you now. Do not forget the prayers that you have been taught, my child."

He put his hand on the lad's head for an instant and turned away, but, before he left the barracks, a hoot of laughter arose, and he heard the lads shouting to their comrade, "Running-dog of a foreigner, are you?"

He had no idea what this meant, and he thought once of going back. He stopped to listen. Someone cried out, laughing like a whip's cut, "Ah, a Christian!" Then he heard the boy's voice raised angrily, half-sobbing: "I hate the priest—I know nothing of his religion. I am a revolutionist! Does anyone dare to question me?"

Father Andrea stood stricken. What words were these to come from his lad's mouth, his lad who had been in his school ever since he was five years old? He trembled a little, and a thought shot into his mind like a pang. "So did Peter deny his Lord!" And he went back into the little mission that was his home and shut himself up in his room and wept bitterly.

After that it seemed to him that he had been standing on the edge of a whirlpool and had not known it. He had said that he must investigate this revolution and see that his boys were not carried away. But there was no need of investigation. Knowledge and experience came pouring over him, and he was caught in a maze of difficulties.

There was so much he had not known. He had never heard of political differences between East and West. He had come only as one who wished to bury himself in his mission to a land where there was not his true Church. In this one spot in an immense crowded city he had lived day after day for twenty-seven years, and his small, black-robed figure had become as much a part of the street as an ancient temple or bridge. Children, as long as they could remember, were accustomed to the sight of him, trudging along in all weathers, his pockets bulging ridiculously with peanuts for them. No one thought of him. Women washing at the well looked up as he came by, knew that it must be an hour after noon and sighed to think of the hours before sunset. Men nodded at him carelessly from the counters of the little shops open to the streets and accepted with good humor his tracts and pictures of the Virgin.

Now this was changed. He was no longer Father Andrea, a harmless, aging priest. He became instead a foreigner.

One day a child refused to take the peanuts he held out to it. "My mother says they may be poisoned," the child said, looking up at Father Andrea with wide eyes.

"Poisoned?" said Father Andrea vaguely and in great surprise.

The next day he returned with his pockets as heavy as when he started, and after that he took no more peanuts. Once a woman spat after him as he passed the well. Then men shook their heads coldly when he smiled and proffered his tracts. He was completely bewildered.

At last one night his native assistant came to him. He was a good old man with a straggling, scanty white beard, honest and a little stupid, so that he never quite got his *Aves* right. Father Andrea had wondered sometimes if he should not find someone more able, but he could never bring himself to tell the old man that he was not perfect. Now he said to Father Andrea, "My Father, do not go out until this madness is past."

"What madness?" asked Father Andrea.

"This talk about foreigners and revolutions. The people are listening to these young men in long black gowns who come from the South, and they say that the foreigners are killing the people and stealing their hearts with new religions."

"New religions?" said Father Andrea mildly. "There is nothing new about mine. I have been here preaching and teaching for more than a quarter of a century."

"Even so, sir, you are a foreigner," replied the old man apologetically.

"Well," said Father Andrea at last, "this astonishes me very much!"

But he listened to the old man after the next day; for, when he stepped from the gate into the street, a great stone flung at him flew against his breast and broke into two pieces the ebony cross that hung there, and, when he put up his hand, aghast, another stone flew against him and cut his hand badly. He turned white and went into the mission house and shut the door and fell upon his knees and looked at the broken cross. For a long time he could say nothing, but at last words came to his lips and he prayed an old prayer. "Father, forgive them; for they know not what they do."

After that he stayed in the compound. Within a few days no one came any more, and he locked the door of the empty schoolroom sadly. It was as if he were in the quiet center of a storm. From outside the lonely compound where he and his old assistant pottered about the garden, strange sounds rose up in confusion from the streets. He locked the gate, opening it only once a day in the evening for the old man to creep out and buy a little food. At last one day the old man came back with his basket empty.

"They will not let me buy food for you," he said piteously. "To save your life I must pretend to leave you, and I must pretend to hate you. But every night I will throw food over the western corner of the garden. And every evening at the hour I will repeat the *Ave*. Our God must look after you beyond this."

Thereafter Father Andrea was quite alone. He spent a great deal of time in the observatory, and he allowed himself to think and remember every evening now. The days were long and solitary, and he missed even the lepers. There was no more need to wash his hands except of the clean garden earth that clung to them after he had been working among the vegetables. And, outside, the noise rose and mounted until he fancied that he was on some small island in the midst of a raging sea and that one day the waves would break over him even there.

He withdrew into his thoughts more and more, and he built little dreams of Italy and of the grape garden where he had played as a boy. He could smell the hot sun on the ripe grapes—incomparable fragrance! Sitting in the old easy chair night after night, he began to reconstruct from the beginning his life. It was May, and the stars were brilliant in a purple sky. But he no longer touched his note-books and pens. He had become indifferent to anything of the stars except their sheer unearthly beauty. Thank God for stars and sky everywhere! These Chinese skies in May were like the skies of Italy in summer, the stars hanging heavy and golden in the dark sky. Once on a night like this in Italy he had leaned from his window and gone suddenly mad with the beauty of the stars, and he had run blindly out of the house to Vitellia. His heart was beating like a great drum, shaking his body with every throb, and he had cried that he must tell her that he loved her. When he had got to his brother's house, his brother had opened the door and said kindly: "We were just about to sleep, Andrea. Is there anything we can do for you?"

Behind his brother he saw Vitellia, shadowy in the room, her face pale and indistinct as a flower in the twilight. She came forward and rested her hand lightly upon her husband's arm and leaned her head upon his shoulder. She was quite content. Passion went out of him.

"No, thank you," he stammered. "I thought—I did not know it was so late—I thought I might come in and talk a little while, perhaps."

"Yes, another day," said his brother gravely. And Vitellia had called, "Good night, brother Andrea!" And the door shut, and he was alone.

That was the night he had stayed in the garden the whole night through, and at dawn he had said at last that he would give himself to the poor, since Vitellia did not need him—the poor of a far country.

Ah, all that passion and pain and the youth he had had to wear down by sheer indomitable will to suffer! He would still never be free of it—never, so long as he lived, quite free. He wondered if there among the stars Vitellia knew—there where surely everything was known. He hoped so. That would mean that he need not tell her of all the pain. She would understand as she had never understood on earth, and they could start in at once on the new heavenly relationship.

He sighed and went down into the garden then, and there at the western end he found a small bundle of cold rice and meat wrapped in a lotus leaf and he ate it and then said his *Aves,* his fingers hovering over the broken cross on his breast.

From outside the wall, in the street, there came the sound of steady, marching feet, thousands upon thousands of feet. He listened awhile, wondering, and then, with a sigh, he went up again to his observatory and sat down, and, looking off into the clear spaces of heaven, he slept lightly.

In the morning he awoke with a start of premonition, as if he had been aroused suddenly by a noise. He could not for an instant collect himself. The stars were weak in the gray light of the dawn, and the roof of the church was dark and wet with dew. From without there came a sound of mad confusion, and shooting and shouts rent the air. He listened. There were several shots in quick succession. He sat up, trying to think what this could be. Was this what had waked him? There was no more marching. A huge blaze lighted up the distant eastern sky. Something was burning—that was the rich quarter of the city, where the streets were hung with the scarlet and yellow banners of the big grain-shops and silk-shops and sing-song houses. But it might be only the sun rising? No, there was no such splendor of sunrise out of this gray sky.

He dragged himself from the chair and went downstairs heavily, with vague alarm. He had not slept restfully, and his mind felt fogged. As he reached the foot of the steps and stood upon the grass, there came a terrific pounding at the gate, and he moved quickly to open it, rubbing his head a little to collect his thoughts. This was the noise he had heard in his sleep! He fumbled at the great wooden bar and withdrew it at last and opened the gate and stared out in amazement. Hundreds of men stood there in a mass—soldiers in gray uniform. Their faces were ferocious as he had not dreamed human faces could be, and he shrank from them as he had never shrunk from his lepers. They leveled their guns at him then with a tigerish shout. He was not afraid, only completely amazed.

"But what do you want, my friends?" he asked in surprise.

A young man, scarcely older than his schoolboy who had run away, stepped forward and tore the rosary from about his neck. The fragment of broken cross, all that was left of the cross he had worn for so many years, fell to the ground.

"We have come to rid the world of imperialists and capitalists!" the young man shouted.

"Imperialists and capitalists?" said Father Andrea, wondering. They were words he had never heard. It had been many years since he had read anything except the ancient Church fathers and his books of astronomy. He did not have the faintest idea what the lad meant.

But the boy cocked his gun and pointed it at Father Andrea. "We are the revolutionists!" he cried. His voice was rough and harsh as if he had been shouting for many hours, and his smooth, youthful face was blotched and red as if with drinking. "We come to set everyone free!"

"Set everyone free?" said Father Andrea slowly, smiling a little. He stooped to pick up his cross from the dust.

But before his hand could touch that cross, the boy's finger moved spasmodically upon the trigger and there was a sharp report, and Father Andrea fell upon the ground, dead.

SIGRID UNDSET

The Death of Kristin Lavransdatter

In Sigrid Undset's trilogy the tumultuous events of the Middle Ages form a
dramatic background for KRISTIN LAVRANSDATTER. Of these events, none was
more terrible, none called more upon the resourcefulness and courage of the
people, than the Pestilence. . . . Kristin's sorrow for her children, and her own
desire for atonement, had brought her at last, as a middle-aged woman, into the
convent of the Rein Cloister. She did not believe she would ever become a good
nun, having "scattered abroad so much of her gift for piety"; but by Yule-tide
of the year 1349 she would be ready to take the veil, and her two sons would be
present for her dedication. Before this time came however, she was called upon
to nurse the sick and dying in the Plague, and in this fatal experience Kristin
reached the moment of her greatest courage.

THERE CAME an evening when they were sitting round the chim-
ney-place in the convent hall—the little flock of folk that were left alive
in Rein cloister. Four nuns and two lay sisters, an old stable-man and a
half-grown boy, two bedeswomen and some children, huddled together
round the fire. On the high-seat bench, where a great crucifix gleamed
in the dusk on the light-hued wall, lay the abbess and Sister Kristin and
Sister Turid sat at her hands and feet.

It was nine days since the last death among the sisters, and five days
since any had died in the cloister or the nearer houses. The pestilence
seemed to be lessening throughout the parish, too, said Sira Eiliv. And
for the first time for near three months something like a gleam of peace
and hope and comfort fell upon the silent and weary folk that sat together there. Old Sister Torunn Marta let her rosary sink upon her lap,
and took the hand of the little girl who stood at her knee:

"What can it be she means? Ay, child, now seems it as we should see
that never for long does God's mother, Mary, turn away her loving-
kindness from her children."

"Nay, 'tis not Mary Virgin, Sister Torunn, 'tis Hel.* She will go from out this parish, with both rake and broom, when they offer up a man without blemish at the graveyard gate—to-morrow she'll be far away—"

"What means she?" asked the nun again, uneasily. "Fie upon you, Magnhild; what ugly heathenish talk is this? 'Twere fit you should taste the birch—"

"Tell us what it is, Magnhild—have no fear"—Sister Kristin was standing behind them; she asked the question breathlessly. She had remembered—she had heard in her youth from Lady Aashild—of dreadful, unnamably sinful devices that the Devil tempts desperate men to practise—

The children had been down in the grove by the parish church in the falling dusk, and some of the boys had strayed through the wood to a turf hut that stood there, and had eavesdropped and heard some men in it laying plans. It seemed from what they heard that these men had laid hold on a little boy, Tore, the son of Steinunn, that lived by the strand, and tonight they were to offer him up to the pest-ogress, Hel. The children talked eagerly, proud that the grown-up folk were paying heed to what they said. They seemed not to think of pitying the hapless Tore—maybe because he was somewhat of an outcast. He wandered about the parish begging, but never came to the cloister, and if Sira Eiliv or any sent by the abbess sought out his mother, she ran away, or she kept a stubborn silence, whether they spoke lovingly or harshly to her. She had lived in the stews of Nidaros for ten years, but then a sickness took hold on her, and left her of so ill a favour that at last she could not win her livelihood as she had used to do; so she had forsaken the town for the Rein parish, and now dwelt in a hut down by the strand. It still befell at times that a chance beggar or some such stroller would take lodging with her for a while. Who was father to her boy she herself knew not.

"We must go thither," said Kristin. "Here we cannot sit, while christened souls sell themselves to the Devil at our very doors."

The nuns whimpered in fear. These were the worst men in the parish; rough, ungodly fellows; and uttermost need and despair must have turned

* In Norse folk-lore the plague was personified as a hideous old woman carrying a rake and a broom. Where she used the rake, some part of the population survived; where she used the broom, she swept the country-side of every living soul. It would be natural, in the fourteenth century, for the popular imagination to identify her with Hel, the death goddess of the old mythology.

them now into very devils. Had Sira Eiliv only been at home, they moaned. In this time of trial the priest had so won their trust, that they deemed he could do all things—

Kristin wrung her hands:

"Even if I must go alone—my mother, have I your leave to go thither?"

The abbess gripped her by the arm so hard that she cried out. The old, tongue-tied woman got upon her feet; by signs she made them understand that they should dress her to go out, and called for her golden cross, the badge of her office, and her staff. Then she took Kristin by the arm—for Kristin was the youngest and strongest of the women. All the nuns stood up and followed.

Through the door of the little room between the chapter-hall and the choir of the church, they went forth into the raw, cold winter night. Lady Ragnhild's teeth began to chatter and her whole frame to shiver— she still sweated without cease by reason of her sickness, and the pest- boil sores were not fully healed, so that it must have wrought her great agony to walk. But she muttered angrily and shook her head when the sisters prayed her to turn, clung the harder to Kristin's arm, and plodded on, shaking with cold, before them through the garden. As their eyes grew used to the darkness, the women made out the dim sheen of the withered leaves strewn on the path beneath their feet, and the faint light from the clouded sky above the naked tree-tops. Cold water-drops dripped from the branches, and puffs of wind went by with a faint soughing sound. The roll of the waves on the strand behind the high ground came to them in dull, heavy sighs.

At the bottom of the garden was a little wicket—the sisters shuddered when the bolt, fast rusted in its socket, shrieked as Kristin withdrew it by main force. Then they crept onward through the grove down towards the parish church. Now they could see dimly the black-tarred mass, darker against the darkness; and against the opening in the clouds above the low hills beyond the lake they saw the roof-top, and the ridge turret with its beasts' heads and cross over all.

Ay—there were folk in the graveyard—they felt rather than saw or heard it. And now a faint gleam of light was to be seen low down, as of a lanthorn set upon the ground. Close by it the darkness seemed moving.

The nuns pressed together, moaning almost soundlessly amid whis- pered prayers, went a few steps, halted and listened, and went on again.

They were wellnigh come to the graveyard gate. Then they heard from out of the dark a thin child-voice crying:

"Oh, oh, my bannock; you've thrown dirt on it!"

Kristin let go the abbess's arm, and ran forward through the church-yard gate. She pushed aside some dark shapes of men's backs, stumbled over heaps of up-turned earth, and then was at the edge of the open grave. She went down on her knees, bent over, and lifted up the little boy who stood at the bottom, still whimpering because the dirt had spoiled the good bannock he had been given for staying quietly down there.

The men stood there frightened from their wits—ready to fly—some stamped about on the same spot—Kristin saw their feet in the light from the lanthorn on the ground. Then one, she made sure, would have sprung at her—at the same moment the grey-white nuns' dresses came into sight —and the knot of men hung wavering—

Kristin had the boy in her arms still; he was crying for his bannock; so she set him down, took the bread, and brushed it clean:

"There, eat it—your bannock is as good as ever now— And now go home, you men"—the shaking of her voice forced her to stop a little. "Go home and thank God you were saved from the doing of a deed 'twere hard to atone." She was speaking now as a mistress speaks to her serving-folk, mildly, but as if it could not cross her mind that they would not obey. Unwittingly some of the men turned toward the gate.

Then one of them shouted:

"Stay a little—see you not our lives at the least are forfeit—mayhap all we own—now that these full-fed monks' whores have stuck their noses into this! Never must they come away from here to spread the tidings of it—"

Not a man moved—but Sister Agnes broke into a shrill shriek, and cried in a wailing voice:

"O sweet Jesus, my bridegroom—I thank Thee that Thou sufferest Thy handmaidens to die for the glory of Thy name—!"

Lady Ragnhild pushed her roughly behind her, tottered forward, and took up the lanthorn from the ground—no one moved a hand to hinder her. When she lifted it up, the gold cross on her breast shone out. She stood propped on her staff, and slowly turned the light upon the ring about her, nodding a little at each man she looked on. Then she made a sign to Kristin to speak. Kristin said:

"Go home peaceably and quietly, dear brothers—be sure that the reverend mother and these good sisters will be as merciful as their duty to God and the honour of his Church will suffer. But stand aside now, that we may come forth with this child—and thereafter let each man go his way."

The men stood wavering. Then one cried out as though in direst need: "Is it not better that *one* be offered up than that we should all perish—? This child here who is owned by none—"

"Christ owns him. 'Twere better we should perish one and all than to hurt one of His little ones—"

But the man who had spoken first shouted again:

"Hold your tongue—no more suchlike words, or I cram them back down your throat with this"—he shook his knife in the air. "Go you home, go to your beds and pray your priest to comfort you, and say naught of this—or I tell you, in Satan's name, you shall learn 'twas the worst thing you ever did to put your fingers into our affairs—"

"You need not to cry so loud for him you named to hear you, Arntor —be sure he is not far from here," said Kristin calmly, and some of the men seemed affrighted, and pressed unwittingly nearer to the abbess, who stood holding the lanthorn. "The worst had been, both for us and for you, had we sat quiet at home while you went about to make you a dwelling-place in hottest hell."

But the man Arntor swore and raved. Kristin knew that he hated the nuns; for his father had been forced to pledge his farm to them when he had to pay amends for man-slaying and incest with his wife's cousin. Now he went on casting up at the sisters all the Enemy's most hateful lies, charging them with sins so black and unnatural that only the Devil himself could prompt a man to think such thoughts.

The poor nuns bowed them terrified and weeping under the hail of his taunts, but they stood fast around their old mother, and she held the lanthorn high, throwing the light upon the man, and looking him calmly in the face while he raved.

But anger flamed up in Kristin like new-kindled fire:

"Silence! Have you lost your wits, or has God smitten you with blindness? Should we dare to murmur under His chastisement—we who have seen His consecrated brides go forth to meet the sword that has been drawn by reason of the world's sins? They watched and prayed while we sinned and each day forgot our Maker—shut them from the world within the citadel of prayer, while we scoured the world around, driven by greed of great and small possessions, of our own lusts and our own wrath. But they came forth to us when the angel of death was sent out amongst us—gathered in the sick and the defenceless and the hungry—twelve of our sisters have died in this plague—that you all know—not one turned aside, and not one gave over praying for us all in sisterly love, till the tongue dried in their mouths and their life's blood ebbed away—"

"Bravely speak you of yourself and your like—"

"*I* am *your* like," she cried, beside herself with anger. "I am not one of these holy sisters—I am one of you—"

"You have grown full humble, woman," said Arntor, scornfully; "you are frighted, I mark well. A little more and you will be fain to call her—the mother to this boy—your like."

"That must God judge—He died both for her and for me, and He knows us both.—Where is she—Steinunn?"

"Go down to her hut; you will find her there sure enough," answered Arntor.

"Ay, truly someone must send word to the poor woman that we have her boy," said Kristin to the nuns. "We must go out to her to-morrow."

Arntor gave a jeering laugh, but another man cried, uneasily:

"No, no— She is dead," he said to Kristin. " 'Tis fourteen days since Bjarne left her and barred the door. She lay in the death-throes then—"

"She lay in—" Kristin gazed at the men, horror-struck. "Was there none to fetch a priest to her—? Is the—body—lying there—and no one has had so much compassion on her as to bring her to hallowed ground—and her child you would have—?"

At the sight of the woman's horror, it was as though the men went clean beside themselves with fear and shame; all were shouting at once; a voice louder than all the rest rang out:

"Fetch her yourself, sister!"

"Ay! Which of you will go with me?"

None answered. Arntor cried:

"You will have to go alone, I trow."

"To-morrow—as soon as 'tis light—we will fetch her, Arntor—I myself will buy her a resting-place and masses for her soul—"

"Go thither now, go to-night—then will I believe you nuns are choke-full of holiness and pureness—"

Arntor had stuck his head forward close to hers. Kristin drove her clenched fist into his face, with a single loud sob of rage and horror—

Lady Ragnhild went forward and placed herself at Kristin's side; she strove to bring forth some words. The nuns cried out that to-morrow the dead woman should be brought to her grave. But the Devil seemed to have turned Arntor's brain; he went on shrieking:

"Go now—then will we believe on God's mercy—"

Kristin drew herself up, white and stiff:

"I will go."

She lifted the child and gave it into Sister Torunn's arms, pushed the men aside, and ran quickly, stumbling over grass tussocks and heaps of earth, toward the gate, while the nuns followed wailing, and Sister Agnes cried out that she would go with her. The abbess shook her clenched hands toward Kristin, beckoning her to stop; but she seemed quite beside herself and gave no heed—

Suddenly there was a great commotion in the dark over by the grave-yard gate—next moment Sira Eiliv's voice asked: who was holding Thing here. He came forward into the glimmer of the lanthorn—they saw that he bore an ax in his hand. The nuns flocked around him; the men made shift to steal away in the dark, but in the gateway they were met by a man bearing a drawn sword in his hand. There was some turmoil and the clash of arms, and Sira Eiliv shouted toward the gate: woe to any who broke the churchyard peace. Kristin heard one say 'twas the strong smith from Credo Lane—the moment after, a tall, broad-shouldered, white-haired man appeared at her side—'twas Ulf Haldorssön.

The priest handed him the ax—he had borrowed it from Ulf—and took the boy Tore from the nun, while he said:

" 'Tis past midnight already—none the less 'twere best you all came with me to the church; I must get to the bottom of these doings this very night."

None had any thought but to obey. But, when they were come out on to the road, one of the light-grey women's forms stepped aside from the throng and turned off by the path through the wood. The priest called out, bidding her come on with the others. Kristin's voice answered from the darkness—she was some way along the track already:

"I cannot come, Sira Eiliv, till I have kept my promise—"

The priest and some others sprang after her. She was standing leaning against the fence when Sira Eiliv came up with her. He held up the lanthorn—she was fearfully white of face, but, when he looked into her eyes, he saw that she was not gone mad, as at first he had feared.

"Come home, Kristin," he said. "To-morrow we will go thither with you, some men—I myself will go with you—"

"I have given my word. I cannot go home, Sira Eiliv, till I have done that which I vowed to do."

The priest stood silent a little. Then he said in a low voice:

"Mayhap you are right. Go then, sister, in God's name."

Like a shadow, Kristin melted away into the darkness, which swallowed up her grey form.

When Ulf Haldorssön came up by her side, she said—she spoke by snatches, vehemently: "Go back—I asked not you to come with me—"

Ulf laughed low:

"Kristin, my lady—you have not learnt yet, I see, that some things can be done without your asking or bidding—nor, though you have seen it many a time, I ween—that you cannot always carry through alone all that you take upon you. But this burden of yours I will help you to carry."

The fir woods sighed above them, and the boom of the rollers away on the beach came stronger or more faint as the gusts of wind rose or died away. They walked in pitch darkness. After a while Ulf said:

"—I have borne you company before, Kristin, when you went out at night—methought 'twere but fitting I should go with you this time too—"

She breathed hard and heavily in the dark. Once she stumbled over somewhat, and Ulf caught her. After that he took her hand and led her. In a while the man heard that she was weeping as she went, and he asked her why she wept.

"I weep to think how good and faithful you have been to us, Ulf, all our days. What can I say—? I know well enough 'twas most for Erlend's sake, but almost I believe, kinsman—all our days you have judged of me more kindly than you had a right to, after what you first saw of my doings."

"I loved you, Kristin—no less than him." He was silent. Kristin felt that he was strongly stirred. Then he said:

"Therefore meseemed 'twas a hard errand, when I sailed out hither to-day—I came to bring you such tidings as I myself deemed it hard to utter. God strengthen you, Kristin!"

"Is it Skule?" asked Kristin softly in a little. "My son is dead?"

"No; Skule was well when I spoke with him yesterday—and now not many are dying in the town. But I had news from Tautra this morning—" He heard her sigh heavily once, but she said naught. A little after he said:

" 'Tis ten days now since they died. There are but four brothers left alive in the cloister, and the island is all but swept clean of folk."

They were come now where the wood ended. Over the flat stretch of land in front the roaring of the sea and the wind came to meet them. One spot out in the dark shone white—the surf in a little bay, by a steep, light-hued sand-hill.

"She dwells there," said Kristin. Ulf felt that long, convulsive shudders went through her frame. He gripped her hand hard:

"You took this on yourself. Remember that, and lose not your wits now."

Kristin said, in a strangely thin, clear voice, that the blast caught and bore away:

"Now will Björgulf's dream come true—I trust in God's and Mary's grace."

Ulf tried to see her face—but it was too dark. They were walking on the shore—in some places so narrow under the bluffs that now and then a wave washed right up to their feet. They tramped forward over tangled heaps of seaweed and great stones. After a while they were ware of a dark hump in against the sandy bank.

"Stay here," said Ulf, shortly. He went forward and thrust against the door—then she heard him hew at the withy bands and thrust at the door again. Then she was ware that the door had fallen inwards, and he had gone in through the black hole.

It was not a night of heavy storm. But it was so dark that Kristin could see naught, save the little flashes of foam that came and vanished the same instant on the lifting sea, and the shining of the waves breaking along the shores of the bay—and against the sand-dune she could make out that black hump. And it seemed to her that she was standing in a cavern of night, and that it was the forecourt of death. The roll of breaking waves and the hiss of their waters ebbing among the stones of the beach kept time with the blood-waves surging through her, though all the time it was as though her body must shiver in pieces, as a vessel of wood falls apart in staves—her breast ached as if something would burst in it sunder from within; her head felt hollow and empty and as if it were rifted, and the unceasing wind wrapped her round and swept clean through her. She felt, with a strange listlessness, that she herself had surely caught the sickness now—but 'twas as though she looked that the darkness should be riven by a great light that would drown the roar of the sea with its thunder, and that in the horror of this she should perish. She drew up her hood, blown back from her head by the wind, wrapped the black nun's cloak close about her, and stood with her hands crossed beneath it—but it came not into her thought to pray; it was as though her soul had more than enough to do to work a way forth from its mansion trembling to its fall, and as though it tore at her breast with every breath.

She saw a light flare up within the hut. A little after, Ulf Haldorssön called out to her: "You must come hither and hold the light for me, Kristin"—he was standing in the doorway—as she came, he reached her a torch of some tarred wood.

A choking stench from the corpse met her, though the hut was so draughty and the door was gone. With staring eyes and mouth half open —and she felt her jaws and lips grow stiff the while and wooden—she looked round for the dead. But there was naught to see but a long bundle lying in the corner on the earthen floor, wrapped in Ulf's cloak.

He had torn loose some long planks from somewhere and laid the door upon them. Cursing his unhandy tools, he made notches and holes with his light ax and dagger, and strove to lash the door fast to the boards. Once or twice he looked up at her swiftly, and each time his dark, grey-bearded face grew more hard set.

"I marvel much how you had thought to get through this piece of work alone," he said as he wrought—then glanced up at her—but the stiff, death-like face in the red gleam of the tar brand was set and unmoved as ever—'twas the face of a dead woman or of one distraught. "Can you tell me that, Kristin?" he laughed harshly—but still 'twas of no avail. "Methinks now were the time for you to say a prayer."

Stiff and lifeless as ever, she began to speak:

"Pater noster qui es in cœlis. Adveniat regnum tuum. Fiat voluntas tua sicut in cœlo et in terra—" Then she came to a stop.

Ulf looked at her. Then he took up the prayer:

"Panem nostrum quotidianum da nobis hodie—" Swiftly and firmly he said the Lord's prayer to the end, went over and made the sign of the cross over the bundle—swiftly and firmly he took it up and bore it to the bier that he had fashioned.

"Go you in front," he said. "Maybe 'tis somewhat heavier, but you will smell the stench less there. Throw away the torch—we can see more surely without it—and see you miss not your footing, Kristin—for I had liefer not have to take a hold of this poor body any more."

The struggling pain in her breast seemed to rise in revolt when she got the bier poles set upon her shoulders; her chest *would* not bear up the weight. But she set her teeth hard. So long as they went along the beach, where the wind blew strong, but little of the corpse smell came to her.

"Here I must draw it up first, I trow, and the bier after," said Ulf, when they were come to the steep slope they had climbed down.

"We can go a little farther on," said Kristin; " 'tis there they come down with the seaweed sleighs—there 'tis not steep."

She spoke calmly, the man heard, and as in her right mind. And a fit of sweating and trembling took him, now it was over—he had deemed she must lose her wits that night.

They struggled forward along the sandy track that led across the flat toward the pine wood. The wind swept in freely here, but yet 'twas not as it had been down on the strand, and, as they drew farther and farther way from the roar of the beach, she felt it as a homefaring from the horror of utter darkness. Beside their path the ground showed lighter—'twas a cornfield that there had been none to reap. The scent of it, and the sight of the beaten-down straw, welcomed her home again—and her eyes filled with tears of sisterly pity—out of her own desolate terror and woe she was coming home to fellowship with the living and the dead.

At times, when the wind was right behind, the fearful carrion stench enwrapped her wholly, but yet it was not so awful as when she stood in the hut—for the night was full of fresh, wet, cold, cleansing streams of air.

And much stronger than the feeling that she bore a thing of dread upon the bier behind her, was the thought that Ulf Haldorssön was there, guarding her back against the black and living horror they were leaving behind—and whose roar sounded fainter and more faint.

When they were come to the edge of the fir woods they were ware of lights: "They are coming to meet us," said Ulf.

Soon after, they were met by a whole throng of men bearing pine-root torches, a couple of lanthorns and a bier covered with a pall—Sira Eiliv was with them, and Kristin saw with wonder that in the troop were many of the men who had been that same night in the churchyard, and that many of them were weeping. When they lifted the burthen from her shoulders she was like to fall. Sira Eiliv would have caught a hold of her, but she said quickly:

"Touch me not—come not near me—I have the pest myself; I feel it—"

But none the less Sira Eiliv stayed her up with a hand below her arm:

"Then be of good cheer, woman, remembering that our Lord has said: 'Inasmuch as ye have done it unto one of the least of these my brethren or sisters, ye have done it unto Me.' "

Kristin gazed at the priest. Then she looked across to where the men were shifting the body from the stretcher that Ulf had fashioned to the bier they had brought. Ulf's cloak slipped aside a little—the point of a worn-out shoe stuck out, dark wet in the light of the torches.

Kristin went across, kneeled between the poles of the bier, and kissed the shoe:

"God be gracious to you, sister—God give your soul joy in His light —God look in His mercy on us here in our darkness—"

Then it seemed to her as if it were life itself that tore its way from out of her—a grinding, inconceivable pain, as though something within her, rooted fast in every outermost fibre of her limbs, were riven loose. All that was within her breast was torn out—she felt her throat full of it, her mouth filled with blood that tasted of salt and foul copper—next moment her whole dress in front was a glistening wet blackness—Jesus! is there so much blood in an old woman? she thought.

Ulf Haldorssön lifted her in his arms and bore her away.

At the gate of the cloister the nuns, bearing lighted candles, came to meet the train of men. Already Kristin scarce had her full senses, but she felt that she was half borne, half helped, through the door, and was ware of the whitewashed, vaulted room, filled with the flickering light of yellow candle flames and red pine torches, and of the tramp of feet rolling like a sea—but to the dying woman the light was like the shimmer of her own dying life-flame, and the footfalls on the flags as the rushing of the rivers of death rising up to meet her.

Then the candlelight spread out into a wider space—she was once again under the open, murky sky—in the court-yard—the flickering light played upon a grey stone wall with heavy buttresses and high, tall windows—the church. She was borne in someone's arms—'twas Ulf again—but now he seemed to take on for her the semblance of all who had ever borne her up. When she laid her arms about his neck and pressed her cheek against his stubbly throat, it was as though she were a child again with her father, but also as though she were clasping a child to her own bosom— And behind his dark head there were red lights, and they seemed like the glow of the fire that nourishes all love.

—A little later she opened her eyes, and her mind was clear and calm. She was sitting, propped up, in a bed in the dormitory; a nun with a linen band over her lower face stood bending over her; she marked the smell of vinegar. It was Sister Agnes, she knew by her eyes and the little red wart she had on her forehead. And now 'twas day—clear, grey light was sifting into the room from the little glass window.

She had no great pain now—she was but wet through with sweat, woefully worn and weary, and her breast stung and smarted when she breathed. Greedily she drank down a soothing drink that Sister Agnes held to her mouth. But she was cold—

Kristin lay back on the pillows, and now she remembered all that had befallen the night before. The wild dream fantasies were wholly gone—her wits must have wandered a little, she understood—but it was good that she had gotten this thing done, had saved the little boy, and hindered these poor folk from burdening their souls with such a hideous deed. She knew she had need to be overjoyed—that *she* had been given grace to do this thing just before she was to die—and yet she could rejoice as it was meet she should; it was more a quiet content she felt, as when she lay in her bed at home at Jörundgaard, tired out after a day's work well done. And she must thank Ulf too—

—She had spoken his name, and he must have been sitting hidden, away by the door and have heard her, for here he came across the room and stood before her bed. She reached out her hand to him, and he took and pressed it in a firm clasp.

Suddenly the dying woman grew restless; her hands fumbled under the folds of linen about her throat.

"What is it, Kristin?" asked Ulf.

"The cross," she whispered, and painfully drew forth her father's gilded cross. It had come to her mind that yesterday she had promised to make a gift for the soul's weal of that poor Steinunn. She had not remembered then that she had no possessions on earth any more. She owned naught that she could give, saving this cross she had had of her father—and then her bridal ring. She wore that on her finger still.

She drew it off and gazed at it. It lay heavy in her hand; pure gold, set with great red stones. Erlend—she thought—and it came upon her now it were liker she should give this away—she knew not wherefore, but it seemed that she ought. She shut her eyes in pain and held it out to Ulf:

"To whom would you give this?" he asked, low, and as she did not answer: "Mean you I should give it to Skule—"

Kristin shook her head, her eyes tight closed.

"Steinunn—I promised—masses for her—"

She opened her eyes, and sought with them the ring where it lay in the smith's dusky palm. And her tears burst forth in a swift stream, for it seemed to her that never before had she understood to the full what it betokened. The life that ring had wed her to, that she had complained against, had murmured at, had raged at and defied—none the less she had loved it so, joyed in it so, both in good days and evil, that not one day had there been when 'twould not have seemed hard to give it back to God, nor one grief that she could have forgone without regret—

Ulf and the nun changed some words that she could not hear, and he went from the room. Kristin would have lifted her hand to dry her eyes, but she could not—the hand lay moveless on her breast. And now the pain within was sore; her hand felt so heavy, and it seemed as though the ring were on her finger still. Her head began to grow unclear again—she *must* see if it were true that the ring was gone, that she had not only dreamed she had given it away— And now too she began to grow uncertain—all that had befallen last night: the child in the grave; the black sea with its swift little flashing waves; the corpse she had borne—she knew not whether she had dreamed it all, or had been awake. And she had no strength to open her eyes.

"Sister," said the nun, "you must not sleep now—Ulf has gone to fetch a priest for you."

Kristin woke up fully again with a start, and fixed her eyes upon her hand. The gold ring was gone, that was sure enough—but there was a white, worn mark where it had been on her middle finger. It showed forth quite clearly on the rough brown flesh—like a scar of thin, white skin—she deemed she could make out two round spots on either side where the rubies had been, and somewhat like a little mark, an M, where the middle plate of gold had been pierced with the first letter of Mary Virgin's holy name.

And the last clear thought that formed in her brain was that she should die ere this mark had time to vanish—and she was glad. It seemed to her to be a mystery that she could not fathom, but which she knew most surely none the less, that God had held her fast in a covenant made for her without her knowledge by a love poured out upon her richly—and in despite of her self-will, in despite of her heavy, earthbound spirit, somewhat of this love had become *part* of her, had wrought in her like sunlight in the earth, had brought forth increase which not even the hottest flames of fleshly love nor its wildest bursts of wrath could lay waste wholly. A handmaiden of God had she been—a wayward, unruly servant, oftenest an eye-servant in her prayers and faithless in her heart, slothful and neglectful, impatient under correction, but little constant in her deeds— yet had he held her fast in his service, and under the glittering golden ring a mark had been set secretly upon her, showing that she was his handmaid, owned by the Lord and King who was now coming, borne by the priest's anointed hands, to give her freedom and salvation—

Soon after Sira Eiliv had given her the last oil and viaticum, Kristin Lavransdatter again lost the knowledge of all around. She lay in the sway of sore fits of blood-vomiting and burning fever, and the priest, who stayed by her, told the nuns that 'twas like to go quickly with her.

—Once or twice the dying woman came so far to herself that she knew this or the other face—Sira Eiliv's, the sister's—Lady Ragnhild herself was there once, and Ulf too she saw. She strove to show she knew them, and that she felt it was good they should be by her and wished her well.

But to those who stood around it seemed as she were but fighting with her hands in the throes of death.

Once she saw Munan's face—her little son peeped in at her through a half open door. Then he drew back his head, and the mother lay gazing at the door—if perchance the boy might peep out again. But instead came Lady Ragnhild and wiped her face with a wet cloth; and that too was good—Then all things were lost in a dark red mist, and a roar, that first grew fearsomely; but then it died away little by little, and the red mist grew thinner and lighter, and at last it was like a fair morning mist ere the sun breaks through, and all sound ceased, and she knew that now she was dying—

Sira Eiliv and Ulf Haldorssön went out together from the room of death. In the doorway out to the cloister yard they stopped short—

Snow had fallen. None had marked it, of them who had sat by the woman while she fought with death. The white gleam from the steep church roof over against the two men was strangely dazzling; the tower shone white against the ash-grey sky. The snow lay so fine and white on all the window-mouldings, and all buttresses and jutting points, against the church's walls of grey hewn stone. And it was as though the two men lingered because they were both to break with their foot-prints the thin coverlid of new-fallen snow.

They drank in the air. After the noisome smell that ever fills the sick-room of one pest-stricken, it tasted sweet—cool, and as it were a little thin and empty; but it seemed as though this snow-fall must have washed the air clean of all poison and pestilence—it was as good as fresh spring water.

The bell in the tower began to ring again—the two looked up to where it swung behind the belfry bars. Small grains of snow loosened from the tower roof as it shook, rolled down, and grew to little balls—leaving spots where the black of the shingles showed through.

"This snow will scarce lie," said Ulf.

"No, 'twill melt, belike, before evening," answered the priest. There were pale golden rifts in the clouds, and a faint gleam of sunshine fell, as it were provingly, across the snow.

The men stood still. Then Ulf Haldorssön said low:

"I am thinking, Sira Eiliv—I will give some land to the church here—

and a beaker of Lavrans Björgulfssön's that she gave me—to found a mass for her—and my foster-sons—and for him, Erlend, my kinsman—"

The priest answered as low, without looking at the man:

"—Meseems, too, you might think you had need to show your thankfulness to Him who led you hither yestereven—you may be well content, I trow, that 'twas granted you to help her through this night."

"Ay, 'twas that I thought of," said Ulf Haldorssön. Then he laughed a little: "And now could I well-nigh repent me, priest, that I have been so meek a man—toward her!"

"Bootless to waste time in such vain regrets," answered the priest.

"What mean you—?"

"I mean, 'tis but a man's sins that it boots him to repent," said the priest.

"Why so?"

"For that none is good saving God only. And we can do no good save of Him. So it boots not to repent a good deed, Ulf, for the good you have done cannot be undone; though all the hills should crash in ruin, yet would it stand—"

"Ay, ay. These be things I understand not, my Sira. I am weary—"

"Ay—and hungry too you may well be—you must come with me to the kitchen-house, Ulf," said the priest.

"Thanks, but I have no stomach to meat," said Ulf Haldorssön.

"None the less must you go with me and eat," said Sira Eiliv—he laid his hand on Ulf's sleeve and led him along with him. They went out into the court-yard and down towards the kitchen-house. Unwittingly, both men trod as lightly and charily as they could upon the new-fallen snow.

—*Translated from the Norwegian by* CHARLES ARCHER

SHOLEM ASCH

A Peculiar Gift

Widely known for his novels of Biblical times, THE NAZARENE and his more recent THE APOSTLE, Sholem Asch has also written many short stories. "A Peculiar Gift" has caught the pioneering spirit of at least one Jew who went to Palestine.

IN THE Valley of Jezreel, within the shadow of Mount Gilboa, a Jew was following a plough pulled by two horses. The Jew guided the plough; his ten-year-old son, Solomon, whipped up the horses, one red and one black; and Sarah, his eight-year-old daughter dropped the seed into the fresh-turned furrow.

"Drop them down straight, little one," he sang to the girl. "Right to the bottom of the furrow. God's over us, and he'll return thirty-fold, forty-fold, fifty-fold. Such returns have been and may be again. Whoa, Solomon, not so fast with the nags! Hold the red one! Hold the black one!" The Jew stopped and peered into the furrow. "Take them, good earth, and multiply them! God gave you to us, and we are back with you. Dear earth, do God's bidding, and you, little seeds, fall in good places where you will not die and rot; fall comfortably and well, so that you may sprout and feed me and my wife and my children. I have prepared a bed for you, a warm, brown bed, a bed that flows with milk and honey, as the great teacher said."

Panting as he followed the plough, the Jew kept up his breathless, ecstatic monologue. He wiped the sweat from his face. The sun blazed down on him, the wind lifted up the corners of his gabardine and the points of his beard; it fluttered the tips of the kerchief round the little girl's head. And all five of them, father, daughter, and son, the red horse and the black, labored joyously along the hard, sloping field, turning up the earth in the ancient Valley of Jezreel.

I, a visitor in this lonely place, sat on a stone and waited for the family to make the last furrow for that afternoon. I was worried for the Jew behind the plough; I was afraid for him. For I knew him from of old, knew the kind of man he had been. Was not this Noah the dry-goods merchant, whom I saw now after many years, Noah who had given up his business in Ekaterinoslav and who now, with son and daughter and two horses, one black and one red, was toiling along the slope of the field, disguised as a farmer? And what a farmer! A lyrical farmer such as never was on land or sea. As he came back toward me his voice was still uplifted.

"It's good, Mr. Jew," he chanted. "Do you hear me? It's good."

"It's good and hot, Reb Noah," I answered.

He halted.

"Hot? Did you say it's hot? Maybe it is. What does the Book say? 'In the summer the heat shall not burn you, and in the winter the cold shall not consume you.' What if it is hot? It's good, I tell you."

In the old days, when I had used to visit him in Ekaterinoslav, Reb Noah had been a merchant of standing, dealing with cities as wide apart as Warsaw, Kishineff, and Lodz. He was said to be worth between fifteen and twenty thousand roubles, and his credit rating was even higher, for who knew as well as Reb Noah the value of a rouble, and who guarded a coin with the same vigilance? When he came to Warsaw as a buyer, he stayed always at a third-rate inn, a rouble a day, meals and all. He welcomed a rouble with jubilation, parted with a kopeck only under duress. He always defended himself by saying that he was saving his money for Palestine; yes, some day he would close his shop, wind up his business, betake himself to the Holy Land, and become a laboring man, a tiller of the soil, which, as all the world knew, was what his ancestors and all the ancestors of the Jews had been. Of course nobody believed him, for if Reb Noah was sparing of his cash, he was most generous of his words. It was remembered, moreover, that in his boyhood Reb Noah had sung in the choir of the famous cantor of Berditchev and had become a business-man against his will; and it is a well-known fact that frustrated singers are the most talkative of mortals. But the unbelievable, or at any rate the unbelieved, came to pass. Noah the dry-goods merchant disappeared from Ekaterinoslav, in the height of the season, and the places of his business knew him no more. They waited for him in vain in the warehouses of Warsaw and Kishineff and Lodz. And soon he was forgotten, as business-men are apt to be. Other customers took his place. Reb Noah had really gone to Palestine; and here he was, in the Valley of Jezreel, wearing, instead of the perky little bowler of the Russian Jew, the stately fez of the Turks, and talking to me as he leaned upon the plough which I had watched him guide.

"But—but—how could you really bring yourself to do it?" I asked, convinced and yet incredulous.

"I'll tell you what it is," he answered, thoughtfully. "I've always believed, deep down, that I was a gifted man, a man of peculiar gifts. My only difficulty was that I didn't know what I was gifted for. Till one day it came to me suddenly that I was *gifted for Palestine.*"

"What's that?" I said. "Gifted for Palestine?"

"Why, certainly. Some Jews have a gift for this, some for that, some for the other—and some for Palestine. Take Baron Edmund Rothschild, for instance. A great man, isn't he? But who knew what he was great *for* until he discovered his peculiar gift? He had a gift for Palestine. And so did I. Not as great a one as Baron Rothschild. I'm gifted for Palestine in a smaller way. But then, I'm a smaller man, and it's all I need."

"It's a laborious talent, Reb Noah," I suggested. "A sweaty talent, if I may say so."

"Not a bit of it," he retorted, and contradicted himself by wiping a freshet of perspiration from his face. "A talent for dry-goods is a lot sweatier. You should have seen me trying to persuade a peasant woman that a length of calico was what she needed, and that she was getting it dirt cheap—which she was. Now, *that* was a sweaty job. But this? Pooh!"

"But the horses, Reb Noah? How do you get along with the horses? I knew you when you wouldn't come within a mile of a horse."

"I daresay you did. And yet—well, how was I to know? See that red nag there? He's the sweetest horse in the world, an absolute saint of a horse. Never kicked anyone in his life. Click your tongue at him, and off he goes; call 'Whoa!' and he stops. A saint, I say. The black one, I admit, was different. A lowdown horse, mean, unfriendly—an anti-Semite of a horse. A grand worker; but he loved to kick. They told me, when I bought him: 'Reb Noah, you'll never manage that horse. You'll never get round him.' 'I won't, won't I?' was all I answered, and took my horse home. And I said to myself: 'Noah, get this into your mind. The first day you handle him, he'll kick you ten times.' But did he? No, he did not. He kicked me only six times. So there I was, four kicks to the good, the very first day. The second day I counted on six, and got away with three.

How's that for progress? Today he doesn't kick any more. He's learned the verse from Isaiah: 'The ox knoweth his master, and the ass his owner's crib.' I'm boss, he's servant, and we're at peace. I give him his food, he gives me his labor."

"And your wife, Yetta," I went on. "How did she take to being a peasant woman?"

"Ah, that now—that was a hard business." Reb Noah became reflective. "Things are brighter today, but the beginning—" and Reb Noah tightened his lips, drew his mouth to one side, closed one eye and nodded several times. "When we came out here, my wife and I and the little ones, the place was a wilderness. *Tohu-u-bohu*. Without form and void. Eight Jewish families in all, in this 'Arab hole' which we took over. That's what my wife called it. 'Noah, you murderer,' she cries, 'what are you doing with me and my little chicks? How do you expect us to live here?' And what could I answer? The first thing I got here was a good dose of malaria. There was no water in the place; you had to bring it by the pailful from the nearest well, miles away. The children were sick, too. And my Yetta! The things she said! And me shivering with the fever. 'Yetta,' I answer, 'don't talk that way! It's blasphemous! This is the Holy Land, of the Prophets and Kings and Priests. It's forbidden to speak evil of it. Wait,' I say, 'this "Arab hole" is a paradise. Wait till the fig trees blossom—our own fig trees now, ours. And wait till we eat the bread of our own planting. Don't you know the story of the twelve spies Moses sent into Palestine, how they brought back an evil report?' No, she knew nothing about the twelve spies. So I told her the story. And soon after that I got better, and took my two horses, and went out to the ploughing, and ploughed all day. And when I come back, she's in tears. 'What is it, Yetta?' She says she's lonely, she hankers for company, the kind she had in Ekaterinoslav. 'What have you done to me and my chicks?' she starts all over again. 'I've done nothing to your chicks,' I says. 'They've been out ploughing the fields with me. And as for your Ekaterinoslav company, a rotten fig for that. Today you're a peasant woman, and peasant women don't have company. And if you're lonely,' I say, further, 'you've only to step out of doors and take a look at our Valley of Jezreel. Look, there's Mount Gilboa, where the glory of the great King, Saul, was brought low; that's where King David pronounced his curse in olden days, no dew and no rain should fall on the hills of Gilboa. And over there is Mount Tabor, where the Prophetess Deborah sang her song of praise to the Lord, for the victory over Sisera. And way up yonder's the summit of Mount Hebron. Isn't that company enough for you? And you talk about that silly Ekaterinoslav company, which always cost money to entertain and wasn't worth a broken eggshell. Why, Yetta,' I say, 'you ought to be ashamed of yourself.' And she answers: 'Oh, you've always had plenty of words to spare. You can talk a stone into a pair of legs, and you've talked me into coming here. God help me, what's going to become of me?' What could you say to a woman like that?"

I could only echo his question: "What *could* you say?"

"Well, there's a God in heaven," he answered, elliptically. "She began to get used to the life. Bit by bit. Bit by bit. One morning I caught her standing at the door, looking out at our little field, shining with dew, and there was a smile on her face—she didn't know I saw her. And then, one evening, I see her go out into the garden, and she's murmuring to herself. And I see her bend down and pull out a weed. And I said to myself, 'Ho, ho, it's getting you, old girl. The soil's getting you, the good mother earth.' And I went out to her and said, 'Pull 'em up, wife, pull 'em up, all the weeds. The mountain up there is still wild, and wild things grow there, and the wind carries the seed of them down, and the wild things grow in our field. But in the time to come our brothers will live up there, on the mountain, and wild things won't grow there any more. So when the wind will blow this way, and bring seed, it'll be the seed of good grain, and we won't have to tear it out.' But she didn't give in so easily, the old woman. She says: 'I wish I could tear you up by the roots, the way I'm tearing these weeds up.' But I knew she was half won over; that's why she talked that way.

"No, after that I wasn't afraid any more. The land got her. There's something in the land that gets everyone. It pulls you. And why? I'll tell you why. You come here in the beginning, and it's a howling wilderness. No people, no friends, no house, no water. Nothing! And you want to run away! You feel you won't be able to stand it twenty-four hours. But if you hold on, till the first things grow in your garden, and you've got the first loaf from your own fields, then you'll never want to leave. All land is like that. And this land of hours, the Holy Land, more than any other land in the world. Think of all the history in it, think of all the blood that's gone into it—think of—"

Reb Noah was becoming rhetorical, and that was a pity. So I interrupted him:

"And how do you get along with the Arabs, Reb Noah? They say, back there in Ekaterinoslav—"

He interrupted me in turn.

"How do I get along with my neighbors? Why, perfectly. Best of friends. When I came out here the young fellows in the neighboring colony said to me; 'Reb Noah, you've got to get yourself a revolver and a knife. If you go without them, the Arabs will find you in the middle of the field, unhitch the horses, and drive them off, leaving you there with the plough.' And what did I answer? 'My lads,' I said, 'I'm not afraid of your Arabs. See this Turkish fez? That's my revolver. And see my little boy Solomon here? That's my knife.' Because the first thing I did when I got to the Holy Land was to buy myself a fez. 'That'll show them,' I said, 'that I'm a Semite, just like them.' I went out into the field, ploughing, and my fez was on my head and my little boy by my side. I'd like to see the Arab who'd attack a father when his six-year-old boy is along with him. There is no such Arab; because the Arabs are Semites, and Semites are merciful. I'll tell you what happened once. I was out there"—he pointed to the furthest end of the field—"I was way out there, one day, under the hill. I was ploughing with my little Solomon, when along comes an Arab on a horse—an Arab with a gun on his shoulder and a sword by his side. When he drew alongside I passed my hand over my forehead and my breast, which is the way they greet each other here, and I said: '*Ni habik said,*' which means, 'Let your day be beautiful.' And he passed his hand over forehead and breast and answered, '*Tahbadnik,*' which means, 'Let your morning be fresh.'

"Because as soon as I came out here I learned to say 'Good morning' in Arabic. I'd like to see the murderer who's going to attack you after you've said 'Good morning' to him. Especially a Semite. Well, the Arab on the horse points to the little boy, and asks me in Arabic whose he is. So I press little Solomon to my heart, to show he's mine. Then the Arab gets off his horse and begins to finger my plough, because he'd never seen one like it before, his people still using wooden ploughs, like our ancestors ages ago. Then I touch the plough, and I point way over the hills, to show that in the place I come from they use iron ploughs. So he shrugs his shoulders, and smiles, and nods. And now, seeing we were good friends, I say to him, 'You, me, *achim,* brothers, Semites'; and he smiles again, showing all his teeth, and bows, and says '*Hawadji,*' which is their word for '*gospodin,*' or mister. Then he jumps on his horse and rides away. So I ask you, do I need a revolver, or a knife?"

I stared at Reb Noah, not knowing what to say now. And he, a little ashamed of his garrulity, said, "One more furrow, there and back," and turned his horses toward the field.

I stood watching him as he steered the plough; I watched the horses pulling, the children helping. It was not too straight a furrow that he drew—but it was a good one, deep and even. And I could not help thinking:

"How did this Jew find it in himself to throw away his comfortable business, his security, his ease, his Ekaterinoslav, and come out here into the wilderness? How did he throw off the habits of the city, the money curse, and take to guiding a plough under a blazing sun?"

Then I remembered what Reb Noah had just said. "I've a special gift. I'm gifted for Palestine." Undoubtedly he was; how else could he have come through? And I reflected further: "Perhaps that gift belongs not only to some Jews, but to all. Perhaps the gift for Palestine slumbers in the whole Jewish people."

—*Translated from the Yiddish by* MAURICE SAMUEL

Redemption

Historians of the science of astronomy are unanimous in holding the encounter of the two great men, Tycho Brahe, the pioneer astronomer (1546-1601) and his pupil, Johann Kepler, to be one of the most pregnant and auspicious events in the development of its teaching.

As is well known, some years after Tycho's death, on the bases of his own observations and those of Tycho, Kepler deduced those famous laws bearing his name, fraught with such revolutionary consequences. In this connection the ever fortunate man derived benefit from the fact that during the interval following the death of Tycho the telescope was invented, rendering possible entirely new modes of apprehending nature.

Kepler, whose character, in integrity and grandeur, did not fall short of his extraordinary intellectual endowments, was always ready to admit with all emphasis his debt to Tycho. Alike in his RUDOLPHINE TABLES and in the actual work of fundamental importance upon the movements of Mars, and also wherever appropriate in other writings, he never forgot to point to Tycho, whom he styled the "phoenix of astronomy," as his master and as the real pioneer.

MAX BROD

PASSING through two dark cabinets, in which guards were on duty, Tycho Brahe reached a small chamber in the castle. It was hung all round with red silk. The Emperor entered it immediately from the other side and came toward him. Tycho bowed low. The Emperor took another step, but still remained standing at some distance from him, without holding out his hand. In this position he moved a little in a sidewise direction and, leaning over a table of gleaming agate, inquired in slow, timid tones: "I hope, Professor Brahe, you are already comfortably installed in our Prague."

Tycho again bowed and remained silent for a space, as if he wished to listen to the dying echoes of the gentle voice. That voice, the sideways movement of the sovereign, and his embarrassed motion over the table all reminded him of the Rabbi's words: "How weak God is! We must support Him. Woe to the father abandoned by his children."

It had been Tycho's intention to pour forth all his sorrows before the Emperor in a wild, reckless statement of grievances. All at once he felt that his misfortune was trifling compared with that of the man who had to support and to guide a whole State, a world full of such misfortunes. And this was the man from whom he had wished to demand help, whom he had almost decided to arraign! Suddenly he felt that he had not the courage to give utterance to his trivial woes. He recounted the story of his removal in brief, matter-of-fact terms, merely observing at its conclusion that he still, of course, had some desiderata.

With what touching attention the Emperor listened! He did not utter a single word of interruption, but kept his great, melancholy eyes steadily fixed upon Tycho. It was obvious that he forced himself to listen. And again when he said in reply that Tycho should draw up his demands in the form of a memorandum and hand it to the Privy Secretary, Barvitius, his words issued forth as if reluctantly and under constraint from lips shaped for silence. One did not see the smile that usually plays when a request is granted. Those lips had assuredly never smiled. . . . Tycho was overcome and wondered how he could even have ventured to force his way into this sphere of majestic seriousness and world domination. He only felt that his audience was over, and once again bowed to the ground.

But the Emperor had not finished. Advancing gently from behind the table, he said that he would be pleased to cultivate closer acquaintance with the great master of the starry lore. He named certain hours at which Tycho should have daily access unannounced.

While he now spoke in greater detail, Tycho respectfully contemplated the monarch's small but well-built figure. Clad from head to foot in radiant black silk, a short jewelled dagger at the side, his form expressed a natural nobility. His face was devoid of colour, the skin soft as buckskin, and the aspect one of infinite melancholy. The loosely hanging under lip and the prominent chin, with its ample, finely curling beard, held fast an unalterable expression of sympathy and compassion. Tycho, in whose excited brain the imperial figure began more and more to blend with the Rabbi's God in His need of help, was quite enraptured at this clear manifestation of sympathy. Soon he answered with the greatest cordiality and joy. And the Emperor, too, seemed to find pleasure in his company. The conversation grew warmer, and finally Tycho followed a

movement of invitation of the Emperor's hand. The discussion continued
while they paced slowly through the adjacent rooms.

They found themselves in the famous imperial art gallery, which it
had never fallen to the lot of any foreigner to behold. Here for the first
time the monarch's face lost its rigid expression. He now behaved with
the complacent bearing of the collector who exhibits his treasures. In
leisurely tones, as if no ministers and visitors were waiting outside, he
interpreted the German, Dutch, and Italian pictures which hung right up
to the ceiling and even along columns and pillars. Some were actually
placed across the windows. Beneath, in numerous glass cases were massed
like sea-foam costly crystal cups, pearls, and silver bowls. The so-called
German room, originally intended for state balls, was also filled with
objets d'art and curiosities. Even the corridors and staircases were radiant
with a dense mass of polished, turned, and embossed work, with mosaic
and ivory, with the glory of stuffed humming-birds, and with furs, so
that at length the silent sheen began to hum in the ears like the sound of
a medley of voices.

"No, God is really not almighty." The words passed through Tycho's
head as he was reminded by this uncontrollable accumulation of the
chaos of the prime. The Emperor, too, in the midst of his treasures,
which he had not perhaps surveyed in their mass for a long time, seemed
to be alarmed. He shook his head like one weary and soon passed silently
back along the exhibits, lacking power to pause by any single object. All
this was calculated to intensify in Tycho's reeling brain the interplay
between imperial and divine lordship over the world, until at length,
giving expression to a doubt which characterized his whole life as an
investigator, he inquired in meek but quite unceremonious tones: "Your
Majesty, is there some law present in all this or none at all?"

The Emperor stood still. "You ask what law I have observed in my
collection? Many have already asked me that, and I have never been able
to answer any of them. I know, too, that many of those outside consider
it a fault that I live here only for these things and look with loathing
upon their disputes. . . ."

"Ah, but they compare you with the Medici princes in Florence, the
patrons of the arts," interjected Tycho in genuine admiration. He was
filled with understanding of the man through whose majestic, composed
tones there trembled an incomprehensible note of weakness.

But Rudolf emphatically repudiated the suggestion. "No, a Medici by no means! They were worldly and found in life itself a meaning which their art was intended merely to adorn. I, however, lock up my art; I keep it pure, for I have found no meaning in life, nothing which must be adorned and honoured. Need I remind you of your coat of arms, Master Brahe: 'Nor power, nor wealth, only the sceptre of the arts'? Some, it is true, come with their religious demands and set them high above everything. Falsehood and deceit! I know my Estates. Freedom of conscience for them is an excuse for extorting liberties of a much coarser sort which have a financial value; they confuse the Holy Spirit with their rubbish. But I—" and here the Emperor raised his head—"I seek perfection in these stones and metals and upon painted canvas, as you seek it in the stars. There is but one thing for the sake of which life is worth living, perfection. . . . There you have the law which governs my collection."

The Emperor had approached a small marble table. It hung over a glass shade which covered a mass of pure gold and indicated that this "alchemical gold" owed its origin to the power of the Pole Sendivoj. The Emperor looked questioningly at Tycho, who maintained an embarrassed silence. Then he continued dejectedly: "Even in the arts we do not often find perfection. I know that I am deceived. That skin you see there was sent me by a Hungarian magnate with a message to the effect that it had fallen from heaven. Herr von Rosenberg has presented me with a stone which grows. I always have the ducal cap of Przemysl and other clumsily forged objects of great rarity. One is taken in; I am well aware of it. In the realm of art it is very much the same as in politics. Thorny is the path of perfection. Ah, if once one could have attained it . . . even as my great-aunt Johanna believed herself to have attained it in her handsome husband!" The Emperor's voice had sunk to a whisper, and Tycho shuddered at the light of madness in his eyes. "Oh, I understand her well. When the perfect dies, the beauty that is irreplaceable, how could one ever forget it? . . . Well might one cause it to be carried about in a glass coffin until the day of one's death. . . ."

They had entered an open gallery. The golden-brown autumnal tops of the acacias in the deer-park brushed against the stone parapet. The chilly odour of decay held Tycho's spirit as in a spell, and the Emperor's confused utterances accorded sorrowfully with this image of decay.

Trembling as in a frosty wind, the Emperor moaned: "I wished to be an example to my subjects. Our time is full of unrest, self-seeking, and vanity. I wished to show that one must observe measure, reflect, live the inward life, be alone rather than amid evil councillors, have but one desire, to discover perfection.—But for that I am too weak."

Too weak!

That was the word for which Tycho had been waiting, and now within him thundered forth a mighty voice: "Yes, God is sick. He is plagued to death; He can do no more.

"And the autumn about us—the perishing and the dropping—that is an illness of God, not His ill will.

"Why have I hated autumn and dying and illness? I held them to be God's ill will. But now I see; they are but His fatigue. His love remains eternal.

"Now I have remorse; now I am reconciled with God! In the gloom of this autumn day He will lead me to Him, of that I am certain."

The Emperor touched Tycho on the shoulder, arousing him at this point from his distraction. They returned to the interior of the palace. There in a well-lighted little room they beheld an easel and beside it a tall man about whose head scanty grey locks hovered. It was the court painter, Bartholomäus Spranger, whom Rudolf esteemed so highly that he always allowed him to work close to his private apartments, indeed under his very eye. The Emperor approached the painter with a lively step in order to touch lightly with the handle of a brush certain places which he wished altered, and to praise others. Tycho, too, drew nearer and greeted the painter.

His attire was disorderly. It consisted of an open, smock-like overall, bespattered with paint-stains and without the customary ruff. His fat, pale face, in which the nose alone had colour, argued many a sleepless night; he might have been taken for a decayed debauchee, although, as was well known, he was a solid Kleinseitner citizen. And this old gentleman sat before a canvas on which he had grouped five or six naked girls and brown, muscular boys in the most indecent postures on the pretext of some allegory: "Virtue Conquers Envy and Pride." In all the flower of their youth, white and with red points upon their breasts, the maidens held weapons and trumpets in their hands. A little Eros was occupied in forcing apart the rounded thighs of one who still resisted the impor-

tunities of her lover. . . . The picture, with its chilly light-blue tints
and its conventional execution, tedious in its complete absence of genuine inspiration and utterly dead, produced upon Tycho a sickly sweet
impression, an impression even as of something vicious. What a morbid
perversion! The worthy burgess, moderation personified, must assume
the mask of immodesty in order to please the virtuous, severe, unsmiling
Emperor! The contrast between these frivolous painted figures and the
two elderly men who examined and fingered them with the air of con-
noisseurs produced upon Tycho, as nothing else could, the impression
of impotence and senility. Suddenly it seemed to him as if here in the
castle there was literally nothing that was young. The dismal chambers
which he had just seen, with their precious and ancient lumber, acquired
while still fresh in his memory a tone of slackness, decay, the aspect of
things shrivelled from age. Did not the caskets totter together like backs
bent in despair, and strange white fungus threads twine themselves along
the damp walls like some enormous white beard? "Oh, God Himself is
a grey-beard!" thought Tycho now. "God is incarcerated here in this
desolate castle of Hradschin as if in His last refuge. Here He awaits His
end. . . ." Tycho hardly observed that he had for a long time been
walking with the Emperor through other rooms. Before his eyes God descended ever lower from the clouds towards him. He had already set
foot upon the woebegone earth and, somewhat like an old beggar whom
he daily encountered opposite the "Greif," stretched towards him, with
a look bordering upon utter despair, red, crooked hands. . . .

At length he started in alarm. Following the Emperor, he had entered
the same chamber, hung in red, in which the audience had begun. And
now he perceived that the audience was really almost at an end. But during
the hours that he had passed in the monarch's company, he had not uttered a single word about the matter on account of which he had come.
He had passed through the rooms like one lost in heaven-sent dreams.
"And yet they say that I am too shrewd," he grumbled to himself. But at
the same moment, even as his visions suddenly faded away, the other, the
matter-of-fact side of his nature asserted itself, and in well-considered
language he reminded the Emperor of his promise regarding an observatory in Prague.

To this, too, the Emperor nodded assent, but not with the decision
and friendliness that Tycho had actually expected after so much confi-

dential discussion. The erection of an observatory, said the ruler, was of course in prospect, but for the immediate future the construction of a pyronomic and alchemical laboratory seemed to him more urgently necessary, setting aside the fact that the latter entailed less expense and even offered some prospect of gain. He would, therefore, desire that for the immediate future Tycho should place his services at his disposal to that end. "Rejected, then, a decisive and final failure," thought Tycho to himself bitterly. The ground trembled under his feet. He could hardly hold out any longer against the rapid change of emotions brought about by this momentous afternoon; he had already begun to stagger towards the door. But through all the excitement within his mind his clear sense of duty still toiled on like a ticking clock reminding him of Kepler. "What a good thing it is, particularly for Kepler, that I am so shrewd!" was the thought that occurred to him. "In my place he would certainly have forgotten me, or rather it would never have struck him to attempt anything on my behalf." And at the same time he thought of all the outrages and finally of that letter which Kepler had written. What heartlessness! But, unaffected by the uproar within him, he set before the Emperor the well-founded, carefully-thought-out request that the young astronomer Kepler might join him to aid him in his work, and that he might be appointed to the now vacant office formerly held by the imperial mathematician, Ursus. He added the request that out of regard for the enhancement of prices in Prague the salary might be increased by a hundred gulden a year.

"Kepler," replied the Emperor, and again leaned on his agate table. "I have heard the name. He is the assistant who lived with you at Benatky. The reports about him are not greatly to his credit."

Tycho listened attentively. "What was that? Not to his credit? Kepler, about whom the whole world is enraptured, whom it places above me?" He thought he had not heard aright and involuntarily took a step nearer to the Emperor. The parquet cracked beneath his hasty tread.

The Emperor continued in his drawling tones: "He has even been accused of taking part in a conspiracy against my government. Your own son-in-law——"

"Tengnagel! Yes. The two had some quarrel. The charges are absolutely unfounded."

"Perhaps so. I only ordered a hurried inquiry and quickly let it drop——

out of regard for you. I could not believe that you would entertain my enemy as your guest."

Tycho was dumb under the Emperor's suspicious look. Only now did he feel the danger of his position. And once more it would have been Kepler to whom he would have owed this most grievous harm, the *coup de grâce,* the loss of the Emperor's favour. This maddening reflection robbed him of all power of speech.

After a pause the Emperor went on: "But more serious than these presumptions is the report that he has expressed himself in terms of coarse contempt concerning astrology and that he does not practise the art at all. You are too tolerant, Master Tycho, and will never speak ill of anyone. You are solicitous on behalf of your pupils, even when they fall away from you. Listen, I have it from people fully deserving of confidence that this Kepler is more attached to the Copernican fancies than to your own excellent *diataxis mundi.*"

Tycho nodded in silence. Was he not to nod? The last sentence which the Emperor had uttered was absolutely correct, was painfully, tormentingly true. Why should he not have nodded? The Emperor's words were correct. There was no doubt that Kepler was Tycho's scientific opponent. And this Kepler, whom all worshipped, was suddenly revealed as not enjoying the Emperor's goodwill. Diabolical fires of malice suddenly flamed up in Tycho. Was not this revenge for all the suffering which Kepler had inflicted upon him, whether consciously or unconsciously, from indifference or from design, in any case so as to penetrate into the most vital part of his whole life's work? In a moment all the good spirits, the vanquishing of self, the triumphs in Tycho's breast, were drowned by a veritable witches' sabbath of loud-voiced temptations. A genuine feeling of voluptuousness had laid hold of him, deep and strong; a burning love of self was kindled within him, gilding everything with its gleams. . . . "A compensation, a compensation for all evil." Tycho exulted. "This, the most exalted moment of my life, compensates me for all the evil that I have suffered. Yes, the whole world pours forth its felicity at Kepler's feet, while I have been overwhelmed with calumnies from the beginning. But as a compensation, out of regard for justice, the highest peak in the world stands out of Kepler's reach and I am welcome there in imperial favour. That, now, is God; that is God's justice; that is the significance of my existence, the justification, the heaven. . . ."

"If you insist upon your request," concluded the Emperor, "I will gladly grant it. But from the first this Kepler has not been agreeable to me, and, as I said, I should do it entirely to please you."

Tycho had involuntarily accompanied the Emperor's remark with a genial murmur of joy. "I need do nothing but keep silent," he said to himself, "I have no need to speak against Kepler. On the contrary, I have done my part and given my recommendation; I could do no more. It would even be dangerous if I were to do more. I can speak no further on his behalf. It would involve me in suspicion myself. No, the Emperor has rejected him—rejected him, moreover, in private conversation; it is no fault of mine. Now it is Kepler's turn to be unlucky. . . ."

The Emperor was really uttering words of farewell. Now he even stretched out his hand. Tycho lightly gripped the white, cold fingers and bent his knee while he kissed them. Then he stepped backwards towards the door, without uttering a single word. The Emperor was already looking down at the shining top of the table, as if Tycho were no longer present in the room. . . .

What now followed was surely something quite contrary to usage. Tycho had already touched the wood of the door when he drew back his hand as if he had laid hold of white-hot steel. At the same moment overwhelming emotion forced him to his knees, so that he fell, weeping, and trembling throughout his whole frame. . . . But in the next instant he had recovered himself; it was just as if he had merely stumbled. With calm aspect and gentle tones he once more approached the Emperor, who raised his eyes in astonishment. "There still remains something that I must set right," wailed Tycho, as if no more master of himself. "I must testify . . . yes, testify."

The Emperor drummed impatiently on his lips with two fingers.

"Your Majesty was not well-informed. Kepler is perfect." As if with these words everything was said, Tycho fell silent; more he could not say.

"So you want to have him, if I understand you aright?"

And now Tycho paid no more heed to the Emperor's wrinkled brow, to the possibility that his whole position might be jeopardized, now that he espoused the cause of the obnoxious Kepler with so much warmth. Without a moment's hesitation the words burst from his lips: "Kepler is the most considerable—no, Your Majesty, that is too mild a term—he is the only considerable scholar of the age. He is simply perfection itself, pure, fruitful, inviolable perfection. It is perfection that Your Majesty seeks. Here it offers itself. And so I ask on his behalf still more than the post of mathematician. Everything must be decided. I feel that I have not much longer to live." Tycho's voice trembled. The Emperor seemed only now to notice that something of vital interest to Tycho was at stake, and his morose expression grew gentler. With kindly eyes he regarded the pallid features of the man who strove with himself and adjured him to banish his sorrowful thoughts.

"It isn't a sorrowful thought," said Tycho, "it is my happiest thought, if I may hope that Your Majesty will hear my request. When I die, I would not have my sons, no, nor the junker Tengnagel—they have all indeed studied the starry lore, but they are nothing in comparison with Kepler's genius—I would have Kepler, Kepler and none else, inherit my position and all that I leave behind in manuscript or print, my instruments and all the scientific equipment that Your Majesty in your graciousness has accorded me. Then I will gladly die, for then I shall know that my work is in good hands, the equal of my own. . . ."

"Kepler, then, upholds your theory, and my information is false?" asked the Emperor, full of interest.

"False and not false. There are difficult questions involved. In some we are not in agreement and I, too, have objections to oppose to him. But these are not of the kind that his traducers allege; they are of a kind that could not arise at all unless he were accorded the fullest recognition." Tycho hesitated. Suddenly the inner voice which had already brought him to this point cried: "Now or never is the time to testify, now or never, to testify and to withhold nothing." And so he continued firmly: "As regards the question of astrology, we are of course entirely of one opinion. One must certainly admit the existence of a general affinity and a divine operation within the cosmos, but it is not enshrined in the naïve prophecies of the horoscope—"

"That is my opinion as well," interrupted the Emperor, speaking more vivaciously than at any time during the whole conversation, and a vast surge of confused ideas, of hopes and curiosity, rose quite visibly upon his features like a cloud in the sky. "Tell me about it. But no—you are tired!"

Tycho's alternately pale and blood-red countenance and the deep rings beneath his moist eyes in fact admitted of no other interpretation. "I beg

Your Majesty to accord me your gracious leave to withdraw," he said, already speaking with difficulty.

"From this moment onwards Kepler is my court mathematician." The Emperor slightly inclined his head and withdrew with measured tread. "We shall see one another again soon," he said, already on the threshold of the next room.

Tycho passed through the two dark cabinets, the white corridor, and the room where the two halberdiers stood. Suddenly it seemed as if he had passed the whole morning between these two gleaming lance-heads, hemmed in between them and whirled about, so that they alternately clashed together and receded with the rise and fall of his emotions. . . . He hastened through the ante-rooms, seeing no one. Already he was in the open air. In his condition of stupor he chose the road leading in the opposite direction from home, passed the cathedral along the inner bastions towards the mighty walls of the fortress. Many acquaintances greeted him in the courts of the burg. He stumbled on in his semi-conscious condition, reaching the George Church and the Daliborka. The autumn rain fell in fine drops. The ivy-stalks, with their yellow and golden leaves waving in the wind like long pendulums, beat upon the castle walls. Tycho observed nothing. Only when he had reached the parapet by the castle steps and saw nothing before him but the grey expanse of the evening sky, did he start up. His whole tension released itself in one mighty cry in this lonely place upon the battlements of the burg.

And now, too, it was also perfectly clear to him that this—and not the earlier infatuation—was the supreme moment of his life. For he now understood for the first time in his life the real reason why he was so shrewd, so capable, and so active, the true significance for him of these seductive and dangerous gifts. Not for himself should he or might he be shrewd—that he now realized amid a rapture that knew no bounds—but in the name of God to establish and redeem the world.

"Oh, this happiness! I have achieved nothing with the Emperor on my own account, but for Kepler everything that I had desired. Ah, how pure that is, how perspicuous, how pregnant with significance: shrewd for others, not for oneself!

"I am upon God's work. I am a servant. I feel the sweet burden of responsibility for everything that happens.

"I am shrewd in the service of God. And to that end it is exceedingly well that I should also feel now how God has heard of my service, how God waits upon me and upon my shrewdness, how He expects sacrifice from me.

"From the clouds on high, God stretches forth His hand, and rising from the earth, I hold my shrewdness high above my head, lifting it up to the aid of my Lord.

"And yet this shrewdness has plagued me throughout my life. It lured me upon false paths, so that I have become weary of it and have learned to curse it.

"Has not shrewdness brought me into insupportable company? Has it not caught me in the toils of weak compliance and compromise? Has it not persuaded me to undertake a thousand useless tasks?

"And yet I have endured it, the evil, the fork-tongued, the poisonous! And yet I have not cast it from me impatiently, like a counterfeit coin. *Nay, I divined that even shrewdness is a sacred thing and that the original nobility of its nature would yet come into prominence! And so I waited and endured amid the tortures that shrewdness inflicted upon me!*

"Oh, praise to the great, eternal shrewdness! Praise to my instinct to bring order to things and to make myself conscious of everything! Praise to my errors and to the right way discovered at long last! For now my shrewdness is in its right place, there where God needs His trusty comrades and can accomplish nothing with such blind Kepler creatures.

"I laud my God. He loves the insensible, but still more those that have within them both impetus and reflection, who would forego neither and who reach His throne panting under the double burden.

"I laud my God. He has led me to Him, stone of offence that I am; He kisses me upon the face, here, right upon my broken nose!

"I laud my God. How could I compare Him with a beggar who supplicates my aid? I do indeed help Him; but who has brought me to His aid if not He Himself?

"Yes, to the governance of the world I lend help with all my strength. But is it my own strength that has made it possible for me to help?

"No, there is God again. God beneath me, who has helped me, even as God above me, whom I help. God everywhere, the powerful no less than the powerless, the helper and he that receives help.

"Hail to myself for that I recognize God is no longer far from me! Alike sublime and needy of help, He stands before me with His tre-

mendous countenance, fierce and gentle, the one eye commanding, while
the other seems to entreat or to thank. Ah, how well I know that countenance! How it has accompanied me throughout life until this present
moment!"

And suddenly Tycho realized what it was that this countenance reminded him of. Of something quite familiar, even intimate. Of his own
father; nay, more, of a particular event, a particular winter evening. For
once—Tycho was then a seven-year-old boy on the estate of Tostrup—his
father had fallen over some newly-frozen snow, and Tycho, who was
smaller even when standing than his gigantic father when kneeling, had
held out his hand to help him. And the very same expression with which
his father had risen to his feet now shone down upon him from God's
halo, an expression which was wrathful and at which one shuddered,
an expression which seemed to say: "Help me, you must help me, it is
your duty to, and you can't do enough for me," and yet at the same time
also: "How fine it is that you do help me! I will never forget it; I rejoice
at it, my good son."

"My good son, my son," sobbed Tycho, striving desperately to fight
down his emotion and to prepare himself for the sharp contest in the
service of God as he now stood before Him. But the idea that God
looked down upon him like a beloved child, that God designed no evil
against him, despite His mighty and terrible aspect, despite His divine
majesty—that God, even in the wondrous manner of a father who, fallen
by accident, needs help, looked forth from eyes enraged and yet at the
same time gentle, eyes humiliated and yet exalted, eyes sternly expectant
and yet filled with a bounteous foreknowledge—this idea was stronger
than his composure. Everything began to dissolve, to form itself into
new shape. And when Tycho looked down upon the city through the
veil of his tears—by the mediation of God, this alien, clamorous, uncomprehending city had also become his friend and confidant. The beautiful river, the pale-hued towers, the streets, and the men—all proceeded
from the Father. That life was so hard and joyless to endure among these
men, who were by no means merely scoundrels, but also honest, gifted,
and earnest people, that injustice should be done to his good intentions
by kindly fellow-creatures, deserving of all respect—even this perplexity
which caused him so much daily disquiet was now completely banished
from him. It was made plain in that paternal aspect which God showed

him, in that strange, unfathomable expression which rejected help, blazed up so proudly, and yet expected help with such ardent longing. . . . Quite enraptured, as if fire were streaming through his being, Tycho looked up to the sky. There aloft through the mist, although the sun had not yet gone down, feeble rays forced a path; and then on a sudden—extraordinary, sublime spectacle!—all, all the stars were there! And this time it was no longer a mocking twinkle and glimmer, as in those recent nights, when he had been compelled to contemplate them without instruments. Like great white flakes of snow all the stars stood in the grey heaven. And by virtue of the same power whereby the light pierced through the veil of evening clouds, they now constantly grew in size and sent forth their white, red, and blue light, first in single rays, then in great fans, which again coagulated like sparks and finally with impetuous movement formed themselves into mighty segments of circles. Nay, the stars began to move along those circles just as Tycho had imagined a thousand times when standing before his celestial charts. He held his breath, while a final feeling of warm exaltation passed through him. Now he saw that for which he had longed and toiled in vain so many years, what was more than astronomical learning: the real course of the stars. It was a clear presentation of the divine law in the ordering of the world, a most exalted harmony, an apprehended unity of creation, inscribed in characters of fire. Like a delighted child Tycho gazed about him upon the ever moving, rolling firmament, resounding in sonorous accord. His eyes could not be satiated. There revolved Mars, whose movements in its simple, beautiful, smooth path he had never been able to penetrate. It was like the peaceful rise and fall in the breathing of a sleeping infant. Near by, constellations which had so often confused him met now in the most entrancing groups. They exchanged places, they glided past one another, they seemed to hold each other by the hand, they sported together and returned once more in wondrous order. The heavens opened with a deeper expanse; the Milky Way stretched itself forth, swelling out like a great white cloth in the wind. Worlds whose existence had never been suspected hastened near. Yet another revolution of the whole, another slight tremor through the cosmos, and then all manifoldness had disappeared; the whole standpoint seemed to have changed. Now all the stars circled round, their stations plotted with an indescribable simplicity in one glowing single ring, the diamond axis of the world.

So it was given to Tycho to see with his own eyes a vision to which he could never have attained by means of his most ingenious instruments: reality, the immortal perfection of his system, the genuine *theatrum astronomicum*. And while ultimate matter, ring, and world-axis dissolved away, he was already caught up into a divine aureole, uniting face to face with the Being he had come to know. A mighty voice resounded through the thundering accords of the spheres: "Tycho, My servant." At that he flung out his arms. "Here am I," he cried, and fell unconscious to the ground.

After midnight the relief guard found him and brought him home, where his anxious family were sitting up for him. Kepler, with his wife and child, had arrived shortly before and had at once betaken himself to Tycho's abode. To his horror he had now to behold his friend and protector carried in on a stretcher.

Tycho was in a high fever. Hagecius, who appeared that night at the sick-bed, ascribed the critical turn to neglected kidney-disorder. He applied leeches and prescribed cooling remedies. Towards morning Tycho recovered somewhat and looked round with tranquil eyes. He greeted Kepler with a friendly nod.

Kepler had brought with him a present for his host, the long-promised apology of Tycho against Ursus, upon which he had bestowed the whole of his time in Graz. Like everything that proceeded from Kepler's pen it had developed into a work of genius, containing startling new vistas upon the future. In Benatky, amid the wealth of suggestions proceeding from Tycho, he had without any ill intent neglected the apology. Just as naturally in Graz, where he lacked the collected material for original investigation, he had flung himself into this, strictly speaking, historical task. He had in fact produced a work entirely after Tycho's mind and indeed surpassing his expectations. But Tycho only regarded the title-page with a gentle smile. Then his fingers, which had already strayed between the pages of the manuscript, slipped back upon the pillows. His thoughts were travelling in another direction: "Blessed, blessed be this hour! Assuredly I greeted you well, my Kepler, when you came to me for the first time. But that hour was not yet the real blessing. Then I was blinded; then I believed that you were come to be my earthly ally and helper of helpers, and on that account I blessed that hour. Now you have by no

means allied yourself with me in earthly matters. On the contrary, you
have but increased my suffering. But it is just by that means that you
have helped me. Yes, now I recognize it; you were the instrument of God
to purify me. Blessed be that hour when you entered my house! Now for
the first time can I say it with a whole and thankful heart! Now and
only now do I see that you have been my best friend! . . ." Tycho was
under the impression that he had actually spoken all these words. In
reality he moved his lips powerlessly, without any sound issuing forth.
Utter impotence had gained upon his senses. . . .

In the mean time the group of relatives round Tycho's bed had been
joined by his more intimate acquaintances, for the report of the great
man's unexpected illness had penetrated the city. The consideration in
which Tycho's name was held among the people was now for the first
time made manifest. By midday the narrow street had become almost
impassable; the crowd pressed together in a dense mass far into the
neighbouring streets and squares, all waiting anxious and solicitous and
whispering in undertones. The courier from the Emperor, who appeared
every hour to obtain intelligence for his master, was respectfully allowed
to pass; behind him the press closed again its iron barriers.

It was significant of Tycho's popularity that very speedily the rumour
circulated that his enemy Raymarus Ursus had poisoned him. Hagecius
himself had to appear at the window and calm the people, reminding
them that Ursus had been long dead.

Tycho several times recovered consciousness, but felt the end near
and desired to take leave of his wife and children. He comforted them
with simple words of faith in God. Then he exhorted his sons, Tengnagel,
and the few pupils who still remained with him to continue their studies
assiduously. . . . This effort seemed to have exhausted all the strength
that was left to him; his breath now came irregularly, its movements
growing tranquil only with difficulty. He did not speak again. It was
with a gesture that he summoned Kepler to his bedside, taking his hand
and continuing to hold it. His eyes remained closed and the fever grew
in strength. But before his inner eye there appeared once more the vision
of the star-set, fiery, agitated heaven as of yesterday. The voice of God
resounded in his ear, and the sublime promise was mingled with kindly
images, recollections of his childhood and of his days of prosperity on
the island of Hveen. Yes, just as formerly he had felt himself happy and

at home in but few regions of the vast earth, and those of restricted area, so now the whole world had become a home for him. Intoxicated and set free, his spirit ranged through distant solar systems, and everywhere he beheld Tostrup and the island of Hveen, everywhere laws disposed themselves in order, everywhere new tasks beckoned to him and new results of wondrous beauty. And so a thousand undreamed-of forces stirred within Tycho, while in the eyes of those who stood around him he lay there expiring, almost without any sign of life. All that he had achieved by his labour seemed small and of no account by comparison with that which he now beheld. Standing upon the boundary of two worlds, the finite and the infinite, he once more became courageous, young, and eager for action. When he looked round upon that which remained behind him as the heritage of a scholar, he was exceedingly discontented. And so it was that once more anxiety snatched him from the divine embrace and forced the cry from him: "If only I have not lived in vain!"

The night of the 24th October fell. Throughout the whole night Tycho, rising out of the death agony, several times repeated the cry: *"Ne frustra vixisse videar!"*

All in the room were upon their knees. From the street there rose the murmurs of the praying multitude, the gleam of torches, and the cries of children. In the half-light of the morning Tycho once more had a moment of freedom; the pain had left him. Then he opened his lips, and to Kepler, who had not stirred from his bedside, he made this request: that everything which he should write in the future might be set forth in his system, the system of Tycho, not in that of Copernicus. As he said these words, his features were lighted up by a peculiar smile. He had assuredly left far behind him all vanity, all paltry weighing of success and failure, and so by his system he naturally no longer meant those earthly experiments, but the all-comprehensive, divine certainty of the true law wherein he now felt himself a blissful participant. In this, too, he wished to make Kepler his pupil, even as in many other matters he had shown him the right way. But his strength did not suffice for him to make this clear, and so Kepler inevitably misunderstood his words.

The words were Tycho's last, words which have descended to posterity with the false interpretation which was so obvious. Soon after, he perished in the arms of Kepler and of his elder son.

His remains were buried at Prague in the Teynkirche on the Grosse

Ring with great pomp and amid a vast assemblage, drawn alike from the court and from the people. There, close by the high altar, his monument may be seen today, a slab in relief, cut out of red marble, bearing the portrait of Tycho in full knightly armour, his left hand caressing a globe, and his right grasping a sword. The device, too, was not wanting: *Nec fasces, nec opes, solum artis sceptre perennant.* "Nor power, nor riches, only the sceptre of the spirit shall prevail."

—*Translated from the German by* FELIX WARREN CROSSE

PIERRE VAN PAASSEN

The New Order

Pierre Van Paassen revisited his native land after the Nazis had taken over. In THAT DAY ALONE, toward the middle of the book, he vividly described some of his observations.

HERR HAUPTMANN Baron Waldemar von Schwabenfels of the Third Prussian Regiment of Death's-Head Hussars, lately mechanized, was sitting in the board room of the orphan asylum. He had personally selected the stately old mansion, with its marble stairway and its high windows, to serve as military headquarters for the occupational forces in the fortress of Gorcum and its environs until the town hall, where everything was still upside down because of the fighting that had taken place there, could be repaired and put in order. On the large oaken table in front of Herr von Schwabenfels stood a gold-framed photograph of Adolf Hitler and a silver coffee set. He had lit a cigar and as he leaned back in a broad red-leather armchair, he raised his brightly polished boots to the table.

The new commander of Gorcum was no longer a young man. Upon first glance one would have put him down as fifty, though he must have been older. He wore the Iron Cross and some other decorations which showed that he had served under the Kaiser in the previous World War. He carried himself well. The recent campaign in Poland had reduced the corpulence that had come upon him in the years he had spent on his estate in East Prussia. The sun had bronzed his features and heightened the vividness of his blue eyes. A close-cropped mustache did not wholly hide his souvenir of Verdun—a livid scar across his upper lip where a piece of shrapnel had struck him. His men said of the *Hauptmann* that he was a good sort. He had a fatherly way with them, a circumstance attested by his kindly, slightly wrinkled face. His first word to Burgomaster Verwey of Gorcum, when he informed that gentleman of his deposition, had been rather in the way of a humble apology. "I

154

beg your worship," he had said, "not to blame me for this rather violent irruption into your community. . . . I am only obeying orders. I assure you that I'd much rather be seeing how the peaches and plums are doing on my farm in Oels."

As he slumped back that June morning and blew out rings of smoke, Baron von Schwabenfels allowed his eyes to travel back and forth along a row of paintings on the wall before him. They were portraits of past regents and donors of the institution in which he had now taken up his abode; full-faced gentlemen in black cloth blouses with high ruff collars, wig-wearing dignitaries of the eighteenth century, and, finally, men in side whiskers and stiff black suits—a procession of Dutch faces and costumes representing four centuries both of change and continuity. He surveyed the pictures casually, but his eyes returned again and again to a Directoire water clock on the mantelpiece. On top of that clock were two metal figures in the costumes of Napoleonic grenadiers, with up- lifted mallets in their hands. The Baron was waiting for the hour of ten, when the two mechanical grenadiers would beat out a tune on the musical bells and then, with a curious gesture of uplifted mallets that made them appear to be saluting the onlooker, switch around and beat out the strokes of the hour on a deeper-toned gong.

As he was anticipating the mechanical play, there was a knock on the door and in strode Herr Stantarttruppenfuehrer Erich Schwartz of the S.S., one of Himmler's Gestapo agents, who had been sent to Gorcum to reorganize Dutch civilian life. The Gestapo man saluted him with outstretched arm and said: *"Heil Hitler!"* Baron von Schwabenfels brought his right arm forward in response and sighed.

"Well, what is it, Schwartz?" he asked.

"I beg to report, *Herr Hauptmann,* that the shops will all be open this morning. The workers have returned to the wharf. The Jews have been assembled in their synagogue. But the schools remain closed until we have examined the teachers. I have ordered the confiscation of all the sugar in the town. We'll need an entire train for it. There are a thousand sacks of flour, too, and several carloads of canned fruit and vegetables and a good stock of cocoa. . . . And then, eh, *Herr Hauptmann,* Gestapo headquarters have ordered that fifty men are to be deported for the out- rage at the mill and three to be executed. The execution will be at three this afternoon. We think it best to have a public execution in order to set an example."

"Have it your own way, Schwartz," said the Baron. "You know what's best. By the way, has Lieutenant Schmidt come in? . . . Oh, there you are, Schmidt," the Baron exclaimed, jumping up from his chair, as a young officer came into the room. "I was just asking for you. You may go now, Schwartz," he added, turning to the Gestapo man. When Schwartz had left, Baron von Schwabenfels fell back into his chair.

"That cursed swine with his Jews and executions gives me the creeps, Manfred," he said. "I was just sizing up that clock on the mantelpiece when he came in. It's mine. I'm shipping it to Silesia. Did you say you wanted the chandelier in the hall? You'd better hurry and get it down. There is apt to be a Gestapo inspector here this afternoon. We're going to have an execution. Get everything packed before that bird arrives. By the way, did you get some good pictures?"

"Yes," laughed Lieutenant Schmidt, reaching for the cigarettes, "I think I have a line of ancestors down to the fourteenth century now. I picked them up in the museum."

"Good, good," beamed the Captain. "I hope you covered up your—ah—little loan."

"Oh, yes," came back the Lieutenant. "I had the vacant spots covered with photographs of him," he pointed to the Fuehrer's photograph on the table, "of him, and Clubfoot, and the Flying Pig."

"Excellent!" returned Captain von Schwabenfels. "Have the pictures put together with your lamp and my clocks, and we'll ship them all out this afternoon before those thieves of the Gestapo arrive. . . . By the way, any news from the front?"

"He went to France this morning!" replied the Lieutenant. "That means it will soon be over, I suppose," Captain von Schwabenfels said. "At least, let us hope so!"

Baron von Schwabenfels dreaded the hours that were to elapse before the execution. Not that he was plagued by any qualms of conscience. A crime had been committed against the German authority and the German army, and that crime was to be punished. If the Dutch would not indicate who the culprit was, that was their affair. In such cases the innocent had to suffer for the guilty. But he looked forward with nervous apprehension to what was to come before the actual shooting, which Lieutenant Schmidt was to supervise. That was all arranged.

The Baron knew from experience in Poland that, as military governor of a newly occupied community, he had to listen to the supplications for reprieve on the part of the relatives of the condemned men.

Why should he have to go through all that torture? It was the most futile gesture of this whole insane business of war, for it was decreed beforehand that, though advocates and relatives of the condemned were permitted to make representations, no mercy was to be shown. But maybe these Dutchmen won't ask for pity. Maybe they won't come whining and wheeping like those horrible Polish priests and women he had been forced to hear in Kalisz last fall. He hoped the Dutch would not make him go through the same ordeal again. He hoped they would let the condemned go to their deaths without a whimper. Then Lieutenant Schmidt would have the pleasure alone. He could have it.

That boy Schmidt had a strong stomach. He came out of the S.A. ranks and had served as supervisor of a concentration camp. He had seen a thing or two. He would not weaken. Schmidt, the Baron thought, actually takes a delight in executions. Had he not finished off those Jews in Kattowitz with his own revolver? *Herr Gott Kreuz noch 'mal!* He had simply waded in their blood!

An orderly, who came to take the water clock away, informed Baron von Schwabenfels that a deputation of burghers was waiting in the ante-chamber.

"Men only?" asked the Captain.

"At your service, men only, *Herr Hauptmann!*" answered the man.

"Show them in!" he added. "I may as well go through with it!"

The delegation consisted of the pastors of the various Reformed churches and three Catholic priests. It was the first time that these men had ever appeared together anywhere. They filed in slowly. Baron von Schwabenfels noticed that not one of them bowed or clicked his heels. Suddenly the thought flashed through his mind that they might have come to murder him. Should he take out his revolver? That would look childish. But still, suppose they intended him harm? You could never be sure. These men were patriots, outraged patriots. They might be desperate. He was alone. The Baron rang the bell. An orderly appeared.

"Let the guard fall in here," he ordered, "and leave the door open.

Heil Hitler," he said, turning to the delegation. "What is it?" They did not answer his salutation. A hard crowd, he thought. It will be a long time before we make Germans and Nazis out of these brethren. They will be hard to break. But that is work for the Gestapo.

"These men are innocent," began the pastor who stood in front, without any preamble. "Is it part of your code to execute innocent men?"

"I do not owe you any explanation, *Herr Pfarrer,"* said the Baron testily. "German soldiers have been killed in your community in a most atrocious, barbaric manner. There is to be punishment for that. If you can name the murderers, we may consent to a revision of the trial. I do not guarantee absolution for those now condemned. There is a bad spirit in your community, a spirit of opposition to the German army, most disgraceful and ungrateful. We came as brothers and liberators, and you received us as enemies. The Fuehrer had the best intentions toward Holland. He gave the German word of honor that no harm would come to your country if there were no resistance. You disregarded the German word. He guaranteed the safety of the dynasty. The dynasty fled. He came to bring you freedom from the English yoke, and what do we find: resistance everywhere, resistance with deadly weapons."

"I never saw an Englishman in all my life," said the pastor curtly.

"That may be true, *Herr Pfarrer,* but the English exercised an occult control over The Netherlands, the English and the Jews. The Fuehrer could no longer permit that." The Baron looked at the gold-framed photograph of Adolf Hitler and wondered if he was saying the right thing. "No man or woman of the German race in this whole world is going to remain in the power of Jews. Neither here, nor in England, nor anywhere in the world. That is Germany's mission. The last century has been the age of the Jews. The next thousand years will be the German epoch. Germany is at last coming into its own. For hundreds of years we Europeans—*was sage ich?*—we Germanic brother peoples, have been kept fighting each other by England. That is the greatest scandal of history. But it is now ended. . . ."

"When did we ever fight before?" asked the pastor dryly. "We, the Dutch and the Germans, or the Germans and the Scandinavians, except at the time of the Reformation, which surely had nothing to do with England?"

"Herr Pfarrer, let us not quibble," came back the Baron. "Germany is victorious, and Germany's will is to rule the Continent now!"

"Quite right," replied the pastor. "But if we are to be brothers, Germanic brothers, as you say, why not deal with us in a more brotherly fashion. Why not spare the lives of the three unfortunate men, who are as blameless of the outrage as I myself or you, *Herr Hauptmann.* . . ."

"You only have to name the culprit's accomplices, and we will surely reconsider our decision."

"We cannot name accomplices when there weren't any," said the pastor. "There are no accomplices, and the men you condemned are surely innocent. We give you our sacred word as Dutchmen," the pastor pleaded.

"Meine Herren, the condemned men must die for the good of Holland."

"For the Holland of the future, *Herr Hauptmann."*

"As you wish, *Herr Pfarrer,"* returned the Baron. "I do not quarrel about words. Facts alone count with us."

The selection of the persons to be executed had been left to the discretion of the Gestapo's representative in Gorcum, Parteigenosse Erich Schwartz. This individual, a tall cadaverous type who had earned his spurs in the early days of the Nazi régime by his iron nerve in administering the most atrocious tortures in the concentration camp of Oranienburg, had not been long in making up his mind. . . . From the moment of his arrival in the town, simultaneously with the troops of the Third Prussian Regiment of Death's-Head Hussars, he had quietly proceeded with the arrest of those Dutch citizens whose names figured on the lists supplied him by the *Ausland Amt,* that branch of the German Secret Police which kept on file the names and activities of every individual in every city, town, and village who is either an active or a potential opponent of German Fascism.

With the aid of certain sympathizers of the Nazi cause in Gorcum— half a dozen men who made up the local membership of the National Socialist Bund—Schwartz had not experienced any difficulty in locating those individuals whom Berlin considered more dangerous than armed troops. He had not arrested them in a single wholesale raid. He had these men placed in custody one by one. So as not to arouse popular indignation or to cause a sensation, they had been quietly removed from their homes in the dead of the night. In this way few in Gorcum were aware of the number of those arrested; fewer still knew where the vanished ones had been taken. The usual commentary on these nocturnal disappearances was that such and such a person had been moved to Germany for a more or less lengthy period of "political education." Relatives who went to inquire about them at the Toll Barracks, a very old building—the remnant of a huge castle—where the Gestapo had established its headquarters, were told that they would soon have their loved ones back. They had merely been sent away, along with intellectuals and radicals from other countries occupied by the German armies, to receive instruction in the duties of the new type of European citizen.

What the relatives were not told, however, was that their husbands, fathers, and brothers were chained up to the walls of the old dungeons of the Toll Barracks and that day after day they were subjected to the brutality and mistreatment of the Gestapo men. It was curious, too, that in rounding up the so-called "dangerous" elements, Schwartz had paid very slight attention to the types who might have been expected to fear Fascist conquest most. . . . None of the men who in the past had been classed as rabble rousers or agitators had been disturbed by the Gestapo.

The men arrested were persons like Kees Boon, the smith and local poet, and his friend Jan Trouw, the house painter, who preached of a Sunday in the chapel of the Darbists. These two men, on whom even the most conservative and reactionary Gorcummers had looked in the past as harmless idealists, incapable of the least act or thought of violence, had been among the first to be taken into custody by the Gestapo, as if the Germans entertained different notions on the subject of their innocence and harmlessness. Not the most vociferous patriotic citizens, who had called for a fight to the death against the invader, were regarded by the Germans as their most determined opponents, but rather, strange as it may seem, the men of peace at any price, the conscientious objectors, the followers of Tolstoy, the believers in nonviolence.

The first to join Boon and Trouw in the dungeon of the Toll Barracks had been the president and officers of the district organization of Kerk en Vrede (Church and Peace), a young pastor from the near-by village of Dalem and his colleagues from the small fortified town of Woercum, across the Merwe River. These men, the fundamental idea of whose preaching had been spiritual defense alone, would have had Holland disarm completely, strip herself of army and navy and face the world as naked as Isaiah of yore, in an attitude of absolute defenselessness. They were willing to face occupation of their country and subjugation of their people without offering the slightest opposition, in the belief that in so doing they carried out Christ's command not to resist evil. Now they were indicted as Germany's worst enemies. Their ideas had not had a wide following, but to the extent that their influence had made itself felt, one might have expected that the Germans would have hailed them as comrades and collaborators in that they had contributed something toward disrupting unanimity on the subject of national defense and so had helped to assure Hitler's victory. These were the men who had been thrown into jail. And it was out of their midst that Parteigenosse Schwartz selected the three who were to pay with their lives for the burning of a mill and its soldier occupants.

But at the last moment, the Gestapo agent changed his plans about having the execution take place in public. He could not keep up the pretense that his prisoners had been sent to Germany for political re-education and yet produce them at so short a notice before the firing squad in the town square or on the bowling green. Moreover, the military commander of Gorcum, Baron von Schwabenfels, had caused the announcement of the forthcoming execution of the three condemned men to be affixed to the billboards as soon as he had learned the names of those selected by Schwartz.

The *Parteigenosse* had decided that the execution was to take place on the rifle range behind the Toll Barracks, an area that was closed to the public. The three men he selected were Sylvan de Wit, a plumber; Jan Trouw, the preacher and painter, and a schoolmaster named Gerrit Jan Strang. The three were informed of their fate at noon, three hours before their death. A request to see their wives and children for a last time, which Baron von Schwabenfels had granted, was later countermanded by Schwartz. The Gestapo man had taken all details of the execution in hand and had even told Lieutenant Schmidt that his presence would not be required.

The only witnesses of the execution were the inhabitants of those houses whose rear garden walls touched on the rifle range. Some of them watched the strange procession that came out of the iron cellar door of the Toll Barracks that afternoon. One of the spectators stood behind the Venetian blinds in his room, looking across his small garden through a pair of binoculars, his attention drawn to the scene by the voices of the condemned.

The three men looked grimy and unkempt. Their faces could be seen plainly. Jan Trouw, the preacher and painter, was almost unrecognizable. His left eye was swollen horribly, and the lower part of his face was covered with a heavy growth of beard. . . . They were chained together. Sylvan de Wit, the plumber, was weeping and had to be assisted by one of the soldiers as the party climbed the stone steps that lead to the rifle range. There were twelve soldiers in the squad. An officer preceded them, while the Gestapo agent, Schwartz, followed behind. The three were placed under an elm tree. Schwartz advanced to read something to them in German, of which, of course, they did not understand a word. The Gestapo man read quickly and in a monotonous tone of voice. Suddenly the sound of the carillon in St. John's tower disturbed the summer afternoon's stillness. Instinctively the three men looked toward the tower. And then, without paying any more attention to Schwartz reading the verdict, the three of them fell in with the tune, singing the words with broken voices: "The Lord is great. His Name is great, the wonder of His works is great, endlessly great His love! . . ."

When the three condemned men began to sing, Schwartz looked at them in surprise and ran back quickly toward the firing squad. . . . At the same moment, the command rang out: "Fire!"

When the smoke had cleared away, the secret onlookers saw that De Wit and Strang had fallen flat on their faces, but Jan Trouw was on his knees, trying to raise himself. Blood was coloring his shirt in dark red blotches. . . . Schwartz walked over swiftly to where Trouw was kneeling. He held a revolver in his right hand. Trouw had almost raised himself, but Schwartz fired, and he fell. Yet again the painter rose to his knees. This time Schwartz kicked him in the face with full force. Sinking back, Jan Trouw pointed a finger at the Gestapo man and called out: *"Toch zijn jullie ook menschen!* And yet you too are human beings!"

For answer Schwartz bent over and, steadying his revolver in the crook of his elbow, fired once more. . . .

The new order had been established in Gorcum!

III

Shadows of Childhood

CLARA LAIDLAW

The Little Black Boys

As to a comment on "The Little Black Boys": It pleases me that it has been chosen as a story of the spiritual life of man. That is what I meant it to be. As I conceived it, the race problem was only an incidental one. The real problem was one of our common stake in humanity, of our reaching out to others in sympathy and love while all the time our pitiful isolation, one from the other, keeps us from ever really touching another life. It was meant to say the same thing Robert Frost has said so much better in his "To a Moth Seen in Winter":

> *But go. You are right. My pity cannot help.*
> *. . . the hand I stretch impulsively*
> *Across the gulf of well nigh everything*
> *May reach to you, but cannot touch your fate.*
> *I cannot touch your life, much less can save,*
> *Who am tasked to save my own a little while.*

CLARA LAIDLAW

THE little black boys, Samuel and Hamuel, were the first, indeed the only Negro children I'd ever had in my classes in Northford. I remember very well the first time I saw them, on Wednesday, the second day of school, when my freshman math class assembled for the first time.

They sidled into the room shyly, after all the white children had rushed in to begin disputing noisily over the choice seats in the back of the room. The black boys hesitated just inside the door, looking around in a bewildered way, and then they slid quickly into two empty front seats. I couldn't help noticing how bent and shriveled and small their bodies were. Obviously they were twins, but even the usual physical retardation of twin children did not explain all their difference from the robust white children. There was hunger in the shallowness of their chests, and their thin, bent shoulders told of hard work beyond their years. When they sat down, the seats were almost ludicrously large for them.

The white children buzzed and tussled until I called them to order, but the little black boys sat like twin statues, their eyes gleaming white as they stared at me, their round, fluted lips sober and still. They had cheap new dime-store tablets before them on their desks, and penny pencils, the dull brown ones with pointed erasers wedged into the tops.

When I asked them, as I had the others, if they wanted to be called by their full names or by nicknames, the frozen stillness of their faces broke for the first time, and the one nearest the blackboard said, his white teeth flashing, "I'm Sammy. He's Hammy."

Some of the little girls behind him began to giggle. I nodded hurriedly and said, "All right, boys. Sammy and Hammy it shall be," and turned quickly to take up the first lesson.

As the days and weeks went by, I paid little attention to the twins. They were quiet and sober and good. They never whispered to anyone and no one whispered to them. I grew used to seeing their black faces staring blankly up at me, or their kinky black heads bent laboriously over their work. With diminished penny pencils clutched tightly in skinny black fingers, they worked hour after hour to produce grubby papers covered with painfully worked problems, all wrong. The class was a slow one; but of all the group, Sammy and Hammy were the slowest. If, after weeks of work, they became finally convinced that if A and B, working alone, could each do a piece of work in six days, working together they could do it in three, then the next day they would be equally certain that, if one tablet cost ten cents, two would cost five.

I used to find myself scolding them occasionally, and they would look up at me with remorse in their liquid black eyes, their mouths drawn down into a mask of guilty grief.

Once I said, "Oh, Sammy and Hammy, what am I to do with you?" and Hammy said, "We're sorry we's so dumb, Miz Carey." Then he smiled and Sammy smiled, like two bad little dogs trying to be ingratiating. So we were friends again, and I began writing on their papers, to their innocent delight, "This is better than yesterday's paper," or "Fine! You had two problems right today" instead of the bare o's and 20's they really earned.

One day I found a paper of Hammy's from which the comment I had written had been neatly cut.

"We saves them," Hammy said shyly when I questioned him. "Our mammy pastes 'em in a big book we got from the tailor shop. She say—

't ain't every boy gets him so many nice words said to him—least, not every black boy."

"Those twins!" the other teachers groaned. Poor little black boys, they couldn't do anything at all. The other children shunned them, too, it seemed, and their days would have been sad indeed had they not had each other for company. Each day they brought their dinners and sat alone on the steps eating their plain bread from a paper sack, while the other children ate and played noisily in the lunchroom.

Sammy and Hammy would sit watching the antics of their fellows with eager interest and delight, whispering to each other, chuckling companionably at whatever pleased them, but never offering to join the fun. Their apparent contentment in their isolation puzzled me until one day Sammy said, concerning another matter, "Our mammy say—you twins, so you be twins together," and I understood what the mother was doing for them: making the gulf between white and black be their choice, guarding them thus from fear and from desire for what they couldn't have, making them self-sufficient in their twoness.

Still, their aloofness bothered me. I didn't want to make an issue of it, but when two or three boys or girls would come in to discuss class politics or the play, or to get news for the paper, or just to visit, I'd begin in a roundabout way to talk about democracy and the American dream and the Golden Rule, and finally, as offhandedly as I could, by way of illustration, I'd bring in Sammy's and Hammy's need of friends. The boys and girls would say, "Yes, Miss Carey," "Of course, Miss Carey," but the shadow would come down over their faces. They would look secretive and stubborn, and I knew they'd been talked to at home.

In a way, you couldn't blame their parents. The twins lived alone with their mother in an old shack 'way down at the shore. At first the black woman had gone about asking for work for herself and her boys, and she had done washing for a few ladies until it had got around that Cash Benson, the town's ne'er-do-well, had been seen hanging around the shack. Now she and the boys managed to live with no apparent means of support, and lately when the woman came to town, everyone could see that she was visibly big with child. "Cash's nigger woman," the men on the street corners called her, guffawing as she passed. No wonder white parents kept their children from making friends with her boys.

She had gone to the Swedish Baptist Church twice when she had first come to town, taking the boys, stiff and clean in their patched Sunday suits. "I been baptized and bred up pure Baptist," she had told Reverend Swanson proudly, hesitantly accepting his proffered hand as he had bade her good day at the door of the church. Behind her the Swedish Baptist ladies had whispered and stared. The next Sunday, when she and the boys had taken their seats humbly in the last pew, there had begun a rustling as, one by one, some irately, some shamefacedly, the white ladies had risen and left the church. The black woman had stayed for the service, though Sammy and Hammy, watching her face, had begun to cry. She had never come again.

The way things were, there didn't seem much I could do except be especially nice to Sammy and Hammy, and that was hard too, because I certainly couldn't praise their work, and to treat them differently from the others would have antagonized the white children and made things still harder for the twins.

Toward spring it came time to have the annual freshman party. We had a class meeting, and the youngsters decided to charge twenty-five cents a ticket to pay for the lunch, and to have dancing and a program. Miss Carey, of course, was to help with the program. I always got that!

"Mr. President," I said. (We try to teach them to observe parliamentary procedure, heaven help us!) "Mr. President, may I say a word?"

"Keep still, you kids," the class president yelled gallantly. "Miss Carey's got sumpin to tell you."

When approximate quiet had finally been achieved, I said, "The program committee and I are going to need help, so if you can play a musical instrument, or sing, or dance, or recite, or stand on your head—" (Hoots from the class. "Miss Carey made a joke! Listen to her!") "why, come and tell us. We need talent for our program."

Then, before the tumult could get under way again, I added, remembering the time I had missed the eighth grade picnic because my mother had been away visiting, and I had been too proud to borrow from the neighbors, "And another thing—sometimes twenty-five cents is hard to get hold of, so if there's anyone who wants to go to the party but who hasn't the money at the time, why, you just come to me, privately, and we'll see if we can't fix it up."

The next day after school, I was correcting papers when the door opened and the twins sidled in. My heart sank. After all, did it matter what one apple cost if a dozen cost twenty-five cents?

Sammy's black face glistened, and he moistened his lips with a pale tongue. "Us—us—," he whispered.

"We's got us each a box," said Hammy quickly from over Sammy's slight shoulder. His eyes rolled toward his brother fearfully. Obviously, it was not what they had intended to tell me.

"A box?" I echoed, a little relieved that the bewildering price of apples was not in question.

"A gittar," explained Sammy, his black face deadly serious. "We each got us a gittar. We plays us gittar music."

"Also, us—we sings," nodded Hammy enticingly. They obviously wanted me to say something. Their eyes begged me to say it, but I could not imagine what it was. It somehow never occurred to me that the two black boys would be coming to see me about the party.

But that was it. Sammy and Hammy wanted to go to the party, and, moreover, they wanted to be on the program.

"But I ain't got no two-bits," said Sammy, his mouth drooping sadly.

"Nor me," echoed Hammy. "You said—come to you, Miz Carey—" His voice died away plaintively.

"We'll work for you—hard," offered Sammy.

Their eyes held mine apprehensively, like spaniels' eyes, hoping for a kind word.

"That's fine," I said with unnecessary vigor. "Fine! I'll put you down for the program. And don't you worry about the money. Your music will pay your way."

It was the wrong thing to say. I knew it when the boys stiffened into black statues and their faces hardened into expressionless masks.

"Our mammy say—work for what you gets," Hammy said at last, adding with sober dignity. "So we works for you."

"Yes," I said quickly, "maybe you'd better, so the others won't be jealous and think I like you best."

A look of blind adoration came into Sammy's face, and Hammy grinned in a pleased sort of way.

So it was fixed. I gave the boys the tickets, ostentatiously taking fifty

cents out of my purse and putting it ceremoniously into the "party box."
The work was to be done later when I needed something done.

As the day for the party approached, excitement began to run high
in the freshman class. The twins whispered to me that they had been
"practicing up," and the sight of their raptly pleased faces intensified
in me a little feeling of doubt I'd been trying to suppress. What, I thought,
if the white children should be unkind to the black boys? What if the
others on the program should refuse to appear with them? And what
about the dance? What little girl would dance with them—and would I
want her to, if she would?

I needn't have worried about the program. Apparently no parental
ultimatum had been laid down. Perhaps no one had mentioned that the
black boys were to make music, or perhaps the hours of the party were
to be a sort of secular Truce of God wherein even black boys with a bad
mother could have their hour of fun.

The party was to begin at eight, and at seven-thirty the gym was almost
filled with children, all the little girls in bright new party dresses, with
their hair tortured into elaborate beauty-parlor curls, sitting shyly on
one side of the decorated gym, while all the little boys, dressed uncomfortably in new suits, with their damp hair brushed to alarming neat-
ness, were seated on the other. The problem of the first half of the evening, as far as we teachers were concerned, was to coax the two groups,
much against their wills, to consent to dance together, while the problem
of the last half was to pry them apart, and get them home before irate
parents began telephoning.

But first came the program. Promptly at eight, since everyone had
already been there for at least a half-hour, the curtain went up, after
several false starts and muffled grunts from the laboring stagehands.

Mary Ellen Adams and Jo Anne Merrill gave their usual military tap-
dance, which, since Mary Ellen is short and fat and lazy, and Jo Anne
tall and thin and active, was rather far from the military effect desired.
Little Genevieve Johnson sang "Ciribiribin," which she pronounced
"See-ree-bee-ree-bean" for some unknown reason, and, with practically
no encouragement, graciously added the encore "Blues in the Night."
Glen Tillman played an excruciating violin solo, during which, mercifully, one string broke, so that the rest of the solo was, by anybody's

mathematics, only three-fourths as bad as the first. Benny Norton gave a reading in Swedish dialect with occasional lapses into Irish, Yiddish, and just plain American.

Then the twins came out from the opposite side of the stage, hesitating, looking dwarfed and lonely under the floodlights, black faces glistening and fearful, patched Sunday best pressed within an inch of its life. They clutched their cheap "gittars," looked out uncertainly at the darkened gym, struck a few chords, and then they sang.

I don't remember much else, not even what they sang. There was stamping of feet when they finished, and shouting. They sang song after song. They sang as the class danced, when it did dance. They sang with the Capehart and without it. They sang while the lunch was passed out until the class president himself brought them two heaped plates and clapped each of the boys on the shoulder by way of congratulation, while the class cheered through mouthfuls of sandwich and cake and waved pop bottles in the air.

They never left the stage all evening. Now, at last, something was well with them: the little black boys, for whom 3×8 was a variable, could sing.

After that, school was their heaven. Boys and girls who couldn't play with them outside of school never failed to call: "Hi, Ham! Hi, Sam!" in school. Math homework papers grew mysteriously accurate though tests still revealed the most abysmal misconceptions concerning mathematical practice. Even the seniors had them sing at their class party. They made the senior glee club, though they had feared before to try out for the junior one.

And they haunted my footsteps with a doglike persistence that came near to wearing me out.

"When we going to work out that fifty cents, Miz Carey, ma'am?"

"When the frost is out of the ground," I explained for the tenth time. "I want you to spade my flower garden."

A day later: "When that frost get outa that ground?"

"Not for two weeks, at least."

Two days later: "That frost gone yet, Miz Carey?"

"Not yet," patiently.

"My! My! Sure stays a long time—that frost!"

When at last the frost did depart, the two black boys attacked my little garden spot with a vigor it had never known before. They trailed quack-grass roots to their remotest hiding places and exterminated them forever. They spaded and weeded and spaded again.

"That's a great deal of work for fifty cents," I teased at last, a little troubled at the sight of their thin bent backs stooping over my garden so long.

"Our mammy say—work good," Sammy said firmly, and Hammy's monkey-thin face echoed the stubborn set of his brother's jaw.

"You give us those seeds—we plant 'em," Hammy called pleadingly.

They planted my seeds, they hovered over the new little shoots, they weeded and watered and tended. I tried to give them extra pay, but they stiffened with hurt pride.

"Our mammy say—you take good care o' Miz Carey's garden, for she been purely good to you."

So I gave up in despair and let them do as they wished. I did all I could to get my neighbors to give them odd jobs, but only a few did, for the black boys' mother had had her baby, a girl baby, almost white, old Dr. Bates said, with hair like Cash Benson's.

In school the boys still haunted my room after class. They'd sit staring at my face, saying never a word until I had finished my work, and then not much unless I set the pace.

One afternoon I'd been reading a volume of Blake's poems, and on an impulse I asked them if they'd like me to read them a poem about a little black boy. I didn't think they'd understand a word of it, but I love to read poetry aloud, even if it's only to myself. Only after I had started to read did it occur to me that the black boys might read into it something that Blake had never intended, that I might be shaking their protective unawareness, might be emphasizing their difference in a way bad for them. But I had started and I had to go on.

They sat still as statues while I read:—

> My mother bore me in the southern wild,
>   And I am black, but O, my soul is white!
> White as an angel is the English child,
>   But I am black, as if bereaved of light.

My mother taught me underneath a tree,
And, sitting down before the heat of day,
She took me on her lap and kissèd me,
And, pointing to the East, began to say:

"Look at the rising sun: there God does live,
And gives His light, and gives His heat away,
And flowers and trees and beasts and men receive
Comfort in morning, joy in the noonday.

"And we are put on earth a little space,
That we may learn to bear the beams of love;
And these black bodies and this sunburnt face
Are but a cloud, and like a shady grove.

"For when our souls have learn'd the heat to bear,
The cloud will vanish, we shall hear His voice,
Saying, 'Come out from the grove, my love and care,
And round my golden tent like lambs rejoice.' "

Thus did my mother say, and kissèd me;
And thus I say to little English boy.
When I from black and he from white cloud free,
And round the tent of God like lambs we joy,

I'll shade him from the heat, till he can bear
To lean in joy upon our Father's knee;
And then I'll stand and stroke his silver hair,
And be like him, and he will then love me.

I watched their faces as I finished. They were still and solemn, but radiant.

"Our mammy say—heaven's like that," Hammy said softly at last.

"Who that man say all that?" Sammy whispered in an awed voice.

"William Blake, a very great poet."

"He a preacher, Miz Carey, I bet?" Hammy asked, looking at me hopefully.

"No, not exactly," I answered, and saw the radiance in their faces dim at my words. Impulsively I added, "But he was a man who thought he spoke with angels, and—and he wrote 'as one having authority, and not as the scribes'!" And I found myself telling them how Blake, dying, sang of the glories of heaven opening before his dimming eyes.

Hammy's face shone, and his teeth flashed in a grin of solemn delight. "He sure knew—that white man!"

"God sure told him sumpin," Sammy affirmed, nodding deeply.

"Read it again, please, Miz Carey," said Sammy suddenly.

I read it again, and they both sighed with one accord.

"That's better'n music," Hammy whispered. "Read it once more again? Huh? Please?"

I laughed and shut the book. "No, twice is enough. Some other day, perhaps."

But I never read it to them again.

As he went out of the door, Sammy turned. "You like rock gardens, Miz Carey?"

"Why, yes, of course," I said, "but if you're thinking— You've done altogether too much—"

"We knows a place," Hammy was saying dreamily, "a place where there's moss like a feather bed an' little white violets that's sweet as Jesus' breath—"

That was the last I was ever to see them. They rowed across to the place they knew after supper that night, a marshy island not very far offshore. Folks who saw them start said the water was choppy as they were going over. Coming back the boat overturned, and before the men could get to them they were drowned.

I heard the next morning in school.

The late May sun was warm on my hair that day, when school was over and I was plodding along the beach toward the Negro woman's shack. The silvery sand filtered into my slippers and dribbled out with each difficult step. Under the slanting sun the smooth blue waves lapped the shore and retreated in little slipping movements, as if they had never known storms or death.

Around the shack the rank shore grasses had been cleared away with scrupulous care, and in the shifting sand a few drooping plants gave evidence of the twins' efforts to make a garden of their own.

She opened the rough, tar-paper covered door when I knocked—a thin, worn woman of about forty, with the fine features and liquid eyes one sometimes sees in people of her race. Her lined black face was mask-like in its calm, but the eyes themselves were alive and tragic.

I don't remember what inadequate thing I said to her, but she must have felt my sorrow reaching out to hers, for she thanked me with something of the boys' doglike look in her eyes.

"They loved you so, Miz Carey," she said strangely, and I had the feeling that behind her simple words there was something strong and seeking, something she wanted of me—wanted badly, if only I could find out what it was.

She asked me in with homely courtesy and pulled out a rough chair for me to sit on.

The one room was painfully neat and bare. In a broken tumbler on the table a small bunch of short-stemmed white violets was beginning to droop, and on the ledge of the one window I saw the purple tulips I had given Hammy two days before. A table, three old chairs,—one with no back,—a small camp stove, and two camp cots were the only furnishings. The floor, rough and splintered from much scrubbing, was immaculate.

That space of floor seemed to me that day to be waiting mutely— waiting for the boys, who hadn't yet been brought back in their cheap little coffins. People never knew until long afterwards that it was Cash Benson who had paid for it all, giving them the best funeral he could afford. That, at least, is to his credit, though he went off the next week and never came back. Reverend Swanson, too, came, the good old man, although he had to face the disapproval of the Swedish Baptist ladies to do it. I've thought of it often since and blessed the kindness of his gentle old heart.

But that day there were just the two of us. I sat by the table, and the afternoon sun through the only window threw the shadow of Hammy's tulips across the bare floor.

The boys' mother stood by the other side of the table, black and monumental and unweeping, staring at me with that queer tense look, seeming about to speak and then closing her lips gravely.

The baby began to cry, and she went over and picked the little thing up from the bed, blindly, as if she hardly knew what she did. After moment she sat down opposite me, rocking the child gently in her arm

Awkwardly I tried to comfort her, saying it was good she had the gi baby to fill a part of her heart. She looked at me strangely across the sur mottled oilcloth, her ugly black face sharp with pain.

"But they was my true-born child'en," she said, as if reasoning wit one who was dull of understanding. Slowly she looked down at th whimpering infant in her arms. "She white man's child, poor little thing.

Then she looked me straight in the eyes, not doglike but womanlik "I was all alone," she said simply.

I tried to speak, but there was nothing to say now.

When I started to go at last, it was with the feeling of how very futi my visit had been, of how empty sympathy and words of sympathy wer to this woman.

She rose reluctantly when I did, saying softly, "You was good as the said you was to come—" Then she added pleadingly, as if she feare I would misunderstand, "But it ain't fitten you come no more. Besides— Her voice caught, but she swallowed and went patiently on, "Besides be best you remember Hamuel and Samuel as they was—yestiday."

I nodded mutely, and she seemed satisfied that I had not misunde stood or taken offense.

But on the doorstep she stopped me again, hesitating, uncertain, an I knew that the thing that was haunting her was still unsaid. I could fe the conflict of urgency and fear in her, the tension and the longing, b I had to watch her helplessly, hoping she would speak, afraid to ask f fear what I might say would be wrong.

She drew a deep breath then, throwing her head back nervously. H eyes were shining and fearful, and the words, when they came, wer slurred and hurried, breathless.

"Last night—suppertime—Hammy 'n Sammy, they full of some wor song you read 'em. They say—it better'n music. They go away singin' to them two— Something about—black boys? You remember, Miz Care ma'am?"

Her breast rose and fell in agitation, and the child, awakening agai began to cry.

"I'll send you a copy," I said thickly. "A poem I read to them."

She shook her head. "You say it to me, please? I never did learn book-reading."

I turned my head away, thinking of the scrapbook of "nice words" she had kept for her boys.

What I could remember, garbled, imperfect, half-forgotten, I tried to say, remembering the two thin, black faces lifted to mine in the quiet of the dusty schoolroom.

She was very still when I had finished, but her face was bright with a faith I could never know.

"My Hammy and Sammy?" she said wonderingly. "Maybe they God's white lambs today?"

And then she wept, putting her face down against the baby in her arms. "Oh, bless God," she whispered brokenly. "Blessed God, make it so. Sweet Jesus, make it so."

I touched her hand silently in farewell and went away. At the gate, when I turned and looked back, she had lifted her head, and I saw that she was looking far out over the water, gazing across at the distant shore-line of that green, marshy island where the moss is like a feather bed and the little white violets are as sweet as Jesus' breath.

MARTHA FOLEY

Martyr

Children, whatever adults forgetting their own childhood may think, want to be good. There are even times, incredible as it may seem, when they want to be holy—and not holy terrors at that!

How I came to write "Martyr" I no longer exactly remember except at the time I was thinking about a lot of things that happened to a little girl in Boston long ago. She was a very serious little girl with pigtails and spectacles. But she had her moments of ecstasy and this story is about one of them.

MARTHA FOLEY

"AND then I'll see visions."

Emily rocked back and forth on the sandpaper that was scratching her bottom.

"Visions? You mean like the Virgin Mary and the Angel Gabriel."

"Yes. Only I won't see an angel. I'll see God himself."

"But God is invisible."

"Not when you're a saint and have visions like me."

Edna stopped flipping the jackstones from the palm of her hand to the back.

"Are you a saint?"

"As soon as I have a vision I'll be."

"How are you going to get a vision?"

"By suffering."

"I know—like a toothache."

"Not exactly. You can't help a toothache but the sufferings a saint does is on purpose. Like my sitting on this sandpaper."

"But that hurts."

"Of course it does. Everything hurts a saint."

"Well, I don't want to be one then. I don't like being hurt."

"You'll never see God then."

"I'll wait until I go to heaven." Edna returned to her jackstones.

"But you can't be sure of going to heaven unless you are a saint."

"Twosy, threesy. I'll pray to God to go there. Foursy. Fivesy."

Emily got up carefully so the sandpaper wouldn't slip out of her drawers. She wished she had enough money to buy a hairshirt. One sheet of sandpaper didn't stay put in place. Perhaps when she got her Christmas money her mother would take her to the big store downtown and she could get one in the shirt department where her mother always bought her underwear. But Christmas was a long way off and she would have to do the best she could till then.

She looked disgustedly at Edna and her jackstones. Edna would never get anywhere always playing. As for herself she was going off to her retreat now for fasting and praying. She walked stiffly across the street and into the next yard. She had to hold her hand on her back to keep the sandpaper in place. She kept hitching it up. If people saw her walking with her hand lower down they might misunderstand and think she was like her little sister who sometimes forgot to go to the bathroom. It was a long time since she had forgot to go to the bathroom. Not since she was in the first grade and Miss Lavey had caught her playing hookey. She hadn't meant to play hookey but she couldn't go into the classroom like that so she just stayed outside looking in Cunningham's. There were lots of things in Cunningham's window, licorice, shoelaces and penholders with colored water and fish in them. But wasn't she silly then, though? All Miss Lavey had to do was look out the school window across the street to Cunningham's and see her. If she ever wanted to play hookey now she wouldn't just hang around the school.

Emily looked all around her back-yard carefully. She couldn't be a hermit and have a retreat in the wilderness if anyone saw her now. Heliotrope was picking her way from picket to picket along the fence, but no one else was in sight. She would have to pretend Heliotrope was a lion infesting the wilderness. God would understand that a cat was the best she could do for wild animals here in Boston. Perhaps when the circus came to town a lion or a tiger would escape. The lives of the Martyrs were full of lions.

She looked all around the yard again. She could hear Delia washing dishes in the kitchen. It was all right then. Everything was a wilderness. She got down on all fours and crept into a hole between the back steps and the wall. This made a much better hut for a hermit than under the syringa bush. No one would spray the hose on the back steps as they had on the syringa bush.

Funny the way the light came through the cracks in the steps. There was a funny smell here too. Closed in and dusty. But she must pray.

Oh, God, in your grace and loving kindness look down on this wretched mortal. Oh sacred heart of Jesus I implore you to forgive me all my wickedness. It was right through that crack there she had lost the ring with the green stone that came around the stick of candy. No matter how much she looked she could never find it. The next time she came into this retreat she would bring Johnny's sand shovel and dig up the dirt around the place. Oh, divine solicitude, extend your infinite mercy to this repentant soul. Oh, heavenly father, heavenly father, heavenly, if she couldn't find the ring perhaps she could ask old Mr. Cunningham if he couldn't get some more of those sticks of candy with rings around them then perhaps she could get a blue or purple stoned one instead oh heavenly father who gave your son for thy people's sake bless me, your erring child. Now three Hail Mary's.

Now let's see. What else was it saints did? Oh, yes. Fasting. She wouldn't go in and ask Delia for a piece of bread and butter. And now she thought of it, she was hungry. All the better. She'd fast all the time between breakfast and luncheon. She had been going to buy one of those nice big three-cent ice cream cones when the hokey-pokey wagon came along too. But she'd rather have a halo than an ice cream cone. Only halos must feel awfully warm on your head all the time blazing away like that on Saint Cecilia's head in the piano picture. How could you wear a hat then? And did saints take off their halos when they went to bed? She would have to ask someone about that.

But she'd better be praying again. She'd say three Our Father's this time. She would like to have a vision this morning if possible. She would pray as hard as she could then perhaps a vision would come. For a vision she would like to see the little angels, the cherrybubs on clouds. She didn't want to see purgatory or hell the way some of the saints did. And she'd just as leave wait awhile before seeing God himself. He might ask her some questions about the catechism and she wasn't sure of the last lesson. The little angels that were always peeking out of clouds in the holy pictures would be very nice to see.

Each time she said an Our Father she would say very hard at the end and please dear God give me a vision of the cherrybubs.

Emily prayed. The hot summer sun beat down on the steps under which she crouched, bees buzzed in nearby shrubs, sounds of domestic endeavor came from the open kitchen window. It was an ordinary Boston back-yard of a warm June morning. Which is the trouble and why I don't get a vision, she thought. I am not even tormented by fiends like Saint Anthony, I must make a great sacrifice for the Lord. He doesn't like just sandpaper.

She took the square of rough paper out of her drawers and put it away in a corner of the wilderness retreat. I'll try it again some other time, she said. She squeezed herself out from under the stoop just as her brother and two other boys came through the back gate.

"Oh, look at Emily! Whatcha doing under there, Emily?"

"Looking for a jackstone I lost." Dear God forgive me for telling a lie. I can't be a hermit if they know where I'm being one. They'll all want to be hermits too and hermits can't play together. Anyway the Herman boys are Protestants. I can't tell Protestants about such sacred things.

"Walter just found something."

"What?"

"Look, he found this medal on the sidewalk."

"Let's see."

"'Tisn't yours."

"Who said it was? I said I wanted to see it."

"Well, you sounded like you were going to say it was."

"Please let me see it. I'm not going to say it's mine. I promise. I don't even know anyone who lost a medal."

"Here then." Walter held out in his hand a bright yellow disc. On one side was a cross. On the other was a picture of the Virgin with the Christ Child.

"Oh Walter. You shouldn't have that. That's a Catholic medal and you're Protestant."

"There! I told you. I knew you'd want it."

"I don't want it. But I know it isn't right for a Protestant to have some-thing that's Catholic."

"Huh! I found it and it's mine. I can do whatever I please with it. I can throw it up in the air or burn it or roll it along the ground."

"Walter! That's sacrilege. You'll go right to hell."

"Who's said so? If anyone'll go to hell it'll be you for telling me what to do with something I find."

"I'm going to tell your mamas on both of you. Talking about hell. I'm going right away and tell your mamas—"

"Tattletale! Tattletale! Carry home the cow's tail! We're not doing anything."

"You are so! You are using the word hell in ordinary conversation. And mama said you can only use it when praying."

"This is not ordinary conversation. This is religious."

"But—"

"You shut up right this minute."

"All right then. I'll sing a hymn and you know you can't interrupt a hymn. Holy God I praise Thy Name, Lord of all above, I praise Thee—"

The three small boys remained quiet until Emily finished the hymn.

"Walter, let me hold the medal."

"No. You'll keep it."

"No, I won't. I promise."

"Cross your heart and hope to die?"

"Yes. Beat me black and blue."

Emily examined the medal on both sides. "This is a holy object."

"Give it back to me."

"I'll give you a cent for it."

"No!"

"Two cents."

"No, can't you see it's bigger than a quarter?"

"Three cents."

"I'll give it to you for a nickel."

"Three cents are all I have. I was saving up for a big cone. Strawberry and chocolate mixed."

"I like chocolate and nut better. All right. Where's your three cents?"

Emily pulled a small imitation silver mesh bag out of her pocket. In it were a handkerchief, some beads and three coppers. It was a very great sacrifice she was making. She hadn't had an ice cream cone since the little one-cent one last Friday and this was Tuesday.

The Protestant heathen took the three cents eagerly.

"Come on. Let's go out on the front sidewalk and wait for the hokey-pokey man."

The boys departed. Holding the medal reverently in an outstretched hand, Emily squeezed her way back under the steps.

"Now, please, dear God, let me have a vision."

FRANZ WERFEL

The Officer Puppet

In the spring of the last year of World War I, the author with his wife—whom he had met only a short time before—visited the famous Wurstelprater in Vienna, that ancient place of popular entertainment, a sort of fun fair, which, in that cruel year of hunger and utter misery made upon the beholder a most ghastly and ghostly impression. The ears were pierced with the squeal of the electric organs; and there were various sorts of crude amusements, among them a dingy shooting-booth, which so affected the author's wife that she was unable to get it out of her mind. Years before, she had gone to the Prater with a group of friends and this same booth had remained her chief memory of the place, for the reason that the dummies were human figures in the round, most lifelike faces expressive of all the misery in the world. Instead of rifles, large hard balls were used as missiles. A freckled half-grown lad served the clients with the balls. In the company that night was an artist with a well-known gift of second sight. He watched for a while the human figures being battered by the balls, then remarked, pointing to the freckled boy: "Some day he will be a murderer."

My wife repeated the comment, which made her uneasy. The war was still going on, and in some fantastic way the booth and the ball-throwing seemed to have some bearing upon it in her mind. She wanted to see the booth again. We could not easily find our direction on the extended meadow and inquired it of an old woman selling tickets at a roundabout. In amazement she answered: "Don't you know? Just follow the crowd; last night the owner of the booth was murdered by his own son."

FRANZ WERFEL

HOW I always envied those boys whose fathers sat of a Sunday afternoon comfortably and cosily smoking their pipes in the porter's lodge or on the bench outside it! Still more the pupils who spent it in their simple civilian homes, with the master of the house in his shirt-sleeves, a Virginia in his mouth and a half-empty beer-glass before him, sitting at the clean white table. Well do I remember my feelings when, as a small cadet, I once happened to pass the open window of a ground-floor flat and saw an elderly man sitting at a piano with an open music-book before him, accompanying his son, a beautiful lad of about eleven, with the pure, unearthly voice of a soprano chorister, in Cherubino's aria, "New Joys, New Sorrows." Never in my life have I wept more bitterly than I did then; for I was on my way back to school from the barracks where I had to go every Sunday to give my father an accounting of the way I had spent the week.

My father smoked cigarettes and he did not play the piano. He smoked cigarettes which my mother, of tragic memory, his cowed and habitual slave, made for him every evening, sometimes until far into the night, for his consumption was enormous. Always he smoked; putting the cigarette to his lips with trembling, fastidious fingers yellowed at the tips: on the parade ground, in the battalion pay-room, or pacing for hours up and down his room while he brooded endlessly over some event which had cost him an outburst of wrath. Even at eight years old it was plain to me that nobody could be a good man who blew such continuous blasts of smoke through his nose. Everything about my father expressed contempt. Anyhow, surely it was only dragons who blew smoke from their nostrils—and there were no dragons any more.

We were stationed in the capital of one of the provinces, a large city with a strong garrison. I remember that my father, as captain, was at first assigned to the household regiment. I myself was a pupil of the cadet school, and as such condemned to penal servitude in any case. But my lot was far harder than that of the other officers' sons.

No one who has not grown up under the inexorable discipline of such an establishment can possibly appreciate the full meaning of the word Sunday. Sunday is the day when the grip of fear on the throat relaxes; when you wake without feeling physically sick; when there are no exams, no punishments, no exasperated masters yelling orders; no shame, no humiliations, no strangled tears. Sunday is the day when one wakes to the surging music of bells, when the trees in the unlovely school garden are trees and not insentient prison guards; the day when every fortunate possessor of the white ticket may pass the sentinel at the gate and issue forth to freedom and joy.

But as for me, not even Sunday could give me what my comrades had. They greeted the dawn with smothered cries of jubilation; they sprang up and held their heads under the thin trickle from the water tap. They might be out all day until nine at night, some of them even until ten or eleven; not until then did the frightful shadow of oncoming Monday fall upon them, with its burden of neglected or unfinished tasks. They escaped from their prison in the morning, trembling and flushed with joy, to go to homes which might be poor but yet which welcomed and cherished them with marks of love. In the afternoon their parents took them to some cake-shop or restaurant garden, where they might sit and let the waves of music from the regimental band crash about their ears.

What was my Sunday like?

I left the school at ten; sick at my stomach, my heart pounding horribly, without having been able to drink the coffee in my battered tin mess-basin. For at half-past ten precisely I had to present myself before my father in the pay-room of the battalion, and feel his eye measure me with a cold official stare as he began:

"Well, Corporal, is that the way to stand?"

So it always began. My knees knocked together, I summoned all my strength to stand erect and rigid. Then followed an inquisition as to the marks which I had received during the previous week. I got no praise, but a full complement of army oaths; that was a blessed Sabbath for me when I came off merely with silent contempt.

While doing execution upon me my father never stopped blowing smoke through his nose (I have never touched a cigarette in my life—smoking is probably the sole vice to which I have not succumbed). When the inquisition was finished, my father bent once more over his papers, beckoned the ensign, who had been standing stiff as a ramrod in the corner all the time, and without looking at me gave the order: "Dismiss."

I went out on the street with a bitter taste in my mouth. My small legs would scarcely carry me further.

Between my fear and the sun in my eyes I was quite dazed; but I had to go on, throwing out my legs and saluting right and left to make sure I did not miss an officer.

Nor was that all. My fellow-pupils wore their own suits on Sunday, made of good worsted and well cut. I alone had to go out in the clumsy uniform with which we were all supplied; how often I blushed for my shapeless trousers!

I arrived towards midday at my parents' house, tired to death. And even here fate still had me in its grip; for it stood within hearing of the retreat and bugle-calls.

My heart always pounded afresh as I rang the bell. My mother herself opened the door—officers' wives cannot afford to keep servants. I kissed her hand; she brushed my forehead with her dry, austere lips. Then I had to take off my tunic, put on a shabby alpaca jacket, short in the sleeves, and sit down with one of my schoolbooks, while my mother bustled about in the kitchen with her curious jerky movements. I used to wonder why she wore such big clumsy flat-heeled boots, so different from the footwear I saw on the pretty ladies in the street, with their bright frocks and high-arched insteps. Why did her footstep not give the same soothed, delightful feeling that I had when I heard their light tap-tap?

At midday my father came home. His patent-leather boots shone. He could walk through the dustiest and dirtiest streets without getting one single spot on their immaculate surface. He always went through the same routine: hung up his shako and shiny nickel-plated dress sword, took out his moustache brush, and put himself in order; then, standing in the doorway, he drew his spurred heels together and saluted my mother and me, who were already waiting with the soup. He gave us the same brusque and formal greeting he gave when he mixed with the junior ranks at the regimental dinners.

There was not much talk. A more silent being than my mother I have never seen; she could speak fluently on but one subject: the Jews and how she hated them. Now and then between bites he made a remark about an officer, referring to his equals or subordinates by their surnames; to his superiors he always gave their proper titles.

He was an excellent officer. The regulations were part of his flesh and blood.

If he spoke to me it was always to test my knowledge. Once, while I was poking away at my stringy beef, he took out of his pocket one of the folded maps used by the General Staff and ordered me to give him a detailed description of the wagon roads in the neighbourhood of Jezierna, a little hole in Galicia. That was too much even for my mother. "Let the child eat, Karl," said she. She said "child"—I never forgot it.

This Sunday dinner was the high spot in my day. At five o'clock I had to be back in the whitewashed room with the ten iron bedsteads, darkly brooding over my arithmetic lesson, consumed by indigestion and dread of the morrow.

Only in the holidays was life any different. To be sure, my father supplied the gap in my instructions by giving me a daily task and making me recite it to him. But I could lie an hour longer in bed, and the bed was softer than the one at school. And I had a little time to myself, to wander about, to play with the dog, or read an Indian story.

When the time for the manœuvres came on and my father left with his regiment for summer quarters, then everything became quite bearable. From the moment of his departure my mother was a different being. She went on long walks with me, and told me stories about her father, who had been an accountant in the Finance Ministry and a famous chess-player. Even her shoes, which had so offended my sense of beauty, seemed gentler and more feminine. She sewed on my buttons, instead of making me do it; she washed my hair and took great pains with the parting.

One day she even took me to a cake-shop, where for the first time in my life I had a taste of chocolate with whipped cream.

Once during my holidays I awoke in the night and saw my mother standing with a candle in her hand by my bed. Her hair was loose and I could see how lovely it was. Tears were running down her face. She sat beside me and began kissing me with a sudden outburst of feeling, whereupon I too sobbed uncontrollably. Next morning, I awoke, for the first time in my young life, with an appetite.

Early in September my father came back from the manœuvres. And I had a pleasant surprise. He did not seem the same man. His face was sunburnt and good-natured, his figure less rigid and pedantic—more like a cavalry than an infantry officer. He had on thin white kid gloves instead of his usual yellow wash-leather ones; and when he came in he slapped me on the shoulder and said: "Well, boy, and how were the holidays?" I turned fiery red and could not believe my ears.

There was good reason for the change in my father's manner. The manœuvres had been a personal success for him. The heir to the throne had mentioned him three times in his report; and he had been advanced to the rank of major over the heads of seven senior captains. Most extraordinary distinction of all, he had received letters patent of nobility, with the title "Edler von Sporentritt." Despite the fact that he had in the past had to break off his studies at the War College, he was now in line to be transferred to the General Staff.

The last week of those holidays were far and away the happiest of all my childhood. My father was fairly jolly; he seemed bent on making

himself over from the regulation army officer into the military diplomat
of the upper ranks.

I had no more holiday tasks, examinations, or barrack-room drill. A
dressmaker came and occupied our back room; my mother had to have a
costume in which she could appear on the street. She flushed like a girl
in her excitement as she bent over patterns in consultation with the old
spinster, or sat at the sewing-machine. And my father, in a uniform
rather better than the regulations prescribed, would come into the room
to be present at a fitting, pronouncing judgment on the drape or a ruffle
in a knowing nasal twang.

One evening we actually entertained the regimental commander and
the brigadier, and their wives. And we had an entrée before the joint:
a French salad served in mussel-shells! I was allowed to sit at table and
nearly died of awe, at the appearance of this choice and outlandish food.

My mother moved about looking most elegant in her fine silk frock,
with her lovely hair showing to full advantage. She wore a thin gold
chain with a turquoise cross, and silver bangles jingled on her wrists.

We had beer and wine to drink. The brigadier, a kindly man, told
Jewish stories, the colonel contributed a few barrack-room jokes. Both of
them addressed my father as "My dear von Sporentritt." They were both
of them middle class, and very proud to have such a distinguished officer
attached to their command. When they said good-night, the general good-
naturedly pinched my cheek as I stood stiffly, like an orderly, at the door.

My parents were greatly pleased with the success of this party. My
father sat rocking himself in a rocking-chair, with his hands clasped
behind his head—an unprecedented thing for him and to me a most
wonderful and aristocratic attitude. Before they went to bed I saw him
kiss my mother's hand. That must have been the happiest moment in her
life.

So came for me the last Sunday of that marvellous holiday; by chance
it fell on my thirteenth birthday—for once in my life I too was a "Sunday
child"!

In the morning I went to my father as he sat at breakfast and he bade
me sit down and share it with him. Despite the friendly atmosphere of
the last few days I should not have dared, for very fear, to obey the command, had he not added:

"Come, come, today is your birthday after all, sit down!" I timidly drank the coffee he poured out. For a long time he said nothing, I felt that he was musing over my case. Then he began:

"You are thirteen today—and youth is soon over. I well remember that on my own thirteenth birthday my father, who was a lieutenant-colonel, made me the present of a special pleasure. I mean to do the same for you, and do you do it in your turn for your son. For you will understand some day that the best thing about a family is its family tradition. Go now, and after luncheon be ready."

The luncheon was a better one than usual. When we had done, my father told me again to make myself presentable; he rose and went into his own room. When he came back, in half an hour, he was quite metamorphosed. He had changed into civilian clothes! And little as I understood such things at the time, I keenly felt the transformation of the stiff and soldierly, spur-ringing apparition into this unimpressive, even poverty-stricken figure, which bore no resemblance to a well-dressed gentleman but was like a poor clerk behind a post-office window.

His sleeves were too short and the loose cuffs showed too much beneath them. The bone collar-button was visible under his made-up tie, his collar was old-fashioned and too tight. His trousers were carefully pressed but the too-short coat betrayed that they were shiny behind. On the other hand, his hair, hat, stick, and gloves were faultless—though contrary to his usual custom, he carried his gloves lightly in his hand.

How quick is the heart of a child!

I understood it all.

The man who was my real father stood revealed, shabby, narrow-chested, and poor; pomp and circumstance hung in the wardrobe and the truth came out. And yet!

A great wave of warmth and sympathy swept over me.

We crossed the street, both with the same absurd knee-jerking military gait.

"Where are we going?" I ventured to ask.

"You will see presently."

But when we had reached the middle of the big bridge I suddenly knew, and my heart stood still with frightened wonder. We were going to the "Bear-Pit." The Bear-Pit was on an island, and served as the amusement park of the town.

I had heard the wildest tales about it from my comrades at school.

There was a panopticon, a scenic railway, an enchanted castle, shooting-booths, photograph galleries, an electric theatre, and roaring merry-go-rounds—I knew that these delights were awaiting me. But an especially sophisticated and initiate schoolfellow had told me of a spot in the very heart of the island, an unspoilt waste, a small Sahara, where every afternoon at half-past three a troop of genuine bedouins performed a "desert ride."

My father and I went down the wide steps at the side of the bridge and passed through a tall arch where a hundred flaming banners flew, into the heart of enchantment.

For the first moment I caught my breath at the din which assailed my ears—used as these were to nothing worse than the shrill piping of the whistle at drill, and the angry shouts of my schoolmasters. I even forgot my awe of my father and involuntarily put out my hand to take his; but my habitual awe came on me again in a flash and made me draw it back.

Hordes of people, in untold hordes of groups, streamed all about and in and out, yet kept the same general direction—like the current of a river on whose surface countless waves and eddies toss to and fro. The frantic music, the jubilant crowd, seemed to enfold me in unexpected kindliness, my downtrodden little spirit took heart and began to mount. I could look almost objectively at this father of mine beside me, and think: This great man, what is he, in his shabby grey coat, that is different from anybody else? Were he to issue orders today, nobody would listen, nobody would obey. No one greets or salutes or troubles himself about him; they look at him disrespectfully and even push him with their elbows.

My father seemed to be having the same ideas.

If anyone shoved him, or trod on his foot, he stamped and gnashed his teeth. His face was wry and chapfallen. Hatred blazed from his eyes, which squinted in the dazzling sunshine. His whole body seemed to realize the bad figure it cut today and to be struggling to create a space about it, free of the crowd, where it could draw itself up in its gold braid and stand in the centre of a hydra-headed silence. How short and sharp the word of command could leap from his throat: "Present! Fire!" But here we were the centre of an irresistible stream of bodies, surrounded by laughter and shrieks; and the more I felt my father's humiliation, the more I tasted the secret sweets of revenge, in that it was I who condemned him to this impotent suffering. How strange, that the hour of my earliest triumph over my father was the very hour in which he first showed kindness towards me!

We had by now got out of the narrow lane, lined by noisy booths, pervaded by the sweaty smell of hosts of people at close quarters and crammed with children blowing trumpets and flying coloured balloons. We emerged into the bustle of a large square, where several orchestrions and electrical organs were filling the air with thunderous noise.

Thirteen years old! And this was the greatest experience of my life so far. It has probably been surpassed by but one other since: when from the deck of the *Great Elector* I heard crashing together the thunderous roar of many bands, welcoming us with a dæmonic music never yet scored, to that land of hope and promise where I now write down this story of my life.

The electric organs brayed, mangling the long-drawn-out strains of the operatic airs they played into horrible, incredible, inextricable confusion.

I stood shattered by this meteoric downpour of sounds. My body felt numb, I could scarcely move.

My father led me to a roundabout and made me sit on a horse with an arching wooden neck. He put the bridle in my hand; there was a smell of wood and leather and warm horse-hair. All the shapes and colours were too gross for me to distinguish them. The organ began to drone "Little Miller's Maiden." The platform moved slowly round, with a man in trunks and a black vest walking recklessly about on it as it revolved. Red canopies waved above the heads of the shouting children. The pace increased, the turn-table with its horses, chariots, dragons, Bengal tigers, lions, and fantastic beasts seemed to be turning into a funnel—I leaned back with glowing cheeks, and gave myself up to the intoxication of speed. But just then I saw my father, topping the crowd, sharp-eyed, his right foot forward and his stick like a training-whip in his hand. He shouted to me in a voice like a ring-master's:

"Sit up! Body well back!"

But I had passed him already, in terrified anticipation of the next round.

"Stick to the saddle!"

I passed him again. As I came round for the third time the old bitter

taste was in my mouth. My father had not moved an inch. Once more
came his voice:

"Grip with your thighs! Point your toes!"

When at length I got down from my wooden steed I felt as dejected
and shattered as after an examination. My father had taken bitter revenge
for my moment of triumph. But he seemed satisfied and made no more
comment. He bought tickets for the grotto, whose barkers were a dwarf
costumed like a jester and a female giant with a kettledrum. This time
my father came with me, wearing a wooden expression. The organ here
was even more powerful; it sent out a mighty wind that seemed to
me like the work of magic. With a rattle and bang we rushed down-
wards into the darksome pit. And in that darkness my father was no
more there, I saw him not, God had taken him from me. My oppression vanished, I gave myself up to dreams. There were many dreams.
Wintry winds tore up the fir trees by the roots and on the whirling
branches rode withered and naked witches with streaming hair. I saw the
floor of the ocean stretching silent, endless, and green, with descending
veils of weed and slowly floating giant jelly-fish; shoals of unnamed fish
drifted on the warm currents, and one great creature rose majestically
upwards, giving off blue rays and looking like a lighted globe with tail
and fins. The floor of the sea was heaped with shells and coral and giant
crabs; rusty anchors and a strew of precious stones; there lay the rotting
corpse of a pilot, half-devoured by fish; and in the distance, where the
deep waters gleamed glassily like unnatural sleep, the wreck of a frigate,
with upturned keel, dipping masts, and square port-holes swayed rhythmically to the motion of invisible waves. From the bowsprit shone a tiny
lantern, still burning after the lapse of centuries, unquenched amid the
waters. And that was not all: I saw the Wolf's Glen as well. The wind
blew down the bridge over the waterfall, owls hovered and hooted, the
wild boar grunted its two notes like a bassoon, Caspar cast the charmed
bullets amid crackling flames, and in a fiery mantle Samiel issued from
the cave.

I knew the story very well. One of my school friends, the only one with
whom I was on good terms, had often told it to me.

"Help, Samiel!" the cry came down the wind. We rattled on into the
darkness. I heard my father's voice.

"What was that?" he asked—not in his examination voice, but as though he really wanted to know. Since we could not see each other at all, he could relax a little.

"That was the *Freischütz*," I answered.

"What do you mean by *Freischütz?*" came his voice, but this time without emphasis.

"The *Freischütz* is an opera," I instructed him, importantly.

"Oh, an opera."

My father tried to speak with careless contempt, but there was no concealing that I knew a world into which he could not enter. I had beaten him. I stiffened with pride. I could even have ridden again now!

Most marvellous of all was the Lisbon earthquake. A fellow-pupil of mine had told me that you saw the end of the world here in this grotto, but I did not believe him.

The houses stood there glaring white under the bluest sky ever seen; the ocean mounted to a sky-line full of red and yellow sails; slowly the loud twittering of the birds was hushed—and though the sun stood high in heaven the world grew slowly dark and dead. All the inhabitants, under the frightful menace of this darkness, fled into houses and cellars. All at once it was pitch-black, a sudden cyclone whirled a great funnel of dust into the blackness, there followed a roar like a million thunderbolts, cannon, hail-storms, and explosions. The invisible ocean in a mighty tidal wave overwhelmed the night and as suddenly retreated. And the darkness? Did it last for days, or years, or only for the half a minute that it actually endured? It lightened a little. Everywhere the glare of fire, the city in flames and smoke sent up a million tongues to heaven, and faint and weak—for how far away in space and time all this was happening!—a hissing and seething and crackling attended the flames.

I came out into the air with a warm and comfortable feeling at my heart. I was supported by the knowledge that I had known about the *Freischütz*, that I had known there was such a thing as opera and had instructed my father about it. Some day I would call him to account; and his lips, knowing only the harsh accents of the service, could only falter.

"Now we will go and have some refreshment," my father said. We entered a coffee-house garden. After all, how kind this stern man was today! "What would you like, Karl?"

I could not utter a word. He bought three pastries from the waiter and laid two of them beside the cup of chocolate he had ordered for me. He kept only one for himself. I felt ashamed in my heart.

This was my Father, here beside me! The great, the all-knowing, the all-powerful, the all-admired! Whom else had I in all the world save him? I did love him! Through long bitter nights I yearned for his love, the pain of all my humiliations was as nothing beside the torture of that recurrent dream wherein I saw him, leading his battalion in a fog of smoke, suddenly clutch at the air and fall!

My small soul was torn by the conflict of my feelings and knew not where to turn.

My father beckoned a waiter. "Where is the shooting-booth?" The man told him.

The parental eye looked sharply at me. "We will do something useful now. I must see what sort of sharp-shooter you are." I was driven out of my paradise of tenderness, and the bitter taste came back in my mouth.

But before we reached the shooting-booth, I had the frightful experience which was to ravage still more my already distracted youth.

We came to a large booth with a crowd in front of it. A comfortable, rather oily voice was making itself heard: "Don't be afraid, ladies and gentlemen, just come along! What better can you do to your enemies than knock off their hats? But you have to be clever, you have to know how to shoot. Just come up, ladies and gentlemen, learn how to knock off their hats! It's the same for everybody—clericals, agrarians, socialists, and all!"

We drew nearer. On the counter of the booth were baskets full of hard felt balls, red, white, and blue. And behind it stood the proprietor, a man with a sly, good-natured face, a military cap, and a red beard. He winked all the time as he gave out the balls and took in the money. "Just learn how to aim, ladies and gentlemen, then you'll be sure to hit." And people took aim and threw their balls, which crossed in the air, and there was a constant stream of laughter.

But what were they aiming at? To my boundless horror they were aiming at human beings! They were stoning human beings! No, that was illusion only. Thank God, they were only puppets, for to such men as these the earth could never have given birth.

But they were moving, and how? Bobbing up and down, up and down. It made me giddy.

The background, which was some distance away, was divided into three parts. Right and left were two rows of benches, one behind the other, and on each three figures bobbed with hypnotic regularity up and down. Twelve in all, with such fiendish expressions that it seemed as though all the furies were after them, they rose and fell—rose and fell.

These distorted visages, rising from the pit to sink again, were so well differentiated that never shall I forget a single one of them. There was a stony-faced Chinese mandarin, an unspeakably Jewish Jew, a horse-toothed officer in the uniform of some imaginary foreign legion, a frightful fiery-faced hangman in a frock coat, a Jesuit father like a straight bad mark, a peasant with a vacuous face and an ulcerous nose which hung down like a bunch of berries, a Negro, a hanged man, a convict, a drunken sailor, a hospital attendant, and a living corpse.

The balls flew about these figures as they rose and fell with their fixed grimaces; hit them in the eye, the chest, the forehead. Now and then somebody achieved the object of the game: the mandarin's cap, the officer's shako, the peasant's three-cornered hat, fell off.

Sometimes I think—and I think often about these puppets still—that they were twelve sinners, condemned by God to inhabit wooden figures in the hateful likeness of their earthly ones and work out their punishment as in a treadmill, on the benches of this booth. I pray that release may come to them.

The middle space of the background had a turn-table, on which a set of quite different figures went round and round. There were twelve of these too, but they were not much differentiated, each one having the same inimitable air of shabby dignity. Their significance was clear: they were usurers, they were mutes and undertakers at low-class funerals, they were dancing-masters and piano-players at proletarian dance-halls. They were all arrayed in long ragged black tailcoats and tall shiny top-hats with long crape weepers. They moved in a slow, measured circle, so that I saw less of their solemn, staring faces than of their backs, which wore the saddest expression in the world.

And they all stood in a crouching posture as though following an invisible coffin; or perhaps as though they saw a door somewhere through which they hoped to escape, but were condemned to be carried eternally past it. And these pathetic figures got hit more often than the demonic puppets to right and left; when a pause came in the bombardment, a boy came out from behind and put their hats on again.

This boy was no older than I myself—perhaps it was his birthday too. His face was as pale and thin as my own; his black eyes shone out of deep hollows.

But even so: how much better off he was than I! He did not have to wear a uniform, he probably went to the regular school, where the boys can come late, or stay away, or play any tricks they like. His father was always laughing heartily, he joked and talked—now he was lighting his Turk's-head pipe and puffing with vast enjoyment.

The balls whizzed past, the malignant faces bobbed up and down, the shabby-respectable old men kept turning round past the door where their salvation lay.

The boy had seen me at once. We were the only children there. And a bond was set up at once between us.

He motioned to me to take a ball; squinted expressively, whistled, made a face, and beckoned with his finger. Often I saw only his hand, stuck out from behind the curtain and signalling spectrally at me.

I on my side responded by signs, the meaning of which I did not know myself. I stared forlornly at the hollow-eyed boy, who seemed to me an embodiment of happiness and freedom.

Then I started as I heard my father's imperious tones: "Now, Karl, show me what a steady hand you have, and if you will be fit one day to wear the Kaiser's coat!"

He put a ball in my hand. What was I to do with it? The demons bobbed up and down, the funeral mutes glided by, the boy nodded and beckoned with his fingers spread out.

All the dolls had their hats on now, for at the sound of my father's rasping voice everybody had ceased throwing. They looked at him with surprise and anger; everybody looked at us two. I held the ball in my hand and trembled. There was silence; then the proprietor said: "Well, young man?"

My father drew himself up. He felt relieved; no longer was he simply one among a crowd, he held one hand on his hip, as a man does who has triumphed over another; or as a vain lieutenant parades in front of his troop. He visibly enjoyed the silence round us.

"Well, be quick about it—throw!" said he, in his loud, barrack-room voice.

My whole body was hot with shame and fear. I lifted my arm and threw the ball with feeble uncertain aim. It fell somewhere about the middle of the booth. The silence was unbroken save for a little laugh raised by the boy behind the curtain.

"Clumsy!" said my father, sternly handing me another ball. "Choose a figure, take good aim at it, and then throw!"

Everything danced before my eyes. The demon figures went up and down. I gathered all my strength to aim; it seemed to me my head would burst into flame. The wrist of the hand that held the ball had a sensation of its own: a venomous feeling, yet sweet. The rhythm of the moving figures became more and more awful—but there! One of them stood out, I saw it quite clearly, gnashing its teeth, opening a mouth closed for all eternity to shriek: "Me, me!" It was the uniformed officer.

I saw him, I saw him! It was my father's horse-teeth that were bared to the gums, his pointed moustache that bristled, the buttons on his epaulets that gleamed. I bent far over the counter and with a little cry flung the ball—which fell quite harmlessly in a corner not far off. And the boy in the background laughed loud and mockingly.

My father came close to me and hissed in my ear:

"Ass! You are making a fool of me. Throw again—and this time hit something, or else . . ."

Another ball was thrust into my hand.

The officer puppet bobbed up and down. At times I saw him very distinctly. But where was my father? Not beside me. He was over there! He was blowing smoke through his nose, as though the rapid motion had affected him not at all. His tunic had not a crease in its faultless blue.

"Corporal! Corporal!" he cried.

Good God, I *will* do it! He himself has commanded me to. He, himself . . . himself!

I strained every muscle; with a wild shriek I flung the ball, flung it with such force that I lost my balance, and fell to the ground.

I must have been unconscious, but I awoke almost at once, to find myself the centre of a crowd, all talking at once. To one side I saw my father, hatless, pressing a blood-stained handkerchief to his nose.

In one frightful moment I saw it all. I had not hit the officer, I had hit my father instead. I saw the blood streaming from his nose. And I was overwhelmed by a wave of sorrow, that mounted and mounted till my heart could bear it no more. My last conscious gaze met the face of the proprietor's boy, leaning over me with a strangely piercing and eager expression.

Then I sank into a swoon, thence into a fever broken by dreams and cries. It lasted three whole months, which for me were but one monstrous night, in which by the light of an infernal lamp Chinamen, Negroes, the hangmen and the hanged, peasants and convicts, swayed up and down on mountains of benches; tottering old men with torches went out a black door and came in through a light one; and the tall, stern, rigid officer who was my father stood immovable among the other forms.

NELLIE MAR YOHANNAN

Holy Day in Persia

When I was a little girl in Persia, one of the biggest occasions of the year was the holy day of Moharam. On this day I could go early in the morning to my father's office in the very heart of the Mohammedan city, and watch the pageant. I watched with both horror and fascination the very pious men and pure boys bleeding and suffering severe pains for their dead Imams. Years later when in America I tried to relive on paper the memories of my home, the holy day was among those that came most vividly to my mind. But now as I looked back the day took its true aspect. I discovered that what had made deep impression on me were the lines of ragged starving men and pitiful-looking, almost naked children bleeding and suffering not for the Imams but for the little food and clothing.

NELLIE MAR YOHANNAN

I T W A S the evening before the great day of Moharam, the holiest of all holy days; the day when the whole country mourned for the beloved Imams who were slaughtered in the wars following the death of the Prophet. For the whole month of Moharam people had been preparing for this great day. The wealthy by wearing black and donating silver for expenses; the poor by shouting and wailing; the middle class by watching and attending the services in the temples, or the most pious among them by taking part with the poor. Evening after evening groups had gathered in the various mosques of the city, from whence they had started for the streets with drums and flutes and wails.

This evening, however, in spite of the people that crowded the many mosques, everything was quiet, as though the sprawling Persian city had already fallen asleep to rest for the great day. Ragged, hungry, filthy men and boys gathered in the temples, for who else would split their heads with swords, tear their backs with chains, slap their breasts or stand before severe whips? Certainly not the rich, who would not even come out to watch; and not the middle class, who had enough to eat; it was only the poor who offered themselves.

Anxiously they waited for the authorities to distribute the white aprons and the swords, the black robes and the chains, the mud and straw. True, the greatest reward that anyone could want came to those who died from the tortures of that day, that of going straight to paradise without the usual forty days' delay in graves while their good deeds were balanced with their bad ones; but very few, probably only the very pious, thought of that. The minds of these poor were only filled with the thought of the food they would receive at the end of the holy day, the one good, satisfying meal that reached their mouths but once a year; and with the thought of the new aprons and the robes which would be turned into shirts for their naked bodies. These thoughts were so intense in their minds that there was no room left for the thought of the pains that the swords and the chains and the whips would inflict upon their bodies the next day. Even the very young ones forgot that.

These were the thoughts that filled Jallal's mind, too, as he stood a little apart from the crowd in the court of one of the mosques. His young head already bore the scars of three previous Moharams. Being an only son, his father, who had loved him more than his own soul, had not let the beloved head be cut before the boy was twelve years of age; in spite of the good food that would have reached his empty stomach on these yearly occasions. No, his father had saved from his own festive plate both rice and meat and brought them in his handkerchief to the boy.

Had he been fed and dressed properly, the boy, no doubt, would have been good looking. His mother's fine, sensitive features, black eyes, that had some sort of sadness in them, her black slender eyebrows and black hair, marked his thin, pale face; and his father's long, bony body was his body.

"What part are you going to take, Jallal?" asked a boy, coming close to him.

"With the split-heads as usual," Jallal answered. Then looking down at his chest, covered with the rags of the shirt made from the apron of last year's Moharam, he added, "I need a shirt badly."

"I shall be with the chain gang," said the other. Then suddenly his eyes brightening, he said, "Did you hear, Jallal? The rich are going to feed us good tomorrow, better than other years. I heard the mullahs have demanded it of them."

His eyes melting in a distance, Jallal said, "They have kind hearts. They have always fed us well."

An older man, who had lent his ear to the boys' talk, came closer.

"Kind hearts?" he said, sneeringly. "They do it for pride, son, and nothing else."

Jallal had heard this from many of the poor ever since he was a little boy. And it might be true, he admitted. Yet he said to the man, "There are kind hearts everywhere, brother."

As they stood there soldiers appeared and began to distribute aprons, robes, swords and chains. As soon as he had received a white apron and a long, sharp butcher's knife—there were not enough swords to supply everyone—Jallal did not wait to speak to anyone, but started back toward his home.

He walked back alone, although swarms of men and boys were going in the same direction. But Jallal had always been a lonely boy, ever since his infancy, when his father had either kept him close to his own bosom or set him in a street corner to play alone and not with other boys. He walked through the roofed streets of the *bazaarchas*, where all the shops were closed by huge wooden gates, so that the street looked as if it had been enclosed by wooden walls. From this dark corner and that, black stray dogs, dozens of them, since dogs must not be killed in those lands, rose and started to follow him. Jallal had heard that on this night the rich were expected by the mullahs to walk in the streets barefooted, carrying lit candles, supposedly in search of the bodies of the Imams. But as he looked about him he saw no one who looked anything but poor. No, Jallal had never seen any of the rich do even this little, and he knew that no one else had seen them and no one dared to ask about it either.

Turning a corner, Jallal entered the Street of the Poor. The early autumn dusk was gathering and enveloping the city. In the dusk Jallal could see the women and children sitting in their doorways waiting for their men folks. Without raising his head to anyone, he walked on to his own home. He did not raise his head to look at anyone or anything, for the sights of this street were familiar to his eyes, as familiar as his own two hands.

It was an ugly, broken, dirty street, this Street of the Poor. It was cast to one side of a large, wealthy city, put there alone as if not to be seen or touched by the rest of the city. On one side a row of shabby, weather-beaten huts clung to a crumbling earthen wall that, in the ancient days when cities were protected by high walls, had been one of the city's mighty walls. These huts clung to it desperately, as a child clings to its mother's veil, as though they received their strength of endurance from it. On the other side of the street the earthen domes of the public baths, baths for shopkeepers and water carriers and such men who had their price, were scattered like round hills in their own ashes. Beyond the baths flowed a stream, supplying these huts and baths with water. The stream started from a natural underground spring about a mile in the heart of the city. There its water was pure and clean. But as it flowed toward this section the stream came to the surface and, passing through many streets and courts, it gathered all the filth that people deposited on its banks, so that a strong odor of rot rose from it and mingled with the many smells of this section where life died and rotted in it day by day.

Naked, filthy children played in this street from dawn to dusk. Children with their bellies swollen before them like drums and their natural dark skin turned to a bluish tint from the half-edible grasses that filled their bodies in the warm seasons. Children whose bellies receded and hung before them like empty water-hides and whose color turned to a ghastly yellow in the cold season, when there were not even the grasses of the fields to fill their bodies. And all year round the little ones' heads were covered with a rash that bled into their faces. A rash that could only be cured by a strong yellow powder sold in the *bazaarchas* for silver. But silver did not reach the hands of the poor so easily.

Jallal, coming almost to the end of the street, where the open country started, turned aside and entered his own home. A little patch of ashes, behind one of the public baths, was his home. The ashes served as its floor, the round stones that he had gathered from the countryside were its walls and the sky above, its ceiling. A ragged, dirty quilt and a few pieces of broken earthenware were the only furnishings.

Jallal put the knife and the apron, the most precious possessions he had, under the broken pieces of earthenware, thus hiding them from the stealing hands of the other orphans who dwelt all around him. Then he pulled his quilt over him and lay on the warm ashes which he had spread on the floor of his shelter that morning from a hot pile that the bath-keepers had emptied out. He closed his eyes and tried to sleep. But sleep would not come to him on this night. It is true he had not had anything to eat all day, but it was not his empty stomach that kept him awake.

No, for there was that good food of tomorrow. Certainly that would keep him, even through many hungry days. It was the memory of the previous Moharams that suddenly filled his mind, stirred his blood and kept him from his sleep.

The boy's mind rushed back over the three years and stopped at the very first Moharam that he had taken part in. That was closest to him, for then his father had been living. His sensitive chin quivered and his eyes filled with tears as he remembered how tenderly his father had held his head between his bony hands and examined the small wounds of the rash to see if his head could stand the scratches of a razor. His father's shaking voice sounded in his ears now as clearly as though he were lying on the ashes by his side, as he had said, then,

"Do not be afraid, *jon ogul*. It will only be scratched a little by a barber's razor." Then he had added, his eyes filled with anxiety, "But do not strike with your own hand. Remember that."

He had remembered that then and on every Moharam after that. He must remember it tomorrow again, Jallal knew.

Such memories of his father were many in the boy's mind. Hardly a day went by that one thing or another did not bring his father back to his thoughts, and seldom his memory did not quiver Jallal's chin and fill his eyes with tears.

But of his mother he remembered nothing. She had died, of starvation, in giving him birth.

The next morning Jallal awoke amid much confusion and noise, for men and boys, dressed in their white aprons and black robes, were rushing to the mosques, as though rushing to a wedding. Jallal jumped up, put on his apron, which covered him from neck to knees, took his sharp knife, and hurried toward the nearest mosque. In spite of the noise and confusion in the city, it was still early in the morning. The sun was just pushing up from behind the mountains, and the melodious voices of a dozen or so muezzins came from the balconies of the temples, giving the call to prayer on this holiest of all holy days.

Jallal crept through the crowd and came close to the steps that led into the mosque. The small carved wooden door was open, but no men entered there. Jallal could see in the dim candle lights the gleaming of the gold and the sharp blackness of the letters of holy verses that covered the white walls. And he could see a few black-veiled women sitting on the colorful carpets, weeping quietly as they listened to the mullah reading, in a sing-song voice, the history of those remote wars when the Imams were slaughtered.

But before the sun had gone very high in the sky the court of this mosque and the courts of all the other mosques had turned to slaughter-houses. Barbers rolled their sleeves to their elbows and shaved a wide circle of hair off the heads of all those who had any hair to be shaved off, and rubbed a spot and made one or two scratches with their sharp razors. Blood oozed out and dripped down their faces and upon the immaculate white aprons. When the barbers had finished with the men they turned to the boys. These little ones, some as young as three years, stood before the barbers' razors like little lambs. When their blood dripped down their faces and neared their mouths they stretched out hungry tongues and licked it.

When Jallal's turn came his heart fluttered a little and he felt his hands perspire, chill and tremble. He knew the razors were sharp and the barbers free with them, not caring how deep they cut. But this barber was careful, as though the dead Akpar were standing there, as he had stood alive and anxious four years before and said to the barber,

"Be a little careful, brother. This son is all I have."

Now the barber made only two small scratches on Jallal's head. He said,

"That did not hurt, did it, son?"

"No," said Jallal.

And it was true. Jallal did not feel the scratches, for the spot was numb from the man's rubbing. He only felt his blood dripping down his cheeks and he saw it on his apron.

While he waited for all the others to be prepared, Jallal raised his eyes and looked at all the sights, although he had seen them many times before.

In one group, standing around a horse covered with a bloody cloth, he saw those who were in the chain gang. Men and boys stood there ready, dressed in black robes with a large opening at their backs and heavy bunches of chains resting on their bare thin shoulders. In another group stood those who had mud and straw, the sign of mourning, on their heads and whose chests were bare and ready for the blows of their own hands. In another group stood those who were dressed in women's clothes. These, Jallal knew, represented the captives in the pageant. Among them red-clad men sat on horses and cracked their whips in the air, as though eager to start beating the captives.

Standing alone, Jallal saw the man who sacrificed the most, his life. He stood quietly with nails hammered into his body and mirrors hung over them, and locks locked into his flesh. Jallal's spine chilled at the sight. How long the man could last in his condition only the man, himself, knew. But the man's thoughts were not on the pains that the nails and the locks inflicted upon his flesh, but on his death that must come sometime that day and take him straight to paradise.

"What a pious man he must be," thought Jallal. "Certainly the rest of us do this only for the food. I know I do it for food."

Yet as he thought this, he felt a little ashamed and looked around him guiltily, as though to make certain that no one had understood his thought.

In contrast to these sad and ugly sights there were lovely ones. When Jallal's eyes found them, they stayed on them. Apart from all, so that these others, the common people, would not touch them, the children of the wealthy, as orphans and brides of the Imams, rested on horses, in boxes decorated with silks, or were carried on the backs of mules. They sat there, beautifully dressed in brocades and velvets, covered with jewels and attended with all the tender care of their servants who must not leave them at any time in the day. The eyes of these pretty ones, Jallal noticed, filled with horror as they fell on the bleeding heads, and their faces soured, as if their stomachs could not stand the sight and smell of hot blood. Among these children colorful banners rose high in the air, amid the gold and silver hands, symbols of the holy hands of the Imams.

When all were ready, for once without much confusion in a land where order is not understood, the drums started, then the sad, beautiful tunes of the flutes, and finally the shouts of the men and boys. Then the procession started, each group moving in its own turn. When shouts rose high many of these poor became hysterical and they struck hard on their own heads with the swords. There were those who fell down and fainted and those who died on the spot. Then the women, who sat on the roofs to watch, whispered to each other,

"There is that one who has gone to paradise."

The women wept, many not knowing whether they wept for the

slaughtered Imams or for their husbands and sons who passed before them thus in torture.

Those in the chain gang did their part. Every now and then they turned in one group and faced the bloody horse, and in one voice shouted words of mourning for its dead master. With the rhythm of their words they raised the chains over their shoulders and struck on their backs. Soon all these backs were black and blue and many were split, as if slashed with sharp razors. Likewise those who slapped their breasts slapped hard, so that their chests turned red as raw meat. And the shrieks of the captives rose high to heaven under the whips of the red-clad men.

But in all this Jallal managed to keep his head. Akpar's words, "Do not strike with your own hand. Remember that," kept sounding in his ears.

Only the children of the wealthy rode through the streets fresh and lovely, as if word had been given, as indeed it had, to their parents that they would be brought back without a single scratch on their noble bodies or a drop of blood on their beautiful clothes. They rode like shahs and princes that Jallal had heard storytellers in the *bazaarchas* tell of. Through the thin streaks of blood that still flowed down over his eyes, Jallal could see these children of the wealthy, and as he looked at them he thought, but not with jealousy. "I wish I were one of them. I would be riding on a horse, fed and clothed like them."

It was nearing noon when suddenly from the head of the procession Jallal heard the shouts of the men rise higher into screams.

"It is another group that has met ours," Jallal heard from the boy next to him, whose belt he was holding with one hand.

Breaking from his line, Jallal ran a little forward. It was true. Another group had come from another direction and had met theirs. And like a sudden storm a fight had started between the two groups. The swords and chains and slaps that so far had turned only on one's own body now turned to another's. In the confusion Jallal saw the children of the wealthy quickly pulled aside, and he knew that he must follow them. Such fights were common in every year's Moharam, but Jallal had never taken a part in them. So now he pulled himself into a corner and snuggled close by a small locked gate. Yet he knew that even there he was not safe. So he joined two or three boys who ran in the streets shouting about the fight, making it ten times as bad as it was. Jallal yelled with the boys to the women on the roofs,

"Men and boys are falling dead fast."

Then the mothers wept even more, wishing that they could rush to the fight and snatch their little boys away, for such little ones were the ones who fell between the swords and were slaughtered worse than any Imams had been.

But when soldiers had come and put an end to the fight, Jallal returned to the procession, found his group and continued on.

At noon the pageant ended, and again quiet filled the city. Jallal followed the crowds of men and boys through the blood-stained streets to the baths to take his free bath before receiving his free meal. The Street of the Poor was thronged. Every one, except the children of the rich, who were rushed back to their homes, was there to take a free bath.

Jallal entered one of the steam-filled baths. The dark, large, smelly room was crowded, and professional bath-givers, naked except for a red bath towel girdled about their loins, worked on bloody heads and filthy bodies. Jallal found a foothold in a corner and stood under the rough hands and rougher scrubbing-bag of the bath-giver. The man washed, then bound, Jallal's head in a red bath towel. Smiling and winking his ugly, sore eye maliciously, he said,

"There isn't much of a wound on your head, son."

"The knife was dull," Jallal answered.

Clean now, as he had not been for a whole year, and his apron washed, Jallal came out and made his way to one of the tearooms. It was a treat for the boy to enter this tearoom and sit down with others to eat and drink tea. All year long he passed by this tearoom, or lingered at its door and gazed into the smoke-filled place, dreaming of this day when he could freely enter it, as freely as if he had silver in his bosom to pay for what he ate.

An oily, dirty servant placed a steaming plate before him, a plate piled with rice—such as the rich ate—meat, vegetables and nuts, fried in oil and spices, and tea which had a tiny portion of opium in it to make it a little intoxicating and pleasure-giving.

In the afternoon Jallal, fed up to his throat, returned to his ashes. He spread his apron over the dome of the bath house to dry in the sun. When it was dry enough he set to work on it, cutting and sewing it into a shirt.

The world was now a comfortable and happy place, as though there were no more hungry days in store for him. He remembered the very first

Moharam that he had taken part in. He had asked his father if the rich ate such food every day. Akpar had smiled at his son's ignorance and said,

"That food which we ate? That is only the food of their servants, my son."

Jallal could not believe it then or now. How could there be food better than that, except probably in heaven? Yes, the world was a contentment-filled place on this day for Jallal, in spite of the wounds on his head which had not yet started to pain severely, for the numbness and the opium had not yet left him. Jallal was so satisfied and happy that he whispered to himself hopefully,

"Who knows, I may be taken in that caravanserai of Ehtimadi Dovlet. They may take me in before the cold days are here. I am older now than when I was there before."

But when he had finished his shirt and drawn it on over his ragged one and had slept for a short while, he awoke with shooting pains in his head. And his happy world crumbled. Although too old for tears, he could not keep from crying. He sat up and unwrapped the bath towel and left his head free of covering. Still the wounds pained, for now both the numbness and the power of opium had gone. For all his efforts to fall asleep and in spite of his filled stomach that must put him to sleep, he could not.

And Jallal knew that he was not the only one up on this night. He knew that many a boy in this section of the poor was up and crying from his pains as he was, and many a mother sat up with her son, trying to soothe a painful head or burning back. Many a mother must say on this night what Akpar had said four years before, as he tried to comfort his son with his long, bony hands.

"Poor boy, he is paying enough for what he ate. Tomorrow he will have forgotten that he ever ate the food, but his pains will still linger on."

"I will never take a part in this Moharam again," Jallal promised himself between tears.

But he remembered that he had said this the previous year, and the year before, just as a woman, suffering from the pains of her child's birth, promises herself that she will never again have another baby. Yet somehow taking heart from his promise, he thought further.

"Certainly I will not," he said to himself, "if I can find some work to do, for my food."

OLIVE SCHREINER

Shadows from Child-Life

The isolation and remoteness of life at an African mission station strongly impressed the imagination of a frail young daughter of a Methodist missionary. In her first and most famous book, *The Story of an African Farm,* Olive Schreiner left a curious record of the inner life of childhood. Olive Schreiner "was never really an inhabitant of the world," Phyllis Bottome once said, "but she was a fighter, an immense force, a great artist."

The farm by daylight was not as the farm by moonlight. The plain was a weary flat of loose red sand, sparsely covered by dry karroo bushes, that cracked beneath the tread like tinder, and showed the red earth everywhere. Here and there a milk-bush lifted its pale-colored rods, and in every direction the ants and beetles ran about in the blazing sand. The red walls of the farmhouse, the zinc roofs of the outbuildings, the stone walls of the kraals, all reflected the fierce sunlight, till the eye ached and blenched. No tree or shrub was to be seen far or near. The two sunflowers that stood before the door, out-stared by the sun, drooped their brazen faces to the sand; and the little cicada-like insects cried aloud among the stones of the kopje.

The Boer-woman, seen by daylight, was even less lovely than when, in bed, she rolled and dreamed. She sat on a chair in the great front room, with her feet on a wooden stove, and wiped her flat face with the corner of her apron, and drank coffee, and in Cape Dutch swore that the beloved weather was damned. Less lovely, too, by daylight was the dead Englishman's child, her little step-daughter, upon whose freckles and low, wrinkled forehead the sunlight had no mercy.

"Lyndall," the child said to her little orphan cousin, who sat with her on the floor threading beads, "how is it your beads never fall off your needle?"

"I try," said the little one gravely, moistening her tiny finger. "That is why."

The overseer, seen by daylight, was a huge German, wearing a shabby suit, and with a childish habit of rubbing his hands and nodding his head prodigiously when pleased at anything. He stood out at the kraals in the blazing sun, explaining to two Kaffer boys the approaching end of the world. The boys, as they cut the cakes of dung, winked at each other, and worked as slowly as they possibly could; but the German never saw it.

Away, beyond the kopje, Waldo, his son, herded the ewes and lambs —a small and dusty herd—powdered all over from head to foot with red sand, wearing a ragged coat and shoes of undressed leather, through whose holes the toes looked out. His hat was too large, and had sunk down to his eyes, concealing completely the silky black curls. It was a curious small figure. His flock gave him little trouble. It was too hot for them to move far; they gathered round every little milk-bush, as though they hoped to find shade, and stood there motionless in clumps. He himself crept under a shelving rock that lay at the foot of the kopje, stretched himself on his stomach, and waved his dilapidated little shoes in the air.

Soon, from the blue bag where he kept his dinner, he produced a fragment of slate, an arithmetic, and a pencil. Proceeding to put down a sum with solemn and earnest demeanor, he began to add it up aloud: "Six and two is eight—and four is twelve—and two is fourteen—and four is eighteen." Here he paused. "And four is eighteen—and four —is—eighteen." The last was very much drawled. Slowly the pencil slipped from his fingers, and the slate followed it into the sand. For awhile he lay motionless, then began muttering to himself, folded his little arms, laid his head down upon them, and might have been asleep, but for the muttering sound that from time to time proceeded from him. A curious old ewe came to sniff at him; but it was long before he raised his head. When he did, he looked at the far-off hills with his heavy eyes.

"Ye shall receive—ye shall receive—shall, shall, shall," he muttered.

He sat up then. Slowly the dulness and heaviness melted from his face; it became radiant. Mid-day had come now, and the sun's rays were poured down vertically; the earth throbbed before the eye.

The boy stood up quickly, and cleared a small space from the bushes which covered it. Looking carefully, he found twelve small stones of somewhat the same size; kneeling down, he arranged them carefully on the cleared space in a square pile, in shape like an altar.

Then he walked to the bag where his dinner was kept; in it was a mutton chop and a large slice of brown bread. The boy took them out and turned the bread over in his hand, deeply considering it. Finally he threw it away and walked to the altar with the meat, and laid it down on the stones. Close by in the red sand he knelt down. Sure, never since the beginning of the world was there so ragged and so small a priest. He took off his great hat and placed it solemnly on the ground, then closed his eyes and folded his hands. He prayed aloud:

"Oh, God my Father, I have made Thee a sacrifice. I have only two-pence, so I cannot buy a lamb. If the lambs were mine, I would give Thee one; but now I have only this meat; it is my dinner meat. Please, my Father, send fire down from heaven to burn it. Thou hast said, Whosoever shall say unto this mountain, Be thou cast into the sea, nothing doubting, it shall be done. I ask for the sake of Jesus Christ. Amen."

He knelt down with his face upon the ground, and he folded his hands upon his curls. The fierce sun poured down its heat upon his head and upon his altar. When he looked up he knew what he should see—the glory of God! For fear his very heart stood still, his breath came heavily; he was half suffocated. He dared not look up. Then at last he raised himself. Above him was the quiet blue sky, about him the red earth; there were the clumps of silent ewes and his altar—that was all.

He looked up—nothing broke the intense stillness of the blue over-head. He looked round in astonishment, then he bowed again, and this time longer than before.

When he raised himself the second time all was unaltered. Only the sun had melted the fat of the little mutton-chop, and it ran down upon the stones.

Then, the third time he bowed himself. When at last he looked up, some ants had come to the meat on the altar. He stood up and drove them away. Then he put his hat on his hot curls, and sat in the shade. He clasped his hands about his knees. He sat to watch what would come to pass. The glory of the Lord God Almighty! He knew he should see it.

"My dear God is trying me," he said; and he sat there through the fierce heat of the afternoon. Still he watched and waited when the sun began to slope, and when it neared the horizon and the sheep began to cast long shadows across the karroo, he still sat there. He hoped when the first rays touched the hills till the sun dipped behind them and was gone. Then he called his ewes together, and broke down the altar, and threw the meat far, far away into the field.

He walked home behind his flock. His heart was heavy. He reasoned so: "God cannot lie. I had faith. No fire came. I am like Cain—I am not His. He will not hear my prayer. God hates me."

The boy's heart was heavy. When he reached the kraal gate the two girls met him.

"Come," said the yellow-haired Em, "let us play 'coop.' There is still time before it gets quite dark. You, Waldo, go and hide on the kopje; Lyndall and I will shut eyes here, and we will not look."

The girls hid their faces in the stone wall of the sheep-kraal, and the boy clambered half way up the kopje. He crouched down between two stones and gave the call. Just then the milk-herd came walking out of the cow-kraal with two pails. He was an ill-looking Kaffer.

"Ah!" thought the boy, "perhaps he will die to-night, and go to hell! I must pray for him, I must pray!"

Then he thought—"Where am I going to?" and he prayed desperately.

"Ah! this is not right at all," little Em said, peeping between the stones, and finding him in a very curious posture. "What are you doing, Waldo? It is not the play, you know. You should run out when we come to the white stone. Ah, you do not play nicely."

"I—I will play nicely now," said the boy, coming out and standing sheepishly before them; "I—I only forgot; I will play now."

"He has been to sleep," said freckled Em.

"No," said beautiful little Lyndall, looking curiously at him: "he has been crying."

She never made a mistake.

THE CONFESSION

One night, two years after, the boy sat alone on the kopje. He had crept softly up the little hill from his father's room and come there. He often did, because, when he prayed or cried aloud, his father might awake and hear him; and none knew his great sorrow, and none knew his grief, but he himself, and he buried them deep in his heart.

He turned up the brim of his great hat and looked at the moon, but most at the leaves of the prickly pear that grew just before him. They glinted, and glinted, and glinted, just like his own heart—cold, so hard, and very wicked. His physical heart had pain also; it seemed full of little bits of glass, that hurt. He had sat there for half an hour, and he dared not go back to the close house.

He felt horribly lonely. There was not one thing so wicked as he in all the world, and he knew it. He folded his arms and began to cry— not aloud; he sobbed without making any sound, and his tears left scorched marks where they fell. He could not pray; he had prayed night and day for so many months; and to-night he could not pray. When he left off crying, he held his aching head with his brown hands. If one might have gone up to him and touched him kindly; poor, ugly little thing! Perhaps his heart was almost broken.

With his swollen eyes he sat there on a flat stone at the very top of the kopje; and the tree, with every one of its wicked leaves, blinked, and blinked and blinked at him. Presently he began to cry again, and then stopped his crying to look at it. He was quiet for a long while, then he knelt up slowly and bent forward. There was a secret he had carried in his heart for a year. He had not dared to look at it; he had not whispered it to himself, but for a year he had carried it. "I hate God!" he said. The wind took the words and ran away with them, among the stones, and through the leaves of the prickly pear. He thought it died away half down the kopje. He had told it now!

"I love Jesus Christ, but I hate God."

The wind carried away that sound as it had done the first. Then he got up and buttoned his old coat about him. He knew he was certainly lost now; he did not care. If half the world were to be lost, why not he too? He would not pray for mercy any more. Better so—better to know certainly. It was ended now. Better so.

He began scrambling down the sides of the kopje to go home.

Better so! But oh, the loneliness, the agonized pain! for that night, and for nights on nights to come! The anguish that sleeps all day on the heart like a heavy worm, and wakes up at night to feed!

There are some of us who in after years say to Fate, "Now deal us your hardest blow, give us what you will; but let us never again suffer as we suffered when we were children."

The barb in the arrow of childhood's suffering is this: its intense loneliness, its intense agony.

Dark Spring

How can one comment on one's own work? Especially when the piece was written so long ago—almost ten years. I was a different person then. I don't even know why I wrote "Dark Spring." I had to, I suppose. I felt it deeply when I wrote it. But to try to comment on it—in any terms that make sense to anyone else—it can't be done. Anything I can say about it now sounds self-conscious and stiff. What did I mean by it? How do I know? It must have grown out of some experience of my own—I recognize fleeting glimpses of myself all through the story—the way I felt about love, the different kinds of love that are so agonizing to you when you're young (I suppose they're always agonizing even when you're no longer young)—spring with its exaltation and its grief and its mysterious stirrings—poetry, that is almost the natural tongue of youth—God and religion that are so close, so real, so urgent to the young—the poignant beauty of sacrifice, of "laying the world away"—everything that makes being alive and seventeen wonderful and tragic and unique.

Maybe it would be better to print the story without comment.

MARY BRINKER POST

SPRING, the burning bush, the voice from heaven, had returned to earth. All along the block women came outside after supper to talk to their men while they sprinkled the grass or stooped over frail green plants in their gardens. The children ran in swift, silent herds playing hide and seek, with wild, sudden outbursts at each capture.

Bliss, who was watering the lawn, stepped lightly on the tender green grass that held the imprint of her feet if she came down hard. She stood under the broad catalpa, a green cave in daylight, a mysterious living cloud at night, and pressed her slender body against its living stem.

All the rowan trees in the parking strip before her house were full and overflowing. Such slender dark boles holding up the bounty of green. "Like small proud women with heavy, heavy hair," whispered Bliss.

Everything turned into poetry this spring. She was like a cup filled to the brim. Was it because she was seventeen? Was it because she had let her hair grow? You felt different with your hair long.

Above the tiny roar of the hose and the children's voices, she could hear the carnival music, like a golden fire of sound across the roofs. Honky-tonk music from a calliope in a cheaply gilded wagon at a tarnished street carnival. She'd seen it setting up its three tents half way downtown in a vacant double lot. The music beat in waves across the house tops. Her heart pounded as she turned off the water and came up the steps.

Her mother sat rocking on the porch, straining her eyes over a pair of socks she was darning.

"Mother," said the girl softly, "do you mind if I go down to see the carnival? It's not far down on Division. I can walk there easily."

"What carnival?" her mother asked, not looking up.

"Oh, Mother, you remember, we saw them putting up tents this morning. It only costs a quarter. But it'd be fun. I feel like a carnival tonight."

"I don't like you to go alone. But Ted's going to a movie with his girl, and your father and I thought we'd drive out in the valley to buy some gladiolus bulbs. If you go, you won't stay late? Just go down for an hour."

"No, I won't stay long."

The dress she had on was clean but that didn't matter. She wanted to put on something different and becoming. She slipped into a new green knitted dress with a short jacket. It made her someone unfamiliar and exciting. Some clothes were like that. It was lovely when they were. As she changed her dress she kept glancing at herself in the long mirror. She liked to look at herself. It was interesting to see what she looked like, to know what other people saw when they looked at her. "Do my eyes really look that deep?" she wondered. "I wonder if people notice how thin my arms are and how bony my wrists. I like them bony, but I don't think other people do." She had to watch her arms sweep up and out as she brushed her hair. "That's the nice thing about long hair. It looks pretty brushing it." At last she had it coiled in soft, snug brown rolls at the back of her neck. While she stood close to the mirror, rubbing on lipstick, the low moan of the golden, insistent music ran through her heart.

She thought, "I could go get Doris to come with me, but I don't think I will. I feel like going alone." When you went with someone else you had to talk and you were as young as they were. Sometimes it was fun to laugh and eat hot dogs with another girl and have people turn around to smile at you. But not tonight.

She went to the door and looked out of the little round window and saw only an interlacing of nodding green boughs and feathery leaves. Her heart leaped. How beautiful it was to look out upon green. She pretended it was a forest out the window and no steps or walks or streets. Everything was so beautiful. She went out and kissed her mother gently because of it.

"Now don't stay late, Bliss. I worry about your going places alone."

"Oh, Mother. Don't be silly and worry all the time. Nothing could happen to anybody on a night like this."

She went swiftly down the street until she came to Division, a main thoroughfare connecting the two parts of town that the river divides. She walked slowly here, watching the lines of cars streaming past, pouring their headlights upon the pale dusk. It was darker with the lights on. These cars, unknown and swift, flashing up and down the big hill, where were all the people going? What thrilling things would they do?

She wondered if the boy she saw that morning putting up tents would be there tonight. She remembered how he had looked up at her and smiled as she and her mother walked past.

Cars were parked solidly for two blocks around the lot where the carnival was pitched. The music was loud and wheezy now. The crowds of people at the ticket office and along the midway stood in a nimbus of light and dust. It was the first carnival of the year and everyone had forgotten the last one of the past year enough to be excited about this.

Bliss paid her quarter at the box office. The ticket seller smiled at her, his cigarette tilted in a long holder at a corner of his mouth. Hamburger stands, orange drink and beer counters jostled the shooting galleries hung high with striped cheap blankets and fatuous Kewpie dolls with headdresses and hula skirts of dyed feathers. There was a side show with a spindly collection of worn-out freaks that Bliss hurried past. Six Oriental dancers chewed gum and waved limp violet veils. Mechanically graceful, a woman trainer in grey tights edged with gold, and a military jacket and hat with a thin aigrette, cracked a whip at two paddy-footed lionesses with opal eyes. Miraculously all this cheapness was strung upon the golden thread of the calliope music and the dark, soft night, the mesmerism of excitement, became enchantment.

Bliss saw the young man who had smiled at her that morning. He stood by a concession where you threw rubber balls at revolving ducks, small and quick, with the blackest eyes. His profile made her think of a dagger, but it was his black, soft eyes that plunged into hers. As she came near he smiled and called to her, "Don't you want to try to hit a duck?"

She shook her head, flushing. She stood in her new, green dress with her thin, young wrists and her mobile mouth, while this young, dark dagger of a boy looked at her. Her lips trembled into a confused smile, and her cheeks got red and hot.

Her smile emboldened the young man. He went over to her and took her arm. "Oh, come on, it won't hurt you. Just try once for luck."

"Oh, I couldn't," she murmured, letting his determined hand guide her through the passing people.

"Yes you can, you've got both hands, haven't you?" He was smiling into her averted face, dark and shadowy. She felt his smile like a soft cloud.

"I can't hit anything. Really I can't," she stammered.

"Here, try it once on me. I bet you'll knock 'em all down. Won't she, Jake?" he said in his peculiar, low voice that cut under the jangle of noise about them.

The chance seller heard him and grinned. "Here," he said gruffly and tossed her a rubber ball. She had to catch it, of course, and throw it at the ducks. The ball hit one, knocked it over. She couldn't keep from laughing, and returned the boy's smile. Then she started off through the crowd, but the boy followed and took her arm.

"Come on over here, they're dancing in this tent," he murmured.

"Oh, no," she protested.

He had the thickest eyelashes she'd ever seen on a man. They were so thick that they made a curved shadow on his cheek bones.

"Wouldn't you dance one dance with me?"

He danced in a shoddy dance-hall way with jiggly broken steps and his hand and hers on his hip. The lesser element at high school dances danced that way.

The minute the music stopped and the clapping began, she slipped outside the tent. He was close behind her and his arm pinned her to his side. His smooth, sharp face hovered over hers like a hawk's. She pushed his arms down from her waist and twisted out of his hard grasp. Something she hadn't known existed in her hated him. It hated her, too, because she wanted to go limp in his arms, wanted to submit to his hawklike insistence.

She ran into the crowd going toward the gate and was lost. The boy looked after her with a funny, contemptuous smile which she didn't see.

Bliss walked home with fast, tense steps. She had had enough of the carnival. Before her house standing dark and patient under the wide, hushed sky, she paused to finger the mountain ash blossoms by the steps. The night breathed quietly and the white blossoms gave out a sharp, sweet sigh. The sound of the calliope had ceased. His face had been smooth, dark and edged as a sword.

The next day was a dark spring Sunday with full green trees at the windows and little girls roller skating on the sidewalks. There was the coolest thing in the world coming in her open bedroom windows, a wind with smell of rain in it. The sky looked full and black with that imminence all day.

Bliss got up early and went alone to church. It was warm and dark, a cave, with candle flames going up straight as a song. The smell of candle wax and communion wine was holy, moving, brought quick tears. The girl made her communion, going to the altar rail with the three faithful elderly ladies and a newly confirmed young boy, but she was alone, wrapped in loneliness as a veil.

She walked home under an overcast sky, between the bright, green lawns. She thought this windy dark day of spring more thrilling and expectant than any sunny, cloudless day. There was a brightness high above in the farthest heavens like the blue beating of angels' wings about the throne.

The only person she met on the way was a boy who lived down the street, a friend of Ted's. He was coming from the direction of the chapel of St. Ignatius' College and he said, "Good morning," to her as they passed.

Her family was getting up lazily, Sunday morning disorder of papers and coffee cups hovering over the front rooms. They had never struck her before as quite so ordinary and spiritless. She looked at them as from afar, but clearly, as from a hilltop one sees the people in the valley just below. Ted's incredible before-breakfast cigarette had smelled up the whole place. Father sat crunching toast and reading out loud from the sports section, "I see Curly Jackson knocked out Bull Morgan in the sixth. Whadd'ye know, Ted?"

Her mother sat comfortable and placid in the midst of it, the sleeves of her lavender bathrobe spotted, her wispy hair streaming down her plump back. "There's toast in the oven, Sweetheart," she called, "and orange juice in the ice box. Come and sit here by the register, it's kind of chilly in the house this morning."

"I don't care for any breakfast," Bliss answered, "I'm not a bit cold either."

She ran upstairs to her own room and lay on the bed, reading poetry until her mother called her to help get the big mid-afternoon orgy of roast, brown potatoes, enormous salads, chocolate cake and pudding that was their Sunday dinner. She dreamed over "When I am dead and over me bright April shakes down her rain-drenched hair—" Sara Teasdale was exquisite. But it was Rupert Brooke, Rupert Brooke who died too young, that she loved. There was a wonderful picture of him in her collection of his poems, a sort of half-tortured, intense profile, with the light falling across his beautiful, strong forehead lifted in such gallant defiance of the world. She looked into his face, at the tenderness of his mouth and chin, his unhappy, fine eyes.

"Oh, why did you die, why did you die?" she whispered, trying to imagine war and a cause great enough to take young immortals and throw them down to death. But at least he had left something behind that was beautiful and good. If she were to die now, there would be nothing to show she had ever lived. She took out a brown notebook from her locked dresser drawer and glanced through the scribbled pages with an expression of pain and disgust on her shadowy face. "They're awful," she cried out loud, tossing the notebook back and locking the drawer.

She opened the book of Brooke's poems again, looked a long time at his picture, then began to read aloud, softly and tensely,

> Blow out, you bugles, over the rich dead,
> There's none of these so lonely and poor of old,
> But dying, has made us rarer gifts than gold.
> These laid the world away; poured out the red,
> Sweet wine of youth, gave up the years to be
> Of worth and joy, and that unhoped serene,
> That men call age; and those who would have been,
> Their sons, they gave, their immortality.

She turned back to his picture. "Their sons! He was so young. He wasn't even married yet. He wasn't even married!" Her mouth trembled and she flung herself on the bed and wept. And then her mother's voice called cheerily from the stairway, "Come and peel the potatoes, Honey, the roast's on."

Dinner lasted until late in the afternoon and after the dishes were done, Mr. Minor got out the car to drive them all to the airport.

"If you don't mind, I'll stay home," Bliss said, watching her mother comb her thin, gray hair again.

"Sis, Dad may let us go up for an hour," Ted boomed from the bathroom.

"I've been up once. I have a book to finish for school."

"Well, if you won't get lonesome," worried her mother.

Bliss only smiled and lay down on the bed, one slender warm arm across her eyes. She lay and listened to them all fussing around and finally going. When the car had gone, silence, holy and sweet, fell upon the house. Bliss lay suspended in quiet and the faint spicy smell of the lemon pudding.

She must have slept because when she opened her eyes the room was dark. It wasn't so dark outside. She put on her white turtleneck sweater and walked up to the store for some candy. She came back home and ate it sitting on the steps. When it was gone she sat with her arms clasped around her knees, looking at the green fountain of the weeping birch. There was a smell of wild roses, damp and secret in some tangle of bushes, coming in a sudden rich perfume. No carnival music rolled over the houses tonight, but from someone's radio there was the prance of a minuet, tiny and metallic on the taut strings of a quartet, coming like a faraway bright tinkle of silver, like a high shaking of stars, into the gathering evening.

Poor Bliss, curled on the steps, her heart pierced by all these fatal lances. It was useless to try to fight the longing, the gnaw of sadness that has no name or cause and so is as sweet as delight or love. She must sit and sigh and give herself completely over.

Some one came up the walk between the mountain ash trees, calling deeply, "Ted, hi, Ted!" He came forward and she saw that he was the boy she'd passed on her way from church, Ted's friend, Gay Kennedy.

"Ted's not here," she said from her steps.

He stopped to recognize her. "Oh, hello, Bliss. I didn't see you there at first. Ted's not here? I wanted to see him about playing tennis in the morning before school. D'ye think he could drag himself out to play at seven? I'd call for him after Mass." He stood with one foot on the lowest step, tall and slight, in tennis flannels and a white sleeveless sweater.

"Did you play today?" she asked idly.

"Jim Scott and I played a couple of the priests from the college."

"Are you going to St. Ignatius this year? I thought you started at the U." She had an instant vision of two priests she had seen walking in the college close in cassocks and birettas. Her imagination animated them suddenly into strange figures with tennis racquets thrust into their hands and cassocks flying.

"I did start at the U. I was taking a pre-medics, but old man depression came along and then the folks kind of wanted me to go to the college anyway. I'm glad I changed." He looked off across the lawn. There was something about his throat and chin seen from the side that reminded her of Rupert Brooke. Something tragic. . . .

"Why are you glad?" she asked. How fine and strong the bones of his face were.

He looked back at her with sudden intentness, and came and sat beside her on the steps, stretching his long, white legs down before him. He laced his fingers together and sat looking at them while he talked to her.

"Because it's changed my whole life, Bliss," he said in his low, masculine voice that was very moving. "I'm a different person now. But—I don't suppose you can understand it—lots of my friends can't."

"Why can't I understand?" she breathed. Here was someone, she felt vaguely, in some kind of inner turmoil, just as she was, and he didn't think she could understand.

Gay Kennedy looked at her over his shoulder. He saw her round, soft face and blurred features and the dark places where her eyes were. "Perhaps you would, I don't know."

"Tell me," she said.

"I'm going to become a priest, Bliss," he answered at last. He breathed very deeply and looked out into the night again.

"Oh," cried Bliss, "oh, Gay, how wonderful." Her eyes were bright and wet and her voice trembled a little. She could feel the sorrow of the spring night flooding up in her again, over and over her heart.

"Do you think so, Bliss? Do you really?" He bent toward her, eager and incredulous.

"Oh, yes." She had to put out her hand to touch his that lay on his knee. His hand caught hers and held it tight. "I saw you coming from Mass this morning, Gay, when I was going home from my church."

"You go to church too? You understand that, too, the secret necessary. . . ."

He bent his head and looked at her. "Why are you crying? Bliss—what a lovely name, Bliss."

"I think it's wonderful for you to give up the world and become a priest, but it makes me sad, too. It's so strange, I've felt a sort of sadness all day, something I couldn't explain. Do you know. . . ."

His face with its beautiful, lifted forehead, was turned to hers. He nodded and held her hand tighter.

"You mustn't be sad because I'm going to become a priest. It's the greatest thing I could do."

"I know it is, but I can't help being sad about it. Though I don't know why I should. I've seen you with Ted a lot, but I've hardly ever spoken to you before."

"I know. I don't know why I told you all this."

They looked into each other's faces and then Gay put his arm around her and kissed her. She did not try to stop him. She sat pressed against his breast and face, her arm held tight to her side. Her heart hurt so she could have cried. She kissed his warm, living face and was lifted out of the world.

They sat for a while on the steps together, but Bliss went in before the folks came back from their drive, because she couldn't bear to see any of them, feeling the way she did. Gay Kennedy went home and she drifted upstairs and got into bed without turning on the lights.

She thought of Gay and cried for a while, not trying to stop. Then she turned her pillow and lay with the night wind coming in from the open window onto her flushed cheeks. After a while she began to feel happy and she smiled in the dark. And suddenly the rain broke out of the sky and pattered upon the screen. The kind, spring rain, so wet and good.

IV

Through a Glass, Darkly

SHERWOOD ANDERSON

The Death of Mrs. Folger

I am very happy that you wish to use "The Death of Mrs. Folger." Sherwood loved to tell that story and it was one of the last things he wrote.

MRS. SHERWOOD ANDERSON

I WENT up the stairs in the little suburban house, her son staying below. It was very cold outside, a stinging wind and drifting snow. It had been a long cold ride out from the city after the phone call came from the son.

He said, "Mother's dying. She keeps asking for you. Will you come?"

I had had to wait for a long time for a street car. I had no money for a taxi. It was one of my hard-up times.

The son was a short, rather fat man with a mustache. He had red cheeks and watery eyes.

As I climbed the stairs I tried to remember what he did.

"Let's see, does he run a store?

"He may be a doctor or a dentist."

I had him connected in my mind with rubber stamps.

"That's it," I told myself. "He makes rubber stamps."

I remembered her speaking of him.

"He's religious," she had said. "My husband was like that too."

I had never seen her husband, had never until that night, when she died, seen her son.

I had a sharp feeling of guilt climbing the stairs.

Why had I so lost touch with her? She had been a sort of second mother, something wonderful for me.

I was remembering her little sharp eyes, so like the eyes of some little wild animal seen at evening at the edge of a wood, her small gray head, alert, alive little body.

I had gone there, to that Middle-Western town, wanting an education. There was a college in the town and she had taken me in.

It was beyond the college, just at the edge of town, a huge old brick
house, a great stretch of lawn, trees, a big barn. Some of the professors
from the college lived there. There were two lawyers, both unmarried, a
newspaper editor, a dentist. There must have been ten or twelve men and
there were three or four women, all schoolteachers, one of them to become
my lifelong friend. She was a big-legged, big-breasted German woman.
She discussed books with me. She brought me books to read.

The little woman with the eyes and the gray hair said, "Look out, boy."

When my work was done in the evening she saw me going off for long
walks with the German woman. She was afraid I might fall in love. She
said she had seen it happen once, there in her own house, a boy like me
had been taken in. He had married a woman much older than himself,
some twenty years older, who was also a schoolteacher.

"Look out, boy."

I was in a room with the little gray one. It was my job at that place to
take care of the yard. I kept the grass mowed. I got my meals and a place
to sleep and there were two others, students, one to take care of her cows
and another to wait on table.

They were both trying to work their way through the college. They
planned to be preachers.

She had taken me into her own room. I had been living there for a
month. She stood before me, such a small alert young old figure.

"Are you also planning to be a preacher? Do you believe in God?"

I had begun trying to explain. I neither believed nor disbelieved. I said
I just went along, didn't try thinking of such things.

"And heaven. Do you believe that, if you are what is called good, you
will go to a place called heaven when you die?"

She was very serious. Her little sharp eyes were peering at me.

"I don't believe," I said, hesitating, "that I will ever be anything of
enough importance to be preserved through what they call 'eternity.'

"It's such a long time," I said. An idea that had got into my boy's
head began to find words.

"It's such an egotistical idea. I can't believe that most people are worth
keeping alive in any form through eternity.

"No, I'm afraid I don't believe."

She came toward me, put up her little old face.

"Kiss me, boy," she said.

We became friends. What talks we had. In the evening we went often into her own room and closed the door. She had helped many boys through college but she had had bad luck. They had all turned out to be preachers or they were religious.

It had been so with her husband who had long been dead. It was so with her son.

"I have always had religious people about me.

"It isn't that I don't like them," she said. "I try to forget what they are."

When she was a child at home, before her marriage, all her people had been pious, but very early in her own life, she declared, she had decided not to believe. It wasn't that she had ever had much impulse to sin. She just didn't want to believe.

"I want to be just the same as a flower or a tree and a house or a dog. I am getting old. Already, a little, I am dying.

"You see my hair is gray. When I awake in my bed in the morning I don't want to get up.

"I can feel death coming. Little bites it takes of me. Now soon it will take me, all of me."

There had been but a few people to whom she had confided her secret. She had never told her husband. When her son, as a young boy, got religion and joined the church she had told him she was glad.

"I don't want to disturb anyone at all by my unbelief," she said.

It was something to which she clung. It was a secret between her and me. In the presence of all the others who lived in her house and when we were all at table and grace was being said . . .

It was said by one of the young boys she had taken in, one who planned to become a minister.

. . . when it was going on she sometimes lifted her head. She sat at the head of the long table and I was far down toward the other end. She winked at me.

She was very ill. She was near death. Because of growing weakness she had long since given up her house.

She had come in to the city to live her last days with her son and her son's children. For a time we had exchanged letters but for several years I had heard nothing of her.

I was at the head of the stairs, near the door of the room where she was lying when a nurse came out. She came and whispered to me:

"She wants you but you mustn't go in. She is very low. She will try to talk. The doctor says she must not talk."

The whispering of the nurse was interrupted by a voice. It was her voice, very small.

It was like the voice of a child.

"It is you," it said. "They will tell you not to come in to me but pay no attention to them." The nurse made a gesture with her hand and followed me into the room.

She was very small. Her body was like that of a very small child.

How small her face, her voice, her little, shrunken hand.

With her hand she made a motion to the nurse.

"Go out."

The nurse went and I was alone with her. I took her little shrunken hand in mine. Only her little sharp eyes seemed alive.

Her little voice seemed coming from far off.

"I wanted you for a moment," she said.

"I did not want them to be hurt.

"They believe and I do not believe. I wanted someone to know that, at the very last, at the edge of the grave, I did not believe."

The effort to speak had seemed to have exhausted her. Her eyes closed, the nurse came into the room and I went softly down the stairs.

The son was there.

"Mother was very fond of you," he said.

"Yes," I said. "She only wanted to say good-by."

I stood with him there in the little hallway of the house, when the nurse came down the stairs.

She said my friend had died. At the very last she had thrust up her little banner.

It was against those who thought they were fit to live through all eternity. She hadn't wanted to hurt them so she had waved the little defiant banner only for me.

AUGUST STRINDBERG

The Votive Offering

With August Strindberg (1849-1912), modern Swedish literature crossed the boundary from the old to the new, and Swedish commentators consider 1879 as the boundary year. That was the year of Strindberg's first notable book, a novel, THE RED ROOM. A "naturalist" in the 80's and a mystic in the 90's, his novels, stories, poems and dramas covered a wide domain.

VESTMAN of Nedergård Island had been on a schooner trip along the coast of Norway, right up to Lofoten. There he had met some whale-catchers and had learnt one or two things about the art of catching whales with the harpoon. So when he came back to his native isle it occurred to him that he might adapt his newly acquired knowledge to the local method of seal-catching, an industry which was steadily on the decline, owing to the terrifying effect which the noise of the guns had on the timid beasts.

With this object he went to work in the following somewhat ill-advised manner, with a result that neither he nor any one else could have reckoned on, and which gave rise to an adventure of which the story still lives among the skerries.

One evening in late spring Vestman took a boy with him in a flat-bottomed boat to the outer skerries, where the seals used to come ashore to bask in the sun. For the carrying out of this remarkable hunting feat he had brought with him an otter-spear, the ordinary purpose of which was the extraction of otters from crevices in the rocks. This weapon, in accordance with the whale-catchers' methods, he had made fast to a windlass in the bows. How he was to get near the timid creatures to catch them with this improvised harpoon, neither he nor any one else knew; but in case things went wrong his friends said one could always catch fish in a water barrel. But the intended plan of campaign was that the boy should come from the shore side with the gun, while Vestman himself crept along in his boat between the ice-floes and there waited for the flying beasts, which wouldn't be able to move very quickly on the rough drift-ice which was heaped up along the shore.

Well, he got the boy ashore just before sunset, and started rowing with a pair of woollen stockings twisted round the looms of his oars to deaden the sound, and with a white shirt over his clothes so as to be less conspicuous. And under cover of the rocky islets and pack-ice he managed to row right up to the foot of the slope, where a gully showed how the beasts had gone up, and how presumably they would have to come down, since there were no holes in the ice.

Vestman sat there, well out of sight, holding aloft the spear at arm's length for such a time that his fingers got frozen and he began to wonder whether the old shot-gun method was not simpler. The seals were there— there was no doubt about that: he heard their cries—but whether they would choose just this risky track for entering the water, that was the great question.

Bang! came the sound from behind the pine-trees on land, and then there was a squeaking in the air and a splashing out at sea, and after that a puffing and a blowing, and then a tapping on the ice like the sound of naked men running along a floor.

Before Vestman had realized how stupid the whole business really was, a shaggy head stuck out through the gap, rose up and plunged into the water, but not before the spear had caught the beast right in the middle. Quick as lightning the rope ran out; the jerk of the boat threw the hunter sprawling over the stern thwarts and off they went at a good round pace for the open sea.

What a lovely ride! Vestman enjoyed the novelty at first, and thought what a splendid hunting story it would make; the booty was already as good as his. But then he saw the boulders dancing past and his own cottage disappear.

"Good-by! So long!" he nodded to the shore. "Back again soon!"

There was jerking and jolting in the boat, but there didn't seem to be any immediate danger till they reached the last rocks and lost sight of land. There was a little sea running, and the sun seemed to have sunk. It looked like a round, black disc on the horizon.

"A bit more," thought Vestman, "and if the worst comes to the worst I shall cut adrift."

So off they went again. But now the boat started rolling; it was meeting the waves and already dipping its nose.

"A little further," thought Vestman. To throw away such a certain catch would be a poor end to such a lovely beginning.

The seas increased and the stars came out. He could still see his axe lying in the bows—his one hope if they went too far.

"On you go, old fellow! You'll soon get tired, if I know you!" muttered the frozen hunter. He was longing to take to the oars and get warm.

At that moment he discovered that his feet were wet and heard the boat's bottom scraping on the rocks.

"Lay off, there!"—the order was to himself—as he got up to cut adrift with the axe. But he promptly sat down again; for just as he was getting up, the seal dragged down the nose of the boat.

After a few unsuccessful attempts to creep forward into the bows he realized the necessity of sitting still; he was at the mercy of the beast, dependent on its whim as to whether he should founder or come home alive.

It was no longer amusing now; a mood of quiet seriousness came over the dispirited hunter. To give himself more courage than he had, he took an oar and stuck it out over the stern, pretending to steer. But he wasn't steering: the beast did that, and always straight out to sea.

"If I ever get out of this, the devil take . . ."

The seal cut a few capers and the oath was broken off; he had to take in the oar and find the bailer to get the water out of the boat.

As soon as he had finished bailing he stuck out the oar again, and at once felt calmer, as though he were really steering.

But by this time the stars had grown dim, and a sprinkle of rain came on, and some snow, so that very soon Vestman could no longer see his axe and found himself completely enveloped in a grey mist. And onward, ever onward, they sped; but the wind seemed on the point of veering, for the seas were now broadside on; and little by little the wind did veer.

And now he began to feel frightened! While he worked the bailer again, he thought of his wife and children, his farm and tools, and then of eternity, which was surely approaching. How he hadn't been to church for—how many years? Well, he couldn't remember, but not since the year of the cholera; and he hadn't been to communion . . . The lee gunwale scraped against the drift ice. "Lord Christ! Poor sinful mortal

that I am!" He had forgotten it all . . . "Our Father which art in
Heaven . . . Thy will be done as in Heaven . . ." even that!

What long hours, and such a lot of them! A few more and they would
be over at Åland, in this wind! But if they came on drift ice they would
have to go down with it to Gothland, or into the Gulf of Finland! Before
that he would be frozen to death.

He snuggled down into the bottom of the boat to try and get shelter
from the icy blast, and as soon as he was on his knees he remembered the
whole of the Lord's Prayer and repeated it a score of times; and every
time he came to the "Amen" he made a notch in the gunwale with his
pocket-knife. And at the sound of his own voice he became calmer; for
it seemed as though he were speaking to some one and some one were
speaking to him; and the words woke the memory of a crowd of people
assembled in church; and he saw them now before him, comforting and
reproaching him. He saw there the Gelings, whom he had recently been
out with picking up coal from the sunken brig—not quite honest, but
perhaps justifiable. He saw there . . . Another jerk of the line! "Lord
Jesus, Son of God, if I get out of this alive, I promise, as God lives, a
new chandelier with seven candlesticks of pure silver, the whole of my
savings for my children—for the church—pure silver! The Lord bless
us and keep us; the Lord lift up the light of His countenance upon us and
be gracious to us. . . ."

A light shone through the mist, straight ahead; a large light, but dim
as a horn lantern.

"It must be Hangö beacon on the Nyland coast," thought Vestman.
"I can quite believe we got there in twelve hours; it seemed like a week!"

Another crash under the boat, which stopped dead; Vestman pitched
forward over the thwarts, and then all was quiet again.

How far now to the beacon, at a guess? Eight miles! and now he
couldn't manage to go either forwards or backwards! It was worse than
ever, for the least movement made the boat rock.

Vestman sat still, waiting for sunrise and daylight in the east, while
he froze and prayed to God. And he promised and vowed, with every
solemn oath, the silver chandelier, hall-marked and costing two hundred
dalers, with seven candlesticks and ornaments on the collars; and a chain
with balls on it to hang from; and when people saw it they would say,
"That is the votive gift of Erik Vestman of Nedergård, whom the Lord

helped so graciously in his hour of need, in the year eighteen hundred and fifty-nine!" "God helped him so graciously and mercifully," he kept on repeating, till at last he believed it and in an exuberance of thankfulness for that gracious help recited the opening words of "Glory, praise and thanks to Thee, O Father dear!" God had helped him—that was quite clear, since the chandelier was hanging there, and the people were saying, or rather would say—they hadn't said it yet . . . And now the beacon went out . . . Lord Jesus, who walked upon the water and bade the billows cease!—They ceased now, they had ceased long ago, for it was perfectly smooth; it was really most strange; for here the sea beat with all its might, and just now had been frightful—yesterday evening, since it was now nearly morning—it must be nearly morning when his feet were so frightfully cold and he felt so hungry—he must get some hot coffee soon if only the pilot boat came out, as it must do, since ships would come at sunrise, which had been lying and cruising about the fairway; but why the dev— why in the world had they gone and put out the beacon fire? Perhaps it was daylight, though one couldn't see it on account of the fog; it must be that, unless the Russian Government had some different rules about their beacons; why, probably they had, and now he remembered as if in a dream that the Russians had a different calendar, in the old style—that was the point—thirty days too early or too late—it didn't matter which, for it must be a difference in time; and it *was* too, since the Finnish boats always came in an hour later than the telegraphed time; so that was why they had put out the beacon an hour before sunrise, which was therefore due in an hour. And now he understood why he felt so frightfully cold; everybody who has had the ague feels that at sunrise; but that seal-beast was keeping so quiet and there was no more jerking at the windlass; perhaps it had broken away and gone! He must see about that anyhow! To sit like this unnecessarily— No, dammit!

Vestman looked out ahead and saw something black and spiky like a forest of masts, rising out of the mist.

"Christ! if that's the Russian Fleet they'll shoot me for a smuggler or send me to Siberia. And what a crowd! Holy Father, it's an entire forest!"

He got up and stretched his knees. The boat rocked sideways only; there was no longer any dipping at the bows. Carefully he climbed forward over the thwarts; saw the line stretched tight as a telegraph wire;

stepped out of the boat; noticed footprints and struck his heel against a stone . . . he was on land! and there stood a pine wood!

"That you, father?" piped a well-known voice from a juniper shrub.

"Ludwig! What the devil are *you* doing here?"

"I was wondering what had become of you, father!"

Vestman rubbed his eyes: "Tell me—what time is it?"

"Getting on for eight: you've been away the best part of an hour! But I see you've brought the beast back all right!"

The creature lay on the rocks, with the otter spear in its back, dead from loss of blood. It had made a trip out to sea and turned back on account of the swell.

And even to-day that adventure is spoken of as the most astonishing in the whole history of the skerries except the story of the sea-serpent. And let him that doubts it go to Nedergård Church and look at the little chandelier hanging beneath the organ gallery in everlasting memory of the merciful rescue of one Vestman, formerly crown pilot, from most unusual peril at sea, when with death before his eyes he promised the Lord, for the benefit and edification of the Christian congregation—this tin chandelier.

—Translated from the Swedish by C. D. LOCOCK

DANA BURNET

Mr. Onion

The primary reason for writing this story was furnished by the fact that my daughter, then five years old, had a toy clown which she had christened "Mr. Onion" and which she dearly loved. This was enough to send me to my typewriter.

A second, and perhaps more compelling reason, was the desire on my part to protest against, or at least to dissent from, the prevailing cynicism of the year 1926, in which the story was composed. That, as readers of my generation will recall, was the height of a godless and undisciplined age which began with the Armistice of 1918 and ended with the Grand Smash of 1929. Possibly I wrote the story as a penance for my participation in that time when license was mistaken for liberty and it was smart to have no faith in anything at all.

At any rate, "Mr. Onion" is a tale of faith. Its simple purpose is to show that love in its pure or child-like form can endow the object on which it is bestowed with an extra-materialistic value that in turn invites faith from others. The completion of this cycle is, I suppose, the sum and substance of religion.

Perfect knowledge may someday make religion superfluous. Till then, it will remain an essential of constructive human living; for it alone can bridge the gap between what we know we are and what we want to be or can conceive ourselves to be. The world today is re-discovering the necessity for faith; and to that re-discovery I am happy to contribute my friend—who is still beloved by one I love—"Mr. Onion."

DANA BURNET

I T W A S when she went to turn out the light back of the sofa that Marian discovered Mr. Onion perched on top of the bookshelves. Dressed in his perennial clown's costume, and holding in his hands the ladder that was an integral part of his character, he stood patiently grinning down at her. His grin was ludicrous. It was also faintly pathetic, as every true clown's grin should be.

Marian thought: Jackie must have climbed up on the sofa last night before he went to bed and put Mr. Onion on top of the bookshelves. . . . Funny that I never noticed him there. . . . But I was so busy with things . . . people. . . . Good Lord! What a party! They must have had a good time. . . . They stayed till daylight. . . . But our crowd always has a good time. . . .

"I'll take Mr. Onion back to the nursery; Jackie adores him. . . . He cares more for that clown than for all his other toys put together. . . ."

But when she reached for the little wooden figure a weakness seized her. She began to laugh hysterically. She was so very tired and Mr. Onion was so very absurd. So unalterably absurd. . . . And so pathetic. . . . It was the way his painted mouth turned up at the corners. . . .

She sank down on the sofa, shaking with uncontrollable laughter. John came stumbling in from their bedroom. His coat was off, and his tie dangled like a wilted purple flag from his loosened collar.

" 'Matter, old girl?"

"Look! F-funny. . . ."

"Oh, Mr. Onion?"

"Y-e-e-s!"

"But what's funny? Where's the joke?"

"I—don't—know. I think it's his grin. . . . No, it's the l-ladder," gasped Marian helplessly. "Why must he always carry a ladder? It's so p-pointless."

"Everything's pointless at five o'clock in the morning," grumbled John, yawning. "Come to bed, Marian. You're worn out. So am I. The damned party lasted too long," he added, with sudden irritability.

"To think of Mr. Onion's standing up there all night watching us!" said Marian, sighing. "I wonder what he thought of us?"

"Sick of parties," said John. "Come to bed—"

But somehow they didn't go to bed just then. The great rush of sunrise across the sea and up the hill and through the windows of their cottage may have struck them all at once as something too precious to be wasted. Or possibly they were still a trifle dizzy from the effects of their own hospitality and wanted to cool their heads in the fresh morning air; or possibly they were just too exhausted to do anything very definite. . . .

They drifted out of doors and sat down on the rustic bench that stood at the edge of the hill, facing the sea. . . . Marian, in her crumpled evening dress, with her hair curling flatly about her pretty, tired face, with something rather strange and crumpled in her eyes, was a mildly fascinating figure to John, her husband. They had been married six years,

reflected remotely. Nice to know that Marian could still turn into a
woman he never had seen before.

But was there, perhaps, a chance, a slight chance, that some day she
might turn into a complete—and permanent—stranger? He had watched
her last night dancing with Tom Nevinson. Nevinson was keen on Marian.
He had fallen for her in the frankly casual way that men these days fell
for other men's wives. It was a case according to the modern code. Also
according to the modern code John Thurston was forbidden the old-
fashioned emotion of jealousy. . . . Besides, wasn't he himself more or
less engaged in making love to Sally Nevinson, Tom's pert, blond wife?
Nevertheless, he recalled, if not with jealousy, at least with amazement,
the difference in Marian when she danced or joked or flirted with Tom.
Or of course she did flirt. All nice women flirted nowadays. . . . Well,
what of it? They always had. . . . Only not so openly.

"I wonder what Mr. Onion *does* think of us?"

"What's on your mind, sweetheart?"

But she didn't answer directly, and his own mind floated off and away
like a bit of cloud—like that fleecy cloud being driven into the sunrise by
the light western breeze. It would be a fine, fair day, said his high-sailing
mind. . . .

He wanted vaguely to ask Marian a question—something that would
involve and bring to an issue all the unasked and unanswered questions
between them. But the only thing he could think of was: Where did Mr.
Onion come from?

He couldn't remember, at the moment, who had given Jackie that
ridiculous clown. His lapse of memory annoyed him. It invested Mr.
Onion with a certain mystery; with a certain importance.

Oh, nonsense! Why not ask Marian? Of course she would know. She
could recite offhand the origin and history of any of Jackie's toys. But
he wouldn't ask her. He wouldn't be so silly. As though there could be
any mystery about a child's plaything!

"By the way, Marian, whoever gave Jackie that darned clown?"

"I don't know," answered his wife absently.

"What? You must know!"

"Well, I don't. We were never able to find out. . . . Don't you remember? He just turned up that Christmas, and we never knew who
sent him. We never found the card. I made quite an effort, too—asked

everyone I could think of—because Jackie adored him so. But I neve
found out. . . ."

"Uh-huh," said John.

"It was Jackie who named him," added Marian, with a sleepy, rem
niscent smile. . . . She could hear, by some mental process that wa
more than memory, little Jackie's grave, childish voice murmuring in he
ears, drumming at her heart. . . . "The clown's name is Mr. Onior
He has a funny name because clowns are funny people. And he has
ladder because he likes it. He can do tricks on it if he wants to. But he'
rather just carry it. It makes him feel like he was going to climb some
thing."

Marian smiled, thinking of Jackie still asleep in his safe, white bed, i
the wing of the cottage which they had built five years before when he wa
born. Safe bed, safe house, safe beautiful country. . . . The Maine shor
in August. . . . No place on earth more perfect for a child!

All safe! Yet, curiously, deep down in her tired body, in her broodin,
mind, she was aware of a blankness, a shadow that was almost fear. Life
in its essence, was so fragile. . . . And there was so much of it that wa
mere doubt and dream and nebulous, swiftly changing chemical read
tion. . . .

"We have no God," she said abruptly, but very simply, as though utte
ing a familiar and commonplace thought.

John stirred beside her. He uncrossed and stretched his long flannel
clad legs. "And what," he asked, "would we be doing with a God if w
had one?"

"Oh, I don't know. Pray to Him. . . . Depend on Him. . . . Hav
Him in for tea—and conversation."

"You've been looking at the sun. It's made you religious," he said.

"The sun's too impersonal," replied Marian. "Sometimes when yo
want it most it goes under a cloud. . . . I'd rather like a God," she con
tinued murmurously, "who would always be on hand in case of—of emer
gency."

John twisted about, with an effort, to look at her.

"Are you serious, old girl?"

"Serious? Yes, I think so."

"How come? What's the big idea? We've got along all right so fa
without any particular household deity."

"Have we?" breathed Marian.

"Well, haven't we?" he countered.

"I don't know," she said again slowly. "I wonder—I can't help wondering whether we, whether people like us—our generation—are as successful at living as we like to think we are. We pretend to a good deal of—advancement. Progress. -. . . But I'm not so sure. We've dragged out a lot of the old bugaboos and made faces at them. We've learned to admit that we have bodies, and we've organized a parade of the senses—with Papa Freud as drum major. We've abolished vice by the simple process of making a virtue of it. And maybe these things help. They're a kind of oil—banana oil—that we keep pouring out to smooth over the surface! But there's something volcanic at the center. I feel it—so often! A kind of restlessness, an uncertainty, as though we were living over a storm that might break at any moment—"

"Don't," said John placidly. "What's the use?"

"You feel it too!"

"Well—yes—in a way. Who doesn't? But—no good expecting things to happen. Besides, what can happen to us? I mean, barring some accident."

"That's just it. Accidents do happen. Oh, why not admit that it's all accident? And—the trouble with us is that we've never been *through* anything. We don't know our own strength or our own weakness—"

"Oh, well," interrupted John, "we've got—anyway—a philosophy. A kind of philosophy. At least I have." He glanced at her rather defiantly, but she was staring at the golden east, at the infinite cobalt sea. "I believe in myself, in my own vitality—"

"Yes, dear, I know." This was the modern credo. She had heard it so many times before.

"Vitality's the only virtue. Be a good animal! Take Jackie, for instance. People are always harping on what a healthy kid he is—as though that were some sort of accident. It makes me sore! Why shouldn't he be healthy?" demanded Jackie's father. "You and I are healthy, decent people. He's our child. There's a kind of reason in it, a kind of logic."

"But life so frequently isn't logical," objected Marian in a voice as distant as her gaze. "There's so often a gap, a vacancy, a lost link in the chain—"

"I don't feel that. I have my work, you know." He was a trifle st
with fatigue.

"Does it satisfy you? Does your painting really satisfy you?"

"If it didn't, why would I go on with it?"

"Why not? One has to do something. . . . I've suspected, at tim
that it was simply a salve to your conscience, an excuse for loafing," s
said with a frankness born, perhaps, of sheer physical exhaustion.

"I see," grunted John. Then he laughed shortly. "Hell! as long
we're telling our real names this morning, I'd like to know—if you dor
mind—just how much that bird Nevinson means in your young life?"

"Tom?" Her voice was a languid note in the increasing breeze. "Do
Tom strike you as being—important?"

"Not as a person, perhaps. But as a symptom—"

"Yes, I grant you that. Tom may be a symptom. . . . Of what,
wonder? Because I really don't know. I'm not a promiscuous sort
woman, am I? Do you think I am?"

"I hope not," answered her husband.

"Why do I bother with Tom at all? Why do you bother with Sally?"

"Oh, Sally. . . ." mumbled John.

"You kissed her last night. I saw you. . . . When you were danci
on the porch. Tom hasn't kissed me—yet. Not really. But he will. I
coming to that. I suppose I'm a fool to tell you this, but I do so want
know why. . . . Because we—you and I—actually care a lot about ea
other, don't we, John dear?"

"Why, sure, a lot! A whole lot! Sure, we do." He was awkward ar
boyish in his desire to be emphatic. He put his hand on her arm. "Le
chuck it," he said. "Let's not play this silly game any more. You're rig
about my work. It *is* an excuse. But I was thinking . . . if I could g
away, go somewhere . . . to Paris, maybe. We've got money enough
do what we please. Let's pull up stakes and beat it—"

She shook briefly her small, dark head.

"Paris is only another place. 'The fault, dear Brutus' . . ." The re
of the quotation was lost in the wind. "You'd find the same silly game
Paris, or wherever you decided to go. . . . Only it isn't silly. It's de
perately serious. . . . The trouble is at the center. . . . What we la
is a faith—some faith—in something—beyond ourselves." Her spee
was broken into staccato bits, and the spaces were filled by the rustling

leaves, by the muffled drumbeat of the surf on the beach a quarter of a mile away. "That's why we go looking into other people. . . . Always prying into other people, hoping, hoping to find the prophet of some true God. . . ."

"You'll find no prophet in Tom Nevinson," growled John.

"Perhaps not. But I'll go on looking just the same. I must look! Don't you see? I can't afford not to. I might be cheated out of some miracle. If only I could find that miracle in you," she said quietly, and turned toward him her strange, searching, weary eyes.

He took her in his arms and kissed her.

"No," he said. "I won't pose. I won't play prophet or promise miracles even to make you happy. I'm not up to a hair shirt and a diet of locusts. If you can't be satisfied with a plain man who—oh, hell!" he broke off sharply. "Let's quit this. We're getting in too deep. It's just because we're so darned tired. What are we sitting out here for, anyway? Let's go in— have some breakfast—go to bed."

Miss Mosby, little Jackie's nurse, appeared in her chaste white as they sat dispiritedly at breakfast on the screened dining porch.

"Jackie has a little cold this morning," said Miss Mosby.

"Don't let him go into the ocean, then," cautioned Marian.

"Very well, Mrs. Thurston."

"How much of a cold?" asked John, stifling a yawn.

"His nose is running," announced Miss Mosby, smoothing her pro-phylactic apron.

"Maybe he oughtn't to go to the beach at all," worried Marian.

"Oh, nonsense!" said her husband. "Beautiful, warm day like this. Do him good to be down there in the sunshine. . . . I'll have a look at him."

He got up and went into Jackie's room.

"Hello, Big Boy! Hear you got the snuffles?"

"But not a cold," quickly replied Jackie, sitting up in bed.

"Well, I don't know. How do you feel?"

"Fine, Daddy! I don't feel sick at all. I guess I can go to the beach all right," added Jackie, and squirmed uneasily as his father seemed to de-liberate. "I guess it would do me a lot of good to go to the beach, all right!"

"Beautiful day," thought John. What could happen to a healthy kid

on a day like this? Well, for the love of Pete, what did he *think* was going
to happen? "My nerves are shot," he decided, "staying up all night,
drinking. . . . I'm jumpy. And, then, that queer talk with Marian! What
was it she'd said about life being so uncertain, so—fragile—?

"Why, sure," he decided finally. "The beach—sure! Only, I wouldn't
go in bathing to-day, if I were you, Big Boy. No ocean, eh? But the beach—
fine! Keep out in the air; keep out in the sunshine. Do you more good
than a lot of foolish medicine."

So Jackie went to the beach that morning as usual. John and Marian
slept till one o'clock. Then John, after luncheon, drove off in the car to
keep a tennis engagement. "Promised Sally last night I'd play dou-
bles. . . ."

Marian shouted after him some casual sporting benediction. She was
in her room, dressing. She herself had a date that afternoon with Tom.
He would arrive shortly in *his* car, and they would drive out to the rocks
at Devil's Cove. . . . She laughed suddenly at the patent absurdity of
this exchange, this almost formal, almost mechanical transfer of interests.
Her husband rushing off to play with Sally, and Sally's husband rushing
off to play with her! How unutterably childish! Yet all the time she was
making herself as attractive as possible, putting on her smartest sport
skirt, her gayest colored sweater, her most fetching hat—the yellow straw
with the sprig of artificial wheat aslant the crown. . . .

Tom Nevinson arrived: a solid, rather boisterous young gallant in white
flannels and a tweed jacket, who smoked an incongruous, delicate-looking
briar pipe.

She listened all the way to Devil's Cove to his breezy protestations of
passion. He was not (he said) the sort of poor fish who went around
making love to every woman he met. Not much! Of course in his college
days (this with a sigh) he'd been—well, the usual sort of indiscriminate
young fool. But he'd learned by bitter experience the value of true emotion. *And* of course he cared a lot for Sally, just as she, Marian, cared a
lot about John. . . . Why, sure? He understood all that. But life was so
short and, er—it was all such a queer jumble, that—well—it seemed just
a darned shame not to be honest and speak out when you met someone
who really meant something to you.

"But that's such an obvious sort of truth," said Marian. "Such an old

truth! And—forgive me—such an unsubstantial one. I want something
more from you, Tom."

"Something more?" He was puzzled, curious, wondering whether he
dared assume that she was deliberately tempting him. . . .

"Yes. You don't happen to have any sort of *divine* truth concealed
about your person, do you?"

"Any sort of what? Divine truth? Are you kidding me, my beautiful?"

"I am not."

"Well, then, I don't get you."

"All right," said Marian serenely.

"My dear girl—"

She stopped him with a quick dart of her hand toward his arm.

"Take me home, Tom."

"Not yet, Marian! Don't spoil things. This is our day, our moment—"

He drew her to him. The delicate-looking pipe was removed, with a
gesture, from his lips. . . . He kissed her, and she made no protest. She
made no comment whatsoever.

She simply got up and started toward the car. He followed her.

"Marian dearest—"

"I must get home, Tom. You've got to take me. Something's happening! Something dreadful's happening— And please—drive fast!"

But when she got home she found that her fear—the black fear that had
seized her so unreasonably—was without justification in fact. Miss Mosby,
to be sure, reported that Jackie had a little fever.

Marian nodded and went into the nursery.

"Well, Jackie boy, how do you feel?"

"Fine, Mother."

"You must keep covered up. . . . You'll be all right to-morrow. . . .
Do you know who's in the living-room?"

"Mr. Nevinson," guessed Jackie, with devastating promptness.

"Yes, he is. . . . But I mean—I meant someone else. A friend of
yours!"

"I don't know."

"Mr. Onion! He's standing up on top of the bookshelves—"

"Oh, yes," said Jackie. "He likes it up there."

"But—shan't I bring him to you?"

"No matter. Because Mr. Onion has to stay there for a special reason. Because if any giants or dragons come in he can see them and then he can climb down and hit them with his ladder and they'll be dead."

"Darling! Where do you get these extraordinary ideas—!"

"There's a dragon 'at lives under the house. Mr. Onion saw him, and he was all black, like when you shut your eyes tight, and Mr. Onion says he might come down the chimney—"

"Jackie! Listen to Mother! There *aren't* any giants or dragons—" blundered Marian; but she was not so sure. Jackie's faintly superior smile made her doubt the rationalistic hypothesis. . . . She leaned down and kissed him. "Blessed baby!" she murmured; and again was strangely humbled by his smile.

Returning to the living-room, she found not only Tom but also Sally and John and several others—all members of the crowd—gathered for cocktails. John was doing the honors. As she came in she caught his eye, and for an instant he stood rigid, with the cocktail shaker poised like a gleaming piston at the top of its stroke. "Anything wrong?" his raised eyebrows telegraphed her. She didn't answer. She couldn't. The moment dragged out and grew thin—grew taut as a stretched fiddle string.

The others felt this tension. Sally Nevinson had been kidding Tom about the extravagant tie he'd put on for his date with Marian. "I can always tell when Tom's hard hit. . . . His tie gives him away. . . . It's an emotional barometer. . . ." But suddenly her shrill voice broke. . . She whirled and stared at Marian. "Good Lord!" She flung out. "What's the matter? You look as though you'd been seeing things!"

"I have," said Marian.

John stepped forward quickly. "What is it?" he asked.

"It's a dragon that lives under the house," replied Marian, and laughed. "Jackie's been telling me about it. . . . Give me a drink, will you, John dear? I need it for my nerves. . . . You see, I'm scared of the dragon."

Her laugh somehow destroyed the charm of the cocktail hour. People drifted away. . . . John and Marian were left alone. "Tell me," he said.

"There's nothing to tell."

"Yes, there is. You know there is! Is it Tom? Is it Sally? Is it—Jackie?" She shook her head.

"It's nothing I can put into words. It's just a feeling. A dragon under the house—"

"What's all this nonsense about a dragon?"

"It's black," said Marian.

"Gosh!" he muttered. "You're getting beyond me, old girl! I can't make you out half the time—"

"Then ask Mr. Onion!" cried Marian, pointing to the little figure on the bookshelves. "He understands—"

"What you need is sleep," decided John. "We'll cut out that dance at the country club to-night. Go to bed early. Get a good night's rest—"

It was well that they did go to bed early that night, for at three o'clock in the morning Miss Mosby woke them to say that Jackie was very ill. He had a temperature of 103 and was breathing hard. He was also coughing a good deal.

"I've already telephoned for the doctor," said the efficient Miss Mosby as Marian struggled into kimono and bedroom slippers. To John, plunging in from the sleeping porch, she said, "You had better put on your heavy dressing gown, Mr. Thurston. There's a chill in the air this morning."

A chill in the air, thought Marian. A dragon under the house. . . . So many things that can't be put into words. . . .

Then it all came down to one word; to one dreadful, ominous word that was like a weight on your heart:

Pneumonia.

Dr. Moulton, the tall, kindly, capable country doctor who had ministered to Jackie's minor summer ailments since he was born, was the first to utter this word. He said it gravely, simply, as one who knows the impossibility of cheating life with accents and inflections. . . . Later, the next afternoon, it was repeated by a locally famous physician, Dr. Hurd, whom Moulton had summoned from Portland. . . . Also from Portland arrived a trained nurse. Miss Mosby hated her on sight. . . .

For three days Jackie's life hung in the balance. Then at noon of the fourth day Dr. Moulton said to Marian, "We're doin' all we can for the boy, Mrs. Thurston. But I must tell you the truth. It looks pretty bad right now. If there's anybody else you'd like to call in—"

"I want the greatest in the country," she said. "There must be some one specialist. . . . Not that I believe he can do any more than they've done. But just because he *is* the greatest. . . ."

John nodded and went to the telephone. For more than an hour he invoked, with the meticulous patience of despair, various distant persons —beings—disembodied voices. Then five minutes of sharp, brisk, businesslike conversation, and the thing was done.

"Dr. Vance," he mumbled to Marian, wiping the sweat from his face, "leaves New York to-night on the *State of Maine,* arrives five-forty tomorrow morning. I mustn't forget to have a car at the station to meet him."

"To-morrow morning may be too late," said Marian, in the queer, hushed voice that had been her voice for the past four days. "If only we had someone here now. . . . If only we had some God to pray to . . ."

Then John cried out, a deep, guttural cry that came from the depths of his tortured soul.

"Well, we haven't! And I refuse to fake one!"

"I would if I could," said Marian. "But I can't. I've tried, and I can't—"

Toward morning they called her. She went into Jackie's room. Dr. Moulton and Dr. Hurd were standing together by the bed. The nurse whom Miss Mosby hated made a pale figure against the wall, and Miss Mosby herself was in the doorway. There was a faint light from the window; a gray hint of dawn. . . .

Marian leaned over her son. Her pose, the maternal brooding of her body, the soft fall of her hands against the mounded bedclothes, served to banish the professional restraint of the sickroom. And when she spoke her simple question seemed somehow to transcend its own scientific futility.

"Jackie darling, when are you going to get well?"

The small figure stirred. It stirred. Then the child's voice came reluctantly—so frail an answer, so light a thread that Marian's heart almost stopped beating.

"I don't know. . . . Mother. . . . You'll have to ask. . . . Mr. Onion. . . ."

She straightened up at once. Miss Mosby, in the doorway, stood aside to let her pass. Miss Mosby thought that Mrs. Thurston was smiling, but she could not be sure. One could not be sure of anything just then.

Marian walked blindly through the silent house to the door of the living-room. There she stopped, aware of some happening that must not be disturbed; aware of something going on in the twilight of the many-windowed room: a sort of birth, a revelation and a renascence that offered high defiance to the pervading thrust of death.

A figure was kneeling before the bookshelves. She knew, of course, that it was John, but the familiar sense of him as flesh and blood was so dimmed by the uncertain light that only his pose mattered. It alone had substance, and that substance was so strange, so blurred with beauty, that she almost cried out. Then she heard his voice and she knew that he was praying.

"Listen, Mr. Onion, don't let him die. Save him, save Jackie. . . . Mr. Onion. . . . He loves you. That makes you alive. He believes in you. That makes you divine. . . . Listen, you've got to! He believes in you. You're his great treasure. You're the wonder of his life. I love him too, but my love isn't enough. . . . Because I've never been more to him than his father. . . . I've never given him magic. . . . I've never given him wonder. . . . Oh, Mr. Onion. . . . Mr. Onion! Oh, God. . . . Save him. . . ."

The strangely articulate, strangely broken voice went on like a groping music that hadn't quite learned to be music. And the light creeping up the hill and warming the windows was like a mute response. . . . Marian turned and ran, sure-footed among shadowy pieces of furniture, among shadowy fears, back to the nursery. The two doctors now were leaning over the bed, but she paid no attention to them. She too leaned down; she would remember this bending of her body all her life long. . . .

"Jackie! Can you hear me?"

The frail voice replied after an interval, "Yes, Mother."

"Then—listen, darling! I asked—Daddy asked Mr. Onion if you were going to get well, and Mr. Onion said 'Yes.' He said—you were to try very hard and then you'd get well—"

"Mr. Onion said—?"

"That it was all right! That you were going to get well!" There was a moment of absolute stillness. Then Jackie sighed—a faint, far sigh of reassurance, of childish contentment and peace. Then, turning on his side, he nestled down comfortably to sleep.

A moment later Marian heard the crunch of car wheels on the drive outside the house and knew that Dr. Vance, the great specialist, had arrived. But she knew also that he was only another lay figure, another supernumerary in the transpired drama that could not be put into words; that could never be put into words. . . .

Dr. Vance appeared, puffing. He was a little, round, fussy man who waddled in and looked at Jackie, and said, "Ah! Hum! Indeed!" and waddled out again, with John and Marian tagging at his heels.

"I want some breakfast. Angels in heaven, what a train! *What* a train! I want some coffee. With hot milk and no sugar. And three eggs boiled four minutes by the clock. By the clock, mind you! I'm very particular about my eggs."

"Jackie!" blurted out John, with a racked smile. "What about Jackie?"

"Going to get well. Well now. Keep him warm. Keep the windows open. Of *course!* Healthy youngster. Good air. *Bound* to pull through. Ask your doctors. I'm not a doctor. I'm a traveling man. Cost you five hundred dollars. Highway robbery. Can't help it. Must keep people in awe of specialists. Only way to do it is to overcharge them. If you have an old-fashioned coffeepot, I prefer it to the modern percolator. And I like my toast just a little bit burned at the edges. . . ."

An hour later John and Marian were sitting on the bench at the edge of the hill, facing the sea. Their bodies a little apart, their hands not touching, they experienced nevertheless that knowledge of each other, that sense of contact which is marriage rarely realized.

"So I prayed," said John. "I had to. If it was cowardice, then it was cowardice. But I had to."

"I know . . . I heard you. . . . I came to the door while you were kneeling there. . . ."

"Funny thing," he said.

"Beautiful thing," said Marian.

"It was real. That's what I mean. And—it's going to make a difference. Can't go on living as we have been. . . . Do the same things, maybe. But there'll be a new element in everything. . . . Always a new element. . . . Only I suspect it's old . . . old and—indispensable. The element of search—man searching for the source of his wonder, man searching for his God. . . ."

"That's what I tried to say to you the other day, the other morning."

"It can't be said," replied John. "It can never be said. Because there's no guide to the search and no definition for the thing found. There's only the necessity—I felt that last night—for man to go beyond himself, to go beyond reason, even beyond truth, as Jackie's young mind went beyond the truth of Mr. Onion. . . . Mr. Onion can be explained, but Jackie's thought of him can never be explained . . . but somewhere along the path of that thought is the power and the glory. . . ."

"We can never tell anyone," said Marian. "This is our secret, and this is . . . our wedding day."

"Happy is the bride the sun shines on," said John.

CLARENCE DAY

My Father's Religion

In my boyhood, I never had a doubt that the beliefs they taught me were true. The difficulty was to live up to them, and to love God. Most of the time I was too busy to think of such things; but then a problem of conduct would face me, or a duty I had forgotten, or my own private feelings at night after saying my prayers, and at such times religion would confront me like a Sphinx in the landscape. I would stand before it like a hypnotized bird before some great ageless serpent, unable to think of or feel any way of escape.

I believed in the Bible. Creation, to me, meant a Creator. And since there was someone so great and powerful that He had created us all, I felt I had better learn His wishes. They were supposed to be good. I wanted to live in harmony with Him—no battle of wills. Yet I also wished greatly to get away and live as I liked.

If I could have been sure that the Creator was my ally, or friend, that would have been a great comfort in those days. It would have not only saved me from worry, it would have set me free to go about my business with confidence, both in Him and myself. Or if I could have surrendered myself to His rather bleak guidance, that again might have been a relief to me. But—I couldn't do it. I didn't quite trust Him or love Him enough to do that.

I thought of God as a strangely emotional being. He was powerful; He was forgiving, yet obdurate, full of wrath and affection. Both His wrath and affection were fitful, they came and they went and I couldn't count on either to continue: although they both always did. In short God was much such a being as my father himself.

What was the relation between them, I wondered—these two puzzling deities?

MY FATHER'S ideas of religion seemed straightforward and simple. He had noticed when he was a boy that there were buildings called churches; he had accepted them as a natural part of the surroundings in which he had been born. He would never have invented such things himself. Nevertheless they were here. As he grew up he regarded them as unquestioningly as he did banks. They were substantial old structures, they were respectable, decent, and venerable. They were frequented by the right sort of people. Well, that was enough.

On the other hand he never allowed churches—or banks—to dictate to him. He gave each the respect that was due to it from his point of view; but he also expected from each of them the respect he felt due to him.

As to creeds he knew nothing about them, and cared nothing either; yet he seemed to know which sect he belonged with. It had to be a sect with the minimum of nonsense about it; no total immersion, no exhorters, no holy confession. He would have been a Unitarian, naturally, if he'd lived in Boston. Since he was a respectable New Yorker, he belonged in the Episcopal Church.

As to living a spiritual life, he never tackled that problem. Some men who accept spiritual beliefs try to live up to them daily; other men, who reject such beliefs try sometimes to smash them. My father would have disagreed with both kinds entirely. He took a more distant attitude. It disgusted him when atheists attacked religion: he thought they were vulgar. But he also objected to have religion make demands upon him—he felt that religion too was vulgar, when it tried to stir up men's feelings. It had its own proper field of activity, and it was all right there, of course; but there was one place religion should let alone, and that was a man's soul. He especially loathed any talk of walking hand in hand with his Saviour. And if he had ever found the Holy Ghost trying to soften his heart, he would have regarded the behavior as distinctly uncalled for; even ungentlemanly.

The only religious leader or prophet I can think of who might have suited my father was Confucius—though even Confucius would have struck him as addled. Confucius was an advocate of peace, and of finding the path; and he enjoined the Golden Rule on his followers long before Christ. My father would not have been his follower in any of these. Finding "the path"? Not even Confucius could have made him see what that meant. He was too busy for that, too hot tempered for peace, and the Golden Rule he regarded as claptrap; how could things work both ways? Whatever he did unto others he was sure was all right, but that didn't mean he would have allowed them to do the same things to him. He saw other men as disorderly troops, and himself as a general; and the Golden Rule was plainly too mushy to apply in such circumstances. He disciplined himself quite as firmly as he tried to discipline others, but it wasn't necessarily by any means the same kind of discipline. There was one saying of Confucius', however, with which he would have agreed:

"Respect spiritual beings—if there are any—but keep aloof from them."
My father would have regarded that principle as thoroughly sound.

When Confucius was asked about the rule to return good for evil, he
said: "What then will you return for good? No: return good for good;
for evil, return justice." If my father had been asked to return good for
evil he would have been even more pithy—his response would have consisted of a hearty and full-throated "Bah!"

If he had been let alone, he would have brought up his sons in this
spirit. But my mother's feelings and teachings were different, and this
complicated things for us. Like my father, she had accepted religion
without any doubtings, but she had accepted more of it. She was far more
devout. And she loved best the kind of faith that comforted her and
sweetened her thoughts. My father didn't object to this at all—it was all
right enough—for a woman; but it led to her giving us instructions that
battled with his.

They both insisted strongly, for example, on our going to church, but
they didn't agree in their reasons. It was the right thing to do, Father
said. "But why do we have to go, Father?" "Because I wish to bring you
up properly. Men who neglect going to church are a lazy, disreputable
lot." A few might be good fellows, he would admit, but they were the
exceptions. As a rule, non-churchgoers were not solid, respectable citizens. All respectable citizens owed it to themselves to attend.

My mother put it differently to us. She said we owed it to God. Church
to her was a place where you worshiped, and learned to be good. My
father never thought of attending for any such reason. In his moral instructions to us he never once mentioned God. What he dwelt on was
integrity. My mother once wrote in my plush-covered autograph album,
"Fear God and keep His commandments"; but the motto that Father had
written on the preceding page, over his bolder signature, was "Do your
duty and fear no one." And nobody could tell him his duty—he knew it
without that, it seemed. It wasn't written down in any book, certainly
not in the Bible, but it was a perfectly definite and indisputable thing
nevertheless. It was a code, a tradition. It was to be upright and fearless
and honorable and to brush your clothes properly; and in general to do
always the right thing in every department of life. The right thing to do
for religion was to go to some good church on Sundays.

When Father went to church and sat in his pew, he felt he was doing
enough. Any further spiritual work ought to be done by the clergy.

When hymns were sung he sometimes joined in mechanically, for the mere sake of singing; but usually he stood as silent as an eagle among canaries and doves, leaving others to abase themselves in sentiments that he didn't share. The hymns inculcated meekness and submission, and dependence on God; but Father was quick to resent an injury, and he had no meekness in him.

> *"Jesus, lover of my soul,*
> *Let me to thy bosom fly,*
> *While the nearer waters roll,*
> *While the tempest still is nigh."*

How could Father sing that? He had no desire to fly to that bosom.

> *"Hide me O my Saviour hide*
> *Till the storm of life be past;*
> *Safe into the haven guide,*
> *Oh receive my soul at last. . . .*
> *All my trust on thee is stayed;*
> *All my help from thee I bring;*
> *Cover my defenceless head*
> *With the shadow of thy wing."*

But Father's head was far from defenceless, and he would have scorned to hide or to ask shelter. As he stood there, looking critically about him, high-spirited, resolute, I could imagine him marching with that same independence through space—a tiny speck masterfully dealing with death and infinity.

When our rector talked of imitating the saints, it seemed drivel to Father. What! imitate persons who gave their whole lives to religion and took only a perfunctory interest in the affairs of this world? Father regarded himself as a more all-round man than the saints. They had neglected nine-tenths of their duties from his point of view—they had no business connections, no families, they hadn't even paid taxes. In a word, saints were freaks. If a freak spent an abnormal amount of time being religious, what of it?

The clergy were a kind of freaks also. A queer lot. Father liked Bishop Greer and a few others, but he hadn't much respect for the rest of them. He thought of most clergymen as any busy man of action thinks of philosophers, or of those scholars who discuss the fourth dimension,

which is beyond human knowing. He regarded the self-alleged intimacy
of our rector with that fourth dimension most sceptically. He himself
neither was nor wished to be intimate with a thing of that sort. But this
didn't mean that he doubted the existence of God. On the contrary, God
and Father had somehow contrived to achieve a serene and harmonious
relation that the clergy themselves might have envied.

How did Father think God felt towards my mother? Why, about the
way he did. God probably knew she had faults, but He saw that she was
lovely and good; and in spite of some mistaken ideas that she had about
money—He doubtless looked on her most affectionately. Father didn't
expect God to regard *him* affectionately—they stood up as man to man
—but naturally God loved my mother, as everyone must. At the gate
of Heaven, if there was any misunderstanding about his own ticket, Father
counted on Mother to get him in. That was her affair.

This idea runs far back, or down, into old human thoughts. "The un-
believing husband is sanctified by the wife." (First Corinthians, vii, 14.)
Medical missionaries report that today, in some primitive tribes, a healthy
woman will propose to swallow medicine in behalf of her sick husband.
This plan seems to her husband quite reasonable. It seemed so—in religion
—to Father.

As to his mental picture of God, I suppose that Father was vague, but
in a general way, he seemed to envisage a God in his image. A God who
had small use for emotionalism and who prized strength and dignity.
A God who probably found the clergy as hard to bear as did Father himself. In short Father and God, as I said, usually saw eye to eye. They
seldom met, or even sought a meeting, their spheres were so different;
but they had perfect confidence in each other—at least at most moments.
The only exceptions were when God seemed to be neglecting His job—
Father's confidence in Him was then withdrawn, instantly. But I'll come
to this later.

As to the nature of God's sphere, namely Heaven, compared to Father's,
the earth, Heaven wasn't nearly so solid and substantial. Father had all
the best of it. Life here on earth was trying, but it shouldn't be—it was
all right intrinsically—he felt it was only people's damned carelessness
that upset things so much. Heaven on the other hand had a more serious
and fundamental defect; the whole place was thin and peculiar. It didn't
inspire much confidence. Father saw glumly that the time would come

when he would have to go there, but he didn't at all relish the prospect. He clung to his own battered realm.

Yet its faults and stupidities weighed on his spirit at times; all the chuckle-headed talk and rascality in business and politics. He was always getting indignant about them, and demanding that they be stamped out; and when he saw them continually spreading everywhere, it was maddening. Nature too, though in general sound and wholesome, had a treacherous streak. He hated and resented decay and failing powers. He hated to see little children or animals suffer. His own aches and pains were an outrage; he faced them with anger. And aside from these treacheries there was a spirit of rebellion in things. He would come in from a walk over his fields—which to me had seemed pleasant—oppressed at the balky disposition of both his fields and his farmer. He would get up from an inspection of his account books with the same irritation; there were always some bonds in his box that had not behaved as they should. And twice a day, regularly, he would have a collision, or bout, with the newspaper: it was hard to see why God had made so many damned fools and democrats.

I would try to persuade him sometimes—in my argumentative years— that it would be better for him to accept the world as it was and adapt himself to it, since he could scarcely expect to make the planet over, and change the whole earth single-handed. Father listened to this talk with suspicion, as to an advocatus diaboli. If he ever was tempted to give in, it was only in his weak moments; a minute later he was again on the warpath, like a materialistic Don Quixote.

There was one kind of depression that afflicted Mother which Father was free from; he never once had any moments of feeling "unworthy." This was a puzzle to Mother, and it made her look at Father with a mixture of awe and annoyance. Other people went to church to be made better, she told him. Why didn't he? He replied in astonishment that he had no need to be better—he was all right as he was. Mother couldn't get over his taking this stand, but she never could get him to see what the matter was with it. It wasn't at all easy for Father to see that he had any faults; and if he did, it didn't even occur to him to ask God to forgive them. He forgave them himself. In his moments of prayer, when he and God tried to commune with each other, it wasn't his own shortcomings that were brought on the carpet, but God's.

He expected a good deal of God, apparently. Not that he wanted God's help, of course; or far less His guidance. No, but it seemed that God—like the rest of us—spoiled Father's plans. Father was always trying to bring this or that good thing to pass, only to find that there were obstacles in the way. These of course roused his wrath. He would call God's attention to such things. They should not have been there. He didn't actually accuse God of gross inefficiency, but when he prayed his tone was loud and angry, like that of a dissatisfied guest in a carelessly managed hotel.

I never saw Father kneel in supplication on such occasions. On the contrary he usually talked with God lying in bed. My room was just above Father's, and he could easily be heard through the floor. On those rare nights when he failed to sleep well the sound of dams would float up—at first deep, tragic and low, then more loud and exasperated. Fragments of thoughts and strong feelings came next or meditations on current bothers. At the peak of these, God would be summoned. I would hear him call "Oh God?" over and over, with a rising inflection, as though he were demanding that God should present himself instantly, and sit in the fat green chair over in the corner and be duly admonished. Then when Father seemed to feel that God was listening, he would begin to expostulate. He would moan in a discouraged but strong voice: "Oh God it's too much. Amen . . . I say it's too damned much . . . No, no, I can't stand it. Amen." After a pause if he didn't feel better, he would seem to suspect that God might be trying to sneak back into Heaven without doing anything, and I would hear him shout warningly: "Oh God! I *won't* stand it! Amen. Oh damnation! A-a-men." Sometimes he would ferociously bark a few extra Amens, and then, soothed and satisfied, peacefully go back to sleep. And one night in the country, when the caretaker of our house in town telephoned to Father that the rain was pouring in through a hole in the roof I heard so much noise that I got out of bed and looked over the banisters, and saw Father standing alone in the hall, shaking his fist at the ceiling, and shouting in hot indignation to Heaven, "What next?"

But Father was patient with God after all. If he didn't forgive, he forgot. His wrath didn't last—he had other things to think of—and he was genial at heart. The very next Sunday after an outburst he would be back in church. Not perhaps as a worshiper or a devotee, but at least as a patron.

IRWIN SHAW

God On Friday Night

Irwin Shaw, playwright and author of some of the most distinguished American short stories of today, is a private with the U. S. Army in Africa.

SOL let himself quietly into the house and walked softly down the long hall toward the kitchen, the only sound the fashionable creaking of his pale tan shoes. He saw his mother bending over the stove, red-faced, peering into the roaster, basting a chicken.

"Ma," he said softly.

Ma grunted, busily pushing the potatoes.

"It's me, Ma. It's Sol."

Ma closed the oven and stood up wearily, her hand pushing helpfully at the hip.

"Kiss Mama," she said.

Sol kissed her and she sat down and looked at him. "You don't look so good, Sol. You don't look the way you looked when you were a young boy."

Every time she saw him she told him the same thing.

"What do you want, Ma?" Sol sighed, voicing the hopeless argument. "I'm not a young boy any more. I'm a man thirty-three years old."

"Even so." Ma wiped her forehead and looked anxiously at him. "The life you lead."

"A man who makes his living entertaining in night clubs can't live like a prize horse," Sol said. He sat down across the table and stretched his hand out tenderly to cover hers. "How're yuh, Ma?"

Ma sighed. "What do you expect? My kidneys. Always my kidneys. A woman with a family gets old like an express train." She looked closely at her son. "Sol, darling," she said, "you wear the worst clothes I've ever seen on a man's back. You belong on a merry-go-round."

"In my profession," Sol said with sober pride, "this is the way they dress."

257

"They should not be allowed out in the daytime." She shook her head. "That tie. That material would be good to line closets with."

"Violet picked out this tie."

"How is Violet? Why can't she come visit her mother-in-law once in a while. Is the Bronx another world?"

"Violet's all right," Sol said flatly, looking at the glitter on his shoe tips. "Only. . . ."

Ma sighed, her large, fashionably supported bosom heaving under the black net. "OK, Baby, tell Mama."

Sol leaned over anxiously. "I must talk to you private."

Ma looked around the kitchen. "Are we in Grand Central Station?"

"Real private, Ma. I don't want *nobody* to hear this. *Nobody*. Not even Pop."

"What've you done, Sol?" There was a note of stern alarm in Ma's voice, and she grabbed Sol's arm tightly. "Tell Mama the truth."

"I ain't done nothing. Honest. At least nothing bad. Don't worry, Ma."

"Nobody's sick?"

"Nobody's sick."

"All right." Ma sat back in her chair, holding her feet off the floor to take the weight off them. "Do you want to stay to dinner? You can always cut an extra portion out of a chicken."

"Lissen, Ma," Sol said intensely, "you got to lissen to me and you got to promise you won't tell nobody."

"I promise. All right, I promise. Will you stay to dinner?"

"Yeah," Sol said. "Well . . ." he hesitated, "this is complicated."

Lawrence came into the kitchen, throwing his books on the floor. "Hiya, Sol. Hello, Mom. Am I hungry, or, Momma, am I hungry. . . . Mom, whatta ye got to eat, or, am I hungry!"

"I'm talkin' to Ma, private," Sol said.

"I'm hungry," Lawrence said, looking in the icebox. "Go ahead and talk. I'll forget it anyway."

"I want to talk to Ma private," Sol said in measured tones.

"What the hell's so private?" Lawrence asked, gesturing with a bottle of milk. "What're you, a German spy? Boy, am I hungry!"

"Don't say 'hell,' Larry," Ma said. "And get out of here."

"I'm taking the bottle with me," Lawrence announced, marching toward the door. He patted his mother on the head. "Mata Hari." He went out.

"A brilliant boy," Ma said. "He leads his class."

Sol cleared his throat.

"Yes, Sol," Ma said, "I'm listening."

"I been thinking, Ma," he began in a low thoughtful voice, twisting his heavy gold ring slowly around on his finger. "I ain't a good boy."

"That's not such private news." Ma laughed at the expression on Sol's face. She pinched his arm. "You got a good heart, Sol," she said. "My baby Sol, with a heart like a house."

"I have done things, Ma," Sol said slowly, choosing his words with great care, "that were not so good."

"If we were all angels, we wouldn't need airplanes," Ma said with finality. "Let me look at the chicken."

She went over and looked at the chicken. "That butcher!" she said. "He is selling me eagles." She closed the oven door and sat down again.

"I have done things," Sol said quietly, "that God wouldn't like."

"I think God has other things on His mind these days, Sol."

"Ma," Sol said, not looking at his mother, "Ma, would you light candles on Friday night and make the prayer?"

There was silence in the kitchen, broken only by the small crackle from the oven, where the chicken was browning.

"I haven't lighted candles for a long time, Sol," Ma said gently. "Ever since the day I married your father. He was a Socialist, your father."

"Would yuh light 'em now, Ma?" Sol pleaded. "Every Friday night?"

"What is it, Sol? Why should I light candles?"

Sol took a deep breath and stood up and walked back and forth in the kitchen. "Violet," he said, "Violet's goin' to have a baby."

"Oh!" Ma gasped, fanning herself. "Oh! Well! That blonde girl! Oh! A grandchild! Oh! Sol, Baby!" She grabbed Sol and kissed him. "My Sol!"

"Don't cry, Ma. Ma, please. . . ." Sol patted her solid wide back. "It's all right."

"It's about time, Sol. I thought you'd never. . . ." She kissed him on the forehead and smiled widely. "I thought Violet was beginning to look very good in the breasts. Congratulations from the bottom of my heart. We'll name him after my father."

"Yeah," Sol said. "Thanks. How about the candles now, Ma?"

"What do you need candles for? I had five children without burning a single candle."

"Violet's different," Sol said uneasily. "She's not like you."

"She is just built for children," Ma declared. "She is built like a horse. When I had you I weighed ninety-five pounds. Including you. She doesn't need candles."

"You don't know, Ma." Sol looked intently into his Mother's eyes. "Today Violet slipped in the bathtub."

"Well?"

"She coulda killed herself. As it is, she fainted."

"So you want me to pray because your wife doesn't know how to take a bath. Sol!" Ma waved him away. "Every day millions of people fall down in bathtubs."

"Lissen, Ma," Sol said, holding both her hands. "Nuthin' can't happen to Violet. And nuthin' can happen to the kid. See, Ma? We been tryin' to have a kid for five years now and. . . ." he stopped.

Ma shook her head in wonderment. "That big blonde horse."

"We want that kid, Ma. We gotta have that kid. Everybody should have a kid. What've I got if I haven't got a son?"

"Sssh, Baby," Ma said. "Sure, you're right. Only don't yell. You're too nervous to yell."

"All right, I won't yell." Sol wiped the sweat off his forehead with a blue silk handkerchief with a green monogram. "All right. What I want to say is, Violet's dumpin' herself in the bathtub was a omen."

"A what?"

"A omen. It's a. . . ."

"I know."

"It shows us we can't take any chances, Ma."

"Loose in the head, my baby Sol," Ma said. "Too much night life."

"We got to pray to God, Ma," Sol said, "that nuthin' happens to that baby."

"If you want to pray to God, go ahead and pray. Did *I* make the baby?" Ma asked. "Let Violet pray."

Sol swallowed. "Violet's not fit to pray," he said gently. "She's a first-class girl and I would lay down on railroad tracks for her, but she ain't fit to pray to God."

"That's no way to talk about your own wife, Solly," Ma said. "Shame on you."

"I love her like she was my right arm," Sol said. "But she's not a very good woman, Ma. What's the sense in kiddin' ourselves? Violet has a weak character, Ma, and she has done two or three or five things. . . . Give Violet four drinks, Ma, and she says, 'Yes' to the man from Macy's. She's young, she'll outgrow it an' settle down, but right now. . . ." Sol nervously lit a cigarette. "Right now, Ma, Violet's prayers'd carry top weight in the field."

"So, Sol," Ma said gravely, "why can't *you* pray?"

Sol sat quietly, observing his cigarette. The blush came up over his purple collar, like dye soaking in cloth. "I am not one hundred percent perfect in any respect, myself," he said. "First of all, Ma, in my business if yuh don't tell the customers dirty jokes, yuh might just as well apply to the WPA."

"You should've been a doctor, like I said."

"I know, Ma," Sol said patiently. "But I'm not. I'm a man who has to play in cheap night clubs in Philadelphia and Lowell, Massachusetts, and Boston, weeks at a time. Yuh don't know how lonely it can get at night in Lowell, Massachusetts."

"A lot, Sol?"

"A lot, Ma, a lot." Sol cast his eyes up at the kitchen ceiling.

"A boy with a face like yours." Ma shrugged. "Girls're funny."

"If I prayed, Ma, the words'd stick in my throat."

"So you want me. I don't even believe in God, Baby."

"That's all right, Ma," Sol said. "You're a good woman. Yuh never hurt anybody in all yer life."

Ma sighed hugely. "I'll have to go down to Mrs. Aaronson and get her to teach me the prayer. Sol, darling, you're a nuisance."

Sol kissed her, his eyes shining.

"I got to see what's happening to that bird," Ma said, bending over the chicken. "I'll pray that it's a boy," she said, "while I'm at it."

Every Friday night the candles were lighted and Ma steadfastly said the old words. . . . *"Burach ee, burach shmoi, Burach ee, burach shmoi. Burach ee, burach shmoi. Burach ata adanoi eluchainu melach huoilom. Lehadleck nar shel shabos."* And then she prayed for a boy.

It was on a Friday night that Sol and Violet brought the baby over to Ma's for the first time.

Sol held the boy, smiling and pink and robust as wood in his arms, before his mother.

"See, Ma?" he said, holding the baby out.

Ma put her hand out slowly and gently rubbed the little soft head. "Hair," she said, "he's got hair." She chuckled and took the baby's hand out and kissed it. "Take him into the bedroom, Violet," she said. "I'm busy here for a minute."

She turned and lighted the seven candles in the window, one by one.

"The last stronghold of religion," Lawrence said. "All of a sudden. This house."

"Shut up," Ma said. "City College philosopher."

And she said, *"Burach ee, burach shmoi, Burach ee. . . ."* as the candles burned.

MANUEL KOMROFF

By the Breath of God

The great mysteries of life lie in that shadowy land removed from all realism. Here in this unknown land are all the mysteries of life and all the great things. Some explorers are quite content with the world that we know. But the great explorers in art and literature have always gone beyond the horizon of reality into the great unknown. In the unknown are hidden the mystery of life and also death. Here too is that citadel dedicated to the soul of man. And courage, blind and proud, is also found in this realm. Is there a better place for adventure? And so, it was these thoughts which prompted the writing of "By The Breath of God."

MANUEL KOMROFF

ONCE the snow has started to fall it is down to stay. It falls gently and usually it begins to fall in the night. The air is still and the flakes are small and very dry and fluffy. That is how it began this year and last year and that year long ago when Napoleon invaded this land.

The snow is dry and sometimes like a very fine white powder. If you were walking out of the door of your hut the little flakes would fly in your face and attach themselves to the lashes of your eyes. You would half-close your eyes but even then a flake or two would get through and melt in your eyes, adding to the fluid of tears. Only the feeling is not sad. It is a happy one and causes a smile to come to your lips. Hundreds of little flakes dash into your face and make a wonderful sensation—a sensation that has been called "the breath of God." It came early to Napoleon when he invaded these parts of Russia. On the night of September 15th it is said he already felt "the breath of God."

The first night the snow falls it is all very pretty, for the flakes join together to make a fine lace—as fine as a bridal veil for a princess—to cover the ugly and sordid world. The stones and stubble in the fields are covered first and then the thatched roofs of the huts and later. . . . Oh! But these days it is different. War makes it different. Artillery cannon is not easily covered. The hungry mouth is always in the air.

Many years have I heard the words "the breath of God" and only yesterday on Christmas eve did I understand its full meaning. And only yesterday did I learn where these words came from. Our colonel Doronov read us a little sermon. You may smile but it is the truth.

As you know, Doronov is a pretty tough boy. And I don't believe he ever went to church in his life. In fact he has at times been very out-spoken against all organized religions and. . . . Well, you know. Every-one knows Doronov. But last night it was Christmas eve and he sent us out to search the abandoned huts for a Bible.

At first we thought he was joking and refused to obey. We had come through two long weeks of hell and at last we were again on the crest overlooking the town of Tommer.

"Here we are again!" exclaimed our colonel as we came to the brow of the hill. "How many times must we take Tommer!"

This was the third time we retook Tommer in six months. The colonel took out his field glasses to get a better view of the besieged town.

"Not much smoke from the chimneys," he said. "The German demons eat raw food and have learnt to hide even the smoke."

In the late spring of the year when we had been on this very spot and looked off toward the town, we saw green fields, black muddy roads, brown thatched huts of the peasants and the stone turret of the old monastery.

In the autumn when we were here, the leaves were falling and the black branches of the trees made a sort of dark hedge about the town. Everything was brown except a spot here and there of a whitewashed hut. But the turret of the monastery no longer stood out as a landmark. The retreating Germans had blown it up.

Now here was Tommer again without the green of spring or brown of autumn, and without the tower. Everything was covered with a deep blanket of snow. It sparkled gaily in the sun. But we knew as we looked out from this place that hidden under this soft feathery blanket was a cruel and merciless enemy. It was they who shot the citizens of Tommer before we retook the village in the spring. They shot every man and woman, and every boy and girl. That was to teach them a lesson for some occurrence that took place while they were there. Or perhaps it was no occurrence at all; merely the fury of an enemy who was being driven back.

Whatever it was, we found the dead when we entered the town. It was all done quickly and they did not bother burying anybody, not even the smallest of the children.

It was then that Doronov swore vengeance. "By God who is in heaven or by the devil who is in hell!" he cried at the top of his voice. "By the last breath of my body, I will exterminate these rats! If the Lord will help me I will take His help. If not, I will sign with the devil!"

The colonel must have remembered his words of last spring, for as he stood there looking through his field glasses, he suddenly turned to me and said: "Vaska, you've got good eyes. See if you can discover anything." He handed me the glasses and then he added: "We are here again and this time I would sign with the devil if only . . ." He made a face and hissed his words. Under his breath flowed a stream of profanity. No tongue could give articulation to such boiling rage.

Our hands and feet were a bit numb and the cold air nipped our cheeks and the tips of our ears, but standing close to the colonel when he was boiling over was like standing near a hot stove. I think he warmed the air for twenty-five feet around. . . . Or at least so it seemed.

The sight of Tommer brought the hot words to the colonel's mouth. But I could see nothing through the field glasses.

"Well?" he asked.

"Nothing."

"Nothing?"

"Not a damn thing."

"They must be there."

"I know, but everything is hidden."

"The snow?"

"Yes."

I handed the field glasses back.

"How does it look to you?" I asked.

"Don't know."

"Last time we were six days on this hill before they would give way."

"We pounded the hell out of them," he added.

"And now?" I asked.

"It all depends. We will know very soon. In an hour or so their scouting planes are sure to discover us. Then after they get the range and open fire in full. . . . Then we can tell perhaps how long we will have to be here. The enemy is better equipped and better supplied, but we have the spirit and right is with us."

"This is a cold hill. It catches the north blasts," I said.

"Not as cold as Tommer," he replied. "It looks sheltered, but it is a hole that catches the worst of the blasts. It was here that Napoleon's men perished by the hundreds. This is one of the campaigns you must study when you go to military school. But war is always different. All you learn is that Tommer is a cold place and that here in Tommer, in the winter of 1812, the peasants rose up suddenly to harry the long lines of retreating soldiers. They sprung from the ground. It was here in Tommer also that the Emperor's gold wagons could go no further. The horses had to be shot and the gold divided among the men. Think of it —a little mistake. It is always a little mistake that lays low a great army. They forgot to put spikes on the horses' shoes. Napoleon depended greatly on his artillery, but he forgot the little spikes on the horses' shoes. Never used spikes in France and never believed they could be necessary. It is always a little thing that loses a campaign. But now we use no horses and there is no need of a treasure wagon. And as for the peasants of Tommer, they were all killed by the enemy. You see, time changes everything and even war is different."

"But the snow is the same and the frost too," I added.

"Yes. Yesterday's snow, wherever it has gone, is the same as to-morrow's snow. But that is about all that has not changed."

We were sort of a ragged little band and certainly not equipped to venture this assault. Nevertheless we knew our land and our snow and were taking a long chance.

While we were talking, men and tanks were coming up behind us to take their new positions on the brow of this ridge. And scouts, covered with white woolen hoods, were going out ahead of us. They were soon lost in that vast feather bed before us. And what looked like little twigs in the distance were the rifles on their backs. But soon these too were lost from sight.

Just as the colonel had predicted, the enemy planes were soon over us. Our range would be recorded and then . . . but no. Nothing happened.

"Well," said Colonel Doronov, "if that is the case, then it is up to us to present our calling cards."

Our artillery opened fire on the little town of Tommer.

And still we waited, but there was no reply.

During this awkward moment of silence I remarked—it just happened into my mind—that it would soon be Christmas eve.

"When is Christmas eve?" asked the colonel.

"Today. Tonight."

"No, it can't be."

"Certainly, Colonel," I said. "Today is the twenty-fourth of the month."

"That's right," he admitted. "So it is. How the days go! My, my!" And then suddenly he exclaimed: "Well, what of it! What is Christmas to you?"

"Well . . ."

"To a soldier all days are alike. Let the victories mark the holidays."

"Nevertheless tonight is Christmas eve."

"Vaska," he said, "you are a good boy, only you are a foolish sentimentalist. Your parents must have been of the old school and filled you full of fairy-stories. Supposing Christ was born on Christmas eve two thousand years ago, well, what of it! Has he ever done you any good?"

I did not reply. There was no use picking an argument with Colonel Doronov. So much difference in rank and age was between us. And also in army experience. He was a veteran from the 1917 Revolution. And at that time I was only in diapers. I was silent.

We all waited in silence for the enemy hidden in Tommer to reply to our volley. But the hot shrapnel answer across a cold winter's sky did not come. Evidently they were in hiding. Or this time, due to the intense cold, they had dug in so deep that it would take them time to get to their guns.

It was a long silence.

Colonel Doronov held his field glasses ready to place to his eye the instant he heard the reply. He had hoped to catch a glimpse of the flashes and learn the position of some of the guns and the type of shell being fired. He knew every hill and field of the landscape before him. The snow covered the roads and fences and some of the low buildings in the valley, but Doronov knew exactly by the general contours where each should be.

This was his land and the very district of his boyhood life. In these fields he played with boys and girls. And in these fields also he hunted small game. But now it was a hunt of a different kind.

As he stood there waiting for the enemy to reply, he thought of his boyhood days, and bringing the glasses to his eyes, looked out. Then he handed the glasses to me.

"There," he said. "Look over this way, Vaska, and you will see two little dots. Very small dots, just below the small group of roofs. See them?"

"No."

"On the right of the telegraph poles."

"Oh, yes!" I exclaimed. "I see them. Very small. One dark on top and the other just a lump of snow."

"That's right. Napoleon's cannon! They are stuck into the ground, mouth down, at the gate of the estate. The estate belonged to my uncle once. And my first sweetheart was my cousin who lived there. Many an evening she would walk me to the gate and there . . . between Napoleon's cannon . . . I wish I now had a rouble for every kiss."

It was cold. He slapped his hands together and smiled. "Yes," he added. "It makes you warm just to think of it."

Then he gave the signal for a second volley. As the shells exploded in Tommer you could see the snow blown high into the air. And so cold it was that, for a short space of time, a fine white dust of snow hung suspended in the air. When you see this, you know it is really cold. And you better take care.

"They are in there," he said. "But they're up to some trick. But trick or no trick . . . I am ready to sign with the devil."

"And tonight will be Christmas eve," I said again.

He looked at me, a full broad glance, but said nothing. And yet in that silent look so much was communicated between us.

All this, as I said before, occurred when we reached the crest of the ridge and got a view of Tommer once more. We had come through a hard winter's road and we had been here before and knew exactly what we could expect. And all this occurred on the ridge where we expected to dig in for at least a week. We knew also that the enemy had brought up strong reinforcements and that this time it would not be quite so easy. . . . And we knew other things which might prevent our ever reaching this town where the innocent citizens—even the children—were slaughtered.

We expected to dig in. And no one in the world would have believed that before the day had closed its dark shutters we would be in the town of Tommer. And no one would ever believe that Colonel Doronov, who said that he signed with the devil, would order us to search in the ruins for a Bible. Of all people in the entire world, he was the very last you would expect to read a sermon on the eve of Christmas.

Having had no reply to our two broadsides, not even a spit of machine-gun fire directed against our forward moving scouts, we started forward, moving slowly and with caution.

As we started down the slope I asked the colonel what he meant when he said he signed with the devil.

"Exactly what I said," he replied.

"But how do you sign with the devil? Does one sign in ink or pencil? Is it a long legal document that you apply your name to or just a motto?"

"I guess it's a motto."

"What motto?"

"You are a fool, Vaska! What difference can words make? Long or short, it's the same thing! It's the devil, that's all. Now do you understand?"

"No."

"Really, Vaska, sometimes I think you are a smart boy and sometimes. . . . First your head is filled with the sentimental pudding of Christmas and the fairy-tales of early miracles; and then suddenly you become very matter-of-fact and want to know fine details—pencil, ink, long, short. . . . You are just plain stupid! The devil is the devil and everyone knows the devil. There are people who say that God is everywhere. And there are people who believe that the devil is everywhere. I am one of those who believe the devil is everywhere."

"Why?"

"Really, Vaska, you are impossible. Why do I belong to those who believe the devil is everywhere! Why? . . . Perhaps it's a good question, after all. Experience! That is the answer. Have we been through hell? Yes. And in hell, what do you find. . . . Well, answer me!"

"You find the devil," I had to admit.

"Experience teaches you not to expect miracles. But you can always expect the devil to turn up. Miracles are very nice but you find them only in books."

We moved on cautiously through the snow, expecting at any moment that enemy fire would break loose. And we knew what we did not want to admit to ourselves or to any of the men, that the enemy in Tommer had been reinforced recently with heavy guns.

The air was cold. Not a shot was fired. The air was so cold that we did not breathe it in too deeply. It made your lungs cold. We took in little breaths only. We went ahead slowly and listened carefully. But not a shot could we hear.

Then it seemed almost too quiet. It was an uncomfortable stillness.

"Watch out for the devil," said the colonel under his breath.

Soon we came along the road to the gate which was marked by two of Napoleon's abandoned cannon. They were covered with about three feet of snow and only the tops projected above the drift.

Doronov stood before them.

"Strange," he said. "Those two dead iron soldiers outlive everybody. I recall in 1912 how my cousin and I decorated them with garlands of flowers to mark the hundred years. My uncle came forward and delivered a little speech to the assembled natives. It was a mild speech filled with nice words. You must remember that we were then living in peace and the first world war had not yet begun. And how much, how much has happened since! Whole empires have cracked and new civilizations have been born. And yet these two iron soldiers stand guard year in and year out. Heat or cold, rain or snow, nothing changes them. But what are they standing for?"

"For one thing, Colonel," I said. "They stand as a reminder. And that is enough."

"Yes, Vaska. That is true. They stand as a reminder. And how you think or how you have been educated, that is the thing you are reminded of. If Napoleon were to pass by now it would remind him of something. And the old Czar would be reminded of victory. And to some of us it might stand for courage. But for me personally it is quite different. I was in love and when it was time for me to go home we would walk out this far together. And here between the two cannon we said good night. And always with a long embrace. It may sound foolish and sentimental, but it is the truth. And yet, what has it to do with what is going on now? Nothing. My dear cousin is long dead. She is buried here near Napoleon's relics, deep under the ice and snow. And in the spring when the snows melt, a new lot of battle relics will be found strewn about this very ground." He paused for a moment, then he added: "Nothing. It all means nothing. The useless iron soldiers will outlive us all. They are the road markers of things that are long past. They will also mark things of the future. Come, let us face the devil!"

Just as we turned to leave we heard the shrill blast of a signalman's whistle. He drew out a small red flag and began to signal to one of the white-hooded scouts ahead.

The colonel looked through his field glasses but could not make out the message.

"Looks like the town of Tommer is deserted," reported the signalman.

"Impossible," replied the colonel. "Watch out for a trick. Proceed with caution."

These were the orders relayed along the entire line.

No shot was fired. We grew bolder.

Soon more signals were received and all seemed to indicate the same strange and mysterious fact. Tommer was deserted. So it seemed, anyway.

An hour later our advance scouts entered the town and raised our flag. It warmed your heart to see this bright bit of cloth climb the mast. But the wind was cold and, as it snapped in the breeze, it looked as though the little flag would be torn to shreds.

Now we moved forward, tanks, artillery, wagons and everything. You could hear nothing by the groaning crunch of hard icy snow under the wheels.

"It is good luck!" I cried. "Soon it will be Christmas eve."

"I suppose you expect a tree with presents on it when we reach Tommer," said Doronov with sarcasm.

"I expect nothing. But if it comes and it is good, then we will all share in its goodness."

To this he did not reply.

Part of the way we rode on one of the trucks, but even then it was more than an hour before we reached the outskirts of the town.

"Here is the hill where last spring we buried the citizens," said Doronov. "It is hard to recognize under snow."

"I remember the singing. The whole division joined in the hymn."

A bright fire was already burning in the yard of the old monastery when we entered the town. We stopped to warm ourselves, as did a hundred others. We made a solid ring around the fire.

The soldiers spoke as they warmed themselves.

"This is Tommer?"

"Yes, Tommer."

"Deserted?"

"Looks that way."

"Completely?"

"Not a shot fired."

"Wait a bit."

"No. They would have started as we came up the slope."

"Funny thing no one's here."

"Yes, strange."

"Must have left in a hurry."

"How do you know?"

"There's one big gun down the street. You can see it from here."

"What else do you know?"

"They are searching the houses now. Perhaps soon we will know."

"These streets are pretty cold."

"Tommer is famous for its cold."

"Yes, true. They say Tommer is colder than Siberia, but no one believes it until they come here."

In this manner words were exchanged between the men who had come into the monastery yard to stand close to the crackling fire.

Soon a young officer arrived and saluting Colonel Doronov, announced that a clue to the mystery had been found and they wanted the colonel to see it with his own eyes. The colonel beckoned to me and I followed along.

We soon came to a stone house, the only house in the town which stood fairly intact. The windows of this house had been repaired with fresh glass or boarded up to keep out the intense cold. Attached to the house and running the full length of the yard was a long low wooden barrack of recent construction.

The door of this wooden shed was open and two of our young officers were standing there awaiting the arrival of Colonel Doronov.

"Here they are," said one.

"What!" exclaimed the colonel.

"Yes. See for yourself."

We looked through the open door. But there was little light within.

"Can't see anything!" exclaimed the colonel. "What have you discovered here?"

"Germans."

"Rout them out! Call the men!"

"No, Colonel. They are already dead."

"Dead?"

"Yes."

"How many?"

"We did not count but there are quite a few. Perhaps four hundred."

"All dead?"

"Yes."

"How?"

"Frozen."

"And what is in the stone house?"

"Officers."

"Also?"

"Yes, also frozen. And there are signs of a hurried departure. Some must have awakened to find this nightmare and attempted. . . . Our scouts are now searching the fields about. They could not have gone far in that weather."

"But how can you explain it?" asked the colonel.

"Their food was low. They were fatigued. They all went to sleep and slept soundly. Each relied on someone else to keep the fires going. And once the fires were low the cold rushed in. Tommer cold runs 40 or more below. Their clothes are thin. They have paper and soft cardboard stuffed underneath their coats. They have thin leather boots, not felt ones as we have. Their blankets are cotton. Cold of this kind does not wake you; in fact it is like an opiate and only brings on a full relaxed sleep."

"Four hundred?" again asked the colonel.

"Yes. We will soon count them. Some are huddled together in groups of six or eight."

We returned to the fire, now burning brighter than before, in the yard of the monastery. I noticed as we walked that the top of the snow was encrusted with a sort of white flower. A beautiful white patterned design, sort of raised up by the great cold from the main body of the snow. It was almost like a magic bridal veil. It must have been very cold to create this wonder.

Soon we received word that some of the German officers who escaped this nightmare from the stone house were found within a league or two from the town. They had made an attempt to get back to the lines but were too weak to go far. The great cold blasts of Tommer brought them down.

"Ah!" I exclaimed. "The Germans are thorough and efficient and they know everything. They have wonderful machines. But they do not understand a good old Russian winter."

"True, Vaska, true," replied the colonel. "They do not even deserve a good honest Russian winter! And if the frost did not get them, then we would have killed them anyway. So you see it is all the same, as far as they are concerned. And this time we took Tommer without the loss of a single man. Is that not a piece of good fortune?"

"Yes," I added, "and tonight good fortune or anything good should be shared with all."

"Very well," he said.

It was then that he ordered us to search the houses for a Bible and at length one was found. The leather back had been split by the frost, but that made no difference.

Now the evening light was falling and we all stood around the big fire. Our feet were thawing out and a nice little tingle was in our toes.

The colonel removed his heavy fur glove and began thumbing the pages, trying to find the right place. At last he found the page he was seeking.

"Men," he said, "I will read you a little sermon. Just a little one. There is no good reading you anything about love and brotherhood and goodwill to men. Our land has been invaded by a cruel and merciless enemy. And there can be no brotherhood or goodwill between such a beastly race and the rest of mankind."

He paused and looked about before he continued:

"But there is a little sermon I would like to read you. The text is from Job, Chapter 37. . . . God thundereth marvellously with his voice; great things doeth he, which we cannot comprehend. For he saith to the snow, Be thou *on* the earth; likewise to the small rain, and to the great rain of his strength. He sealeth up the hand of every man; that all men may know his work. Then the beasts go into dens, and remain in their places. Out of the south cometh the whirlwind: and cold out of the north."

He paused again. The sky overhead was dark as a sheet of slate. And then he continued in a strong loud voice:

"By the breath of God frost is given."

He closed the book.

"Now it is Christmas," he added. "Let each man speak what he has in his heart."

HONORÉ DE BALZAC

The Atheist's Mass

Balzac, it must always be remembered, was himself pretty definitely "on the side of the angels." As a Frenchman, as a man with a strong 18th-century tincture in him, as a student of Rabelais, as one not too much given to regard nature and fate through rose-colored spectacles, as a product of more or less godless education (for his school days came before the neo-Catholic revival) and in many other ways, he was not exactly an orthodox person. But he had no ideas foreign to orthodoxy; and neither in his novels, nor in his letters nor elsewhere, would it be possible to find a private expression of unbelief. And such a story as this is worth a bookseller's warehouse full of tracts, coming as it does from Honoré de Balzac.

GEORGE SAINTSBURY

BIANCHON, a physician to whom science owes a fine system of theoretical physiology, and who, while still young, made himself a celebrity in the medical school of Paris, that central luminary to which European doctors do homage, practised surgery for a long time before he took up medicine. His earliest studies were guided by one of the greatest of French surgeons, the illustrious Desplein, who flashed across science like a meteor. By the consensus even of his enemies, he took with him to the tomb an incommunicable method. Like all men of genius, he had no heirs; he carried everything in him, and carried it away with him. The glory of a surgeon is like that of an actor: they live only so long as they are alive, and their talent leaves no trace when they are gone. Actors and surgeons, like great singers too, like the executants who by their performance increase the power of music tenfold, are all the heroes of a moment.

Desplein is a case in proof of this resemblance in the destinies of such transient genius. His name, yesterday so famous, to-day almost forgotten, will survive in his special department without crossing its limits. For must there not be some extraordinary circumstances to exalt the name of a professor from the history of Science to the general history of the human race? Had Desplein that universal command of knowledge which makes a man the living word, the great figure of his age? Desplein had a godlike eye; he saw into the sufferer and his malady by an intuition, natural or acquired, which enabled him to grasp the diagnostics peculiar to the individual, to determine the very time, the hour, the minute when an operation should be performed, making due allowance for atmospheric conditions and peculiarities of individual temperament. To proceed thus, hand in hand with nature, had he then studied the constant assimilation by living beings, of the elements contained in the atmosphere, or yielded by the earth to man who absorbs them, deriving from them a particular expression of life? Did he work it all out by the power of deduction and analogy, to which we owe the genius of Cuvier? Be this as it may, this man was in all the secrets of the human frame; he knew it in the past and in the future, emphasising the present.

But did he epitomise all science in his own person as Hippocrates did and Galen and Aristotle? Did he guide a whole school towards new worlds? No. Though it is impossible to deny that this persistent observer of human chemistry possessed the antique science of the Mages, that is to say, knowledge of the elements in fusion, the causes of life, life antecedent to life, and what it must be in its incubation or ever it *is,* it must be confessed that, unfortunately, everything in him was purely personal. Isolated during his life by his egoism, that egoism is now suicidal of his glory. On his tomb there is no proclaiming statue to repeat to posterity the mysteries which genius seeks out at its own cost.

But perhaps Desplein's genius was answerable for his beliefs, and for that reason mortal. To him the terrestrial atmosphere was a generative envelope; he saw the earth as an egg within its shell; and not being able to determine whether the egg or the hen first was, he would not recognise either the cock or the egg. He believed neither in the antecedent animal nor the surviving spirit of man. Desplein had no doubts; he was positive. His bold and unqualified atheism was like that of many scientific men, the best men in the world, but invincible atheists—atheists such as religious people declare to be impossible. This opinion could scarcely exist otherwise in a man who was accustomed from his youth to dissect the creature above all others—before, during, and after life; to hunt through all his organs without ever finding the individual soul, which is indispensable to religious theory. When he detected a cerebral centre, a nervous centre, and a centre for aerating the blood—the two first so perfectly

complementary that in the latter years of his life he came to a conviction
that the sense of hearing is not absolutely necessary for hearing, nor the
sense of sight for seeing, and that the solar plexus could supply their
place without any possibility of doubt—Desplein, thus finding two souls
in man, confirmed his atheism by this fact, though it is no evidence against
God. This man died, it is said, in final impenitence, as do, unfortunately,
many noble geniuses, whom God may forgive.

The life of this man, great as he was, was marred by many meannesses,
to use the expression employed by his enemies, who were anxious to
diminish his glory, but which it would be more proper to call apparent
contradictions. Envious people and fools, having no knowledge of the
determinations by which superior spirits are moved, seize at once on
superficial inconsistencies, to formulate an accusation and so to pass sentence on them. If, subsequently, the proceedings thus attacked are crowned
with success, showing the correlation of the preliminaries and the results,
a few of the vanguard of calumnies always survive. In our own day, for
instance, Napoleon was condemned by our contemporaries when he
spread his eagle's wings to alight in England: only 1822 could explain
1804 and the flat boats at Boulogne.

As, in Desplein, his glory and science were invulnerable, his enemies
attacked his odd moods and his temper, whereas, in fact, he was simply
characterised by what the English call eccentricity. Sometimes very hand-
somely dressed, like Crébillon the tragical, he would suddenly affect
extreme indifference as to what he wore; he was sometimes seen in a
carriage, and sometimes on foot. By turns rough and kind, harsh and
covetous on the surface, but capable of offering his whole fortune to his
exiled masters—who did him the honour of accepting it for a few days
—no man ever gave rise to such contradictory judgments. Although to
obtain a black ribbon, which physicians ought not to intrigue for, he was
capable of dropping a prayer-book out of his pocket at Court, in his heart
he mocked at everything; he had a deep contempt for men, after studying
them from above and below, after detecting their genuine expression
when performing the most solemn and the meanest acts of their lives.

The qualities of a great man are often federative. If among these co-
lossal spirits one has more talent than wit, his wit is still superior to that
of a man of whom it is simply stated that "he is witty." Genius always
presupposes moral insight. This insight may be applied to a special sub-

ject; but he who can see a flower must be able to see the sun. The man who on hearing a diplomate he had saved ask, "How is the Emperor?" could say, "The courtier is alive; the man will follow!"—that man is not merely a surgeon or a physician, he is prodigiously witty also. Hence a patient and diligent student of human nature will admit Desplein's exorbitant pretensions, and believe—as he himself believed—that he might have been no less great as a minister than he was as a surgeon.

Among the riddles which Desplein's life presents to many of his contemporaries, we have chosen one of the most interesting, because the answer is to be found at the end of the narrative, and will avenge him for some foolish charges.

Of all the students in Desplein's hospital, Horace Bianchon was one of those to whom he most warmly attached himself. Before being a house surgeon at the Hôtel-Dieu, Horace Bianchon had been a medical student lodging in a squalid boarding-house in the *Quartier Latin,* known as the Maison Vauquer. This poor young man had felt there the gnawing of that burning poverty which is a sort of crucible from which great talents are to emerge as pure and incorruptible as diamonds, which may be subjected to any shock without being crushed. In the fierce fire of their unbridled passions they acquire the most impeccable honesty, and get into the habit of fighting the battles which await genius with the constant work by which they coerce their cheated appetites.

Horace was an upright young fellow, incapable of tergiversation on a matter of honour, going to the point without waste of words, and as ready to pledge his cloak for a friend as to give him his time and his night hours. Horace, in short, was one of those friends who are never anxious as to what they may get in return for what they give, feeling sure that they will in their turn get more than they give. Most of his friends felt for him that deeply-seated respect which is inspired by unostentatious virtue, and many of them dreaded his censure. But Horace made no pedantic display of his qualities. He was neither a puritan nor a preacher; he could swear with a grace as he gave his advice, and was always ready for a jollification when occasion offered. A jolly companion, not more prudish than a trooper, as frank and outspoken—not as a sailor, for nowadays sailors are wily diplomates—but as an honest man who has nothing in his life to hide, he walked with his head erect, and a mind content. In short, to put the facts into a word, Horace was the Pylades of more

than one Orestes—creditors being regarded as the nearest modern equiva-
lent to the Furies of the ancients.

He carried his poverty with the cheerfulness which is perhaps one of
the chief elements of courage, and, like all people who have nothing, he
made very few debts. As sober as a camel and active as a stag, he was
steadfast in his ideas and his conduct.

The happy phase of Bianchon's life began on the day when the famous
surgeon had proof of the qualities and the defects which, these no less
than those, make Doctor Horace Bianchon doubly dear to his friends.
When a leading clinical practitioner takes a young man to his bosom,
that young man has, as they say, his foot in the stirrup. Desplein did not
fail to take Bianchon as his assistant to wealthy houses, where some com-
plimentary fee almost always found its way into the student's pocket, and
where the mysteries of Paris life were insensibly revealed to the young
provincial; he kept him at his side when a consultation was to be held,
and gave him occupation; sometimes he would send him to a watering-
place with a rich patient; in fact, he was making a practice for him. The
consequence was that in the course of time the Tyrant of surgery had a
devoted ally. These two men—one at the summit of honour and of his
science, enjoying an immense fortune and an immense reputation; the
other a humble Omega, having neither fortune nor fame—became intimate friends.

The great Desplein told his house surgeon everything; the disciple
knew whether such or such a woman had sat on a chair near the master,
or on the famous couch in Desplein's surgery, on which he slept; Bianchon
knew the mysteries of that temperament, a compound of the lion and
the bull, which at last expanded and enlarged beyond measure the great
man's torso, and caused his death by degeneration of the heart. He studied
the eccentricities of that busy life, the schemes of that sordid avarice, the
hopes of the politician who lurked behind the man of science; he was
able to foresee the mortifications that awaited the only sentiment that lay
hid in a heart that was steeled, but not of steel.

One day Bianchon spoke to Desplein of a poor water-carrier of the
Saint-Jacques district, who had a horrible disease caused by fatigue and
want; this wretched Auvergnat had had nothing but potatoes to eat during
the dreadful winter of 1821. Desplein left all his visits, and at the risk
of killing his horse, he rushed off, followed by Bianchon, to the poor

man's dwelling, and saw, himself, to his being removed to a sick house, founded by the famous Dubois in the Faubourg Saint-Denis. Then he went to attend the man, and when he had cured him he gave him the necessary sum to buy a horse and a water-barrel. This Auvergnat distinguished himself by an amusing action. One of his friends fell ill, and he took him at once to Desplein, saying to his benefactor, "I could not have borne to let him go to any one else!"

Rough customer as he was, Desplein grasped the water-carrier's hand, and said, "Bring them all to me."

He got the native of Cantal into the Hôtel-Dieu, where he took the greatest care of him. Bianchon had already observed in his chief a predilection for Auvergnats, and especially for water-carriers; but as Desplein took a sort of pride in his cures at the Hôtel-Dieu, the pupil saw nothing very strange in that.

One day, as he crossed the Place Saint-Sulpice, Bianchon caught sight of his master going into the church at about nine in the morning. Desplein, who at that time never went a step without his cab, was on foot, and slipped in by the door in the Rue du Petit-Lion, as if he were stealing into some house of ill fame. The house surgeon, naturally possessed by curiosity, knowing his master's opinions, and being himself a rabid follower of Cabanis (*Cabaniste en dyable,* with the *y,* which in Rabelais seems to convey an intensity of devilry)—Bianchon stole into the church, and was not a little astonished to see the great Desplein, the atheist, who had no mercy on the angels—who give no work to the lancet, and cannot suffer from fistula or gastritis—in short, this audacious scoffer kneeling humbly, and where? In the Lady Chapel, where he remained through the mass, giving alms for the expenses of the service, alms for the poor, and looking as serious as though he were superintending an operation.

"He has certainly not come here to clear up the question of the Virgin's delivery," said Bianchon to himself, astonished beyond measure. "If I had caught him holding one of the ropes of the canopy on Corpus Christi day, it would be a thing to laugh at; but at this hour, alone, with no one to see—it is surely a thing to marvel at!"

Bianchon did not wish to seem as though he were spying the head surgeon of the Hôtel-Dieu; he went away. As it happened, Desplein asked him to dine with him that day, not at his own house, but at a restaurant. At dessert Bianchon skilfully contrived to talk of the ass, speaking of it as mummery and a farce.

"A farce," said Desplein, "which has cost Christendom more blood than all Napoleon's battles and all Broussais' leeches. The mass is a papal invention, not older than the sixth century, and based on the *Hoc est corpus*. What floods of blood were shed to establish the Fête-Dieu, the Festival of Corpus Christi—the institution by which Rome established her triumph in the question of the Real Presence, a schism which rent the Church during three centuries! The wars of the Count of Toulouse against the Albigenses were the tail end of that dispute. The Vaudois and the Albigenses refused to recognise this innovation."

In short, Desplein was delighted to disport himself in his most atheistical vein; a flow of Voltairian satire, or, to be accurate, a vile imitation of the *Citateur*.

"Hallo! where is my worshipper of this morning?" said Bianchon to himself.

He said nothing; he began to doubt whether he had really seen his chief at Saint-Sulpice. Desplein would not have troubled himself to tell Bianchon a lie, they knew each other too well; they had already exchanged thoughts on quite equally serious subjects, and discussed systems *de natura rerum*, probing or dissecting them with the knife and scalpel of incredulity.

Three months went by. Bianchon did not attempt to follow the matter up, though it remained stamped on his memory. One day that year, one of the physicians of the Hôtel-Dieu took Desplein by the arm, as if to question him, in Bianchon's presence.

"What were you doing at Saint-Sulpice, my dear master?" said he.

"I went to see a priest who has a diseased knee-bone, and to whom the Duchesse d'Angoulême did me the honour to recommend me," said Desplein.

The questioner took this defeat for an answer; not so Bianchon.

"Oh, he goes to see damaged knees in church!—He went to mass," said the young man to himself.

Bianchon resolved to watch Desplein. He remembered the day and hour when he had detected him going into Saint-Sulpice, and resolved to be there again next year on the same day and at the same hour, to see if he should find him there again. In that case the periodicity of his devotions would justify a scientific investigation; for in such a man there ought to be no direct antagonism of thought and action.

Next year, on the said day and hour, Bianchon, who had already ceased to be Desplein's house surgeon, saw the great man's cab standing at the corner of the Rue de Tournon and the Rue du Petit-Lion, whence his friend jesuitically crept along by the wall of Saint-Sulpice, and once more attended mass in front of the Virgin's altar. It was Desplein, sure enough! The master-surgeon, the atheist at heart, the worshipper by chance. The mystery was greater than ever; the regularity of the phenomenon complicated it. When Desplein had left, Bianchon went to the sacristan, who took charge of the chapel, and asked him whether the gentleman were a constant worshipper.

"For twenty years that I have been here," replied the man, "M. Desplein has come four times a year to attend this mass. He founded it."

"A mass founded by him!" said Bianchon, as he went away. "This is as great a mystery as the Immaculate Conception—an article which alone is enough to make a physician an unbeliever."

Some time elapsed before Doctor Bianchon, though so much his friend, found an opportunity of speaking to Desplein of this incident of his life. Though they met in consultation, or in society, it was difficult to find an hour of confidential solitude when, sitting with their feet on the fire-dogs and their head resting on the back of an arm-chair, two men tell each other their secrets. At last, seven years later, after the Revolution of 1830, when the mob invaded the Archbishop's residence, when Republican agitators spurred them on to destroy the gilt crosses which flashed like streaks of lightning in the immensity of the ocean of houses; when Incredulity flaunted itself in the streets, side by side with Rebellion, Bianchon once more detected Desplein going into Saint-Sulpice. The doctor followed him, and knelt down by him without the slightest notice or demonstration of surprise from his friend. They both attended this mass of his founding.

"Will you tell me, my dear fellow," said Bianchon, as they left the church, "the reason for your fit of monkishness? I have caught you three times going to mass— You! You must account to me for this mystery, explain such a flagrant disagreement between your opinions and your conduct. You do not believe in God, and yet you attend mass? My dear master, you are bound to give me an answer."

"I am like a great many devout people, men who on the surface are deeply religious, but quite as much atheists as you or I can be."

And he poured out a torrent of epigrams on certain political personages, of whom the best known gives us, in this century, a new edition of Molière's *Tartufe*.

"All that has nothing to do with my question," retorted Bianchon. "I want to know the reason for what you have just been doing, and why you founded this mass."

"Faith! my dear boy," said Desplein, "I am on the verge of the tomb; I may safely tell you about the beginning of my life."

At this moment Bianchon and the great man were in the Rue des Quatre-Vents, one of the worst streets in Paris. Desplein pointed to the sixth floor of one of the houses looking like obelisks, of which the narrow door opens into a passage with a winding staircase at the end, with windows appropriately termed "borrowed lights"—or, in French, *jours de souffrance*. It was a greenish structure; the ground floor occupied by a furniture dealer, while each floor seemed to shelter a different and independent form of misery. Throwing up his arm with a vehement gesture, Desplein exclaimed—

"I lived up there for two years."

"I know; Arthez lived there; I went up there almost every day during my first youth; we used to call it then the pickle-jar of great men! What then?"

"The mass I have just attended is connected with some events which took place at the time when I lived in the garret where you say Arthez lived; the one with the window where the clothes line is hanging with linen over a pot of flowers. My early life was so hard, my dear Bianchon, that I may dispute the palm of Paris suffering with any man living. I have endured everything: hunger and thirst, want of money, want of clothes, of shoes, of linen, every cruelty that penury can inflict. I have blown on my frozen fingers in that *pickle-jar of great men,* which I should like to see again, now, with you. I worked through a whole winter, seeing my head steam, and perceiving the atmosphere of my own moisture as we see that of horses on a frosty day. I do not know where a man finds the fulcrum that enables him to hold out against such a life.

"I was alone, with no one to help me, no money to buy books or to pay the expenses of my medical training; I had not a friend; my irascible, touchy, restless temper was against me. No one understood that this irritability was the distress and toil of a man who, at the bottom of the social scale, is struggling to reach the surface. Still, I had, as I may say to you, before whom I need wear no draperies, I had that ground-bed of good feeling and keen sensitiveness which must always be the birthright of any man who is strong enough to climb to any height whatever, after having long trampled in the bogs of poverty. I could obtain nothing from my family, nor from my home, beyond my inadequate allowance. In short, at that time, I breakfasted off a roll which the baker in the Rue du Petit-Lion sold me cheap because it was left from yesterday or the day before, and I crumbled it into milk; thus my morning meal cost me but two sous. I dined only every other day in a boarding-house where the meal cost me sixteen sous. You know as well as I what care I must have taken of my clothes and shoes. I hardly know whether in later life we feel grief so deep when a colleague plays us false, as we have known, you and I, on detecting the mocking smile of a gaping seam in a shoe, or hearing the armhole of a coat split. I drank nothing but water; I regarded a café with distant respect. Zoppi's seemed to me a promised land where none but the Lucullus of the *pays Latin* had a right of entry. 'Shall I ever take a cup of coffee there with milk in it?' said I to myself, 'or play a game of dominoes?'

"I threw into my work the fury I felt at my misery. I tried to master positive knowledge so as to acquire the greatest personal value, and merit the position I should hold as soon as I could escape from nothingness. I consumed more oil than bread; the light I burned during these endless nights cost me more than food. It was a long duel, obstinate, with no sort of consolation. I found no sympathy anywhere. To have friends, must we not form connections with young men, have a few sous so as to be able to go tippling with them and meet them where students congregate? And I had nothing! And no one in Paris can understand that nothing means *nothing*. When I even thought of revealing my beggary, I had that nervous contraction of the throat which makes a sick man believe that a ball rises up from the œsophagus into the larynx.

"In later life I have met people born to wealth who, never having wanted for anything, had never even heard this problem in the rule of three: A young man is to crime as a five-franc piece is to *x*.—These gilded idiots say to me, 'Why did you get into debt? Why did you involve yourself in such onerous obligations?' They remind me of the princess who, on hearing that the people lacked bread, said, 'Why do not they buy cakes?' I should like to see one of these rich men, who complain that I charge too much for an operation,—yes, I should like to see him alone in Paris without a sou, without a friend, without credit, and forced to work with his five fingers to live at all! What would he do? Where would he go to satisfy his hunger?

"Bianchon, if you have sometimes seen me hard and bitter, it was because I was adding my early sufferings on to the insensibility, the self-ishness of which I have seen thousands of instances in the highest circles; or, perhaps, I was thinking of the obstacles which hatred, envy, jealousy, and calumny raised up between me and success. In Paris, when certain people see you ready to set your foot in the stirrup, some pull your coat-tails, others loosen the buckle of the strap that you may fall and crack your skull; one wrenches off your horse's shoes, another steals your whip, and the least treacherous of them all is the man whom you see coming to fire his pistol at you point blank.

"You yourself, my dear boy, are clever enough to make acquaintance before long with the odious and incessant warfare waged by mediocrity against the superior man. If you should drop five-and-twenty louis one day, you will be accused of gambling on the next, and your best friends will report that you have lost twenty-five thousand. If you have a head-ache, you will be considered mad. If you are a little hasty, no one can live with you. If, to make a stand against this armament of pigmies, you collect your best powers, your best friends will cry out that you want to have everything, that you aim at domineering, at tyranny. In short, your good points will become your faults, your faults will be vices, and your virtues crimes.

"If you save a man, you will be said to have killed him; if he reappears on the scene, it will be positive that you have secured the present at the cost of the future. If he is not dead, he will die. Stumble, and you fall! Invent anything of any kind and claim your rights, you will be crotchety, cunning, ill-disposed to rising younger men.

"So, you see, my dear fellow, if I do not believe in God, I believe still less in man. But do not you know in me another Desplein, altogether different from the Desplein whom every one abuses?—However, we will not stir that mud-heap.

"Well, I was living in that house, I was working hard to pass my first examination, and I had no money at all. You know. I had come to one of those moments of extremity when a man says, 'I will enlist.' I had one hope. I expected from my home a box full of linen, a present from one of those old aunts who, knowing nothing of Paris, think of your shirts, while they imagine that their nephew with thirty francs a month is eating ortolans. The box arrived while I was at the schools; it had cost forty francs for carriage. The porter, a German shoemaker living in a loft, had paid the money and kept the box. I walked up and down the Rue des Fossés-Saint-Germain-des-Prés and the Rue de l'Ecole de Médicine without hitting on any scheme which would release my trunk without the payment of the forty francs, which of course I could pay as soon as I should have sold the linen. My stupidity proved to me that surgery was my only vocation. My good fellow, refined souls, whose powers move in a lofty atmosphere, have none of that spirit of intrigue that is fertile in resource and device; their good genius is chance; they do not invent, things come to them.

"At night I went home, at the very moment when my fellow lodger also came in——a water-carrier named Bourgeat, a native of Saint-Flour. We knew each other as two lodgers do who have rooms off the same landing, and who hear each other sleeping, coughing, dressing, and so at last become used to one another. My neighbour informed me that the landlord, to whom I owed three-quarters' rent, had turned me out; I must clear out next morning. He himself was also turned out on account of his occupation. I spent the most miserable night of my life. Where was I to get a messenger who could carry my few chattels and my books? How could I pay him and the porter? Where was I to go? I repeated these unanswerable questions again and again, in tears, as madmen repeat their tunes. I fell asleep; poverty has for its friend heavenly slumbers full of beautiful dreams.

"Next morning, just as I was swallowing my little bowl of bread soaked in milk, Bourgeat came in and said to me in his vile Auvergne accent——

" '*Mouchieur l'Etudiant,* I am a poor man, a foundling from the hospital at Saint-Flour, without either father or mother, and not rich enough to marry. You are not fertile in relations either, nor well supplied with the ready? Listen, I have a hand-cart downstairs which I have hired for two sous an hour; it will hold all our goods; if you like, we will try to find lodgings together, since we are both turned out of this. It is not the earthly paradise, when all is said and done."

" 'I know that, my good Bourgeat,' said I. 'But I am in a great fix. I have a trunk downstairs with a hundred francs' worth of linen in it, out of which I could pay the landlord and all I owe to the porter, and I have not a hundred sous."

" 'Pooh! I have a few dibs,' replied Bourgeat joyfully, and he pulled out a greasy old leather purse. 'Keep your linen.'

"Bourgeat paid up my arrears and his own, and settled with the porter. Then he put our furniture and my box of linen in his cart, and pulled it along the street, stopping in front of every house where there was a notice board. I went up to see whether the rooms to let would suit us. At midday we were still wandering about the neighbourhood without having found anything. The price was the great difficulty. Bourgeat proposed that we should eat at a wine shop, leaving the cart at the door. Towards evening I discovered, in the Cour de Rohan, Passage du Commerce, at the very top of a house next the roof, two rooms with a staircase between them. Each of us was to pay sixty francs a year. So there we were housed, my humble friend and I. We dined together. Bourgeat, who earned about fifty sous a day, had saved a hundred crowns or so; he would soon be able to gratify his ambition by buying a barrel and a horse. On learning my situation—for he extracted my secrets with a quiet craftiness and good nature, of which the remembrance touches my heart to this day, he gave up for a time the ambition of his whole life; for twenty-two years he had been carrying water in the street, and he now devoted his hundred crowns to my future prospects."

Desplein at these words clutched Bianchon's arm tightly. "He gave me the money for my examination fees! That man, my friend, understood that I had a mission, that the needs of my intellect were greater than his. He looked after me, he called me his boy, he lent me money to buy books, he would come in softly sometimes to watch me at work, and took a mother's care in seeing that I had wholesome and abundant food, instead of the bad and insufficient nourishment I had been condemned to. Bourgeat, a man of about forty, had a homely, mediæval type of face, a prominent forehead, a head that a painter might have chosen as a model for that of Lycurgus. The poor man's heart was big with affections seeking an object; he had never been loved but by a poodle that had died

some time since, of which he would talk to me, asking whether I thought
the Church would allow masses to be said for the repose of its soul. His
dog, said he, had been a good Christian, who for twelve years had accompanied him to church, never barking, listening to the organ without opening his mouth, and crouching beside him in a way that made it seem as
though he were praying too.

"This man centred all his affections in me; he looked upon me as a
forlorn and suffering creature, and he became, to me, the most thoughtful
mother, the most considerate benefactor, the ideal of the virtue which
rejoices in its own work. When I met him in the street, he would throw
me a glance of intelligence full of unutterable dignity; he would affect to
walk as though he carried no weight, and seemed happy in seeing me in
good health and well dressed. It was, in fact, the devoted affection of the
lower classes, the love of a girl of the people transferred to a loftier level.
Bourgeat did all my errands, woke me at night at any fixed hour, trimmed
my lamp, cleaned our landing; as good as a servant as he was as a father,
and as clean as an English girl. He did all the housework. Like Philopœ-
men, he saved our wood, and gave to all he did the grace of simplicity
while preserving his dignity, for he seemed to understand that the end
ennobles every act.

"When I left this good fellow, to be house surgeon at the Hôtel-Dieu,
I felt an indescribable, dull pain, knowing that he could no longer live
with me; but he comforted himself with the prospect of saving up money
enough for me to take my degree, and he made me promise to go to see
him whenever I had a day out: Bourgeat was proud of me. He loved me
for my own sake, and for his own. If you look up my thesis, you will see
that I dedicated it to him.

"During the last year of my residence as house surgeon I earned
enough to repay all I owed to this worthy Auvergnat by buying him a
barrel and a horse. He was furious with rage at learning that I had been
depriving myself of spending my money, and yet he was delighted to see
his wishes fulfilled; he laughed and scolded, he looked at his barrel, at
his horse, and wiped away a tear, as he said, 'It is too bad. What a splendid
barrel! You really ought not. Why, that horse is as strong as an Auvergnat!'

"I never saw a more touching scene. Bourgeat insisted on buying for
me the case of instruments mounted in silver which you have seen in my

room, and which is to me the most precious thing there. Though enchanted with my first success, never did the least sign, the least word, escape him which might imply, 'This man owes all to me!' And yet, but for him, I should have died of want; he had eaten bread rubbed with garlic that I might have coffee to enable me to sit up at night.

"He fell ill. As you may suppose, I passed my nights by his bedside, and the first time I pulled him through; but two years after he had a relapse; in spite of the utmost care, in spite of the greatest exertions of science, he succumbed. No king was ever nursed as he was. Yes, Bianchon, to snatch that man from death I tried unheard-of things. I wanted him to live long enough to show him his work accomplished, to realise all his hopes, to give expression to the only need for gratitude that ever filled my heart, to quench a fire that burns in me to this day.

"Bourgeat, my second father, died in my arms," Desplein went on, after a pause, visibly moved. "He left me everything he possessed by a will he had had made by a public scrivener, dating from the year when we had gone to live in the Cour de Rohan.

"This man's faith was perfect; he loved the Holy Virgin as he might have loved his wife. He was an ardent Catholic, but never said a word to me about my want of religion. When he was dying he entreated me to spare no expense that he might have every possible benefit of clergy. I had a mass said for him every day. Often, in the night, he would tell me of his fears as to his future fate; he feared his life had not been saintly enough. Poor man! he was at work from morning till night. For whom, then, is Paradise—if there be a Paradise? He received the last sacrament like the saint that he was, and his death was worthy of his life.

"I alone followed him to the grave. When I had laid my only benefactor to rest, I looked about to see how I could pay my debt to him; I found he had neither family nor friends, neither wife nor child. But he believed. He had a religious conviction; had I any right to dispute it? He had spoken to me timidly of masses said for the repose of the dead; he would not impress it on me as a duty, thinking that it would be a form of repayment for his services. As soon as I had money enough I paid to Saint-Sulpice the requisite sum for four masses every year. As the only thing I can do for Bourgeat is thus to satisfy his pious wishes, on the days when that mass is said, at the beginning of each season of the year, I go for his sake and say the required prayers; and I say with the good faith of a sceptic—'Great God, if there is a sphere which Thou hast appointed after death for those who have been perfect, remember good Bourgeat; and if he should have anything to suffer, let me suffer it for him, that he may enter all the sooner into what is called Paradise.'

"That, my dear fellow, is as much as a man who holds my opinions can allow himself. But God must be a good fellow; He cannot owe me any grudge. I swear to you, I would give my whole fortune if faith such as Bourgeat's could enter my brain."

Bianchon, who was with Desplein all through his last illness, dares not affirm to this day that the great surgeon died an atheist. Will not those who believe like to fancy that the humble Auvergnat came to open the gate of heaven to his friend, as he did that of the earthly temple on whose pediment we read the words—"A grateful country to its great men."

—*Translated from the French by* CLARA BELL

V

The Inward Vision

ERNEST HEMINGWAY

The Snows of Kilimanjaro

Kilimanjaro is a snow-covered mountain 19,710 feet high, and is said to be the highest mountain in Africa. Its western summit is called the Masai "Ngàje Ngài," the House of God. Close to the western summit there is the dried and frozen carcass of a leopard. No one has explained what the leopard was seeking at that altitude.

E. H.

"THE marvellous thing is that it's painless," he said. "That's how you know when it starts."

"Is it really?"

"Absolutely. I'm awfully sorry about the odor though. That must bother you."

"Don't! Please don't."

"Look at them," he said. "Now is it sight or is it scent that brings them like that?"

The cot the man lay on was in the wide shade of a mimosa tree and as he looked out past the shade onto the glare of the plain there were three of the big birds squatted obscenely, while in the sky a dozen more sailed, making quick-moving shadows as they passed.

"They've been there since the day the truck broke down," he said. "Today's the first time any have lit on the ground. I watched the way they sailed very carefully at first in case I ever wanted to use them in a story. That's funny now."

"I wish you wouldn't," she said.

"I'm only talking," he said. "It's much easier if I talk. But I don't want to bother you."

"You know it doesn't bother me," she said. "It's that I've gotten so very nervous not being able to do anything. I think we might make it as easy as we can until the plane comes."

"Or until the plane doesn't come."

"Please tell me what I can do. There must be something I can do."

"You can take the leg off and that might stop it, though I doubt it. Or you can shoot me. You're a good shot now. I taught you to shoot didn't I?"

"Please don't talk that way. Couldn't I read to you?"

"Read what?"

"Anything in the book bag that we haven't read."

"I can't listen to it," he said. "Talking is the easiest. We quarrel and that makes the time pass."

"I don't quarrel. I never want to quarrel. Let's not quarrel any more. No matter how nervous we get. Maybe they will be back with another truck today. Maybe the plane will come."

"I don't want to move," the man said. "There is no sense in moving now except to make it easier for you."

"That's cowardly."

"Can't you let a man die as comfortably as he can without calling him names? What's the use of slanging me?"

"You're not going to die."

"Don't be silly. I'm dying now. Ask those bastards." He looked over to where the huge, filthy birds sat, their naked heads sunk in the hunched feathers. A fourth planed down, to run quick-legged and then waddle slowly toward the others.

"They are around every camp. You never notice them. You can't die if you don't give up."

"Where did you read that? You're such a bloody fool."

"You might think about some one else."

"For Christ's sake," he said, "that's been my trade."

He lay then and was quiet for a while and looked across the heat shimmer of the plain to the edge of the bush. There were a few Tommies that showed minute and white against the yellow and, far off, he saw a herd of zebra, white against the green of the bush. This was a pleasant camp under big trees against a hill, with good water, and close by, a nearly dry water hole where sand grouse flighted in the mornings.

"Wouldn't you like me to read?" she asked. She was sitting on a canvas chair beside his cot. "There's a breeze coming up."

"No thanks."

"Maybe the truck will come."

"I don't give a damn about the truck."

"I do."

"You give a damn about so many things that I don't."

"Not so many, Harry."

"What about a drink?"

"It's supposed to be bad for you. It said in Black's to avoid all alcohol. You shouldn't drink."

"Molo!" he shouted.

"Yes Bwana."

"Bring whiskey-soda."

"Yes Bwana."

"You shouldn't," she said. "That's what I mean by giving up. It says it's bad for you. I know it's bad for you."

"No," he said. "It's good for me."

So now it was all over, he thought. So now he would never have a chance to finish it. So this was the way it ended in a bickering over a drink. Since the gangrene started in his right leg he had no pain and with the pain the horror had gone and all he felt now was a great tiredness and anger that this was the end of it. For this, that now was coming, he had very little curiosity. For years it had obsessed him; but now it meant nothing in itself. It was strange how easy being tired enough made it.

Now he would never write the things that he had saved to write until he knew enough to write them well. Well, he would not have to fail at trying to write them either. Maybe you could never write them, and that was why you put them off and delayed the starting. Well he would never know, now.

"I wish we'd never come," the woman said. She was looking at him holding the glass and biting her lip. "You never would have gotten anything like this in Paris. You always said you loved Paris. We could have stayed in Paris or gone anywhere. I'd have gone anywhere. I said I'd go anywhere you wanted. If you wanted to shoot we could have gone shooting in Hungary and been comfortable."

"Your bloody money," he said.

"That's not fair," she said. "It was always yours as much as mine. I left everything and I went wherever you wanted to go and I've done what you wanted to do. But I wish we'd never come here."

"You said you loved it."

"I did when you were all right. But now I hate it. I don't see why that had to happen to your leg. What have we done to have that happen to us?"

"I suppose what I did was to forget to put iodine on it when I first scratched it. Then I didn't pay any attention to it because I never infect. Then, later, when it got bad, it was probably using that weak carbolic solution when the other antiseptics ran out that paralyzed the minute blood vessels and started the gangrene." He looked at her. "What else?"

"I don't mean that."

"If we would have hired a good mechanic instead of a half baked kikuyu driver, he would have checked the oil and never burned out that bearing in the truck."

"I don't mean that."

"If you hadn't left your own people, your goddamned Old Westbury, Saratoga, Palm Beach people to take me on——"

"Why, I loved you. That's not fair. I love you now. I'll always love you. Don't you love me?"

"No," said the man. "I don't think so. I never have."

"Harry, what are you saying? You're out of your head."

"No. I haven't any head to go out of."

"Don't drink that," she said. "Darling, please don't drink that. We have to do everything we can."

"You do it," he said. "I'm tired."

Now in his mind he saw a railway station at Karagatch and he was standing with his pack and that was the headlight of the Simplon-Orient cutting the dark now and he was leaving Thrace then after the retreat. That was one of the things he had saved to write, with, in the morning at breakfast, looking out the window and seeing snow on the mountains in Bulgaria and Nansen's Secretary asking the old man if it were snow and the old man looking at it and saying, No, that's not snow. It's too early for snow. And the Secretary repeating to the other girls, No, you see. It's not snow and them all saying, It's not snow we were mistaken. But it was the snow all right and he sent them on into it when he evolved exchange of populations. And it was snow they tramped along in until they died that winter.

It was snow too that fell all Christmas week that year up in the Gauertal, that year they lived in the woodcutter's house with the big square porcelain stove that filled half the room, and they slept on mattresses filled with beech leaves, the time the deserter came with his feet bloody in the snow. He said the police were right behind him and they gave him woolen socks and held the gendarmes talking until the tracks had drifted over.

In Schrunz, on Christmas day, the snow was so bright it hurt your eyes when you looked out from the weinstube and saw every one coming home from church. That was where they walked up the sleigh-smoothed urine-yellowed road along the river with the steep pine hills, skis heavy on the shoulder, and where they ran that great run down the glacier above the Madlener-haus, the snow as smooth to see as cake frosting and as light as powder and he remembered the noiseless rush the speed made as you dropped down like a bird.

They were snow-bound a week in the Madlener-haus that time in the blizzard playing cards in the smoke by the lantern light and the stakes were higher all the time as Herr Lent lost more. Finally he lost it all. Everything, the skischule money and all the season's profit and then his capital. He could see him with his long nose, picking up the cards and then opening, "Sans Voir." There was always gambling then. When there was no snow you gambled and when there was too much you gambled. He thought of all the time in his life he had spent gambling.

But he had never written a line of that, nor of that cold, bright Christmas day with the mountains showing across the plain that Barker had flown across the lines to bomb the Austrian officers' leave train, machine-gunning them as they scattered and ran. He remembered Barker afterwards coming into the mess and starting to tell about it. And how quiet it got and then somebody saying, "You bloody murderous bastard."

Those were the same Austrians they killed then that he skied with later. No not the same. Hans, that he skied with all that year, had been in the Kaiser-Jägers and when they went hunting hares together up the little valley above the saw-mill they had talked of the fighting on Pasubio and of the attack on Pertica and Asalone and he had never written a word of that. Nor of Monte Corno, nor the Siete Commum, nor of Arsiedo.

How many winters had he lived in the Voralberg and the Arlberg? It was four and then he remembered the man who had the fox to sell when they had walked into Bludenz, that time to buy presents, and the cherry-pit taste of good kirsch, the fast-slipping rush of running powder-snow on crust, singing, "Hi! Ho! said Rolly!" as you ran down the last stretch to the steep drop, taking it straight, then running the orchard in three turns and out across the ditch and onto the icy road behind the inn.

Knocking your bindings loose, kicking the skis free and leaning them up against the wooden wall of the inn, the lamplight coming from the window, where inside, in the smoky, new-wine smelling warmth, they were playing the accordion.

"Where did we stay in Paris?" he asked the woman who was sitting by him in a canvas chair, now, in Africa.

"At the Crillon. You know that."

"Why do I know that?"

"That's where we always stayed."

"No. Not always."

"There and at the Pavillion Henri-Quatre in St. Germain. You said you loved it there."

"Love is a dunghill," said Harry. "And I'm the cock that gets on it to crow."

"If you have to go away," she said, "is it absolutely necessary to kill off everything you leave behind? I mean do you have to take away everything? Do you have to kill your horse, and your wife and burn your saddle and your armour?"

"Yes," he said. "Your damned money was my armour. My Swift and my Armour."

"Don't."

"All right. I'll stop that. I don't want to hurt you."

"It's a little bit late now."

"All right then. I'll go on hurting you. It's more amusing. The only thing I ever really liked to do with you I can't do now."

"No, that's not true. You liked to do many things and everything you wanted to do I did."

"Oh, for Christ sake stop bragging, will you?"

He looked at her and saw her crying.

"Listen," he said. "Do you think that it is fun to do this? I don't know why I'm doing it. It's trying to kill to keep yourself alive, I imagine. I was all right when we started talking. I didn't mean to start this, and now I'm crazy as a coot and being as cruel to you as I can be. Don't pay any attention, darling, to what I say. I love you, really. You know I love you. I've never loved any one else the way I love you."

He slipped into the familiar lie he made his bread and butter by.

"You're sweet to me."

"You bitch," he said. "You rich bitch. That's poetry. I'm full of poetry
now. Rot and poetry. Rotten poetry."

"Stop it. Harry, why do you have to turn into a devil now?"

"I don't like to leave anything," the man said. "I don't like to leave
things behind."

*   *   *

It was evening now and he had been asleep. The sun was gone behind
the hill and there was a shadow all across the plain and the small animals
were feeding close to camp; quick dropping heads and switching tails,
he watched them keeping well out away from the bush now. The birds
no longer waited on the ground. They were all perched heavily in a tree.
There were many more of them. His personal boy was sitting by the bed.

"Memsahib's gone to shoot," the boy said. "Does Bwana want?"

"Nothing."

She had gone to kill a piece of meat and, knowing how he liked to
watch the game, she had gone well away so she would not disturb this
little pocket of the plain that he could see. She was always thoughtful, he
thought. On anything she knew about, or had read, or that she had ever
heard.

It was not her fault that when he went to her he was already over. How
could a woman know that you meant nothing that you said; that you
spoke only from habit and to be comfortable? After he no longer meant
what he said, his lies were more successful with women than when he
had told them the truth.

It was not so much that he lied as that there was no truth to tell. He
had had his life and it was over and then he went on living it again with
different people and more money, with the best of the same places, and
some new ones.

You kept from thinking and it was all marvellous. You were equipped
with good insides so that you did not go to pieces that way, the way most
of them had, and you made an attitude that you cared nothing for the
work you used to do, now that you could no longer do it. But, in yourself,
you said that you would write about these people; about the very rich;
that you were really not of them but a spy in their country; that you
would leave it and write of it and for once it would be written by
some one who knew what he was writing of. But he would never do it,
because each day of not writing, of comfort, of being that which he de-

spised, dulled his ability and softened his will to work so that, finally, h
did no work at all. The people he knew now were all much more com
fortable when he did not work. Africa was where he had been happiest i
the good time of his life, so he had come out here to start again. The
had made this safari with the minimum of comfort. There was no hard
ship; but there was no luxury and he had thought that he could get bacl
into training that way. That in some way he could work the fat off hi
soul the way a fighter went into the mountains to work and train in orde
to burn it out of his body.

She had liked it. She said she loved it. She loved anything that wa
exciting, that involved a change of scene, where there were new peopl
and where things were pleasant. And he had felt the illusion of returnin
strength of will to work. Now if this was how it ended, and he knew i
was, he must not turn like some snake biting itself because its back wa
broken. It wasn't this woman's fault. If it had not been she it would hav
been another. If he lived by a lie he should try to die by it. He heard
shot beyond the hill.

She shot very well this good, this rich bitch, this kindly caretaker an
destroyer of his talent. Nonsense. He had destroyed his talent himself
Why should he blame this woman because she kept him well? He ha
destroyed his talent by not using it, by betrayals of himself and what h
believed in, by drinking so much that he blunted the edge of his percep
tions, by laziness, by sloth, and by snobbery, by pride and by prejudice
by hook and by crook. What was this? A catalogue of old books? Wha
was his talent anyway? It was a talent all right but instead of using it
he had traded on it. It was never what he had done, but always what h
could do. And he had chosen to make his living with something els
instead of a pen or a pencil. It was strange, too, wasn't it, that when h
fell in love with another woman, that woman should always have mor
money than the last one? But when he no longer was in love, when h
was only lying, as to this woman, now, who had the most money of al
who had all the money there was, who had had a husband and children
who had taken lovers and been dissatisfied with them, and who loved
him dearly as a writer, as a man, as a companion and as a proud posses
sion; it was strange that when he did not love her at all and was lying
that he should be able to give her more for her money than when he ha
really loved.

We must all be cut out for what we do, he thought. However you make your living is where your talent lies. He had sold vitality, in one form or another, all his life and when your affections are not too involved you give much better value for the money. He had found that out but he would never write that, now, either. No, he would not write that, although it was well worth writing.

Now she came in sight, walking across the open toward the camp. She was wearing jodhpurs and carrying her rifle. The two boys had a Tommy gun and they were coming along behind her. She was still a good-looking woman, he thought, and she had a pleasant body. She had a great talent and appreciation for the bed, she was not pretty, but he liked her face, she read enormously, liked to ride and shoot and, certainly, she drank too much. Her husband had died when she was still a comparatively young woman and for a while she had devoted herself to her two just-grown children, who did not need her and were embarrassed at having her about, to her stable of horses, to books, and to bottles. She liked to read in the evening before dinner and she drank Scotch and soda while she read. By dinner she was fairly drunk and after a bottle of wine at dinner she was usually drunk enough to sleep.

That was before the lovers. After she had the lovers she did not drink so much because she did not have to be drunk to sleep. But the lovers bored her. She had been married to a man who had never bored her and these people bored her very much.

Then one of her two children was killed in a plane crash and after that was over she did not want the lovers, and drink being no anæsthetic she had to make another life. Suddenly, she had been acutely frightened of being alone. But she wanted some one that she respected with her.

It had begun very simply. She liked what he wrote and she had always envied the life he led. She thought he did exactly what he wanted to. The steps by which she had acquired him and the way in which she had finally fallen in love with him were all part of a regular progression in which she had built herself a new life and he had traded away what remained of his old life.

He had traded it for security, for comfort too, there was no denying that, and for what else? He did not know. She would have bought him anything he wanted. He knew that. She was a damned nice woman too. He would as soon be in bed with her as any one; rather with her, be-

cause she was richer, because she was very pleasant and appreciative an
because she never made scenes. And now this life that she had built agai
was coming to a term because he had not used iodine two weeks ago whe
a thorn had scratched his knee as they moved forward trying to photo
graph a herd of waterbuck standing, their heads up, peering while thei
nostrils searched the air, their ears spread wide to hear the first noise tha
would send them rushing into the bush. They had bolted, too, before h
got the picture.

Here she came now.

He turned his head on the cot to look toward her. "Hello," he said.

"I shot a Tommy ram," she told him. "He'll make you good broth an
I'll have them mash some potatoes with the Klim. How do you feel?"

"Much better."

"Isn't that lovely? You know I thought perhaps you would. You wer
sleeping when I left."

"I had a good sleep. Did you walk far?"

"No. Just around behind the hill. I made quite a good shot on th
Tommy."

"You shoot marvellously, you know."

"I love it. I've loved Africa. Really. If *you're* all right it's the most fu
that I've ever had. You don't know the fun it's been to shoot with you
I've loved the country."

"I love it too."

"Darling, you don't know how marvellous it is to see you feeling better
I couldn't stand it when you felt that way. You won't talk to me like tha
again, will you? Promise me?"

"No," he said. "I don't remember what I said."

"You don't have to destroy me. Do you? I'm only a middle-aged woma
who loves you and wants to do what you want to do. I've been destroye
two or three times already. You wouldn't want to destroy me again, woul
you?"

"I'd like to destroy you a few times in bed," he said.

"Yes. That's the good destruction. That's the way we're made to b
destroyed. The plane will be here tomorrow."

"How do you know?"

"I'm sure. It's bound to come. The boys have the wood all ready an
the grass to make the smudge. I went down and looked at it again today

here's plenty of room to land and we have the smudges ready at both
nds."

"What makes you think it will come tomorrow?"

"I'm sure it will. It's overdue now. Then, in town, they will fix up
our leg and then we will have some good destruction. Not that dreadful
talking kind."

"Should we have a drink? The sun is down."

"Do you think you should?"

"I'm having one."

"We'll have one together. *Molo, letti dui whiskey-soda!*" she called.

"You'd better put on your mosquito boots," he told her.

"I'll wait till I bathe . . ."

While it grew dark they drank and just before it was dark and there
was no longer enough light to shoot, a hyena crossed the open on his way
round the hill.

"That bastard crosses there every night," the man said. "Every night
for two weeks."

"He's the one makes the noise at night. I don't mind it. They're a
filthy animal though."

Drinking together, with no pain now except the discomfort of lying in
the one position, the boys lighting a fire, its shadow jumping on the tents,
he could feel the return of acquiescence in this life of pleasant surrender.
She *was* very good to him. He had been cruel and unjust in the afternoon.
She was a fine woman, marvellous really. And just then it occurred to
him that he was going to die.

It came with a rush; not as a rush of water nor of wind; but of a sudden
evil-smelling emptiness and the odd thing was that the hyena slipped
lightly along the edge of it.

"What is it, Harry?" she asked him.

"Nothing," he said. "You had better move over to the other side. To
windward."

"Did Molo change the dressing?"

"Yes. I'm just using the boric now."

"How do you feel?"

"A little wobbly."

"I'm going in to bathe," she said. "I'll be right out. I'll eat with you and
then we'll put the cot in."

So, he said to himself, we did well to stop the quarrelling. He had nev‹ quarrelled much with this woman, while with the women that he love‹ he had quarrelled so much they had finally, always, with the corrosi‹ of the quarrelling, killed what they had together. He had loved t‹ much, demanded too much, and he wore it all out.

He thought about alone in Constantinople that time, having quarrell‹ in Paris before he had gone out. He had whored the whole time an‹ then, when that was over, and he had failed to kill his loneliness, b‹ only made it worse, he had written her, the first one, the one who le‹ him, a letter telling her how he had never been able to kill it. . . . Ho‹ when he thought he saw her outside the Regence one time it made hi‹ go all faint and sick inside, and that he would follow a woman wh‹ looked like her in some way, along the Boulevard, afraid to see it was n‹ she, afraid to lose the feeling it gave him. How every one he had sle‹ with had only made him miss her more. How what she had done cou‹ never matter since he knew he could not cure himself of loving her. H‹ wrote this letter at the Club, cold sober, and mailed it to New Yor‹ asking her to write him at the office in Paris. That seemed safe. And th‹ night missing her so much it made him feel hollow sick inside, he wan‹ dered up past Taxim's, picked a girl up and took her out to supper. H‹ had gone to a place to dance with her afterward, she danced badly, and le‹ her for a hot Armenian slut, that swung her belly against him so it almo‹ scalded. He took her away from a British gunner subaltern after a row‹ The gunner asked him outside and they fought in the streets on th‹ cobbles in the dark. He'd hit him twice, hard, on the side of the jaw an‹ when he didn't go down he knew he was in for a fight. The gunner h‹ him in the body, then beside his eye. He swung with his left again an‹ landed and the gunner fell on him and grabbed his coat and tore th‹ sleeve off and he clubbed him twice behind the ear and then smashe‹ him with his right as he pushed him away. When the gunner went dow‹ his head hit first and he ran with the girl because they heard the M. P.‹ coming. They got into a taxi and drove out to Rimmily Hissa along th‹ Bosphorus, and around, and back in the cool night and went to bed an‹ she felt as over-ripe as she looked but smooth, rose-petal, syrupy, smooth‹ bellied, big-breasted and needed no pillow under her buttocks, and h‹ left her before she was awake looking blousy enough in the first da‹

ght and turned up at the Pera Palace with a black eye, carrying his coat
ecause one sleeve was missing.

That same night he left for Anatolia and he remembered, later on that
rip, riding all day through fields of the poppies that they raised for
pium and how strange it made you feel, finally, and all the distances
eemed wrong, to where they had made the attack with the newly arrived
Constantine officers, that did not know a god-damned thing, and the artil-
ery had fired into the troops and the British observer had cried like a
hild.

That was the day he'd first seen dead men wearing white ballet skirts
nd upturned shoes with pompons on them. The Turks had come steadily
nd lumpily and he had seen the skirted men running and the officers
hooting into them and running then themselves and he and the British
bserver had run too until his lungs ached and his mouth was full of
he taste of pennies and they stopped behind some rocks and there were
he Turks coming as lumpily as ever. Later he had seen the things that
e could never think of and later still he had seen much worse. So when
e got back to Paris that time he could not talk about it or stand to have
t mentioned. And there in the café as he passed was that American poet
vith a pile of saucers in front of him and a stupid look on his potato face
alking about the Dada movement with a Roumanian who said his name
vas Tristan Tzara, who always wore a monocle and had a headache,
nd, back at the apartment with his wife that now he loved again, the
quarrel all over, the madness all over, glad to be home, the office
ent his mail up to the flat. So then the letter in answer to the one he'd
vritten came in on a platter one morning and when he saw the hand-
vriting he went cold all over and tried to slip the letter underneath
nother. But his wife said, "Who is that letter from, dear?" and that was
he end of the beginning of that.

He remembered the good times with them all, and the quarrels. They
lways picked the finest places to have the quarrels. And why had they
lways quarrelled when he was feeling best? He had never written any
f that because, at first, he never wanted to hurt any one and then it
eemed as though there was enough to write without it. But he had
lways thought that he would write it finally. There was so much to write.
Ie had seen the world change; not just the events; although he had seen
nany of them and had watched the people, but he had seen the subtler

*change and he could remember how the people were at different times. H
had been in it and he had watched it and it was his duty to write of it; bu
now he never would.*

"How do you feel?" she said. She had come out from the tent nov
after her bath.

"All right."

"Could you eat now?" He saw Molo behind her with the folding tabl
and the other boy with the dishes.

"I want to write," he said.

"You ought to take some broth to keep your strength up."

"I'm going to die tonight," he said. "I don't need my strength up."

"Don't be melodramatic, Harry, please," she said.

"Why don't you use your nose? I'm rotted half way up my thigh now
What the hell should I fool with broth for? Molo bring whiskey-soda.

"Please take the broth," she said gently.

"All right."

The broth was too hot. He had to hold it in the cup until it coole
enough to take it and then he just got it down without gagging.

"You're a fine woman," he said. "Don't pay any attention to me."

She looked at him with her well-known, well-loved face from *Spu*
and *Town and Country*, only a little the worse for drink, only a littl
the worse for bed, but *Town and Country* never showed those goo
breasts and those useful thighs and those lightly small-of-back-caressin
hands, and as he looked and saw her well known pleasant smile, he fe
death come again. This time there was no rush. It was a puff, as of a win
that makes a candle flicker and the flame go tall.

"They can bring my net out later and hang it from the tree and buil
the fire up. I'm not going in the tent tonight. It's not worth moving. It'
a clear night. There won't be any rain."

So this was how you died, in whispers that you did not hear. Wel
there would be no more quarrelling. He could promise that. The on
experience that he had never had he was not going to spoil now. H
probably would. You spoiled everything. But perhaps he wouldn't.

"You can't take dictation, can you?"

"I never learned," she told him.

"That's all right."

There wasn't time, of course, although it seemed as though it tel

scoped so that you might put it all into one paragraph if you could get
it right.

There was a log house, chinked white with mortar, on a hill above the
lake. There was a bell on a pole by the door to call the people in to meals.
Behind the house were fields and behind the fields was the timber. A line
of lombardy poplars ran from the house to the dock. Other poplars ran
along the point. A road went up to the hills along the edge of the timber
and along that road he picked blackberries. Then that log house was
burned down and all the guns that had been on deer foot racks above the
open fireplace were burned and afterwards their barrels, with the lead
melted in the magazines, and the stocks burned away, lay out on the
heap of ashes that were used to make lye for the big iron soap kettles,
and you asked Grandfather if you could have them to play with, and he
said, no. You see they were his guns still and he never bought any others.
Nor did he hunt any more. The house was rebuilt in the same place out
of lumber now and painted white and from its porch you saw the poplars
and the lake beyond; but there were never any more guns. The barrels of
the guns that had hung on the deer feet on the wall of the log house lay
out there on the heap of ashes and no one ever touched them.

In the Black Forest, after the war, we rented a trout stream and there
were two ways to walk to it. One was down the valley from Triberg and
around the valley road in the shade of the trees that bordered the white
road, and then up a side road that went up through the hills past many
small farms, with the big Schwarzwald houses, until that road crossed
the stream. That was where our fishing began.

The other way was to climb steeply up to the edge of the woods and
then go across the top of the hills through the pine woods, and then out
to the edge of a meadow and down across this meadow to the bridge.
There were birches along the stream and it was not big, but narrow, clear
and fast, with pools where it had cut under the roots of the birches. At
the Hotel in Triberg the proprietor had a fine season. It was very pleasant
and we were all great friends. The next year came the inflation and the
money he had made the year before was not enough to buy supplies to
open the hotel and he hanged himself.

You could dictate that, but you could not dictate the Place Contre-
scarpe where the flower sellers dyed their flowers in the street and the
dye ran over the paving where the autobus started and the old men and

the women, always drunk on wine and bad marc; and the children with their noses running in the cold; the smell of dirty sweat and poverty and drunkenness at the Café des Amateurs and the whores at the Bal Musette they lived above. The Concierge who entertained the trooper of the Garde Republicaine in her loge, his horse-hair-plumed helmet on a chair. The locataire across the hall whose husband was a bicycle racer and her joy that morning at the Cremerie when she had opened L'Auto and seen where he placed third in Paris-Tours, his first big race. She had blushed and laughed and then gone upstairs crying with the yellow sporting paper in her hand. The husband of the woman who ran the Bal Musette drove a taxi and when he, Harry, had to take an early plane the husband knocked upon the door to wake him and they each drank a glass of white wine at the zinc of the bar before they started. He knew his neighbors in that quarter then because they all were poor.

Around that Place there were two kinds; the drunkards and the sportifs. The drunkards killed their poverty that way; the sportifs took it out in exercise. They were the descendants of the Communards and it was no struggle for them to know their politics. They knew who had shot their fathers, their relatives, their brothers, and their friends when the Versailles troops came in and took the town after the Commune and executed any one they could catch with calloused hands, or who wore a cap, or carried any other sign he was a working man. And in that poverty, and in that quarter across the street from a Boucherie Chevaline and a wine co-operative he had written the start of all he was to do. There never was another part of Paris that he loved like that, the sprawling trees, the old white plastered houses painted brown below, the long green of the autobus in that round square, the purple flower dye upon the paving, the sudden drop down the hill of the rue Cardinal Lemoine to the River, and the other way the narrow crowded world of the rue Mouffetard. The street that ran up toward the Pantheon and the other that he always took with the bicycle, the only asphalted street in all that quarter, smooth under the tires, with the high narrow houses and the cheap tall hotel where Paul Verlaine had died. There were only two rooms in the apartments where they lived and he had a room on the top floor of that hotel that cost him sixty francs a month where he did his writing, and from it he could see the roofs and chimney pots and all the hills of Paris.

From the apartment you could only see the wood and coal man's place

He sold wine too, bad wine. The golden horse's head outside the Bou-
cherie Chevaline where the carcasses hung yellow gold and red in the
open window, and the green painted co-operative where they bought
their wine; good wine and cheap. The rest was plaster walls and the win-
dows of the neighbors. The neighbors who, at night, when some one lay
drunk in the street, moaning and groaning in that typical French ivresse
that you were propaganded to believe did not exist, would open their
windows and then the murmur of talk.

"Where is the policeman? When you don't want him the bugger is
always there. He's sleeping with some concierge. Get the Agent." Till
some one threw a bucket of water from a window and the moaning
stopped. "What's that? Water. Ah, that's intelligent." And the windows
shutting. Marie, his femme de menage, protesting against the eight-hour
day saying, "If a husband works until six he gets only a little drunk on
the way home and does not waste too much. If he works only until five
he is drunk every night and one has no money. It is the wife of the work-
ing man who suffers from this shortening of hours."

"Wouldn't you like some more broth?" the woman asked him now.

"No, thank you very much. It is awfully good."

"Try just a little."

"I would like a whiskey-soda."

"It's not good for you."

"No. It's bad for me. Cole Porter wrote the words and the music. This
knowledge that you're going mad for me."

"You know I like you to drink."

"Oh yes. Only it's bad for me."

When she goes, he thought, I'll have all I want. Not all I want but all
there is. Ayee he was tired. Too tired. He was going to sleep a little while.
He lay still and death was not there. It must have gone around another
street. It went in pairs, on bicycles, and moved absolutely silently on the
pavements.

No, he had never written about Paris. Not the Paris that he cared
about. But what about the rest that he had never written?

What about the ranch and the silvered gray of the sagebrush, the
quick, clear water in the irrigation ditches, and the heavy green of the

alfalfa. The trail went up into the hills and the cattle in the summer wer
as shy as deer. The bawling and the steady noise and slow moving mas
raising a dust as you brought them down in the fall. And behind th
mountains, the clear sharpness of the peak in the evening light and
riding down along the trail in the moonlight, bright across the valle
Now he remembered coming down through the timber in the dar
holding the horse's tail when you could not see and all the stories tha
he meant to write.

About the half-wit chore boy who was left at the ranch that time and
told not to let any one get any hay, and that old bastard from the Fork
who had beaten the boy when he had worked for him stopping to ge
some feed. The boy refusing and the old man saying he would beat hir
again. The boy got the rifle from the kitchen and shot him when he trie
to come into the barn and when they came back to the ranch he'd bee
dead a week, frozen in the corral, and the dogs had eaten part of him
But what was left you packed on a sled wrapped in a blanket and rope
on and you got the boy to help you haul it, and the two of you took it ou
over the road on skis, and sixty miles down to town to turn the boy over
He having no idea that he would be arrested. Thinking he had done hi
duty and that you were his friend and he would be rewarded. He'
helped to haul the old man in so everybody could know how bad the ol
man had been and how he'd tried to steal some feed that didn't belon
to him, and when the sheriff put the handcuffs on the boy he couldn'
believe it. Then he'd started to cry. That was one story he had saved t
write. He knew at least twenty good stories from out there and he ha
never written one. Why?

"You tell them why," he said.

"Why what, dear?"

"Why nothing."

She didn't drink so much, now, since she had him. But if he lived h
would never write about her, he knew that now. Nor about any of them
The rich were dull and they drank too much, or they played too mucl
backgammon. They were dull and they were repetitious. He remembere
poor Julian and his romantic awe of them and how he had started a stor
once that began, "The very rich are different from you and me." An
how some one had said to Julian, Yes, they have more money. But tha

as not humorous to Julian. He thought they were a special glamorous
ce and when he found they weren't it wrecked him just as much as any
ther thing that wrecked him.

He had been contemptuous of those who wrecked. You did not have
o like it because you understood it. He could beat anything, he thought,
ecause no thing could hurt him if he did not care.

All right. Now he would not care for death. One thing he had always
readed was the pain. He could stand pain as well as any man, until it
ent on too long, and wore him out, but here he had something that had
urt frightfully and just when he had felt it breaking him, the pain had
opped.

*He remembered long ago when Williamson, the bombing officer, had
een hit by a stick bomb some one in a German patrol had thrown as he
as coming in through the wire that night and, screaming, had begged
very one to kill him. He was a fat man, very brave, and a good officer,
though addicted to fantastic shows. But that night he was caught in the
ire, with a flare lighting him up and his bowels spilled out into the wire,
 when they brought him in, alive, they had to cut him loose. Shoot me,
arry. For Christ sake shoot me. They had had an argument one time
bout our Lord never sending you anything you could not bear and some
ne's theory had been that meant that at a certain time the pain passed
ou out automatically. But he had always remembered Williamson, that
ight. Nothing passed out Williamson until he gave him all his morphine
blets that he had always saved to use himself and then they did not
ork right away.*

Still this now, that he had, was very easy; and if it was no worse as it
ent on there was nothing to worry about. Except that he would rather
e in better company.

He thought a little about the company that he would like to have.

No, he thought, when everything you do, you do too long, and do too
te, you can't expect to find the people still there. The people all are
one. The party's over and you are with your hostess now.

I'm getting as bored with dying as with everything else, he thought.

"It's a bore," he said out loud.

"What is, my dear?"

"Anything you do too bloody long."

He looked at her face between him and the fire. She was leaning bac in the chair and the firelight shone on her pleasantly lined face and h could see that she was sleepy. He heard the hyena make a noise just ou side the range of the fire.

"I've been writing," he said. "But I got tired."

"Do you think you will be able to sleep?"

"Pretty sure. Why don't you turn in?"

"I like to sit here with you."

"Do you feel anything strange?" he asked her.

"No. Just a little sleepy."

"I do," he said.

He had just felt death come by again.

"You know the only thing I've never lost is curiosity," he said to he

"You've never lost anything. You're the most complete man I've eve known."

"Christ," he said. "How little a woman knows. What is that? You intuition?"

Because, just then, death had come and rested its head on the foot c the cot and he could smell its breath.

"Never believe any of that about a scythe and a skull," he told her. " can be two bicycle policemen as easily, or be a bird. Or it can have a wid snout like a hyena."

It had moved up on him now, but it had no shape any more. It simpl occupied space.

"Tell it to go away."

It did not go away but moved a little closer.

"You've got a hell of a breath," he told it. "You stinking bastard."

It moved up closer to him still and now he could not speak to it, an when it saw he could not speak it came a little closer, and now he trie to send it away without speaking, but it moved in on him so its weigl was all upon his chest, and while it crouched there and he could nc move, or speak, he heard the woman say, "Bwana is asleep now. Tak the cot up very gently and carry it into the tent."

He could not speak to tell her to make it go away and it crouched nov heavier, so he could not breathe. And then, while they lifted the co suddenly it was all right and the weight went from his chest.

It was morning and had been morning for some time and he heard the plane. It showed very tiny and then made a wide circle and the boys ran out and lit the fires, using kerosene, and piled on grass so there were two big smudges at each end of the level place and the morning breeze blew them toward the camp and the plane circled twice more, low this time, and then glided down and levelled off and landed smoothly and, coming walking toward him, was old Compton in slacks, a tweed jacket and a brown felt hat.

"What's the matter, old cock?" Compton said.

"Bad leg," he told him. "Will you have some breakfast?"

"Thanks. I'll just have some tea. It's the Puss Moth you know. I won't be able to take the Memsahib. There's only room for one. Your lorry is on the way."

Helen had taken Compton aside and was speaking to him. Compton came back more cheery than ever.

"We'll get you right in," he said. "I'll be back for the Mem. Now I'm afraid I'll have to stop at Arusha to refuel. We'd better get going."

"What about the tea?"

"I don't really care about it you know."

The boys had picked up the cot and carried it around the green tents and down along the rock and out onto the plain and along past the smudges that were burning brightly now, the grass all consumed, and the wind fanning the fire, to the little plane. It was difficult getting him in, but once in he lay back in the leather seat, and the leg was stuck straight out to one side of the seat where Compton sat. Compton started the motor and got in. He waved to Helen and to the boys and, as the clatter moved into the old familiar roar, they swung around with Compie watching for wart-hog holes and roared, bumping, along the stretch between the fires and with the last bump rose and he saw them all standing below, waving, and the camp beside the hill, flattening now, and the plain spreading, clumps of trees, and the bush flattening, while the game trails ran now smoothly to the dry waterholes, and there was a new water that he had never known of. The zebra, small rounded backs now, and the wildebeeste, big-headed dots seeming to climb as they moved in long fingers across the plain, now scattering as the shadow came toward them, they were tiny now, and the movement had no gallop, and the plain as far as you could see, gray-yellow now and ahead old Compie's tweed back

and the brown felt hat. Then they were over the first hills and the wildebeeste were trailing up them, and then they were over mountains with
sudden depths of green-rising forest and the solid bamboo slopes, and
then the heavy forest again, sculptured into peaks and hollows until
they crossed, and hills sloped down and then another plain, hot now, and
purple brown, bumpy with heat and Compie looking back to see how he
was riding. Then there were other mountains dark ahead.

And then instead of going on to Arusha they turned left, he evidently
figured that they had the gas, and looking down he saw a pink sifting
cloud, moving over the ground, and in the air, like the first snow in a
blizzard, that comes from nowhere, and he knew the locusts were coming up from the South. Then they began to climb and they were going
to the East it seemed, and then it darkened and they were in a storm, the
rain so thick it seemed like flying through a waterfall, and then they
were out and Compie turned his head and grinned and pointed and
there, ahead, all he could see, as wide as all the world, great, high, and
unbelievably white in the sun, was the square top of Kilimanjaro. And
then he knew that there was where he was going.

Just then the hyena stopped whimpering in the night and started to
make a strange, human, almost crying sound. The woman heard it and
stirred uneasily. She did not wake. In her dream she was at the house
on Long Island and it was the night before her daughter's début. Some
how her father was there and he had been very rude. Then the noise the
hyena made was so loud she woke and for a moment she did not know
where she was and she was very afraid. Then she took the flashlight and
shone it on the other cot that they had carried in after Harry had gone
to sleep. She could see his bulk under the mosquito bar but somehow
he had gotten his leg out and it hung down alongside the cot. The dressing
had all come down and she could not look at it.

"Molo," she called, "Molo! Molo!"

Then she said, "Harry, Harry!" Then her voice rising, "Harry! Please
Oh Harry!"

There was no answer and she could not hear him breathing.

Outside the tent the hyena made the same strange noise that had
awakened her. But she did not hear him for the beating of her heart.

A Still Moment

I am sorry but I haven't any sort of note I could add to my story, "Still Moment."

EUDORA WELTY

LORENZO DOW rode the Old Natchez Trace at top speed upon a race horse, and the cry of the itinerant Man of God, "I must have souls! And souls I must have!" rang in his own windy ears. He rode as if never to stop, toward his night's appointment.

It was the hour of sunset. All the souls that he had saved and all those he had not took dusky shapes in the mist that hung between the high banks, and seemed by their great number and density to block his way, and showed no signs of melting or changing back into mist, so that he feared his passage was to be difficult forever. The poor souls that were not saved were darker and more pitiful than those that were, and still there was not any of the radiance he would have hoped to see in such a congregation.

"Light up, in God's name!" he called, in the pain of his disappointment.

Then a whole swarm of fireflies instantly flickered all around him, up and down, back and forth, first one golden light and then another, flashing without any of the weariness that had held back the souls. These were the signs sent from God that he had not seen the accumulated radiance of saved souls because he was not able, and that his eyes were more able to see the fireflies of the Lord than His blessed souls.

"Lord, give me the strength to see the angels when I am in Paradise," he said. "Do not let my eyes remain in this failing proportion to my loving heart always."

He gasped and held on. It was that day's complexity of horse-trading that had left him in the end with a Spanish race horse for which he was bound to send money in November from Georgia. Riding faster on the beast and still faster until he felt as if he were flying he sent thoughts of love with matching speed to his wife Peggy in Massachusetts. He found it effortless to love at a distance. He could look at the flowering trees and love Peggy in fullness, just as he could see his visions and love God. And Peggy, to whom he had not spoken until he could speak fateful words ("Would she accept of such an object as him?"), Peggy, the bride, with whom he had spent a few hours of time, showing of herself a small round handwriting, declared all in one letter, her first, that she felt the same as he, and that the fear was never of separation, but only of death.

Lorenzo well knew that it was Death that opened underfoot, that rippled by at night, that was the silence the birds did their singing in. He was close to death, closer than any animal or bird. On the back of one horse after another, winding them all, he was always riding toward it or away from it, and the Lord sent him directions with protection in His mind.

Just then he rode into a thicket of Indians taking aim with their new guns. One stepped out and took the horse by the bridle, it stopped at a touch, and the rest made a closing circle. The guns pointed.

"Incline!" The inner voice spoke sternly and with its customary light-ning-quickness.

Lorenzo inclined all the way forward and put his head to the horse's silky mane, his body to its body, until a bullet meant for him would en-danger the horse and make his death of no value. Prone he rode out through the circle of Indians, his obedience to the voice leaving him almost fearless, almost careless with joy.

But as he straightened and pressed ahead, care caught up with him again. Turning half-beast and half-divine, dividing himself like a heathen Centaur, he had escaped his death once more. But was it to be always by some metamorphosis of himself that he escaped, some humili-ation of his faith, some admission to strength and argumentation and not frailty? Each time when he acted so it was at the command of an instinct that he took at once as the word of an angel, until too late, when he knew it was the word of the devil. He had roared like a tiger at In-dians, he had submerged himself in water blowing the savage bubbles of the alligator, and they skirted him by. He had prostrated himself to ap-pear dead, and deceived bears. But all the time God would have protected him in His own way, less hurried, more divine.

Even now he saw a serpent crossing the Trace, giving out knowing glances.

He cried, "I know you now!", and the serpent gave him one look out of which all the fire had been taken, and went away in two darts into the tangle.

He rode on, all expectation, and the voices in the throats of the wild beasts went, almost without his noticing when, into words. "Praise God," they said. "Deliver us from one another." Birds especially sang of divine love which was the one ceaseless protection. "Peace, in peace," were their words so many times when they spoke from the briars, in a courteous sort of inflection, and he turned his countenance toward all perched creatures with a benevolence striving to match their own.

He rode on past the little intersecting trails, letting himself be guided by voices and by lights. It was battlesounds he heard most, sending him on, but sometimes ocean sounds, that long beat of waves that would make his heart pound and retreat as heavily as they, and he despaired again in his failure in Ireland when he took a voyage and persuaded with the Catholics with his back against the door, and then ran away to their cries of "Mind the white hat!" But when he heard singing it was not the militant and sharp sound of Wesley's hymns, but a soft, tireless and tender air that had no beginning and no end, and the softness of distance, and he had pleaded with the Lord to find out if all this meant that it was wicked, but no answer had come.

Soon night would descend, and a camp-meeting ground ahead would fill with its sinners like the sky with its stars. How he hungered for them! He looked in prescience with a longing of love over the throng that waited while the flames of the torches threw change, change, change over their faces. How could he bring them enough, if it were not divine love and sufficient warning of all that could threaten them? He rode on faster. He was a filler of appointments, and he filled more and more, until his journeys up and down creation were nothing but a shuttle, driving back and forth upon the rich expanse of his vision. He was homeless by his own choice, he must be everywhere at some time, and somewhere soon. There hastening in the wilderness on his flying horse he gave the night's torch-lit crowd a premature benediction, he could not wait. He spread his arms out, one at a time for safety, and he wished, when they would all be gathered in by his tin horn blasts and the inspired words would go out over their heads, to brood above the entire and passionate life of the wide world, to become its rightful part.

He peered ahead. "Inhabitants of Time! The wilderness is your souls on earth!" he shouted ahead into the treetops. "Look about you, if you would view the conditions of your spirit, put here by the good Lord to show you and afright you. These wild places and these trails of awesome loneliness lie nowhere, nowhere, but in your heart."

A dark man, who was James Murrell the outlaw, rode his horse out of a cane brake and began going along beside Lorenzo without looking at him. He had the alternately proud and aggrieved look of a man believing himself to be an instrument in the hands of a power, and when he was young he said at once to strangers that he was being used by Evil, or sometimes he stopped a traveler by shouting, "Stop! I'm the Devil!" He rode along now talking and drawing out his talk, by some deep control of the voice gradually slowing the speed of Lorenzo's horse down until both the horses were softly trotting. He would have wondered that nothing he said was heard, not knowing that Lorenzo listened only to voices of whose heavenly origin he was more certain.

Murrell riding along with his victim-to-be, Murrell riding, was Murrell talking. He told away at his long tales, with always a distance and a long length of time flowing through them, and all centered about a silent man. In each the silent man would have done a piece of evil, a robbery or a murder, in a place of long ago, and it was all made for the revelation in the end that the silent man was Murrell himself, and the long story had happened yesterday, and the place *here*—the Natchez Trace. It would only take one dawning look for the victim to see that all of this was another story and he himself had listened his way into it, and that he too was about to recede in time (to where the dread was forgotten) for some listener and to live for a listener in the long ago. Destroy the present!— that must have been the first thing that was whispered in Murrell's heart —the living moment and the man that lives in it must die before you can go on. It was his habit to bring the journey—which might even take days—to a close with a kind of ceremony. Turning his face at last into the face of the victim, for he had never seen him before now, he would tower up with the sudden height of a man no longer the tale teller but the speechless protagonist, silent at last, one degree nearer the hero. Then he would murder the man.

But it would always start over. This man going forward was going backward with talk. He saw nothing, observed no world at all. The two ends of his journey pulled at him always and held him in a nowhere, half asleep, smiling and witty, dangling his predicament. He was a murderer whose final stroke was over-long postponed, who had to bring himself through the greatest tedium to act, as if the whole wilderness, where he was born, were his impediment. But behind him and before him he kept in sight a victim, he saw a man fixed and stayed at the point of death—no matter how the man's eyes denied it, a victim, hands spreading to reach as if for the first time for life. Contempt! That is what Murrell gave that man.

Lorenzo might have understood, if he had not been in haste, that Murrell in laying hold of a man meant to solve his mystery of being. It was as if other men, all but himself, would lighten their hold on the secret, upon assault, and let it fly free at death. In his violence he was only treating of enigma. The violence shook his own body first, like a force gathering, and now he turned in the saddle.

Lorenzo's despair had to be kindled as well as his ecstasy, and could not come without that kindling. Before the awe-filled moment when the faces were turned up under the flares, as though an angel hand tipped their chins, he had no way of telling whether he would enter the sermon by sorrow or by joy. But at this moment the face of Murrell was turned toward him, turning at last, all solitary, in its full, and Lorenzo would have seized the man at once by his black coat and shaken him like prey for a lost soul, so instantly was he certain that the false fire was in his heart instead of the true fire. But Murrell, quick when he was quick, had put his own hand out, a restraining hand, and laid it on the wavelike flesh of the Spanish race horse, which quivered and shuddered at the touch.

They had come to a great live-oak tree at the edge of a low marshland. The burning sun hung low, like a head lowered on folded arms, and over the long reaches of violet trees the evening seemed still with thought. Lorenzo knew the place from having seen it among many in dreams, and he stopped readily and willingly. He drew rein, and Murrell drew rein, he dismounted and Murrell dismounted, he took a step, and Murrell was there too; and Lorenzo was not surprised at the closeness, how Murrell in his long dark coat and over it his dark face darkening still, stood beside him like a brother seeking light.

But in that moment instead of two men coming to stop by the great forked tree, there were three.

From far away, a student, Audubon, had been approaching lightly on the wilderness floor, disturbing nothing in his lightness. The long day of beauty had led him this certain distance. A flock of purple finches that he tried for the first moment to count went over his head. He made a spelling of the soft *pet* of the ivory-billed woodpecker. He told himself always: remember.

Coming upon the Trace, he looked at the high cedars, azure and still as distant smoke overhead, with their silver roots trailing down on either side like the veins of deepness in this place, and he noted some fact to his memory—this earth that wears but will not crumble or slide or turn to dust, they say it exists in one other spot in the world, Egypt—and then forgot it. He walked quietly. All life used this Trace, and he liked to see the animals move along it in direct, oblivious journeys, for they had begun it and made it, the buffalo and deer and the small running creatures before man ever knew where he wanted to go, and birds flew a great mirrored course above. Walking beneath them Audubon remembered how in the cities he had seen these very birds in his imagination, calling them up whenever he wished, even in the hard and glittering outer parlors where if an artist were humble enough to wait, some idle hand held up promised money. He walked lightly and he went as carefully as he had started at two that morning, crayon and paper, a gun, and a small bottle of spirits disposed about his body. (*Note: "The mocking birds so gentle that they would scarcely move out of the way."*) He looked with care; great abundance had ceased to startle him, and he could see things one by one. In Natchez they had told him of many strange and marvelous birds that were to be found here. Their descriptions had been exact, complete, and wildly varying, and he took them for inventions and believed that like all the worldly things that came out of Natchez, they would be disposed of and shamed by any man's excursion into the reality of Nature.

In the valley he appeared under the tree, a sure man, very sure and tender, as if the touch of all the earth rubbed upon him and the stains of the flowery swamp had made him so.

Lorenzo welcomed him and turned fond eyes upon him. To transmute

a man into an angel was the hope that drove him all over the world and
never let him flinch from a meeting or withhold good-byes for long.
This hope insistently divided his life into only two parts, journey and
rest. There could be no night and day and love and despair and longing
and satisfaction to make partitions in the single ecstasy of this alternation.
All things were speech.

"God created the world," said Lorenzo, "and it exists to give testimony. Life is the tongue: speak."

But instead of speech there happened a moment of deepest silence.

Audubon said nothing because he had gone without speaking a word for
days. He did not regard his thoughts for the birds and animals as suscepti-
ble, in their first change, to words. His long playing on the flute was not
in its origin a talking to himself. Rather than speak to order or describe,
he would always draw a deer with a stroke across it to communicate his
need of venison to an Indian. He had only found words when he discovered that there is much otherwise lost that can be noted down each
item in its own day, and he wrote often now in a journal, not wanting
anything to be lost the way it had been, all the past, and he would write
about a day, "Only sorry that the Sun Sets."

Murrell, his cheated hand hiding the gun, could only continue to smile
at Lorenzo, but he remembered in malice that he had disguised himself
once as an Evangelist, and his final words to this victim would have been,
"One of my disguises was what you are."

Then in Murrell Audubon saw what he thought of as "acquired sorrow"—that cumbrousness and darkness from which the naked Indian,
coming just as he was made from God's hand, was so lightly free. He
noted the eyes—the dark kind that loved to look through chinks, and saw
neither closeness nor distance, light nor shade, wonder nor familiarity.
They were narrowed to contract the heart, narrowed to make an averting
plan. Audubon knew the finest-drawn tendons of the body and the working of their power, for he had touched them, and he supposed them that in
man the enlargement of the eye to see started a motion in the hands to
make or do, and that the narrowing of the eye stopped the hand and
contracted the heart. Now Murrell's eyes followed an ant on a blade of
grass, up the blade and down, many times in the single moment. Audubon
had examined the Cave-In Rock where one robber had lived his hiding
life, and the air in the cave was the cavelike air that enclosed this man,

the same odor, flinty and dark. O secret life, he thought—is it true that the secret is withdrawn from the true disclosure, that man is a cave man, and that the openness I see, the ways through forests, the rivers brimming light, the wide arches where the birds fly, are dreams of freedom? If my origin is withheld from me, is my end to be unknown too? Is the radiance I see closed into an interval between two darks, or can it not illuminate them both and discover at last, though it cannot be spoken, what was thought hidden and lost?

In that quiet moment a solitary snowy heron flew down not far away and began to feed beside the marsh water.

At the single streak of flight, the ears of the race horse lifted, and the eyes of both horses filled with the soft lights of sunset, which in the next instant were reflected in the eyes of the men too as they all looked into the west toward the heron, and all eyes seemed infused with a sort of wildness.

Lorenzo gave the bird a triumphant look, such as a man may bestow upon his own vision, and thought, Nearness is near, lighted in a marshland, feeding at sunset. Praise God, His love has come visible.

Murrell, in suspicion pursuing all glances, blinking into a haze, saw only whiteness ensconced in darkness, as if it were a little luminous shell that drew in and held the eyesight. When he shaded his eyes, the brand "H.T." on his thumb thrust itself into his own vision, and he looked at the bird with the whole plan of the Mystic Rebellion darting from him as if in rays of the bright reflected light, and he stood looking proudly, leader as he was bound to become of the slaves, the brigands and outcasts of the entire Natchez country, with plans, dates, maps burning like a brand into his brain, and he saw himself proudly in a moment of prophecy going down rank after rank of successively bowing slaves to unroll and flaunt an awesome great picture of the Devil colored on a banner.

Audubon's eyes embraced the object in the distance and he could see it as carefully as if he held it in his hand. It was a snowy heron alone out of its flock. He watched it steadily, in his care noting the exact inevitable things. When it feeds it muddies the water with its foot. . . . It was as if each detail about the heron happened slowly in time, and only once. He felt again the old stab of wonder—what structure of life bridged the reptile's scale and the heron's feather? That knowledge too had been lost. He watched without moving. The bird was defenseless in the world except for the intensity of its life, and he wondered, how can heat of blood and speed of heart defend it? Then he thought, as always as if it were new and unbelievable, it has nothing in space or time to prevent its flight. And he waited, knowing that some birds will wait for a sense of their presence to travel to men before they will fly away from them.

Fixed in its pure white profile it stood in the precipitous moment, a plumicorn on its head, its breeding dress extended in rays, eating steadily the little water creatures. There was a little space between each man and the others, where they stood overwhelmed. No one could say the three had ever met, or that this moment of intersection had ever come in their lives, or its promise fulfilled. But before them the white heron rested in the grasses with the evening all around it, lighter and more serene than the evening, flight closed in its body, the circuit of its beauty closed, a bird seen and a bird still, its motion calm as if it were offered: Take my flight. . . .

What each of them had wanted was simply *all*. To save all souls, to destroy all men, to see and to record all life that filled this world—all, all—but now a single frail yearning seemed to go out of the three of them for a moment and to stretch toward this one snowy, shy bird in the marshes. It was as if three whirlwinds had drawn together at some center, to find there feeding in peace a snowy heron. Its own slow spiral of flight could take it away in its own time, but for a little it held them still, it laid quiet over them, and they stood for a moment unburdened. . . .

Murrell wore no mask, for his face was that, a face that was aware while he was somnolent, a face that watched for him, and listened for him, alert and nearly brutal, the guard of a planner. He was quick without that he might be slow within, he staved off time, he wandered and plotted, and yet his whole desire mounted in him toward the end (was this the end—the sight of a bird feeding at dusk?), toward the instant of confession. His incessant deeds were thick in his heart now, and flinging himself to the ground he thought wearily, when all these trees are cut down, and the Trace lost, then my Conspiracy that is yet to spread itself will be disclosed, and all the stone-loaded bodies of murdered men will be pulled up, and all everywhere will know poor Murrell. His look pressed upon Lorenzo, who stared upward, and Audubon, who was taking out his gun, and his eyes squinted up to them in pleading, as if to say, "How soon may I speak, and how soon will you pity me?" Then he looked back to the bird, and he thought if it would look at him a dread penetration would fill and gratify his heart.

Audubon in each act of life was aware of the mysterious origin he half-concealed and half-sought for. People along the way asked him in their kindness or their rudeness if it were true, that he was born a prince, and was the Lost Dauphin, and some said it was his secret, and some said that that was what he wished to find out before he died. But if it was his identity that he wished to discover, or if it was what a man had to seize beyond that, the way for him was by endless examination, by the care for every bird that flew in his path and every serpent that shone underfoot. Not one was enough; he looked deeper and deeper, on and on, as if for a particular beast or some legendary bird. Some men's eyes persisted in looking outward when they opened to look inward, and to their delight, there outflung was the astonishing world under the sky. When a man at last brought himself to face some mirror-surface he still saw the world looking back at him, and if he continued to look, to look closer and closer, what then? The gaze that looks outward must be trained without rest, to be indomitable. It must see as slowly as Murrell's ant in the grass, as exhaustively as Lorenzo's angel of God, and then, Audubon dreamed, with his mind going to his pointed brush, it must see like this, and he tightened his hand on the trigger of the gun and pulled it, and his eyes went closed. In memory the heron was all its solitude, its total beauty. All its whiteness could be seen from all sides at once, its pure feathers were as if counted and known and their array one upon the other would never be lost. But it was not from that memory that he could paint.

His opening eyes met Lorenzo's, close and flashing, and it was on seeing horror deep in them, like fires in abysses, that he recognized it for the first time. He had never seen horror in its purity and clarity until now, in bright blue eyes. He went and picked up the bird. He had thought it to be a female, just as one sees the moon as female; and so it was. He put it in his bag, and started away. But Lorenzo had already gone on, leaning a-tilt on the horse which went slowly.

Murrell was left behind, but he was proud of the dispersal, as if he had done it, as if he had always known that three men in simply being together and doing a thing can, by their obstinacy, take the pride out of one another. Each must go away alone, each send the others away alone.

He himself had purposely kept to the wildest country in the world, and would have sought it out, the loneliest road. He looked about with satisfaction, and hid. Travelers were forever innocent, he believed: that was his faith. He lay in wait; his faith was in innocence and his knowledge was of ruin; and had these things been shaken? Now, what could possibly be outside his grasp? Churning all about him like a cloud about the sun was the great folding descent of his thought. Plans of deeds made his thoughts, and they rolled and mingled about his ears as if he heard a dark voice that rose up to overcome the wilderness voice, or was one with it. The night would soon come; and he had gone through the day.

Audubon, splattered and wet, turned back into the wilderness with the heron warm under his hand, his head still light in a kind of trance. It was undeniable, on some Sunday mornings, when he turned over and over his drawings they seemed beautiful to him, through what was dramatic in the conflict of life, or what was exact. What he would draw, and what he had seen, became for a moment one to him then. Yet soon enough, and it seemed to come in that same moment, like Lorenzo's horror and the gun's firing, he knew that even the sight of the heron which surely he alone had appreciated, had not been all his belonging, and that never could any vision, even any simple sight, belong to him or to any man. He knew that the best he could make would be, after it was apart from his hand, a dead thing and not a live thing, never the essence, only a sum of parts; and that it would always meet with a stranger's sight, and never be one with the beauty in any other man's head in the world. As he had seen the bird most purely at its moment of death, in some fatal way, in his care for looking outward, he saw his long labor most revealingly at the point where it met its limit. Still carefully, for he was trained to see well in the dark, he walked on into the deeper woods, noting all sights, all sounds, and was gentler than they as he went.

In the woods that echoed yet in his ears, Lorenzo riding slowly looked back. The hair rose on his head and his hands began to shake with cold, and suddenly it seemed to him that God Himself, just now, thought of the Idea of Separateness. For surely He had never thought of it before, when the little white heron was flying down to feed. He could understand God's giving Separateness first and then giving Love to follow and heal in its wonder; but God had reversed this, and given Love first and then Separateness, as though it did not matter to Him which came first. Perhaps it was that God never counted the moments of Time; Lorenzo did that, among his tasks of love. Time did not occur to God. Therefore—did He even know of it? How to explain Time and Separateness back to God, Who had never thought of them, Who could let the whole world come to grief in a scattering moment?

Lorenzo brought his cold hands together in a clasp and stared through the distance at the place where the bird had been as if he saw it still; as if nothing could really take away what had happened to him, the beautiful little vision of the feeding bird. Its beauty had been greater than he could account for. The sweat of rapture poured down from his forehead, and then he shouted into the marshes.

"Tempter!"

He whirled forward in the saddle and began to hurry the horse to its high speed. His camp ground was far away still, though even now they must be lighting the torches and gathering in the multitudes, so that at the appointed time he would duly appear in their midst, to deliver his address on the subject of "In that day when all hearts shall be disclosed."

Then the sun dropped below the trees, and the new moon, slender and white, hung shyly in the west.

WHIT BURNETT

Sherrel

"Sherrel" is that not unfamiliar kind of story, a story growing out of conscience. It was written in Paris in 1925 by a young man considerably under thirty, recollecting an age of seventeen or eighteen and first love, recollecting an age of nine or ten and first tragedy.

WHIT BURNETT

I DO not know whether I can do this thing or not. Maybe it is just a thought, maybe I just think it is necessary to do it. I mean about the name. I have thought about it a lot though and it keeps urging at me. It is not easy to understand. But I must try to understand and explain it.

You see, I actually did have a brother. People sometimes asked me, Are you the only boy in the family? And I've said, Yes. This wasn't a lie wholly. I was the first born in my family. But there were others, two others. One died in long clothes. We have his picture at home. The other was named Sherrel.

It is easy to remember him. My mother had us photographed together, for instance. And one especial print was transferred onto little smooth discs the size of a saucer. The discs fit into small twisted wire easels and my brother and I used to sit on the easel like that on my mother's bureau in the bedroom.

He was, as I said, younger than I. This is important. The neighbors used to say, It's the difference in their ages. They tried to explain in that way why I was so mean. And you can see the difference clearly enough on the picture discs. We both stood by the photographer's chair, a plush chair. But I was up to the top of it. My brother's hand rested on the arm. It looks pretty small to me now because I'm twice as old as I was then. We both wore black velvet tam-o'-shanters and dark red velvet coats and pants. My mouth was a little open, too, looking at the photographer. I did not touch my brother. He had one hand, which was very small, on the chair, and the other one had hold of me. His hair was lighter than mine and softer and his eyes wider and bluer. He had a small mouth like a flower and it was smiling. He was a beautiful child. This was the brother I killed.

I am not telling you about a melodrama. I won't be arrested and hanged. I did not kill him yesterday. It was a long time ago, in fact, and I do not remember it all the time, only sometimes when something suggests the way I was then or when someone asks, Have you any other brothers? And I say, No. And here too in this other town at this school except for a girl I know I am quite alone in certain ways and in the winter as now I have seen any number of things to remind me. There is, for example, an epidemic of smallpox here and instead of smooth fast automobile hearses they still have funeral carriages that drag along slowly through the streets. Only once have I ridden in such a carriage. And that was then.

There are some things difficult to remember out of childhood. I do not remember when my brother was born. There was not so much difference then. Only four years before, I had been born. But I remember clearly when I was nine. My brother then was five. And we were two in the family. But I was the first.

Do you know how this is? Nine and five? Well, nine is somebody. Five is still curls. At nine I have seen something of the world. What have you seen at five? Go on, you can't come with us! Go on back to the house! We're going down to the store. You'll get run over. Go on, you can't play with us. You ain't big enough. Go on, grow up some before you come tagging around after us. Who asked you along? Beat it! I know how that is. I said all that, more brutally even. He didn't say anything. He didn't cry or whine or crab. I probably would have. He stopped following simply, and stood there. And then we ran off. He stood alone. Sometimes I found him other places alone, sitting still in a corner thinking quietly about something. I am always a little puzzled now I am older. I have talked it over with others. He would have been important. . . . But at nine one is a weed, growing wild. Five is still in the hothouse.

We lived near the sand hills. It wasn't until several years later that I really got into the hills exploring them with a cousin of my own age. Sherrel never did get there. And there was a great liking in both of us for the hills, his maybe different from mine. I often found him sitting dreaming looking at them. But one day late in the spring the hills in a way came down to our house. A cloudburst drenched them, rolling down soft sand, cutting great ditches in the road in front of our place. We weren't long in discovering that, I'll tell you. When Sherrel wandered out of the kitchen the ditch was full of us kids. It was a peach of a ditch as high as our head, gnawed with caves and dangers.

I started the discoveries. There's some hole, I yelled. And down I had gone, doing what the others wanted to do, the first to absorb their wishes. Then they followed, yelling too. Sherrel, I suppose, could hear my voice coming up out of the ground. He came over to the ditch and looked down, standing alone above us. Go on back, I shouted, you'll fall in. He moved away. I paid no more attention then to him and the rest of us ran racing, hiding, searching, together in the wash.

And then, separated from the others for a moment or so, I noticed something odd about my hands. Hey, kids, I cried, lookee! Look at my hands! They looked. They stood back in wonderment. They looked at their own hands. No, they couldn't, they said. It was something funny. Look what Martin can do! Lookee, he can peel off his hands! It was true, something had happened to my hands. I took hold and pulled off long shreds of skin. I amazed them all. They stood astounded.

Let me see, said somebody. It was Sherrel.

Say, I yelled, didn't I say not to come down here? You ain't big enough to be in this here ditch. Let me see your hands, he said. The kids were all looking at me. I'll let you see, all right! I said. He stood his ground and didn't go. That makes me mad, I felt. No, I said. I took him by the shoulder and talked straight in his face, hard. How many times do I have to tell you to get out of this ditch! He turned around and walked up the gorge to a shallower spot and climbed slowly out.

A day or so later Sherrel stayed in bed. There's something the matter with him, my mother said. She didn't know what. Then he took a high fever, they said, and was delirious. I thought it was strange about delirious. Sherrel's eyes were shut and he looked as if he was sleeping but he was talking without any sense. We'll have to have a doctor, my mother said. And that afternoon the doctor came to our house, wiping his feet at the door and entering with a serious look. Let's see the other young fellow, he said. Anything wrong with him? He had a little sore throat, my mother said, but he's all right. He looked down my throat. Look at my hands, I said, ain't they funny?

What I thought, he said.

The same afternoon a man from downtown came and nailed up a yellow flag. It was a cloth sign saying, black on orange, Scarlet Fever. I couldn't go out of the yard. That's sure tough, the kids said, peering through the pickets. I even had to keep back from the fence, too. It was catching.

I sat on the steps fronting north from our bare two-room brick house and looked at the hills. I had had the Scarlet Fever and hadn't even known it. Why, my mother said, he was playing around all the time. Why, he was out there playing in the ditch with all those children. That's bad, said the doctor. But my brother was worse. He had it good.

I remember the windows in the front room were darkened and my mother never went to bed. She never took her clothes off. And my father didn't go to work. My aunt came to the fence with a bag of oranges and bananas. How is he? she asked. If he isn't any better Dr. Anderson says he'd better have a consultation, said my mother. How is Dr. Anderson? asked my aunt. He is the best doctor in town, my mother said.

I sat in the sun all tired now and weak. But I wasn't sick. I was big and nine.

I remember the consultation. There were four doctors in the kitchen standing around and talking low and sitting down and getting up. I could see in from outside. My mother was nervous and walking around and my father, who was a big heavy man, stood around too and sat down and then got up. They were waiting for something definite they spoke of that I could not understand. It was the Crisis. I asked what it was, and my mother had said, Sherrel will get better then. I didn't know what a Crisis would be like and I opened the door slowly and got into the house quietly, past the doctors.

My father and mother were in the front room by the bed where Sherrel lay. He was still and wasn't talking deliriously. And then my mother, who was standing by him with my father waiting, suddenly cried terribly for a minute or so, and then she took hold of my father and pulled him down by the bed to the floor. I didn't know what was happening. I was frightened, too. Pray, she sobbed. Pray, if you never prayed before. O God, she began . . . and she was crying more and more. My father was kneeling heavily and strangely in a big dark bulk. He put his arm around my mother. There, there, he said. I never saw them like that before. My father is English, my mother is German, I did not think about that though then. I thought, I am scared; this is all different, and dark. I stood in the doorway, too frightened to move.

Come in, Martin, my mother suddenly cried out to me. Come in to your brother. Come here with us. I came over, and there we were all kneeling down together.

Do you want your brother to die? she asked. No, I said. I was frightened at her, at the strange heavy silence on my father, at my brother even. Go and look at him, she told me.

I got up and looked at my brother's white face. It was like a face of ivory with pale lips. I looked hard. He was different too. What do I do? I thought. I am rough, not like that. My mother is looking at me terribly. Kiss him. I bent over and touched his face. His lips opened with a quiet breath, like a little flower bursting on my cheek.

The crisis came and passed. It came while we were in the room there. My mother could not wait. She went to the bed, trying to wake up my brother. Look, Sherrel, she whispered, we are going to get you the nice pearl-handled pocketknife to-morrow. You won't have to wait till Christmas. To-morrow. You just get well, now. Sherrel! Do you hear me, Sherrel?

Or, he can have mine, I thought.

But he didn't hear us. He didn't hear anybody. Then my mother went to sleep suddenly, it seemed, and drooped down by the bed and they put her in the other room on a couch.

I stood in the dark by a curtain when the doctors came in. Too bad, said Dr. Anderson. He leaned over my brother. Remarkable head, said one of the others. Isn't it! spoke up another one. Artist's head, said the one with the beard. Yes . . . Then the doctors walked out together into the room where my mother was and in a little while they all left the house.

A few days later there were the strange preparations for the funeral. I don't want to dwell on the funeral. That is not the point. But we rode in a carriage shut in by ourselves, still quarantined, the others following slowly behind us. I remember we passed the Watson's place. They were standing at the gate, the family, staring stupidly at the procession as the horse carriages jogged down the hilly street rolling off to the cemetery.

This is all strange, I thought, riding along past the Watson's house in a carriage like this. My mother and my father and myself. I was taken up with the thought and looked back out of the carriage window now and then at the carriages behind me. My mother pulled me back to sit up straight. My mother's face was drawn and tired and she was crying. My father's eyes had tears in them too. I could not cry. I thought, I ought to cry. How can I cry? I am not hurt any place where I can feel. I squeezed

into the corner of the carriage opposite them, pressing up against on
hand hard to make it hurt. It turned numb and pained but not in a cryin
way. You cry easy differently, I thought. Onions, for instance, make yo
cry. Would it have been a trick, I thought, or right and honest if I ha
put an onion in my handkerchief, no one seeing me, and then smelt i
now and then in the curtained shadows of the carriage? I would hav
cried then. I wanted to cry. But all I could think was, Sherrel was a quee
kid. Were we brothers sure enough? Am I anybody's brother? Why don'
I cry? . . .

You see, he would sit in a corner quiet and frailly beautiful. I wa
nine and active. It's the difference in their ages. Maybe so. There wer
the Elwell brothers, now. They were twins. They had a carpenter's shop
It was a peach of a shop, down in a cellar, and they worked together great
making book-ends and rabbit hutches and things like that.

I gave him that sickness. I knew that. That killed him. That is why
my brother is dead. But I am trying to remember, to clear things up.
am trying to remember if I thought that then. I remember I thought, It'
funny just he got it. Why not Leona Eads, Ed or Billy Simons? The
touched my hands. I wondered if I hadn't forced my sickness on my
brother out of hatred for him, out of my own peculiar older-brothe
hatred. Did I slap him, maybe strike him in the face with my peelin
hand? Perhaps I did. I wondered over this for many weeks now and then

I'm not even sure now. I might have. It's funny how mean, you see, a
person can be. I've thought of that. I've got a girl. I've talked things ove
with her, not everything, but generally you know. She doesn't like meanness either. I remember when I was about twelve, my sister was just coming along then. She was about two and I had to tend her occasionally.
didn't like it. Once my mother said to me, Do you want your little siste
to die too? Well, no, I said. She might even have said, Do you want t
kill your little sister too? Maybe this was it, because I asked myself tha
a lot later, trying to be better. I said, Do you want to kill your sister too?
No, I said.

I didn't, either. But I remembered what I'd said when she was born.
said, There's enough in this family already. But I didn't want to kill her.
Still I had killed my brother. I had killed Sherrel. Not only by giving him
sickness. But by meanness.

This is how I figure it now. I killed my brother by meanness. And it is too bad. I wouldn't do it now. I am not that way. I could have got him a job here in this other town where I am now after he got out of school. I'll be out of school here pretty soon. I'm eighteen next week. Then I'll go on a paper where I've got a stand-in. I'd have said, Now you keep on at school and read a lot of good things, good books you know, poetry and good things and learn how to write. You've got good stuff in you, I can tell. You're going to be an artist. So am I. We'll be two artists, brothers, maybe different, but we can help each other. You've got a poetic style, and I've got a stronger style. I see things more as they are. I'm a little tougher. I can digest more. But that's all right. When I get going, I'll help you. You've got fine things in you. I'll help you bring them out.

That's the kind of a person he would have been. He would have been an artist. There's nothing any bigger than that. Nothing finer. It's the best, in a holy way. It has to be in you first. It hides sometimes and doesn't get a chance to come out where people are.

I've talked that over with people, with that girl I spoke of. I want to be an artist. A writer. I can see back from where I am, though. I've been pretty mean, pretty contemptible. It's funny to look back like that and see yourself in old pictures and things. It's hard to think you had the same name, even.

And that's what I'm puzzling over now. There's nothing wrong with my name, actually. Mark. Mark Stowe. It was first Martin. It was even Martin Tilton Stowe. I didn't like it. All that, I mean. I cut it down to Mark Stowe. It made me feel surer, quicker, stronger.

But even that doesn't quite go. It doesn't all fit. I'm not all blunt, like that. Mark. Mark Stowe. I've got other things. I've written poems, even, and I wouldn't kiss a girl hard. I know how my brother was. He would have been like that too, only a lot more.

And, you know, about the name . . . My folks are getting along now. Sisters don't count, the way I mean, that is. I'm the only boy in the family. And I've been thinking, what if I should write a poem, a long, good one—here I am, alive and everything—and sign it not Mark Stowe but, well, Sherrel Stowe? Do you see what I mean? And then by and by there would be another poem, and after a while I would just go ahead and use it right along. Can you understand that? How I would be more him too, then—Sherrel?

WARREN BECK

Between Two Worlds

"Between Two Worlds," being fiction, must speak for itself conclusively within its artistic design. Yet beyond its agnosticism (neither bitter nor frivolous) it suggests broader questioning, whether men can live without illusions of accessible immutable absolutes, can cheerfully face relativity. Humanism, basic to democracy, proposed rational, responsible behavior; but naturalism claimed to make freedom easy. Humanism requires self-discipline and renunciation beyond most religious practice; naturalism's fiascoes admit new illusions of socioeconomic heavens. Humanism and democracy are "found difficult and not tried." Between Catholicism and communism, and jostled by everyman's chaotic pleasures or resentments, stand maturing, ethical individuals in melancholy isolation.

WARREN BECK

THE bench was of iron, wrought into extravagant curves and scrolls that emphasized its rigidity. Its coating of white paint had weathered to a gray almost like the tombstones. Of its own weight it had sunk its legs into the sod. He remarked that it would be hard, and folded his topcoat upon it for her to sit on. She settled herself, leaned back, and said she was very comfortable. He sat down beside her, on the bare iron.

"I suppose it had to be something like granite," he said, "to have lasted all these years, until I found my way back again."

She nodded companionably. They sat and looked out over the close rows of stone blocks, large and small, the narrow streets of that pine-shaded hillside city of the dead; they saw the broad fresh-ploughed fields below, the new green of the river willows, and further still the roofs of the town, daubed yellow by the slanting sun or streaked with shadow, and St. Andrew's steeple rising in their midst over all, confronting the sky with a glittering cross.

"How long has it been?" she said, at last.

"Since I was a senior in college," he answered, "and that's fourteen years. I haven't come back since my father's funeral. This bench was here then. It had been here two years then. My father had it put out just

after my mother died. He used to come and sit on Sunday afternoons—
in all but the very worst weather."

Fourteen and two—sixteen years. She laid her bare hand on the ornate
bench-arm and just could feel the touch of warmth taken from the spring
sunshine. She thought it was like fingering the slow pulsebeat of time
itself through these atoms of iron, sixteen times warmed and sixteen
times chilled in the systole and diastole of those years of weather. Like
a human heart this ironbound rhythm labored on toward its own release
through disintegration, but much more slowly. This bench would endure
centuries of alternate scorching and congealing, if sixteen years had left
no mark upon its stoutness. Years during which with more rapid pulses
they two had put their first youth behind, had moved unknown to each
other in their separate ways across the same small section of the earth's
surface, had slept and wakened, eaten and drunk, danced and mourned,
had loved otherwise and had forgotten, had worked ambitiously and with
success, and altogether had laid up a store of experience at the expense
of life itself, paid out by installments, until only last autumn, no longer
ago than this phlegmatic iron's last contraction under the encroaching
frost, they had found each other. She took his hand and held it between
hers, for its human softness and sustained warmth.

"This place is like a stage for the seasons, isn't it?" she said. " 'The
heat o' the sun, the furious winter's rages'—and April afternoons like
this."

He smiled at her, and told himself for the thousandth time that it
was no wonder he loved her. He said, "If a fellow were looking for a
hole in the hedge—to peep through into infinity, you know—this might
be the spot."

"I never realized before," she said, "how good it is to have cemeteries,
for those who come and sit in them. It sets something inside you by a
kind of standard time again."

"That's a slow old pendulum," he added. "Something more deliberate
than our private syncopations."

"It's soothing," she agreed.

"I wonder if it's really more meaningful too," he mused. "I wonder
if whatever it is that steps along in the seven-league boots of the seasons
is getting anywhere."

She stared out over the town.

"God knows about that," she said. "All I know is that it has its rhythm and we have ours and ours is somehow relative to it, if we stop to notice. Out here today life seems so brief and so sweet."

He nodded.

"You're right about this too," he said. "We wouldn't be thinking or talking this way if we hadn't lingered here."

He moved and bent to straighten the pot that held the Easter lily he had brought to his father's grave, and then rising and dusting his hands, he squinted to see that it was exactly in line with the one by his mother's headstone. Watching his filial intentness, she felt the sweet pang of a new intimacy with him. She was glad that when he came and sat again, he wanted to put his arm around her.

"Darling," he said, "I'm afraid it was selfish of me to lug you out here to Waynesville. Maybe we should have stayed in the city for the week end so you could have seen the fashion parade."

She smiled and shook her head.

"Or maybe," he said, "we should have driven out three hundred miles in some other direction, where the scenery is more high-powered and abounding."

"No," she said, "I like these dear scenes of your childhood; and I know you've brought me here—to your parents, Andy. It was sweet of you to want me to come, and I'm very happy."

He kissed her and pulled her close under his arm.

"You know," he said, "being in love this way, and contemplating the good estate of matrimony till death do us part, it makes me want to put my life together, in one piece. I suppose that's really why I brought you down here—I suppose I wanted to turn my past over to you."

"I know just what you mean," she said. "It must be a common feeling. Perhaps that's why some people are such insistent fools about confessing all the bygones."

"It is foolish," he said, "but in a way it's right too. You can't hold cards in this game without betting all your chips."

"That's what's wonderful about it," she murmured. "Flying the Pacific is nothing compared to it."

"I know it sounds trite," he said, "but my mother would have liked you."

"It is trite," she answered, "but I'm so glad it occurred to you. Isn't it nice how all the old sayings keep bobbing up and fitting in?"

"All right, then," he said, "so my dad would have liked you too."

They smiled into each other's eyes.

"I'm so sorry they aren't here now," she said, "for your sake."

His face took on a stricken look, and he nodded silently. She squeezed his hand and tried to be cheerful.

"And for my sake, Andy," she went on quickly. "They could tell me about the darker side of your youth and warn me what lapses to expect."

He smiled his appreciation before he went on in the soft tone of reminiscence.

"My mother would have asked you to call me Andrew," he said, "out of respect—for the saint I was named after."

She took off her hat and laid it beside her on the bench. With both hands twice she smoothed her black hair from its precise part, that middle line which Andrew said he loved for the symmetry it gave her head, and loved too for its even symbol of her fastidious mind. She turned her dark eyes to him in a serious gaze.

"I shall try to call you Andrew, all this week end while we are here," she said. "And now may I ask a question?"

He nodded.

"How have you stayed away for so long?" she said. "Why haven't you come back, ever, until now?"

He bent over, picked a young blade of grass, bit off a piece, and blew it from the tip of his tongue.

"I can't tell you," he said at last. "It's one of those things you just don't quite know about yourself. My staying away wasn't exactly neglect. I didn't forget. I not only had this lot cared for; I had a friend in town report on its condition, regularly. But I definitely decided, again and again, that I wouldn't come myself. I suppose . . . well, I've been afraid, perhaps."

"Is . . . that what you were afraid of?" she said, and pointed across the tombstones to the central junction of cemetery roads, where a stone pedestal supported a great cross, on which hung a more than man-sized Christ.

"I wonder," he said. "It's a tall tree. It casts a long shadow."

"I thought you had moved out of its range," she said. "I never saw

that shadow fall on you before. Not until just now, when you wondere
about something purposeful behind all this passing time."

He smiled at her and took her hand.

"That shadow isn't falling on me, darling," he said. "Or if it is, I'r
not myself. Not my present self. Maybe out here I am a bit ridden b
the ghost of what I was. Maybe that's what I've had an instinct for stayin,
away from."

She leaned over and kissed his cheek.

"I'm sorry I bothered you about it," she said. "Let's table it. Let's jus
sit and look at things."

And so they did, while the spring wind hummed in the pines and th
mourning doves that haunt those trees sobbed with quick inhalatio
and long-expiring lament. The increasingly yellow sunlight of late after
noon slid from one facet to another on the houses of the town. Andrev
pointed about at the topography of Waynesville. They could see the roo
of the parochial school he had attended, close under the church steeple
From that point he traced a line to a gable and a chimney, on the hous
where he and his parents had lived. She demanded nearer views, and s
they rose from the bench. Before they went, he knelt to straighten th
lilies once more, and while he did, she strolled away slowly to his car
feeling at every step the spell of that place, and wondering how differentl
he felt it.

They came first to the school. The building was of brick grown shabby
with large vacant windows, in a few of which were pasted irregular frieze
of paper daffodils and tulips.

"Authentic first grade," she said. "I'll stake my rep as a critic on that."

"Judging by dead reckoning rather than the canons of art, I'd sa
you're right," he remarked. "That should be the corner room where
first learned to look out through glass at the sky and wait for the clocl
to strike."

Inside the iron fence, all around the schoolyard, was a strip of grass, a
struggling growth. It was set off from the expanse of playground grave
by a low flat wooden railing. Andrew stepped up on this, teetered a mo
ment, and then ran along on it, balancing himself with outstretched arm
flapping more and more violently until he jumped off to one side.

"Hell," he said, returning, "I could do better than that when I was ten."

They sat down on the railing with their heels in the gravel. He scooped up a handful of pebbles and tossed them from him slowly, one by one. She scrutinized the whole scene closely.

"I don't much like this for the little Andrew," she remarked. "It must have been rather barren and gloomy."

"Oh, it wasn't too bad," he told her. "The lessons were a lot of abra-cadabra, and the nuns used to smack our knuckles with rulers, but we managed to improve each shining hour."

"Was little Andy a little devil?" she asked.

"What do you think?" he said.

"I wouldn't be surprised," she told him, and smiled.

Behind them, across the street, the heavy doors of St. Andrew's church squeaked open and thumped shut, again and again. Andrew looked back over his shoulder.

"Confession," he remarked. "They're going to confession today. To-morrow they'll make their Easter communions."

He turned, stared at the ground, and meditatively shook his head several times. He picked up another handful of pebbles and began tossing them across the schoolyard. Then he grinned and spoke again.

"You've heard the one about the old priest advising the young priest on hearing confessions? He said to say *Tsch, Tsch!* instead of *Whew!*"

"Don't strain yourself, Andrew," she whispered, "you're with friends."

Slowly he dropped the rest of the pebbles through the funnel of his hands. He gave her a cigarette and took one himself.

"You know, Pat," he began, reflectively, "a lot of people think it's just machinery, all that"—and he jerked his head toward the church behind him. "But it isn't—that is, not for those who believe in it. It's pretty important for them. It's like a circle all around—it's out beyond everything else, whichever way they look."

"Even from where I stand I can see something of what it must be like," she murmured. "Honestly, I can't help wondering how a person like you escapes, after he's been brought up in it."

He looked down at his cigarette and turned it in his fingers.

"Oh," he said, slowly, "it's just like anything else—you live and learn. The other customs of other men, you know, begin to make your own fixed beliefs look as provincial and temporary as theirs. Then it seems to dawn on you that these systems are erected on a few very arbitrary interpreta-tions. And as you wangle your way along, you realize that the angels and ministers of grace you had thought some of leaning back on really aren't there. It isn't as if somebody moved a chair from behind you; it's just that all at once you know it isn't there, and never was there, and that the whole place isn't furnished at all as you were led to believe. Then —if you're not too egotistical—you allow that this universe may have no plans for you beyond your possible threescore years and ten, and may have no help for you except what you're welcome to through your own sense. You don't exactly give up God necessarily, but this attempt to read his mind and to contract for his special favors begins to seem kind of presumptuous, just as the records of his direct manifestations have begun to seem—well, legendary, mythical."

"And then how do you feel?" she said. "I understand this point of view, of course; it's the one I've always had. But how do you feel when you've come over to it, all the way over from its complete opposite?"

He grinned at her.

"Let me see," he drawled, "how can I explain that to a born and bred heathen? Well, put it this way—it's as if at first you had thought you were at home with your parents, and then you realize it isn't home, but a boarding school, where you are promoted from one temporary footing to another, for reasons not entirely revealed, by a headmaster—no, that's too paternal—by an educator. I suppose educator's a cold enough word. After all, some educators choose white mice to work on."

She looked intently at his face.

"But then how do you feel about it?" she insisted.

He stared off at the school building.

"Oh," he said, with a barely perceptible sigh, "at first the sun seems to have gone under a cloud, and it gets kind of chilly, but you turn up your coat collar and tell yourself you're a big boy now, and you fellows have your traditions, and if this isn't home but just a school, at least you can keep going and needn't ever return to any of the rooms you've passed out of."

"Unless you want to," she said. "Like today."

"But then only as a visitor, like today," he added.

"Suppose he isn't even a kind of orphan schoolboy," she said. "Suppose he's just one of these white mice in an educational experiment."

"Oh, then he just tries to be a smart mouse," Andrew went on. "He tries to find the cheese and avoid the blind alleys and electric shocks. And he tries to find a lady-mouse for a friend."

"Yes," she said, "and then perhaps there are some new little white mice."

"That depends," he said. "You know that—you're in here in this maze with me. It depends on whether the mouse and his lady-friend think the whole experiment is fair to mice. It depends on the ratio of handicaps to cheese. Oh, I see what you're driving at, darling; you're wondering just how much everyday faith a man dispenses with when he loses his capital-F faith."

She rose and looked down at him, and took him fondly by the ear.

"Maybe I am wondering, darling," she said, "but I understand how that's a question you can't answer right off. And you don't need to, darling. So come along; I want to see the house where you were born, and the little window where the sun came peeping in at morn. What's the rest of it? Oh, yes. Were the trees then dark and high, and did you think their slender tops were close against the sky?"

"I don't remember, I don't remember," he responded. "But I suppose I did. And I'm surprised at your knowing that jingle."

She smirked at him.

"In *my* youth, darling," she said, "I was taught a lot of bad poetry."

He took her arm as they started to the car.

"And what," he asked, "would we teach the little new white mouse or mice, if any?"

"Oh," she answered, "I suppose we could whip up some sort of decalogue on the general subject of blind alleys and cheese."

They drove slowly down streets familiar to him. He drew up before a large frame house and shut off his motor.

"There it is," he announced. "And it needs paint, sure enough."

"Where was your room?" she asked, eagerly.

"You can't see it from here," he said. "It's around on the other side."

A small girl came skipping down the street, stopped and investigated them with a steady eye, and then turned and ran into the house. Andrew touched the starter and let the motor idle.

"That bay window is in the living room," he told her. "There's a fireplace there—if they haven't closed it up. That's where we used to sit at nights, reading. I do wish they'd paint it."

"It's still a very nice house," she said. "Don't worry, dear, they'
probably paint it when they put up that bronze tablet saying here yo
were born."

He laughed as he moved the gear-shift and started off.

"If that's meant the way I think it is," he said, "I wouldn't blame you
This pilgrimage has been plenty solemn. You deserve some relief, an
I'm going to hunt it up right now."

What he found was a new restaurant-bar of the most chromium-plate
kind, on the high banks of the river, three miles out from town. The
had cocktails and danced to the nickel-in-the-slot phonograph. The
after dinner they drank coffee on a balcony overlooking the moonlit rive
The scene revived his reminiscences. He pointed out Bell's Island, a na
row wooded strip in mid-channel, and told her what a perfect privat
resort for boys it had been, for fishing and swimming and camping-ou
because no adult would trouble to row over to that insignificant place
He told her how he used to go over there by himself sometimes, to savo
the rich sense of battling the wilderness single-handed, and once, for
whole afternoon, in the summer of his fourteenth year, to ponder th
solemn question of whether or not he had a vocation for the priesthood
She wanted to hear more about that, and could it mean he was a particu
larly pious child; and he said no, but just that his mother had got th
idea and made it the daily intention of her prayers, and now and the
asked him to keep his mind open to the thought, and to lift up his heart
that it might be more nearly fit for the Holy Ghost to enter in.

Patricia remembered the mother's picture, the gentle face with th
serene eyes, and thought she could imagine the quiet earnestness of tha
appeal heavenward and to the son's spirit. The years to come opene
before her; she wondered whether she would ever know any such ma
ternal devotion and hope.

"Andrew, I'm glad you told me," she said. "It helps me see things."

"My dear mother," he went on, "would rather have seen her son
priest standing at the altar than in any other position of honor amon
men."

"And what happened?" asked Patricia. "Did you ever agree to do wha
she wanted?"

"Oh, no," he said, "I shied off from it, by a kind of instinct, and sh
saw that, and gradually the matter was dropped. I think, though, sh

was still hoping and praying for my vocation when I went to college, and perhaps right up to the time of her death, two years later."

"She must have been terribly disappointed," said Patricia.

"Not the way you'd suppose," he said, in a low voice. "Not the way lots of women we know would be irritated or crushed or bitter if they didn't get what their hearts were set on. No, it must have been a disappointment, but she took it quietly. It was God's will, she thought, and that made it right to her. You know, she always warned me not to think of becoming a priest just to please her, but only if I myself wanted to, because I felt God wanted me."

They both stared out toward the uninhabited blackness of Bell's Island, a streak on the silver of the river. Patricia had a sense of pulling herself together to speak, carefully, as befits important things.

"That was rather wonderful of her, wasn't it?" she said. "You know, Andrew, I keep thinking what a large world she lived in, really."

"Did I ever tell you," he said, "that every night before she went to bed she'd go out, if the weather were clear, and look at the stars?"

"Somehow at the moment it makes me feel like a child," said Patricia.

He took her hand and kissed it.

"It's sweet to have you understand so well," he said. "I've left it behind, but it's still part of me, I suppose—the way all memories are. You've never believed any of it, I know, but you understand better than some who think they believe, or think they once believed."

"I don't know that you could call it understanding," she said. "But it is respect. I don't mean the kind of respect you have for a good opponent, for I'm nobody's opponent in this. I suppose it's like the respect you'd feel for a strange nation who spoke a language you didn't know and lived by an economy different from yours. You couldn't stop among them and still be yourself, but you could hail them in passing. You could salute them for their purpose and their dignity."

They smoked another cigarette in silence, holding hands. She was thinking that it seemed the most mysterious moment in her experience, and that she had never had a deeper glimpse into lives of others. He suddenly declared that she had had enough of his past life and times for one installment, and he would take her to a movie.

Next morning by their agreement she telephoned him as soon as she wakened, and met him half an hour later in the hotel lobby. They noticed

that it was the earliest they had ever been together, and agreed they like
it very much. He asked what she was going to give him for Easter break
fast, and when she ordered strawberries, broiled ham, hot biscuits, an
coffee, he said he admired her housekeeping. Over the last bites he tol
her the day was entirely hers. If they waited until afternoon to start, the
could still get back to the city comfortably by bedtime; or they coul
start now and poke about on the way home, or even take the longer loo
back through the hill country. Suddenly she looked earnestly at him.

"Why don't you take me to church?" she suggested. "I mean here, t
St. Andrew's, where you used to go. I've never been to church. Perhap
this is the week end for it."

He stared at her in surprise.

"Well!" he drawled. "I haven't been going myself any more, yo
know."

"Yes, I know that," she said.

"Not for years," he said.

Feeling all at once that she had been tactless out of sheer ignoranc
she apologized.

"I'm sorry, Andy. If you'd rather not. . . ."

"I wouldn't mind," he put in quickly. "Not at all. That is, if you war
to see what it's like."

She looked at him and nodded, but still she studied his face in silenc
trying to determine his feeling. He laughed at her and patted her chee

"Come along, then, darling, let's go," he said. "What it's like mean
high mass."

They started in time to walk the seven blocks to St. Andrew's. Th
sunshine was warm and bright. All along the street were pleasant peopl
in new clothes. Andy said again that he liked her new hat. He admitte
he liked her too, and liked to take her places. And they decided h
wouldn't try to tell her anything about high mass, but she'd just look an
listen, and try to use her college Latin for whatever she could hear. The
also decided to sit as far back as possible.

Coming in out of brightness, she was dazzled. Her first impression wa
of the sweet smell of incense. Then she saw dimly that the church wa
full of people. Andy led her along and found seats for them in the nex
to-last row, on the side aisle. A fat man sat there, and Andrew went i

first, to protect her from crowding and to give her the end of the bench, with its better view. They sat down.

Discreetly she looked around. She was bemused by the many strange details. Small flames, red and yellow, singly and in designs and patches, flickered at the other end of the interior. Farthest of all, central and commanding, the altar stood on its tier of red-carpeted steps, thrusting its many spires high in an eruption of intricate design, with niches peopled by carved figures richly colored. There were other figures elsewhere about the church, and paintings on all the walls. In the crowded pews most of the people were on their knees. Rows of pillars stood over this irregular surface of human beings and branched into the lofty vaulted ceiling. Shafts of sunlight thrust through clerestory windows, showing in the upper air a thin haze of drifting smoke.

The organ was playing now. A little boy in long vestments came out before the altar with a flaming taper on a pole, bent one knee, and then began to light rows of candles there. Patricia watched him, anxious with him when a wick was slow to catch. She wondered if little Andrew ever had to do that. She turned her head and glanced at Andy. His face was as of one in a dream. She could not look away. Then she noticed that his eyes moved, rested briefly upon a point on the opposite wall, moved again, rested again. Her eyes followed, and she saw the carved figures, group after group, in each of them Christ and his cross. Via Dolorosa, she remembered. These then were "the stations of the cross"?

Now men and boys in vestments had entered before the altar and were beginning intricate ceremonies. She saw the priest's hand making the repeated gesture of sprinkling, over the altar, and over those around him. Above the organ's rich accompaniment she made out some intoned words . . . *Vidi aquam . . . de templo* . . . I saw water . . . from the temple. The priest came down the middle aisle of the church, and she saw that he was flinging drops of water over the congregation. As these drops fell upon them, the people touched forehead and breast, in the sign of the cross. The choir was singing now . . . *et omnes ad quos pervenit aqua ista salvi facti sunt* . . . all to whom that water came were saved . . . *et dicent alleluia, alleluia* . . . and they shall say *alleluia, alleluia.*

The clear voices of boys soared through the vaulted space. She wondered whether little Andrew had sung Latin from that loft. She looked at Andy again and saw him leaning slightly forward in his seat, with his hands clenched between his legs, and with his eyes fixed upon the priest and his attendants, now kneeling before the altar. The priest stood, his arms stretched wide, and in a resonant voice that filled the church he intoned *Oremus,* and ascended the steps before the altar.

Incense had been kindled, and as its container was swung back and forth on a long chain, the sweet-smelling smoke floated out over the congregation. She turned to Andy again, but he did not look at her; his brooding face was set as in a trance. She heard the choir chanting . . . *Resurrexi et adhuc tecum sum* . . . I have risen and I am with thee still . . . *posuisti super me manum tuam* . . . thou hast placed thy hand over me . . . *Domine, probasti me et cognovisti me* . . . Lord, thou hast tested me and known me . . . *tu cognovisti sessionem meam et resurrectionem meam* . . . thou hast known my sitting down and my arising.

At the altar the mysterious observances were proceeding with a rapidity and mechanical precision that Patricia recognized as of the highest ceremonial dignity. She sensed a growing intensity in this throng of people around her. It was like the mood of an audience at a play, she thought, no, it was deeper, and in a more definite, sustained crescendo. *Kyrie eleison* . . . Lord, have mercy, sang the choir softly . . . *Christe eleison.* Her imagination fumbled along a strange new way. Then she was aware that Andrew was moving forward. Slowly he went upon his knees, like all the others. She did not turn toward him, but she could see him touch forehead and breast, as the others had done, and then fold his hands and bow his head. Then she looked and saw that tears were running down his cheek.

Her heart tightened and stumbled. She felt she had blundered to the edge of an abyss, over which only a winged creature could go, and she knew herself to be without wings. And Andy, what had happened to him? What had she done to Andy? Her mind calmly took control, as always. She decided at once there was but one course for her. From her purse she took an old envelope and a pencil; she wrote, "Darling, I'll be waiting at the hotel." She reached and tucked the message loosely inside his coat. As she hurried out of the church alone, she heard behind her the priest's full-voiced intonation to the people . . . *Dominus vobiscum* . . . The Lord be with you.

In the sunlight she blinked and went slowly, cautiously down the wide stone steps. The street was empty now; all the smiling people were in the

shadowy church, all kneeling, and the faces of some were now more lit
with reverence than they had been with smiles. She knew herself to be
quite apart from them, and alone. She felt desperately that Andy had
gone a long way from her, without her having time to say good-by,
without her knowing how to get any word to him again, ever. Her heels
clicked as she nervously quickened her step, the sparrows bounced and
chattered in the gutter, and these slight sounds and motions in the vacant
street increased her desolation. How long would it last, that high mass,
she wondered, and when would he come? And then what would she and
Andrew have to say to each other?

She feared what she foresaw—a black crowded mood of emotional
blockade, an awful shared paralysis of intimacy. Yet she felt she could
not bear her solitude another moment. Now she heard some one running
up behind her. It was Andy. He seized her arm.

"Darling," he said gravely, "you're wrong."

They stopped in the middle of the sidewalk and stood holding each
other's hands between them, looking steadily at each other.

"The hotel is back the other way," he said, trying to smile.

"Then I was walking away from everything," she said. "Wasn't I?"

He shook his head slowly.

"Not from me," he said. "You're just a lone woman on foot, and you
can't get away from me, sweetheart."

She bit her lip and looked down at the sidewalk, and at the glistening
tips of Andy's shoes, with the dulled spots that had rubbed when he knelt.

"I didn't mean to have you leave and follow me," she whispered. "I
don't want to take you away from anything, Andrew, just to follow a
girl who—doesn't know her directions."

"Listen," he said gravely. "You can understand this, I know. You
needn't be disturbed. You're not taking me away from anything, and
nothing is taking me away from you. When you left, I was as alone in
there as you were out here. Look, I can't put it into words, but it was as
if all my life had come together there in one moment, and then when
you went away, it all fell apart again."

"And now?" she said, raising her eyes almost wonderingly.

"You've always been such a smart woman," he chided gently. "Need
you ask?"

"No," she answered, and held his hands close up to her breast. "No, darling. But don't call me a smart woman. I may know what I think, but this week end my stock of ideas seems so insignificant. Except what I think of you, Andy."

"Me too, sweetheart," he said.

He linked his arm in hers and turned her toward the church. They walked close to each other, slowly and in silence. Faintly came a swelling roll from St. Andrew's organ. They came to the broad steps of the church. They passed the great middle doors, and went on.

"Dearest," she said, "I'm afraid I shall always wonder whether I . . . prevented . . ."

"No," he said. "I'm with you, remember. And as for wondering—we shall always wonder, both of us, about everything—except each other."

Suddenly the long-forbidden tears brimmed in her eyes; and she was happy, knowing them to be a bond with Andrew's. They walked on steadily, arm in arm, silent, looking ahead up the vacant street, where in the almost noontime light the shadows paused shrunken before the slow beginning of their augmentation with the day's decline.

ANTON CHEKHOV

The Black Monk

"The Black Monk" was one of the favorite stories of Edward J. O'Brien, the short story anthologist. It has been interpreted as a thesis for and against delusions of grandeur, but Chekhov himself specifically wrote once to his friend Souvorin: "It by no means follows that whenever a writer describes a character who is mentally deranged that he also is deranged. I wrote 'The Black Monk' without any personal melancholy in a mood of cool reflection. I simply wished to portray megalomania. The monk floating over the country was a dream and when I woke I told my brother Misha about it."

Mr. O'Brien has pointed out that in Chekhov's stories each character is a soul in isolation, living in a self-created world. The core of Chekhov's philosophy of life was expressed by himself: "Everything in nature has a meaning, and everything is forgiven, and it would be strange not to forgive."

I

ANDREY VASILYEVICH KOVRIN, *Magister,* had worn himself out, and unsettled his nerves. He made no effort to undergo regular treatment; but only incidentally, over a bottle of wine, spoke to his friend the doctor; and his friend the doctor advised him to spend all the spring and summer in the country. And in the nick of time came a long letter from Tanya Pesotzky, asking him to come and stay with her father at Borisovka. He decided to go.

But first (it was in April) he travelled to his own estate, to his native Kovrinka, and spent three weeks in solitude; and only when the fine weather came drove across the country to his former guardian and second parent, Pesotzky, the celebrated Russian horticulturist. From Kovrinka to Boriskova, the home of the Pesotzkys, was a distance of some seventy versts, and in the easy, springed calêche the drive along the roads, soft in springtime, promised real enjoyment.

The house at Borisovka was large, faced with a colonnade, and adorned with figures of lions with the plaster falling off. At the door stood a servant in livery. The old park, gloomy and severe, laid out in English fashion, stretched for nearly a verst from the house down to the river, and ended there in a steep clay bank covered with pines whose bare roots resembled shaggy paws. Below sparkled a deserted stream; overhead the snipe circled about with melancholy cries—all, in short, seemed to invite a visitor to sit down and write a ballad. But the gardens and orchards, which together with the seed-plots occupied some eighty acres, inspired very different feelings. Even in the worst of weather they were bright and joy-inspiring. Such wonderful roses, lilies, camellias, such tulips, such a host of flowering plants of every possible kind and colour, from staring white to sooty black,—such a wealth of blossoms Kovrin had never seen before. The spring was only beginning, and the greatest rareties were hidden under glass; but already enough bloomed in the alleys and beds to make up an empire of delicate shades. And most charming of all was it in the early hours of morning, when dewdrops glistened on every petal and leaf.

In childhood the decorative part of the garden, called contemptuously by Pesotzky "the rubbish," had produced on Kovrin a fabulous impression. What miracles of art, what studied monstrosities, what mockeries of nature! Espaliers of fruit trees, a pear tree shaped like a pyramidal poplar, globular oaks and lindens, apple-tree houses, arches, monograms, candelabra—even the date 1862 in plum trees, to commemorate the year in which Pesotzky first engaged in the art of gardening. There were stately, symmetrical trees, with trunks erect as those of palms, which after examination proved to be gooseberry or currant trees. But what most of all enlivened the garden and gave it its joyous tone was the constant movement of Pesotzky's gardeners. From early morning to late at night, by the trees, by the bushes, in the alleys, and on the beds swarmed men as busy as ants, with barrows, spades, and watering-pots.

Kovrin arrived at Borisovka at nine o'clock. He found Tanya and her father in great alarm. The clear starlight night foretold frost, and the head gardener, Ivan Karlych, had gone to town, so that there was no one who could be relied upon. At supper they spoke only of the impending frost; and it was decided that Tanya should not go to bed at all, but should inspect the gardens at one o'clock and see if all were in order, while Yegor Semionovich should rise at three o'clock, or even earlier.

Kovrin sat with Tanya all the evening, and after midnight accompanied her to the garden. The air already smelt strongly of burning. In the great

orchard, called "the commercial," which every year brought Yegor Semionovich thousands of rubles profit, there already crept along the ground
the thick, black, sour smoke which was to clothe the young leaves and
save the plants. The trees were marshalled like chessmen in straight rows
—like ranks of soldiers; and this pedantic regularity, together with the
uniformity of height, made the garden seem monotonous and even tiresome. Kovrin and Tanya walked up and down the alleys, and watched
the fires of dung, straw, and litter; but seldom met the workmen, who
wandered in the smoke like shadows. Only the cherry and plum trees and
a few apple trees were in blossom, but the whole garden was shrouded
in smoke, and it was only when they reached the seed-plots that Kovrin
was able to breathe.

"I remember when I was a child sneezing from the smoke," he said,
shrugging his shoulders, "but to this day I cannot understand how smoke
saves plants from the frost."

"Smoke is a good substitute when there are no clouds," answered
Tanya.

"But what do you want the clouds for?"

"In dull and cloudy weather we have no morning frosts."

"Is that so?" said Kovrin.

He laughed and took Tanya by the hand. Her broad, very serious,
chilled face; her thick, black eyebrows; the stiff collar on her jacket which
prevented her from moving her head freely; her dress tucked up out of
the dew; and her whole figure, erect and slight, pleased him.

"Heavens! how she has grown!" he said to himself. "When I was here
last time, five years ago, you were quite a child. You were thin, long-
legged, and untidy, and wore a short dress, and I used to tease you. What
a change in five years!"

"Yes, five years!" sighed Tanya. "A lot of things have happened since
then. Tell me, Andrei, honestly," she said, looking merrily into his face,
"do you feel that you have got out of touch with us? But why do I ask?
You are a man, you live your own interesting life, you . . . Some es-
trangement is natural. But whether that is so or not, Andriusha, I want
you now to look on us as your own. We have a right to that."

"I do, already, Tanya."

"Your word of honour?"

"My word of honour."

"You were surprised that we had so many of your photographs. But surely you know how my father adores you, worships you. You are a scholar, and not an ordinary man; you have built up a brilliant career, and he is firmly convinced that you turned out a success because he educated you. I do not interfere with his delusion. Let him believe it!"

Already dawn. The sky paled, and the foliage and clouds of smoke began to show themselves more clearly. The nightingale sang, and from the fields came the cry of quails.

"It is time for bed!" said Tanya. "It is cold too." She took Kovrin by the hand. "Thanks, Andriusha, for coming. We are cursed with most uninteresting acquaintances, and not many even of them. With us it is always garden, garden, garden, and nothing else. Trunks, timbers," she laughed, "pippins, rennets, budding, pruning, grafting. . . . All our life goes into the garden, we never even dream of anything but apples and pears. Of course this is all very good and useful, but sometimes I cannot help wishing for change. I remember when you used to come and pay us visits, and when you came home for the holidays, how the whole house grew fresher and brighter, as if someone had taken the covers off the furniture. I was then a very little girl, but I understood . . ."

Tanya spoke for a time, and spoke with feeling. Then suddenly it came into Kovrin's head that during the summer he might become attached to this little, weak, talkative being, that he might get carried away, fall in love—in their position what was more probable and natural? The thought pleased him, amused him, and as he bent down to the kind, troubled face, he hummed to himself Pushkin's couplet:

> *"Oniegin, I will not conceal*
> *That I love Tatyana madly."*

By the time they reached the house Yegor Semionovich had risen. Kovrin felt no desire to sleep; he entered into conversation with the old man, and returned with him to the garden. Yegor Semionovich was tall, broad-shouldered, and fat. He suffered from shortness of breath, yet walked so quickly that it was difficult to keep up with him. His expression was always troubled and hurried, and he seemed to be thinking that if he were a single second late everything would be destroyed.

"There, brother, is a mystery for you!" he began, stopping to recover breath. "On the surface of the ground, as you see, there is frost, but raise

the thermometer a couple of yards on your stick, and it is quite warm. . . .
Why is that?"

"I confess I don't know," said Kovrin, laughing.

"No! . . . You can't know everything. . . . The biggest brain cannot comprehend everything. You are still engaged with your philosophy?"

"Yes . . . I am studying psychology, and philosophy generally."

"And it doesn't bore you?"

"On the contrary, I couldn't live without it."

"Well, God grant . . ." began Yegor Semionovich, smoothing his big whiskers thoughtfully. "Well, God grant . . . I am very glad for your sake, brother, very glad. . . ."

Suddenly he began to listen, and making a terrible face, ran off the path and soon vanished among the trees in a cloud of smoke.

"Who tethered this horse to the tree?" rang out a despairing voice. "Which of you thieves and murderers dared to tether this horse to the apple tree? My God, my God! Ruined, ruined, spoiled, destroyed! The garden is ruined, the garden is destroyed! My God!"

When he returned to Kovrin his face bore an expression of injury and impotence.

"What on earth can you do with these accursed people?" he asked in a whining voice, wringing his hands. "Stepka brought a manure cart here last night and tethered the horse to an apple tree . . . tied the reins, the idiot, so tight, that the bark is rubbed off in three places. What can you do with men like this? I speak to him and he blinks his eyes and looks stupid. He ought to be hanged!"

When at last he calmed down, he embraced Kovrin and kissed him on the cheek.

"Well, God grant . . . God grant! . . ." he stammered. "I am very, very glad that you have come. I cannot say how glad. Thanks!"

Then, with the same anxious face, and walking with the same quick step, he went round the whole garden, showing his former ward the orangery, the hothouses, the sheds, and two beehives which he described as the miracle of the century.

As they walked about, the sun rose, lighting up the garden. It grew hot. When he thought of the long, bright day before him, Kovrin remembered that it was but the beginning of May, and that he had before him a whole summer of long, bright, and happy days; and suddenly through him pulsed the joyous, youthful feeling which he had felt when as a child he played in this same garden. And in turn, he embraced the old man and kissed him tenderly. Touched by remembrances, the pair went into the house and drank tea out of the old china cups, with cream and rich biscuits; and these trifles again reminded Kovrin of his childhood and youth. The splendid present and the awakening memories of the past mingled, and a feeling of intense happiness filled his heart.

He waited until Tanya awoke, and having drunk coffee with her, walked through the garden, and then went to his room and began to work. He read attentively, making notes; and only lifted his eyes from his books when he felt that he must look out of the window or at the fresh roses, still wet with dew, which stood in vases on his table. It seemed to him that every little vein in his body trembled and pulsated with joy.

II

But in the country Kovrin continued to live the same nervous and untranquil life as he had lived in town. He read much, wrote much, studied Italian; and when he went for walks, thought all the time of returning to work. He slept so little that he astonished the household; if by chance he slept in the daytime for half an hour, he could not sleep all the following night. Yet after these sleepless nights he felt active and gay.

He talked much, drank wine, and smoked expensive cigars. Often, nearly every day, young girls from the neighbouring country-houses drove over to Borisovka, played the piano with Tanya, and sang. Sometimes the visitor was a young man, also a neighbour, who played the violin well. Kovrin listened eagerly to their music and singing, but was exhausted by it, so exhausted sometimes that his eyes closed involuntarily, and his head drooped on his shoulder.

One evening after tea he sat upon the balcony, reading. In the drawing-room Tanya—a soprano, one of her friends—a contralto, and the young violinist studied the well-known serenade of Braga. Kovrin listened to the words, but though they were Russian, could not understand their meaning. At last, laying down his book and listening attentively, he understood. A girl with a disordered imagination heard by night in a garden some mysterious sounds, sounds so beautiful and strange that she was forced to recognise their harmony and holiness, which to us mortals are incomprehensible, and therefore flew back to heaven. Kovrin's eyelids drooped. He rose, and in exhaustion walked up and down the drawing-room, and then up and down the hall. When the music ceased, he took Tanya by the hand and went out with her to the balcony.

"All day—since early morning," he began, "my head has been taken up with a strange legend. I cannot remember whether I read it, or where I heard it, but the legend is very remarkable and not very coherent. I may begin by saying that it is not very clear. A thousand years ago a monk, robed in black, wandered in the wilderness—somewhere in Syria or Arabia. . . . Some miles away the fishermen saw another black monk moving slowly over the surface of the lake. The second monk was a mirage. Now put out of your mind all the laws of optics, which legend, of course, does not recognise, and listen. From the first mirage was produced another mirage, from the second, a third, so that the image of the Black Monk is eternally reflected from one stratum of the atmosphere to another. At one time it was seen in Africa, then in Spain, then in India, then in the Far North. At last it issued from the limits of the earth's atmosphere, but never came across conditions which would cause it to disappear. Maybe it is seen to-day in Mars or in the constellation of the Southern Cross. Now the whole point, the very essence of the legend, lies in the prediction that exactly a thousand years after the monk went into the wilderness, the mirage will again be cast into the atmosphere of the earth and show itself to the world of men. This term of a thousand years, it appears, is now expiring. . . . According to the legend we must expect the Black Monk to-day or to-morrow."

"It is a strange story," said Tanya, whom the legend did not please.

"But the most astonishing thing," laughed Kovrin, "is that I cannot remember how this legend came into my head. Did I read it? Did I hear it? Or can it be that I dreamed of the Black Monk? I cannot remember. But the legend interests me. All day long I thought of nothing else."

Releasing Tanya, who returned to her visitors, he went out of the house, and walked lost in thought beside the flower-beds. Already the sun was setting. The freshly watered flowers exhaled a damp, irritating smell. In the house the music had again begun, and from the distance the violin produced the effect of a human voice. Straining his memory in an attempt to recall where he had heard the legend, Kovrin walked slowly across the park, and then, not noticing where he went, to the river-bank.

By the path which ran down among the uncovered roots to the water's edge Kovrin descended, frightening the snipe, and disturbing two ducks. On the dark pine trees glowed the rays of the setting sun, but on the surface of the river darkness had already fallen. Kovrin crossed the stream. Before him now lay a broad field covered with young rye. Neither human dwelling nor human soul was visible in the distance; and it seemed that the path must lead to the unexplored, enigmatical region in the west where the sun had already set—where still, vast and majestic, flamed the afterglow.

"How open it is—how peaceful and free," thought Kovrin, walking along the path. "It seems as if all the world is looking at me from a hiding-place and waiting for me to comprehend it."

A wave passed over the rye, and the light evening breeze blew softly on his uncovered head. Yet a minute more and the breeze blew again, this time more strongly, the rye rustled, and from behind came the dull mur-mur of the pines. Kovrin stopped in amazement. On the horizon, like a cyclone or waterspout, a great, black pillar rose up from earth to heaven. Its outlines were undefined; but from the first it might be seen that it was not standing still, but moving with inconceivable speed towards Kovrin; and the nearer it came the smaller and smaller it grew. Involun-tarily Kovrin rushed aside and made a path for it. A monk in black cloth-ing, with grey hair and black eyebrows, crossing his hands upon his chest, was borne past. His bare feet were above the ground. Having swept some twenty yards past Kovrin, he looked at him, nodded his head, and smiled kindly and at the same time slyly. His face was pale and thin. When he had passed by Kovrin he again began to grow, flew across the river, struck inaudibly against the clay bank and pine trees, and, passing through them, vanished like smoke.

"You see," stammered Kovrin, "after all, the legend was true!"

Making no attempt to explain this strange phenomenon; satisfied with the fact that he had so closely and so plainly seen not only the black cloth-ing but even the face and eyes of the monk; agitated agreeably, he re-turned home.

In the park and in the garden visitors were walking quietly; in the house the music continued. So he alone had seen the Black Monk. He felt a strong desire to tell what he had seen to Tanya and Yegor Semiono-vich, but feared that they would regard it as an hallucination, and decided to keep his counsel. He laughed loudly, sang, danced a mazurka, and felt in the best of spirits; and the guests and Tanya noticed upon his face a peculiar expression of ecstasy and inspiration, and found him very inter-esting.

III

When supper was over and the visitors had gone, he went to his own room, and lay on the sofa. He wished to think of the monk. But in a few minutes Tanya entered.

"There, Andriusha, you can read father's articles . . ." she said. "They are splendid articles. He writes very well."

"Magnificent!" said Yegor Semionovich, coming in after her, with a forced smile. "Don't listen to her, please! . . . Or read them only if you want to go to sleep—they are a splendid soporific."

"In my opinion they are magnificent," said Tanya, deeply convinced. "Read them, Andriusha, and persuade father to write more often. He could write a whole treatise on gardening."

Yegor Semionovich laughed, blushed, and stammered out the conven-tional phrases used by abashed authors. At last he gave in.

"If you must read them, read first these papers of Gauché's, and the Russian articles," he stammered, picking out the papers with trembling hands. "Otherwise you won't understand them. Before you read my re-plies you must know what I am replying to. But it won't interest you . . . stupid. And it's time for bed."

Tanya went out. Yegor Semionovich sat on the end of the sofa and sighed loudly.

"Akh, brother mine . . ." he began after a long silence. "So you see, my dear *Magister,* I write articles, and exhibit at shows, and get medals sometimes. . . . Pesotzky, they say, has apples as big as your head. . . . Pesotzky has made a fortune out of his gardens. . . . In one word:

" *'Rich and glorious is Kochubey.'* "

"But I should like to ask you what is going to be the end of all this? The gardens—there is no question of that—are splendid, they are models. . . . Not gardens at all, in short, but a whole institution of high political importance, and a step towards a new era in Russian agriculture and Russian industry. . . . But for what purpose? What ultimate object?"

"That question is easily answered."

"I do not mean in that sense. What I want to know is what will happen with the garden when I die? As things are, it would not last without me a single month. The secret does not lie in the fact that the garden is big and the workers many, but in the fact that I love the work—you understand? I love it, perhaps, more than I love myself. Just look at me! I work from morning to night. I do everything with my own hands. All grafting, all pruning, all planting—everything is done by me. When I am helped I feel jealous, and get irritated to the point of rudeness. The whole secret is in love, in a sharp master's eye, in a master's hands, and in the feeling when I drive over to a friend and sit down for half an hour, that I have left my heart behind me and am not myself—all the time I am in dread that something has happened to the garden. Now suppose I die to-morrow, who will replace all this? Who will do the work? The head gardeners? The workmen? Why the whole burden of my present worries is that my greatest enemy is not the hare or the beetle or the frost, but the hands of the stranger."

"But Tanya?" said Kovrin, laughing. "Surely she is not more dangerous than a hare? . . . She loves and understands the work."

"Yes, Tanya loves it and understands it. If after my death the garden should fall to her as mistress, then I could wish for nothing better. But suppose—which God forbid—she should marry!" Yegor Semionovich whispered and looked at Kovrin with frightened eyes. "That's the whole crux. She might marry, there would be children, and there would be no time to attend to the garden. That is bad enough. But what I fear most of all is that she may marry some spendthrift who is always in want of money, who will lease the garden to tradesmen, and the whole thing will go to the devil in the first year. In a business like this a woman is the scourge of God."

Yegor Semionovich sighed and was silent for a few minutes.

"Perhaps you may call it egoism. But I do not want Tanya to marry. I am afraid! You've seen that fop who comes along with a fiddle and makes a noise. I know Tanya would never marry him, yet I cannot bear the sight of him. . . . In short, brother, I am a character . . . and I know it."

Yegor Semionovich rose and walked excitedly up and down the room. It was plain that he had something very serious to say, but could not bring himself to the point.

"I love you too sincerely not to talk to you frankly," he said, thrusting his hands into his pockets. "In all delicate questions I say what I think, and dislike mystification. I tell you plainly, therefore, that you are the only man whom I should not be afraid of Tanya marrying. You are a clever man, you have a heart, and you would not see my life's work ruined. And what is more, I love you as my own son . . . and am proud of you. So if you and Tanya were to end . . . in a sort of romance . . . I should be very glad and very happy. I tell you this straight to your face, without shame, as becomes an honest man."

Kovrin smiled. Yegor Semionovich opened the door, and was leaving the room, but stopped suddenly on the threshold.

"And if you and Tanya had a son, I could make a horticulturist out of him," he added. "But that is an idle fancy. Good night!"

Left alone, Kovrin settled himself comfortably, and took up his host's articles. The first was entitled "Intermediate Culture," the second "A Few Words in Reply to the Remarks of Mr. Z. about the Treatment of the Soil of a New Garden," the third "More about Grafting." The others were similar in scope. But all breathed restlessness and sickly irritation. Even a paper with the peaceful title of "Russian Apple Trees" exhaled irritability. Yegor Semionovich began with the words "*Audi alteram partem,*" and ended it with "*Sapienti sat*"; and between these learned quotations flowed a whole torrent of acid words directed against "the learned ignorance of our patent horticulturists who observe nature from their academic chairs," and against M. Gauché, "whose fame is founded on the admiration of the profane and *dilletanti.*" And finally Kovrin came across an uncalled-for and quite insincere expression of regret that it is no longer legal to flog peasants who are caught stealing fruit and injuring trees.

"His is good work, wholesome and fascinating," thought Kovrin, "yet in these pamphlets we have nothing but bad temper and war to the knife. I suppose it is the same everywhere; in all careers men of ideas are nervous, and victims of this kind of exalted sensitiveness. I suppose it must be so."

He thought of Tanya, so delighted with her father's articles, and then of Yegor Semionovich. Tanya, small, pale, and slight, with her collar-bone showing, with her wildly-opened, her dark and clever eyes, which it seemed were always searching for something. And Yegor Semionovich with his little, hurried steps. He thought again of Tanya, fond of talking, fond of argument, and always accompanying even the most insignificant phrases with mimicry and gesticulation. Nervous—she must be nervous in the highest degree.

Again Kovrin began to read, but he understood nothing, and threw down his books. The agreeable emotion with which he had danced the mazurka and listened to the music still held possession of him, and aroused a multitude of thoughts. It flashed upon him that if this strange, unnatural monk had been seen by him alone, he must be ill, ill to the point of suffering from hallucinations. The thought frightened him, but not for long.

He sat on the sofa, and held his head in his hands, curbing the inexplicable joy which filled his whole being; and then walked up and down the room for a minute, and returned to his work. But the thoughts which he read in books no longer satisfied him. He longed for something vast, infinite, astonishing. Toward morning he undressed and went unwillingly to bed; he felt that he had better rest. When at last he heard Yegor Semionovich going to his work in the garden, he rang, and ordered the servant to bring him some wine. He drank several glasses; his consciousness became dim, and he slept.

IV

Yegor Semionovich and Tanya often quarrelled and said disagreeable things to one another. This morning they had both been irritated, and Tanya burst out crying and went to her room, coming down neither to dinner nor to tea. At first Yegor Semionovich marched about, solemn and dignified, as if wishing to give everyone to understand that for him justice and order were the supreme interests in life. But he was unable to keep this up for long; his spirits fell, and he wandered about the park and sighed, "Akh, my God!" At dinner he ate nothing, and at last, tortured by his conscience, he knocked softly at the closed door, and called timidly:

"Tanya! Tanya!"

Through the door came a weak voice, tearful but determined:

"Leave me alone! . . . I implore you."

The misery of father and daughter reacted on the whole household, even on the labourers in the garden. Kovrin, as usual, was immersed in his own interesting work, but at last even he felt tired and uncomfortable. He determined to interfere, and disperse the cloud before evening. He knocked at Tanya's door, and was admitted.

"Come, come! What a shame!" he began jokingly; and then looked with surprise at her tear-stained and afflicted face covered with red spots. "Is it so serious, then? Well, well!"

"But if you knew how he tortured me!" she said, and a flood of tears gushed out of her big eyes. "He tormented me!" she continued, wringing her hands. "I never said a word to him. . . . I only said there was no need to keep unnecessary labourers, if . . . if we can get day workmen. . . . You know the men have done nothing for the whole week. I . . . I only said this, and he roared at me, and said a lot of things . . . most offensive . . . deeply insulting. And all for nothing."

"Never mind!" said Kovrin, straightening her hair. "You have had your scoldings and your cryings, and that is surely enough. You can't keep this up for ever . . . it is not right . . . all the more since you know he loves you infinitely."

"He has ruined my whole life," sobbed Tanya. "I never hear anything but insults and affronts. He regards me as superfluous in his own house. Let him! He will have cause! I shall leave here to-morrow, and study for a position as telegraphist. . . . Let him!"

"Come, come. Stop crying, Tanya. It does you no good. . . . You are both irritable and impulsive, and both in the wrong. Come, and I will make peace!"

Kovrin spoke gently and persuasively. But Tanya continued to cry, twitching her shoulders and wringing her hands as if she had been overtaken by a real misfortune. Kovrin felt all the sorrier owing to the smallness of the cause of her sorrow. What a trifle it took to make this little creature unhappy for a whole day, or, as she had expressed it, for a whole life! And as he consoled Tanya, it occurred to him that except this girl and her father there was not one in the world who loved him as a kinsman; and had it not been for them, he, left fatherless and motherless in early childhood, must have lived his whole life without feeling one sincere caress, or tasting ever that simple, unreasoning love which we feel only for those akin to us by blood. And he felt that his tired, strained nerves, like magnets, responded to the nerves of this crying, shuddering girl. He felt, too, that he could never love a healthy, rosy-cheeked woman; but pale, weak, unhappy Tanya appealed to him.

He felt pleasure in looking at her hair and her shoulders; and he pressed her hand, and wiped away her tears. . . . At last she ceased crying. But she still continued to complain of her father, and of her insufferable life at home, imploring Kovrin to try to realise her position. Then by degrees she began to smile, and to sigh that God had cursed her with such a wicked temper; and in the end laughed aloud, called herself a fool, and ran out of the room.

A little later Kovrin went into the garden. Yegor Semionovich and Tanya, as if nothing had happened, were walking side by side up the alley, eating rye-bread and salt. Both were very hungry.

v

Pleased with his success as peacemaker, Kovrin went into the park. As he sat on a bench and mused, he heard the rattle of a carriage and a woman's laugh—visitors evidently again. Shadows fell in the garden, the sound of a violin, the music of a woman's voice reached him almost inaudibly; and this reminded him of the Black Monk. Whither, to what country, to what planet, had that optical absurdity flown?

Hardly had he called to mind the legend and painted in imagination the black apparition in the rye-field when from behind the pine trees opposite to him, walked inaudibly—without the faintest rustling—a man of middle height. His grey head was uncovered, he was dressed in black, and barefooted like a beggar. On his pallid, corpse-like face stood out sharply a number of black spots. Nodding his head politely the stranger or beggar walked noiselessly to the bench and sat down, and Kovrin recognized the Black Monk. For a minute they looked at one another, Kovrin with astonishment, but the monk kindly and, as, before, with a sly expression on his face.

"But you are a mirage," said Kovrin. "Why are you here, and why do you sit in one place? That is not in accordance with the legend."

"It is all the same," replied the monk softly, turning his face toward Kovrin. "The legend, the mirage, I—all are products of your own excited imagination. I am a phantom."

"That is to say you don't exist?" asked Kovrin.

"Think as you like," replied the monk, smiling faintly. "I exist in your imagination, and as your imagination is a part of Nature, I must exist also in Nature."

"You have a clever, a distinguished face—it seems to me as if in reality you had lived more than a thousand years," said Kovrin. "I did not know that my imagination was capable of creating such a phenomenon. Why do you look at me with such rapture? Are you pleased with me?"

"Yes. For you are one of the few who can justly be named the elected of God. You serve eternal truth. Your thoughts, your intentions, your astonishing science, all your life bear the stamp of divinity, a heavenly impress; they are dedicated to the rational and the beautiful, and that is, to the Eternal."

"You say, to eternal truth. Then can eternal truth be accessible and necessary to men if there is no eternal life?"

"There is eternal life," said the monk.

"You believe in the immortality of men?"

"Of course. For you, men, there awaits a great and a beautiful future. And the more the world has of men like you the nearer will this future be brought. Without you, ministers to the highest principles, living freely and consciously, humanity would be nothing; developing in the natural order it must wait the end of its earthly history. But you, by some thousands of years, hasten it into the kingdom of eternal truth—and in this is your high service. You embody in yourself the blessing of God which rested upon the people."

"And what is the object of eternal life?" asked Kovrin.

"The same as all life—enjoyment. True enjoyment is in knowledge, and eternal life presents innumerable, inexhaustible fountains of knowledge; it is in this sense it was said: 'In My Father's house are many mansions. . . .'"

"You cannot conceive what a joy it is to me to listen to you," said Kovrin, rubbing his hands with delight.

"I am glad."

"Yet I know that when you leave me I shall be tormented by doubt as to your reality. You are a phantom, a hallucination. But that means that I am physically diseased, that I am not in a normal state?"

"What if you are? That need not worry you. You are ill because you have overstrained your powers, because you have borne your health in sacrifice to one idea, and the time is near when you will sacrifice not merely it but your life also. What more could you desire? It is what all gifted and noble natures aspire to."

"But if I am physically diseased, how can I trust myself?"

"And how do you know that the men of genius whom all the world trusts have not also seen visions? Genius, they tell you now, is akin to insanity. Believe me, the healthy and the normal are but ordinary men— the herd. Fears as to a nervous age, over-exhaustion and degeneration can trouble seriously only those whose aims in life lie in the present—that is the herd."

"The Romans had as their ideal: *mens sana in corpore sano.*"

"All that the Greeks and Romans said is not true. Exaltations, aspirations, excitements, ecstasies—all those things which distinguish poets, prophets, martyrs to ideas from ordinary men are incompatible with the animal life, that is, with physical health. I repeat, if you wish to be healthy and normal go with the herd."

"How strange that you should repeat what I myself have so often thought!" said Kovrin. "It seems as if you had watched me and listened to my secret thoughts. But do not talk about me. What do you imply by the words: eternal truth?"

The monk made no answer. Kovrin looked at him, but could not make out his face. His features clouded and melted away; his head and arms disappeared; his body faded into the bench and into the twilight, and vanished utterly.

"The hallucination has gone," said Kovrin, laughing. "It is a pity."

He returned to the house lively and happy. What the Black Monk had said to him flattered, not his self-love, but his soul, his whole being. To be the elected, to minister to eternal truth, to stand in the ranks of those who hasten by thousands of years the making mankind worthy of the kingdom of Christ, to deliver humanity from thousands of years of struggle, sin, and suffering, to give to one idea everything, youth, strength, health, to die for the general welfare—what an exalted, what a glorious ideal! And when through his memory flowed his past life, a life pure and chaste and full of labour, when he remembered what he had learnt and what he had taught, he concluded that in the words of the monk there was no exaggeration.

Through the park, to meet him, came Tanya. She was wearing a different dress from that in which he had last seen her.

"You here?" she cried. "We were looking for you, looking. . . . But what has happened?" she asked in surprise, looking into his glowing, enraptured face, and into his eyes, now full of tears. "How strange you are, Andriusha!"

"I am satisfied, Tanya," said Kovrin, laying his hand upon her shoulder. "I am more than satisfied; I am happy! Tanya, dear Tanya, you are inexpressibly dear to me. Tanya, I am so glad!"

He kissed both her hands warmly, and continued:

"I have just lived through the brightest, most wonderful, most unearthly moments. . . . But I cannot tell you all, for you would call me mad, or refuse to believe me. . . . Let me speak of you! Tanya, I love you, and have long loved you. To have you near me, to meet you ten times a day, has become a necessity for me. I do not know how I shall live without you when I go home."

"No!" laughed Tanya. "You will forget us all in two days. We are little people, and you are a great man."

"Let us talk seriously," said he. "I will take you with me, Tanya! Yes? You will come? You will be mine?"

Tanya cried "What?" and tried to laugh again. But the laugh did not come, and, instead, red spots stood out on her cheeks. She breathed quickly, and walked on rapidly into the park.

"I did not think . . . I never thought of this . . . never thought," she said, pressing her hands together as if in despair.

But Kovrin hastened after her, and, with the same glowing, enraptured face, continued to speak.

"I wish for a love which will take possession of me altogether, and this love only you, Tanya, can give me. I am happy! How happy!"

She was overcome, bent, withered up, and seemed suddenly to have aged ten years. But Kovrin found her beautiful, and loudly expressed his ecstasy:

"How lovely she is!"

VI

When he learned from Kovrin that not only had a romance resulted but that a wedding was to follow, Yegor Semionovich walked from corner to corner, and tried to conceal his agitation. His hands shook, his neck seemed swollen and purple; he ordered the horses to be put into his racing droshky, and drove away. Tanya, seeing how he whipped the horses and how he pushed his cap down over his ears, understood his mood, locked herself into her room, and cried all day.

In the orangery the peaches and plums were already ripe. The packing and despatch to Moscow of such a delicate load required much attention, trouble, and bustle. Owing to the heat of the summer every tree had to be watered; the process was costly in time and working-power; and many caterpillars appeared, which the workmen, and even Yegor Semionovich and Tanya, crushed with their fingers, to the great disgust of Kovrin. The autumn orders for fruit and trees had to be attended to, and a vast correspondence carried on. And at the very busiest time, when it seemed no one had a free moment, work began in the fields and deprived the garden of half its workers. Yegor Semionovich, very sunburnt, very irritated, and very worried, galloped about, now to the garden, now to the fields; and all the time shouted that they were tearing him to bits, and that he would put a bullet through his brain.

On top of all came the bustle over Tanya's trousseau, to which the Pesotzkys attributed infinite significance. With the eternal snipping of scissors, rattle of sewing-machines, smell of flat-irons, and the caprices of the nervous and touchy dressmaker, the whole house seemed to spin around. And, to make matters worse, visitors arrived every day, and these visitors had to be amused, fed, and lodged for the night. Yet work and worry passed unnoticed in a mist of joy. Tanya felt as if love and happiness had suddenly burst upon her, although ever since her fourteenth year she had been certain that Kovrin would marry nobody but herself. She was eternally in a state of astonishment, doubt, and disbelief in herself. At one moment she was seized by such great joy that she felt she must fly away to the clouds and pray to God; but a moment later she remembered that when August came she would have to leave the home of her childhood and forsake her father; and she was frightened by the thought—Go

nows whence it came—that she was trivial, insignificant, and unworthy
f a great man like Kovrin. When such thoughts came she would run up
 her room, lock herself in, and cry bitterly for hours. But when visitors
ere present, it broke in upon her that Kovrin was a singularly handsome
1an, that all the women loved him and envied her; and in these moments
er heart was as full of rapture and pride as if she had conquered the
hole world. When he dared to smile on any other woman she trembled
ith jealousy, went to her room, and again—tears. These new feelings
ossessed her altogether; she helped her father mechanically, noticing
either papers nor caterpillars, nor workmen, nor how swiftly time was
assing by.

Yegor Semionovich was in much the same state of mind. He still
orked from morning to night, flew about the gardens, and lost his tem-
er; but all the while he was wrapped in a magic reverie. In his sturdy
ody contended two men, one the real Yegor Semionovich, who, when
e listened to the gardener, Ivan Karlovich's report of some mistake or
isorder, went mad with excitement, and tore his hair; and the other the
nreal Yegor Semionovich—a half-intoxicated old man, who broke off
1 important conversation in the middle of a word, seized the gardener
y the shoulder, and stammered:

"You may say what you like, but blood is thicker than water. His
1other was an astonishing, a most noble, a most brilliant woman. It was
 pleasure to see her good, pure, open, angel face. She painted beauti-
1lly, wrote poetry, spoke five foreign languages, and sang. . . . Poor
1ing, Heaven rest her soul, she died of consumption!"

The unreal Yegor Semionovich sighed, and after a moment's silence
ontinued:

"When he was a boy growing up to manhood in my house he had just
1ch an angel face, open and good. His looks, his movements, his words
ere as gentle and graceful as his mother's. And his intellect! It is not
or nothing he has the degree of *Magister*. But you just wait, Ivan Karlo-
ich; you'll see what he'll be in ten years' time. Why, he'll be out of
ght!"

But here the real Yegor Semionovich remembered himself, seized his
ead and roared:

"Devils! Frost-bitten! Ruined, destroyed! The garden is ruined; the
arden is destroyed!"

Kovrin worked with all his former ardour, and hardly noticed the bustle about him. Love only poured oil on the flames. After every meeting with Tanya, he returned to his rooms in rapture and happiness, and set to work with his books and manuscripts with the same passion with which he had kissed her and sworn his love. What the Black Monk had told him of his election by God, of eternal truth, and of the glorious future of humanity, gave to all his work a peculiar, unusual significance. Once or twice every week, either in the park or in the house, he met the monk, and talked with him for hours; but this did not frighten, but on the contrary delighted him, for he was now assured that such apparitions visit only the elect and exceptional who dedicate themselves to the ministry of ideas.

Assumption passed unobserved. Then came the wedding celebrated by the determined wish of Yegor Semionovich with what was called *éclat*, that is, with meaningless festivities which lasted for two days. Three thousand rubles were consumed in food and drink; but what with the vile music, the noisy toasts, the fussing servants, the clamour, and the closeness of the atmosphere, no one appreciated the expensive wines or the astonishing *hors d'œuvres* specially ordered from Moscow.

VII

One of the long winter nights. Kovrin lay in bed, reading a French novel. Poor Tanya, whose head every evening ached as the result of the unaccustomed life in town, had long been sleeping, muttering incoherent phrases in her dreams.

The clock struck three. Kovrin put out the candle and lay down, lay for a long time with closed eyes unable to sleep owing to the heat of the room and Tanya's continued muttering. At half-past four he again lighted the candle. The Black Monk was sitting in a chair beside his bed.

"Good night!" said the monk, and then, after a moment's silence, asked, "What are you thinking of now?"

"Of glory," answered Kovrin. "In a French novel which I have just been reading, the hero is a young man who does foolish things, and dies from a passion for glory. To me this passion is inconceivable."

"Because you are too clever. You look indifferently on fame as a toy which cannot interest you."

"That is true."

"Celebrity has no attractions for you. What flattery, joy, or instruction can a man draw from the knowledge that his name will be graven on a monument, when time will efface the inscription sooner or later? Yes, happily there are too many of you for brief human memory to remember all your names."

"Of course," said Kovrin. "And why remember them? . . . But let us talk of something else. Of happiness, for instance. What is this happiness?"

When the clock struck five he was sitting on the bed with his feet trailing on the carpet and his head turned to the monk, and saying:

"In ancient times a man became frightened at his happiness, so great it was, and to placate the gods laid before them in sacrifice his beloved ring. You have heard? Now I, like Polycrates, am a little frightened at my own happiness. From morning to night I experience only joy—joy absorbs me and stifles all other feelings. I do not know the meaning of grief, affliction, or weariness. I speak seriously, I am beginning to doubt."

"Why?" asked the monk in an astonished tone. "Then you think joy is a supernatural feeling? You think it is not the normal condition of things? No! The higher a man has climbed in mental and moral development the freer he is, the greater satisfaction he draws from life. Socrates, Diogenes, Marcus Aurelius knew joy and not sorrow. And the apostle said, 'rejoice exceedingly.' Rejoice and be happy!"

"And suddenly the gods will be angered," said Kovrin jokingly. "But it would hardly be to my taste if they were to steal my happiness and force me to shiver and starve."

Tanya awoke, and looked at her husband with amazement and terror. He spoke, he turned to the chair, he gesticulated, and laughed; his eyes glittered and his laughter sounded strange.

"Andriusha, whom are you speaking to?" she asked, seizing the hand which he had stretched out to the monk. "Andriusha, who is it?"

"Who?" answered Kovrin. "Why, the monk! . . . He is sitting there." He pointed to the Black Monk.

"There is no one there, . . . no one, Andriusha; you are ill."

Tanya embraced her husband, and, pressing against him as if to defend him against the apparition, covered his eyes with her hand.

"You are ill," she sobbed, trembling all over. "Forgive me, darling, but for a long time I have fancied you were unnerved in some way. . . . You are ill, . . . physically, Andriusha."

The shudder communicated itself to him. He looked once more at the chair, now empty, and suddenly felt weakness in his arms and legs. He began to dress.

"It is nothing, Tanya, nothing, . . ." he stammered, and still shuddered. "But I am a little unwell. . . . It is time to recognise it."

"I have noticed it for a long time, and father noticed it," she said, trying to restrain her sobs. "You have been speaking so funnily to yourself, and smiling so strangely, . . . and you do not sleep. O, my God, my God, save us!" she cried in terror. "But do not be afraid, Andriusha, do not fear, . . . for God's sake do not be afraid. . . ."

She also dressed. . . . It was only as he looked at her that Kovrin understood the danger of his position, and realised the meaning of the Black Monk and of their conversations. It became plain to him that he was mad.

Both, themselves not knowing why, dressed and went into the hall, she first, he after her. There they found Yegor Semionovich in his dressing-gown. He was staying with them, and had been awakened by Tanya's sobs.

"Do not be afraid, Andriusha," said Tanya, trembling as if in fever. "Do not be afraid . . . father, this will pass off . . . it will pass off."

Kovrin was so agitated that he could hardly speak. But he tried to treat the matter as a joke. He turned to his father-in-law and attempted to say,

"Congratulate me . . . it seems I have gone out of my mind." But his lips only moved, and he smiled bitterly.

At nine o'clock they put on his overcoat and a fur cloak, wrapped him up in a shawl, and drove him to the doctor's. He began a course of treatment.

VIII

Again summer. By the doctor's orders Kovrin returned to the country. He had recovered his health, and no longer saw the Black Monk. It only remained for him to recruit his physical strength. He lived with his father-in-law, drank much milk, worked only two hours a day, never touched wine, and gave up smoking.

On the evening of the 19th June, before Elijah's day, a vesper service was held in the house. When the priest took the censer from the sexton, and the vast hall began to smell like a church, Kovrin felt tired. He went into the garden. Taking no notice of the gorgeous blossoms around him he walked up and down, sat for a while on a bench, and then walked through the park. He descended the sloping bank to the margin of the river, and stood still, looking questioningly at the water. The great pines, with their shaggy roots, which a year before had seen him so young, so joyous, so active, no longer whispered, but stood silent and motionless, as if not recognising him. . . . And, indeed, with his short-clipped hair, his feeble walk, and his changed face, so heavy and pale and changed since last year, he would hardly have been recognised anywhere.

He crossed the stream. In the field, last year covered with rye, lay rows of reaped oats. The sun had set, and on the horizon flamed a broad, red afterglow, foretelling stormy weather. All was quiet; and, gazing towards the point at which a year before he had first seen the Black Monk, Kovrin stood twenty minutes watching the crimson fade. When he returned to the house, tired and unsatisfied, Yegor Semionovich and Tanya were sitting on the steps of the terrace, drinking tea. They were talking together, and, seeing Kovrin, stopped. But Kovrin knew by their faces that they had been speaking of him.

"It is time for you to have your milk," said Tanya to her husband.

"No, not yet," he answered, sitting down on the lowest step. "You drink it. I do not want it."

Tanya timidly exchanged glances with her father, and said in a guilty voice:

"You know very well that the milk does you good."

"Yes, any amount of good," laughed Kovrin. "I congratulate you, I have gained a pound in weight since last Friday." He pressed his hands to his head and said in a pained voice: "Why . . . why have you cured me? Bromide mixtures, idleness, warm baths, watching in trivial terror over every mouthful, every step . . . all this in the end will drive me to idiocy. I had gone out of my mind . . . I had the mania of greatness. . . . But for all that I was bright, active, and ever happy. . . . I was interesting and original. Now I have become rational and solid, just like the rest of the world. I am a mediocrity, and it is tiresome for me to live. . . . Oh, how cruelly . . . how cruelly you have treated me! I had hallucinations . . . but what harm did that cause to anyone? I ask you what harm?"

"God only knows what you mean?" sighed Yegor Semionovich. "It is stupid even to listen to you."

"Then you need not listen."

The presence of others, especially of Yegor Semionovich, now irritated Kovrin; he answered his father-in-law drily, coldly, even rudely, and could not look on him without contempt and hatred. And Yegor Semionovich felt confused, and coughed guiltily, although he could not see how he was in the wrong. Unable to understand the cause of such a sudden reversal of their former hearty relations, Tanya leaned against her father, and looked with alarm into his eyes. It was becoming plain to her that their relations every day grew worse and worse, that her father had aged greatly, and that her husband had become irritable, capricious, excitable, and uninteresting. She no longer laughed and sang, she ate nothing, and whole nights never slept, but lived under the weight of some impending terror, torturing herself so much that she lay insensible from dinner-time till evening. When the service was being held, it had seemed to her that her father was crying; and now as she sat on the terrace she made an effort not to think of it.

"How happy were Buddha and Mahomet and Shakespeare that their kind-hearted kinsmen and doctors did not cure them of ecstasy and inspiration!" said Kovrin. "If Mahomet had taken potassium bromide for his nerves, worked only two hours a day, and drunk milk, that astonishing man would have left as little behind him as his dog. Doctors and kind-hearted relatives only do their best to make humanity stupid, and the time will come when mediocrity will be considered genius, and humanity will perish. If you only had some idea," concluded Kovrin peevishly, "if you only had some idea how grateful I am!"

He felt strong irritation, and to prevent himself saying too much, rose and went into the house. It was a windless night, and into the window was borne the smell of tobacco plants and jalap. Through the windows of the great dark hall, on the floor and on the piano, fell the moonrays. Kovrin recalled the raptures of the summer before, when the air, as now, was full of the smell of jalap and the moonrays poured through the window. . . . To awaken the mood of last year he went to his room, lighted a strong cigar, and ordered the servant to bring him wine. But now the cigar was bitter and distasteful, and the wine had lost its flavour of the year before. How much it means to get out of practice! From a single cigar, and two sips of wine, his head went round, and he was obliged to take bromide of potassium.

Before going to bed Tanya said to him:

"Listen. Father worships you, but you are annoyed with him about something, and that is killing him. Look at his face; he is growing old, not by days but by hours! I implore you, Andriusha, for the love of Christ, for the sake of your dead father, for the sake of my peace of mind—be kind to him again!"

"I cannot, and I do not want to."

"But why?" Tanya trembled all over. "Explain to me why!"

"Because I do not like him; that is all," answered Kovrin carelessly, shrugging his shoulders. "But better not talk of that; he is your father."

"I cannot, cannot understand," said Tanya. She pressed her hands to her forehead and fixed her eyes on one point. "Something terrible, something incomprehensible is going on in this house. You, Andriusha, have changed; you are no longer yourself. . . . You—a clever, an exceptional man—get irritated over trifles. . . . You are annoyed by such little things that at any other time you yourself would have refused to believe it. No . . . do not be angry, do not be angry," she continued, kissing his hands, and frightened by her own words. "You are clever, good, and noble. You will be just to father. He is so good."

"He is not good, but merely good-humoured. These vaudeville uncles—of your father's type—with well-fed, easy-going faces, are characters in their way, and once used to amuse me, whether in novels, in comedies, or in life. But they are now hateful to me. They are egoists to the marrow of their bones. . . . Most disgusting of all is their satiety, and this stomachic, purely bovine—or swinish—optimism."

Tanya sat on the bed, and laid her head on a pillow.

"This is torture!" she said; and from her voice it was plain that she was utterly weary and found it hard to speak. "Since last winter not a moment of rest. . . . It is terrible, my God! I suffer . . ."

"Yes, of course! I am Herod, and you and your papa the massacred infants. Of course!"

His face seemed to Tanya ugly and disagreeable. The expression of hatred and contempt did not suit it. She even observed that something was lacking in his face; ever since his hair had been cut off, it seemed changed. She felt an almost irresistible desire to say something insulting, but restrained herself in time, and overcome with terror, went out of the bedroom.

IX

Kovrin received an independent chair. His inaugural address was fixed for the 2nd of December, and a notice to that effect was posted in the corridors of the University. But when the day came a telegram was received by the University authorities that he could not fulfill the engagement, owing to illness.

Blood came from his throat. He spat it up, and twice in one month it flowed in streams. He felt terribly weak, and fell into a somnolent condition. But this illness did not frighten him, for he knew that his dead mother had lived with the same complaint more than ten years. His doctors, too, declared that there was no danger, and advised him merely not to worry, to lead a regular life, and to talk less.

In January the lecture was postponed for the same reason, and in February it was too late to begin the course. It was postponed till the following year.

He no longer lived with Tanya, but with another woman, older than himself, who looked after him as if he were a child. His temper was calm and obedient; he submitted willingly, and when Varvara Nikolayevna—that was her name—made arrangements for taking him to the Crimea, he consented to go, although he felt that from the change no good would come.

They reached Sevastopol late one evening, and stopped there to rest, intending to drive to Yalta on the following day. Both were tired by the journey. Varvara Nikolayevna drank tea, and went to bed. But Kovrin remained up. An hour before leaving home for the railway station he had received a letter from Tanya, which he had not read; and the thought of this letter caused him unpleasant agitation. In the depths of his heart

he knew that his marriage with Tanya had been a mistake. He was glad
that he was finally parted from her; but the remembrance of this woman,
who towards the last had seemed to turn into a walking, living mummy,
in which all had died except the great, clever eyes, awakened in him only
pity and vexation against himself. The writing on the envelope reminded
him that two years before he had been guilty of cruelty and injustice, and
that he had avenged on people in no way guilty his spiritual vacuity, his
solitude, his disenchantment with life. . . . He remembered how he
had once torn into fragments his dissertation and all the articles written
by him since the time of his illness, and thrown them out of the window,
how the fragments flew in the wind and rested on the trees and flowers;
in every page he had seen strange and baseless pretensions, frivolous irritation, and a mania for greatness. And all this had produced upon him
an impression that he had written a description of his own faults. Yet
when the last copybook had been torn up and thrown out of the window,
he felt bitterness and vexation, and went to his wife and spoke to her
cruelly. Heavens, how he had ruined her life! He remembered how once,
wishing to cause her pain, he had told her that her father had played in
their romance an unusual rôle, and had even asked him to marry her; and
Yegor Semionovich, happening to overhear him, had rushed into the
room, so dumb with consternation that he could not utter a word, but only
stamped his feet on one spot and bellowed strangely as if his tongue had
been cut out. And Tanya, looking at her father, cried out in a heart-rend-
ing voice, and fell insensible on the floor. It was hideous.

The memory of all this returned to him at the sight of the well-known
handwriting. He went out on to the balcony. It was warm and calm, and
a salt smell came to him from the sea. The moonlight, and the lights
around, were imaged on the surface of the wonderful bay—a surface of
a hue impossible to name. It was a tender and soft combination of dark
blue and green; in parts the water resembled copperas, and in parts,
instead of water, liquid moonlight filled the bay. And all these combined in a harmony of hues which exhaled tranquillity and exaltation.

In the lower story of the inn, underneath the balcony, the windows
were evidently open, for women's voices and laughter could plainly be
heard. There must be an entertainment.

Kovrin made an effort over himself, unsealed the letter, and, returning to his room, began to read:

"My father has just died. For this I am indebted to you, for it was you who killed him. Our garden is being ruined; it is managed by strangers; what my poor father so dreaded is taking place. For this also I am indebted to you. I hate you with all my soul, and wish that you may perish soon! Ah, how I suffer! My heart burns with an intolerable pain! . . . May you be accursed! I took you for an exceptional man, for a genius; I loved you, and you proved a madman. . . ."

Kovrin could read no more; he tore up the letter and threw the pieces away. . . . He was overtaken by restlessness—almost by terror. . . . On the other side of the screen, slept Varvara Nikolayevna; he could hear her breathing. From the story beneath came the women's voices and laughter, but he felt that in the whole hotel there was not one living soul except himself. The fact that wretched, overwhelmed Tanya had cursed him in her letter, and wished him ill, caused him pain; and he looked fearfully at the door as if fearing to see again that unknown power which in two years had brought about so much ruin in his own life and in the lives of all who were dearest to him.

By experience he knew that when the nerves give way the best refuge lies in work. He used to sit at the table and concentrate his mind upon some definite thought. He took from his red portfolio a copybook containing the conspect of a small work of compilation which he intended to carry out during his stay in the Crimea, if he became tired of inactivity. . . . He sat at the table, and worked on this conspect, and it seemed to him that he was regaining his former peaceful, resigned, impersonal mood. His conspect led him to speculation on the vanity of the world. He thought of the great price which life demands for the most trivial and ordinary benefits which it gives to men. To reach a chair of philosophy under forty years of age; to be an ordinary professor; to expound commonplace thoughts—and those thoughts the thoughts of others—in feeble, tiresome, heavy language; in one word, to attain the position of a learned mediocrity, he had studied fifteen years, worked day and night, passed through a severe psychical disease, survived an unsuccessful marriage—been guilty of many follies and injustices which it was torture to remember. Kovrin now clearly realised that he was a mediocrity, and he was willingly reconciled to it, for he knew that every man must be satisfied with what he is.

The conspect calmed him, but the torn letter lay upon the floor and

hindered the concentration of his thoughts. He rose, picked up the fragments, and threw them out of the window. But a light wind blew from
the sea, and the papers fluttered back onto the window sill. Again he
was overtaken by restlessness akin to terror, and it seemed to him that
in the whole hotel except himself there was not one living soul. . . .
He went on to the balcony. The bay, as if alive, stared up at him from
its multitude of light- and dark-blue eyes, its eyes of turquoise and fire,
and beckoned him. It was warm and stifling; how delightful, he thought,
to bathe!

Suddenly beneath the balcony a violin was played, and two women's
voices sang. All this was known to him. The song which they sang told
of a young girl, diseased in imagination, who heard by night in a garden
mysterious sounds, and found in them a harmony and a holiness incomprehensible to us mortals. . . . Kovrin held his breath, his heart ceased
to beat, and the magical, ecstatic rapture which he had long forgotten
trembled in his heart again.

A high, black pillar, like a cyclone or waterspout, appeared on the
opposite coast. It swept with incredible swiftness across the bay towards
the hotel; it became smaller and smaller, and Kovrin stepped aside to
make room for it. . . . The monk, with uncovered grey head, with
black eyebrows, barefooted, folding his arms upon his chest, swept past
him, and stopped in the middle of the room.

"Why did you not believe me?" he asked in a tone of reproach, looking
caressingly at Kovrin. "If you had believed me when I said you were a
genius, these last two years would not have been passed so sadly and so
barrenly."

Kovrin again believed that he was the elected of God and a genius; he
vividly remembered all his former conversation with the Black Monk,
and wished to reply. But the blood flowed from his throat on to his chest,
and he, not knowing what to do, moved his hands about his chest till
his cuffs were red with the blood. He wished to call Varvara Nikolayevna,
who slept behind the screen, and making an effort to do so, cried:

"Tanya!"

He fell on the floor, and raising his hands, again cried:

"Tanya!"

He cried to Tanya, cried to the great garden with the miraculous flowers,
cried to the park, to the pines with their shaggy roots, to the rye-field, cried

to his marvellous science, to his youth, his daring, his joy, cried to the life which had been so beautiful. He saw on the floor before him a great pool of blood, and from weakness could not utter a single word. But an inexpressible, infinite joy filled his whole being. Beneath the balcony the serenade was being played, and the Black Monk whispered to him that he was a genius, and died only because his feeble, mortal body had lost its balance, and could no longer serve as the covering of genius.

When Varvara Nikolayevna awoke, and came from behind her screen, Kovrin was dead. But on his face was frozen a smile of happiness.

HALLIE SOUTHGATE

Barren to the Stars

This is a story about a man I had forgotten I knew, and was never aware I felt sympathy for. It is strange to me how real and important his problem seems now, remembering it twenty years later.

HALLIE SOUTHGATE

THE Reverend Mr. Trask looked small and old as he stood beside Bishop Matthews in the vestibule of the tiny Episcopal church. The wide white sleeves under the Bishop's cassock fell back in ecclesiastical grace from his lace cuffs and large, well-cared-for hands, and a look of power was upon him. Mr. Trask had none of this; in his worn black frock he seemed withdrawn and tired, and it was as if the years of his calling had taken much from him.

It was the first Sunday after Easter and the two clerics could look back now toward the nave and watch Mr. Trask's parishioners flow into the aisle like little tributaries emptying into a main and troubled stream, where they were propelled onward by the force of the Bishop's attraction. "Good to see you again—fine—fine—" Bishop Matthews murmured greetings in such a way that they passed out into the April sunshine smiling, pleased with themselves, and knowing they were honoured by his visit. Mr. Trask could not avoid the thought that once they had approached *him* with the same air of expectancy, but he had lacked the grace to fold his hands over theirs as the Bishop did with such assurance, nor had he ever possessed the deep and booming voice to stir them with. It was not unnatural that a man so young, with this manner, had been made a Bishop.

That was never my ambition, reflected Mr. Trask. I only desired to remain in one place and be needed there. It is regrettable that I have found so little to admire in these people I was cast among. I have been with them for many years, and I have learned not to like them, he thought coldly, dispassionately. I was not surprised when things turned out as they did. . . . Now that he was leaving he could remember his first day, knowing that it is the end of anything that gives shape to its beginning. He had been young then, and hopeful for their love; thinking, surely the church was an expression of a larger generosity, a need to share—which was love in its essence—that brought them together under one roof every Sunday, that bent them to their knees in prayer, and lifted their heads in song. . . .

But he had seen them begin to nod their heads in drowsiness a moment after the services had begun; he had noticed how their knees bent in prayer with less urgency than when they climbed the steps to their offices, or their homes; and their heads were unlifted, and their voices tuneless when they sang, as if they had not known they were singing for the Lord. And, they would be glad to see him go.

Bowing soberly to his parishioners, he could see himself as he was now. With a painful honesty he admitted that he lacked completely this grace that was so apparent even in the turn of the young Bishop's head; that it was not only a physical lack but a mental one as well. He knew his beliefs were angular and sometimes harsh, but he had not the gift to mold them into something different. And when he had found himself unable to meet the rising cost of living within his frugal salary, he had felt right (so seldom before had he thought of money) in asking for the small increase; he had asked as if he had the right to expect it. It was that which had given them the opportunity to say, Times are hard for us all. We will have to get a young man, unmarried, who can live on your salary. We can't hold you from some parish that will give you more . . .

Now they were making a great fuss, as if they did not want to see him go. The Bishop's fine talk this morning about their regrets was fine and eloquent. The Bishop as always was the image of tact, and affability—his own requests would be subtly phrased when he made them, or not at all.

Just as the bitterness began to flicker again, Mr. Trask saw old Mrs. Johnson approaching, and he was glad he had been told she was not present at the meeting that decided his fate. Now she moved slowly as she had in the past year, so that her natural dignity seemed to grow greater as her strength grew less. She was not one of those nervous ones, he reflected, who fight against weakness in the sight of all; rather, she was accepting the gradual defeat of her body with a grace as timeless as the slow pounding of waves upon a rock.

And he felt tender toward her as he recalled her indignation because he was leaving, but she had not insulted him by offering to change things then. He also knew the purse the congregation would give him tonight was four-fifths filled by her. If it had not been, he could not take it, and yet he must, as it was in this way he had to permit his "flock" to salve their consciences.

There was an element of real sincerity in Bishop Matthews' manner now, in the lifting of his hand.

"Mrs. Johnson," he said in his deep fine voice, "I have thought so often of our charming evening in your home last winter."

Mrs. Johnson nodded, with the pleasant formality that seemed to intimidate no one, not even her grandchildren. "We expect you with us today, Bishop Matthews. Mr. Trask has promised to bring you for luncheon."

And she went on as though with no impulse to linger as had the others.

This pleased Mr. Trask. He had been in an oddly unpredictable state of mind for the past week when strange things pleased him, and others could fill him with an almost Biblical rage. He did not recognize himself drawn thus into the stress of living; the outer layers of his being seemed wrapped in the many garments of his errors, and it was as if he could not remove them, as yet unmoistened by his tears. He had been angry; he had known bitterness; he had failed to reach his people, and he had nursed his vanity in this failure like an open wound. Still he permitted himself a fleeting touch of amusement because Mrs. Johnson had said so little to the Bishop!

Walking across the grass to the rectory after the service Bishop Matthews no longer talked; his quick and well-phrased words rested behind a thoughtful smile, which was his way of communicating with lesser people. But he did say,

"Reverend, it is a pity you find you must leave here when Mrs. Johnson is obviously so very fond of you."

Coldly, Mr. Trask walked beside him, his lean nervous face controlled by habit, and also at this moment by his own anger.

"I shall miss Mrs. Johnson," he said, "she has been kind, always."

He knew what the Bishop meant; it was the very reason he had not gone to see her more often, had, with her, kept at a distance he did not wish. He had suffered when he had to ask her help for other members of the congregation, because she was a very rich woman, and because of this he must pretend not to love her, for fear she might think he cared for this. This too, perhaps, was a part of his failure as a man and as a leader among them; and yet, deeply, he felt that she understood.

Genevieve met them at the door. He saw his wife again now as she must look to the Bishop—a square, Germanic looking woman with protruding teeth, and he hurried quickly into the house. It was not that he wanted to escape her—he had never been aware of this as a desire—but because he felt he did not please her now more than he did the others. Because she was another part of his life that he had fitted into without grace, without understanding, and without enough love; and which, foolishly, he did not want to leave. His marriage, as his years here in Leesville, had meant no lifting of a veil on beauty, upon the rewards of a deeper life, a finer consciousness; in both cases the original outline had been superior to the finished work.

"I was just saying," repeated the Bishop as if continuing a long conversation, "that Mrs. Johnson seems to have a real fondness for your husband, Mrs. Trask. It is a pity—perhaps—"

Genevieve of course could see what the Bishop was getting at, and Mr. Trask watched her apprehensively. He had not believed her own sparse way of meeting people was the best, but at least she had not toadied to the important ones either, she had been firm and righteous with all— even the children of the parishioners and he reflected wryly how she made them eat everything on their plates when the young people had dined at the rectory. "It is a pity there were not more like her," said Genevieve acidly, unexpectedly, and although it was this thought that had been in Mr. Trask's mind, he looked at her with distaste.

"There are many fine people here," he said, hurriedly, but Bishop Matthews did not appear to hear him, nor had he seemed to understand Genevieve.

"It is quite possible, Reverend," he went on, "that an adjustment could still be made. I understand Mrs. Johnson was not advised earlier—and that it is not easy at this time to spare a young man for this post, so many of them are doing God's work in other ways, helping the boys in the trenches—"

"No adjustment is possible, I am afraid," said Mr. Trask, quickly, and, whereas the anger before had been like a small flame that suddenly licked forth from a nest of coals, now it was detached and blue.

At last the Bishop did understand, and he must have been puzzled how two people could stand before him with the same reactions, and yet seem so far apart in relation to each other, as if, absurdly, each somehow had wished for the other to be different.

Bishop Matthews went to his room to rest, and Mr. Trask started for his study. As he made his way up the worn stairs, he thought of his house and how it must seem to the Bishop. The Mission furniture had endured and would have endured until he himself was dust. And the meals Genevieve served the Bishop had been well-cooked, well-balanced. "Oh, now, Philip," she would say before anyone—"but this is *good* for you." Perhaps if there had been some taste to the food, or to the house. Just taste, he thought, I don't even ask for beauty—perhaps with a little of that *I* might have been different.

In the study he thought in this way for a while, but there was a pattern here that sooner or later got such digressions under control. The groove of dogma was strong in this room, and his thoughts quite naturally were drawn to a more orderly plane, and thus, a controlled one. And he fell then to completing plans to move to the little village thirty miles away, which was to be the scene, as here he could admit almost disdainfully, of his final defeat among the living.

At luncheon Mr. Trask had a small triumph when Mrs. Johnson asked him to confer the blessing. It was such a small thing, and it did not really move him at all, but he could see the schemes start again in Bishop Matthews' head like a hive of bees set in motion by the wind. The Bishop even looked at him with a little nod, not resenting this, but as if to say, You see, you do have her interest. Genevieve looked at her plate, her lips compressed; he knew her impulse was to speak, and say it was proper that the Bishop ask grace, and before a member of the congregation younger than Mrs. Johnson she would have spoken.

So with a quite irreverent feeling of amusement Mr. Trask bent his head and began, "Oh, heavenly Father—"

When he had finished, he caught a twinkle in the eye of Mrs. Johnson, as if together they had shared a joke. And for the first time in his

life Mr. Trask recognized the impulse to wink; he even tried to, un-
successfully, looking down on his plate, but he fancied Genevieve was
leaning over, about to speak, and he quickly recovered himself.

This one small incident, however, had set off something within him
so that he felt rather giddy, as if his depression had been suddenly lifted,
too suddenly. That this was largely due to Mrs. Johnson he understood,
and that it was fleeting, he knew also. But today somehow he did not
bother as before to fear the ogre of privilege; he was enjoying things
he had not even noticed before. From the moment he had come in, he
had been surprised to find that he was looking at things with a new appreciation, even as a few hours ago he had been too poignantly aware of
the ugliness in his own home. He let the golden lights on the silver
candlesticks please him, disproportionately, he noticed the intricate floral
design on the fine old bone china, and he held the wine for an instant
on the back of his tongue, tasting it, as he had once been taught to do
by a Catholic priest. And he did not once look at Genevieve, but frequently at Mrs. Johnson, lovely in gray, with a creamy lace collar, and
he thought her eyes were the most gracious he had ever seen. He thought
if she were a young woman, and he a different kind of a man, this was
the feeling he would like to have had in love! And he knew all this was
because tomorrow he would die, and recklessness is a privilege of the
damned. And he knew also that one of the hard things he had to face
was knowing he would not see Mrs. Johnson again.

Later she took them all for a drive into the hills, and he was startled
to find that the buds were already green and the earth black and moist
for growth and he felt regret that the pending event of his leaving had
not permitted him the freedom of impulse to walk into the country and
see these things. He felt slightly feverish about everything and exhilarated
in a way he knew would not last, but which he clung to as long as he
dared.

It was not until Bishop Matthews had been put on the train, and he
and Genevieve were left at their own door that he also recalled something he had been aware of earlier: a feeling of excitement, of anticipation in Mrs. Johnson, as if she knew something that perhaps he did
not know. And occasionally she had a look of being faintly puzzled also;
but he thought he understood. She knew him, he felt, hopefully, and
she was happy about the purse they were to give him as any generous

person was about a gift: and she felt a sense of anticipation for the pleasure of it. As for being puzzled, why then how could she know yet if he could accept this, being as he was? She did not know he had forced himself to recognize that he must.

There was a knock on the study door, and he knew it was Genevieve. Sitting very still in his old leather chair, his eyes closed, his hands folded over his vest, he waited, in case she should look in; but after a moment he heard her go away.

And then a great tiredness came over him, and he did not move again for a long time.

He and Genevieve came out of the rectory just at dusk, and the tiny steeple of his church rose above them, and he thought that has been called a finger pointing to God. But it is perhaps in reality only an extremity erected by the architect to rise above the houses around—remote from them, it does not contain apples and potatoes like a cellar, it contains only a bell that arouses them from their slumbers on Sunday morning, their suppers on Sunday night. Otherwise, I do not think it has any significance for them. But he thought this mildly, for now that the time was near, he was moved only by a feeling of sadness. The anger had been broken somewhere between lunch and sleep. My youth is gone, he thought, my hopes, my fine sermons that were never so eloquent as I wished, but which I thought would sometimes, if only by the law of averages, reach my people. Perhaps I have never reached them, he thought, sadly; I doubt if I was ever able to speak the words they wanted to hear.

They separated, and he went into the little vestry and put on his frock, while Genevieve entered the church from the front and sat down in the same pew she had occupied for so long.

They were all there, and now in his sadness he thought he could detect, if not regret, at least embarrassment, on some faces. That there is also regret in embarrassment he acknowledged to himself, as he noticed the silence that hung over the church.

"Oh Lord, my God, in thee have I put my trust," he began the ritual to the bowed heads.

The responses were soft to his listening ears, and the singing also. And when the banker, Mr. Gow, got to his feet at the appointed time, and

cleared his throat, it was almost as if there was a presence in the church
that had not been there before.

"We—the people of this congregation, would like to make this little
gift of appreciation to the Reverend Trask for his services during these
years and to wish him and Mrs. Trask a lot of luck on their new under-
taking."

The banker was flushed, and his words were spoken gruffly, because he
knew no other way, but at least now he was wide awake, and even mildly
moved, if only by the solemnity of his own mission.

The purse was brought to Mr. Trask by the banker's daughter, Nellie,
whose small face was very serious. He felt tender toward her for a moment, so that he could accept the gift better than he had thought he
would. Holding the little bag in his hand, with the lettering First National
Bank of Leesville on one side, he felt the bills and the silver, just as it
had been collected, and it burned in his hands, so that he wanted to thrust
it aside; but at this moment he found he could draw on some resource of
graciousness he had not known, or had forgotten, that he possessed.

"Mrs. Trask and I accept this offering with deep gratitude," he said,
and if his voice sounded remote even in his own hearing, he knew he
was saying the words they wanted him to say, and perhaps had not been
quite sure he would. "Our years among you have been rich and rewarding
ones, we have gone through much together, war, the loss of friends,
anxiety for the future—and we have, I hope, shared the same faith."

He looked toward Mrs. Johnson sitting upright, majestic in her pew,
and her look of attention was a reward. He said another word or two, and
looked back at her. And as his eyes passed over the congregation for a
moment he had a strange feeling of triumph. I have reached them at last,
he thought, here, in this hour of my defeat, I am at last among them. He
felt a strange stirring in his breast, and when he lifted his hands above
them for the Benediction the feeling flooded through him, so that his
voice did not sound remote any longer, but strangely moved and resonant.

Abruptly he drew back into himself as they filed out; the weakness he
had shown now embarrassed him. And he had seen also that Mrs. Johnson had been the first to leave, going down the aisle alone, and it had
reminded him more forcibly than ever of all that he was losing.

She does not want to say goodbye, he thought. I believe that is it. She
is moved, and perhaps sorry I must go. And this came as a surprise to

him, for he had not for many years considered the possibility that one should feel so personally toward him.

The church was cleared quickly after this, and when he saw Genevieve waiting he told her that she was to go home alone, he would be with her soon. She did not speak, only nodded, and he saw that she also could have wept if she had been less strong. *We have been too strong,* he thought, *we have not let them be easy in this House.* But it is too late now, you can not undo the error of having expected too much from anyone. He and Genevieve were, in a sense, alike; only he had asked for more, and Genevieve did not question what the Lord had given her, or rather failed to give her. There had been no children. She had not even questioned the Lord's decision in this.

And perhaps, if we had been parents, we would have made the same mistakes, he admitted, painfully, sitting alone in the front pew, facing the tiny baptismal font on the right of the altar. We would have kept too much to the letter, and it may be, they also would have felt we did not understand and would have rejected us.

Where had it all gone wrong?

He had been thirty-two when he came to Leesville, feeling not young then except in his hope for a place in this new parish. Before that he had been in Minnesota, where the winters were cold and the land barren for long months of the year, and, in his section, intellectually barren as well. The parish here had not been much larger but it was the East, where, he always believed, the mind could feast with the body. He had spread the spiritual food before his people, gladly drawing on all the resources of his intellect—but he had stopped there, when he found they were not reaching out for it, for he had not known how to make them eat. And so, he had gone back into himself again, forgetting his failure after a time, taking it for granted in the cold pleasure of his own interior nourishment. And his years between thirty-two and forty-five had passed, and he had just learned, as each man does for himself how fast in time these years go.

It was too late now to retrieve what he had lost. It was too late, his heart cried, to start again, and perhaps fail as before. The ties that bind one person to others must be started early, begun with a small invisible thread, adding others, so that in time they become visible, and a pattern is made—

He felt like a man who has been long crippled, and now must walk by faith alone. Or not walk; perhaps even this did not matter now.

His loneliness suddenly became so acute, and his sorrow so deep that he got up quickly, and a few moments later was outside, the church darkened, and the night still, around him. The street lamp burned brightly on the corner, and the living rooms of the houses around him were warm pink glows of comfort; but outside where he stood was black solitude and he felt lost in misery. The barrenness of the world, he thought; and remembered a bitter phrase from some closed book—"the barrenness of the world extends even to the stars."

He felt his hand cold against his clothes, and his legs were so tired and heavy that if his will power had not been strong, they would have failed him as he stumbled up the dark walk, away from the rectory.

He must have walked for hours, his mind searching, condemning himself, and even when the moon came up full and glowing, he did not find an answer. He did not tire, and he did not stop; but the heavy weight of his own failure kept pressing in like a suffocation, and he could not escape it. The moon is the Bishop, he thought once, trying to lighten his mood, and I am but one of the little stars whose light grows dim as his light grows brighter. The strong ones, like Venus, survive.

The moon is Faith, some soberer answer came from his brain. Perhaps the stars, then, are one's problems, to be lost in the glow—

He did not know where to turn after awhile, and it was then he let his feet lead him, willing them not at all. They kept going, like the knees of his parishioners, he thought, in robot fashion. So the bitterness is still there, he admitted; if only I could expel that, it would be easier to find my way. But the two extremes, his failure and the failure of others, kept swinging pendulum-wise within the confines of his mind.

It was not until he saw the lights in Mrs. Johnson's house that he realized how late it was. Some warning came into his consciousness, then, and he thought, although he had not known he was aware of the passing time, *Why it is late for her to be still awake!* And then he saw the doctor's car at the curb, and the maid in a wrapper suddenly drawing aside the lace curtains, roughly, as though she were frightened, and peering out into the night. He thought, She is ill!

His legs now carried him to the front door, and the maid flung it wide for him.

"Oh Mr. Trask," she cried, and her homely face was distorted with crying. "She was took so bad—I just got him here, the doctor— He don't leave the room, he don't open the door. I don't know what it is— She called me, Mary, she says—I was in my bed and she says, Oh, Mary— And I phoned the doctor. Oh—" The girl began crying loudly now, so that Mr. Trask tried to comfort her. "Maybe she'll *die*—" she moaned.

"She has lived many useful years, Mary," he said, and pushed her aside, gently. "Try to be calm. I will go and see." But once on the stairs, his own calm left him, and he moved quickly, so that in an instant he was outside the bedroom door, listening. For a long moment he heard nothing, and then there was a sigh, a long, tired sound like the brushing of a hand in a pile of dead leaves; and it struck him poignantly as he recognized even in this the peculiar quality of personality that was Mrs. Johnson's. Softly he touched the door with his knuckles, and the doctor called sharply.

"Who's there?"

"It is I, Mr. Trask—"

When the door was opened, he looked quickly, apprehensively, to the bed, not knowing what he would see. He had never before feared impending death, but he knew what death could be, and he could not bear to see disintegration in *her*.

She did not fail him. Propped high on her big pillows and breathing sharply, her fine white hair hung in serene and lovely braids over the coverlet. Even her eyes smiled for him, although he saw at a glance they were veiled by a sedative. But one side of her mouth was paralyzed, and a fold of gray-white flesh hung sadly over her chin.

"So—glad," he understood her to say. "You—were fine—".

She could not go on, but her eyes continued to look at him with the same sense of sharing he had felt earlier. It was as if they were both going away now, and she was encouraging him to look for what she seemed sure to find.

The doctor spoke. "She wanted you," he said. "We called, but Mrs. Trask said you were out—Mrs. Johnson asked for you."

"For me?" Deeply moved, Mr. Trask looked at the face on the pillows. *Me?*

"You were—fine," she whispered. "Tonight—you made them feel— you had courage."

"I have no courage," he had to say, softly, sorrowingly. "And no gift to give it to others—"

She tried to nod her re-assurance, but she did not speak again, she could not. But what she had said! Did she know the power of what she had said now! Was it more than kindness, more than last hour prescience that had let her speak? Perhaps, he thought suddenly, I have reached them.

Mr. Trask dropped to his knees beside her, and taking her long warm hand in his he began to pray. "Our Father, who art in heaven, Hallowed be thy Name," and he felt the doctor tiptoe from the room. The door closed softly. When he had finished, he felt his own tears on her hand, undrying, and looked up, wondering if she felt them, the first he had shed. But Mrs. Johnson was not living now, although on her face was a look as though she had been listening to the end.

He got to his feet stiffly, as if he had been there a long time, and yet he was able to move with more ease, and the tiredness seemed less. And he thought, gratefully, I was here with her up to the very last. I *was* able to reach her!

Slowly, he left the room, giving it over once again to the doctor, and he thought, It will not be so hard to go, now that she is no longer here.

And he thought also, tenderly, hurrying home to Genevieve—she would be worried that he was gone so long—how this day had been so important, perhaps the most important in his life. He could go now to the smaller parish with hope, for even there quite possibly would be other Mrs. Johnsons. At least he knew now he had touched one person deeply, a beautiful and gracious one, and in time he might reach others, even as she said he had tonight.

And he thought quite humbly that it would be fine to try again, after all. He knew better how it was done, now.

JEAN TOOMER

Fern

Jean Toomer's stories, sketches and poems have gone beyond the superficial aspects of Negro life in America. "Fern" is perhaps his best-known story.

FACE flowed into her eyes. Flowed in soft cream foam and plaintive ripples, in such a way that wherever your glance may momentarily have rested, it immediately thereafter wavered in the direction of her eyes. The soft suggestion of down slightly darkened, as the shadow of a bird's wing might, the creamy brown color of her upper lip. Why, after noticing it, you sought her eyes, I cannot tell you. Her nose was aquiline, Semitic. If you have heard a Jewish cantor sing, if he has touched you and made your own sorrow seem trivial when compared with his, you will know my feeling when I follow the curves of her profile, like mobile rivers, to their common delta. They were strange eyes. In this, that they sought nothing—that is, nothing that was obvious and tangible and that one could see, and they gave the impression that nothing was to be denied. When a woman seeks, you will have observed, her eyes deny. Fern's eyes desired nothing that you could give her; there was no reason why they should withhold. Men saw her eyes and fooled themselves. Fern's eyes said to them that she was easy. When she was young, a few men took her, but got no joy from it. And then, once done, they felt bound to her (quite unlike their hit-and-run with other girls), felt as though it would take them a lifetime to fulfill an obligation which they could find no name for. They became attached to her, and hungered after finding the barest trace of what she might desire. As she grew up, new men who came to town felt as almost everyone did who ever saw her: that they would not be denied. Men were everlastingly bringing her their bodies. Something inside of her got tired of them, I guess, for I am certain that for the life of her she could not tell why or how she began to turn them off. They began to leave her, baffled and ashamed, yet vowing to themselves that some day they would do a fine thing for her: send her candy every week and not let her know whom it came from, watch out for her wedding day and give her a magnificent something with no name on it, buy a house and deed it to her, rescue her from some unworthy fellow who had tricked her into marrying him. As you know, men are apt to idolize or fear that which they cannot understand, especially if it be a woman. She did not deny them, yet the fact was that they were denied. A sort of superstition crept into their consciousness of her being somehow above them. Being above them meant that she was not to be approached by anyone. She became a virgin. Now a virgin in a small southern town is by no means the usual thing, if you will believe me. That the sexes were made to mate is the practice of the South. Particularly, black folks were made to mate. And it is black folks whom I have been talking about thus far. What white men thought of Fern I can arrive at only by analogy. They let her alone.

Anyone, of course, could see her, could see her eyes. If you walked up Dixie Pike most any time of day, you'd be most like to see her resting listless-like on the railing of her porch, back propped against a post, head tilted a little forward because there was a nail in the porch post just where her head came which for some reason or other she never took the trouble to pull out. Her eyes, if it were sunset, rested idly where the sun, molten and glorious, was pouring down between the fringe of pines. Or maybe they gazed at the gray cabin on the knoll from which an evening folk-song was coming. Perhaps they followed a cow that had been turned loose to roam and feed on cotton stalks and corn leaves. Like as not they'd settle on some vague spot above the horizon, though hardly a trace of wistfulness would come to them. If it were dusk, then they'd wait for the search-light of the evening train which you could see miles up the track before it flared across the Dixie Pike, close to her home. Wherever they looked, you'd follow them and then waver back. Like her face, the whole countryside seemed to flow into her eyes. Flowed into them with the soft listless cadence of Georgia's south. A young Negro, once, was looking at her, spellbound, from the road. A white man passing in a buggy had to flick him with his whip if he was to get by without running him over. I first saw her on the porch. I was passing with a fellow whose crusty numbness (I was from the North and suspected of being prejudiced and stuck-up) was melting as he found me warm. I asked him who she was. "That's Fern," was all that I could get from him. Some folks already thought that I was given to nosing around; I let it go at that, so far as questions were concerned. But at first sight of her I felt as if I heard a Jewish cantor sing. As if his singing rose above the unheard chorus of a folk-song. And I felt bound to her. I too had my dreams: something I would do for her. I have knocked about from town to town too much not to know the futility of mere change of place. Besides, picture if you can, this cream-colored solitary girl sitting at a tenement window looking down on the indifferent throngs of Harlem. Better that she listen to folk-songs at dusk in Georgia, you would say, and so would I. Or, suppose she came up North and married. Even a doctor or a lawyer, say, one who would be sure to get along—that is, make money. You and I know, who have had experience in such things, that love is not a thing like prejudice which can be bettered by changes of town. Could men in Washington, Chicago, or New York, more than the men of Georgia, bring her something left vacant by the bestowal of their bodies? You and I who know men in these cities will have to say, they could not. See her out and out a prostitute along State Street in Chicago. See her move into a Southern town where white men are more aggressive. See her become a white man's concubine. . . . Something I must do for her. There was myself. What could I do for her? Talk, of course. Push back the fringe of pines upon new horizons. To what purpose? and what for? Her? Myself? Men in her case seem to lose selfishness. I lost mine before I touched her. I ask you, friend (it makes no difference if you sit in the Pullman or the Jim Crow as the train crosses her road), what thoughts would come to you—that is, after you'd finished with the thoughts that leap into men's minds at the sight of a pretty woman who will not deny them; what thoughts would come to you, had you seen her in a quick flash, keen and intuitively, as she sat there on her porch when your train thundered by? Would you have got off at the next station and come back for her to take her where? Would you have completely forgotten her as soon as you reached Macon, Atlanta, Augusta, Pasadena, Madison, Chicago, Boston, or New Orleans? Would you tell your wife or sweetheart about a girl you saw? Your thoughts can help me, and I would like to know. Something I would do for her. . . .

One evening I walked up the Pike on purpose, and stopped to say hello. Some of her family were about, but they moved away to make room for me. Damn if I knew how to begin. Would you? Mr. and Miss So-and-So, people, the weather, the crops, the new preacher, the frolic, the church benefit, rabbit and possum hunting, the new soft drink they had at old Pap's store, the schedule of the trains, what kind of town Macon was, Negro's migration north, boll-weevils, syrup, the Bible— to all these things she gave a yassur or nassur, without further comment. I began to wonder if perhaps my own emotional sensibility had played one of its tricks on me. "Let's take a walk," I at last ventured. The sugges- tion, coming after so long an isolation, was novel enough, I guess, to surprise. But it wasn't that. Something told me that men before me had said just that as a prelude to the offering of their bodies. I tried to tell her with my eyes. I think she understood. The thing from her that made my throat catch, vanished. Its passing left her visible in a way I'd thought, but never seen. We walked down the Pike with people on all the porches gaping at us. "Doesn't it make you mad?" She meant the row of petty gossiping people. She meant the world. Through a canebrake that was ripe for cutting, the branch was reached. Under a sweet-gum tree, and where reddish leaves had damned the creek a little, we sat down. Dusk, suggesting the almost imperceptible procession of giant trees, settled with a purple haze about the cane. I felt strange, as I always do in Georgia, particularly at dusk. I felt that things unseen to men were tangibly im- mediate. It would not have surprised me had I had a vision. People have them in Georgia more often than you would suppose. A black woman once saw the mother of Christ and drew her in charcoal on the court-house wall. . . . When one is on the soil of one's ancestors, most anything can come to one. . . . From force of habit, I suppose, I held Fern in my arms, that is, without at first noticing it. Then my mind came back to her. Her eyes, unusually weird and open, held me. Held God. He flowed in as I've seen the countryside flow in. Seen men. I must have done something—what, I don't know, in the confusion of my emotion. She sprang up. Rushed some distance from me. Fell to her knees, and began swaying, swaying. Her body was tortured with something it could not let out. Like boiling sap it flooded arms and fingers till she shook them as if they burned her. It found her throat, and spattered inarticulately in plaintive, convulsive sounds, mingled with calls to Christ Jesus. And then she sang, brokenly. A Jewish cantor singing with a broken voice. A child's voice, uncertain, or an old man's. Dusk hid her; I could hear only her song. It seemed to me as though she were pounding her head in anguish upon the ground. I rushed to her. She fainted in my arms.

There was talk about her fainting with me in the canefield. And I got one or two ugly looks from town men who'd set themselves up to protect her. In fact, there was talk of making me leave town. But they never did. They kept a watch-out for me, though. Shortly after, I came back North. From the train window I saw her as I crossed her road. Saw her on her porch, head tilted a little forward where the nail was, eyes focused on the sunset. Saw her face flow into them, the countryside, and something that I call God, flowing into them. . . . Nothing ever really happened. Nothing ever came to Fern, not even I. Something I would do for her. Some fine unnamed thing. . . . And, friend, you? She is still living, I have reason to know. Her name, against the chance that you might happen down that way, is Fernie May Rosen.

RAINER MARIA RILKE

A Story Told to the Dark

If you want something idyllic, I think you should look into Rilke, particularly the *"Geschichten von dem Lieben Gott,"* Stories of God.

GEORGE N. SHUSTER
*President, Hunter College
of the City of New York*

I WANTED to put on my coat and go to my lame friend Ewald. But I had lingered over a book, an old book at that, and evening had come, as in Russia spring comes. A moment ago the room had been distinct, even to its remotest corners, and now all the things in it were as though they had never known anything but twilight; everywhere large dark blossoms opened, and luminous gleams slipped about their velvet calyxes as on dragonfly wings.

The lame man would surely no longer be at his window. So I stayed at home. What was it I had wanted to tell him? I no longer knew. But after a while I felt that someone was entreating me for this lost story —some lonely soul, perhaps, standing far away at the window of his dusky chamber, or perhaps this very darkness itself, that surrounded me and him and all things. So it happened that I told my story to the dark. And it leaned ever closer to me so that I could speak more and more softly, quite as befits my story. It takes place in the present and begins:

After a long absence Doctor Georg Lassmann was returning to the home of his birth. He had never possessed much there, and now he had only two sisters left in his native city, both married, apparently well married; to see them again after twelve years was the purpose of his visit. So he himself believed. But in the night, unable to sleep in the overcrowded train, it became clear to him that he was really going for the sake of his childhood, hoping to rediscover something in those old streets: a doorway, a tower, a fountain, anything to induce some joy or

some sorrow by which he might recognize himself again. One gets so
lost in life. And then he remembered many things: the little apartment in
the Heinrichsgasse with the shiny door-latch and the dark-coated tiles,
the well-cared-for furniture and his parents, those two threadbare beings,
standing almost awed beside it; the swift and harassed week-days and
the Sundays that were like emptied rooms, the rare visitors whom one
received laughing and embarrassed, the out-of-tune piano, the old canary,
the heirloom armchair in which one might not sit, a birthday, an uncle
who came from Hamburg, a puppet-show, a barrel-organ, a children's
party, and someone calling: "Klara." The doctor had almost dropped
off. They were in a station, lights went by and the listening hammer
went ringing along the wheels. And that was like: Klara, Klara. "Klara,"
the doctor reflected, now wide awake, "who was Klara anyway?" And
immediately he became aware of a face, a child's face with blond, straight
hair. Not that he could have described it, but he had a sense of something quiet, helpless, resigned, and of a pair of narrow childish shoulders
drawn still more together by a washed-out little dress, and he began to
imagine a face to go with them—but then he knew that he need not
imagine it. It was there—or rather, it had been there, then. So the doctor
recalled his single playfellow Klara, not without effort. Until the day he
went to boarding-school, at the age of about ten, he had shared with
her everything that happened to him, little that it was (or was it much?).
Klara had no sisters or brothers, and he had as good as none; for his
older sisters did not concern themselves with him. But since then he
had never asked anyone about her. How had that been possible?—He
leaned back. She had been a pious child, he still remembered, and then
he asked himself: "What can have become of her?" For a time the thought
frightened him that she might have died. An immeasurable dread overcame him in the closely packed compartment; everything seemed to
confirm this assumption: she had been a sickly child, she hadn't been
very well off at home, she had often cried; undoubtedly, she was dead.
The doctor could not stand it any longer; he disturbed certain of the
sleepers, shoving his way between them into the corridor of the car.
There he opened a window and gazed out into the blackness with the
dancing sparks. That quieted him. And when he returned to the compartment later, despite the uncomfortable position, he soon went to sleep.

The reunion with his two married sisters passed off not without embarrassment. The three had forgotten how far apart, notwithstanding their close relationship, they had always remained, and endeavored for a while to act like brother and sisters. But they soon silently agreed to take refuge behind that polite mediate tone which social intercourse has invented for all occasions.

He dined at his younger sister's, whose husband was in particularly comfortable circumstances, a manufacturer with the title of Imperial Councilor; and it was after the fourth course that the doctor asked:

"Tell me, Sophie, what's become of Klara?"

"Klara who?"

"I don't remember her name. The little one, you know, a neighbor's daughter, with whom I played as a child."

"Oh, you mean Klara Söllner?"

"Söllner, that's it, Söllner. Now I remember: old Söllner was that awful old man—but what of Klara?"

His sister hesitated. "She married—and now she lives altogether in retirement."

"Yes," went on the Imperial Councilor, and his knife slid rasping across his plate, "quite retired."

"You know her too?" The doctor turned to his brother-in-law.

"Y-ye-es—just slightly; she's pretty well known here, of course."

Husband and wife exchanged a look of understanding. The doctor noticed that for some reason they did not care to say more on the subject, and he let it drop.

The more eagerness to pursue it did the Councilor show when the lady of the house had left them to their coffee.

"This Klara," he asked with a sly smile, watching the ash that fell from his cigar into a silver bowl, "wasn't she supposed to be a quiet child, and homely too?"

The doctor said nothing. The Councilor moved confidentially closer.

"That was a story!—Did you never hear of it?"

"But I haven't seen anybody to talk to."

"Talk to?" the Councilor laughed cunningly. "You could have read it in the papers."

"What?" asked the doctor nervously.

"Why, she ran off and left him—" From behind a cloud of smoke the manufacturer discharged this astonishing sentence and waited in un-confined well-being for the effect. But the effect did not seem to please him. He took on a businesslike manner, sat up straight and began to re-port in another, an injured tone, as it were: "Well, they had married her to Lehr, of the building council. You wouldn't have known him. Not an old man—my age. Rich, thoroughly respectable, you know, thoroughly respectable. She hadn't a penny and in addition she had no looks, no bringing-up, etc. Still, Lehr didn't want a great lady, just a modest house-keeping wife. But Klara—she was taken into society all over, everybody was kindly disposed towards her—really, they acted—well, you know, she could easily have made a position for herself—when one day, hardly two years after the wedding, off goes Klara. Can you imagine it: gone. Where? To Italy. A little pleasure-trip, not alone, naturally. All that last year we hadn't invited them—as though we had suspected! Lehr, a good friend of mine, a man of honor, a man—"

"And Klara?" the doctor broke in, rising.

"Oh, yes—well, the chastisement of heaven fell upon her. You see, the man in question—an artist, they say, you know—a casual sort of bird, naturally, just—well, when they got back from Italy, to Munich: good-bye, and she saw him no more. Now she's sitting there with her child!"

Doctor Lassmann strode excitedly up and down: "In Munich?"

"Yes, in Munich," replied the Councilor and also rose. "They say she's having a pretty miserable time—"

"How miserable?"

"Well," the Councilor gazed at his cigar, "peculiarily, and then any-how—God, what an existence—"

Suddenly he laid his well-groomed hand on his brother-in-law's shoul-der and clucked with pleasure: "You know they also used to say that she lived on—"

The doctor turned short about and walked out of the door. The Coun-cilor, whose hand had fallen from the other's shoulder, needed ten min-utes to recover from his astonishment. Then he went in to his wife and said angrily:

"I've always said so, your brother is decidedly queer."

And she, having just dozed off, yawned lazily: "Oh, Lord yes."

A fortnight later the doctor departed. He knew all at once that he must seek his childhood elsewhere. In the Munich directory he found:

Klara Söllner, the name of a suburb, the street and number. He announced his coming and drove out. A slender woman greeted him in a room full of light and kindliness.

"Georg, and you remember me?"

The doctor stood still in amazement. At last he said: "So this is you, Klara."

She held her calm face with its clear brow quite still, as though to give him time to recognize her. It took long. Finally the doctor seemed to have found something that proved to him that his old playfellow really stood before him. He sought her hand again and pressed it; then slowly let it go and looked about the room. It seemed to contain nothing superfluous. At the window a desk with papers and books, at which Klara must just have been sitting. The chair had been pushed back.

"You were writing?". . . and the doctor felt how silly the question was.

But Klara answered, unconcernedly: "Yes, I'm doing some translating."

"For publication?"

"Yes," Klara said simply, "for a publishing house."

Georg noticed some Italian photographs on the walls. Among them Giorgione's "Concert."

"You are fond of this?" He stepped nearer to the picture.

"And you?"

"I have never seen the original; it's in Florence, isn't it?"

"In the Pitti. You must go there."

"For the purpose?"

"For the purpose." There was a free and simple serenity about her. The doctor looked up thoughtfully.

"What's the matter, Georg? Won't you sit down?"

"I'm upset," he faltered. "I thought—but you aren't in the least miserable—!" he suddenly exclaimed.

Klara smiled. "You have heard my story?"

"Yes, that is—"

"Oh," she interrupted quickly, as she saw his brow darken, "it's not people's fault if they speak differently of it. The things we experience are often inexpressible, and any one who insists on telling them nevertheless, necessarily makes mistakes—" A pause.

And the doctor: "What has made you so kind?"

"Everything," she said softly and warmly. "But why do you say: kind?"

"Because—because you really ought to have grown hard. You were such a weak, helpless child; children of that sort later either grow hard or—"

"Or they die, you mean. Well, I died too. I died for many years. From the time I last saw you at home, until—" She took up something from the table. "See, this is his picture. It flatters him a little. His face is not so clear-cut, but—nicer, simpler. I'll show you our child in a moment, it's asleep in the next room. It's a boy. Called Angelo, like him. He is away now, traveling, far away."

"And you are all alone?" asked the doctor absently, still absorbed in the photograph.

"Yes, I and the child. Isn't that enough? I will tell you how it is. Angelo is a painter. His name is little known; you would never have heard it. Until lately he had been struggling with the world, with his plans, with himself and with me. Yes, with me too; because for a year I've been begging him to travel. I felt how much he needed it. Once he asked jokingly: 'Me or a child?' 'A child,' said I, and then he went."

"And when will he come back?"

"When the child can say his name, that's how we arranged it." The doctor was about to say something, but Klara laughed: "And as it's a difficult name, it will take a while yet. Angelino won't be two till summer."

"Extraordinary," said the doctor.

"What, Georg?"

"How well you understand life. How big you have grown, how young! What have you done with your childhood? We were both such—such helpless children. But that can't be altered or made never to have happened."

"You mean, we ought to have suffered from our childhood, by rights?"

"Yes, I mean just that. From that heavy darkness behind us with which we preserve such feeble, vague relations. There comes a time when we deposit in it all our firstlings, all beginning, all confidence, the seeds of all that which might perhaps some day come to be. And suddenly we realize that the whole thing has sunk in a deep sea, and we don't even know just when. We never noticed it. As though some one were to gather in all his money and buy with it a feather to stick in his hat: whish!—the first breeze carries it away. Naturally he arrives home without his feather, and nothing remains for him but to look back and think when it could have flown off."

"You are thinking of that, Georg?"

"Not any more. I've given it up. I begin somewhere behind my tenth year, at the point where I stopped praying. The rest doesn't belong to me."

"And how is it, then, that you remember me?"

"That is just why I have come to you. You are the only witness to that time. I believed I could find again in you—that which I cannot find in myself. Some gesture, some word, some name, that has significance— some enlightenment—" The doctor's head sank into his cold, uneasy hands.

Frau Klara pondered. "I remember so little of my childhood, as though there were a thousand lives between. But now that you remind me of it so, something comes back to me. One evening. You came to us, un- expectedly; your parents had gone out, to the theater or something of the sort. Our house was all lit up. My father was expecting a guest, a relative, a distant wealthy relative, if I remember rightly. He was coming from, from—I don't know where, but in any case from some distance. We had already been awaiting him for two hours. The doors were open, the lamps were burning, my mother went over from time to time and smoothed an antimacassar on the sofa, father stood at the window. No- body dared sit down for fear of displacing a chair. As you happened to come, you waited with us. We children listened at the door. And the later it grew, the more marvelous a guest did we expect. Yes, we even trembled lest he come before he should have attained that last degree of gloriousness to which with every minute of his not-coming he drew nearer. We were not afraid that he might not appear at all; we knew for certain he would come, but we wanted to leave him time to grow great and mighty."

Suddenly the doctor raised his hand and said sadly: "So we both know that—that he didn't come. I had not forgotten it either."

"No," Klara corroborated, "he didn't come—" And after a pause: "But it was lovely all the same!"

"What?"

"Oh, well—the waiting, the many lamps—the stillness—the festive spirit."

Something stirred in the next room. Frau Klara excused herself for a moment; and as she came brightly and serenely back, she said: "We can go in now. He's awake and smiling.—But what was it you wanted to say just now?"

"I was just wondering what could have helped you to—to yourself, to this calm possession of yourself. Life certainly hasn't made it easy for you. Evidently something helped you that I haven't got?"

"What might that be, Georg?" Klara sat down beside him.

"It is strange; when I first remembered you again, one night, three weeks ago, on the train, I thought: She was a pious child. And now, since I have seen you, although you are so entirely different from what I had expected—in spite of that, and yet, I would like to say, only the more surely, I believe I feel that what led you through all dangers was—your piety."

"What do you call piety?"

"Well, your relation to God; your love of God, your belief."

Frau Klara closed her eyes. "Love of God? Let me think." The doctor watched her tensely. She seemed to speak her thoughts slowly, as they came to her: "As a child—did I love God? I don't believe so. Why, I never even—it would have seemed to me insane presumption—that isn't the right word—like the worst sin, to think: *he is*. As though I had thereby compelled him to be in me, in that weak child with the absurdly long arms, in our poor apartment where everything was imitation and false, from the bronze wall-plaques of papier mâché to the wine in the bottles that bore such expensive labels. And later—" Klara made a defensive gesture with her hands, and her eyes closed tighter, as though she feared to see something dreadful through the lids—"why, I would have had to drive him out of me if he had been living in me then. But I knew nothing about him. I had quite forgotten him. I had forgotten everything.—It was in Florence, when for the first time in my life I saw, heard, felt, realized and simultaneously learned to be thankful for all those things, that I first thought of him again. There were traces of him everywhere. In all the pictures I found bits of his smile, the bells were still alive with his voice, and on the statues I saw the imprints of his hands."

"And you found him there?"

Klara looked at the doctor with large, happy eyes: "I felt that he had been—somewhere, once, had been . . . why should I have felt more? That was already more than enough."

The doctor got up and went to the window. From it one could see a stretch of field and the little old village church, and above it sky, no longer quite untouched by evening. Suddenly Doctor Lassmann asked, without turning round:

"And now?"

Receiving no answer, he came softly back again.

"Now—" Klara faltered as he stood before her, and then raised her eyes full to his face, "now I sometimes think: he will be."

The doctor took her hand and kept it a moment. He seemed to gaze into the unknown.

"What are you thinking of, Georg?"

"I'm thinking that it's like that evening once more: you are again waiting for the wonderful guest, for God, and know that he will come. And I have joined you by chance—"

Klara rose, calm and happy. She looked very young. "Well, this time we'll really wait until it happens." She said it so joyfully and so simply that the doctor had to smile. And so she led him into the adjoining room, to her child—

In this story there is nothing that children may not know. Still, the children haven't heard it. I have told it only to the dark, to no one else. And the children are afraid of the dark, and run away from it, and if some time they have to stay in it, they press their eyes shut and put their fingers in their ears. But for them also the time will come when they love the dark. From it they will learn my story, and then they will understand it better, too.

—Translated from the German by M. D. HERTER NORTON
AND NORA PURTSCHER-WYDENBRUK

VI

City of God

FRANZ KAFKA

The Builders

Many complain that the words of the wise are always merely parables and of no use in daily life, which is the only life we have. When the sage says: "Go over," he does not mean that we should cross to some actual place, which we could do anyhow if the labour were worth it; he means some fabulous yonder, something unknown to us, something too that he cannot designate more precisely, and therefore cannot help us here in the very least. All these parables really set out to say merely that the incomprehensible is incomprehensible, and we know that already. But the cares we have to struggle with every day: that is a different matter.

Concerning this a man once said: Why such reluctance? If you only followed the parables you yourselves would become parables and with that rid of all your daily cares.

Another said: I bet that is also a parable.

The first said: You have won.

The second said: But unfortunately only in parable.

The first said: No, in reality; in parable you have lost.

FRANZ KAFKA

THE CITY COAT OF ARMS

AT FIRST all the arrangements for building the Tower of Babel were characterized by fairly good order, indeed the order was perhaps too perfect, too much thought was taken for guides, interpreters, accommodation for the workmen and roads of communication, as if there were centuries before one to do the work in. In fact the general opinion at that time was that one simply could not build too slowly; a very little insistence on this would have sufficed to make one hesitate to lay the foundations at all. People argued in this way: The essential thing in the whole business is the idea of building a tower that will reach to heaven. In comparison with that idea everything else is secondary. The idea, once seized in its magnitude, can never vanish again; so long as there are men on the earth there will be also the irresistible desire to complete the building. That being so, however, one need have no anxiety about the future; on the contrary, human knowledge is increasing, the art of building has made progress and will make further progress, a piece of work which takes us a year may perhaps be done in half the time in another hundred years, and better done, too, more enduringly. So why exert oneself to the limit of one's present powers? There would be some sense in doing that only if it were likely that the tower could be completed in one generation. But that is beyond all hope. It is far more likely that the next generation with their perfected knowledge will find the work of their predecessors bad, and tear down what has been built so as to begin anew. Such thoughts paralysed people's powers, and so they troubled less about the tower than the construction of a city for the workmen. Every nationality wanted the finest quarter for itself, and this gave rise to disputes, which developed into bloody conflicts. These conflicts never came to an end; to the leaders they were a new proof that, in the absence of the necessary unity, the building of the tower must be done very slowly, or indeed preferably postponed until universal peace was declared. But the time was spent not only in conflict; the town was embellished in the intervals, and this unfortunately enough evoked fresh envy and fresh conflict. In this fashion the age of the first generation went past, but none of the succeeding ones showed any difference; except that technical skill increased and with it occasion for conflict. To this must be added that the second or third generation had already recognized the senselessness of building a heaven-reaching tower; but by that time everybody was too deeply involved to leave the city. All the legends and songs that came to birth in that city are filled with longing for a prophesied day when the city would be destroyed by five successive blows from a giant fist. It is for that reason too that the city has a closed fist on its coat of arms.

THE GREAT WALL OF CHINA

The Great Wall of China was finished off at its northernmost corner. From the southeast and the southwest it came up in two sections that finally converged there. This principle of piecemeal construction was also applied on a smaller scale by both of the two great armies of labour, the eastern and the western. It was done in this way: gangs of some twenty workers were formed who had to accomplish a length, say, of five hundred yards of wall, while a similar gang built another stretch of the same length to meet the first. But after the junction had been made the construction of the wall was not carried on from the point, let us say, where this thousand yards ended; instead the two groups of workers were transferred to begin building again in quite different neighbour-hoods. Naturally in this way many great gaps were left, which were only filled in gradually and bit by bit, some, indeed, not till after the official announcement that the wall was finished. In fact it is said that there are gaps which have never been filled in at all, an assertion, how-ever, which is probably merely one of the many legends to which the building of the wall gave rise, and which cannot be verified, at least by any single man with his own eyes and judgment, on account of the extent of the structure.

Now on first thoughts one might conceive that it would have been more advantageous in every way to build the wall continuously, or at least continuously within the two main divisions. After all the wall was intended, as was universally proclaimed and known, to be a protection against the peoples of the north. But how can a wall protect if it is not a continuous structure? Not only cannot such a wall protect, but what there is of it is in perpetual danger. These blocks of wall left standing in deserted regions could be easily pulled down again and again by the nomads, especially as these tribes, rendered apprehensive by the building operations, kept changing their encampments with incredible rapidity, like locusts, and so perhaps had a better general view of the progress of the wall than we, the builders. Nevertheless the task of construction probably could not have been carried out in any other way. To under-stand this we must take into account the following: The wall was to be a protection for centuries: accordingly the most scrupulous care in the building, the application of the architectural wisdom of all known ages and peoples, an unremitting sense of personal responsibility in the build-ers, were indispensable prerequisites for the work. True, for the more purely manual tasks ignorant day labourers from the populace, men, women and children who offered their services for good money, could be employed; but for the supervision even of every four day labourers an expert versed in the art of building was required, a man who was capable of entering into and feeling with all his heart what was involved. And the higher the task, the greater the responsibility. And such men were actually to be had, if not indeed so abundantly as the work of construction could have absorbed, yet in great numbers.

For the work had not been undertaken without thought. Fifty years before the first stone was laid the art of architecture, and especially that of masonry, had been proclaimed as the most important branch of knowledge throughout the whole area of a China that was to be walled round, and all other arts gained recognition only in so far as they had reference to it. I can still remember quite well us standing as small children, scarcely sure on our feet, in our teacher's garden, and being ordered to build a sort of wall out of pebbles; and then the teacher, girding up his robe, ran full tilt against the wall, of course knocking it down, and scolded us so terribly for the shoddiness of our work that we ran weeping in all directions to our parents. A trivial incident, but significant of the spirit of the time.

I was lucky inasmuch as the building of the wall was just beginning when, at twenty, I had passed the last examination of the lowest grade school. I say lucky, for many who before my time had achieved the highest degree of culture available to them could find nothing year after year to do with their knowledge, and drifted uselessly about with the most splendid architectural plans in their heads, and sank by thousands into hopelessness. But those who finally came to be employed in the work as supervisors, even though it might be of the lowest rank, were truly worthy of their task. They were masons who had reflected much, and did not cease to reflect, on the building of the wall; men who with the first stone which they sank in the ground felt themselves a part of the wall. Masons of that kind, of course, had not only a desire to perform their work in the most thorough manner, but were also impatient to see the wall finished in its complete perfection. Day labourers have not this impatience, for they look only to their wages, and the higher supervisors, indeed even the supervisors of middle rank, could see enough of the manifold growth of construction to keep their spirits confident and high. But to encourage the subordinate supervisors, intellectually so vastly superior to their apparently petty tasks, other measures must be taken. One could not, for instance, expect them to lay one stone on another for months or even years on end, in an uninhabited mountainous region, hundreds of miles from their homes; the hopelessness of such hard toil,

which yet could not reach completion even in the longest lifetime, would
have cast them into despair and above all made them less capable for
the work. It was for this reason that the system of piecemeal building
was decided on. Five hundred yards could be accomplished in about five
years; by that time, however, the supervisors were as a rule quite exhausted and had lost all faith in themselves, in the wall, in the world.
Accordingly, while they were still exalted by the jubilant celebrations
marking the completion of the thousand yards of wall, they were sent
far, far away, saw on their journey finished sections of the wall rising
here and there, came past the quarters of the high command and were
presented with badges of honour, heard the rejoicings of new armies of
labour streaming past from the depths of the land, saw forests being
cut down to become supports for the wall, saw mountains being hewn
into stones for the wall, heard at the holy shrines hymns rising in which
the pious prayed for the completion of the wall. All this assuaged their
impatience. The quiet life of their homes, where they rested some time,
strengthened them; the humble credulity with which their reports were
listened to, the confidence with which the simple and peaceful burgher
believed in the eventual completion of the wall, all this tightened up
again the cords of the soul. Like eternally hopeful children they then
said farewell to their homes; the desire once more to labour on the wall
of the nation became irresistible. They set off earlier than they needed;
half the village accompanied them for long distances. Groups of people
with banners and scarfs waving were on all the roads; never before had
they seen how great and rich and beautiful and worthy of love their
country was. Every fellow-countryman was a brother for whom one was
building a wall of protection and who would return lifelong thanks for
it with all he had and did. Unity! Unity! Shoulder to shoulder, a ring
of brother, a current of blood no longer confined within the narrow circulation of one body, but sweetly rolling and yet ever returning throughout
the endless leagues of China.

Thus, then, the system of piecemeal construction becomes compre-
hensible; but there were still other reasons for it as well. Nor is there
anything odd in my pausing over this question for so long; it is one of
the crucial problems in the whole building of the wall, unimportant as
it may appear at first glance. If I am to convey and make understandable

the ideas and feelings of that time I cannot go deeply enough into this very question.

First then, it must be said that in those days things were achieved scarcely inferior to the construction of the Tower of Babel, although as regards divine approval, at least according to human reckoning, strongly at variance with that work. I say this because during the early days of building a scholar wrote a book in which he drew the comparison in the most exhaustive way. In it he tried to prove that the Tower of Babel failed to reach its goal, not because of the reasons universally advanced or at least that among those recognised reasons the most important of all was not to be found. His proofs were drawn not merely from written documents and reports; he also claimed to have made enquiries on the spot, and to have discovered that the tower failed and was bound to fail because of the weakness of the foundation. In this respect at any rate our age was vastly superior to that ancient one. Almost every educated man of our time was a mason by profession and infallible in the matter of laying foundations. That, however, was not what our scholar was concerned to prove; for he maintained that the Great Wall alone would provide for the first time in the history of mankind a secure foundation for a new Tower of Babel. First the wall, therefore, and then the tower. His book was in everybody's hands at that time, but I admit that even today I cannot quite make out how he conceived this tower. How could the wall, which did not form even a circle, but only a sort of quarter or half-circle, provide the foundation for a tower? That could obviously be meant only in a spiritual sense. But in that case why build the actual wall, which after all was something concrete, the result of the lifelong labor of multitudes of people? And why were there in the book plans, somewhat nebulous plans, it must be admitted, of the tower, and proposals worked out in detail for mobilising the people's energies for the stupendous new work?

There were many wild ideas in people's heads at that time—this scholar's book is only one example—perhaps simply because so many were trying to join forces as far as they could for the achievement of a single aim. Human nature, essentially changeable, unstable as the dust, can endure no restraint; if it binds itself it soon begins to tear madly at its bonds, until it rends everything asunder, the wall, the bonds and its very self.

It is possible that these very considerations, which militated against the building of the wall at all, were not left out of account by the high command when the system of piecemeal construction was decided on. We—and here I speak in the name of many people—did not really know ourselves until we had carefully scrutinised the decrees of the high command, when we discovered that without the high command neither our book learning nor our human understanding would have sufficed for the humble tasks which we performed in the great whole. In the office of the command—where it was and who sat there no one whom I have asked knew then or knows now—in that office one may be certain that all human thoughts and desires were revolved, and counter to them all human aims and fulfilments. And through the window the reflected splendours of divine worlds fell on the hands of the leaders as they traced their plans.

And for that reason the incorruptible observer must hold that the command, if it had seriously desired it, could also have overcome those difficulties which prevented a system of continuous construction. There remains, therefore, nothing but the conclusion that the command deliberately chose the system of piecemeal construction. But the piecemeal construction was only a makeshift and therefore inexpedient. Remains the conclusion that the command willed something inexpedient. Strange conclusion!—True, and yet in one respect it has much to be said for it. One can perhaps safely discuss it now. In those days many people, and among them the best, had a secret maxim which ran: Try with all your might to comprehend the decrees of the high command, but only up to a certain point; then avoid further meditation. A very wise maxim, which moreover was elaborated in a parable that was later often quoted: Avoid further meditation, but not because it might be harmful; it is not at all certain that it would be harmful. What is harmful or not harmful has nothing to do with the question. Consider rather the river in spring. It rises until it grows mightier and nourishes more richly the soil on the long stretch of its banks, still maintaining its own course until it reaches the sea, where it is all the more welcome because it is a worthier ally.— Thus far may you urge your meditations on the decrees of the high command.—But after that the river overflows its banks, loses outline and shape, slows down the speed of its current, tries to ignore its destiny by forming little seas in the interior of the land, damages the fields, and yet cannot maintain itself for long in its new expanse, but must run back between its banks again, must even dry up wretchedly in the hot season that presently follows.—Thus far may you not urge your meditations on the decrees of the high command.

Now though this parable may have had extraordinary point and force during the building of the wall, it has at most only a restricted relevance for my present essay. My enquiry is purely historical; no lightning flashes any longer from the long since vanished thunder clouds, and so I may venture to seek for an explanation of the system of piecemeal construction which goes further than the one that contented people then. The limits which my capacity for thought imposes upon me are narrow enough, but the province to be traversed here is infinite. Against whom was the Great Wall to serve as a protection? Against the people of the north. Now, I come from the southeast of China. No northern people can menace us there. We read of them in the books of the ancients; the cruelties which they commit in accordance with their nature make us sigh beneath our peaceful trees. The faithful representations of the artist show us these faces of the damned, their gaping mouths, their jaws furnished with great pointed teeth, their half-shut eyes that already seem to be seeking out the victim which their jaws will rend and devour. When our children are unruly we show them these pictures, and at once they fly weeping into our arms. But nothing more than that do we know about these northerners. We have not seen them and if we remain in our villages we shall never see them, even if on their wild horses they should ride as hard as they can straight toward us,—the land is too vast and would not let them reach us, they would end their course in the empty air.

Why, then, since that is so, did we leave our homes, the stream with its bridges, our mothers and fathers, our weeping wives, our children who needed our care and depart for the distant city to be trained there, while our thoughts journeyed still farther away to the wall in the north? Why? A question for the high command. Our leaders know us. They, absorbed in gigantic anxieties, know of us, know our petty pursuits, see us sitting together in our humble huts, and approve or disapprove the evening prayer which the father of the house recites in the midst of his family. And if I may be allowed to express such ideas about the high command, then I must say that in my opinion the high command has existed from old time, and was not assembled, say, like a gathering of mandarins summoned hastily to discuss somebody's fine dream in a conference as hastily terminated, so that that very evening the people are drummed out of their beds to carry out what has been decided, even if it should be nothing but an illumination in honour of a god who may have shown great favour to their masters the day before, only to drive them into some dark corner with cudgel blows tomorrow, almost before the illuminations have died down. Far rather do I believe that the high command has existed from all eternity and the decision to build the wall likewise. Unwitting peoples of the north, who imagined they were the cause of it! Honest, unwitting Emperor, who imagined he decreed it! We builders of the wall know that it was not so and hold our tongues.

During the building of the wall and ever since to this very day I have occupied myself almost exclusively with the comparative history of races —there are certain questions which one can probe to the marrow, as it were, only by this method,—and I have discovered that we Chinese possess certain folk and political institutions that are unique in their clarity, others again unique in their obscurity. The desire to trace the causes of these phenomena, especially the latter, has always teased me and teases me still, and the building of the wall is itself essentially involved with these problems.

Now one of the most obscure of our institutions is that of the empire itself. In Pekin, naturally, at the imperial court, there is some clarity to be found on this subject, though even that is more illusive than real. Also the teachers of political law and history in the high schools claim to be exactly informed on these matters and to be capable of passing on their knowledge to their students. The farther one descends among the lower schools the more, naturally enough, does one find teachers' and pupils' doubts of their own knowledge vanishing, and a superficial culture mounting sky high round a few precepts that have been drilled into peoples' minds for centuries, precepts which, though they have lost nothing of their eternal truth, remain eternally invisible in this fog of confusion.

But it is precisely this question of the empire which in my opinion the common people should be asked to answer, since after all they are the empire's final support. Here, I must confess, I can only speak once more for my native place. Except for the nature gods and their ritual, which fills the whole year in such beautiful and rich alternation, we think only about the Emperor. But not about the present one; or rather we

would think about the present one if we knew who he was or knew anything definite about him. True—and it is the sole curiosity that fills us—
we are always trying to get information on this subject, but, strange as it
may sound, it is almost impossible to discover anything, either from pilgrims, though they have wandered through many lands, or from near or
distant villages, or from sailors, though they have navigated not only our
little stream, but also the sacred rivers. One hears a great many things,
true, but can gather nothing definite.

So vast is our land that no fable could do justice to its vastness, the
heavens can scarcely span it,—and Pekin is only a dot in it, and the
imperial palace less than a dot. The Emperor as such, on the other hand,
is mighty throughout all the hierarchies of the world: admitted. But the
existent Emperor, a man like us, lies much like us on a couch which is of
generous proportions perhaps, and yet very possibly may be quite narrow
and short. Like us he sometimes stretches himself and when he is very tired
yawns with his delicately cut mouth. But how should we know anything
about that—thousands of miles away in the South—almost on the borders
of the Tibetan Highlands? And besides, any tidings, even if they did reach
us, would arrive far too late, would have become obsolete long before
they reached us. The Emperor is always surrounded by a brilliant and yet
ambiguous throng of nobles and courtiers—malice and enmity in the
guise of servants and friends—who form a counter-weight to the Imperial power and perpetually labour to unseat the ruler from his place
with poisoned arrows. The Empire is immortal, but the Emperor himself
totters and falls from his throne, yes, whole dynasties sink in the end
and breathe their last in one death-rattle. Of these struggles and sufferings the people will never know; like tardy arrivals, like strangers in a
city, they stand at the end of some densely thronged side street peacefully
munching the food they have brought with them, while far away in front,
in the market square at the heart of the city, the execution of their ruler
is proceeding.

There is a parable that describes this situation very well: The Emperor,
so it runs, has sent a message to you, the humble subject, the insignificant
shadow cowering in the remotest distance before the Imperial sun; the
Emperor from his death-bed has sent a message to you alone. He has
commanded the messenger to kneel down by the bed and has whispered
the message to him; so much store did he lay on it that he ordered the

messenger to whisper it back into his ear again. Then by a nod of the
head he has confirmed that it is right. Yes, before the assembled spectators
of his death—all the obstructing walls have been broken down, and on
the spacious and loftily-mounting open staircases stand in a ring the
great princes of the Empire—before all these he has delivered his message. The messenger immediately sets out on his journey; a powerful, an
indefatigable man; now pushing with his right arm, now with his left,
he cleaves a way for himself through the throng; if he encounters resistance
he points to his breast, where the symbol of the sun glitters; the way,
too, is made easier for him than it would be for any other man. But the
multitudes are so vast; their numbers have no end. If he could reach the
open fields how fast he would fly, and soon doubtless you would hear
the welcome hammering of his fists on your door. But instead how vainly
does he wear out his strength; still he is only making his way through
the chambers of the innermost palace; never will he get to the end of
them; and if he succeeded in that nothing would be gained; he must fight
his way next down the stairs; and if he succeeded in that nothing would
be gained; the courts would still have to be crossed; and after the courts
the second outer palace; and once more stairs and courts; and once more
another palace; and so on for thousands of years; and if at last he should
burst through the outermost gate—but never, never can that happen—
the imperial capital would lie before him, the centre of the world, crammed
to bursting with its own refuse. Nobody could fight his way through
here even with a message from a dead man.—But you sit at your window
when evening falls and dream it to yourself.

Just so, as hopelessly and as hopefully, do our people regard the Emperor. They do not know what emperor is reigning, and there exist doubts
regarding even the name of the dynasty. In school a great deal is taught
about the dynasties with the dates of succession, but the universal uncertainty in this matter is so great that even the best scholars are drawn
into it. Long-dead emperors are set on the throne in our villages, and
one that only lives in song recently had a proclamation of his read out
by the priest before the altar. Battles that are old history are new to us,
and one's neighbour rushes in with a jubilant face to tell the news. The
wives of the emperors, pampered and overweening, seduced from noble
custom by wily courtiers, swelling with ambition, vehement in their greed,
uncontrollable in their lust, practise their abominations ever anew. The

more deeply they are buried in time the more glaring are the colours in which their deeds are painted, and with a loud cry of woe our village eventually hears how an Empress drank her husband's blood in long draughts thousands of years ago.

Thus, then, do our people deal with departed emperors, but the living ruler they confuse among the dead. If once, only once in a man's lifetime, an imperial official on his tour of the provinces should arrive by chance at our village, make certain announcements in the name of the government, scrutinise the tax lists, examine the school children, enquire of the priest regarding our doings and affairs, and then, before he steps into his litter, should sum up his impressions in verbose admonitions to the assembled commune,—then a smile flits over every face, each man throws a stolen glance at his neighbour, and bends over his children so as not to be observed by the official. Why, they think to themselves, he's speaking of a dead man as if he were alive, this Emperor of his died long ago, the dynasty is blotted out, the good official is having his joke with us, but we will behave as if we did not notice it, so as not to offend him. But we shall obey in earnest no one but our present ruler, for to do so would be a crime. And behind the departing litter of the official there rises in might as ruler of the village some figure fortuitously exalted from an urn already crumbled to dust.

Similarly our people are but little affected by revolutions in the state or contemporary wars. I recall an incident in my youth. A revolt had broken out in a neighbouring, but yet quite distant, province. What caused it I can no longer remember, nor is it of any importance now; occasions for revolt can be found there any day, the people are an excitable people. Well, one day a leaflet published by the rebels was brought to my father's house by a beggar who had crossed that province. It happened to be a feast day, our rooms were filled with guests, the priest sat in the chief place and studied the sheet. Suddenly everybody started to laugh, in the confusion the sheet was torn, the beggar who, however, had already received abundant alms, was driven out of the room with blows, the guests dispersed to enjoy the beautiful day. Why? The dialect of this neighbouring province differs in some essential respects from ours, and this difference occurs also in certain turns of the written speech, which for us have an archaic character. Hardly had the priest read out two lines before we had already come to our decision. Ancient history told long ago, old sorrows long since healed. And though—so it seems to me in recollection—the gruesomeness of the living present was irrefutably conveyed by the beggar's words, we laughed and shook our heads and refused to listen any longer. So eager are our people to obliterate the present.

If from such appearances any one should draw the conclusion that in reality we have no Emperor, he would not be far from the truth. Over and over again it must be repeated: There is perhaps no more people more faithful to the Emperor than ours in the south, but the Emperor derives no advantages from our fidelity. True, the sacred dragon stands on the little column at the end of our village, and ever since the beginning of human memory it has breathed out its fiery breath in the direction of Pekin in token of homage—but Pekin itself is far stranger to the people in our village than the next world. Can there really be a village where the houses stand side by side, covering all the fields for a greater distance than one can see from hills, and can there be dense crowds of people packed between these houses day and night? We find it more difficult to picture such a city than to believe that Pekin and its Emperor are one, a cloud, say, peacefully voyaging beneath the sun in the course of the ages.

Now the result of holding such opinions is a life on the whole free and unconstrained. By no means immoral, however; hardly ever have I found in my travels such pure morals as in my native village. But yet a life that is subject to no contemporary law, and attends only to the exhortations and warnings which come to us from olden times.

I guard against large generalisations, and do not assert that in all the countless villages in my province it is so, far less in all the five hundred provinces of China. Yet perhaps I may venture to assert on the basis of the many writings on this subject which I have read, as well as from my own observation—the building of the wall in particular, with its abundance of human material, provided a man of sensibility with the opportunity of traversing the souls of almost all the provinces—on the basis of all this, then, perhaps I may venture to assert that the prevailing attitude to the Emperor shows persistently and universally something fundamentally in common with that of our village. Now I have no wish whatever to represent this attitude as a virtue; on the contrary. True, the essential responsibility for it lies with the government which in the most ancient empire in the world has not yet succeeded in developing, or has neglected to develop, the institution of the empire to such precision that its workings extend directly and unceasingly to the farthest frontiers of the land. On the other hand, however, there is also involved a certain feebleness of faith and imaginative power on the part of the people, that prevents them from raising the empire out of its stagnation in Pekin and clasping it in all its palpable living reality to their own breasts, which yet desire nothing better than but once to feel that touch and then to die.

This attitude then is certainly no virtue. All the more remarkable is it that this very weakness should seem to be one of the greatest unifying influences among our people; indeed, if one may dare to use the expression, the very ground on which we live. To set about establishing a fundamental defect here would mean undermining not only our consciences, but, what is far worse, our feet. And for that reason I shall not proceed any further at this stage with my enquiry into these questions.

—*Translated from the German by* WILLA AND EDWIN MUIR

ALDOUS HUXLEY

On the Road to Rome

This is an episode from the tragic story of a man who tried to make the best of two worlds, situated at the extreme polar limits of human experience—the world of pure Christian spirituality, and the world of power politics. The biography of Father Joseph reads like a parable specially composed to illustrate the truth that it is impossible for a man to serve both God and Mammon.

ALDOUS HUXLEY

THE friar had kilted up his habit, and his bare legs were muddy to the knees. After the spring rains, the road was like a swamp. It had been like a lime kiln, he reflected, last time he walked this way. He recalled the poem he had written on another of his journeys.

> *Quand au plus chaud du jour l'ardente canicule*
> *Fait de l'air un fourneau,*
> *Des climats basanés mon pied franc ne recule,*
> *Quoy que je coule en eau.*[1]

That summer of 1618, when the three of them had taken the road for Spain! Poor Brother Zeno of Guingamp had died of sunstroke at Toulouse. And a week later, near Burgos, Father Romanus had fallen sick with dysentery. In three days it was all over. He had limped into Madrid alone. And alone he was now to limp into Rome. For Father Angelus had had to be left behind with the Capuchins of Viterbo, too sick of the ague to walk another step. God bring him soon to health again!

> *Ni des Alpes neigeux, ni des hauts Pirénées*
> *Le front audacieux*
> *N'a pu borner le cours de mes grandes journées,*
> *Qui tendent jusqu'aux cieux.*[2]

---

[1] When, at day's hottest hour, the burning Dog Star makes a furnace of the air, my roving feet affront the swarthy regions of the earth, though I be streaming with sweat.

[2] The aspiring crests of the snowy Alps and Pyrenees have not sufficed to limit my long marches that aim at the very heavens.

Cher Seigneur, si ta main m'enfonça la blessure
De ce perçant dessein,
J'ay droit de te montrer ma tendre meurtrissure
Et descouvrir mon sein.[3]

"La blessure de ce perçant dessein," he repeated to himself. The phrase was particularly felicitous. Almost Latin in its pregnancy—like one of those phrases of Prudentius. . . .

The Capuchin sighed profoundly. That wound, he reflected, was still open, and, goaded by the barb of God's piercing design, he was still hurrying, at the rate of fifteen leagues a day, across the face of Europe. When would that design be carried into execution? When would it be granted to another Godefroy of Bouillon to storm Jerusalem? Not yet awhile, to all appearances—not till the wars were over, not till the House of Austria should be humbled and France grow strong enough to lead the nations on the new Crusade. How long, Oh Lord, how long?

He sighed again, and the sadness of his thoughts was reflected upon his face. It was the face of a man in middle life, weathered, gaunt with self-inflicted hardship, lined and worn with the incessant labour of the mind. Beneath the broad, intellectual forehead, the prominent blue eyes were widely opened, almost staring. The nose was powerfully aquiline. Long and unkempt, a reddish beard already grizzled, covered his cheeks and chin; but the full-lipped, resolute mouth suggested a corresponding firmness of the jaw beneath. It was the face of a strong man, a man of firm will and powerful intelligence; a man also, under the second nature imposed by a quarter-century of the religious life, of powerful passions and a fierce intensity of feeling.

Barefooted—for he had taken off his sandals and was carrying them in his hand—he walked on through the mud, engrossed in his melancholy thoughts. Then, recollecting himself, he suddenly realized what he was doing. Who was *he* to criticize God's ways? His sadness was a recrimination against Providence, a flying in the face of that divine will, to obey which was the only purpose of his life. And it must be obeyed without reluctance, whole-heartedly, joyfully. To be sad was a sin and, as such, an obstacle between his soul and God. He halted and for more than a

[3] Dear Lord, if it is Thy hand which has penetrated me with the wound of this piercing design, I have the right to show Thee my tender hurt and to unveil my breast.

minute stood there in the road, covering his face with his hands. His lips moved; he was praying to be forgiven.

When he walked on, it was in a contrite mood. The natural man, he was thinking, the old Adam—what a sleepless hostility to God one carried about in the depths of one's own mind and body! What a fixed resolve to sin! And what resourcefulness in the art of sinning, what skill, when one temptation had been overcome, in discovering another and more subtle evil to surrender to! There was no remedy but in perpetual vigilance. Sentinels for ever on guard against the stratagems of the enemy. *Timeo Danaos et dona ferentes.* But there was also the great ally—the Divine friend, without whose aid the garrison must infallibly be destroyed. Oh, ask him in! Open the gates! Sweep clean the streets and garnish the town with flowers!

The sun came out from behind the clouds. The Capuchin looked up and, from its position in the sky, calculated that the time must be a little after two o'clock. Rome was still three leagues away. There was no time to stop. He would have to practise his annihilation in the Essential Will as he walked. Well, it would not be the first time.

He repeated the Lord's Prayer slowly and aloud; then addressed himself to the opening phase of his exercise, the act of pure intention. To do the will of God, the exterior will, the interior will, the essential will. To do it for the sake of God alone, and without reference to what he himself desired, or hoped, or might gain in this world or the next. . . . To annihilate himself in all he thought and felt and did, so that there should be nothing left but the instrument of God's will and a soul united by God's grace with that divine substance, which was identical with the divine, essential will. He held his mind unwaveringly upon that resolution, while he walked a furlong or more. Then words came once again. "To expose myself to God, to prepare my soul for his coming, watchfully and with reverence. To turn myself, naked of every other design, every other feeling and thought and memory, towards such radiance of divine love and knowledge as God may vouchsafe to give. And even if he should vouchsafe to give me nothing, even if it should be his will to leave me without light or consolation, to turn towards him none the less with thankfulness and in perfect faith. *Qui adhaeret Deo, unus spiritus est.*" He who adheres to God, is one spirit with God.

To adhere, he repeated, to adhere. . . .

From the act of pure intention he passed to that of adoration and humility. "God for his own sake and not with any thought of myself." For what was this self of his? A nothing—but an active nothing, capable of sin and therefore capable of cutting itself off from the All. An active nothing that had to be annihilated into passive nothingness, if God's will was to be done.

He had worked hard to annihilate that active nothing, and God in his great mercy had granted him many favours—strength to control at least the grosser impulses of nature, sensible consolations, visions and revelations, access at moments to the outskirts of the divine presence. But for all that his active nothingness still persisted; he was still capable of negligence and imperfection, even of such downright wickedness as complacency in the recollection of his own work and God's past favours. The Old Adam knew how to make use even of the soul's efforts to annihilate the Old Adam and, by taking pride in those efforts, was able to undo their results and strengthen his own resistance to God. Nay, the very graces of God could be turned, unless the soul was unremittingly on guard, into a stumbling block and a source of grievous sins and imperfection. The Son of God, the incarnate source of all grace—how had *he* proclaimed his divinity? By humility, by adoration and love of God.

"Love, love, love," the Capuchin repeated, "humility and love, humility of the nothing before the all, love and adoration of the all by the nothing, love . . ."

Horny like a savage's from their incessant marching and countermarching across the face of Europe, his bare feet splashed through the puddles, stepped unflinching on the stones, treading the beat of the reiterated words. "Love, Christ's love, love . . ." It was said that the Cardinal Nephew had been offended by the behaviour of His Catholic Majesty's ambassador. "Christ's love, Christ's love . . ." These Spaniards were forever undoing themselves by their stupid arrogance. "Love, love, love . . ." Well, so much the better for France. All at once he perceived that the words he was still repeating to himself had become separated from his thoughts, that the flame he had been cherishing was extinguished.

"Martha, Martha, thou art careful and troubled about many things; but one thing is needful." He excluded the Cardinal Nephew and the Spanish ambassador, and reestablished the connection between his thoughts and his words. "Love, love, love, Christ's love . . ." The little flame was alight again. He kept it burning unwaveringly while he walked a quarter of a mile. Then it was time to pass on to operation—the repudiation of distracting thoughts and the resolve to banish them from the mind.

The Cardinal Nephew and the Spanish ambassador . . . More than five and twenty years had passed since Father Benet of Canfield had taught him how to pray. More than five and twenty years—and his mind was not yet completely under control, the devils of distraction still had power, sometimes, to intrude even into the sanctuary of orison. There was no final remedy but the grace of God. Meanwhile, one could only resolve to banish the distracting thoughts each time they found their way past the defences. If one persisted in the struggle, if one worked hard and patiently, it would be counted, no doubt, as a merit. God knew one's weaknesses and the efforts one made to overcome them.

Headed in the opposite direction, a train of pack animals from the City jingled slowly past him. The muleteers interrupted their talk for a moment and respectfully doffed their hats. Half blind, as he was, with too much straining over books and documents, the friar saw their gesture as a blur of movement against the sky. Recognizing its intention, he raised a hand in blessing; then went back once again to his orison.

In the form of prayer he was accustomed to use, an act of discursive meditation succeeded the preparatory exercises. Today the perfection he had chosen as his theme was love. Following the established order of his discourse, he addressed himself first of all to the consideration of God as the source of love. *Pater noster, qui es in coelis. Qui ES in coelis.* God, the eternal and Infinite Being. But when a finite being abandoned itself to the Infinite Being, Infinite Being was apprehended as Love. Thus, Infinite Being was at the same time a loving Father—but of children so rebellious and ungrateful that they were for ever doing all in their power to shut themselves out from his love. They shut themselves out from his love and, by that act, cut themselves off from their own happiness and salvation.

"All manner of virtue and goodness," the Capuchin repeated in a whisper, "and even that Eternal Good which is God Himself, can never make a man virtuous, good, or happy, so long as it is outside the soul."

He raised his head for a moment. In the blue gap of rain-washed sky between the clouds, the sun was gloriously bright. But if one chose to drop one's eyelids against the light, so—why, then one was blind, one walked in darkness. God was love; but the fact could be fully known only to one who himself loved God.

This thought served as a bridge between the first stage of his meditation and the second, between God as the source of love and his own shortcomings as a lover of God.

He loved God insufficiently because he was insufficiently detached from the world of creatures in which he had to do his work. *Factus est in pace locus ejus.*[4] God can be perfectly loved only by a heart that has been sanctified by the divine presence; and God is present only in a heart at peace. He is excluded by anxiety, even when that anxiety is a concern about the works of God. God's work must be done; but if it is not done in the peace of perfect detachment, it will take the soul away from God. He himself had come nearest to that perfect detachment in the days when he had worked at preaching and spiritual instruction. But now God had called him to these more difficult tasks in the world of great events, and the peace of detachment had become increasingly difficult of achievement. To dwell in the essential will of God while one was negotiating with the Duke of Lerma, say, or the Prince of Condé—that was hard indeed. And yet those negotiations had to be undertaken; they were a duty, and to do them was God's exterior will. There could be no shrinking from such tasks. If peace eluded him while he undertook them, it was because of his own weakness and imperfection. That highest degree of orison—the active annihilation of self and all creatures in the essential will of God—was still beyond him. There was no remedy but God's grace, and no way to earn God's grace but through constant prayer, constant humility, constant love. Only so could God's kingdom come in him, God's will be done.

It was time to pass to the third phase of his meditation—reflection on the Saviour's acts and sufferings as related to the love of God. *Fiat voluntas tua.*[5] Once in the world's history God's will had been done, fully and completely; for God had been loved and worshipped by one who, being himself divine, was able to give a devotion commensurate with its object.

The image of Calvary rose up before the friar's mind—the image that had haunted him ever since, as a tiny child, he had first been told of what wicked men had done to Jesus. He held the picture in his imagination,

[4] In peace is his place established.
[5] Thy will be done.

nd it was more real, more vivid than what he actually saw of the road
t his feet. "Father, forgive them, for they know not what they do." Pity
nd love and adoration suffused his whole being, as with a sensible warmth
hat was at the same time a kind of pain. Deliberately, he averted the eyes
f his mind. The time had not yet come for such an act of affection and
vill. He had still to consider, discursively, the ends for which the Saviour
ad thus suffered. He thought of the world's sins, his own among them,
nd how he had helped to hew the cross and forge the nails, to plait the
scourge and the crown of thorns, to whet the spear and dig the sepulchre.
And yet, in spite of it, the Saviour loved him and, loving, had suffered,
suffered, suffered. Had suffered that the price of Adam's sin might be
paid. Had suffered that, through his example, Adam's children might
learn how to conquer evil in themselves. "Her sins, which are many, are
forgiven; for she loved much." Loving, one was forgiven; forgiven, one
became capable of forgiving; forgiving, one could open one's soul to
God; opening one's soul to God, one could love yet more intensely; and
so the soul could climb a little higher on the ascending spiral that led
towards perfect union. *Ama, et fac quod vis.* Love, and do what thou wilt.

"Let there be love," he repeated, modulating his orison out of Meditation into Affection, transforming it from an act of the discursive intellect
into an act of loving, self-renouncing will. "Let there be love." And taking his own lovelessness, taking the malignantly active nothing that was
himself, he offered it up as a sacrifice, as a burnt offering to be consumed
in the fire of God's love.

Lose life to save it. Die, that life may be hid with Christ in God. Die,
die, die. Die on the cross of mortification, die in the continuous and
voluntary self-noughting of passive and active annihilation.

Die, die, die, die . . . In an act of pure contrition he begged God's
forgiveness for being still himself, Joseph of Paris, and not yet wholly
the instrument of the divine will, at peace even in action, detached even
in the turmoil of business.

Die, help me to die, help me to love so that I may be helped to die.
He laid lovelessness upon an inward altar and prayed it might be consumed, prayed that from its ashes might arise a new birth of love.

Trotting up from behind, came a young horseman, gaily plumed, with
a silver-studded saddle and the damascened butts of two fine pistols in

his holsters. He interrupted his whistling to shout a friendly good day
The other did not answer, did not even raise his bowed head.

"What, is he deaf?" cried the horseman, as he drew up level with the
friar. Then, for the first time, he saw the face under the grey hood. The
spectacle of those lowered lids, those lips almost imperceptibly moving
in prayer, that expression of intense and focussed calm, abashed the young
man into silence. He mumbled a word of apology, raised his hat, as though
to the image in a wayside shrine, and crossed himself; then set spurs to
his horse and cantered away, leaving the friar to perfect his act of self
immolation undisturbed.

How delicately the sacrifice had to be performed! How subtly, effort
lessly, unabruptly! There were occasions when violence might be used to
take the kingdom of heaven; but this was not one of them. Violent annihi
lation of the self would defeat its own purpose; for such violence be
longed to the merely human will, and to make use of it would only
strengthen that will against the will of God. In this act of self-abnegation
a man must somehow operate without effort; or rather he must permi
self to be operated, passively, by the divine will. . . .

In the matter of the Valtelline, of course, His Holiness had more rea
son to fear the closer union between Spain and Austria than to be angry
with the French for ousting a papal garrison. The Cardinal Nephew
would probably. . . .

The friar became aware, once again, that concern with God's work had
drifted like a dark eclipsing cloud between himself and God. Checking
his first movement towards a passionate self-reproach that would only
have made the eclipse completer, he gently changed the focus of his inner
vision, looking past the Cardinal Nephew, past the Valtelline and Spain
and France towards the pure will of God beyond and above and within
them. The cloud drifted away; he was exposed once more to the light
Patiently, delicately, he opened himself to its purifying and transforming
radiance.

Time passed, and a moment came at length when it seemed to him
that he was fit to go on to the next stage of contemplation. The mirror
of his soul was cleansed; the dust and vapours that ordinarily intervened
between the mirror and that which it was to reflect had been laid to rest
or dissolved. If he now turned his soul to Christ, the divine form would
be reflected clearly and without blasphemous distortion; the image of the

crucified Saviour would be within him, imprinting itself upon his will, his heart, his understanding, a divine model to be imitated, a spirit to inform and quicken.

Tenaciously he held the beloved image behind his half-closed eyelids; and this time he permitted himself the happiness of that adoration, intense to the point of physical pain, that boundless bliss and agony of compassion, from which he had had to turn in the earlier, discursive part of his exercise. Suffering, suffering. . . . Tears filled his eyes. Suffering of the Son of God, of God himself incarnate as man. Suffering endured by the loving Saviour of all sinners, this darkest sinner among them. *Recede a me, quia homo peccator sum.*[6] And yet the Saviour came, and took this leper in his arms, and knelt before him, and washed his feet. Dost Thou wash my feet? These feet that have walked in wickedness, that are all caked with the filth of sin and ignorance? Yes, and not only washes his feet, but, for the sinner's sake, permits himself to be taken, judged, mocked, scourged and crucified. He came back to the Calvary in his heart, to the suffering, the suffering of his God. And the annihilation for which he had striven seemed now to be consummated in a kind of rapture of devotion and compassion, love and pain. He was absorbed into a blissful participation in the sufferings of God incarnate—of God incarnate and therefore at the same time of the pure essential godhead out of which the God-Man had proceeded. That body upon the cross was the invisible made visible. Calvary was bathed in the uncreated light, irradiated by it, consubstantial with it. Absorbed into his source and ground, the crucified Christ was annihilated in the light, and there was nothing but the shining rapture of love and suffering. Then, as it were, re-condensing, the light took form again in Jesus crucified, until a new transfiguration once more assimilated Calvary with the glory that surrounded it.

Striding along, the friar's body measured out with its bare feet the furlongs and the minutes, the hours and the miles. Within, his soul had reached the fringes of eternity and, in an ecstasy of adoration and anguish, contemplated the mystery of the incarnation.

A donkey brayed; the outriders in front of a coach sounded their bugles; someone shouted and there was a sudden outburst of women's laughter.

Under the Capuchin's hood, there was a distant consciousness of these

[6] Depart from me, for I am a sinful man.

things. Eternity receded. Time and self came gliding in again to take its
place. Reluctantly, the friar raised his head and looked about him. His
myopic eyes discerned a house or two and the movement of men and
animals on the road before him. He looked down again and, to cushion
the shock of this abrupt return from one world to another, reverted to a
discursive meditation on the Word made Flesh.

At the Milvian Bridge a group of soldiers had been posted to keep check
on all incoming travellers from the North. The Capuchin answered their
questions fluently, but with a foreign accent that automatically aroused
suspicion. He was taken to the guard room to give an account of himself. The officer in charge touched his hat as the friar entered, but did not
rise or remove his booted feet from the table on which he had propped
them. Standing before him his hands crossed over his breast, the traveller
explained that his name was Father Joseph, that his convent was in Paris,
that he had been sent by his superiors to attend a meeting of the Chapter
General of his order. The officer listened, picking his teeth, as he did so,
with a silver-gilt toothpick. When the Capuchin had finished, he touched
his hat again, belched and said that, while of course he had no reason
whatever to doubt the truth of the Reverend Father's words, the existence
of certain malefactors, certain brigands, certain (he made an emphatic
flourish with the toothpick), certain enemies of God and man, who did
not scruple to hide their wickedness under the Franciscan habit, made it
necessary for him to ask for the Reverend Father's papers. The Capuchin
hesitated for a moment, then inclined his head in acquiescence. Opening
his habit at the neck, he reached into an inner pocket. The packet which
he brought out was wrapped in blue damask and tied with a white silk
ribbon. The officer raised his eyebrows as he took it, then smiled. Undoing
the ribbon, he remarked facetiously that there had been a time when he
carried his mistresses' love letters in just such a packet as this. Now, with
a jealous wife in his bed and his mother-in-law actually living in the
house . . . Suddenly the smile on his fat face was replaced by a look
of astonishment that gave place to one positively of alarm. The object
he had extracted from the packet was a letter sealed with the royal arms
of France and addressed, with the most magnificent flourishes, to His
Holiness, Urban VIII. He glanced apprehensively at the friar, then back
again at that formidable superscription, that portentous seal; then with

a great jingling and clatter he took his feet off the table, sprang out of his chair and, removing his hat, made a deep bow.

"Forgive me, Reverend Father," he said. "If I had only known . . . If only you had made it clear from the outset. . . ."

"There is also a letter to His Eminence, the Cardinal Nephew," said the Capuchin. "And another, if you will give yourself the trouble of looking, to His Most Christian Majesty's ambassador. And finally a passport delivered to myself and signed by His Eminence, the Cardinal Minister . . ."

At each name the officer made another obeisance.

"If I had known," he kept on repeating, while the friar gathered up the letters, "if I had only known . . ."

Breaking off, he rushed to the door and began shouting furiously at his men.

When the Capuchin left the guard room, he found his way across the bridge lined on either side by a company of papal musketeers. He halted for a moment, humbly acknowledged the officer's salute, raised a hand in blessing and then crossing his arms on his breast, he bowed his head and, without looking to right or left, hurried forward noiselessly on his bare feet between the double row of pikes.

WILLIAM ZUKERMAN

The Refugee From Judea

"The Refugee from Judea" is to be taken as a reflection of the profound scepticism bordering on despair which had swept Europe during that dark period between the rise of Naziism and the outbreak of the Second World War. Not only was Naziism then young, lusty and vigorous, promising to sweep the world, but the world did not seem to mind being overrun. Civilized humanity was listless and indifferent and seemed to have made peace with the evil force not only politically, but also spiritually and morally. In an atmosphere such as that scepticism cut deeply into faith and reached the lowest depths of the abyss. The "Refugee" touched that point. The hero not only questions the most fundamental bases of our moral life and all our spiritual values, but he doubts also the life and character of Christ. He imagines Him as fleeing from the Garden of Gethsemane on the night of the Passion. Instead of remaining in the Garden to take upon Himself the Cross, he sees Christ escaping to Egypt as a refugee and becoming there a popular and successful preacher.

WILLIAM ZUKERMAN

WHAT strange thoughts pass through one's mind while sitting alone on a cold night in front of an open hearth fire! The thin, blue flames leap up and wreathe around the dark, cold lumps of coal, as if engaged in some mysterious sacred dance to drive away chill, and resurrect the frozen dead with quick, fiery kisses. They invite one to fantastic daydreaming; and in these days when humanity is not dreaming but acting out a horrible nightmare, the day-dreams of one man sitting before a hearth fire often intermingle with wisps of the universal nightmare that constantly float about in our consciousness; and together they form a strange dark tangle of fact and fancy, truth and lies, hope and despair, that settles heavily on the heart, and makes a man's thought toss about restlessly like a child in fever.

Yet the little dancing flames have also a curiously soothing effect on the troubled spirit. Or is it the soft, crackling voice of the fire? It is a quiet, rich, mellow voice slow and unhurried, the voice of a kind, old Nanny who lulls frightened children to sleep by telling them a long, long tale of the triumph of good over evil, of the handsome Prince over the ugly witch.

"Once upon a time . . . ," the gentle voice begins. But—but suppose the story did *not* happen as the good Nanny used to tell it? Suppose virtue did *not* triumph? Courage did *not* win the day? Truth did *not* prevail? The forces of love did *not* rout the forces of hatred? Suppose the man who had set out in search of the Holy Grail came back empty-handed, tired, disillusioned, bored and indifferent to everything but a good meal and a warm bed? After all, is not this what usually happens in real life? Why, then, should it not happen also in man's dreams which he dreams for the soothing of his spirit? Why should his dreams be so distant from his reality? Perhaps, if the creations of his longing were nearer to his real life, his world might not be as dark as it is now?

Outside, the black night presses itself against the window like a lost soul in search of salvation. Out there, on the other side of the window, all is darkness and cold: a bitter wind, soaked through with rain, viciously bends the bare trees almost to the ground. But here, in this little room, all the meanness, the inexplicable cruelty and darkness which oppress the world so heavily, is barred out by a small attic window. Strange how the whole of that heavy power, which seems to crunch over life like a steam-roller leaving men mangled beyond recognition, can be stopped by one small window-pane. Yet so it is. An entire universe is gathered into this small warm room, thickly populated with lilting little flames and leaping shadows that are able, in some mysterious manner, to pierce into the deep and devious caverns of thought and lead it to the surface.

"Suppose, in these days of nightmare and darkness," the thought insinuates itself softly, "some of the most beautiful stories which have sustained mankind for centuries were to be retold? Suppose they were retold more truthfully, nearer to reality, as the events they relate in all probability happened, and not as human imagination has embellished them? Would it not be more likely to bring to troubled spirits the comfort and peace they now lack? Would it not lull to sleep the many frightened children who find no rest? For what frightens children most in nightmares is that these are so different from the beautiful stories of love and valor with which they were lulled to sleep. Perhaps what we need is to make our day dreams more like reality, instead of continually flogging our poor nag of reality to reach the heights of our dreams?

"Suppose Jesus ran for his life on the night of Gethsemane instead of remaining in the Garden to pray and then die."

The voice of the fire is so soft it does not frighten thought, nor ever startle it. "Suppose that, instead of accepting his Father's will, he had insisted on his own. Would not that have been the perfectly natural and human way? Would it not have been the sane, the practical, and in the long run even the best thing to do? Is not life sweet? Is not life the most precious gift received from our Father? Why should we give it up for something which may be nothing but a chimera? At best a thought, an idea, a vision? And even if this something is indeed the truth, is it more true than life itself? Jesus knew the great value of life. He taught its sacredness. What, then, would have been more natural than that he should wish to preserve it? All the accounts of the awful scene in the Garden testify that he thought of this possibility, that throughout the long terrible night of his passion he struggled with this temptation. Why should he not have yielded to it? How easy it would have been if, instead of remaining there to pray in an agony of sweating blood, he had taken with him Peter and the two sons of Zebedee and had escaped into the dark night and hidden in the hills of Galilee which they knew so much better than the Roman soldiers. A little later he might easily have slipped across the frontier into the neighboring Alexandria, and become a refugee in Egypt, instead of a martyr in Judea."

The fire on the hearth is now in full blaze. The hard, cold, black lump of coal have yielded to the fiery embraces of the flames; have opened their hearts, and reveal to amazed eyes the buried treasures of centuries. What fantastic and unearthly beauty! Strange castles with towers and spires all burning in a glory the like of which can be seen only in the sky when the sun takes leave of the earth. The little fireplace is a throne of gold standing on a mountain of amber and rubies. The blue flames continue their sacred dance around the golden throne, writhing lively in an ecstasy of passion. The crackle of the fire continues the tale.

"Alexandria of those days was a great and flourishing city, next to Athens the center of Greek culture. Its people were not as drunk with religion as were those of Judea, not as fanatical. Like all peoples under the influence of Greece, their spiritual interests were more philosophic than religious, and they were tolerant of unconventional thoughts and deas. The city also had a rich and influential Jewish community; but it oo was Greek rather than Judean in its outlook. The Alexandrian Jews were out of sympathy with the long-bearded fanatical priests of Jerusa-em, even disliked them, and a victim of their persecution would have been given refuge, if not a warm welcome. Jesus would hardly have found any followers among them. For, in the first place, they were mostly well-to-do merchants and artisans to whom the idea of a kingdom of the poor would not have appealed. Secondly, they were under the influence of the rationalist philosopher Philo; and the simple truths of the Galilean refugee, which flowed from a source deeper than reason, would not have attracted their sophisticated minds. Above all, they had themselves too much contempt for Jews in general and Jews from Judea in particular to be influenced by anything that came from one of them, unless it was first accepted and praised by the Egyptians. But, in the old tradition of their race, they certainly would not have let the Galilean exile fall a financial burden on the non-Jews of Alexandria.

"There were, in fact, many other such refugees in Egypt then, and the rich Alexandrian Jews had in all probability formed a Refugee Committee to look after them. In that Committee, young Jesus, after being cross-examined by a number of supercilious young women and inspected by a still larger number of overbearing middle-aged and elderly men, would be sternly admonished not to attract too much attention to himself in the streets of Alexandria, not to speak Hebrew or Aramaic, and above all to emigrate as soon as possible to some distant part of the Roman Empire, like the newly discovered lands of the Teutons, the Gauls, the Angels, and other barbarians. Nevertheless, he would be given a meager subsidy to keep him from starvation in the meantime. As his physical needs were very small, he would have been satisfied.

"With time, indeed, he might even have begun to find followers: these would come, in the first instance, from the poorer Egyptians and the slaves of all nationalities who thronged the docks of Alexandria. For not all the people of Egypt in those days were under the influence of Greek rationalist philosophy. Still very strong in the masses were the traditions of old Egypt and the Orient; and there was a longing in the air for a truth which the teaching neither of Philo nor of Aristotle could satisfy. At any rate, slaves and freemen who worked like slaves might have collected around the refugee from Judea. The ardor of his faith,

the charm of his personality, his limpid simplicity, and the colorful con
trast between his beautiful parables and the dry rationalism of the Greek
philosophers, might well have increased his following. So a new sect
would gradually be formed; it might find adherents not only in Alex
andria and in the rest of Egypt, but also across the frontiers, in Greece
in Rome, even in Judea where it would come with the new irresistible
prestige of the non-Jewish world, and hence would be eagerly accepted
by those who had rejected it when first preached by an unknown Galilean
Jew.

"The fame of the new teaching might also reach the ears of those
practical and energetic people, present in all ages, whose business it is
to materialize visions and to convert dreamers' dreams into practical prop
ositions. It might have attracted a terrific fanatic and organizer like
Paul of Tarsus, who would come to Alexandria to sit at the feet of the
new teacher. With his coming, the new sect would be transformed beyond
all recognition. The apostles, the dreamers, the doubters, the simple fishermen and dockers who first took up the new teaching, would be swept
aside. Their place would be taken by sleek and fashionable preachers
who knew everything and never had a doubt about anything. The teacher
himself would lose all influence on the movement. He would become
in his lifetime an almost legendary figure in whose name all the work
of the preachers would be done.

"There would develop a feverish activity of organization and propaganda. A net of cells would be established. Contacts would be formed
with governments, with important institutions, with men of wealth and
influence. The word of God would be preached in a highly scientific
manner according to the latest laws of psychology. It would penetrate
into the most exclusive salons of Alexandrian society where the richly
coiffured, painted and perfumed Egyptian ladies would speak daintily
of the Kingdom of the Meek, and their young offspring would be among
the most ardent admirers of the new teacher.

"After the Roman War in Judea and the destruction of the Temple,
Jesus would return home, for his heart had always been in his native
hills. There he would pick up the threads where he left them on the night
of Gethsemane, now no longer as an obscure and persecuted preacher
of the Galilean hills forever in danger of crucifixion, but as a famous
exile who had returned to his native land and had been received with

universal acclamation. He would begin to build his Kingdom of God on the very ruins of the destroyed Temple where the priests who had sought to have him crucified once ruled. He might even become a ruler himself, and his first act as ruler might be to strengthen the guard in the mountain passes of Galilee to prevent men under sentence of crucifixion from escaping to Egypt . . ."

At this moment the heart of the brightly burning coal suddenly caved in with a crash. In an instant all the fantastic castles, towers, spires, thrones of gold, mountains of rubies and emeralds lay in fiery fragments around the ruins. The sound of the crash interrupted the quiet flow of the story and startled the fire-gazer's thought into reality.

"Come to your senses!" whispered a frightened thought in his mind. 'Do you realize what blasphemy you have just dreamed? Just think what the world would have lost if your horrible supposition were true! Lost not merely in goodness, in moral values, but in the grandeur of faith and in beauty. Think of the drabness of the life of a great portion of humanity without the somber grandeur of Calvary, without the austere beauty of the dark Cross standing out in sharp relief against a copper sky. Can you grasp the magnitude of the loss to the world of the suffering of this lonely, deserted and mocked man staggering up a dusty hill on a hot day, deliberately to lay down his life for his faith? Think of the millions oppressed, persecuted, tortured on the rack, who were enabled to live and to bear their pain and sorrow by the thought of his suffering, his loneliness, his anguish. Think of the millions who died on battle-fields, of the innumerable slaves in galleys and under the yoke, of the legions in prisons, concentration camps, torture chambers and execution places, of the poor, the hounded and driven, of the mocked and insulted, of all the hopeless and despairing who throughout nineteen centuries found solace in the thought of him who also was driven and tortured, mocked and insulted, and abandoned by all, even by his Father. Think, think, and be horrified into silence!"

A sudden hush did fall in the room, as if the garrulous voice that was telling the tale was shamed by the outburst of outraged piety. For a moment the fire-place was dark, and it looked as if the tale was at an end. But the fire on the hearth was not extinguished; only dimmed by the caving-in of the coal; nor was the bitterness and defiance of the human imagination exhausted. Soon the fire resumes building its magic fairy land with its streets of gold and houses of emeralds and rubies. And the fire-gazer's imagination, stirred again by this magic, rises in a new hot and defiant rejoinder.

"For almost two thousand years," he begins, "men have died on battle fields, in prisons, in concentration camps, by the hands of the executioner and on beds of pain, and many have indeed found solace in the though of the suffering which the Son of Man willingly took upon himself. Al most two thousand years have passed since he shot up his life like a rocke into the dark sky to lighten humanity's night and to illumine the road for the suffering children of men. Yet now the darkness is thicker than ever, the end to the night is not in view, and the road to salvation ha not yet been described, still less followed. After two thousand years of pain and suffering immeasurable, of faith in his words which for pathos depth and sincerity has no equal in the history of this world, his promise is no more fulfilled today than it was during his lifetime. Men still die in agony on the battle-fields, in prisons and concentration camps; they still groan under the yoke of slavery; they are still oppressed and down trodden; they are still mocked, humiliated, spat upon and crucified, al though he gave his life that all these things should be no more. Two thousand years of the preaching of the word of love, and the anguish of the night of Gethsemane still drags on; the shadow of Calvary ha spread over the whole face of the world; humanity lies crushed under the cross; and the groans of the dying, the oppressed and humiliated go up to Heaven in such volume that they drown out every other sound in creation."

Now the shadows on the wall stood still as if they, too, were shocked by the fire-gazer's thoughts. Big, heavy, and warm, they no longer moved lithely and vivaciously as before, but bent their heads slowly like a group of hooded monks repeating in a whisper the dreadful blasphemy they had just heard. The man at the fire looked at them long and silently, as if he expected an answer from them. Failing to receive it, he suddenly turned upon them fiercely and spoke with great vehemence:

"Tell me, you who have served him all your lives, tell me, were the Son of Man to come down to the earth now, this very night, what would happen to him? Would he not be promptly clapped into a concentration camp, flogged, beaten, kicked, spat upon and crucified more surely and more brutally than in the days of Pilate? Would he not be subjected to greater indignities and humiliations? Would he not be driven off the Prater and every park in Vienna? Would he not be made to dance and to crawl in the gutter in the very shadow of the great Cathedral which was erected in his name? Would he not be deprived of a bench when weary, of a drink when thirsty, of food when hungry, of medicine when sick? Would he not be avoided as a leper; and if he came into a public place, would he not be kicked out amidst the jeering of the crowd? Would he not be thrown out of his home, deprived of his work and livelihood, sentenced to starvation, driven from his homeland and not admitted into any other? Would he not be declared a louse, a rat, a verminous parasite who must be exterminated without mercy? Tell me, was there ever a time in history since his own days when he was crucified more readily and with greater sadistic joy than he is being crucified now, every day and every hour? When was he and his teaching more deliberately trampled under foot, jeered at and degraded, than now? What was the scoffing of the Roman soldiers on Calvary as compared with the jeering of the mobs in Vienna and Berlin? The horrors of Golgotha compared with the horrors of the bombing of Guernica and Warsaw and London? The whole world now is one big deliberate mockery of him. Yes, a mockery, more than a cruelty. It is as if some infernal imagination had deliberately invented the whole of the present scene for the sole purpose of jeering and mocking at God and of showing the utter futility and failure of Calvary. And yet, you continue to whisper your prayers and to pour out sermons about the coming of the Kingdom of God upon the earth and about the victory of the Cross. Where is that victory? Where is the glory, strength and beauty of that Kingdom? Why does it not rise from the gutters of Vienna and Prague, of Warsaw and Berlin, to strike terror into the hearts of its blasphemers? Why do not its defenders come forth to smite those who drag the dignity of Man through the mud and humiliate God as He has never been humiliated before?"

The silence in the room was heavy now and oppressive, laden with that heaviest of all loads, the anguish of a human soul. Not only the voice of the fire, but the movement of the shadows on the wall and the very whisper of the man's bitter thoughts, seemed to have stopped. The entire

world gathered in this little room was hushed in stupefied despair; wa
this man's destiny upon the earth?

"Something is wrong somewhere," the man at the hearth groaned i
the confusion of his mind. "Was it all a mistake: Golgotha, Calvary, th
Cross? Did the Son of Man err on the eve of his passion and throw awa
his life for nothing? Perhaps, had he really become a refugee in Egyp
and experienced the long-drawn-out agony of being pulled up by th
roots; had he felt his sap drying up, his roots shrivelling, his whole sel
withering and dying without yet being physically dead; had he sat lon,
and wearily in the anterooms of the Refugee Committees, seen the loo
of contempt in the eyes of the supercilious young women and heard th
loud rebuffs of the overbearing smug men; had he been made to fee
continually that he was a stranger, an alien, living on the mercy an
generosity of others, that he was taking away someone else's job, eatin,
someone else's bread, treading on someone else's soil, breathing some
one else's air; had it been dinned into him that he was a failure, that hi
life was superfluous, and that he was probably more responsible himsel
for his situation than the brutes who had caused it; had he dragged o
for many dreary years an existence which was neither life nor death; ha
he known longing which finally exhausts itself as a child sobs itself t
sleep; had he had all faith in men, hope in life, and belief in himsel
stamped out in him; were he able to survive only by forgetting his realit
in front of a dying fire—then, perhaps, the Son of Man would hav
known more of human misery than he ever knew on Calvary, and histor
might have taken a different course."

Defiance suddenly began to ooze out from the fire-gazer's thoughts
like air from a punctured tire. Having hurled his greatest challenge int
the heavy silence and shadows of the room, he became calm, and hi
pensive mood returned. Once more his old doubts and regrets, drive
off by his outbursts like a flock of frightened birds, were coming bac
and settling comfortably again on their usual perch in his mind.

"Surely, we cannot escape our fate," he mused, but no longer wit
bitterness. "We only think we can escape by crossing frontiers an
oceans. But in reality we never escape, for we all carry our cross withi
ourselves, and when we think that we have left it far behind us, w
suddenly find it rising before us from the fire on an open hearth."

The fire-gazer suddenly realized with a familiar pang that his elab

rate dream of the evening had petered out like everything else in his
life. At the beginning, it was to be a bitter revolt, a mighty call for a
new and brave Gethsemane; but it was turning out to be a poor little
whimper of a naked soul which had ventured for a moment into the raging storm outside, and had turned quickly back into the warmth of an
attic room with a faithful coal fire. Even in his growing drowsiness he
could not help but see clearly that the fine web he had woven all evening, out of the phantoms of his mind with the shadows of the night,
was nothing but a screen behind which he had sought to hide regrets and
sorrows he feared to face. He saw the tenuous fabric of his fanciful screen
breaking in many places, and through the rifts dreaded monsters pushed
ugly wagging heads, demanding: "What right have you to be warm and
snug in front of a fire while out there the others are trudging through
deep snow on wintry roads, are huddled into ghettos and driven through
the streets with a badge of shame? What right has one part of mankind
to enjoy a single ray of light and happiness while the other is steeped so
deeply in darkness and in pain?"

Quickly and deliberately he switches off the flow of his thoughts, as
one switches off an electric light, and sinks into a heavy, silent reverie,
his eyes blankly fixed on the fire. The drowsiness gets bigger and heavier;
it is now like a big, kind, pregnant woman, moving softly and gathering
into its apron everything in the room: the shadows on the walls, the
leaping flames on the hearth, the castles, the spires, the domes, the fairy-
land with streets of gold, the weird fancies and visions of man, and the
soft, mellow voice of the fire crackling its long tale of wisdom and error,
regret and grief. Only the human mind, still struggling weakly, resists
the sweet sensation of rest and peace that is descending slowly upon a
tired spirit worn out by a long night of its own Gethsemane. It is as if
man's mind alone, of all things in the world, is not yet fully convinced
that the greatest and sweetest of all human truths is sleep, and is still
restlessly seeking some other answer. But finally he too sees that there
is no other solution to the torturing problems of men; and waving a faint
little good-bye to the waking, warring world, he too sinks into the sweet
bosom of merciful sleep.

VII

The Green Bough

STEPHEN VINCENT BENÉT

The Barefoot Saint

This lyrical little story by the late Stephen Vincent Benét was, curiously, first published in the boom year in America, 1929. The story constituted a volume by itself in a high-priced and limited edition. This is its first general publication.

AT CHEZERAY, the fertile, high-lying table-land between the Seine and the Eure, the whole town smells like a cider-press, in the Fall. They make good calvados in that neighborhood; they know how to cook and eat. They know the tricks of the rose, the horse and the spaniel, but they are not voluble people, and it takes a magician to cheat them in a bargain. They know how to keep their money warm, and they are hard to change. The priest rides a bicycle, with his black skirts tucked up to his knees; the radio at the Café des Sports gets the programs from the Eiffel Tower every night; but the striped fields beyond the town are the fields of generations of infinitely patient farmers, and the old mortar is still as hard as iron in the ruins of the old walls.

It is only a score of miles to the Deauville road, but Paris is another country, for all of that. This is France, or a stubborn part of it—the snail on the wall has its own house; the trees are knotted with bearing, but they continue to bear. The crypt of the little chapel goes back to Rome and in the chapel itself you will find the statue of a saint who is not in any calendar—a small saint, carved from grey stone. Her smile is decided and courteous, her hand extended to bless, but she has no name and her feet have never worn shoes. Nevertheless, there is always a candle before her. They can pray to Ste. Thérèse at Lisieux or to Ste. Jeanne at Rouen, if they like, and as much as they like. Chezeray has a saint of its own.

And for how this barefoot and nameless saint first came to her town of Chezeray, the tale tells this, in black-letter, written with a monk's pen. When the Great Fear of the Year 1000 had passed from Christendom and a man could go to sleep at night without hearing the knock of the

447

Last Judgment in every beat of his heart, many learned doctors looked for a new earth, taught its lesson by shame and terror, turning away from Satan as the burnt child turns from the fire. Alas, it was not to be so. Never had the Devil and his angels been more active, never were the black arts more highly regarded, or practised with such appalling craft. In every nation, sorcerers and magicians flourished; burn one at the stake and a whole coven sprang up from the ashes; cast one in the river and the waters themselves were attaint. It was a time of prodigies and searchings and tribulations. In France, after many years, this evil matter came to a head at last in Gilles de Rais, that notable wizard, and was ended. But long before Gilles had said his first prayer backward at his familiar's knee, there were men in our country fully as evil as he. There was, for example, the man called Gui Bastide.

His true name was Ormastes, and he was a magician from Persia. Why he came from Persia the tale does not tell—perhaps even the earth of that hot, corruptible country of enchanters sickened of him at last. But come he did, and he travelled into France as a rat slips down the cable of some ship come into port, bringing the plague in its coat. And with all France open before him, the Devil brought him to settle in our own village of Chezeray. They say that the Devil loves a thriving town. But, after Gui Bastide had been with us some few months, the town ceased to thrive.

He said that he was a retired merchant and that his mother had been Simone Bastide, a poor widow of Chezeray. He must have thrown some sort of spell over the older folk—for when he spoke, they remembered him, a little boy, picking up sticks in the forest and playing boys' games. He was a good fellow, always ready to pay for the wine. He gave greatly to the Church—it was, doubtless, permitted him by his allies, for the sake of the terrible things he was to bring to pass. The first sign of his power and intentions was the death of Angelique Ourcq. She was not more than fourteen and as good as bread. He had given her a ribbon once on Market Day because he said it suited her pretty hair, and would talk to her now and then on grave, instructive subjects. One morning she arose and went into the middle of the market-place and began to scream in a loud voice, cursing God and all His angels. They tried to restrain her, but she foamed at the lips and fought, and one of the women she scratched with her fingers died in two days. Nor would she leave off blaspheming the whole company of Heaven—even when they gagged her, she made signs with her hands. So Chezeray knew that the Devil had come to Chezeray and entered into her. She was tried and condemned and burnt in the public square.

There had never been such sorrow in the town since the Great Fear. Through a crowd of which not even the most pious reviled her, she was led to her fire. At the last, they say, she was like the good girl she had always been—for the ribbon had been taken from her when they dressed her in her shift for execution—and only cried pitifully and uncomprehendingly, like a beaten child. After that, there was a smoked place in the square, and people passed by it sickly, making the sign of the cross, while each man looked from the corner of his eye at his neighbor, afraid to think.

There were long, hot rains all summer. No one could remember such rains—and the crops that were not rotted, ripened too early, a grain full of bad, small ears. Fat, silly Jean Doumic killed Pierre Quervel with a cleaver in a squabble about nothing at all. They hanged him over the East Gate; and after that the children did not play games there. Two charcoal burners were eaten by wolves—not in the forest, but in the cleared fields, as they were bringing their load to town. And to cap things, the great bell of the chapel, Anne, the bell with the voice of a young boy, cracked into two pieces one day as the sexton was ringing her and so crippled him that he had to walk with two sticks the rest of his life.

A cloud lay on the countryside—a cloud that did not lift. The Bishop came in his mitre to drive the invisible evil away, with relics and a saint's thighbone. But, after he had left, things were worse than before. Gui Bastide walked about in a Turkey gown and was foremost in pious suggestions for exorcising the trouble, for, unlike most demons, he could pronounce the name of God without burning pains.

After the birth of a child with horns who prophesied unceasingly for three days in its cradle and then vanished, leaving a heap of dried leaves where it had lain, the town was like a colony of ghosts or lepers. No man would speak to another except by signs—and, when they were not in the chapel, the families were shut up in their houses, hardly daring even to eat or drink for fear the meat on the plate might become alive. The winter came on early, whetting a knife, and men began to draw in their belts about their stomachs. There was so little grain. As for the poor, who were few, they died like May flies, for a rumor had got about that some vagabond from another town was responsible for these terrors, and no one would feed them.

The priest prayed for hours to every saint in Heaven—but Ormastes, the magician, knew every saint by name, and, as soon as a prayer would rise as high as the chimney pots, he would send his familiars to take from it the name to which it was addressed so that it wandered like a senseless thing to the gates of Paradise, and could not ask admittance. To God, also, the priests prayed, and fervently—but there were three wars in Christendom then, besides the constant trouble of the Turks, and the Grand Seigneur cannot always attend to all his million petitions in person at times like those. These things are sometimes permitted—that we may know what cup was drunk by the saints.

So the priest only wearied his knees till the bone began to rub through them—and still no succor came. I have said that he implored every saint in Paradise—that is not so. He did not call on the Saint With the Bare Feet—the Saint Who Has No Name. And this was because, in the first place, he did not know that she existed and in the second, if he had, he would not have known how to address her respectfully—for he was a rather literal man. And how she came to be nameless fell about thus.

She was French, but she had been stolen when she was two years old, when a raid of barbarians came over the Rhine. This was in the wrecked time before Charlemagne. The barbarians brought her up as a scullion among the camp followers and she could not remember the name that had been given her—it was not a Christian name. As for her new masters —all they ever called her was "Here, you!" or "You there with the stubby nose!" She accepted this fact as a condition of her servitude, and by the grace in her that God grants to the defenceless, she remained a clean virgin in her life among those heathen.

Now, when she was about sixteen, St. Avennel of Lorraine came seeking martyrdom among the pagans of Germany, and, after escaping many deaths, he arrived at the camp of her army and preached to the soldiers —after which he broke their idol, which was a wooden goat, into three pieces with a stone. So they bound him and made preparations by bending down the tops of two strong saplings that grew at some distance from each other, intending, in the morning, to tie one of his arms to one sapling and one to the other, and then release the saplings. But this girl had seen St. Avennel and taken pity on him and in the night, when the camp was asleep she crept between the sentries to bring him a cup of water. And St. Avennel blessed her, and, finding her ready and eager for the knowledge of God, in the three hours before dawn, he explained God and all His mysteries to her and baptized her in the water she had brought him, naming her Claire, in the name of the Father and the Son and the Holy Ghost. Next morning she informed the heathen of these matters, and after St. Avennel had died, they bent down two other saplings, and she perished so, praising God.

When she arrived in Heaven at the heels of St. Avennel, she was very warmly received, you may be sure. As you know, though, martyrdoms were rather more common in those days than they are now. So, while she was given much praise for the directness and consistency of her actions, it was hardly to be expected that she should enjoy such an ovation as Ste. Geneviève, for instance, received on the occasion of her entrance—for, though she had done her uttermost, she had not the incessant years of mortification and service on earth behind her of such Saints as Ste. Hilarius, or Ste. Bridget or Ste. Simeon Stylites. Still, she was treated, she thought, very much beyond her deserts, for all that, and instantly given a fitting place in the heavenly hierarchy, with all its rights, powers, immunities and privileges.

But then the terrible question of her name came up. "What is this child's name?" said St. Peter, in his capacity as interlocutor, with a kindly glance at the barefoot saint's bent head, as yet unaccustomed to its halo. She was too embarrassed to answer. Besides, she had her name for such a short while. "Claire is her name," St. Avennel answered rather proudly. "For it was nearly my last act on earth to baptize her Claire." And at this both Ste. Claire of Auxerre and Ste. Claire of Amphipolis arose.

"There are already two Ste. Claires in Heaven," remarked the first, looking coldly at her neighbor, and St. Eustace muttered, "Three is for the Holy Trinity, to whom be all praise and laud but three Ste. Claires in Heaven like the two we have already and I, for one, should be inclined to ask for my caldron of boiling lead again."

"If she is to be Ste. Claire as well as myself and my sister," put in Ste. Claire of Amphipolis, with a side glance at Ste. Claire of Auxerre that had more woman than saint in it—for even in Heaven the blessed know their own minds—"it is necessary to find out where she comes from— for it is evident that she cannot be merely Ste. Claire."

"That is true," said St. Peter. "Child, what is the name of the place where you were martyred?" The barefoot saint felt more embarrassed than ever.

"I don't know," she said, timidly, after a long time. "If you please— I don't think it has any name."

This created a slight commotion in Heaven. St. Peter turned to St. Avennel. Heaven's gatekeeper was beginning to feel worried, but he dealt with the matter tactfully.

"Do you know the name of the place, St. Avennel?" he queried.

"Certainly not," said St. Avennel crisply. "All I know is that I christened this child Claire and that she is Ste. Claire."

"She cannot be simply Ste. Claire," said Ste. Claire of Auxerre, and for the first time since the two had met in Heaven, Ste. Claire of Amphipolis agreed with her.

"She is Ste. Claire," said St. Avennel, annoyed, and it almost seemed as if a personal dispute were about to develop between himself and the two Ste. Claires who were already Ste. Claires.

"I will send a cherub to make inquiries," said St. Peter, soothingly. "The place undoubtedly has a name—all places have."

When the council was reconvened the cherub made his report. He seemed rather tired. As far as could be ascertained, by methods human and divine, the place of the two saints' martyrdom was a large waste camp field which had no name in any language.

"Well, call her Ste. Claire of the Barbarians!" said Ste. Claire of Amphipolis, with a rustle of her garments. "That will be very well for the present."

"She shall not on any account be called Ste. Claire of the Barbarians!" said St. Avennel, passing a reminiscent hand over his principal scars. And St. Avennel's services had been so recent and so spectacular that no one dared contradict him.

"Ste. Claire of the Bare Feet is a pretty name," broke in St. Peter, hurriedly. "Well now—Ste. Claire of the Bare Feet—"

"Is childish, ridiculous, and derogatory to the dignity of Heaven," pronounced St. Paul, weightily. "I must enter my voice in protest against any such scheme."

There was a painful silence in Heaven for several minutes. St. Avennel looked intensely displeased with the whole affair.

Now the barefoot saint raised her head again. She looked St. Peter squarely in the beard.

"If you please," she said, modestly, but with some firmness, "I don't want any name, really. I shouldn't know what to do with a name if I had it."

"What?" said St. Avennel.

"You see, I never had a name in my life, except for six hours," said the barefoot saint, "and it takes a good deal longer than that to get used to such things."

"It was a very nice name I gave you," said St. Avennel, aggrievedly.

"It is," said his disciple, "but here are two people who have it already."

"That makes no difference at all," said St. Avennel, glaring at the other Ste. Claires.

"It makes all the difference in the world," said his godchild, "for I would not offend either of these ladies for my seat in Heaven. In fact, I will not have a name."

"But, my dear child," argued St. Peter, "the prayers—the petitions—how will people on earth know how to find you up here if you insist on having no name?"

"They will know," said the barefoot saint.

So it was settled. And, in the angelic countries, time passes like a minute and is scarcely perceived at all, so that it was several centuries before the barefoot saint had reason or opportunity to regret her decision.

But, one morning, Ste. Claire of Amphipolis passed her on the golden streets. "Have you had many petitions to-day, sister?" she said, her eyes glinting sharply under her aureole.

"Why, no," said the barefoot saint, quite truthfully—then later, a little sadly, "not one."

"That seems curious," chattered Ste. Claire of Amphipolis, "for to-day —I have given sight to two blind beggars and healed a goitre and saved a whole shipful of sailors who cried to me out of the middle of the blackest storm on the Atlantic. Their praises go up to God the Father like the smoke of sanctified candles—and I feel sure He must be very pleased with me, though he does say so little. But you must excuse me, my dear, for these are busy days—and I have to chastise a king and scare four heretics out of their wits with a rain of frogs before four o'clock this afternoon, mortal time—Good-bye . . ." And she swept away, in a great hurry of holiness, and left the barefoot saint wondering why alone of all the saints of Heaven she had no human petitioners—for she had always been a dutiful girl.

And one evening—or it may have been fifty years later—Ste. Claire of Auxerre passed her near the jasper walls, where she was watching the younger seraphs play at quoits with their halos, flinging them from comet to tasseled comet.

"Good evening, sister!" said Ste. Claire of Auxerre—and she seemed to be in a great hurry, for she had tucked up her nimbus about her knees— "and how goes the task of aiding the distressed on earth? Have a score appealed to you to-day, or only a dozen—for you look tired and seem to be taking a much-needed rest?"

"Neither a score nor a dozen," answered the barefoot saint, very sorrowfully this time, but as truthfully as ever. "Not one."

"Well, well, well, times are changed to be sure!" said Ste. Claire of Auxerre, sardonically, "for these new saints that come into Heaven and do nothing but enjoy themselves! And when I was a girl! But I really must hurry along, dear, for I have so many affairs on hand that I hardly know where to turn. There were eleven requests for happy delivery in childbirth only this morning—and I have to stop a little war and appear to a pagan philosopher in the form of a cross of white roses before I can call myself really settled for the night. Still, live and learn, my dear, live and learn, and when you're a little older and a great deal wiser, people may—" but Ste. Claire's last words were cut off as if a hand had snatched them out of her mouth, for she rushed away so fast that she looked like a meteor, and then she was a sparkling speck, and then nothing whatever.

But the barefoot saint hid herself in a cloud and wept, for it seemed to her that she had missed her vocation and was of no use in Heaven.

Then, because it is never permitted to be quite unhappy in Heaven, God blew the cloud beyond the shining gates, and she looked down and saw the earth. And it happened that the very first glance she saw was her own land, France, and in it Chezeray and the very bad state of Chezeray. After a short while, she dried her eyes and looked upon Chezeray more intently. She began to smile.

"There seems to be something for me to do after all," she said. "Yes, there seems to be something that I can do rather well." She had faults enough, no doubt, but false modesty was not among them.

"It is hard," said a quiet voice in her ear. "It is very hard, Ste. Barefoot."

"I don't care how hard it is," said the barefoot saint with a chuckle. "When the pot's dirty, it takes hot water to clean it." Then she straightened her robe, smoothed back her hair, and descended to the earth with rapid invisibility.

It was a rigid December evening, howling with wind, and Ormastes sat alone in his room, smiling at himself and his triumph. After a while, he hid that smile with his hand, for even he did not like to see it reflected in the tall yellow mirror in front of him. Outside, the flurries of the snow fought like pallid lions, tearing at each other and at the fronts of the houses and even at the windows of Ormastes, their master. He had brought the storm. After a while, he roused himself and began a minor incantation. But he had hardly said the Lord's Prayer backward twice and the chalk marks inside the red circle at his feet had not yet begun to glow like foxfire, when he heard a sound at his door that was neither wind nor snow, a sound like human speech and a weak hand tapping for entrance. It broke his mood for a moment, and the room, that had been heavy with magic, cleared. Then he shook himself and began again, but, before his sorceries took hold of the air once more, the sound was repeated.

"What the devil can that be?" said Ormastes aloud, and as he said it a shudder went through him as if he had been touched with hot iron, for if those who have sold their souls to evil will not wince at the name of God, they must at that of their Master. That is the bargain.

Again he began—and again there was a sound. This time it was impatient and yet, no mortal but he could live within that storm. He hid his apparatus, he put his skeleton and his crocodile in their cupboard and turned the yellow mirror with its face to the wall. Then he went to the door and opened it.

Crouched up on the sill, like a frozen squirrel, was a girl about sixteen years old. She was dressed in one poor garment that the wind tugged away from her, and her feet were bare as shells and blue with the cold.

"Fire," she said, faintly. "Help." And Ormastes lifted her in. He dried her feet and ankles with his own napkins. He put her before the fire and gave her wine. Then he smiled again, and this time his smile was grey as ashes and deadly as yewberries, for he could tell by his arts that she was Christian and a clean virgin—and it was of such that he stood in great need at this time.

The girl revived with the wine and the heat. She began to stir a little and moan. Ormastes put a fur cloak about her and, taking a little rosy vial from his breast, gave her three drops of the clear liquid within it. Then she seemed to come to herself and sat up dazedly.

"I was lost," she said, "I was dying. And who are you?"

"I am Gui Bastide, well known in Chezeray, a solid citizen," he answered. "And you, my child?"

"I am Claire Nupieds, and Mother keeps the wine shop by the East Gate," she answered innocently. "Only nobody ever comes there any more because of the trouble, and we must have bread. So I went out to beg some from Simon the baker, we are so hungry. But I did not know the storm was so fierce, and when the cold had caught me, I lost my way. The last thing I can remember is falling against someone's door—"

She was telling lies as fast as an ass can trot—but nearly anything is permitted in a good cause.

"It was my door," said Ormastes, "and you are a lucky child and your mother a lucky woman, for though I am not Simon the baker, my heart is as soft as cheese when it comes to helping the necessitous—and I can give you all the bread you want and to spare."

Well, then there were thanks to be sure, and between the gratitude of the saint and Ormastes' expostulations that it was nothing at all for an honest fellow to do for his neighbor, they took up quite a quarter of an hour between them.

But, finally, "I am very tired," said the saint, drooping her head, "and if you will give me a sack to cover me, I will lie down here till morning, when I must get back to Mother, for she will be nearly mad thinking I have been frozen in the storm."

"In a little while I will give you a whole room to yourself and the best bed in Chezeray," Ormastes answered, "but meanwhile—I have some little tricks I should like to show you—things that amused my nephews and nieces when we are—" and he coughed "—at home, around the fire. Just something to interest the children, but rather neat in their way. Would you like to see them, little Claire?"

"Oh, yes, yes, yes!" said the saint sitting bolt upright and trying to look as stupid as she possibly could.

Then Ormastes cracked his fingers behind his back till his great rings hurt him, for he felt that the game and the soul of the child before him were delivered into his hands.

He began mildly. There was nothing he showed at first that would have disquieted a nervous boy. He made shadows dance on the wall and pictures come in the fire, and brought out a box of wonderfully carved wooden toys from a red chest, and struck them with a wand, and made them jig and play with each other like tadpoles. Of course, each new pastime that he presented was a trifle odder than the last, and that with a strain an indefinably unpleasant oddity. Not one of the wooden kings and queens, for instance, had five whole fingers to a hand. But the saint played her part and gaped like a servant on Fair Day. She laughed and clapped her hands and asked for more.

Then Ormastes redrew his circle and turned the mirror towards it. He proceeded admirably in the path of his sorceries—never had the spirits been so eager to come. Soon there were three large murmuring skulls, with eyes like phosphorus, in the center of the circle, and a crowd of twisted devilkins hopped about them, going through such mimicries as made the saint wish herself safely back on her cloud. All the bones in the skeletons shook as if it were bitter cold, and the mirror was full of vague and deadly shapes. Ormastes watched the child as a cat watches a mousehole—for this was a strong and subtle destruction that he had prepared, and his body and mind were all one starving lust for her soul.

But the saint plucked up heart and said, with an evident yawn, that it was strange how the days kept drawing in. She picked up one of the skulls as a bowler picks up a ball and threw it idly at a devilkin. It caught him square and he yelped, for it hurt him very badly. And with that the whole phantasmagoria blew away like foggy weather. The fire died out of the floor—the mirror shuddered back into peace again—the circle was broken in three places.

"That was very funny indeed. Do it again, please," said the saint, approvingly.

Ormastes looked at her as if he could not believe in sight.

Still, he knew in the caverns of his heart that he was the most skilled magician in all Persia, and, while he had been beaten once, he thought that it had been by a mortal innocence and he had arts unexercised that

could corrupt the egg in the nest and the seed under the ground. This
time he made his preparations with almost excessive care.

He filled a crystal bowl with new blood—explaining to the saint that
it was wine—crucified a lizard on the small portable altar that accompanied him in all his travels, and arranged seven black candles so that
they formed the Unspeakable Figure. He filled the room with narcotic
incense till he could hardly breathe in it, brought out his crocodile, and
began to bound up and down the length of the chamber, gashing himself
with a curved knife and uttering short, blasphemous cries. The crocodile
moved, its eyes opened, it placed its head in the saint's white lap. And
then the whole room seemed to coagulate into a single drop of cold,
venomous oil, and through the weaving of the smoke and the ravings of
Ormastes, a voice and a form took shape. The form was princely to look
upon, and the first notes of the voice had a singular sweetness. But if
they and Death both beckoned a man, a man would run to Death and hide
under his ragged cloak.

The voice spoke. "I am here," it said, "and who calls me from Hell?"

Then Ormastes fell on his face like a dead body, for he had seen his
Master. And, lying there in such abominable shock and terror of soul
as he had never known, he heard only one sound, a sound that followed
the whirlwind of that Voice and broke it to pieces, an unbelievable sound
—the clear, pleased laughter of the saint.

When he opened his eyes again and knew that he was still alive, there
was neither incense nor Presence in the room. The crocodile had rolled
over on its back, a stuffed, pitiful figure. The yellow mirror was abolished
as if it had been beaten on an anvil—the sacrilegious pentacles of Ormastes were gone with the crystal bowl, and lizard and candles were a
pool of black wax. Also the floor was carpeted with a fine grey ash like
the dust of ground bones. These things he did not seem to mind.

He staggered to his feet. The saint stood facing him, and, as he looked
at her, he saw that she shone.

"I will repent!" he croaked hoarsely. "I submit. I ask pardon of God."

She smiled and stretched out her hand. Within it were half a dozen
flakes of white snow that lay there, unmelting. They seemed to Ormastes,
gazing at them, the coolest and most peaceful things he had ever seen.

"Is there still time?" he asked, and now his voice was that of a man
who has been tortured beyond the last extremity of the flesh.

For answer, the saint laid the flakes of snow upon his parched mouth and, suddenly, there was no more Ormastes—only a small boy child about five years old, weeping and naked except for a Turkey gown that was much too big for it. The saint smiled modestly, yet with a touch of pardonable pride. Then she knitted her brows. The boy was well enough—but she had forgotten to provide him with a family. Still, it only needed another miracle for that, and she was in the vein. She picked up the child in her arms, and comforted him.

"You are little Gui Bastide, son of Simone Bastide, the widow," she told him. "And it's high time I took you home, for your people will be wondering where you are."

"Yes," said the child, "that is right." And he curled up in her arms and slept as if he had not been to sleep for twenty years. So they left the house of Ormastes the magician. The town was brilliant with frost, and clean with bright, biting air. People stirred in the streets and the market-place. Already they were talking and disputing like neighbors. The Terror had passed. She carried the child to a poor house. There was a smell of hot cabbage soup from the door. When the child sniffed it, he woke and sprawled out of the saint's embrace like a starfish, all arms and legs and hunger. He ran to the door and beat upon it.

"Mother!" he piped, impatiently, "Mother! Is breakfast ready? I'm here, but I don't know what I've done with my clothes!" The door opened. A woman's face looked out. "Ready and boiling and waiting!" she answered impatiently. Then she saw that her son stood before her stark naked and her mouth fell open and hung like a gate ajar.

"Great merciful Lord on High!" she said in a whisper and, grabbing hold of Ormastes the magician by the scruff of his neck, ran him into the house. The door slammed. From within, a little later, came the sound of slaps.

JOAN VATSEK

The Vigil of Brother Fernando

Stories can grow slowly in the imagination, almost by themselves, from some strong impression. Such an impression I had in the little church of the skulls in Rome. One cannot readily forget the half-playful *memento mori* of the monks, the repetitive "Alas, poor Yorick" ensconced in the walls of their crypts. The setting haunted me for a long time, and then one day Brother Fernando stepped out of it and after him Father Jerome.

JOAN VATSEK

BROTHER FERNANDO stood near the church door, in the side chapel where Guido Reni's painting had hung for the last hundred and fifty years. Just now it was a little dusty, but the blue of St. George's tunic still held its original soft hue, hanging in Grecian brevity below the breastplate which seemed made of gray velvet scales rather than hard metal. The dragon under his feet writhed with unfaded, greenish contortions, bright gore spumed from its wounds, and the flying draperies, that somehow managed to be there in the background, wind-blown and billowing, glowed with color.

The head of St. George was really the head of Lucrezia, who had gone to visit Guido in prison. Even if one did not know that she had been his model, it was evident that the head was out of proportion, reflected Brother Fernando. It perched, in small blonde glory, on a massive warrior's neck, over a gigantic masculine torso with one muscled, sandaled leg held straight, like a piece of bronze, and the other gouging into the dragon's side.

Yes, one would have surely known the head was the head of a woman. It was delicate and dreamy, with blue eyes that gazed out, blandly unaware of the dragon's twisting, and her own enormous hand that poised negligently, holding a slim, wand-like spear, in preparation to plunging it once more into the dragon's many-tinted flesh.

It was obvious that when Guido had come to the head of St. George, he forgot all the extravagant paraphernalia of dragon and spear and blood, and painted Lucrezia as he saw her, looking at him.

Brother Fernando was not primarily concerned with this curious effect, he had observed it before. Neither was he praying before this attractive and ineffectual tableau, to be delivered from evil. As a matter of fact, he was trying to get some joy out of the color. For the singular thing had happened to him, that all colors seemed the same.

Now in the years that had hurried him so imperceptibly and quietly toward forty, color had been one of his greatest pleasures. The mellow splendor of stained glass windows were a continual joy to him. He had spent hours toiling through difficult old Latin books, for the illumination —the tiny, miraculously clear figures, the gay unstinted splattering of gold leaf and minute flowers—electrified his labors.

He was not given to moods. Occasionally someone of his pupils chafed at him for his lack of imagination, but this did not disturb him in the least. He had originally entered orders because a regulated, religious and scholarly life was the only one that appealed to him. This was the first time that anything had gone wrong, and Brother Fernando would far rather have lost his imperturbable capacity for sleep, or his equable temper, or his appetite, than his appreciation of color.

It was not that his eyes were growing weak. His eyes were clear, and fine. His eyes saw sharply everything that passed in the classroom.

But instead of being glad when he got up in the morning and looked out of his tight little window, and saw the clipped, gem-like green of the hedges, and the crowding fertility of the grass, it seemed to him that grass and trees and sky, all shared the same dreadful abnegation of color.

He greeted his companions at the refectory, and noted with an unfamiliar sourness, that their faces all looked the same, and that the dark carved woodwork of the panels, which had seemed to him always unobtrusively magnificent, was drab, uninspiring and dull.

He walked along the aisle among the congregation, and thought how heavy and cloddish they were. The rainbow of hats the women wore, in which he had always taken a half humorous interest, with the unpredictable conceits that varied from season to season—for it was a fashionable church, one of the richest little churches in Rome, in fact—the whole crowd looked to him a vague, dark gray.

And now, even Guido's picture, to which Brother Fernando had come as a last resort, for all its soft gaudiness, had failed him. The oil was certainly a little mottled, he admitted to himself reluctantly. Odd that he had never thought so before.

The tall, bronze-studded church door was heaved open just then, and a little group of tourists was ushered in by one of the innumerable cocky guides who lead strangers like sheep about Rome.

"And this great masterpiece," declared the guide at once, in spluttering English, "is by Guido Reni. By Guido Reni, ladies and gentlemen, the same who painted 'Aurora.'"

Brother Fernando moved off in solitary scorn, his brown robes lightly brushing his bare legs as he moved, his sandals making a little echo on the stone.

The guide suddenly left his charges and began to pursue him. Brother Fernando covered distance swiftly, and the rather stout guide had a hard time to catch him before he entered the sacristy.

"*Ecco!*" exclaimed the guide. "How fast you hurry, Father! Would the sacristan take us below? I have promised these people that they should see the place of skulls. They will put something in the box," he added placatingly.

"The sacristan is at dinner," replied Brother Fernando shortly. "Let them come back later, if they wish."

"But—but this tour is all arranged!" exclaimed the guide. "We cannot come back to the same place twice! There is no time! We are going to the Coliseum now, and the baths, and the Vatican"—he checked them off on his pudgy fingers.

"What is that to me?" said Brother Fernando.

"But they will be angry! I promised them this, and they won't be satisfied if they don't have it! I beg of you, Father!"

Brother Fernando shrugged.

"Oh, very well. I will get the keys."

The guide, beaming, returned to his flock.

They were waiting when Brother Fernando returned. He could not help smiling a little, tourists had always struck him as so childish.

"Tell them to be careful of their heads," he said to the guide.

"Be careful!" cried the guide. "*Prenez garde!*"

They all obediently ducked, when they entered the winding passage which led to the vaults below.

"Now, I am telling you," said the guide, "you are about to see the most unique, the most extraordinary curiosity in Rome. I am telling you."

The place which was usually kept for the special tombs of prelates and for monuments was, instead, crowded with little chapels side by side, like booths. Brother Fernando led them to the first one and there was a gasp of astonishment from the group behind him. He turned and looked at their faces with ironical amusement. Horror, shock, disbelief, and the kind of unnatural smile that is struck from the face by strong and unexpected emotion, were all present, in varying degrees.

Then they all broke out in exclamations, and laughter burst from them. It was too grotesque to take seriously.

Skulls were placed, with meticulous exactitude, into the plaster of the wall. They formed a geometrical design, varied with a nice eye for effect, by cross-bones and hip bones and collarbones, and, in fact, by every bone in the human anatomy. During the Middle Ages a monk, with a penchant for the unusual, had begun the game and it was kept up by generation after generation of the order, with a scrupulous perseverance and ever growing rivalry.

The first chapel was quite modest in its basic pattern; the next was more ambitious, attempting a little flourish with ribs; the third had a rather terrifying pyramid effect; the fourth had managed two great rosettes of skulls, and a circular design, and so on, sixteen in all.

"Tell them these are the heads of my predecessors," said Brother Fernando.

The guide translated with gusto, into three languages.

There was a little flurry, and Brother Fernando could feel that they were looking at him for the first time as a living man, instead of an impersonal brown robe.

"Yes," said Brother Fernando, "these are all the bodies of monks. They are piled here, in this offhand manner, to remind us that we must die also. Have your charges examined them to their satisfaction?"

The guide said, a little nonplussed, that they had.

And so, thanking Brother Fernando with nods and rather hesitant smiles, the visitors were herded up again, and whisked off by their competent manager, presumably to the Coliseum, the baths, and the Vatican.

Brother Fernando followed them slowly, locked the door, and went to take a short rest before going to his class of eager and argumentative theological students.

But he had no spirit for argument that day, his research, his knowledge, his insight, seemed things of the past. He listened to the words falling drearily from his own lips, and longed to escape from the eyes that fastened on him first with expectation, then with puzzled disappointment. In the end he apologized, before leaving them.

"Brother Fernando is not well," said one to the other, in explanation.

Brother Fernando, indeed, felt like a ghost. Intensity had left him, there was nothing to be explored, or learned, or discovered. Vaguely he wandered up to his room, looked around, and wandered disconsolately down again, into the courtyard. There he stood for a moment in the sunshine, looking at the small fountain that had seemed so peaceful to him a short time ago. Now the continuous trickle of water made him irritable.

Across the courtyard, on a stone bench under the portico, he could see Brother Luigi sitting, reading. It seemed peculiarly fitting that he should be there, in just that position, with his delicate and noble head like a fine fresco against the wall. His tonsure had grown over again, and his head was a mass of brown curls. His body, young and supple, showed its elasticity beneath the graceful folds of his robe. As Brother Fernando's glance rested on him, he looked up and waved his hand cheerfully. He yawned and got up.

"I don't believe him for a moment," he said, coming to join Brother Fernando.

"Who?"

"This man. He is all mixed up. He doesn't know enough history to put in a teaspoon."

"Well," said Brother Fernando.

They began to walk up and down, under the eaves, and around the courtyard, getting the most out of the little square of space.

Suddenly Brother Luigi began to talk about the Last Judgment.

It was evident that he had been reading heavily on the subject, for his phantasy caught fire as he spoke, and described the coming of the angels and the rising of the dead.

"Do you think it will be so?" he asked at last.

"I don't know," said Brother Fernando, and left him abruptly.

For many days after that, Brother Fernando looked for color, but could

not find it. He became more and more morose. At last he decided to go
to his superior, a man whom he did not care for, whom in fact he despised
a little, for certainly his erudition was not equal to Brother Fernando's
own, and he had a rough manner that was more becoming a butcher
than a monk.

When Brother Fernando knocked and entered he did not alter his
comfortable slump in an old easy chair.

"What is it, Brother?" he asked. Brother Fernando looked at his florid
face over his large and well-fed paunch, and felt unable to begin.

He stood silent for a moment, his rather long and earnestly enquiring
face unrelieved by any trace of his usual half ironical smile.

"Father," he said, "I am at the end of my usefulness."

"Indeed?" said Father Jerome. He did not move, only his eyes narrowed a little, shrewdly. "I would say that you were at the height of it:
active, healthy—how old are you, forty, forty-two?—at any rate, you
have always seemed to me one of our best men."

"Thank you. At this moment, I am no good to anybody, least of all
to myself."

"Well, well," said Father Jerome, and he got up and began to stump
about the room. "It is a pity you had to disturb my siesta with this unpleasant news," he said with a grimace.

"I am sorry." Brother Fernando wished he could explain more fully.
He could not state, bluntly, that he could not see color any more.

"Yes, now I shan't be able to sleep as well as usual. It is a great pity."

Brother Fernando smiled slightly, apologetically. His lips felt quite
strange when he did so: he realized that he had not smiled for a long time.

"Now, if it were another man," said Father Jerome, talking to himself
and gesticulating with his heavy, ham-like hands, "I would dismiss it as
temperament, and humor him out of it. Or I would bully him a little,"
he added, reflectively. "But you, now, that's a different case." He sighed.
"What is the matter?" he asked.

Brother Fernando shook his head. "That's what I should like to know,"
he said. "I've never been depressed before—I don't know what to do
about it."

Father Jerome sat down again, puffing a little in annoyance. But he
was not unkindly, in fact he had already rather lifted the weight from
Brother Fernando.

"Sit down, sit down," he said, motioning. "Why can't you sit down by yourself? Are you a little boy?"

Brother Fernando sat down. This time he laughed a little. "Forgive my saying so, Father," he remarked, "but I have never appreciated you before."

"You did not need me before," retorted his superior. "Well, I shall tell you something at which you will laugh, but all the same, I suggest that you try it. Spend a night in the chapels below, as I did once. There is nothing like death to make you enjoy life. It is since then that I have taken on so much weight."

Brother Fernando stared, frankly astonished.

"I know, I know!" said Father Jerome, shaking one hand dismissively, "I know what you are thinking! An old fool if there ever was one! Well, well. But try it. Spend tonight down there, and let me know in the morning how you fare."

Brother Fernando shrugged. "I will fall asleep," he said, "and that is all." He got up. "But," he added, "I shall certainly do as you say. I am under your orders." And he made a rather questionable bow. It was a little too humble.

He was deeply annoyed with Father Jerome. What idiocy! he thought, as he took his leave.

But at nine o'clock he said good night gravely, took a blanket, a flashlight, and the keys, and locked himself in the underground chapels. He wrapped himself in the blanket, lay down on the cold stone floor, and fell promptly asleep, in spite of the dank chilliness.

At night he awoke with a start, and sat up. He was perfectly convinced that he was not alone. He groped for the flashlight, and turned it on, sweeping the bright arc into every one of the little chapels set with skeletons. There was nothing, nobody. He lay down and tried to go to sleep again, but his senses were keenly awake. He listened, and listening made him sweat a little, for it was so quiet.

He felt helpless, lying straight on his back, as though he were being kept down by a stone on his chest. So he sat up again, cross-legged, turned on his flashlight dimly, and waited. He wondered what he was waiting for. What were the dead waiting for? There was certainly something disconcertingly expectant in the way a skull faced your gaze, with sockets just as good as yours, except that they were empty.

He was sitting up opposite the third chapel, with the heads placed in a rising pile. The one at the summit was of singularly fine structure. It looked familiar, and Brother Fernando could not imagine why. It reminded him of someone.

He got up, and went into the small enclosure, going quite close to the central skull. It had a high brow, narrow cheekbones, and gave the impression, even in that stark state, of having contained a highly intelligent brain. But when he was near it, the familiarity vanished. He went further away again, experimentally. Again it seemed as if he had known the man, as if he had seen him often. But bones look much alike, and perhaps it was only the dominant position, enjoyed by the central skull, that made it stand out so.

His thoughts slipped into the past, when the monks were, say, halfway through this very chapel. Did some artistic fingers itch for just one more bone to complete a design? He smiled at the thought. Were any of the monks disturbed at the idea that, when their bones were blanched enough, they would be dug up again and apportioned a place in the wall?

His mind began to play with words, conversationally, in his solitude. Entertaining custom, he thought—undress burial. Three or four centuries ago, they enjoyed such things.

Perhaps it is Brother Luigi, he thought suddenly, for his eyes were drawn again to the central skull, and he remembered Brother Luigi's fine contour against the shadowed wall that afternoon. But concentrating on the skull, he saw that it was much longer, and guessed, at a hazard, that it had belonged to an older man.

He had an impulse to examine some of the other chapels, but hesitated. He had become used to this one. There's nothing to look at anyway! he thought crossly.

But after a little while, since he felt no hint of sleepiness, he got up and looked at some length, at each design, weighing their relative merits.

One could see the historic deterioration from the primal simple arrangement, no more than an array of heads, to a veritable orgy of Byzantine curlicues and complications. He preferred the third chapel, with his friend at the top of the pyramidal pattern. His friend was really a royal conclusion; the monk who unearthed him must have been very well pleased.

It struck Brother Fernando that even for as large an order as it had been, there were a few too many well-preserved remains. He laughed a little to himself, and his laughter was scattered softly in the silence. He was laughing at the creative eagerness of his colleagues that had made them rob graves.

"Weren't you afraid," he asked out loud, in a mild bantering tone, "that a few murderers would slip into the company?"

"Imagine, my friends," he went on, finding it a relief to talk, "imagine if, as Brother Luigi believes, the dead will rise? What a scrambling for bones there will be! And what a surprise to find, perhaps, a woman or two in your midst?" He laughed again.

He thought of Lucrezia's head, on the body of St. George. It was a pity that it, too, had not a niche somewhere. He looked at his watch. "Witching hour," he remarked.

Of course he did not expect anything to happen, but once he had spoken, it was more than ever as though he were waiting for something. He became annoyed. He began to stalk up and down, angrily. Tomorrow he would be exhausted, not having slept all night. What a fool Father Jerome was. It was really a pity that Brother Fernando was not in his shoes—he would be so much more dignified, and give so much better advice. He wondered what Father Jerome had thought about when he spent the night in the chapels. He had probably had lugubrious thoughts about death. Brother Fernando sneered. "This has no power over me," he said coldly, and as he spoke more loudly than before, the words were thrown back at him, startlingly.

When, at that moment, a bit of bone, loosened from the plaster, crumbled away and fell, making a tiny noise, Brother Fernando was seized with a fit of shuddering. Even his teeth chattered. He sat down, and put the blanket around his shoulders.

For distraction, he decided to go over the theological lesson he was planning for the next day. He did not often do this, formally, but it was as good a way to spend the time as any.

"Now, class," he began, with jesting bravado, and choked. All the white skulls gleamed at him.

"There is heaven and earth," he whispered, and paused for a long time.

He could say nothing that the gathering before him did not question, though listening quietly enough.

He recalled his powerful sensation of not being alone when he woke up. This feeling had not been dispelled, but he had grown used to it. He realized now that it was not a single presence, but made up by the piles and piles of chalky remains, which appealed to him mutely, making his bones ache in sympathy.

He thought with wistful longing, of the sunny garden in the afternoon, and the blades of pushing, crowding grass.

"My poor friend," he said to the skull on top of the pyramid, "you won't know the sun's brave warmth again."

Suddenly, with a horror-stricken shriek, he leaped up. He knew who the skull reminded him of—it was himself.

His hands went to his head in a wild gesture, and he tried to press its warmth in, to catch it and hold it there forever. He fell on his knees.

Father Jerome always had his breakfast brought to him in his room. It began with pale purple smoked ham and fresh canteloupe. He was just beginning on the sweet, flushed orange of the canteloupe, when Brother Fernando entered, looking haggard and woebegone.

Father Jerome put down his fork, regretfully but firmly.

"Well, my son," he said, "what did you find in the chapels?"

"Nothing," replied Brother Fernando.

Because Father Jerome's eyes looked at him so piercingly, and he felt so weak, he turned and went to the window, which was as small as his own and latticed. But it was open, and the balmy air of Rome blew in lazily, bringing the smell of grass from the garden plot below. A few doves had settled by the fountain, and were ruffling their white feathers in the morning sun, and darting their pink bills into the clear water.

He saw that Brother Luigi was out early, walking up and down the narrow pebbled path—under the eaved porticos, and that he had pulled a little blue gentian, from the border of carefully planted flowers, and was swinging it in one hand in an inconsequential manner and looking at the sky—which, as Brother Fernando noted with a start, was certainly blue. Every wisp of cloud had been melted against its deep dye, and it stretched in lazy and casual perfection before his unexpectedly delighted eyes.

He turned back to Father Jerome slowly, and looked at his red, round face worriedly gazing at him, and the smoked ham and juicy canteloupe on his plate, untouched. It struck him as very funny.

"Eat, Father," he said. He sat down on the window ledge, and threw back his head in a long, refreshing laugh. The sun was very warm on his back. "It is certainly good to be alive," he remarked lightly.

Then he jumped up. "I must have a look at St. George's mantle," he said.

ISAAC PERETZ

Bontshe the Silent

Peretz is the father of modern Yiddish literature. His masterly work, woven on the rich traditional religious life of the Jew, always has through it a shining thread of gold—the Jewish mysticism which is a support and hope to the millions of simple souls like Bontshe. Peretz had no illusions of the feeling of this materialistic world toward the poor Wandering Jew, and with unique foresight he has created an escape in the great mystic universe. The work of Peretz will always stand as a monument to the common and forgotten people so murderously being slaughtered in the European ghettos.

RUBIN, *Palestine artist*

HERE, in this world below, the death of Bontshe produced no impression whatever. In vain you will ask: "Who was Bontshe? How did he live? What did he die of? Was it his heart that burst, his strength that gave out, or his dorsal spine that broke under a burden too heavy for his shoulders?" No one knows. Maybe it was hunger that killed him.

Had a dray horse fallen dead in the street, people would have displayed much more interest than they did in this case of a poor man. The newspapers would have reported the incident, and some of us would have hurried to the spot to look at the carcass and examine the place where the accident had occurred. But were there as many horses as there were men—a thousand millions—then even a horse would not have received such distinction.

Bontshe had lived quietly, and quietly died; like a shadow he passed over the face of the earth. At the ceremony of his circumcision no wine was drunk and no clinking of glasses was heard. When he celebrated his confirmation he made no brilliant speech. He lived, a grain of sand on the sea shore, among the millions of its kind. And when the wind at last carried him off to the other side, no one noticed it. In his life-time the dust of the roads kept no impression of his footsteps, and after his death the wind swept away the small board over his grave. The gravedigger's wife found it at some distance from the grave and made a fire with it to boil a pot of potatoes. Three days after Bontshe's death you would ask the grave-digger in vain to show you the spot where he had buried him.

Had there been a tombstone over Bontshe's grave, a learned archaeologist might have discovered it after a century, and once more the name of Bontshe would have been heard among us. He was only a shadow. No head or heart preserved his image, and no trace remained of his memory.

He left behind neither child nor property. He had lived miserably, and miserably he died. Had it not been for the noise of the crowd, someone might, by accident, have heard how Bontshe's vertebral column was snapping under a too heavy burden. Had the world had more time, someone might have noticed that during his life Bontshe's eyes were already dim and his cheeks terribly hollow. He might have noticed that even when he was not carrying loads on his shoulders his head was always bent to the ground, as if he were looking for his grave. Had there been as few poor people as there are horses someone might, perhaps, have asked: "What has become of Bontshe?"

When they took him to the hospital, Bontshe's corner in his basement hovel did not for long remain unoccupied; ten people of his kind were already waiting for it, and they knocked it down among themselves to the highest bidder. When they carried him from his hospital bed to the mortuary chamber, twenty poor patients were already waiting for the place vacated. And scarcely had Bontshe left the morgue, when twenty corpses extricated from underneath the ruins of a fallen house were brought in.

Who knows how long he will remain undisturbed in his grave? Who knows how many corpses are already waiting for the piece of ground he is buried in? Born quietly, he lived in silence, died in silence, and was buried in a silence even greater.

But it was not thus that things happened in the *other* world. There, the death of Bontshe produced a deep impression, a veritable sensation. The bugle-call of the Messiah, the sound of the ram's horn, was heard throughout the seven heavens: "Bontshe the Silent has died." Broad-winged archangels were flying about, announcing to each other that Bontshe had been summoned to appear before the Supreme Judgment Seat. In Paradise there was a noise, an excitement, and one could hear the joyful shout: "Bontshe the Silent! Just think of it! Bontshe the Silent!"

Very young angels, with eyes of diamond, gold-threaded wings, wearing silver slippers, were rushing out, full of joy, to meet Bontshe. The buzzing of their wings, the clatter of their small slippers, and the merry laughter of those dainty, fresh, and rosy little mouths, filled the heavens and reached the throne of the Most High. God himself knew that Bontshe was coming—

The Patriarch Abraham stationed himself at the gate of heaven, stretching out his right hand to Bontshe in cordial welcome: "Peace be with you," a sweet smile illuminating his delighted old countenance.

What means this rumbling and rolling here in heaven? Two angels were rolling an armchair of pure gold for Bontshe. Whence this luminous flash of light? It was a golden crown, set with the most precious stones, that they were carrying—for Bontshe!

"But the Supreme Court has not yet pronounced judgment?" ask the astonished saints, not without a tinge of jealousy.

"Bah!" reply the angels, "that will only be a formality. Against Bontshe, even the attorney for the prosecution himself will not find a word to say. The case will not last five minutes. Don't you know who Bontshe is? He is of some importance, this Bontshe."

When the little angels seized Bontshe in mid-air and played a sweet tune to him; when the Patriarch Abraham shook hands with him as if he had been an old comrade; when he learned that his chair was ready for him in Paradise and that a crown was waiting for his head, that before the Celestial Tribunal not one superfluous word would be spoken in his case, Bontshe, as once upon earth, was frightened into silence. He was sure that it could only be a dream from which he would soon awake, or simply a mistake.

He was used to both. More than once, when he was still on earth, he had dreamed of picking up money from the ground. Veritable treasures were lying there!—and yet—when he awoke in the morning, he was more miserable and poorer than ever. More than once it had happened to him that someone in the street had smiled at him and spoken a kind word to him. But when he found out his mistake, the stranger turned and spat out in disgust, full of contempt. "Just my luck," thought Bontshe, scarcely daring to raise his eyes, afraid lest the dream should disappear. He trembles at the thought of suddenly waking up in some horrible cavern full of serpents and lizards. He is careful not to let the slightest sound escape his mouth, to stir or move a limb for fear of being recognized and hurled into the abyss. He trembles violently, and does not hear the compliments paid him by the angels, nor does he notice how they are dancing around him. He pays no heed to the Patriarch's cordial "Peace be with you," nor does he even wish good-morning to the celestial court when he is at last brought in. He is simply beside himself with fear.

His fear increased greatly when his eyes involuntarily fell upon the flooring of the Supreme Court of Justice. It was of pure alabaster, inset with diamonds. "And my feet," thought Bontshe, "are treading such a floor!" He grew quite rigid. "Who knows," he thought, "what rich man, what Rabbi, what saint they are expecting? He will soon arrive and mine will be a sad end!"

Terror-stricken, he did not even hear the President of the Court call out in a loud voice: "The case of Bontshe the Silent!" He did not hear how, handing over a dossier to the counsel for the defence, he commanded: "Read, but briefly." All around Bontshe the whole hall seemed to be turning. A muffled noise reached his ears, but in the midst of the din he began to distinguish more clearly and sharply the voice of the angelic advocate—a voice as sweet as a violin:

"His name," the voice was saying, "suited him even as a gown made by an artist's hand suits a graceful body."

"What is he talking about?" Bontshe asks himself. And then he heard an impatient voice interrupting the speaker:

"No metaphors, please."

"Never," continues the advocate, "never has he uttered a complaint against God or men. Never has a spark of hatred flamed up in his eyes, never has he lifted his eyes with pretensions to heaven."

Again Bontshe fails to understand what it is all about, but once more the stern voice interrupts the speaker:

"No rhetoric, please."

"Job succumbed, but Bontshe has suffered more than Job."

"Facts, bare facts, please," the President emphatically calls again.

"He was circumcised on the eighth day."

"Yes, yes, but no realism, please."

"The clumsy barber-surgeon could not stanch the blood—"

"Go on, go on."

"He was always silent," the advocate proceeds, "even when his mother died and at the age of thirteen there came a stepmother, a serpent, a wicked woman."

"Perhaps after all he means me," thinks Bontshe to himself.

"No insinuations, please, against third persons," angrily says the President.

"She used to begrudge him a piece of bread; throw him a few musty crusts three days old and a mouthful of gristle for meat, whilst she herself drank coffee with cream."

"Come to business!" cries the President.

"She never spared him her fingernails, blows, or cuffs, and through the holes of his miserable musty rags there peeped out the blue and black body of the child. Barefooted he used to chop wood for her in winter, in the biting frost. His hands were too young and too weak to wield the dull ax, and the blocks were too big. More than once did he sprain his wrists, more than once were his feet frozen, but he remained silent. He was silent even before his father——"

"Oh, yes, the drunkard," laughs the accusing attorney, and Bontshe feels cold all over.

"Even to his father he never complained," the advocate concludes.

"He was always miserable and alone, had no friends, no schooling, no religious instruction, no decent clothes and not a minute of respite."

"Facts, facts," the President once more interrupts.

"He was silent even later, when his own father, the worse for drink, seized him by the hair and threw him out of the house on a bitterly cold and snowy winter night. He picked himself up from the snow, without weeping, and ran whither his eyes carried him. He was silent during his lonely walk, and when the pangs of hunger began to torture him, he begged only with his eyes.

"On a wet and foggy spring night he reached a large town. He entered it like some drop of water that is falling into the ocean, but he nevertheless passed his first night in the police jail. He was silent, without asking the why or wherefore. Set free, he started to look for work, for the hardest work possible; but he was silent. What was even harder than work itself, was the finding of it, and he was silent. He was always silent. Splashed by the mud thrown at him by strangers, spat upon by strangers, driven with his heavy load from the sidewalk into the midst of the road, among cabs, cars, coaches, and vehicles of every sort—at every instant looking death in the face, he remained silent. Bathed in a cold sweat, crushed under the heavy loads he was carrying, his stomach empty and tortured, he was silent.

"He never calculated how many pounds he was carrying for a farthing, how often he stumbled for a penny and how many errands he had to run, how many times he almost breathed his last when going to collect his pay. He was always silent. He never dared to raise his voice when asking for his pay, but like a beggar or a dog he stood at the door and his dumb and humble request could only be read in his eyes. 'Come later,' he was told, and he disappeared like a shadow until later, when he would ask even more quietly, nay *beg* for his due. He was silent even when people haggled over his pay, knocked off something from it, or slipped a counterfeit coin into his hand. He was always silent!"

"Then after all it is me that they mean," Bontshe consoles himself.

"One wonderful day Bontshe's fortune changed," proceeded the advocate, after taking a drink of water. "Two spirited, frightened, runaway horses were rushing by, dragging a rich coach with rubber wheels. With a broken skull the driver lay way back on the pavement. Foam was spurting from the mouths of the animals, sparks flew from their hoofs, and their eyes shone like glowing coals on a dark night. In the coach, there sat a man, more dead than alive. Bontshe stopped the runaway horses. The man whose life he had thus saved was a Jew; he proved to be of a charitable disposition and was grateful to Bontshe. He handed over to him the whip of his dead coachman, and Bontshe became a coachman. The charitable man even found him a wife. He did more: he provided Bontshe with a child. And Bontshe always kept silent."

"They mean me; they mean me!" thought Bontshe, strengthening himself in his belief; but nevertheless he dared not raise his eyes on the august tribunal. Still he listened to his angelic advocate.

"Bontshe was silent," continued the latter, "even when his benefactor became bankrupt and neglected to pay Bontshe his wages. He was silent when his wife ran away from him, leaving him alone with an infant in arms. He was silent even fifteen years later, when the same child grew up till he was strong enough to throw the father out of his own house."

"They mean me, they mean me!" Bontshe thinks joyfully.

"He was silent," continued the defending angel, as his voice grew still softer and more sad, "when his former benefactor paid all his creditors except Bontshe, to whom he did not give a penny. And when, riding again in his coach with rubber tires and with horses like lions, the benefactor one day ran over him, Bontshe still kept silent. He did not even tell the police. Even in the hospital where one is allowed to cry, he kept silent! He was silent even when the house physician refused to approach his bed unless he had paid him fifteen coppers, or when the attendant refused to change his bed linen unless he gave him five coppers.

"He was silent in his death agony, he was silent in his last hour. Never did he utter a word against God, never a word against man. . . . I have spoken!"

Bontshe began to tremble in his whole body. He knew that after the speech for the defence it was the turn of the prosecution. "What will the prosecuting counsel say now?" Bontshe did not remember his life. Down *below* he used to forget everything the moment it occurred. The angel advocate had recalled to his mind all his past. Who knows what the prosecuting angel will recall to his memory?

"Gentlemen judges," begins a strident, incisive, and stinging voice—but stops short.

"Gentlemen," he begins again, this time more softly but once more he interrupts himself.

And at last, very soft, a voice issues from the throat of the accuser:

"Gentlemen judges! He was silent! I shall be silent too."

Profound silence fell over the assembly. Then from above a new soft, sweet, and trembling voice is heard:

"Bontshe, my child, Bontshe," said the voice, and it sounded like a harp. "Bontshe, my well-beloved child."

And Bontshe's heart begins to weep for joy. He would like to raise his eyes, but they are dimmed by tears. Never in his life had he felt such joy in weeping.

"My child, my well-beloved!" Since his mother's death he had never heard such a voice or such words.

"My child," continues the President of the Celestial Tribunal, "you have suffered everything in silence. There is not a limb in your body that is whole, not a bone that is intact, not a corner in your soul that is not bleeding—and you have always kept silent.

"Down below upon the earth they never understood such things. You yourself were not aware of your power; you did not know that you could

cry and that your cries would have caused the very walls of Jericho
tremble and tumble down. You yourself did not know what stren
lay hidden in you. Down below your silence was not rewarded, but do
below is the world of delusion, whilst here in heaven is the world of tr
here you will reap your reward.

"The Supreme Tribunal will never pass sentence against you; it
never judge and condemn you, nor will it mete out to you such and s
a reward. Everything here belongs to you; take whatever your h
desires."

For the first time Bontshe ventures to lift his eyes. He is dazzle
so much light and splendor. Everything is sparkling, everything aro
him is flashing, beams are issuing from all sides, and he droops his w
eyes once more.

"Really?" he asks, still doubting and embarrassed.

"Yes, really," replies the President of the Celestial Tribunal; "v
I tell you that it is so indeed, and that everything here is yours; everyth
in heaven belongs to you. All the brightness and the splendor you
ceive is only the reflection of your own silent goodness of heart,
reflection of your own pure soul. You will only be drawing from y
own source."

"Really?" Bontshe asks again, but this time his voice sounds more
and assured.

"Certainly, certainly, certainly," he is assured on all sides.

"Then, if such is the case," says Bontshe with a happy smile, "I sh
like to have every morning a hot roll with fresh butter."

Abashed, angels and judges drooped their heads; while the acc
burst out into loud laughter.

—*Translated from the Yiddish by* DR. ANGELO S. RAPPOP

RUTH DOMINO

The Wonderful White Paper

A Story of Spain Before the Civil War

There was always a passionate love for books in my surroundings and there were always cool, meditative libraries wherever I went, from Hamburg southward or westward, to Vienna and Paris—as a student and later as an expatriate. And ever since my early childhood I wondered how much these thoughts and dreams preserved on white pages could influence the minds of people driven into battle by the most primitive urges of life; would they have any effect at all? Whether this question grew out of one memorable impression, I do not know. As a child, my father would take me by the hand to see the soldiers returning from the first World War. The books I had been reading at the time were visions of peace and happiness, but the faces of the soldiers were wretched. This contrast troubled me, and from then on whenever I touched a book, I felt both a repulsion and attraction towards it.

That I overcame this doubt I owe to many different impressions, to many people.

There came a time when I did not touch any book for weeks. Seventeen days of flight before Hitler's men, seventeen days and nights on motor lorries, peasant cars, bicycles, with nights spent in ditches or abandoned barns, tended to make me forget, in June, 1940, that there were such things as books and cool meditative libraries, The Sorbonne, the seminaries about the Place de Panthéon, lay behind me like a dream from another life. Realities were the sweaty, hunted faces of the fugitives on the roads.

We came to the foot of the Pyrenees, to a little old city. We had plenty of time and so had the thousands of other fugitives from Belgium and the North of France. In this city was a little library, "Bibliothéque populaire," founded in a liberal impulse of the seventies, open twice a week for a few hours. In other days only the school children had come and gone, carrying the books in their childish book-bags; now came men with heavy hands, laborers, and soldier-fugitives, and wrapped the books carefully in newspapers before they entrusted them to the great pockets of their rough clothes.

I read Anatole France's REVOLTE DES ANGES, and a Spanish refugee who had been reading it over my shoulder begged me to save it for him. He had learned to read and write during the civil war and was doubtless attracted by the word *"Revolte."*

And then I remembered: once, at the time of the Spanish civil war, a book came into my hands which was supposed to teach the illiterate republican soldiers reading and writing in their spare time. The colorful letters illustrated by common subjects were gradually combined into words, and finally into sentences which made a social appeal.

Who knows, I thought then, in what form printed words may not come to life again in the hearts and minds of men?

RUTH DOMINO

AT THE edge of the province of La Mancha, on one of the huge sandy plains somewhat withdrawn from the great highways leading to Madrid, stood a little village called Cueva. On the horizon before and behind it rose bald mountains of reddish stone which, toward evening when the sun went down, shone in lilac hues.

The village was exactly like every other poor village in the land. The houses were small and white with flat roofs; and in summer when the heat seemed inescapable, they had sackcloth curtains instead of doors. The biggest space in every house was the courtyard which, enclosed by the henhouses and goatsheds and living quarters, was like a room surrounded by four walls. This courtyard had the same trampled clay floor as that in the living quarters. The peasants, too, were exactly like those in the other villages. They wore black shirts which hung over their trousers. In summer they wore large broadbrimmed straw hats, and the whole year round canvas sandals with matted soles and a cloth around their neck.

The women had black dresses and black headcloths. It was as if they went constantly in mourning in their white houses because hundreds of years since the water had dried from their fields together with the trees in the woods. On the other side of the village was a small river whose bed was usually dried up in summer, exposing gray rocks like weatherbeaten tombstones.

The priests had told the people that the dearth of water came from their sins. So they bore the heat, the drought, the flies and their poverty as the curse of God, and thought no more about it; they sinned and brought children into the world who, as long as they were tiny, crept about naked on the courtyard clay.

The peasants had dark brown faces, the older ones with many wrinkles and deeply wrought furrows. Their skin hung like supple leather, though not like tired flesh, about their joints. And in that, too, they were exactly like poor peasants the world over whose fat poured from their bodies, together with their sweat, as they bent over the earth. And finally—like peasants everywhere—they had a passion: they sang. They sang after their work when they sat by the side of the road; the women sang in the evenings in their tiny rooms, and the young girls on Sundays when they tied a colored ribbon in their hair. Their songs were called *flamencos*. They were wild monotonous melodies that suddenly soared and swelled out of their throats. The heads of the singers lifted high as if about to fly from their necks. Then the voices would subside again. The more suddenly and fiercely the song mounted, the more highly esteemed was the singer's art. On Sundays the people of the village would sit about such a leader and as he sang shrill and loud, they would clap hands and cry, *"Olè, olè, olè!"*

The words of the songs were very simple, generally only one short sentence, "The landlord is powerful, he does with us what he pleases." Or, "The earth is dry and quivers like a fish on dry land." And the young girls sang that they were so poor the sun and the moon belonged to them, but nothing on earth; there was no man who would look upon them.

Only one thing was more remote from these peasants' imagination than a moist earth with constantly flowing streams: that was a land without colors, in which the sky did not appear blue and the earth was neither red nor violet. Faced with such a prospect they would certainly have replied that the people who lived there must be much, much poorer even than themselves.

Though the rich gentlemen still sat in their castles, the King had already been turned out of the country. Gradually teachers went into the districts to instruct the children; and to Cueva there came a young man, Fernando.

Before this when the monastery was still occupied, a few children had gone there to study, but they were the exception. Fernando brought with him maps that were very colorful. The children realized with astonishment that the land on the maps was only a plain without mountains. Moreover the mountains were shown in folds, brown like the earth; the rivers were as blue as the heavens and as sinuous as a goat's limb; the cities were thick black points like goat droppings and the villages little black points like flyspecks.

The children learned that on the map their village lay directly to the right of the capital of Madrid, that the land near Valencia looked so green because it was a valley with abundant water and many green plants and that behind it, like unending and multitudinous confluent rivers, was the sea. And the teacher taught those who already knew a few letters that the various curves and lines in the letters of the alphabet imitated objects in nature; and that when, for example, they placed a large O on its back or stomach, it resembled the shape of a lemon, only without the little nose. And he taught those who knew no letters that, conversely, lines and curves could be joined together to form letters. He distributed colored crayons, water colors and paintbrushes to the children.

For their first lesson they all drew a lemon which the teacher had laid on his desk as a model.

Suddenly a titter swept over the class. The teacher, who was reading a book, looked up in surprise. Then the children held their painted lemons high and waved them like yellow drapes toward the desk. Fernando laughed too. There was not a child in the class who was bored.

After a few drawing and painting lessons the teacher divided his class. He asked his most diligent pupils to set down on paper objects out of their own imagination. He told them also that in the evening their older brothers and sisters, if they had time, could come to school. A few of the children tried to portray Bible stories in pictures, others attempted to make maps.

At home the mothers clad in black made the sign of the cross when they saw the paintings. To be sure, they had learned how to embroider in their youth but they had not drawn objects from nature. They had made patterns which had no meaning, or which depicted the cross of Christ and the loose swaddling-clothes of a Christ child on his Mother's lap. The fathers, for their part, gazed long at the maps. The children explained that the blue lines represented flowing water and that where there was much water everything was green, and that near Valencia there were three crops in the year.

To reproduce mountains, rivers and fruits on a small white piece of paper so that one could recognize and find meaning in colors and spaces as easily as in words, even if one could not read and write, that fascinated everyone. But then began what the authorities later called "the plague."

In the houses where there were boys, a colored map soon hung next to the oil painting of the Virgin Mother and the calendar of the Saints. Water-color paintings of biblical events were pasted over the sleeping-places of the girls. And where there were both boys and girls, colored drawings were grouped both to the right and the left of the Virgin.

Little Juanita wanted to show the rain of manna in the wilderness. But since she was unfamiliar with manna and tomatoes seemed to her good, tasty food, a gift of God worthy of the unfortunate Jews, she let tomatoes rain down from heaven. So her paper was filled with many beautiful, red tomato plants. Nine-year-old Angelita had a weakness for matches so she made an angel walk from star to star, at the coming of night, with a burning match in order to light the star spots which by day were colorless.

Not far from the village lay the landlord's house. The peasants had to bring payments to him for the arid little fields they rented from him. The tribute consisted of vegetables, eggs and a little wine. But the vine-yards bore badly in the years of drought and exacted much toil. The landlord's house stood on the same broad expanse as the village; white rectangular, it faced the high red mountains. It had an outer courtyard and an inner courtyard around which the living quarters were grouped. At each of its corners there was a spire. The peasants knew only the outer courtyard where the bailiff stripped them of their food payments. But once little Pedro, peering from behind his father's black shirt, had glimpsed the inner court. There in the center stood a well with magnifi-cently embossed iron troughs. A stream of water jetted forth and fairly flooded the surrounding flower beds. It struck him as the height of earthly splendor: water which was not laboriously drawn by bending over a thousand times, water which did not have to be stolen from the sparse rains, water which poured lavishly forth and yet was neither river nor rain!

When the teacher placed colored crayons at Pedro's desk, he chose a blue one. Then he drew a white, wavy rectangle with pointed spires at the corners. And in the middle he drew a blue stream gushing high and away over the walls and over the brown fields, right into the middle of the village. At home he laid the sheet of paper on the table. His mother wrung her hands; his father took the picture in his hands and murmured in his black beard, "Is this not the landlord's castle?" His wife asked, "What are you saying, husband?" But Pedro's father fell silent again, so the matter was left as if unspoken.

And therewith, the authorities later said, sin came to the village because of the plague of the drawings.

In the evening before the sun had completely set, the father said to Pedro, "Give me a piece of paper and the drawing pencil!" And he sat himself in the yard, not by the edge of the road as was his custom, and drew his house and the blue stream of water which he let fall on his field behind the house.

That night it rained mightily, and the pails that had been set out were filled to the brim with water. The next morning the leaves were crisp and green.

"The Holy Virgin is pleased with the picture," said little Pedro's mother. Word spread throughout the village. "The Holy Virgin grants us water and painting to the children," the people said. Pedro's father did not listen to the women's prattle; and before the sun went down he again sat in his courtyard and painted a garden to his house, and colored his field green, red and blue. The blue came from the water of a little river which he depicted leading through canals and then flowed richly through all his fields. He painted the red of tomatoes and the green of the vine and the onion plant. The next day he sat down again and added a few more hills covered with vineyards, to which a little path led from his house.

The news of the painting by Pedro's father did not remain secret, and the neighbors with whom he used to sit before the house now came and watched over his shoulder. They liked the joyous colors of the garden and especially the water in it; and since their children also had crayons at home, one after the other began to sketch and paint his house with a big garden beside it and much water—in short, everything which did not in reality exist. And since they did not have much water, they copied from the stream which Pedro had sketched in his painting of the landlord's house. They made their little fields and gardens abundant in water and added vineyards which rose higher and higher, almost as high as the red mountains but in green. They extended their painted fields so much that they soon came close to the landlord's house. And now instead of singing *flamencos,* the peasants sat on Sundays before their houses and painted. Even those who could not write thus gave expression in paint to their desires on this earth. Fernando the teacher, who sometimes strolled in the evening through the village streets, would correct here and there an uneven line by one of the artists. He also showed them how to use water colors.

Then one evening a peasant said, "Yes, we're really painting our fields too big; the land no longer belongs to us."

Pedro's older brother sketched a white rectangle with spires and made it quite small next to the many-colored fields and blue canals. But no one yet said aloud to whom the great fields really belonged and what kind of a house that white rectangle with the ornamental spires was.

It seized them like a wild wind from the fields. Almost everyone painted; and if it was not a father, then it was his sons and small daughters who painted the white rectangle with spires as well as they could. Some painted the Egyptian plagues, and huge grasshoppers rained down over the little white rectangle with spires. The rectangle remained unchanged, as little Pedro had first drawn it. Some painted the Flood like a mighty blue pinion which started in one corner of the paper and moved down to the other where stood a small white rectangle with spires, tottering and wavelike. And there was a second picture, "After the Flood," in which green plots of ground with houses and fruit orchards rose up; one who could also write drew an inscription on the green plot of land, "Fields of the peasants of Cueva, the village is swimming far behind."

After two months the supply of drawing crayons and paper was exhausted, so the teacher went into the city to get new materials. The proprietor of the stationery store told Fernando that he did not have so many supplies in stock and asked him what he was doing with so much paper and so many crayons. Fernando replied that he was only the teacher of the village of Cueva and that his pupils and several of the peasants were now actively painting.

"And what do they paint all the time?"

"They paint water, always water, so much water that it almost drowns out the landlord's house," smiled Fernando.

But the merchant did not smile. He remarked that that was very serious, but Fernando did not agree with him.

In the evening at the tavern the tradesman told the mayor and the doctor of the town, and they all shook their heads. They had never bothered with the village of Cueva because none of the peasants there had ever brought them any money. But now times were uncertain in the country, they said, and even churches and monasteries had been burned.

The monks had long since been driven from the district of Cueva and undoubtedly the peasants no longer went to church, and now this young and worldly teacher—the authorities should really begin to pay attention to the village now that insubordination was so rife among the people. On Sunday they even voiced their opinions to the priest.

And that Sunday the peasants of Cueva sat before their houses and Pedro's older brother sang a *flamenco* with a new text. He sang, "Oh wonderful white paper, you are getting fruits and fields! Oh wonderful little white paper, the water flows blue on you and the vineyards grow. Little white paper, you will be bigger than the house with the spires facing the red mountains!"

The peasants were silent a moment after the song had ended, then they cried loudly, "*Olè, olè, olè!*" They clapped their hands and sang, "Little white paper, oh wonderful white paper."

The next week a city clerk visited the schoolhouse and inspected the children's paintings on the walls. He wrung his hands and hastened back to the city.

The next Sunday there came four men of the *Guardia Civil*. It was about noon. They had revolvers and swords in their belts. They strode through the village streets until they came to the schoolhouse which was closed. They knocked. The young teacher looked out of the window. What did they want? Just let him open the door, he'd see soon enough! He opened the schoolroom. The many pictures of the children and grown ups hung roundabout on large thick nails.

"Who has painted these pictures?"

"The children," answered the teacher.

Didn't he know that the pictures were subversive? And they placed handcuffs on him. Two of them began to tear the pictures down from the walls. The children came running to the schoolhouse. They pressed themselves against the classroom door. Suddenly little Pedro sprang forward and cried, "Leave our pictures alone!" And he grasped the gendarme by the arm to stop him. When the man tried to shake him off, Pedro bit hard into his arm.

"*Now* will you!" the gendarme roared.

A gust of wind blew into the schoolroom and drove the pile of pictures into the street. The children watched with eyes wide open. Now the men of the village stood behind them; they too stood silent, their eyes staring.

Meanwhile the soldier had hurled the child from him with a powerful blow. The small body fairly flew across the room and lay on the threshold, stunned by the impact of his fall. His head hung down, his eyes were closed.

"That is my son," said Pedro's father taking a step toward the child.

"And so much the worse for you," shouted the soldier, "for he is the son of a dog!" Provoked by the silence of the children and the men, he kicked the senseless child from the threshold.

At that Pedro's father clenched his fist and held it ready for a blow. But the gendarme drew his saber and made as if to strike the peasant over the head. Perhaps he meant to use only the flat side. Pedro's father tried with his other hand to ward off the upstretched arm, but the blade turned and fell downward, slashing him right across the face. Blood spurted forth and gushed on his new sandals. He staggered toward his son. The gendarme, still more infuriated, pointed to the red drops in the sand. "There you have colors to paint with!" Then all four of the *Guardia Civil* turned to go, dragging the handcuffed teacher after them. A cry arose from the crowd of peasants. But the four men soon disappeared around a bend of the village street.

Perhaps it was this cry, a long echo, grown audible, of the drops of blood in the sand—all of them suddenly had the oppressive feeling that they had been robbed, and that still more would be stolen from them. So they went swiftly home, and those who had paintings took them from their walls and hid them in the darkest corners of their closets.

Early next morning a party of horsemen drew near the village. A few children, seeing the glint of harnesses in the sun, ran into the fields to tell their fathers. The peasants dropped their implements at once and ran back with their children. The vanguard of the riders had already entered the village. They rode on beautiful white horses that shimmered even more brightly than the little white houses. Then they shouted to the men and women that they must hand over those accursed pictures or else they would soon see what would befall them. And they set about searching the bedding and the few pieces of furniture, smashing them to bits. The men stood silently by but when a soldier found a picture, they would unfold their arms and leap furiously at him.

That lasted about an hour. When the soldiers left the village, they dragged behind them ten peasants in chains.

In the afternoon three dead men lay outstretched on the square before the schoolhouse. Among them was Pedro's father. The blackclad women stood at the foot of the biers staring into the faces of the dead. Then Pedro's mother and another woman stepped forth and loosened something from the stiff hands of the corpses. They were fragments of the torn pictures. They smoothed them with loving care and brought them home. Then they again hid the bits of paper in the darkest corners of their closets.

MARY WEBB

Many Mansions

The stories of Mary Webb were suggested for this volume by several readers. Her followers were not as numerous as those of some more popular writers, but those who read her loved her and after her death in England in 1927, her five novels were reprinted with introductions by Stanley Baldwin, John Buchan, G. K. Chesterton, Robert Lynd, and others.

HIS NAME—John Lloyd. His age—something verging on one hundred years. His home—a dusky cottage in an ancient borough. The cottage had one room below, very silent, full of shadows and soft lights from the low wood fire. An open staircase went up to the bedroom, so that when John Lloyd had supped, said his prayers and doused his fire, he could climb without much difficulty to his bed. In the corner by the fire stood his beadle's staff, painted in bands of black and yellow. For that ancient borough kept its old customs. It was a very Rip-van-Winkle of a borough. Somewhere in the Middle Ages it had fallen asleep, and if you should wonder at the fashion of its garments, you must remember that it had not, since the day it fell asleep, changed its coat, its hosen or its hat. So John Lloyd kept his staff, and in his hale years he would rap unruly lads on their round heads till you would think a woodpecker had come to church. Old folks, also, should they become too emotional in their prayers, did not escape his vigilant eye: but he would not touch them with his staff, only he would lay a reminding hand upon their shoulders. If the old lady whom he judged to have the right to communicate first was absorbed in prayer, he would gently insinuate his staff into her pew and give three little taps to her hassock. *Noblesse oblige*. She must not forfeit her prerogative, nor must she keep the congregation waiting.

But when I remember him, John was almost too feeble for his beadle's work. I was sent once a week as a small child to read the Bible to him. That was a great adventure! There was the walk of a mile down the country road, beside which ran a thread of a brook, except in the summer. In the hedgebanks grew a few sweet violets, and there you might find the largest, most brightly-coloured snail-shells I have ever seen. But one must not linger too long, for down there, in the pool of hyacinth made by the valley shadows and the gentle smoke of hearth fires, John Lloyd waited to hear about the Many Mansions.

On then, down the brown road between its sloping fields of miraculous green, past the roaring smithy, past—if possible—the small square window which had the splendid glass marbles. (But it could be passed if one remembered that the person who painted the marbles was really not half so good an artist as the person who painted the snail-shells.) Down the street of blue shadows, past the church with its needling spire, with just one glance through the wrought-iron gates beyond which lived a lady in a garden of lilies—the most beautiful of ladies she seemed to me, white and gold like her flowers, so that when I read to John Lloyd about Mary of Galilee pondering things in her heart, I always saw her beyond gates of wrought iron, walking in a garden of lilies. But this was seldom, because John liked what he called "the Many Mansions piece," and when it was his turn to choose, he chose that. And when it was my turn to choose, remembering that this was John's party, I was in honour bound to choose that also.

Up three hollow steps, into the dusky room, silent as one of the porches of eternity, and there was John in his Windsor chair, his black and yellow wand beside him, his great black Bible, so heavy that it made my arms ache, ready on the deal table.

"Come thy ways in, my dear," he would say. "And God be with ye. A grand morning, seemingly?"

"Grand, John. And here's a snail-shell in case you'd like a game of conker."

"Nay, my dear, I be past conker. You keep it."

"Then I'll put it in my faery house."

"Ah. You do."

"What shall I read, John?"

He made a great show of considering, saying, "Well, there's a good few nice pieces. There's 'The greatest of these.' Then there's 'The pitcher be broken at the fountain,' and 'I will give you rest.' Then he would pause and in a moment say, as if it were a totally new idea:

"How about the Many Mansions piece, my dear?"

I had no need to look for it; the book always fell open just there.

"In my Father's house are many mansions. . . . If it were not so, I would have told you."

John would strike his palm upon the table.

"Ah! Fair and square, He'd ha' told us," he would. say. "If so be it was only a tuthree housen for the grand folk, and no room for us, He'd ha' said so, straight. But there's room for all, and He's gone to get it ready."

"Shall you like going there, John?"

"Surely I shall, my dear."

"Shall you go by train, or shall you get the cab from the *Arms?*"

He laughed at that, with a sound like the stirring of dry rushes.

"I doubt Tom Ostler would be put about to find that road."

"Train, then?"

"No station!" said John tersely.

"Oh," I said, "I know! They're going to send for you!"

For I remembered how the lady of the garden once sent for me, and how I drove in unwonted glory past the violets and the snail-shells.

"Got it!" said John. "Ah, they'll send."

"A carriage?" I was glad for John.

"Horses of fire, and a chariot of fire!" said he, and the soft lights from the burning wood lit his old eyes to splendour.

"I'll come too!" I cried.

"You mun multiply by ten first."

"How?"

"Ten tens a hunderd."

"Wait for me, John!"

"Not to be done, my dear. They send when they've a mind."

It is a long time now since they had a mind to send for John Lloyd, but I shall never forget the simple goodness of his seamy face, his inexpressive righteousness, his bantering affection.

LUIGI PIRANDELLO

The Captive

Richly representative of the great Sicilian writer's style and viewpoint, "The Captive" depicts a man in a situation, the solution of which forces him to a consideration of reality as a whole and his place in life and death.

I T looked as if old Vicé Guarnotta were walking along the road—so regularly did his body sway from side to side with the movements of the little donkey on which he sat. His legs dangled outside the stirrups and nearly dragged along the dusty highway. He was returning, as he did every day at that hour, from his holding on the edge of the plateau, almost overhanging the sea. The aged donkey, even more tired and melancholy than her master, had begun to pant from the effort of ascending the interminable road, which wound its way up the mountain in a succession of steep curves and hairpin bends. At the summit of the spur stood the ramshackle houses of the little town, huddled closely together, one above another. It was so late that the peasants had all returned home from the countryside and the road was deserted. If Guarnotta did happen to meet anyone, he always received a friendly greeting, for—God be thanked—they all thought well of him.

In the old man's eyes, the whole world was now as lonely as that highway, and his own life gray as that twilight. He glanced at the bare branches projecting over the low, cracked walls, the tall dusty cacti, and the heaps of road metal lying here and there—which some one really might have thought of spreading over the numerous holes and ruts. Everything about him was still, silent and deserted, as if, like him, oppressed by a sense of infinite boredom and futility. Even the silence seemed to have turned into dust—dust that lay so thick that he could not hear the footsteps of his donkey.

What quantities of that road dust had the old man carried home every evening! Whenever he took off his coat, his wife seized it and held it out at arm's length. To relieve her feelings, she displayed it round the room—to the chairs and the wardrobe, the bed and the coffer, exclaiming, "Just look at it! Look! Why, you could write on it with your finger!"

If only he would yield to her persuasion and not wear his black suit of broadcloth out on the farm. Hadn't she ordered three corduroy suits for him, for that very purpose—three of them? And while she raged and angrily gesticulated, Guarnotta, sitting in his shirt sleeves, often felt tempted to sink his teeth into the three stumpy fingers which she brandished in front of his eyes; but, like a well-behaved dog, he confined himself to giving her a side glance of dissatisfaction and let her continue her nagging. Fifteen years before—on the death of his only son—had he not vowed that he would dress in black for the rest of his life? So, therefore. . . .

"But why d'you want to wear black out in the fields? I'll put crepe bands on the sleeves of your corduroy coats. That and a black tie will be quite enough—after fifteen years!"

He let her nag. Was he not out on his holding by the sea the whole blessed day? For years past, he had never been seen in the town. Therefore, if he did not wear mourning for his son out on the countryside, where was he to wear it? Why, in God's name, didn't she think a little before opening her mouth then she would leave him in peace. . . . Oh! so he was to wear mourning in his heart, was he? Indeed! And who said that he didn't wear it in his heart? But he wanted people to see some external sign of it. Let the trees see it, and the birds of the air—since the boy, alas! was unable to see that he wore it for him. . . . Why on earth was his wife grumbling so about it? Was it because she had to shake and brush the clothes every evening? Why not let the servants do it? There were three of them to wait upon only two persons. Was it for economy's sake? Come, what nonsense! One black suit a year cost only eighty or ninety lire. She ought to realize that it wasn't right—it wasn't kind of her to go on like that. She was his second wife: the son, who had died, had been by the first one. He had no other relatives—even distant ones; therefore, on his death, all his property (and it was no small amount) would pass to her and to her nephews and nieces. She should keep quiet then, if only for decency's sake. . . . Ah well! Being the sort of woman she was, she didn't, of course, see it in that way.

So that was why he stayed out all day, alone on his land, alone with his trees and the panorama of the sea spread just below him; and, as he listened to the continuous gentle rustling of the foliage and the sad little song of the waves—which seemed to float up to him from an endless distance—his soul was constantly oppressed by a sense of the vanity of all things and the insufferable boredom of life.

He had reached a point less than half a mile from the little town and could hear the soft chimes of the Ave Maria from the chapel of the Addolorata on the top of the hill, when at a sharp bend in the road, there came a shout, "Face to the ground!"

Three men, who had lain ambushed in the shadow, sprang out upon him; he noticed that they wore masks and carried guns. One seized his ass's bridle, while the others, in the twinkling of an eye, dragged him from the saddle and threw him on the road; one man knelt on his legs and fastened his wrists together, the other meanwhile bandaging his eyes with a folded handkerchief tied tightly round his head.

He had barely time to say, "But what do you want, my lads?"—when he was forced to his feet, pushed and hustled off the road, and dragged violently down the stony hillside toward the valley.

"But, my lads. . . ."

"Silence or you're a dead man!"

He was frightened by their rough handling, but still more so by the state of terror that the three men were in—obviously on account of their deed of violence. He could hear them panting like wild beasts. They were going to do something horrible to him.

But perhaps they did not mean to kill him—at any rate not at once. If they had been paid to murder him, or were carrying out a vendetta, they would have despatched him up there on the highroad, from their ambush in the shadows. So it must be that they were carrying him off for a ransom.

"My lads. . . ."

They gripped his arms more tightly, shook him, and told him again to be silent.

"But at least loosen the bandage a little. It's very tight on my eyes. . . . I can't. . . ."

"Go on! Move."

First down, then up, now straight on, then turning back; down again, then up and up and up. Where could they be taking him?

Sinister imaginings haunted his mind on that terrible, blind march over rocks and thorns, pushed and pulled along in total darkness. And then, suddenly, he saw the lights—the lights of the little town on top of the ridge—the oil lamps shining from the houses and streets—just as he had seen them round the bend a moment before he was attacked, just as he had seen them again and again on his way home from his holding at that evening hour. How strange! He saw them plainly through the tight bandage over his eyes—as clearly as before when his eyes were open. How strange. . . . As he stumbled on and on, savagely pulled and pushed by his captors, so that his heart filled with terror, he took the little lamps with him; and not only those soft, sad little lamps, but the whole of the mountain spur with the town on its summit—the town whose other inhabitants went safely and peacefully about their business, unconscious of his horrible adventure.

At one point he caught the sound of the hurried patter of his ass's hoofs.

Oh! So they were dragging his weary old donkey along, too! She, poor beast, could not understand. All she would notice would be the unwonted hurry and rough treatment, but she would go where she was taken, without any idea of what had happened. If only they would stop a moment and let him speak, he would tell them quietly that he was ready to pay whatever they demanded. He had not long now to live, and it really was not worth while suffering such hideous treatment just for the sake of a little money—money which brought him no satisfaction.

"My lads. . . ."

"Silence! Go on!"

"I can't imagine it. . . . Why are you doing this to me? I'm ready to. . . ."

"Silence! We'll talk later. Go on!"

They made him trudge like that for what seemed eternity. At last, overcome by weariness and sick and giddy from the tight bandage, he fainted and remained unconscious.

He recovered his senses next morning and found himself lying, utterly exhausted, in a low cavern.

A strong, musty smell seemed to emanate from the first light of dawn, which entered wanly through the winding entrance to the chalky grotto. Faint though it was, that light comforted him in his pain—the pain he felt from the rough handling he had undergone. He remembered that brutal violence as if it had been a nightmare—remembered how, when he had been unable to keep on his feet, he had been carried, first on one man's back and then on another's, dropped on the ground and dragged along, then held up by his arms and legs.

Where was he now? He listened attentively: from the stillness outside, he imagined that he was high on some lofty peak. The idea made him feel quite giddy. He was unable to move, for his hands and feet were tied, and he lay stretched on the ground like a dead animal. His limbs and head were so heavy that they seemed made of lead. He wondered whether he was wounded. Perhaps they had left him there for dead.

No. There they were, discussing something outside the cave. So his fate was not yet settled. . . . He considered what had happened, and found that he had no longer any thought of attempting to escape from his position of danger. He knew that he could not escape, and he had almost lost the will to do so. The disaster was accomplished—it was as if it had happened a long time ago, almost in a previous life. That life had been a miserable affair, and he had left it far, far away, down below in the valley, where they had captured him. Now he had only the silence of that high place—a void in which the past was forgotten. Even if they set him free, he no longer had the strength, perhaps not even the desire, to go down and restart the old life.

Suddenly a wave of self-pity swept over him, and he began to shudder with horror at the fate awaiting him, as he saw one of his captors crawling into the cave on all fours. The man's face was concealed by a red handkerchief with holes made in front for the eyes. Guarnotta looked quickly at his hands. They carried no weapons, only a new pencil—the kind you buy for a penny—not yet sharpened. In his other hand was a crumpled sheet of common note paper, with an envelope held in its fold.

The old man felt reassured. He smiled involuntarily. At that moment, the other two—also masked—entered the cave on their hands and knees. One of them came up to him and undid his hands, but not his feet. Then the first to enter spoke, "Now have some sense! You must write as we tell you."

Guarnotta thought he recognized the voice. Yes, of course! It was Manuzza—so-called because he had one arm shorter than the other. But was it really he? A glance at the man's left arm confirmed his suspicion. He felt sure that he would recognize the other two, if they removed their masks, for he knew everyone in the town.

He replied, "Have some sense, indeed! It's you, my lads, who ought to have some sense. To whom do you want me to write? And what am I to write with? That thing?" He pointed to the pencil.

"Why not? It's a pencil, isn't it?"

"Yes, it's a pencil, all right. But you don't even understand how such things are used."

"What d'you mean?"

"Why! You must sharpen it first!"

"Sharpen it?"

"Yes, sharpen it, with a penknife, there—at the tip."

"Penknife—I haven't got one," said Manuzza, and added, "Have some sense, now—here, have some sense!" followed by a string of oaths.

"Yes, I've got sense, all right, Manuzza . . ."

"Oh!" shouted the fellow. "So you've recognized me?"

"What else can you expect, when you hide your face and leave your left arm exposed? Take off that handkerchief and look me straight in the eyes. Why are you doing this . . . to me?"

"Stop all that chatter!" bellowed Manuzza, pulling the handkerchief from his face. "I've told you to have some sense. Either you write or I'll kill you!"

"Yes, yes! I'm ready to write," rejoined Guarnotta, "when you've sharpened the pencil. But—if you don't mind my asking—it's money you want, my lads, isn't it? How much?"

"Three thousand florins!"

"Three thousand? That's no small sum."

"You're worth that much! Let's have no nonsense about it!"

"Three thousand florins?"

"Yes, and more too! More than that!"

"Quite true. I am worth more than that, but I've not got that sum at home, in ready money. I should have to sell some houses and fields. D'you think that can be done at a day's notice and without my presence there?"

"Tell them to borrow the money!"

"Tell who?"

"Your wife and nephews!"

Guarnotta smiled bitterly and tried to raise himself up on one of his elbows. "That's just the point I wanted to explain," he answered. "My lads, you have made a great mistake. Are you counting on my wife and her nephews? If you're bent on killing me, kill me. Here I am! Kill me and no more said about it. But if it's money you're after, you can only get the money from me, on condition that you let me return home so I can raise it."

"What are you talking about? Let you go home? Do you think we're mad? You're joking!"

"Well, then. . . ." began Guarnotta, with a sigh.

Manuzza snatched the sheet of writing paper angrily from his companion's hand and repeated, "Stop all that chatter, as I told you—just you write! The pencil . . . Oh God, yes! . . . it has to be sharpened. . . . How's that done?"

Guarnotta explained the way and the men exchanged glances and left the cave. As he saw them crawl out, on all fours—looking like three animals—he could not refrain from smiling once more. He reflected that they were now engaged in trying to sharpen the pencil, and that perhaps, by dint of pruning it like a branch of a tree, they would fail in their attempts. That was what might well happen, and he smiled at the idea, at the thought that, at that moment, his life depended on the absurd difficulty which those three men would be up against, in trying to carry out an operation they had never performed before. Perhaps, when they saw the pencil growing smaller and smaller they would be so annoyed that, on their next entry, they would show him that though their knives might be no good for sharpening a pencil, they were quite good for cutting his throat. . . . He had been a fool and had committed an unpardonable mistake in letting that fellow Manuzza know that he had recognized him. . . . Yes, he could hear them all talking at once—outside the cave, shouting and cursing. He was sure they were passing that wretched penny pencil from one to another and that it was growing shorter and shorter under their clumsy treatment. Heaven knows what kind of knives they held in their great chalky fists. . . . There they were, crawling back in single file, having failed in their endeavor.

"The wood's rotten," said Manuzza. "That pencil's no good. As you know how to write, haven't you got a decent pencil in your pocket, properly sharpened?"

"No, I haven't, my lads," replied Guarnotta. "And anyhow it would be useless, I assure you. I would have written if you'd given me a pencil and paper. But to whom should I write? To my wife and nephews? They are her nephews, not mine—d'you understand that? You may be quite sure that none of them would have answered. They'd have pretended that they never received the threatening letter, and wash their hands of me. If you want money from them, you shouldn't have begun by falling on me. You should have made terms with them—say a thousand florins— for killing me. But they wouldn't even have paid that much. . . . I quite admit that they look forward to my death, but—you see—I'm an old man, and they expect that God will very soon grant it to them free of expense and in that way there'll be no feeling of remorse. You surely don't imagine they'd pay you a *centesimo*, one single *centesimo*, to *save* my life? You have muddled the whole business. My life is only of interest to myself; and it isn't of much interest even to me—that's the truth. Still, I admit, I don't want to die like this—it's a horrible death. And therefore, simply to escape that kind of end, I promise and swear to you, by the soul of my dear son, that, as soon as I possibly can—within two or three days—I myself will bring you the money to the place you appoint."

"Yes! After you've already reported us!"

"I swear that I will not do so. I swear that I will not breathe a word of this matter to anyone. Remember, my life is at stake!"

"It is at present, but will it be when you are free? Why, even before going home, you'll report us to the police!"

"I swear to you that I will not! You really ought to trust me. Remember that I go out every day into the country, and my life, out there, is in your hands. And have I not always been a father to you boys? God knows, you have always looked up to me and respected me. . . . Do you think that I'm anxious to expose myself to the danger of a vendetta? No, you ought to trust my word and let me return home, and you can be sure that you'll have the money."

They said no more to him, but exchanged glances and left the cave crawling away on hands and knees.

All day long he did not see them again. At first he could hear them engaged in discussion outside; after a while, no further sound reached him.

He lay there, turning over in his mind all the probabilities, and wondering what decision they would come to. One thing seemed clear to him—that he had fallen into the hands of three stupid fellows, mere amateurs, and that this was probably their first essay in crime. They had entered on it blindly, thinking solely of his money, without giving any previous consideration to their position as married men with families. Now that they realized their blunder, they did not know what to do next, and could see no way out of their difficulties. As for his oath that he would not denounce them, none of the three would trust in it, least of all Manuzza, who had been recognized. What was to happen then?

His only hope was that it would not occur to anyone of them to feel repentance for their stupid, unreasonable act, and a consequent desire to wipe out every trace of this first offence. If they decided to continue brigandage as outlaws, they might as well spare his life and set him free, without worrying about his denouncing them; but, if they repented and wanted to return to an honest livelihood, they must necessarily prevent the denunciation which they were convinced would follow on his freedom, and therefore they must murder him.

It followed from this that God might, he hoped, come to his assistance by enlightening them—by bringing them to see that it would not profit them to live an honest life. It should not be difficult to persuade them of this, seeing that they had already shown, by kidnapping him, that they were prepared to imperil their immortal souls. But he was very anxious about the disillusionment which they must have experienced when their eyes were opened to the great blunder they had committed, at the outset of a career of crime; for disillusionment is very apt to turn into repentance and into a desire to abandon a path which had begun badly. To withdraw from it, obliterating every trace of their previous steps, they might logically hold that they had no alternative but to commit a crime; for if they were willing to set him free, would they not, with equal logic, be forced to go on committing crimes? They would conclude then that it was better to commit that one crime at the outset—a deed which would remain secret, entirely untraced—than to commit any number of crimes, done openly as outlaws. At the cost of one misdeed, they could still hope to save themselves, not indeed as far as their consciences were concerned, but in the sight of men: if they were to release him—they would argue—they would be irretrievably lost.

As a result of these harassing reflections, he arrived at the conclusion that on that day or on the morrow, perhaps that very night while he slept, they would assassinate him.

He waited until it grew dark inside the cave. Then, overcome with terror at the thought of falling asleep in that silent and dreadful place, he determined to crawl outside the cave, even though his hands and feet were still tied. He moved forward with infinite difficulty, wriggling along like a worm, restraining his instinctive fears in an endeavor to make the least possible noise. What could he possibly hope for in trying to poke his head out, like a glowworm from its hole? Nothing. But at least he would see the sky and meet his death in the open, face to face, and not have it come upon him treacherously in his sleep. That was something.

Ah! there he was, at last . . . Quietly. . . . Was that moonlight? Yes, there was the young moon, and countless stars. . . . What a splendid night! Where was he? . . . On some mountaintop—the air and the silence proved that . . . Perhaps that was Monte Caltafaraci over there, or San Benedetto. . . . Then what was that valley? Either the plain of Consolida or the valley of Clerici? Yes, and that mountain to the west must be the Carapezza. But if so, what were those twinkling lights over there, glittering like clusters of fireflies in the opal moonlight? Were they the lights of Girgenti? Why then—good God!—then he was quite near! And it had seemed as if they had made him walk so far, so far. . . .

He looked anxiously round him, as if the possibility that they might have gone off, leaving him there, aroused his fear rather than hope. Dark and motionless, squatting like a great owl on a bank of chalk, sat one of the three men, left on guard; he showed plainly in the faint, pale light of the moon. Was he asleep?

The old man tried to squirm his way out a little farther, but all at once his arms lost all their power, as he heard a voice saying quite calmly, "I'm watching you, Don Vicé. Back you go, or I shoot!"

He held his breath and lay motionless, looking out. Perhaps the man might think that he had made a mistake.

"I am watching you."

"Let me have a breath of fresh air," he then begged. "I'm suffocated inside there. D'you mean to keep me like this? I'm dying of thirst—"

The man made a threatening gesture. "Well, you can stay there, but only on condition you don't utter a sound. I'm hungry and thirsty too, as well as you. Keep silent or I make you go back inside."

Silence . . . But at least he had the moon, revealing all those quiet valleys and mountains . . . and the relief of the fresh air . . . and the sad glimmer of those distant lights shining from his native town.

Where had the other two gone? Had they left to this third man the task of despatching him during the night? If so, why did he not do it at once? What was he waiting for? Was he perhaps waiting for the other two to come back that night?

Again he felt tempted to speak, but restrained himself. Well, if that was what they had decided to do . . .

He looked again at the slope where the man had been squatting and saw that he had resumed his former position. Judging from his voice and accent, Guarnotta concluded that he came from Grotte, a large village among the sulphur mines. Could it possibly be Fillico, a quiet, kindly fellow, a regular beast of burden, strong as a horse? If it really was he— if that silent, hard-working man had left the straight path, it was a bad business.

He could not stand it any longer, but spoke almost automatically, not as a question, in fact without any clear intention—it seemed as if he meant the name to sound as if uttered by some one else. "Fillico . . ." The man did not stir.

Guarnotta waited, then repeated it in the same tone, as if it were some other person talking; as he spoke, he gazed intently at his finger with which he was drawing marks on the sand.

"Fillico."

This time a shudder ran down his spine at the thought that his obstinacy in repeating that name—almost involuntarily—was likely to be paid for by a gunshot in return.

But again the man made no movement. Then Guarnotta gave a loud sigh of despair; suddenly his head was a dead weight which he could no longer support. He lay like a dying animal, with his face in the sand— the sand running into his open mouth—and, in spite of the prohibition against speaking and the threat of shooting, he began to rave—to rave interminably. He spoke of the beautiful moon—he cried a farewell to it, for it had by this time set; he spoke of the stars which God had created and placed in the distant heavens, so that the brute creation could not know that they were really countless worlds, much larger than this earth; he spoke of the earth, saying that everyone who is not a brute—a mere animal—knows that it spins like a top; it seemed to relieve his feelings

to declare that at that very moment there were men on it with their heads
pointing downward, and that they did not fall off into the sky for reasons which everyone ought to take the trouble to find out, unless he were
the lowest of the low—a mere clod into which our Lord God has not
breathed the divine spirit.

In the midst of all his wild raving, he suddenly found that he was
talking astronomy, expounding it like a professor; and the man who had
gradually drawn nearer to him, was now sitting beside him there, close
to the mouth of the cave; and it actually was as he had guessed—Fillico
from Grotte; and that it so happened that Fillico had wanted to know
about these matters for many years—all about the zodiac, the Milky Way,
the nebulae. . . . But he was not easy to convince; he did not think the
explanations given were true.

It was a strange situation. It was strange, too, that though he was at
the end of his strength, exhausted by despair, though he had a gun barrel
pointing at him—yet he was able to devote great attention to cleaning his
fingernails with a stalk of grass, taking care that it did not break or bend.
He also examined his remaining teeth—only three incisors and one canine
—and devoted much consideration to the problem whether his neighbor,
the maker of wine jars, who had lost his wife a fortnight back, was left
with three children or with four. . . .

"Now, let's talk seriously. Just tell me, what d'you think I am? By the
Madonna! D'you think I am a blade of grass—that blade of grass, there,
which you can pluck like this, just as if it were nothing? Feel me! By the
Madonna, I'm made of flesh and blood, and I have a soul, which God
gave me, just as He has given you one. Yet you mean to cut my throat
while I'm asleep? No . . . don't go . . . wait here, listen to me. . . .
What? You're not going? Oh! I see—as long as I was speaking of the
stars. . . . Listen to what I've got to say. Cut my throat here while I'm
awake—not treacherously while I'm asleep . . . d'you hear? What d'you
say to that? You won't answer? But why are you putting it off? What are
you waiting for, I want to know? If it's money you're after, you won't
get it. You can't keep me here and you don't want to let me go . . . you
mean to kill me? Well, for God's sake do it and get it over!"

But he was talking to empty space. The man had gone off and was
again squatting like an owl on the slope, to show him that it was quite
useless to speak on that subject—he would not listen to a word.

After all, thought Guarnotta, how stupid it was to worry like that. If he had to be murdered, was it not better to be murdered during his sleep? He even decided that if he was still awake when he heard them crawl into the cave later on, he would shut his eyes and pretend to be sleeping. Not that there was any need to shut his eyes, really—it would be dark and he could keep them open. All he had to do was to make no movement when they came close and were feeling for his throat, to cut it like a sheep's.

So he simply said, "Good night," and crawled away inside the cave.

They did not, however, murder him. They admitted their blunder; but were unwilling either to free him or to kill him. They would keep him there.

"What! Forever?"

For as long as God saw fit. They placed themselves in His hands. The captivity would terminate sooner or later, according as He wished to impose upon them a short or a long expiation for their fault in taking Guarnotta captive.

What was their intention then? That he should die a natural death up there? Could that be their intention? he asked.

Yes, that was it.

"But by all that is holy, can't you silly idiots see that it's not God, in the least, who is going to kill me? It's you who will be doing it, keeping me here in this cave, dying of hunger and thirst and cold, tied up like an animal, sleeping on the ground, easing myself here on the ground like an animal."

His protest was in vain: they had placed the matter in God's hands and their prisoner might as well have been talking to the stones. They pointed out to him, however, that as for dying of starvation, it was not true; neither was it true that he would have to sleep on the ground. They had brought him up three bundles of straw for his bed and, to keep off the cold, there was an old cloak padded with cotton wool, which belonged to one of them. And, moreover, there would be his daily bread and something to eat with it. They took it out of their own mouths and from the mouths of their wives and children to give it to him. It was bread which cost them much toil to procure, for one of them would have to keep guard over him, taking it in turns, while the other two went out to work. In the earthen pitcher was drinking water—and God only knew how hard it was to find water in that thirsty tract. As for his having to ease himself on the floor of his cave, he could go outside at night into the open.

When he found that he could make no impression on this stupid obduracy, he began to stamp his feet like a child. Were they brutes, then, with hearts of stone?

"Look here! Do you admit you've made a grave mistake—yes or no?"
Yes, they admitted it.

"Do you admit that you've got to pay for that mistake?"

Yes, they would pay for it by refraining from killing him, by waiting till God granted them his death and by endeavoring to alleviate, to the utmost of their power, the suffering which they had brought upon him.

"Very good. Oh, very good indeed! That's your expiation—you blockheads—for the sin you yourselves confess that you've committed? But what about me? Where do I come in? What sin did I commit? Am I, or am I not, the victim of your mistake? Why should you make me pay the penalty for the sin which you committed? Since I had nothing to do with it, why should I suffer in this way—for your fault? How can you justify that?"

No, they did not attempt any justification, but simply listened to him—their harsh, strained features impassive, their eyes dull and fixed. There was the straw—there was the overcoat . . . and there the pitcher of water . . . and the bread which they had earned with the sweat of their brows . . . and he could come outside when he had to.

They persisted in their expiation, taking it in turns to remain behind on guard over him. When keeping him company, they made him tell them about the stars and about all manner of things in town and country—what splendid harvests there were in former times when people were truly religious and how certain diseases of plants were not known in those good old days when there was more religion. They brought him an old almanac picked up somewhere, so that he could beguile his leisure by reading it, and stood around him watching, full of envy at his being able to read.

"Do tell us what it means—this printed sheet with that moon and the scales and those fish and the scorpion?"

His words stimulated their curiosity and they were gluttons for further knowledge, listening to him with childlike wonder and uttering low grunts of amazement. Little by little, he came to enjoy his talks with them.

In telling of so much that was new to them, it almost seemed to be new to him too, as if something alive were stirring within him, as if his soul were awakening after long years of torpor in his former distressful existence. Once his anger had subsided, he found that a new life was beginning for him and tried to adapt himself to it. As time passed, he bowed before the inevitable. Though his surroundings were strange and devoid of interest, he was no longer under the threat of a horrible end.

By this time, he reflected, he was already dead to everyone, on his distant farm overlooking the sea and in the town whose lights he could see at night. Perhaps no one had bothered to search for him after his mysterious disappearance; even if they had searched, they would not have put much energy into the task, as there was nobody keenly interested in finding him.

Since his heart had withered long years ago, what object was there now in returning to life—to that life which he had been leading? He felt that he had no real ground for complaint at his deprivations; for if he could recover his former comfort, he would recover also the terrible depression of his former life—a life that dragged its weary way through years of intolerable boredom! There was this to be said for his captivity, that although he spent his time merely lying on the ground, he did not feel the hours drag so wearily. Day followed day on the silent mountain spur, devoid of all sense and purpose, and it seemed to him as if time had ceased. In that extreme seclusion, even the consciousness of his own existence dropped away from him. He would look round at his shoulders and the chalk wall of the cave beside him, as the only things which had a real existence; or his hand, if his eyes rested on it—yes, that too was real and lived just on its own account; or it might be that rock or twig—they existed in a world of frightful isolation.

As the old man's anger at his unjust treatment died down, and he came gradually to the conclusion that what had befallen him was not such a disaster as had at first appeared, he began to perceive that it was indeed a very severe punishment that those three men had inflicted upon themselves—the task of keeping him there as a prisoner. Dead though he already was to everyone else, he remained alive solely for them, and they had taken on the entire burden of his support. They could have freed themselves from that burden without the slightest difficulty, since his person no longer possessed value to anyone, since nobody took any interest in him. But, on the contrary, they continued to bear it, and carried through with resignation their self-imposed punishment. Not only did they complain, but they even did their best to render their task still more arduous by the little attentions which they lavished on him. For, quite apart from the duty imposed by their consciences, they had, all three of them, become genuinely attached to the old man, regarding him as their own private property in which no one else had any claim. In some mysterious manner, they derived a great satisfaction from this—a satisfaction which they would miss for the rest of their lives, when the time came to lose him.

One day, Fillico brought his wife to the cave. She had her baby at her breast and was holding a little girl by the hand; the child had carried up a fine homemade cake as a gift for "granddad."

How they stared at him—the mother and daughter. He reflected that by then he must have been several months in captivity and presented a lamentable appearance—dirty, ragged, and with tufts of bushy hair on his chin and cheeks. Pleased at their visit, he received them with a friendly smile. Perhaps it was the sight of a smile on the emaciated face which so startled the good woman and her daughter.

"Don't be afraid, my darling! Come here, little one . . . that's right. See, there's a bit for you. Yes, you eat it. So Mummy made it, did she?"

"Mummy."

"That's lovely. Have you got any little brothers? . . . Three? Oh! Poor Fillico! Four children already. . . . Bring the boys up here to me. I'd like to see them. Next week, yes, that's right—only I hope there won't be any next week for me. . . ."

The next week duly arrived: in truth God wished the three men's expiation to last a long time, for it dragged on for over two months more.

He died on a Sunday, on a splendid evening when it was still bright as day, up on the heights. Fillico had brought his children to see old granddad and Manuzza his also. He died while he was playing with the children, behaving like a boy himself, wearing a red handkerchief over his head to cloak his bushy hair. While amusing the children and laughing at his own antics, he suddenly collapsed on the ground; the men rushed forward to pick him up and found him dead.

They put the children on one side and sent them and the women down from the mountain. Kneeling around the corpse, the three men burst into floods of tears, with fervent prayers for his soul and for their own salvation. They then buried him in the cave.

The rest of their lives, if anyone happened to mention Guarnotta in their presence and speak of his mysterious disappearance, they would say, "He was a saint, that man. . . . . I'm sure he was admitted straight to paradise."

—*Translated from the Italian by* ARTHUR AND HENRI MAYNE

MARY AUSTIN

The Green Bough

I believe that the ills of this world are remediable while we are in the world
by no other means than the spirit of truth and brotherliness working their
lawful occasions among men. I believe in Here and Now. I believe in Man,
the Friend of the Soul of Man, and I am unconvinced of Death.

MARY AUSTIN

I T W A S the season of the green bough. On into the night, emanations
from the warm, odorous earth kept the chill from the air, and the sky,
steeped in the full spring suns, retained, almost until dawn, light enough
to show the pale undersides of the olive branches where they stirred with
the midnight currents. It was not until the hours fell into the very pit of
the night that the morning coolness began to strike shivers along the
bodies of those whose business kept them sleeping on the open slopes
outside the city walls.

It would have been about that time that he awoke. For more than an
hour past he had swung from point to point of consciousness on successive waves of pain; now he was carried almost to the verge of recovery,
and now he felt the dragging clutch of the Pit from which hardly he had
escaped. By degrees as he was borne toward life his passages in and out
of insensibility began to approach more nearly the normal phases of
waking and sleeping; the pangs of his body separated from the obsessions
of spiritual distress, and recurrent memory began to ply.

It began with the agony in the garden and the falling away of all
human support from that inexplicable wrestling of great souls with foreknowledge, which must always seem to the generality, unnecessary if not
a little absurd. More pitiably than all that had rolled between, he felt the
empty reach of his affections toward the uncomprehending sleep of his
companions. . . . Could ye not watch one little hour! He remembered
the futility of trial, the scoffing and the betrayals, through the crisis of
which his quick spirit had lived so long before, that at last it broke upon

him harmlessly. Pain by pain, his body picked out for him other memories of the way, the cross, the tearing nails . . . more than all else the impotence of purely human impulses under the larger vision which kept him even in the midst of anguish, profoundly aware of how little they knew the thing they did. It came back upon him as the stiffness of his wounds, the burden of understanding that loses even the poor human relief of bitterness and blame. As he fell away again into the trough of bodily pain it was to measure the full horror of that drop, which, when the racked consciousness that had sustained him in the knowledge of Fatherliness, had failed like a splitten sail and left him beating blindly in the void. "My God, my God, why hast thou forsaken me?" He came strangely up to life in the anguish of that cry. . . . Suddenly he put up his hand and touched the cold stones of his sepulchre. He was dead then, and was alive. Lying very still for pure weakness, his spirit returned half unwittingly by the old track and travelled toward God. . . . fumblingly, as a drowsy child at the breast, he sucked comfort, the ineffable, divine support. It flowed. Slowly the slacked spirit filled. . . . Power came upon him. God was not dead . . . nor forsaking. . . . He hung upon that and waited for a word. Outside in the dawn dusk a bird, hung awakened by the swaying of his bough in the first waft of the morning, bubbled over with the joyous urge of the spring. The sound of it filtered through the rock crevices in a thin, clear trickle of song. He laid off the grave cloth and began to feel for the round stone which he knew should close the mouth of the grave. Wounded as he was, it was still no more than many suffer in battle, with the cheerful promise of recovery; calling on those reserves of power for which he had always been remarkable, he applied his shoulder to the stone . . . it yielded to the pressure and slid along the groove.

He made out the soft bulk of the olive trees, all awake and astir to catch the first streak of morning, and the *tink tink* of water falling from a pipe into a stone basin. Following it he came to the fountain from which the garden was watered, and drank and bathed his wounds. He was startled for a moment by the swaying of a garment against him, and then he perceived it to be the gardener's cloak left hanging in the tree, the long, brown hooded garment of the time. He drew its folds around him as a protection against the warning chill of dawn. He was a workingman also, and knew the ways of working folk; he groped in the split hollow of the

ancient olive tree, and far under the roots behind the gardener's spade he
found a lump of figs tied in a cloth and a common flask which had yet a
few swallows of wine in it. When he had eaten and drunk he bound up
his side with the cloth and sat down on the stone bench of the fountain
to think what had befallen him.

He was dead—else why had they buried him?—and he was alive again.
This then was the meaning of those glimmers and intimations of a life so
abundant that he could not imagine even the shock of death to separate
him from it. . . . For a long time he had known what he must face if
he came up to Jerusalem, yet he had faced it, urged by that inward impulse
too deep and imperative for human withstanding . . . and he had died
. . . witness the aching wound in his side . . . and now he walked
among the olives. Vestiges and starts of the broken images of pain and
returning consciousness advised where he had been. He turned his mind
deliberately away from that and laid hold on God . . . he was alive
again. . . . The currents of the Eternal Being circulated through him
with peace and healing.

The dusk of the dawn cleared to blueness, in which the domes and
towers of Jerusalem swam, islanded in light. Round about, single high
peaks, which still retained the winter whiteness, glowed like outposts of
the heavenly host. The gates of the city clattered to let in the hordes of
market gardeners with their donkeys, camped since the night before outside the walls, and presently in the cool dimness he saw the woman stealing out by a postern and beginning to climb the hill path toward the place
of sepulchres. They came peering through the dawn, for they were not
certain of any mark by which they should know it, except that it was a
new tomb wherein never man was laid. Their voices came up to him
clearly through the morning stillness, and he knew at once what their
errand was when he heard them troubling lest they had come so early
there would be no one about to take away the stone from the door; but
when they came to the place where it should be, and saw that it was already rolled away, they were amazed and a little afraid. Then Mary the
mother of James and Salome, and the other Mary, put down the spices
they had brought, to go and carry word to the disciples, but Mary Mag-
dalene stayed weeping by the sepulchre.

When he saw that she was alone he went to her and inquired why she
wept. She, supposing him to be the gardener, for she saw little because

of her weeping and it was not yet full light—"Oh, Sir," she said, "if you have borne him hence, tell me where you have laid him that I may take him away."

"Mary!" he said, and as he spoke he put back the gardener's hood from his head.

"Rabboni," the old title came back half consciously in answer to the tone, and suddenly she saw that it was he and fell in trembling for she could not understand but that he was a spirit. She sunk in the wet grass of the orchard, for the quaking of her limbs would not sustain her.

"Why seek ye the living among the dead?" he questioned with the old tender irony, but she scarcely heard him. She worked toward him on her knees; tremblingly her hands went out to touch the beloved feet, half to prove it were his very self or a vision of thin air.

"Nay, touch me not, Mary." He drew back with the sensitiveness of the newly wounded. "I am not ascended to my Father," he assured her as he raised her from the ground.

Louder now they heard the stir of Jerusalem awake, and knew that the broadening day might soon bring the rabble about them. When he had questioned her a little hurriedly concerning the state of the city and his disciples, he bade her tell them to come to him in Galilee in a place known to them of old, and so saying drew the folds of his cloak about him and went down by the hill trail away from Jerusalem.

It was twilight of the same day when he came near to the village of Emmaus and heard the cheerful barking of the dogs and the lowing of the cattle at the byres. There was a good spring smell of tillage in the inlets of the hills and the cry of the night-jar shaken out over the stony places in a shrill fine spray of sound. Half an hour from the village he came upon two who had followed him up to Jerusalem in the beginning of the Passover, and as they walked they reasoned together concerning the things that had come to pass there. When he had entered into conversation he saw that they were sad, and inquired of them the reason for it; and they, taking him for a stranger, told him how but a short time since there had gone a man up to Jerusalem with a great company, preaching the Kingdom of Heaven at hand, and what had been done to him by the authorities.

"But," said they, "we trusted it had been he should redeem Israel."

"O slow of heart," cried he, "that you believe not all that the prophets have spoken!"

All day as he had come, against the pangs of his torn body, his spirit had beat up toward God with the rhythm of his walking, calling on Power by all the names of Jehovah until he went veiled in it as in a cloud, which now, by the mere added effort of communication burst into splendor. But a few days since he had walked up to Jerusalem, battling, in the midst of the presages of betrayal and disaster, with the incomplete revelation of Messiahship. This morning waking at once to a knowledge of the practical defeat and to a new and extraordinary security of Divine continuance, he had felt his way, like a true Hebrew, back through the maze of intimations by the words of the Prophets; starlighted sayings shot like meteors across the dark of Israel's history. They lit far inward past the shames and consternations of the crucifixion.

This, then, was the Kingdom; not the overthrow of one form by another, but the flux of all forms, empires, pomps, societies, in the eternal facts of existence . . . the redemption of life from the bondage of things. He was dead and was alive again.

How indeed was a Messiahship to prove its divine origin by merely setting up in the room of thrones and principalities, say rather, the last word as to the futility of the Kingdoms of the world was pronounced when they wrecked themselves against his immortal quality.

As he held up the events of the last few days to the familiar scriptures, new meanings came out in them like secret writing held before a flame, and as he talked the hearts of his companions burned within them. As they drew near to their house, the speaker made as if he would have gone further, but they urged that he should come in to supper, for the way was hard and the dark had fallen. So as they sat at table, still talking, the mistress of the house set food before them and a little oil-fed lamp. Then the guest put back the hood from his head and stretching forth his hand broke the bread and blessed it, as was his custom, and at once they knew him, but for very fear and astonishment they spoke neither to him nor to one another. As soon as he saw that he was recognized he rose and went forth from them, disappearing in the night.

So little anticipated by his disciples had been the overthrow of the Messianic Hope that the stroke of it fell upon them like a wolf upon the flock. It scattered them into nooks and corners, into the hill places and villages around about Jerusalem, there to huddle, pressing together for relief from consternation, loath to believe that the miraculous powers, which had so often served them, had failed him on his own account, and wholly unable to accept the whispered word brought by the women from the sepulchre. He was gone; power and personality, his body even risen or spirited away. All during that day there had been fearful stealers about the precincts of the burial place for a view of the deserted tomb, stealing back again to whisper and wonder or to handle the dropped grave cloth which lay treasured in the house of Mary.

And now, here came two back from Emmaus with extraordinary new proof of a resurrection, which when they had heard it neither did they believe. But as some few of them sat together talking of these things, secretly behind shut doors for fear of authorities, he of whom they spoke, advised by that mysterious inward leading that his name passed among them with the old reverent tenderness, sought them out by it, and while they were yet speaking appeared among them. Wounded and pale from his vigils and his pains, the voice of his customary salutation struck terror through them. There were men there who had unbound him dead, as they believed, from the cross and bestowed him in the tomb!

"Behold my hands and my feet," he said; "handle me and see; for a spirit hath not flesh and bones." But seeing they hung between terror and wonder, he understood that they still supposed they had seen a spirit. Then he sat at table and asked that he be served with what food they had, the broiled fish and honey in the comb, upon which they had been at supper, talking quietly the while. Seeing him eat they grew secure, and as they began to realize that he was with them in flesh they were glad.

So by such simple means as they were able to receive he made them to know that he was the very man whom with their own hands they had laid away, in no wise changed or altered; but of the new meaning which his life had taken on by the fact, he spoke very little, for their minds were not opened to it; neither was it at all times and altogether plain to himself.

In the hills beyond the Sea of Tiberias there was a hut built in a secret and solitary place by one of those wild anchorites not infrequently met with in the borders of Judea. None knew of it except perhaps a runaway slave or two, and shepherds who used it at lambing time. Here in the beginning of his ministry he had drawn apart for seasons of prayer and meditation, that the Word might be plain to him; here, then, he remained resting of God, subsisting in the body by what the hills afforded him and by the gifts of a few poor followers who had their homes hereabout, as yet scarcely apprised of the tragic termination of his mission to Jerusalem. Here he saw the passing of the rains, and flowers come out, flame-like, on low piney shrubs; wandering shepherds went by him with their new-washed flocks, and whiter clouds led flockwise in the draws between the hills. . . . By all these things knowledge flowed into him.

He saw with chastening how it was that he, so near at all times to the Divine mind, should suffer these things. Lying so close there, as a child to its parent, he had been pushed off the better to measure its reach and fullness. He had clung to that breast which in his ministry had nourished him, until torn from it by betrayals, mockings, tortures of his body, he had dropped despairingly into the gulf of death, and lo, he was fallen into the lap of God! "The Kingdom of Heaven is in the midst of you," he had said to his disciples, and now suddenly he had discovered it in the midst of himself! this profound inward clutch upon Being, from which not the breaking of his Body could divide him.

Here in the weakness of shock and wounds, much that had perplexed him in his own life, the fullness of Power straining at his human imitations, came out clearly like the contour of a coast at ebb, but it left him more than ever groping for that communicating touch by which the gained knowledge could be made serviceable to men.

"As my father hath sent me," he had said to his disciples when his newfound resistance to wounding and the malice of men was at flood, "even so I send you." Now, as his body frailed before the inundation of revelation, he yearned for Peter and that John whom he had loved; all the company of humble folk who had heard him gladly, following up to Jerusalem as trustfully as the great bands of sheep that passed him almost daily, roving the Galilean hills at the heels of the shepherd.

How was he to reach them now, scattered and leaderless, with the significance of his persistence in the body which he accepted at its humanest interpretation? Lying close in the cover of the hills he sent out his thoughts in a strong cry toward his best loved disciples, and Peter and John and the others picking up again the dropped thread of their humble avocations about Gennesareth, heard him. They heard him inwardly, but read it so

humanly awry that they made excuse to one another that they went a fishing. They entered into the fishing boats and all night, though they caught
nothing, they beat toward the coast where the cry was; and when it was
early light they heard his very voice calling to them that they should cast
in their net on the side where he had seen the silver schools floating under
the morning mist. When Peter knew the voice he girt on his fisher's coat
and came ashore through the shallows, for they were close in, and he had
the quickest faith of all the twelve.

Then the others came in with the nets full to breaking, and found that
he had made a fire, for the nights along the lake borders were chill, and
prepared bread. So they took fish and broiled it and broke their fast
together as they had done so many times before when in the beginning of
his ministry he had often no other food than the shared bread of the working people. The naturalness of the morning meal restored to them a little
of their former reverent familiarity, and served as the medium by which
he undertook to lay upon them the obligation of the gospel which he
could now no more in this frame and presence preach about the world.

Of this he seems to have been certain. Daily as he reached inward on
great tides of prayer for the word born of his late experience, he was
aware of being carried so far out of his wracked body that it was inevitable
that he should finally leave it there tumbled like weed along the shore of
Things. Beyond that episode lay the full light for which he panted more
than a hart for the water brook.

He had known, evidently, how his visit to Jerusalem must terminate, he
seems now to have understood that his further usefulness must wait upon
the dropping off of the tortured frame which he had brought up through
the tomb with him, but he missed knowing how to convey to the remnant
of his disciples, who came together about him in the hills, the spiritual
values of his return.

He failed, perhaps, because he was not himself yet sure that it might
not come that way, to rid them of the expectation of Jewish Autonomy;
he was concerned, as always, with the preaching of his Word, rather than
what came of it. On this morning the flocks rounding the lake-fronting
hills furnished the figure of his admonition.

"Feed my sheep," he said to Peter, and again; and then, "Feed my
lambs." One thing he had not brought back out of the tomb with him was

the fear by which his church was afterward corrupted, that the Truth of God could not be trusted to do its Perfect Work in man.

On a mountain in a place appointed for them, he flamed forth for the last time, with that message, the faint, misread recollection of which as it lay in the minds of his disciples, has become the ultimate hope of all our science and all untoward questionings—the assurance of the supremacy of the Spirit. What they got from it chiefly was the certainty of the continuance of his personal power. It was the green bough preserved to them among the desolating blasts of human experience. "For, lo, I am with you always," he said, "even to the end of the world."

That they did not treasure more these last words, preserve them with that meticulous accuracy for which that body of religionists, from whom they were shorn by the sword of Christ's teaching, were notable, was due in part to their having no apparent belief in this being the last. They had seen him in the flesh and they expected to see him in the flesh again. Nothing else could account for the boldness with which these timid and easily shaken peasant souls faced so soon again the possibility of persecution and death in that Jerusalem whither he had told them to await the confirming visitation of the Spirit. They faced it. They went, while the city still rang with the story of his defeat, to confirm his triumph; they preached what they had known and seen.

It seems likely then, that on that last occasion when he went with them a little way on the road toward Jerusalem, they had no notion that it was the last they should see of him in the body. They said unto him, "Lord, dost thou at this time restore the Kingdom to Israel?"

"It is not for you," said he, "to know times and seasons." In his own time he should come again and in no other guise than Counsellor and Friend. When he had blessed them they saw him pass up the hill trail toward his chosen place and the mountain mists receive him.

Afterward in the long time when they expected him in vain, they said, in the manner of speaking of that country, that he had ascended to Heaven, so that long afterward it came to be reported that they had seen him ascending there in the company of clouds of angels. But so long as they lived who had seen him they looked out for him every day . . . any knock at the door . . . any solitary figure on the hill paths about Bethany. . . . For they had laid him in the tomb, and he had come to them in the very flesh.

VIII

Testament

WILLIAM SAROYAN

Leaning on the Everlasting Arms

In these times the opportunity (and necessity) for dynamic dramatic religious experience is tremendously increased, and already the chronicling of these experiences has begun. Before the war is over there will be a great body of it. Faith seems to spring from two opposite emotions: adoration and fear. There is no time now for adoration and there appears to be no escape from fear—for anyone—it is purely a matter of degree. Helplessness (as much if not more than fear) turns the vision of some men to the vastness and benignity of God, or of things, or of the universe, or of whatever order moves things in and out of being. . . . You have surely heard the sorrowful expression which sums up a good deal of this kind of religious experience: "There are no atheists in fox-holes." As a matter of fact, there probably are a few—but in all probability fewer than there are in other places. The little poem of the flier, published or reprinted in *Time Magazine* three or four months ago, is an example. In the hope of saving his hide, man is swift to drop his ten cents' worth of pride, his ignorant-intelligence, and the other things which help to make a fool of him in normal times. Essentially, though, no man endures without faith—again it is a matter solely of degree, of extent of faith. If you dismiss the large order of things, you cannot dismiss the small order of them. And so on, all of which is by way of letting you know I have been wondering what to send you for your anthology, which I think is an excellent idea.

WILLIAM SAROYAN

AN AMERICAN passenger train moved swiftly over American earth through an American night. The train was filled with American boys, among them Marcus and his friend Tobey—all of them dressed as soldiers and trained for war. But from their eyes, from their high spirits, and from their laughter and shouting and singing, you knew this was not an army alone, but a nation, and surely a good and great one. You knew that while they had been taught to stand in line and to behave on schedule with no personal rights beyond the needs of the unit, they had not become a machine and were still good human beings with at least average intentions. You knew that if they were noisy and perhaps unaware of their own importance, they were not without dignity. You knew surely that while their noise came from deep inner fear, they were still utterly unafraid. You knew they had accepted for no terribly pompous or false reasons the necessity to dismiss their fear, and if it so happened, to die. You knew they were American boys, some of them past forty even, but most of them kids—kids from big cities and little towns, from farms and offices, from rich families and poor families, kids lifted out of great worlds and kids lifted out of small worlds, some moved away from magnificent dreams of action and some from humble dreams of peace—kids brilliant and swift in spirit and kids slow and steady. In the midst of the clamor, the laughter, the excitement, the confusion, the eagerness, and the magnificent combination of profound ignorance and profound wisdom, Marcus Macauley and his friend Tobey George talked quietly.

"Well,'" Tobey said, "I guess we're on our way."

"That's right," Marcus said.

"You know, Marcus," Tobey said, "I feel lucky, because if it hadn't been for this War I wouldn't have run into you and I would never have found out about your family."

Marcus felt embarrassed. "Thanks," he said. "I feel the same way about you." He stopped a moment and then asked the question that every man exposed to unknown danger must ask himself again and again. "I want you to tell me the truth," he said. "Are you going to care much if you're killed?"

The other could not answer the question immediately, but at last he said, "Sure. I *could* bluff, I guess, and *pretend* that I wouldn't care. Of course I'm going to care. Aren't you?"

"Yes," Marcus said. "I'm going to care very much. I just wanted to know." He stopped a moment and then said, "What do you *think* about? What do you want to get back to?'

"I don't know," Tobey said, because he didn't know. "I guess I want to get back to—well, anything—whatever it happens to be. I haven't got a family as you have. I haven't anybody to go back to, but whatever it is, that'll be O.K. with me. I want to get back to whatever it turns out to be. I haven't got a girl waiting for me like your girl Mary, but I know I want to get back just the same—if I can."

"Sure," Marcus said.

Again they were silent a moment and then Marcus said, "How does it happen that you like to sing?"

"How should I know?" Tobey said. "I just like to sing, that's all." They listened to the train and to the noise inside the train and then Tobey said, "What do *you* think about?"

Marcus took a little time before beginning to answer this question. "I think about my father," he said, "and my mother, and my sister Bess and my brother Homer and my brother Ulysses. And I think about Mary and her father, Mr. Arena. I think about the whole neighborhood, the empty lot, the kids, the houses, Ara's Market, and Ara himself. The railroad tracks where I used to watch the trains go by, the Sunday School, the church, the courthouse park, the Public Library, the old teachers, the kids who used to be in my life—some of them dead already, but not from this War—just dead."

"It's a funny thing," Tobey said. "Maybe you won't understand a thing like this, but I feel that Ithaca is *my* home town, too." He waited a moment and then said, "If we get through all right, if we come out of this O.K., will you take me with you to Ithaca? Will you show me the places you knew, and tell me about them, what happened at this place and what happened at that place?"

"Sure," Marcus said, "sure. I *want* to do that. And I want you to meet my family, too. We're poor, always have been—my father was a *great* man. He was not a successful man. He didn't make any more money than what we needed—ever."

"Matthew Macauley?" Tobey said.

"Yes," Marcus said. "Matthew Macauley, my father. He worked in the vineyards, in the packing houses, and in the wineries. He did plain, ordinary, everyday work. If you saw him in the street you would think he was nobody. He looked like anybody else and acted like anybody else— but even so he was a great man. He was my father and I know he was great. The only thing he cared about was his family—my mother and his children. He saved money for months and made a down payment on a harp—yes, a harp—I know nobody plays a harp any more but that's what my mother wanted, so my father saved up money and made a down payment on a harp for her. It took him five years to pay for the harp. It was the most expensive harp you could buy. We used to think every house had a harp just because we had one. Then he bought a piano for my sister Bess—that didn't cost so much. I thought everybody was great like my father—until I got out and met some of the rest of the people. They're all right, they're fine—but I don't think they're great. Well, maybe they *are* and I just don't know them very well. You've got to know people real well to know whether they're great or not. A lot of people are great that nobody ever thinks are great."

"I wish I knew a man like your father," Tobey said. "Of course he wouldn't have to be *my* father. He could be anybody, just so I *knew* him. I guess I'm lucky in a way, not knowing who my father was, because, not knowing, I can *believe* he was great, just like your father."

"Maybe he *was* great," Marcus said.

"Maybe," Tobey said. "I hope so. You know, I didn't know kids had mothers and fathers until I went to school and heard the other kids talk about them." Tobey laughed with embarrassment. "I couldn't understand it," he said. "I thought every man was in the world alone—the same as me —to start out all by himself. I guess I felt bad for a long time, after I found out. It made me lonely. I mean it made me *lonelier*. Maybe *that's* the reason I like to sing. You don't feel your loneliness so much when you're singing." Then shyly, almost timidly, he said, "What kind of a girl is Bess?"

Marcus knew his friend was uncomfortable asking this question and he didn't want him to be uncomfortable. "That's all right," Marcus said. "You can ask me about my sister. I want you to meet her. I think she will like you."

"Me?" Tobey said.

"Yes, I have an idea she might like you very much," Marcus said. "I want to take you back and have you stay at our house. If you like each other—well, I guess Bess is just about—well, anyway, even if she *is* my sister—well, I just think she'll like you very much, that's all."

Now Marcus began to speak very swiftly, because while he knew it was almost impossible to speak of such a thing at all, he also knew it was necessary to *try* to do so at least. Therefore he wanted to get the words spoken and their meaning established as swiftly as possible so that his embarrassment would not endure too long. "Marry her and live in Ithaca," he said. "It's a good town. You'll be happy there. Now, here. I'm going to give you her picture—to keep." He handed Tobey a little snapshot of his sister Bess. "Keep it in your identification folder where I keep Mary's picture. See?"

Tobey George took the photograph of his friend's sister and looked at it for a long time, while Marcus looked at him. At last he said, "Bess sure is beautiful. I don't know if a guy can fall in love with a girl without meeting her, but I feel in love with Bess already. I feel sick. I'll tell you the truth. I was afraid to talk to you about Bess until now. But I figured, well, maybe as long as we're on our way, and there's no telling, you might not mind so much. I can't help it, but I always feel I haven't the same kind of rights that other people have—you know, a guy who is given his name by an orphanage, not by his mother and father—who doesn't even know who his mother and father were—who doesn't even know what nationality they were—or what nationality *he* is. Some people say I'm Spanish and French, and some people say I'm Italian and Greek, and some people say I'm English and Irish. Almost everybody gives me a different nationality."

"You're an American," Marcus said. "That's all. Any man can see that."

"Sure," Tobey said. "I guess that's right, all right. I guess I'm an American all right. But I sure would like to know *which* American."

"You're the American whose name is Tobey George," Marcus said. "That's good enough for anybody. Now keep that picture. We'll go back to Ithaca and you'll raise a family and I'll raise a family, and we'll visit each other once in a while, have some music and songs—pass the time of life."

"You know, Marcus," Tobey said, "I *believe* you. I swear to God I believe you. I don't think you're saying this just because we happen to be friends, on our way. I believe you, and more than anything else in the world I want to go to Ithaca with you. I want to live there and I want to do all the things you said." He stopped a moment to try to imagine what might go wrong to keep him from doing these things, and then he said, "If Bess doesn't like me—if she falls in love with somebody else—if she's married when we get there—I'm going to live in Ithaca anyway. I don't know, but Ithaca seems to be *my* home now, too. For the first time in my life I feel that I belong somewhere and—I hope you won't mind—I feel that my family is the Macauley family, because that's the kind of family I'd want for myself if I could choose. I hope to God Bess likes me or doesn't fall in love with someone else, because I *know* I like *her*." Now he spoke very softly, and even though the train was full of noise, Marcus could hear the words, "Even though Bess doesn't know it yet, she's mine. And from now on, every breath I take will be to keep me alive until I get to Ithaca and her. Ithaca's my home. That is where I live. That's where I want to be when I die—if I can."

"We'll get back," Marcus said. "We'll be in Ithaca some day, Bess and you and Mary and me, and my mother and Homer and Ulysses. You wait and see."

Now the two friends did not talk for a long time. They were greeted by other boys in the train and shouted with the others and even sang a song which these boys had themselves invented, a song about women of the streets and what they were good for. And then in the midst of this song, as if what he was saying was altogether appropriate, Tobey said very simply, "Do you pray?" And Marcus replied, almost swiftly, "Always —always."

"At the orphanage," Tobey said, "we were *forced* to pray. It was a rule there. Whether we wanted to pray or not, we prayed."

"Maybe it's not such a bad rule," Marcus said, "but prayer is one thing you can't force. It's not a prayer if it's forced."

"I know," Tobey said. "That's why I quit praying when I left the orphanage. I don't think I've said a prayer since I was thirteen years old. But I'm starting all over again—right now—and this is it." He waited a moment and then, without closing his eyes, without bowing his head, without folding his hands, he began to pray, and what he said was unmistakably a prayer. "Just get me to Ithaca," he said, "if You can. Anything You say, but if You can, get me to Ithaca. Let me get home. Protect everybody. Keep everybody from pain. Find homes for the homeless. Get the traveler home and get me to Ithaca." He stopped and began singing again the words of the ribald song. Suddenly he stopped singing and shouted, "Amen!"

"That's a good prayer," Marcus said. "I hope it's answered."

The orphan decided that he had left a few things out of the prayer. Therefore, he continued. "Keep the town there," he said. "Let me walk through its streets. Keep the Macauleys there—all of them. Keep Bess. Let her know I love her. Keep Marcus—and Mary. Keep his mother and his brother Homer and his brother Ulysses. Keep the house and the empty lot next door. Keep the harp and the piano and the songs. Keep the railroad tracks so I can see the trains go by. Keep the world where it is, and give me a chance to get to it—where I want to be—in Ithaca. Get me there —to Ithaca—if You can. That's all." And again he shouted, "Amen!"

Now the soldiers were singing another song which they had made up for themselves. This song had to do with the impermanence of all things, particularly a woman's love, and the boys delighted in the cynical wisdom of the song. Tobey and Marcus joined in the singing. Tobey stopped singing to say, "What do *you* pray for, Marcus?"

Marcus stopped singing to say, "I pray for the same things you pray for—the very same things." And again the two friends took up the song with the cynical wisdom.

After the song the whole train became silent. There was no reason for this silence and yet every man on the train was hushed and for a moment deeply solemn. At last a soldier named Joe Higgins came to Marcus and Tobey and said, "What's the matter, what's everybody so quiet about? How about a song, Tobey? How about playing for us on the accordion, Marcus?"

"What would you like to hear, Joe?" Marcus said.

"Oh, I don't know," Joe said. "We've sung all the dirty songs, maybe we ought to sing something old—you know, something, well, something *good!* Why don't we sing a good old-time church song—something we all know and used to sing as kids?"

"Why not?" Marcus said. "What church song do you like, Joe?"

"Well," Joe said, "now don't you guys laugh at me—I'd sure like to hear *Leaning*. You know—*Leaning on the Everlasting Arms.*"

Marcus turned to Tobey. "Do you know the words of that song, Tobey?" he said. "If you don't, I can help you."

"Do I *know* them?" Tobey said. "I guess I sang that song almost every Sunday for ten years."

"All right," Marcus said, "let's do it for Joe." Marcus turned to Joe. "If you feel like joining in, Joe," he said, "you don't have to know how to sing. Just join in, that's all."

"Sure," Joe said, "I'm going to sing—sure."

Marcus began to play the old hymn, and soon Tobey began to sing:

> *"What a fellowship, what a joy divine,*
> *Leaning on the everlasting arms;*
> *What a blessedness, what a peace is mine,*
> *Leaning on the everlasting arms."*

Now in a strong, unmusical but nevertheless pleasant voice, Joe began to sing with Tobey, and soon everyone in the train was listening. After a moment everyone gathered around Marcus and Tobey and Joe to be nearer the music and the words of the wonderful old hymn. Joe and Tobey sang:

> *"Leaning, leaning, safe and secure from all alarms;*
> *Leaning, leaning, leaning on the everlasting arms."*

By this time everybody gathered around the singers was singing.

GLENNYTH M. WOODS

The Last Mass

This is my tribute to our secular priesthood—to those soldiers in Christ who are neither saints nor supermen, but only very human individuals doing a hard job, for the most part consummately well, often heroically. The wonder to me is not that there *are* bad priests, but that there are so few of them.

GLENNYTH M. WOODS

"INTROIBO AD ALTARE DEI—I will go unto the altar of God. To God, Who gives joy to my youth. . . ."

The familiar words scraped like sand along his bruised and aching throat, as he thought with a surge of fresh pain: This is the end.

And it seemed to him that the lilies banked against the marble altar had the chill pallor of death.

This was the moment he had always subconsciously dreaded. He knew now that in the secret recesses of his mind there had always existed a feeling of transience, of impermanence; a sense of ever-impending separation. This, in itself, was not unnatural for a priest is always subject to sudden transfer at the order of his superior. His difficulty was in never being able wholly to resign himself to the possibility. During the four years while the Church was in the building, and in all the years that followed, he never lost his original almost hurting wonder at the beauty which had been achieved of cold insensate stone. Something of his very being had gone into that building; something of himself was immolated in its marble blocks, its sturdy, graceful columns. And always the little haunting fear to intensify his attachment. Certainly his relations with his people during the sixteen years of his pastorate had attained an added poignance because of that sense of inevitable parting.

Now the actual parting had come at last. He had been transferred quickly, almost without warning, away from his people, out of the city into a remote country parish. He suspected, though numbly and without resentment, political machination, for though the Church herself is divine, her members are frequently only too human. And he had made enemies, both lay and clergy. He recognized, yet without ever successfully correcting it, that he was too forthright and outspoken, wanting in a certain quality of self-restraint which no priest should lack.

The Bishop, brisk, business-like and not unkindly, pointed out the reasons for the change. His parish here was running smoothly. . . .

"I've worked very hard to build up this parish, sir."

"And you've done an excellent job." The Bishop was quick to forestall him. "An excellent job. That's exactly why I've chosen you for this work. Simonetta, as you know, is located in a section of the state which is predominantly non-Catholic. A parish in such a community requires a strong hand. Father Lawrence has been ill so long that he's rather let the reins slip. The people are becoming indifferent and drifting away. It's no easy assignment I'm handing you, but I think you're equal to it."

He thought resentfully:

"You don't have to give me a sales talk."

And aloud he said:

"I'll do my best, Bishop."

The Bishop favored him with one of his surprisingly pleasant, but infrequent, smiles; far back in his eyes there was a glint of not unsympathetic amusement.

"I know you will. And you'll find it will be good for you. Give you a new perspective."

However, what lay behind the move was immaterial; it was not open to appeal in any event. He at least knew the value of obedience.

"For thou, O God, art my strength . . . Hope in God, for Him will I praise forever; the salvation of my countenance and my God . . ."

Yes, he knew that love for God must come first; that God alone is the true and lasting reality; and that he, a priest, was the servant of God. That should be his consolation. Only—only it wasn't! His heart was as bleak and desolate as though it had been stripped of its last hope. And there was no use lying about it—at least not to himself. He would have let himself be chopped into dice before the world should know how he felt, but he refused, in his hour of sorrow, to try to deceive himself.

And the Mass went on.

He read the Epistle and the Gospel, kissed the Missal; then, slowly and majestically in his white and gold robes, advanced to the pulpit. There he again read the Lesson and Gospel in English, laid down the book, and looked out upon his people.

" 'Nevertheless, I tell you the truth; it is expedient for you that I go away.' The words are taken from today's Gospel. In the name of the Father, the Son and the Holy Ghost. Amen. Dearly beloved . . ."

He heard detachedly his own voice in its smooth, unhurried delivery of the farewell sermon he had so carefully prepared. His eyes and tortured heart strayed restlessly over the pulpit rail out into the congregation who had gathered to offer up with him this last (so far as he and they were concerned) sacrifice of the Mass.

Over to the left sat Doc—quiet, dependable, good old Doc! They'd come through some times together. And without reason, as scraps of remembrance will, a certain vivid memory returned to him of a summer afternoon many years ago when the two of them lay on the grass of the high school grounds, keenly aware, though anticipatorily, not nostalgically, that a certain phase of their lives was ended forever, and another beginning, with their graduation in June. They were discussing a variety of subjects related only to the mind of seventeen. Doc—only it was Pete then—had asked lazily, munching on a piece of clover:

"Well, have you decided between teaching and your music yet?"

And he heard in retrospect his own slow answer:

"I don't think it's going to be either. I've just about decided that I want to study for the priesthood."

He almost laughed now at the recollection of Pete, shocked up on one elbow, and looking at him as though he had lost his mind, while every freckle stood out distinct and clear on a face suddenly gone a shade

"Are you crazy!" demanded Pete in horror.

"No," he replied. "No—I don't think so. . . ."

But not even to Pete could he explain those nebulous yet definite longings which urged him along the road he was to follow.

The outlines of the mental image blurred and faded.

So long, Doc, old boy . . .

In one of the front pews he saw Felicia, slim and tall as young willows in the spring. He had known her since her grade-school days, and from the beginning there had been a rare and fragile sympathy between them which had deepened into genuine friendship as she grew older. He liked her enormously; felt at ease and relaxed in her company. She had an active, independent mind and strong convictions, which she defended ably and courageously. Even while still a child he had had occasion to take her to task for open rebellion against one of the Sisters.

"Mother Superior tells me that you were impertinent to Sister Jeanne Therese and now refuse to apologize. Is that right?"

"Yes," she answered, sullenly but with determination.

He frowned slightly.

"You know I won't tolerate impudence."

Her mouth set more stubbornly, and abruptly he tried another tack.

"Felicia, you're usually moderately well-behaved. Tell me why you were rude to Sister Jeanne Therese. Perhaps there's something to be said for your side."

She responded, as always, to fairness and reason.

"Well," she answered candidly, "when we lose our temper we have to say the Act of Contrition, but when Sister Jeanne Therese loses hers she calls it holy anger. I don't think it's very holy to bang a ruler on the desk and shout."

With difficulty he kept his lips from twitching. The word-picture she painted of the volatile little French nun was unflatteringly accurate. He managed to reply gravely:

"I see your point. But," here his voice sharpened, "Sister Jeanne Therese's temper is her own personal problem. It has no bearing on your behavior at all. Remember, Felicia, our Lord didn't tell us to be as perfect as the Saints or even as the angels. He said, 'Be perfect as I am perfect.' Your task is to emulate Christ, not Sister Jeanne Therese. And you see you itating Sister when you let her loss of temper make you lose yours. understand?"

She nodded.

"Yes, Father. And I'll remember."

She had remembered. But once in high school, during an unusually hot discussion, when she became in his eyes somewhat impudent, he suddenly lost his own temper and rebuked her, severely and publicly. Afterwards, with hurt, angry tears sparkling in her eyes, she asked:

"Why do we always quarrel?"

His anger had faded as abruptly as it had been aroused, leaving him faintly ashamed at having been unable to control it. Also, her slight display of emotion embarrassed him.

"Oh, I don't know," he said uncomfortably. "Perhaps it's because we're so much alike."

She leveled one of her direct looks at him.

"Yes," she agreed, "we *are* alike. Only I didn't think you realized it so clearly."

The maddening, endearing omniscience of extreme youth!

She was steadfastly loyal, but he was not aware to what an extent adverse criticism of him had rankled in her until one day she burst out:

"They say you're just a social priest; that you cater to people with money and influence who can push you along. I hate for them to say things like that. You're not a social priest!"

He was furious, the more so because the accusation contained a germ of truth. He did have snobbish impulses, but God and he knew that he fought them to the death. Because he had a convivial nature; because he liked people and liked to have them around him; because he enjoyed parties and dances and gay social affairs, why must tongues always be wagging and dropping their bitter venom on his doings? To be a priest is not to be an anchorite. Christ spent three years in public ministry and the record is dotted with dinners, feasts and happy gatherings. Do people mourn while the bridegroom is still with them? So he reasoned, and in a measure rightly, for his hour of agony had not yet come.

Toward the rear of the Church he recognized Bill Malone, morose and taciturn, who had once been possessed of the blithest good spirits and bonhomie; Bill, who had married the wrong kind of girl. He remembered her—a pert, pretty little thing with a roving eye and no sense of responsibility. The marriage had lasted a couple of years during which Bill's nature changed steadily and for the worse; then she was off with another man. And later, when she had come back whining for forgiveness, Bill had come to him.

"What'll I do, Father? She wants to come back. She says she's learned her lesson; that it'll be different from now on."

"Do you think it will be?"

"No." Bill's negative was flat and disillusioned. "She'll never really change; she's made that way. But what I want to know is, shall I take her back? After all, I did marry her, and that means something to me even if it doesn't to her."

He framed his answer slowly:

"Well, Bill, that's up to you. If her character is fundamentally un-changed, you'll probably be up against the same problem again. It depends on whether you want to take the chance. Of course, you remember our Lord's words on forgiveness."

"Yes, Father, but He also gave one cause for which a man might put away his wife."

"That's true."

"Well, Father, in my place what would *you* do?"

The vivacious doll's face with its wanton eyes rose up before him. He said after a pause:

"I think I'd be inclined to call it quits."

And Bill had followed his implied advice. But sometimes—and at the most unexpected moments, when his mind should have been filled with thoughts of God; when he knelt to say his daily office, or during the most sacred parts of the Mass—sometimes the memory of that conversation would return to him and he wondered . . .

Charity is long suffering . . . is kind . . . seeketh not her own . . . thinketh no evil . . . beareth all things; believeth all things; hopeth all things; endureth all things . . . Charity never faileth. . . .

God—he prayed—forgive me . . . if I was wrong. And forgive me, too, Bill's wife. . . .

Off to the right sat Thurlow Reed III, on one of his rare public appear-ances in the bosom of his eminently respectable family—a rake and a sot if ever there was one. His lip curled a little. And quite involuntarily he recalled the occasion when young Reed, lying drunk and ill in a disrepu-table hotel, had burned up the telephone wire, alternately cursing and slobbering in a maudlin fear of death:

"I tell you, Father, I'm dying. You've got to come! For Christ's sake don't let me die like this—outside the Church. Damn it—you've got to come. Now look—"

In disgust, he slammed down the receiver and boiled over to the group of friends who happened to be with him when the call came, finishing with an angry:

"I'll not go down to that drunken sot again! Let him get another priest."

But little old Mrs. Bascomb laid a gentle hand on his arm and said in her tired, kind voice:

"You can't do that, Father. You're a priest and you've taken certain vows. You've got to go."

All at once he capitulated and patted her hand:

"All right, you win—I'll go."

Because he had suddenly remembered that old Mrs. Bascomb's youngest son had died in delirium tremens. . . .

If you forgive others their trespasses, so will your heavenly Father forgive your trespasses. . . .

His tormented spirit twisted in sick pain under the weight of old memories.

Scattered throughout the congregation his restless gaze picked out first one boy and then another whom he had taught in school, who had been his altar boy, who had been on his debating team. Here was Ty Slater whom he had helped out secretly more than once in a money crisis; further back Jim Booth looked so suspiciously innocent and virtuous that he found himself wondering what the young devil had been up to this time. And in the foremost pew directly facing the pulpit, sat Red and Hank, his two blackest sheep, for whom he had an open, shameless and abiding affection.

He would never forget his first glimpse of them at the New York docks, grimy and belligerent, in the hands of an officer, after being hauled from hiding on the liner where they had tried to stow away. He was in his usual hurry, but the picture of boys in trouble was too much for him, and he elbowed his way through the curious crowd.

"What's the matter, officer? Boys had a brush with the law?"

"That's right. They caught the young bast—sorry, Father. They were trying to stow away. They're Reds—want to get to Russia."

"They're not of age, are they?"

"No. Just kids. Ran away from home; we're holding 'em till we can notify their parents."

"Where are they from?"

The officer told him. To his surprise they were from his own state. He said:

"Why, that's my state. Look here—may I talk to them?"

"Sure, Father, but you won't get much out of 'em. They're kind of unsociable. And you two," he turned to the boys, "keep a civil tongue in your heads."

"We'll get on all right."

The crowd, seeing that there was to be no excitement, drifted off. He eyed the sulky pair appraisingly; they didn't look vicious, and it had been his experience that when the Red virus infected them this young, they were rather touchingly sincere. He made a tentative conversational sally:

"I understand you want to get to Russia."

The look they gave him was beneath contempt. One of them commented briefly but expressively:

"So what?"

He took off his hat and ran a hand through thick, unruly hair:

"Well," he reflected aloud, "Russia's a great country. I was there myself last year."

Sneering and hostile, they tried to remain indifferent and aloof, but they were very young and the bait was too tempting. Russia seen through the eyes of the clergy—here was an opportunity to carry the war against effete and decadent clericalism into the very camp of the enemy. They looked at one another; then Red fired the first shot.

Some hours later, having been released into his custody, which he had agreed to assume—wholly against his better judgment, he assured the boys—until arrangements could be made to turn them over to their parents; and over a dinner which went a long way toward smoothing the path to friendship, they relaxed and became somewhat expansive.

"You know," Red remarked, "you don't talk much like a priest."

He replied with a touch of irony:

"I question whether you're a competent judge. How did you expect a priest to talk?"

"Oh, you know what I mean. Most of them are stuffed shirts, and so down on Communism that they begin foaming at the mouth at the mention of it."

He permitted a slight smile.

"Is that so? Well, I've always been a fairly good Communist myself—it has its points. But it has a lot of weaknesses too."

"How do you mean?" Hank bristled to the defense.

"Well, for instance—human nature. Communism simply leaves it out of the equation. You know, there's nothing new about Communism. For as long as we have any knowledge men have been trying to build a perfect state—one that would work like a well-oiled machine. Ever read Plato? It's a swell idea; I'm all for it. Only a human being isn't a mechanical automaton which never makes mistakes, and that's where all these 'perfect' economic systems slip up. Communism talks a lot about the brotherhood of man and love of humanity, but the Church is the only institution throughout the ages which has upheld and stood for the freedom and dignity of the individual as against the majority."

"The Church!" Red was primed for that. For fifteen minutes he held forth on the iniquities of ecclesiastics in all ages and the picture he drew was not a pretty one.

He had listened in silence to the indictment, and when Red ran down at last, he made a wry face.

"Truth certainly doesn't appear synonymous with beauty in this case, does it?" he observed with a rueful laugh. Both Red and Hank pounced on that.

"Then you admit the charges are true?"

"True—of course they're true. We gave up long ago trying to deny that there have been bad priests and faithless nuns—in fact I can give you a good many more instances you've missed entirely. But it shows you've been doing a lot of reading and thinking on the subject. That's good. Only it's one-sided. You're like a steak that's burned on one side and raw on the other."

They were won then, only they didn't know it. It had been one of his happiest experiences to administer to them that rite which in early Christian times was naively referred to as the "washing." It rather amused him to see them as hotly champion the Church now as they had formerly attacked it.

He was going to miss their visits, infrequent though they were; the brazen squawk of their aged jalopy, the gay and breezy: "H'ya, Padre!"

Suddenly they were all—even the weakling, Reed, even gossiping Miss Williams and miserly Mr. Hughes—all inexpressibly, unbearably dear. They were his people and this was his Church, and both were being taken away from him.

Holy Mary, Mother of God!—cried his soul in voiceless anguish.

At the same time he was aware with a sick self-contempt that he was reacting like an adolescent. He finished his address in a carefully emotionless voice:

". . . with this in mind, I bid you all a fond good-bye."

But he stumbled a little as he descended the steps from the pulpit, and he realized that his eyes were blind with tears.

I mustn't let go—he thought in momentary panic—I've got to get a grip on myself.

And he found that his vision had cleared by the time he ascended the altar, where he chanted strongly and steadily the first words of the Credo:

"Credo in unum Deum—I believe in one God, the Father Almighty . . ."* finishing it inaudibly as the choir took it up in a mighty swell of sound.

While he sat waiting on the choir the memory of his ordination Mass returned to him vividly—the scarlet and white of the altar boys, moving in a haze of incense; the faint clinking of the censer as they swung it to and fro; the old Bishop, benign and saintly, in a blaze of gold, like a king upon his throne; the deep organ tones of the men's voices and the shrill sweetness of the little choir boys. And crowding hard upon this scene, he relived briefly the ecstasy of that moment in his own first High Mass when, with bridal eagerness, tempered with a deep sense of his own unworthiness—a kind of exalted humility—lifting the sacred Host, he spoke the mystic words by which through some alchemy of the Spirit mere bread becomes Flesh and Blood. The savor of that holy and eternal moment was on his lips; his whole being thirsted to taste again its fresh and matutinal sweetness. But the picture dissolved and he choked instead on the bitter ash of the present.

He went through the Offertory automatically. The pain seemed to ebb and flow in great waves over his soul, which, receding, left him wooden and lifeless, a robot performing dead acts mechanically. But at the washing of the hands feeling and the capacity to suffer again swept over him.

". . . O Lord, I have loved the beauty of thy house. . . ."

And involuntarily his eyes sought the proud symmetry of the multi-colored marble pillars; the domed and vaulted roof; the chapel of the Sacred Heart where crimson roses throbbed and flamed with life; the image of Our Lady, chaste and chill; while his sick heart cried mutely: My God, how can I bear it?

Then his gaze fell upon the figure of the Crucified, and a measure of calm descended upon him. He felt almost happy at the Elevation, but it was the happiness of a momentary exaltation which faded, and the old aching misery engulfed him once more.

"*Agnus Dei . . . qui tollis . . . peccata mundi. . . .*"

High and clear rose the voice of the soloist above the muted undertone of the choir. Another time it would have been simply Miss Hurlock sing-ing—plain, middle-aged, spinsterish. Now for the first time he noticed that her voice had the virginal freshness of a young girl's as though welling up from deep springs of eternal youth. And he remembered having noticed once or twice that her face when she sang was touched with a fleeting look of youth and innocence.

"*. . . miserere . . . miserere . . . miserere nobis. . . .*"

He faced his people holding aloft the sacred species.

"*Ecce Agnus Dei . . . Domine, non sum dignus . . .* Lord, I am not worthy that thou shouldst enter under my roof . . ." And he descended from the altar, the Incarnate Word in his hands.

It was over. He pronounced the final, irrevocable words:

"*Ite—Missa est.*"

It is finished . . . This is the end.

Oh, my people—he thought; and could go no further. His suffering had reached its peak. He had seen other priests leave their parishes—parishes where they had served far longer than he—and he had thought he understood their pain, but he realized now that he had never even remotely gauged it. Why, this was the agony of birth; the separation of a woman and her child, but more terrible, for this was also the parting of death. And with that thought there came to him one of those flashes of spiritual illumination which sometimes climax periods of intense pain. Suddenly he comprehended, perfectly and completely, the agony of the Garden. It was like the opening of a door.

Here lay the answer to the mystery of birth and death. They are in-separable: twin faces of the same disk. The child dies to the womb that it may live to the world; a man must die to the world in order to live to God. Strange—he thought—I've talked about it all these years, but I never really knew what it meant.

Outwardly serene he stood at the foot of the altar while the choir filed slowly past him into the sacristy, but in reality he was shaken and stunned. He felt a curious inner upheaval as though he were about to cry, and a great longing for the relief of tears swept over him. He remem-bered having heard that boys studying for the priesthood often wept bit-terly before taking the final irrevocable step. At the time this had been

incomprehensible to him. Once having made up his mind to be a priest
there had been no qualms, no waverings, no tortured self-examination.
The call of the world had not existed for him. But he knew now that it
was because he had never left the world. The words "secular priesthood"
took on new and poignant meaning.

Father—he prayed suddenly and spontaneously—I want to come home!

It was the first time he had ever experienced that exact feeling; so lost
and nostalgic a longing for God. For the first time in an active aggressive
life he felt oddly helpless and at a loss. Momentarily, at least, his self-
assurance was shaken; almost non-existent. He had always taught the
virtue of humility as a matter of doctrine and had taken it for granted
that he believed in and practiced it. He perceived now with a flash of
true humbleness that it had had no real significance for him at all. The
Bishop's last remark recurred to him: It will be good for you. He had
resented it at the time; he did not resent it now. A deep desire, almost a
need, for prayer swept through him.

In the sacristy the boys were divesting themselves of robes and surplices
with their customary clatter. As each one left he shook hands saying:

"Good-bye, Father. Sorry you're leaving."

A few of the older boys, most of whom he had known all their lives,
lingered and he knew they wanted to talk to him, but he felt that he
could not talk to anyone now. He said:

"You'd better run along, boys. You can tell me good-bye this afternoon. I'm not leaving right away. I'm going to say my office in the Church."

There must have been something unusual in his voice or manner because they looked at him quickly with that mixture of curiosity and shyness
characteristic of youth. Finally one of the boys asked, casually, yet with
underlying affection and concern:

"Is anything the matter, Father?"

But he had recovered sufficient poise to smile naturally and reply:

"Matter? Why no, Jimmy. As far as I know, everything's all right.
Everything's fine."

And walking with firm step back into the almost empty Church he discovered, somewhat to his own surprise, that it was true.

Over Arras

Of St. Exupéry it has been said, "He sails between the limits of earth and sky." An airplane pilot in peace and war, a man of a meditative and sensitive nature to whom the experience of flight has provided poetry, St. Exupéry is a new kind of man, a product, at least in part, of an experience that has only been possible in our times. A philosopher, the air has offered to him a lesson, it has been said, in man's fate. This contribution is embodied in his book FLIGHT TO ARRAS which tells of his last hopeless reconnaissance flight in May, 1940, when France was beaten and to go into the air meant almost certain death.

THERE is a verity that is higher than the pronouncements of the intelligence. There is a thing which pierces and governs us and which cannot be grasped by the intelligence. A tree has no language. We are a tree. There are truths which are evident, thought not to be put into words. I do not die in order to obstruct the path of the invasion, for there is no shelter upon which I can fall back with those I love. I do not die to preserve my honor, since I deny that my honor is at stake, and I challenge the jurisdiction of my judge. Nor do I die out of desperation.

And yet Dutertre, looking at his map, having pin-pointed the position of Arras somewhere round the one hundred and seventy-fifth degree of the compass, is about to say to me—I can feel it:

"175° captain."

And I shall accept.

"172°."

"Right! 172°."

Call it one seventy-two. Epitaph: "Maintained his course accurately on 172°." How long will this crazy challenge go on? I am flying now at two thousand three hundred feet beneath a ceiling of heavy clouds. If I were to rise a mere hundred feet Dutertre would be blind. Thus we are forced to remain visible to the anti-aircraft batteries and play the part of an archer's target for the Germans. Two thousand feet is a forbidden altitude. Your machine serves as a mark for the whole plain. You drain the cannonade of a whole army. You are within range of every calibre. You dwell an eternity in the field of fire of each successive weapon. You are not shot at with cannon but beaten with a stick. It is as if a thousand sticks were used to bring down a single walnut.

I had given a bit of thought to this problem. There is no question of a parachute. When the stricken plane dives to the ground the opening of the escape hatch takes more seconds than the dive of the plane allows. Opening the hatch involves seven turns of a crank that sticks. Besides, at full speed the hatch warps and refuses to slide.

That's that. The medicine had to be swallowed some day. I always knew it. Meanwhile, the formula is not complicated: stick to 172°. I was wrong to grow older. Pity. I was so happy as a child. I say so; but is it true? For already in that dim hall I was moving on this same course, 172°. Because of my uncles.

Now is the time when childhood seems sweet. Not only childhood, but the whole of my past life. I see it in perspective as if it were a landscape.

Despite my lack of altitude, I had been hoping. Despite the tank parks, despite the flame over Arras. Desperately, I had been hoping. I had escaped into a memory of early childhood in order to recapture the sense of sovereign protection. For man there is no protection. Once you are a man you are left to yourself. But who can avail against a little boy whose hand is firmly clasped in the hand of an all-powerful Paula? Paula, I have used thy shade as a shield.

I have used every trick in my bag. When Dutertre said to me, "It's getting worse," I used even that threat as a source of hope. We were at war: necessarily, then, there had to be evidence of war. The evidence was no more than a few streaks of light. "Is this your terrible danger of death over Arras? Don't make me laugh!"

The man condemned had imagined that the executioner would look like a pallid robot. Arrives a quite ordinary decent-appearing fellow who is able to sneeze, even to smile. The man condemned clings to that smile as to a promise of reprieve. The promise is a wraith. The headsman sneezes —and the head falls nevertheless. But who can reject hope?

I myself could not but be deceived by the smile I saw—since this whole world was snug and verdant, since the wet slate and tile shone so cordially, since from minute to minute nothing changed nor promised to change. Since we three, Dutertre, the gunner, and I, were men walking across fields, sauntering idly home without so much as the need to raise our collars, so little was it raining. Since here at the heart of the German zone nothing stood forth that was really worth telling about, whence it must follow that farther on the war need not of necessity be different to this. Since it seemed that the enemy had scattered and melted into the wide and rural plain, standing perhaps at the rate of one soldier to a house, one soldier to a tree, one of whom, remembering now and then the war, would fire. The order had been drummed into the fellow's ears: "Fire on all enemy planes." But he had been daydreaming, and the order had been dimmed by the dream. He let fly his three rounds without much expectation of results. Thus at dusk I used to shoot ducks that meant very little to me if the evening invited my soul. I would fire while talking about something else. It hardly disturbed the ducks.

It is so easy to spin fine tales to oneself. The enemy takes aim, but without firm purpose; and he misses me. Others in turn let us pass. Those who might trip us up are perhaps at this moment inhaling with pleasure the smell of the night, or lighting cigarettes, or finishing a funny story —and they let us pass. Still others, in the village where they are billeted, are perhaps dipping their tin cups into the soup. A roar rises and dies away. Friend or enemy? There isn't time for them to find out: their eyes are on the cup now filling—they let us pass. And I, whistling a tune and my hands in my pockets, do my best to walk as casually as I can through this garden forbidden to trespassers where every guard, counting on the next guard, lets us pass.

How vulnerable I was! Yet it seemed to me that my very vulnerability was a trap, a means of cajoling them: "Why fire? Your friends are sure to bring me down a little farther on." And they would shrug their shoulders: "Go break your neck somewhere else." They were leaving the chore to the next battery—because they were anxious not to miss their turn at the soup, were finishing their funny story, or were simply enjoying the evening breeze. I was taking advantage of their negligence, and I was saved by the seeming coincidence that all of them at once appeared to be weary of war. And why not? Already I was thinking vaguely that from soldier to soldier, squad to squad, village to village, I should get through this sortie. After all, what were we but a passing plane in the evening sky? Not enough to make a man raise his eyes.

Of course I hoped to get back. But I could feel at the same time that something was in the air. You are sentenced: a penalty hangs over you; but the gaol in which you are locked up continues silent. You cling to that silence. Every second that drops is like the one that went before. There is no reason why the second about to drop should change the world. Such a task is too heavy for a single second. Each second that follows safeguards your silence. Already this silence seems perpetual.

But the step of him who must come sounds in the corridor.

Something in this countryside suddenly exploded. So a log that seemed burnt out crackles suddenly and shoots forth its sparks. How did it happen that the whole plain started up at the same moment? When spring comes, all the trees at once drop their seed. Why this sudden springtime of arms? Why this luminous flood rising towards us and, of a sudden, universal?

My first feeling was that I had been careless. I had ruined everything. A wink, a single gesture is enough to topple you from the tight-rope. A mountain climber coughs, and he releases an avalanche. Once he has released the avalanche, all is over.

We had been swaying heavily through this blue swamp already drowned in night. We had stirred up this silent slime; and now, in tens of thousands, it was sending towards us its golden bubbles. A nation of jugglers had burst into dance. A nation of jugglers was dribbling its projectiles in tens of thousands in our direction. Because they came straight at us, at first they appeared to be motionless. Like colored balls which jugglers seem not so much to fling into the air as to release upwards, they rose in a lingering ascension. I could see those tears of light flowing towards me through a silence as of oil. That silence in which jugglers perform.

Each burst of a machine gun or a rapid-fire cannon shot forth hundreds of these phosphorescent bullets that followed one another like the beads of a rosary. A thousand elastic rosaries strung themselves out towards the plane, drew themselves out to the breaking point, and burst at our height. When, missing us, the string went off at a tangent, its speed was dizzying. The bullets were transformed into lightning. And I flew drowned in a crop of trajectories as golden as stalks of wheat. I flew at the center of a thicket of lance strokes. I flew threatened by a vast and dizzying flutter of knitting needles. All the plain was now bound to me, woven and wound round me, a coruscating web of golden wire.

I leant towards the earth and saw those storied levels of luminous bubbles rising with the tardy movement of veils of fog. I saw as I stared the slow vortex of seed, swirling like the husks of threshed grain. And when I raised my head I saw on the horizon those stacks of lances. Guns firing? Not at all! I am attacked by cold steel. These are swords of light. I feel . . . certainly not in danger! Dazzled I am by the luxury that envelopes me.

What's that!

I was jolted nearly a foot out of my seat. The plane has been rammed hard; I thought. It has burst, been ground to bits. . . . But it hasn't; it hasn't. . . . I can still feel it responsive to the controls. This was but the first blow of a deluge of blows. Yet there was no sign of explosion below. The smoke of the heavy guns had probably blended into the dark ground.

I raised my head and stared. What I saw was without appeal.

I had been looking on at a carnival of light. The ceiling had risen little by little and I had been unaware of an intervening space between the clouds and me. I had been zigzagging along a line of flight dotted by ground batteries. Their tracer bullets had been spraying the air with wheat-colored shafts of light. I had forgotten that at the top of their flight the shells of those batteries must burst. And now, raising my head, I saw around and before me those rivets of smoke and steel driven into the sky in the pattern of towering pyramids.

I was quite aware that those rivets were no sooner driven than all danger went out of them, that each of those puffs possessed the power of life and death only for a fraction of a second. But so sudden and simultaneous was their appearance that the image flashed into my mind of conspirators intent upon my death. Abruptly their purpose was revealed to me, and I felt on the nape of my neck the weight of an inescapable reprobation.

Muffled as those explosions reached me, their sound covered by the roar of my engines, I had the illusion of an extraordinary silence. Those vast packets of smoke and steel moving soundlessly upward and behind me with the lingering flow of icebergs, persuaded me that, seen in their perspective, I must be virtually motionless. I was motionless in the dock before an immense assizes. The judges were deliberating my fate, and there was nothing I could plead. Once again the timelessness of suspense seized me. I thought—I was still able to think—"They are aiming too high," and I looked up in time to see straight overhead, swinging away from me as if with reluctance, a swarm of black flakes that glided like eagles. Those eagles had given me up. I was not to be their prey. But even so, what hope was there for me?

The batteries that continued to miss me continued also to readjust their aim. New walls of smoke and steel continued to be built up round me as I flew. The ground-fire was not seeking me out, it was closing me in.

"Dutertre! How much more of this is there?"

"Stick it out three minutes, Captain. Looks bad, though."

"Think we'll get through?"

"Not on your life."

There never was such muck as this murky smoke, this mess as grimy as a heap of filthy rags. The plain was blue. Immensely blue. Deep-sea blue. What was a man's life worth between this blue plain and this foul sky? Ten seconds, perhaps; or twenty. The shock of the exploding shells set all the sky shuddering. When a shell burst very near, the explosion rumbled along the plane like rock dropping through a chute. And when for a moment the roar stopped, the plane rang with a sound that was almost musical. Like a sigh, almost; and the sigh told us that the plane had been missed. Those bursts were like the thunder: the closer they came, the simpler they were. A rumble meant distance, a clean *bang!* meant that we had been squarely hit by a shell fragment. The tiger does not do a messy job on the ox it brings down. The tiger sets its claws into the ox without skidding. It takes possession of the ox. Each square hit by a fragment of shell sank into the hull of the plane like a claw into living flesh.

"Anybody hurt?"

"Not I!"

"Gunner! You all right?"

"O.K., sir!"

Somehow those explosions, though I find I must mention them, did not really count. They drummed upon the hull of the plane as upon a drum. They pierced my fuel tanks. They might as easily have drummed upon our bellies, pierced them instead. What is the belly but a kind of drum? But who cares what happens to his body? Extraordinary, how little the body matters.

There are things that we might learn about our bodies in the course of everyday living if we were not blind to patent evidence. It takes this rain of upsurging streamers of light, this assault by an army of lances, this assizes set up for the last judgment, to teach us those things.

I used to wonder as I was dressing for a sortie what a man's last moments were like. And each time, life would give the lie to the ghosts I evoked. Here I was, now, naked and running the gauntlet, unable so much as to guard my head by arm or shoulder from the crazy blows raining down upon me. I had always assumed that the ordeal, when it came, would be an ordeal that concerned my flesh. My flesh alone, I assumed, would be subjected to the ordeal. It was unavoidable that in thinking of these things I should adopt the point of view of my body. Like all men, I had given it a good deal of time. I had dressed it, bathed it, fed it, quenched its thirst. I had identified myself with this domesticated animal. I had taken it to the tailor, the surgeon, the barber. I had been unhappy with it, cried out in pain with it, loved with it. I had said of it, "This is me." And now of a sudden my illusion vanished. What was my body to me? A kind of flunkey in my service. Let but my anger wax hot, my love grow exalted, my hatred collect in me, and that boasted solidarity between me and my body was gone.

Your son is in a burning house. Nobody can hold you back. You may burn up; but do you think of that? You are ready to bequeath the rags of your body to any man who will take them. You discover that what you set so much store by is trash. You would sell your hand, if need be, to give a hand to a friend. It is in your act that you exist, not in your body. Your act is yourself, and there is no other you. Your body belongs to you: it is not you. Are you about to strike an enemy? No threat of bodily harm can hold you back. You? It is the death of your enemy that is you. You? It is the rescue of your child that is you. In that moment you exchange yourself against something else; and you have no feeling that you lost by the exchange. Your members? Tools. A tool snaps in your hand: how important is that tool? You exchange yourself against the death of your enemy, the rescue of your child, the recovery of your patient, the perfection of your theorem. Here is a pilot of my Group wounded and dying. A true citation in general orders would read: "Called out to his observer, 'They've got me! Beat it! And for God's sake don't lose those notes!'" What matters is the notes, the child, the patient, the theorem. Your true significance becomes dazzlingly evident. Your true name is duty, hatred, love, child, theorem. There is no other you than this.

The flames of the house, of the diving plane, strip away the flesh; but they strip away the worship of the flesh too. Man ceases to be concerned with himself: he recognizes of a sudden what he forms part of. If he should die, he would not be cutting himself off from his kind, but making himself one with them. He would not be losing himself, but finding himself. This that I affirm is not the wishful thinking of a moralist. It is an everyday fact. It is a commonplace truth. But a fact and a truth hidden under the veneer of our everyday illusion. Dressing and fretting over the fate that might befall my body, it was impossible for me to see that I was fretting over something absurd. But in the instant when you are giving up your body, you learn to your amazement—all men always learn to their amazement—how little store you set by your body. It would be foolish to deny that during all those years of my life when nothing insistent was prompting me, when the meaning of my existence was not at stake, it was impossible for me to conceive that anything might be half so important as my body. But here in this plane I say to my body (in effect), "I don't care a button what becomes of you. I have been expelled out of you. There is no hope of your surviving this, and yet I lack for nothing. I reject all that I have been up to this very instant. For in the past it was not I who thought, not I who felt: it was you, my body. One way and another, I have dragged you through life to this point; and here I discover that you are of no importance."

Already at the age of fifteen I might have learnt this lesson. I had a younger brother who lay dying. One morning towards four o'clock his nurse woke me and said that he was asking for me.

"Is he in pain?" I asked.

The nurse said nothing, and I dressed as fast as I could.

When I came into his room he said to me in a matter-of-fact voice, "I wanted to see you before I died. I am going to die." And with that he stiffened and winced and could not go on. Lying in pain, he waved his hand as if saying "No!" I did not understand. I thought it was death he was rejecting. The pain passed, and he spoke again. "Don't worry," he said. "I'm all right. I can't help it. It's my body." His body was already foreign territory, something not himself.

He was very serious, this younger brother who was to die in twenty minutes. He had called me in because he felt a pressing need to hand on part of himself to me. "I want to make my will," he said; and he blushed with pride and embarrassment to be talking like a grown man. Had he been a builder of towers he would have bequeathed to me the finishing of his tower. Had he been a father, I should have inherited the education of his children. A reconnaissance pilot, he would have passed on to me the intelligence he had gleaned. But he was a child, and what he confided to my care was a toy steam engine, a bicycle, and a rifle.

Man does not die. Man imagines that it is death he fears; but what he fears is the unforeseen, the explosion. What man fears is himself, not death. There is no death when you meet death. When the body sinks into death, the essence of man is revealed. Man is a knot, a web, a mesh into which relationships are tied. Only those relationships matter. The body is an old crock that nobody will miss. I have never known a man to think of himself when dying. Never.

"Captain!"

"What's up?"

"Getting hot!"

"Gunner!"

"Er . . . yes, sir."

"What—"

My question vanished in the shock of another explosion.

"Dutertre!"

"Captain?"

"Hurt?"

"No."

"You, gunner!"

"Yes, sir."

"I wa—"

I seemed to be running the plane into a bronze wall. A voice in my ear said, "Boy! oh, boy!" as I looked up to measure the distance to the over-hanging clouds. The sharper the angle at which I stared, the more densely the murky tufts seemed to be piled up. Seen straight overhead, the sky was visible between them, and they hung curved and scattered, forming a gigantic coronet in the air.

A man's thigh muscles are incredibly powerful. I bore down upon the rudder bar with all my strength and sent the plane shuddering and skidding at right angles to our line of flight. The coronet swung overhead and slid down on my right. I had got away from one of the batteries and left it firing wasted packets of shell. But before I could bring my other thigh into play the ground battery had set straight what hung askew— the coronet of smoke was back again. Once more I bore down, and again the plane groaned and swayed in this swampy sky. All the weight of my body was on that bar, and the machine had swung, had skidded squarely to starboard. The coronet curved now above me on the left.

Would we last it out? But how could we! Each time that I brought the ship brutally round, the deluge of lance-strokes followed me before I could jerk back again. Each time the coronet was set back into place and the shell bursts shook up the plane anew. And each time, when I looked down, I saw again that same dizzyingly slow ascension of golden bubbles that seemed to be accurately centered upon my plane. How did it happen that we were still whole? I began to believe in us. "I am invulnerable, after all," I said to myself. "I am winning. From second to second, I am more and more the winner."

"Anybody hurt yet?"

"Nobody."

They were unhurt. They were invulnerable. They were victorious. I was the owner of a winning team. And from that moment each explosion seemed to me not to threaten us but to temper us. Each time, for a fraction of a second, it seemed to me that my plane had been blown to bits; but each time it responded anew to the controls and I nursed it along like a coachman pulling hard on the reins. I began to relax, and a wave of jubilation went through me. There was just time enough for me to feel fear as no more than a physical stiffening induced by a loud crash, when instantly after each buffet a wave of relief went through me. I ought to have felt successively the shock, then the fear, then the relief; but there wasn't time. What I felt was the shock, then instantly the relief. Shock, relief. Fear, the intermediate step, was missing. And during the second that followed the shock I did not live in the expectancy of death in the second to come, but in the conviction of resurrection born of the second just passed. I lived in a sort of slipstream of joy, in the wake of my jubilation. A prodigiously unlooked-for pleasure was flowing through me. It was as if, with each second that passed, life was being granted me anew. As if with each second that passed my life became a thing more vivid to me. I was living. I was alive. I was still alive. I was the source of life itself. I was thrilled through with the intoxication of living. "The heat of battle" is a familiar phrase; the heat of living is a truer one. "I wonder," I said to myself, "if those Germans below who are firing at us know that they are creating life within us?"

All my tanks had been pierced, both gas and oil. Otherwise we seemed to be sound. Dutertre called out that he was through, and once again I looked up and calculated the distance to the clouds. I raised the nose of the ship, and once again I sent the plane zigzagging as I climbed. Once again I cast a glance earthwards. What I saw I shall not forget. The plain was crackling everywhere with short wicks of spurting flame—the rapid-fire cannon. The colored balls were still floating upward through an immense blue aquarium of air. Arras was glowing dark red like iron on the anvil, a flame fed by subterranean stores, by the sweat of men, the inventions of men, the arts of men, the memories and patrimony of men, all these braided in the ruddy ascension of that single plume that changed them into fire and ash, borne away on the wind.

Already I was flying through the first packets of mist. Golden arrows still rose and pierced the belly of the cloud, and just as the cloud closed round me I caught through an opening my last glimpse of that scene. For a single instant the flame over Arras rose up glowing in the night like a lamp in the nave of a cathedral. The lamp that was Arras was burning in the service of a cult, but at a price. By tomorrow it would have consumed Arras and itself have been consumed.

"Everything all right, Dutertre?"

"First rate, Captain. Two-forty, please. We shan't be able to come down out of this cloud for about twenty minutes. Then I'll pick up a landmark along the Seine somewhere."

"Everything all right, gunner?"

"Everything fine, sir."

"Not too hot for you, was it?"

"No, I guess not, sir."

Hard for him to tell. But he was feeling fine. I thought of Gavoille's gunner. In the days when this was still a very odd war, we used to do long-distance reconnaissance over Germany. There was a night over the Rhine when eighty searchlights picked up Gavoille's plane and built a giant basilica round it. The anti-aircraft began to fire, and suddenly Gavoille heard his gunner talking to himself—for the inter-com is hardly a private line. The man was muttering a dialogue of one: "Think you've been around, do you? I'll tell you something you've never seen!" He was feeling fine, that gunner.

I flew on, drawing deep slow breaths. I filled my lungs to the bottom. It was wonderful to breathe again. There were many things I was going to find out about. First I thought of Alias. No, that's not true. I thought first of my host, my farmer. I still looked forward to asking him how many instruments he thought a pilot had to watch. Sorry, but I am stubborn about some things. One hundred and three. He would never guess. Which reminds me. When your tanks have been pierced, it does no harm to have a look at your gauges. Wonderful tanks! Their rubber coatings had done their job; automatically, they had contracted and plugged the holes made by bullets and shell splinters. I had a look at my stabilizers too. This cloud we flew in was a storm cloud. It shook us up pretty badly.

"Think we can come down now?"

"Ten minutes more. Better wait another ten minutes."

Of course I could wait another ten minutes. . . . Yes, I had thought of Alias. Was he still expecting us, I wondered? The other day we had been half an hour late. A half hour is generally longer than you ought to be: it means trouble. I had landed and run to join the Group, who were at table. I had opened the door and fallen into a chair beside Alias. At that moment he had a cluster of spaghetti on his fork and was preparing to tuck it away. He jumped, took a good look at me, and sat perfectly still, the noodles hanging from his fork.

"Well, I . . . Glad to see you," he said.

And he stuffed the noodles into his mouth.

The major has one serious fault, to my mind. He insists stubbornly on examining his pilots about their sorties. He will examine me. He will sit looking at me with embarrassing patience, waiting for me to spin out my commonplace observations. He will have armed himself with paper and pencil, determined not to lose a single drop of the elixir I shall presumably have brought back.

I thought of school: "Saint-Exupéry, how do you integrate Bernoulli's equations?"

"Er . . . er."

Bernoulli, Bernoulli. Let me see. . . . And you stiffened under the teacher's gaze, motionless, fixed in place like an insect on a pin.

Intelligence is Dutertre's business, not mine. He is the observer; I am the pilot. From where he sits he can see straight below. He sees lots of things—lorries, barges, tanks, soldiers, cannon, horses, railway stations, trains, station masters. From where I sit I see the world at an angle. I see clouds, sea, rivers, mountains, sun. I see roughly, and get only a general impression.

"Major, you know as well as I do that a pilot . . ."

"Come, come, Saint-Ex! You do see some things, after all."

I . . . Oh, yes! Flames. Villages burning. Doesn't the major think that interesting?

"Nonsense! The whole country is on fire. What else?"

Why must Alias be so cruel?

—*Translated from the French by* LEWIS GALANTIERE

LOUIS PAUL

Five Lie Dying

The novel of which "Five Lie Dying" is a part was written out of pity and sympathy and love for all the dying soldiers of America who ask, "Why?" Conceived as a dramatic poem by a writer who is not a poet and in a time when dramatic poetry rarely appears on publishers' lists, it was inevitable that it should take the form of fiction. In one form or another, it made imperative demands on its author to be written. Obviously it is not enough. Whatever it is, it could never be enough.

LOUIS PAUL

PERHAPS I write as an escape, the ideas I pursue a figurative whistling in the dark. I grow old in a week. It seems a long time since I started this record of my thoughts. No doubt I have been inconsistent a hundred times. Night comes to interrupt my scribbling. The wings of death hover darkly over me. I have only memory to nourish my shrinking body; I think in terms of the man I used to be. With the cataclysm of war I became a soldier; I lost the voluntary solitude of the poet. No longer had I the privilege of my peacetime pre-occupations. Affirm or negate, affirm or negate. No longer am I one man, but a member of an army on the march. This is a revolution, and of course I am confused. Love and hate, life and death, freedom or tyranny, kill or be killed, these are the primary alternatives.

And yet I am not discouraged. I died when young Lenn Morrow fell beside me, his fingers senselessly smashed, his throat pierced with a bullet hole. A bit of me died when I learned the truth of Pearl Harbor. I died when I knew our forces were defeated, when our captain cried, when the few planes we owned flew up valiantly into the blue sky, never again to return. I died when America allowed me to be beaten with Japanese whips, when I groveled in the dirt at the feet of my inferiors. One day our bombers will fly in great fleets to drop patterns of death upon their cities; our tanks will roll over their prostrate bodies, our guns will pound them to fleshless rubble. But meanwhile I have died a dozen deaths. I died when

I watched my comrades suffer, when Gabowitz was clubbed to earth, when Nishi Inaki laughed at me. But I shall persist in spite of these little deaths. I and my comrades shall persist until they stop our hearts with bullets.

Lately I have become subject to a new kind of illness. When I lie stretched out motionless for a while my nerves begin to hum. Strange nervous vibrations are set up within me. A hum like the distant roar of ten thousand bees goes on inside me, my whole body becomes light and aërial, I seem to float suspended in some hitherto undiscovered dimension of space. My sensation is quite physical, sometimes being accompanied by a peculiar ballooning of the feet. I don't like this. It is unpleasant; the terrible humming inside me wears me out. Usually I am able, with an effort of will, eventually to regain control of myself. But now and then my sensation exerts a complete mastery over me, and I think this is the way it first feels when one is dying.

Release from pain is having its effect upon Evans. He is weak, he still experiences his little shivery spasms, but they are less frequent, and he now converses almost normally again. Peters appears cured of his dysentery. He is extraordinarily frail, a mere wisp of a body, looking like pictures I once saw of starving Chinese children. Gabowitz has become groggy. He staggers when he tries to walk, and this annoys him. Gabowitz has lost his capacity to remain sullen, but hour by hour his gloom deepens. Beneath his brooding melancholy there exists a kind of grim satisfaction, as though our predicament were a final confirmation of his belief in the malignance of nature. Sachs must be called remarkable. Never especially healthy-looking, he appears less changed than any of us.

Our minds are still clear. This never fails to surprise and gratify me. By now, I thought, one or the other of us must have gone mad. Rather, it seems to me that our faculties have in some fashion increased their sensitivity. We have crowded the tremendous experiences of a lifetime into a few weeks. I rememberd about Oriental somnambulists and how, by extremes of asceticism, they induced a Nirvana in which their minds are supposed to be capable of snatching out of the void the answers to life's enigmas. I don't mean that we have suddenly become clairvoyant. It is merely that we realize our situation clearly. We are without the egotisms and illusions of an everyday existence. The little conceits it is so natural and yet so useless to cultivate have atrophied in us. Only a few bitter hours of life are left. Because we face eternity we seem now thoroughly to understand for the first time the absurdities of human vanity.

The evenings are still lovely with starlit skies. The earth, as always, is beautiful. As my life draws to a close I now perceive the very one-ness of time and earth. My mind is peopled with the folk of history; I know now that Chaucer was a virtual contemporary of John Keats, Attila of Adolf Hitler. A grain of corn found in an Egyptian crypt is planted and grows. A manuscript of Virgil is discovered, and learning revives. "World conquest" strikes me as a fatuous phrase. Our Japanese friends cannot conquer five starving men, much less the stars. No one can conquer courage or beauty or love or the starlit night; no one can conquer truth or learning or time, for these are an essence, an essence that slips through the fingers of barbarians and fools. Time and the earth are history, and history is what the dead take with them. Time belongs to St. Paul and Homer, to Giotto and Rembrandt, to Burke and George Washington, and soon a tiny little part of it will belong to me.

An apprehension such as this, because somehow it must be contained in words, might once have seemed to me a verbal fancy. A prayer to some seems suspect, as are all attempts to give meaning to the human spirit. Well, I am no reformer. Words are unwieldy to convey a vision. I can only describe, and hope. Sometimes in the night, when sleep will not come to me, I think harsh thoughts: I think the loyal fight and die for the unscrupulous. I think that men exploit the justness of their cause for private profit. I think that liberty with some is a synonym for self-preservation. I think that decency and human affection, like prayers, are suspect; ideals are generally suspect to narrow and vulgar minds. I am incapable of reforming such people if I would. But while the five of us lie dying there are those who callously pursue their private interests, and I think it is such as they who would look on my view of history with contempt, who would laugh at Evans's prayers.

They are not the prayers of our clergymen back home, Evans's prayers. Neither do they resemble the importunities of the poor for food, the rich for grace, the smug for divine justification, the sniveling of the sinner for absolution. I remember Evans when his legs were whole. We used to call him "Big Evans." Smiling, fearless, clear-headed, he seemed to me like the idealization of a soldier on enlistment posters. Now he sits, dirty and helpless, a heap of dying bones in the corner of an enemy prison. Big Evans is gone, and all the physical excellence he once possessed. He evokes in this dark hour the spiritual identity of his God. Calmly he communes with this image in his heart, and I think I would not like to have his death upon my conscience.

Inaki, the Japanese interpreter, looks in on us now and then. He is fast reverting to the anthropological type he represents. Once he seemed a mere polite little Japanese, unctuous and hypocritical. Little by little he is acquiring the jungle characteristics. His face seems cruel and moronic, small dark hairs straggle on his upper lip, his eyes appear vacant, he looks like a minion of Genghis Khan. I can't help it—I hate his race. I hate the imitative little monkeys that people Japan.

It is unintelligent blindly to hate, but I hate these chattering half civilized animals. They make me feel uncomfortable, like chimpanzees well-trained and clever and walking about in ill-fitting human clothing. They are physically sturdy and blindly courageous; they have learned to fly and sail ships, they've mastered the mechanical arts of war. My head tells me that our revolutionary colonials loathed the smug Tory redcoats as bitterly as I hate these Japanese; that the secessionist in our Civil War detested the "nigger-lovin' " Northerner, that we could violently despise the Russians or the Chinese were we at war with them. I know hate is conflict-inspired and proceeds from no dependable historical judgment. But anyway I hate the god-damned Japanese, for I am only human. I question, as I have a right to do, the complex social processes which ordain my death; categorically do I abominate the savages who accomplish it.

Hate and love—perhaps I simplify. I, who toil with the last moments of my life to reason with a deadly fact, produce in myself these elementary emotions. Do I arrive at the point where reason evaporates? Is truth no more than affirmation or negation? Painfully I record our conduct. I am like a prospector who roams the wild fastnesses, feebly pecking at the rocky surface of the earth for precious metals. It is all sweat and lonely toil, this prospecting for precious truth. As miners sometimes grow a little mad with inbred thoughts, it may be that I think grotesquely.

Yes, Inaki has been here often. If perseverance is a virtue our friends will be difficult to defeat. Inaki reminds me of a bug trying to climb out of a bathtub. The tension in the atmosphere increases. There is reason to believe our end is near. The great assault will soon begin. A soldier intuitively feels the coming of a battle. We know the Jap has been momentarily frustrated. All the while we've been imprisoned we clearly understood the nature of the siege. When they've gathered sufficient men and planes and artillery they will attack. Our position is untenable. Food and ammunition finally exhausted, lacking air support and reinforcement, we shall surrender. All this has been building up for days about us. And although we ourselves are no longer part of the final battle we are depressed by the inevitability of our defeat. Each man of a beaten army experiences this melancholy, a sadness which is inconsolable. Soon the guns will begin to fire, the troops to move forward. I know our sparse artillery will take its toll of enemy lives before it is finally destroyed. In a way we fight on the sidelines, but still we fight. Incapable of perceiving the existence of any value but the materialistic, Inaki cannot reason why we should still refuse to divulge our information. When it was he came and offered us freedom I cannot now remember—perhaps it was this morning.

"I want to come in," said Nishi Inaki through the window.

Why should he speak thus, as though cautious of us? For a brief moment I was sure he knew we had discussed the possibility of killing him. Then I worried. Sachs had the makeshift knife. I'd given it to him for some reason or other. I worried that perhaps he would attack the interpreter in a sudden frenzy. Sachs's anger was of the violent sort; he always wanted an axe to use on our jailers. I knew that Johnny was not likely to succeed in so desperate an attempt, that Inaki could kill him quite easily and would. The thought made me nervous.

"Good morning," said Inaki. The sentry had opened our door, and Inaki involuntarily recoiled from the sight of us and the stench of our prison. In spite of our attempts at sanitation our success in this direction is limited. Ever since Inaki watched me work on Evans's leg I seem to detect a concealed distaste for his appointed task.

"Good morning, my friend," I said.

"Now you tell me about the artillery."

I thought I would stand up. My head had begun to spin with vertigo. Only a little while ago I had endured another spell of nervous humming inside me.

"No, Inaki. Why doesn't your aviation get reconnaissance pictures from the air?" We both knew our anti-aircraft had been knocking their reconnaissance planes out of the sky like clay pigeons.

"Your comrades very ill."

Johnny Sachs edged closer to the Japanese. "Nobody wants to talk to you, you son of a bitch."

"That's all right, Johnny. Don't mind Inaki."

"No, don't mind me," the interpreter said.

"We're all pretty sick," I said. "But we agreed long ago among ourselves to tell you nothing."

"I know. It is difficult for me. Our lieutenant has become very angry. The general knows we have this means of getting information, and makes us much trouble. I am very sincere in please asking for it."

"I can still laugh."

"Then I don't put it right," said Inaki. "How could we know you make a matter of importance of it? We are military, taking orders. We are just soldiers, like you. We have patriotism, too. I think our respected lieutenant makes a mistake."

"Yes. He beat us and clubbed us, and that isn't our idea of war. He trumped up a lying charge against us of being spies. He starved us and deprived us of humane treatment for our wounds. Your lieutenant has tried to make animals of us. Animals cannot talk, my friend."

"I am sincerely sorry, take my word for it."

"Once I permitted myself to talk to you, and I was whipped. You can whip me again if you please, Inaki, because I can't live much longer anyway."

"Beg to contradict, Corporal. Confess to a desperate desire to have information. Our lieutenant does not know your ways, he makes a mistake. Very humbly implore—"

"Get that bastard out of here," said Sachs, grunting. "I'll kill him."

I placed myself between Johnny and the interpreter. Fear danced in my head, fear of the outcome of this conversation.

"We give you back your liberty, dismiss charges of spying, send you with escort to your lines. Humbly apologize for mistaken manner of carrying out military duties."

Fear shivered all through me. I couldn't help it, I turned to Johnny and I said, "Give me the knife, boy."

For a long time we looked into each other's eyes. Imperceptibly his resolution died. Finally he held his hand out to me and dropped the knife into mine. It was hot and wet with sweat. I turned to Inaki. "My friend was going to kill you."

"Ah." He stared strangely at Johnny Sachs. *"Sore ni soi nai n'desu,"* he said.

"We do not understand Japanese."

"I say I believe it." He shook himself. "I am empowered to offer you your freedom."

"I heard you. Your offer to capitulate comes too late. We're incapable of moving."

"You will be given transportation."

"And the condition of our release?"

"The information concerning the location of artillery in Sector M."

My dizziness had left me. I think my chest swelled and I know I smiled. "I'll convey your offer to our sergeant."

"You needn't bother," said Evans from his place on the floor. "I heard what the Jap said. But I'm no longer able to discharge the duties of a sergeant properly. From now on each soldier here will make his own decisions. A man has a right to save his life if he can." Then he began calling our names. "Hilton, do you want to accept the interpreter's offer?"

"No."

"Peters, do you want to accept the interpreter's offer?"

"No."

"Gabowitz?"

"No."

"Sachs?"

"No."

We were all smiling now, looking at Nishi Inaki. I will admit the Japanese is persistent. "You make very interesting gesture, gentlemen. One time somebody here request of me where I attend school. My education in America is far from perfect. I notice the very selfish, the very stupid, the very childish there. At Pearl Harbor we surprise the United States. But you also have methods of surprise strange to us. How can anybody tell that among five soldiers we do not find a weakling? We are sorry we misjudge. Now we admire, we frankly confess want of information. Much face is lost, but we implore very humbly. I am asked by our commanding officer to make any offer within our power."

This language seemed curious coming from Nishi Inaki. He is a barbarian who was never made to think, and his reasoning roused my risibility. He was like an orang-outang arguing evolution with Darwin. I couldn't control myself. I began laughing, uncontrollably, hysterically.

Inaki shrugged. "You wish to force more torture upon yourselves, I think?"

"We're sick, Inaki. I didn't mean to laugh. You've broken us, and degraded us before your men. We realize we have to die, that there's nothing to laugh at. You've made a war on the United States of America, and our deaths are only the beginning of the lives we will spend to annihilate your nation. I know it's a speech I'm making, but I'm entitled to it. Good-bye and god damn you, my friend. We'll never tell you anything, never."

I had become excited, my face flushed hotly, I was making a fool of myself. Unnerved, I sank down beside my comrades.

"Not sensible, this attitude." Inaki was smiling again, a smile of cold superiority. He always smiled when he saw our emotions getting the better of us. "Not sensible. We make an argument, and all arguments most unrealistic. Everything is a bargain in this world, gentlemen. Everything give and take, like buying shoes or ladies or farmhouse or freedom. Purchaser sometime make mistake trying to buy lady's honor too cheap. We learn honor of five Americans comes high. Very well. Purchaser wants to give greatest value for goods received. Name price."

Evans said, "You've got a queer slant on things, Inaki. But maybe you're right. I've been trying to think of what you could pay that would be worth the information you want. How about the life of your commanding general?"

Inaki straightened imperceptibly. "I don't come to joke, Sergeant Evans."

"Well, that's our price. Execute your commanding general in front of our door. Then we'll tell you what you want to know. Everything give and take, everything a bargain in this world, Inaki."

"American fools!"

"You got his goat that time, Marty," said Sachs. "I'd've settled for Inaki and the lieutenant."

"You see it's no use, my friend," I said. "We know you're a liar. The moment we gave you the information you want you'd shoot us in the back. There's no way of doing business with a liar. So we'll never tell you anything, Inaki. Never."

"That is your final word?"

"It was always our final word."

Were these mock heroics? On paper they seem so. Yet nothing could have summed up better what all of us felt than Evans's commonplace remark after Inaki had gone. He smiled almost happily from his helpless position on the prison floor. "If five half-dead guys like us can outsmart those monkeys, imagine what our army and navy'll do to them one of these days." And then Evans added, "My only regret is that I may not be alive to see it."

Maybe, I thought, our sergeant has hit upon the truth of Nathan Hale's regrets. Whether this is so or not, it was his admission that he is dying. It will be an anonymous fame he enjoys. He'll have no legend on the bottom of an idealized statue. He will not find himself dramatized in the hearts of his countrymen, nor will he be sentimentalized for the ears of radio listeners. Posterity will never know how Evans died for his country. He'll have accomplished nothing except to prove that men are still unselfish and brave.

Night comes at last. Still strong enough to clamber upon the shaky box and look outdoors, I attempt to translate for Evans my impressions of the exterior world. A foolish artificial excitement has taken hold of my senses. In my calmer moments the lines seem silly to me. I report our conversation because this is the way it happened, these are the things I said. I am feverish. I know Evans's life ebbs away and so I try with my febrile thoughts to hide our fears. We are all dying now and I want to conceal the knowledge in unreal words.

"The sky isn't any single color tonight, Marty. It changes from moment to moment, pink and blue and purple. It's one of those Maxfield Parrish skies all dabbed up with paintbox colors."

"Never . . . never heard of the guy." Evans pretends he is in excellent health and that what I say amuses him.

"The wind's coming now. It feels like a lady's veil accidentally blown across one's face."

"You're nuts, kid."

"I know. When I was a youngster the laundryman used to give us a handful of leechee nuts. They had a sort of unconvincing taste. There's a fat moon tonight, Marty. He looks like a Chinese laundryman, yellow and moon-cheeked and imperturbable."

"We used to . . ." Evans stops to catch his breath. "We used to think the Chink restaurant made chop suey out of rats."

"Propaganda, Marty. Race prejudice stirred up by commercial competition. In the light of experience I'm convinced that rats could furnish only an expensive and unsatisfactory dish. Kids are a funny race of creatures. What were you like when you were a youngster, Marty?"

"Me? I was a little stinker." Marty's eyelids blink. "Once I caught a fish and tied a tin can to its tail and threw it back in the water. I sure thought it was funny to see that can movin' around the bay."

"Only a kid could think up a trick like that."

"Yeah." Evans coughs a little, painfully, then looks up at me again. "What's the moon look like now?"

"Still like a fat Chinaman. The stars are beginning to brighten. The trees around the Jap's encampment remind me of a fisherman's beard. The stars are tremendous, I can't describe them, Marty. They create an emotion in my belly."

"Can you see the Big Dipper?"

"Yes. But it's a fake. It hasn't the remotest resemblance to a dipper. It never did look like a big dipper to me."

"Me either. I guess probably lots of things in the world are fakes."

"Oh, I don't know. It isn't anybody's fault if we start off with naïve minds and then need disillusioning."

"You wanted to be an author or a writer or something, didn't you?"

"Something like that."

Evans smiles wanly. "All the things we used to think and do seem kind of silly now, I guess. I used to be in love with a girl. She wanted to marry me. I figure girls have a talent for makin' mistakes. I'm damn glad I talked this one out of it. A corpse isn't exactly the ideal bridegroom."

"You always was a selfish bastard at heart," Sachs says gruffly. "She could of collected your life's insurance and went out with some other guy and had herself some fun."

"I never thought of that, Sachsy." An emotional little pain gathers inside my chest to see him trying to the last to be gay. "I—I never looked at it that way."

"Maybe I would of turned up to be a comedian in later life," Sachs adds with a melancholy little sigh.

"There's a bird out there that makes a sound like the first three notes of a ballet suite by a guy named Stravinsky. Can you hear it?"

"It wouldn't do me any good if I could. There's a thing I always wanted to find out," says Evans. His breathing is becoming more difficult all the time. "Do people really like music by this Bach or Back and those other guys, or is it just something phony they put on?"

"I'm afraid they really like it."

"Oh." After a moment Evans says, "I had a kid sister who took violin lessons for a while. She got pretty good at it. When I left home she was keepin' company with a fellow who'd just graduated from law school. He's probably drafted by this time."

"Do you remember things from your childhood, Marty?"

"Sure. I remember a kid who bet me a new ruler I couldn't lick him." Phlegm has collected in his throat and he turns his head to clear it. "It— it was a swell ruler, so I licked him, and he was very surprised."

"Did you ever walk in a dark country lane at night, Marty, and wonder what part you were made to play in the world?"

"No."

"I've done that."

"And what happened?"

"Nothing. It was a crazy dream."

"How's that fat Chinaman?"

"Still beaming, Marty. He probably learned from his ancestors to smile like that. When you're old, like a Chinaman, you become stylized. Your laughter is the symbol of all laughter. Everything old resembles one of those fragile ancient prints with Chinese characters written on it. Why is that, Marty?"

"How the hell should I know?"

"There goes that nightingale again, or whatever it is. The evening's tremendous out there."

"Is it?"

"When you're cooped up in a little space the world seems incredibly big. I always used to pity convicts. How do you feel?"

Marty says, "I feel like the buzzards have been feastin' off the little that's left of me. You sound pretty crazy, Bill. Hey, Gabby. Don't Bill sound like he's gone crazy?"

Gabowitz gazes at me stolidly, attempting to arrive at a fair decision. "A little," he says at last.

"You're mistaken, my friends. My brain is clear and everything seems very bright. I don't mean I'm clairvoyant, but I feel things keenly, the way they say a man does when he's eaten hashish. The night's really tremendous. Our Japanese hosts are preparing a war out there. I get glimpses of detachments moving ammunition. We and our dreams, they and their dreams—you can't imagine how silly it is. Silly, I mean, compared with the night. And the stars, they're so god damned beautiful I want to cry." I cannot any longer prevent myself from saying what is on my mind. "Evans, you're dying."

"What?"

"You're dying."

"I know, kid. And Sachs there told me I was losing a leg. You don't look any further than your nose, you guys. You miss the point. A battle is coming off in a little while. Suppose our men counterattack. This sector's a weak spot. Why shouldn't they drive these bastards back and find us here?"

"Why?"

"That's right. Why. Today I'm dying. Tomorrow I'm back in the base hospital playing casino with a pretty nurse."

"How about it, Gabby—who's crazy, Evans or me? You're a wonderful man, Marty. But it's my turn now."

Gabby shakes his head. "I don't know. I hear you talk all around something, but I'm not payin' attention. It's the Jap I'm thinkin' of. He's the craziest of anybody. When he comes back, look out."

I have one of my dizzy spells. I think I fell off the box. Sachs gives me some water. The feverish artificial brightness in my mind dissipates. Again we are five dying men stumbling weakly about in the dark. Evans watches me, his eyes reflecting the moonlight. My nerves stiffen. An army marches to the roll of drums. The feet of a million hobnailed men thunder in my brain.

"What were you saying, kid?" asks Sergeant Evans.

"Will we ever stop them, Marty?"

"Who?"

"The Japs."

"What's the matter with you, boy?"

"I can feel their feet grinding my body into a bloody pulp."

"Too much imagination. I have a hunch about this battle that's coming off. Our fellows will push out somewhere along the line. This sector's thinly defended. It'll bend back like a pretzel. Just wait and see."

"But first they'll kill us, won't they?"

"The Jap gets confused if he has to think of two things at once."

"It's a hell of a spot to be in, isn't it, Marty?"

"There are probably. . . ."

"What?"

"Worse."

Little by little I recover control of my nerves. The shack has stopped spinning. "Marty?"

"Yeah?"

"How do you feel?"

"Feel."

"How do you feel, Marty?"

"Feel fine."

"Gabby. Sachs. Peters!" I know what is happening. We crawl to Evans's side.

"What were you saying?" Evans asks. He speaks with difficulty, his throat seems stopped up with phlegm.

"Nothing," says Gabowitz.

"What—what about that ole Chinaman, Bill?"

"He's out there."

"It's kind of dark. Our guys . . . our guys'll be coming soon."

"They'll be coming soon."

"Give me your hand, Bill. Hello, Johnny. Hello, Gabowitz."

"Hello."

"Who's doing that?"

"That's Peters, crying."

"All right. A kid as brave as Dink Peters can. . . ."

My throat hurts. "There's a secret I've been keeping from you, Marty. I guess I should have told you sooner, but—"

"What, kid?"

"You know I used to be a great reader. Used to read right through a whole library without stopping. Scientific books, history books, religious books. I've been thinking hard, Marty, and I've got it all down pat in my brain, word for word. Extreme unction. I wanted to wait—"

"You know it?"

"I'm no priest. I'm not even a Catholic, Marty. But I can say the words."

"The Latin ones?"

"The Latin ones."

"How do they go, Bill?"

"*In freta dum fluvii current, dum montibus umbrae, Lustrabunt convexa, polus dum sidera pascet, Semper honos nomenque tuum laudesque manebunt . . .*"

"You're a good kid," Evans sighs. "But it's no— In the real ceremony he keeps saying '*Sanctus.*' What do the ones you said mean, Bill?"

My tongue is hard and dry. " 'While the rivers run to the ocean and the shadows move in the mountain valleys and the sky feeds the stars, always will your honor and your name and your glory remain.' He was a sweet poet, Virgil. They were the best I could remember. I'm sorry, Marty."

"Will you stop them noises now?" Sachs inquires of Peters.

"It's all right, Dink. It's what a fellow would want from his friends, some Latin words and a little crying. I—I sure had a swell life, you know that? What's—what's. . . ."

"Yes, Marty?"

"What's the moon doing now, Bill?"

"Still smiling the same old wise smile."

"He doesn't know from nothing. Wait and see. Wait'll our boys bust through this sector. Some of us'll make it, just wait and see."

"Sure, Marty."

"How is it you never went to officer's training school?"

"Just never wanted to."

"Dark, isn't it?"

"Yes, it's dark now, Marty."

"Were you afraid of the dark when you were a kid?"

"Yes."

"Bill?"

"Yes?"

"Say that little poem over. In English."

" 'While the rivers run to the ocean and the shadows move in the mountain valleys and the sky feeds the stars, always will your honor and your name and your glory remain.' "

"What's the guy's name again?"

"Virgil."

"Fellows . . ."

"Yes?"

"We held out, didn't we?"

"We sure did."

"Gabby, are you there? Hello, Gabby."

"Hello."

"Hello, Sachs."

"Hello, Marty. How do you feel?"

"Marty?"

I have been holding his hand. The pulse in it has stopped. "It's all right now, fellows," I remember saying.

KAHLIL GIBRAN

Testament: From Three

I

A MAN OUTSIDE OF JERUSALEM

A master stylist, Kahlil Gibran is represented here by three pieces from his book, JESUS, SON OF MAN, which was an attempt to show Christ through the consciousness of his immediate contemporaries, friends and enemies.

J U D A S came to my house that Friday, upon the eve of the Passover; and he knocked at my door with force.

When he entered I looked at him, and his face was ashen. His hands trembled like dry twigs in the wind, and his clothes were as wet as if he had stepped out from a river; for on that evening there were great tempests.

He looked at me, and the sockets of his eyes were like dark caves and his eyes were blood-sodden.

And he said, "I have delivered Jesus of Nazareth to His enemies and to my enemies."

Then Judas wrung his hands and he said, "Jesus declared that He would overcome all His foes and the foes of our people. And I believed and I followed Him.

"When first He called us to Him He promised us a kingdom mighty and vast, and in our faith we sought His favor that we might have honorable stations in His court.

"We beheld ourselves princes dealing with these Romans as they have dealt with us. And Jesus said much about His kingdom, and I thought He had chosen me a captain of His chariots, and a chief man of His warriors. And I followed His footsteps willingly.

"But I found it was not a kingdom that Jesus sought, nor was it from the Romans He would have had us free. His kingdom was but the kingdom of the heart. I heard Him talk of love and charity and forgiveness,

and the wayside women listened gladly, but my heart grew bitter and I
was hardened."

My promised king of Judea seemed suddenly to have turned flute-
player, to soothe the mind of wanderers and vagabonds.

"I had loved Him as others of my tribe had loved Him. I had beheld
in Him a hope and a deliverance from the yoke of the aliens. But when
He would not utter a word or move a hand to free us from that yoke,
and when He would even have rendered unto Caesar that which is Caesar's,
then despair filled me and my hope died. And I said, 'He who murders
my hopes shall be murdered for my hopes and expectations are more
precious than the life of any man.'"

Then Judas gnashed his teeth; and he bent down his head. And when
he spoke again, he said, "I have delivered Him up. And He was crucified
this day . . . Yet when He died upon the cross, He died a king. He died
in the tempest as deliverers die, like vast men who live beyond the shroud
and the stone.

"And all the while He was dying, He was gracious and He was kindly;
and His heart was full of pity. He felt pity even for me who had delivered
Him up."

And I said, "Judas, you have committed a grave wrong."

And Judas answered, "But He died a king. Why did He not live a
king?"

And I said again, "You have committed a grave crime."

And he sat down there, upon that bench, and he was still as a stone.

But I walked to and fro in the room, and once more I said, "You have
committed a great sin."

But Judas said not a word. He remained as silent as the earth.

And after a while he stood up and faced me and he seemed taller, and
when he spoke his voice was like the sound of a cracked vessel; and he
said, "Sin was not in my heart. This very night I shall seek His kingdom,
and I shall stand in His presence and beg His forgiveness.

"He died a king, and I shall die a felon. But in my heart I know He will
forgive me."

After saying these words he folded his wet cloak around him and he
said, "It was good that I came to you this night even though I have
brought you trouble. Will you also forgive me?

"Say to your sons and to your sons' sons: 'Judas Iscariot delivered Jesus of Nazareth to His enemies because he believed Jesus was an enemy to His own race.'

"And say also that Judas upon the selfsame day of his great error followed the King to the steps of His throne to deliver up his own soul and to be judged.

"I shall tell Him that my blood also was impatient for the sod, and my crippled spirit would be free."

Then Judas leaned his head back against the wall and he cried out, "O God whose dreaded name no man shall utter ere his lips are touched by the fingers of death, why did you burn me with a fire that had no light?

"Why did you give the Galilean a passion for a land unknown and burden me with desire that would not escape kin or hearth? And who is this man Judas, whose hands are dipped in blood?

"Lend me a hand to cast him off, an old garment and a tattered harness.

"Help me to do this tonight.

"And let me stand again outside of these walls.

"I am weary of this wingless liberty. I would a larger dungeon.

"I would flow a stream of tears to the bitter sea. I would be a man of your mercy rather than one knocking at the gate of his own heart."

Thus Judas spoke, and thereupon he opened the door and went out again into the tempest.

Three days afterwards I visited Jerusalem and heard of all that had come to pass. And I also heard that Judas had flung himself from the summit of the High Rock.

I have pondered long since that day, and I understand Judas. He fulfilled his little life, which hovered like a mist on this land enslaved by the Romans, while the great prophet was ascending the heights.

One man longed for a kingdom in which he was to be a prince.

Another man desired a kingdom in which all men shall be princes.

II

CYBOREA THE MOTHER OF JUDAS

MY SON was a good man and upright. He was tender and kind to me, and he loved his kin and his countrymen. And he hated our enemies the cursed Romans, who wear purple cloth though they spin no thread nor sit at any loom; and who reap and gather where they have not ploughed nor sowed the seed.

My son was but seventeen when he was caught shooting arrows at the Roman legion passing through our vineyard.

Even at that age he would speak to the other youths of the glory of Israel, and he would utter many strange things that I did not understand.

He was my son, my only son.

He drank life from these breasts now dry, and he took his first steps in this garden, grasping these fingers that are now like trembling reeds.

With these selfsame hands, young and fresh then like the grapes of Lebanon, I put away his first sandals in a linen kerchief that my mother had given me. I still keep them there in that chest, beside the window.

He was my first-born, and when he took his first step, I too took my first step. For women travel not save when led by their children.

And now they tell me he is dead by his own hand; that he flung himself from the High Rock in remorse because he had betrayed his friend Jesus of Nazareth.

I know my son is dead. But I know he betrayed no one; for he loved his kin and hated none but the Romans.

My son sought the glory of Israel, and naught but that glory was upon his lips and in his deeds.

When he met Jesus on the highway he left me to follow Him. And in my heart I knew that he was wrong to follow any man.

When he bade me farewell I told him that he was wrong, but he listened not.

Our children do not heed us; like the high tide of today, they take no counsel with the high tide of yesterday.

I beg you question me no further about my son.

I loved him and I shall love him forevermore.

If love were in the flesh I would burn it out with hot irons and be at peace. But it is in the soul, unreachable.

And now I would speak no more. Go question another woman more honored than the mother of Judas.

Go to the mother of Jesus. The sword is in her heart also; she will tell you of me, and you will understand.

III

MATTHEW: THE SERMON ON THE MOUNT

ONE HARVEST DAY Jesus called us and His other friends to the hills. The earth was fragrant, and like the daughter of a king at her wedding-feast, she wore all her jewels. And the sky was her bridegroom.

When we reached the heights Jesus stood still in the grove of laurels, and He said, "Rest here, quiet your mind and tune your heart, for I have much to tell you."

Then we reclined on the grass, and the summer flowers were all about us, and Jesus sat in our midst.

And Jesus said:

"Blessed are the serene in spirit.

"Blessed are they who are not held by possessions, for they shall be free.

"Blessed are those who remember their pain, and in their pain await their joy.

"Blessed are they who hunger after truth and beauty, for their hunger shall bring bread and their thirst cool water.

"Blessed are the kindly, for they shall be consoled by their own kindliness.

"Blessed are the pure in heart, for they shall be one with God.

"Blessed are the merciful, for mercy shall be in their portion.

"Blessed are the peacemakers, for their spirit shall dwell above the battle, and they shall turn the potter's field into a garden.

"Blessed are they who are hunted, for they shall be swift of foot and they shall be winged.

"Rejoice and be joyful, for you have found the kingdom of heaven within you. The singers of old were persecuted when they sang of that kingdom. You too shall be persecuted, and therein lies your honor, and therein your reward.

"You are the salt of the earth; should the salt lost its savor wherewith shall the food of man's heart be salted?

"You are the light of the world. Put not that light under a bushel. Let it shine rather from the summit, to those who seek the City of God.

"Think not I came to destroy the laws of the scribes and the Pharisees; for my days among you are numbered and my words are counted, and I have but hours in which to fulfil another law and reveal a new covenant.

"You have been told that you shall not kill, but I say unto you, you shall not be angry without a cause.

"You have been charged by the ancients to bring your calf and your lamb and your dove to the temple, and to slay them upon the altar, that the nostrils of God may feed upon the odor of their fat, and that you may be forgiven your failings.

"But I say unto you, would you give God that which was His own from the beginning; and would you appease Him whose throne is above the silent deep and whose arms encircle space?

"Rather, seek out your brother and be reconciled unto him ere you seek the temple; and be a loving giver unto your neighbor. For in the soul of these God has builded a temple that shall not be destroyed, and in their heart, He has raised an altar that shall never perish.

"You have been told, an eye for an eye and a tooth for a tooth. But I say unto you: Resist not evil, for resistance is food unto evil and makes it strong. And only the weak would revenge themselves. The strong of soul forgive, and it is honor in the injured to forgive.

"Only the fruitful tree is shaken or stoned for food.

"Be not heedful of the morrow, but rather gaze upon today, for sufficient for today is the miracle thereof.

"Be not overmindful of yourself when you give but be mindful of the necessity. For every giver himself receives from the Father, and that much more abundantly.

"And give to each according to his need; for the Father gives not salt to the thirsty, nor a stone to the hungry, nor milk to the weaned.

"And give not that which is holy to dogs; nor cast your pearls before swine. For with such gifts you mock them; and they also shall mock your gift, and in their hate would fain destroy you.

"Lay not up for yourselves treasures that corrupt or that thieves may steal away. Lay up rather treasure which shall not corrupt nor be stolen, and whose loveliness increases when many eyes behold it. For where your treasure is, your heart is also.

"You have been told that the murderer shall be put to the sword, that the thief shall be crucified, and the harlot stoned. But I say unto you that you are not free from the wrongdoing of the murderer and the thief and the harlot, and when they are punished in the body your own spirit is darkened.

"Verily no crime is committed by one man or one woman. All crimes are committed by all. And he who pays the penalty may be breaking a link in the chain that hangs upon your own ankles. Perhaps he is paying with his sorrow the price for your passing joy."

Thus spake Jesus, and it was in my desire to kneel down and worship Him, yet in my shyness I could not move nor speak a word.

But at last I spoke; and I said, "I would pray this moment, yet my tongue is heavy. Teach me to pray."

And Jesus said, "When you would pray, let your longing pronounce the words. It is in my longing now to pray thus:

"Our Father in earth and heaven, sacred is Thy name.
Thy will be done with us, even as in space.
Give us of Thy bread sufficient for the day.
In Thy compassion forgive us and enlarge us to forgive one
    another.
Guide us towards Thee and stretch down Thy hand to us in
    darkness.
For Thine is the kingdom, and in Thee is our power and our
    fulfillment."

And it was not evening, and Jesus walked down from the hills, and all of us followed Him. And as I followed I was repeating His prayer, and remembering all that He had said; for I knew that the words that had fallen like flakes that day must set and grow firm like crystals, and that the wings that had fluttered above our heads were to beat the earth like iron hoofs.

Contributors

SHERWOOD ANDERSON, who died March 8, 1941, was the author of several novels and volumes of short stories the deep inner quality of which became immediately manifest when they began appearing in 1919. His influence deepened the content of the American short story for a couple of decades. He was born September 13, 1876 in Camden, Ohio and, after a spotty schooling and a brief attendance at Wittenberg College, he served in the Spanish-American War and settled down to become the manager of a paint factory in Ohio, but one day walked out of the job and the state and into literature. He was associated with the "Chicago Group" of writers, lived for some time in New Orleans and various parts of Europe. "The Death of Mrs. Folger" appeared in his final book, his Memoirs.

SHOLEM ASCH, who has been called "a seeker after revelation" and "a great seer of reality," is the author of The Nazarene, The Apostle and many other books. He was born November 1, 1880, in Kutno, Poland, of Jewish parents. At present, he is living in Connecticut. "A Peculiar Gift" appears in his collection of short stories Children of Abraham.

MARY AUSTIN. Mrs. Mary (Hunter) Austin, American novelist and essayist, was born in Carlinville, Illinois, September 9, 1868, and spent her last sixteen years in Santa Fé, particularly interesting herself in the civilization and the mystical life o fthe American Indians. It has been said of her that "she found peace only in a mystical fusion with nature and primitive humanity.

HONORÉ DE BALZAC born at Tours May 16, 1799, died August 18, 1850. He began writing at the age of twenty. The Atheist's Mass is from one of the volumes in Scènes de La Vie Privee, in his forty-volume Human Comedy.

WARREN BECK is a professor of English and a tutor of literary composition at Lawrence College, Appleton, Wisconsin, and has been reprinted in the Best American Short Stories series.

STEPHEN VINCENT BENÉT, whose recent death robbed American literature of a valuable spirit, was born July 22, 1898. He was a Pulitzer Prize winner and came from a writing family. He was a brother of William Rose Benét, the poet, and Laura Benét, the husband of Rosemary Carr and, until her death, he was a brother-in-law of Elinor Wylie. He has published many volumes of poetry and prose.

MAX BROD, poet, novelist and essayist, was born in Prague, Czechoslovakia, then part of the Austro-Hungarian Empire, May 27, 1884, the son of a Jewish banker. He spent some years in journalism and government and was an active Zionist, founder of the National Jewish Council of Austro-Hungary. He was a lifelong friend of Franz Kafka, and his literary executor, and wrote his biography, as well as one of Heine. After the Nazi conquest of Austria, Dr. Brod went to Palestine, where he now lives. His best known novel is The Redemption of Tycho Brahe.

MRS. PEARL (SYDENSTRICKER) BUCK (June 26, 1892—), American lovelist and winner of the Nobel Prize for literature, was born in Hillsboro, West Virginia, but was taken to China at an early age. She is the daughter of American missionaries and has spent a good deal of her life in China. She taught English literature in the University of Nanking and in Southeastern University. Her books, most of them laid in China, have had a very wide distribution. She lives on a farm in Perkasie, Pennsylvania, with her two daughters and four adopted children. She was married in China to a young American, Dr. John Lossing Buck, an agricultural missionary, but in 1934 she came to New York alone, joined the editorial staff of John Day Co., her publishers, and secured a divorce. In 1935, she married Richard J. Walsh, president of the publishing company and editor of *Asia*.

DANA BURNET was born in Cincinnati, Ohio, July 3, 1888. He has written several plays and has contributed extensively to magazines.

WHIT BURNETT is a native of Salt Lake City, Utah, born there among the Mormons August 14, 1899, and until the age of thirty was in newspaper work on the West Coast, in New York City, Paris and the Balkans. In 1931, he and Martha Foley founded the magazine *Story*, devoted solely to contemporary short stories. He is still editor of that publication and has done one volume of his own short stories THE MAKER OF SIGNS, one volume of essays, THE LITERARY LIFE AND THE HELL WITH IT, a fictionalized life of Robert Burns (with John Pen), IMMORTAL BACHELOR, and is the editor of THIS IS MY BEST and TWO BOTTLES OF RELISH. In 1942 he was divorced and married Hallie Southgate, who is also a writer.

ANTON CHEKHOV, born at Taganrog, Russia, in 1860 and died in 1904, was one of the world's greatest writers in the short story form. He took up writing in order to support himself while studying to be a doctor. He was a grandson of a serf and son of a poverty-stricken shopkeeper.

JOHN COURNOS, Russian-American novelist, born in Kiev, March 6, 1881, writes in English although he did not hear English until the age of ten when his parents came to America and settled down in Philadelphia. His first job was selling newspapers on the Philadelphia streets. He began novel-writing at the age of thirty-five and his first book was THE MASK published

in 1919. He has written many since, as well as his autobiography, and has translated extensively from the Russian and edited several short story anthologies.

CLARENCE (SHEPARD) DAY, JR. was a writer who became immortal through immortalizing an incredible father. He was born in 1874 and died December 22, 1935, and wrote always as Clarence Day, Jr. The elder Day was a stockbroker and a governor of the Stock Exchange. From the time of the Spanish-American War, which he entered when he withdrew from partnership with his father in Wall Street, Mr. Day was a cripple and unable to leave his bed or move more than a finger. He was a sufferer from arthritis. His writings were always characterized by humor and irony. His most popular books were LIFE WITH FATHER and LIFE WITH MOTHER.

RUTH DOMINO came to the United States in 1941 and is now a teaching fellow of Bryn Mawr College. She was born in 1908 in Austria where she studied at the University and received her LL.D. After occupation of Austria in 1938 by the Nazis she went to Paris and later, when the Germans came, fled to the Pyrenees.

LLOYD (CASSEL) DOUGLAS was born August 27, 1877, in Columbia City, Indiana ,the son of the Reverend Alexander Jackson Douglas and Sara Jane (Cassel) Douglas. He was ordained as a Lutheran minister in 1904. In 1908 he was Chaplain of the First Infantry, District of Columbia, and from 1911 to 1915 the Director of Religious Work at the University of Illinois. After serving as minister in Ann Arbor, Akron, and in Los Angeles and Montreal, he retired from the ministry in 1933 to devote his time to writing. His first novel was THE MAGNIFICENT OBSESSION, which he wrote after he was fifty. He has said that his novels were not written so much for entertainment as for inspiration.

DOROTHY CANFIELD FISHER. Mrs. Dorothea Frances (Canfield) Fisher was born February 17, 1879, in Lawrence, Kansas, the daughter of an educator and an artist. She has always been interested in education and although she trained to be a teacher never has served as one. In 1907 she married James Redwood Fisher and has a son and daughter and, with Mr. Fisher, who was in the ambulance corps, she was active in refugee work in the First World War. She lives in Vermont. She translated Papini's widely read LIFE OF CHRIST. Since her first novel, THE SQUIRREL CAGE in 1912, she has built up a large following for her books which are notable for their deep understanding of human beings.

MARTHA FOLEY, who was born in Boston, the daughter of a doctor and a poet, was an active newspaperwoman from 1918 until the early 1930's when, with Whit Burnett, she was co-founder of the magazine *Story* in Vienna and, until 1940, its co-editor. She is the co-editor of several anthologies and has lectured on the short story at several universities. She is now the editor of the Best Short Stories series, having succeeded the late Edward J. O'Brien. She has written many stories. She is the mother of David Foley Burnett, twelve, and lives in Connecticut.

KAHLIL GIBRAN (1883-April 10, 1931), Syrian-American mystical writer and artist, was born in Bechari, Lebanon, of Nordic stock. His parents were affluent and his mother a noted musician. He studied in the United States as a child and entered a Syrian college at fourteen. He also studied the arts at the Ecole des Beaux Arts in Paris. His first literary work was written in Arabic, prose poems which became known throughout the Arabic world for their mystical vision and metrical beauty. At twenty, he began to write in English and continued to do so throughout the rest of his life. One of his most well-known books was JESUS, SON OF MAN. He died in New York City at the age of forty-eight.

ERNEST HEMINGWAY, born July 21, 1898, the son of a doctor of Oak Park, Illinois, began newspaper work on the Kansas City *Star* at the age of nineteen but a few months later left to serve as an ambulance driver in the First World War, transferring later to the Italian infantry. For several years, beginning in 1921, he lived in Paris.

He has written many notable short stories of which "The Snows of Kilimanjaro" is considered one of his best. His FAREWELL TO ARMS and FOR WHOM THE BELL TOLLS are perhaps his most widely read novels.

ALDOUS (LEONARD) HUXLEY (July 26, 1894—), is the son of Leonard Huxley, elder son of T. H. Huxley, the biologist. His mother was the daughter of Thomas Arnold, a brother of Matthew Arnold, the poet. His early intention was to become a doctor and, after specializing in medicine at Eton, he contracted keratitus and became almost completely blind. He learned to read books and music in Braille and to use a typewriter and continued his education with tutors. His eyes improved and, after work at Oxford, he abandoned a scientific career because of his defective vision, and went into journalism and criticism. He has traveled extensively throughout the world, has regained his eyesight, and now lives in Southern California. He has written a great many works of fiction, poetry and essays, one play, and a biography of Father Joseph, a 17th Century French mystic.

FRANZ KAFKA was born July 3, 1883 and died June 3, 1924. He was an Austrian novelist and short story writer, son of a wealthy family of Czech Jews of Prague. His literary career began about 1912, and his most ambitious works were THE TRIAL and THE CASTLE. He died after a short and ailing life, his end brought about by consumption contracted during the starving days during the First World War. He was a friend of Franz Werfel and Max Brod, and his influence on writers has been admitted by many in several countries, although his actual output was relatively small. His literary work was preoccupied with problems involving moral and spiritual issues.

MANUEL KOMROFF was born in New York September 7, 1890 and went to Yale to study engineering but left in 1912 and became art critic for the New York *Call*. He spent several years in journalism, covering the first Russian Revolution and worked for a time on the *China Press* in Shanghai. In

1924 he was a member of the Liveright Publishing organization which brought out his first book of short stories THE GRACE OF LAMBS. His novel CORONET, in 1929, had a public estimated at one million readers. He lives in New York, is married, and devotes most of his time to writing. He also conducts a class in the novel at Columbia University.

SELMA (OTTILIANA LOISA) LAGERLÖF (November 20, 1858-March 16, 1940), Swedish novelist and the first woman to win the Nobel Prize for Literature, was the daughter of a man descended from a long line of army officers and a mother whose people were clergymen. She began her literary career as a verse writer in local papers in a small town in Southern Sweden. A delicate child, lamed for a lifetime as a result of an early attack of infantile paralysis, she spent many years as a teacher in comparative obscurity, but at the end of her life had become the most popular author Scandinavia ever had, except for Hans Christian Andersen. Her best known work in English was GÖSTA BERLING'S SAGA.

CLARA LAIDLAW, who was born in Gladstone, Michigan, is a teacher of high-school English in Michigan where she has won three Avery Hopwood Awards, two in fiction and one in the essay, at the University of Michigan. "The Little Black Boys," awarded the Avery Hopwood Award for 1942, was Miss Laidlaw's first published story, and it appeared in the *Atlantic Monthly*.

THOMAS MANN, who now lives in California, came to the United States in 1938 where he has been active in the anti-Fascist cause. Dr. Mann was born June 6, 1875, in Lübeck. His people were a prosperous mercantile family. Author of THE MAGIC MOUNTAIN, BUDDENBROOKS, and numerous extensive works, he has received the Nobel Prize for Literature.

LOUIS PAUL, like Manuel Komroff, is a native of New York City. He was born December 4, 1901, the son of a French wood carver and sculptor, while his mother's ancestors migrated from Boston to Albany in pre-Revolutionary

times. After a public school education in New York, he went into the Army, under age, in the First World War, and after the Armistice, decided to become a writer. His first short story was published in *Esquire* and won the 1934 O. Henry Memorial Award. Ten years earlier, he married Mary Engargiola, daughter of an Italian ship captain, and, although he had lived for several years in California, he now makes his home in New York City.

ISAAC (LOEB) PERETZ, who was born in Poland May 25, 1851, died there March, 1915. He is considered the most powerful and the most European of Yiddish authors. He wrote first in Hebrew but is best known as an author in Yiddish or Judeo-German, the dialect of Jews in Russia and Poland.

LUIGI PIRANDELLO was born in Sicily on June 28, 1867, but left there at eighteen for Rome. He took his degree in literature and philosophy at the University at Bonn, Germany. Up to the time of his death on December 10, 1936, he had written and published in Italy seven volumes of poetry, seven novels, twenty-eight plays and thirteen volumes of short stories. In 1934 he received the Nobel Prize for Literature. He married in January 1894 and had three children. A local colorist so far as stories are concerned about his native Sicily, an ironist and a metaphysicist in his plays, much of his creative writing drew upon material from a tormented life. For fourteen years he lived with a wife who had become insane.

MARY BRINKER POST, who lives in Connecticut, is the wife of the Rector of a Connecticut Episcopal Church. She is the mother of three children and has written frequently for the magazines.

RAINER MARIA RILKE (December 4, 1875-December 29, 1926), of whom the English poet Auden has said, "Rilke is almost the first poet since the 17th century to find a fresh solution of how to express abstract ideas in concrete terms," was born in Prague. His parents intended him for a military career but his physical frailty prevented this. For a time he served as secretary to the sculptor, Rodin. He translated Paul Valéry into German and spent the last years of his life in comparative solitude in a 13th century tower in a Swiss canton. He died as the result of a festered wound in a finger caused by a thorn of a rose he picked one day for a young woman visitor. His most popular book was THE LOVE AND DEATH OF CORNET CHRISTOPHER RILKE but his most influential books among the literary were his two volumes of poems in 1907 and 1908.

ANTOINE DE ST. EXUPÉRY, who has written poetically of war-flying and who has been called the "Joseph Conrad of the air" is the French novelist and essayist. He was born in Lyons in 1900, was educated at the Jesuit schools and was trained as a military flyer at Strasbourg, went to Morocco as a cadet and returned an officer, and, in 1926, became a commercial aviator in Africa. He established an airmail route to South America and, in an attempt in 1935 at a long distance flight from Paris to Sargon, Africa, he nearly died when forced down in the desert. His plane was shot down by Nazis in the Battle of France and he has recorded some of his war-flying in FLIGHT TO ARRAS, 1942. It has been said of him that he "came to aviation through poetry." He has received the Prix Femina and the Grand Prize of the French Academy. He is married and lives in the United States.

WILLIAM SAROYAN was born in Fresno, California, August 31, 1908, of Armenian parents. His father was a Presbyterian minister, but died when his son was two years old. He acquired his first fame through a short story "The Daring Young Man on the Flying Trapeze" which appeared in the magazine Story in 1934, although he had written earlier under the pseudonym of Sirak Goroyan for the Armenian magazine Hairenik of Boston. He has written several hundred short stories, traveled to Armenia, Russia, Scotland and in 1939 became a playwright with several successful plays including MY HEART'S IN THE HIGHLANDS, TIME OF YOUR LIFE, etc. He is also the author of the motion picture script of THE HUMAN COMEDY. Edmund Wilson, the critic, has referred to him as "an agreeable mixture of San Francisco bonhomie and Armenian Christianity." He married a young actress in 1943 and is now a private in the United States Army, in the motion picture branch of the Signal Corps.

OLIVE (EMILIE ALBERTINA) SCHREINER was still in her teens when she began her first famous book THE STORY OF AN AFRICAN FARM. She was born March 24, 1855, at Wittenbergen Mission Station in Basutoland, the sixth of twelve children of Gottlob Schreiner, a Methodist missionary of German descent and Rebecca Lyndahl, an Englishwoman. She was self-educated and spent some of her childhood as a nursery governess in a Boer family on the edge of the Karoo desert. She died December 12, 1920. THE STORY OF AN AFRICAN FARM was published first in London under the pseudonym of Ralph Iron, after many years of efforts to find a publisher.

IRWIN SHAW, a native New Yorker and an author of many short stories, is also the playwright-author of BURY THE DEAD and SONS AND SOLDIERS. He is at present a private in the United States Army somewhere in Africa.

HALLIE SOUTHGATE, whose "Eighteenth Summer," a short story in the magazine Story in 1941, was one of the O. Henry Memorial Award prize winners of that year, was born in St. Louis, Missouri, in December, 1908, has been writing for some years and was for a time on the staff of the Junior League Magazine. Her stories have appeared under the name of Hallie Southgate Abbett, the name of her first husband, and later Hallie Southgate Burnett. She married Whit Burnett in 1942. She has a sixteen-year-old son, William Abbett and another, a few months old, John Burnett.

AUGUST STRINDBERG is the Swedish dramatist. He was born in Stockholm in 1849 and died in 1912.

HENRY DAVID THOREAU, called the genius of Concord and America's "poet-naturalist," was born July 12, 1817, in Concord, and died May 6, 1862. His most famous work is WAL-

DEN, his life as a hermit beside the banks of a little New England pond to which he retired to think, and contemplate nature. His life was a devotion to nature. Although he lived at Walden Pond only two years, this experiment in isolation colored all the remainder of his life.

COUNT LEO TOLSTOY (September 9, 1828-November, 1920) came to a crisis in his life at about the age of fifty when nothing in the world seemed to him to have any zest or meaning. When a young man, he served in the Crimean War. After 1861 and the freeing of the serfs he retired to his country estate and devoted much of his time to bettering conditions. He was the father of thirteen children, eight of whom survived infancy. His novels and short stories constitute a library in themselves.

JEAN TOOMER was born in Washington, D. C., and educated there and at the University of Wisconsin and the College of the City of New York. His first book of stories and poems appeared in 1923 under the title CANE. Its presentation of the moods and characters of his Negro people won high critical acclaim.

SIGRID UNDSET, Norwegian novelist and Nobel Prize winner, now lives in Brooklyn, following her escape from her native land in April, 1940, when the Germans overran Norway. She is the daughter of a distinguished archaeologist. Her best known work was the trilogy KRISTIN LAVRANSDATTER for which she received the Nobel Prize in 1928. Its setting was the Middle Ages in Scandinavia. She was born in Kalundborg, Denmark, May 20, 1882. Her mother was Danish and her father Norwegian. She was brought up and educated in Oslo. In 1912 she married a painter, S. V. Svarstad, whom she divorced in 1925. They had three sons. The eldest, Anders, was killed defending his country against the Germans in 1940. On the first of November, 1924, after many years of studying the origins of Christianity, she was received into the Catholic Church.

PIERRE VAN PAASSEN was born in 1895 in Gorcum, a town in Holland, of mixed Dutch and Flemish descent. He studied in Holland, Canada and Paris and came to Canada with his family in 1911, when he was seventeen, where he studied for the ministry and became assistant pastor in a Ruthenian Mission (Methodist) in Alberta. He served in France with the Canadian Army in the First World War and, with peace, entered journalism where he has remained since. He has been twice married. He has been expelled from nearly every country in Europe, chiefly due to his being such a vigorous opponent of Fascism and advocate of Democracy. His sympathy for the Jews caused him to join the Zionists and it is said he is the only Gentile Zionist alive. In college he specialized in New Testament Greek. His DAYS OF OUR YEARS and THAT DAY ALONE have had very wide circulation.

JOAN VATSEK lives in New York City and is the daughter of a Hungarian Consulate official. She lived for five years in Egypt before going with her family to Canada where she attended McGill University. In Cairo, she taught school in a convent. She is now connected with the New York Public Library. Her first stories appeared in the magazine *Story,* her poetry in the *Catholic World.*

MARY WEBB. Mrs. Mary Gladys (Meredith) Webb (March 25, 1881-October 8, 1927), the English novelist, came to her greatest fame, after her death, through the praise of her Shropshire stories and novels. She was awarded the Prix Femina in 1924 for her novel PRECIOUS BANE.

EUDORA WELTY, who was born in Jackson, Mississippi, and attended the University of Wisconsin and Columbia, lives in her native state where she devotes all her time to fiction. Her books are THE ROBBER BRIDEGROOM, A CURTAIN OF GREEN and THE WIDE NET.

FRANZ WERFEL, born September 10, 1890 in Prague of a wealthy Jewish family, wrote his first play in 1910 when he left his paternal home, abandoning the possibilities of a business career in his father's glove factory, and went to work in a Hamburg shipping house. After his compulsory military service in 1911 he joined a Leipzig publishing house. During World War I he was actively pacifist, an attitude deriving from his "mystical belief in a community of souls in all living things." He married in 1918 and in 1919 brought out his book NOT THE MURDERER, involving the conflict of father and son. He has written many plays and novels, including THE FORTY DAYS OF MUSA DAGH, EMBEZZLED HEAVEN, etc. In 1940 he escaped from a part of Nazi-held Europe, an experience which indirectly gave birth to his novel THE SONG OF BERNADETTE.

THOMAS WOLFE (born October 3, 1900 —died September 15, 1938), entered the University of North Carolina at the age of fifteen, attended Harvard where he studied in George Pierce Baker's Drama Workshop and, after receiving his M.A. from Harvard, became an instructor in English at Washington Square College in New York University. His first novel writing was influenced by James Joyce. His first published book was LOOK HOMEWARD, ANGEL, which was edited by Maxwell Perkins of Scribner's. He wrote nine books, the later ones being published by Harper's.

GLENNYTH M. WOODS, who works in the office of the Coordinator of Inter-American Affairs, went to Washington about five years ago from Denver, Colorado, where she had previously been in school. Her hobby is the bal-

let. Her stories have been published in the *Catholic World*.

NELLIE MAR YOHANNAN is the daughter of native Presbyterian missionaries and was born in Rizaia, Persia, in 1906 and, as soon as she was born was given to a peasant family in her grandfather's village to rear, following native customs. At three her parents took her to Russia and at five they returned to Persia and settled down in Tabriz where her father took over the Presbyterian church and worked for many years among the Mohammedans. She came to America in 1923, graduated from Rockford College in 1927, is married to a Persian and lives in America. Her story in this volume was her first published work.

WILLIAM ZUKERMAN is an American newspaper man who was for twenty years the European correspondent for a New York daily newspaper. He has lived in most of the European countries but chiefly in England. He has contributed many articles and stories to leading American and British magazines, such as *Harper's, The London Quarterly Review, The Nation, The Menorah Journal, Antioch Review* and others. He is the author of a book, THE JEW IN REVOLT, published in England before the war, in which he deals with the Jewish problem from the point of view of the Internationalist. Mr. Zukerman has been back in the United States since the summer of 1940 and is on the staff of a New York newspaper.

Acknowledgments

The editors and publishers wish to express their gratitude for the courteous permission of the publishers, authors and literary agents whose cooperation made this book possible. The material, except in those cases where the stories have never appeared in type before, has been taken from the sources listed as follows:

Anderson, Sherwood: From SHERWOOD ANDERSON'S MEMOIRS. 1942. Harcourt, Brace & Co. By permission of Eleanor Anderson.

Asch, Sholem: CHILDREN OF ABRAHAM. G. P. Putnam's Sons. Copyright 1942 by Sholem Asch.

Austin, Mary: THE GREEN BOUGH. Copyright 1913 by Doubleday, Doran and Company, Inc.

Balzac, Honoré De: THE ATHEIST'S MASS AND OTHER STORIES. Everyman's Library. Translated by Clara Bell, preface by George Saintsbury. Reprinted by permission of E. P. Dutton & Co., Inc.

Beck, Warren: From *Story* Magazine, 1941. By permission of author. Copyright 1941 by Story Magazine, Inc.

Benét, Stephen Vincent: Copyright 1929 by Stephen Vincent Benét.

Brod, Max: Reprinted from THE REDEMPTION OF TYCHO BRAHE by Max Brod, by permission of Alfred A. Knopf, Inc. Copyright 1928 by Alfred A. Knopf, Inc.

Buck, Pearl S.: THE FIRST WIFE AND OTHER STORIES. The John Day Co. Copyright 1933 by Pearl S. Buck.

Burnet, Dana: From *Colliers* 1926. By permission of the author and Brandt & Brandt.

Burnett, Whit: From *Story* Magazine, June-July 1931. By permission of the author.

Chekhov, Anton: THE STORIES OF CHEKHOV. Copyright 1932 by Modern Library. Random House, Inc.

Cournos, John: From THE DEVIL IS AN ENGLISH GENTLEMAN. By permission of the author. Copyright 1932 by Farrar and Rinehart, Inc.

Day, Clarence: Reprinted from GOD AND MY FATHER. By permission of Alfred A. Knopf, Inc. Copyright 1931, 1932 by Clarence Day.

Domino, Ruth: From *Story* Magazine, March-April 1943. By permission of the author. Copyright 1943 by Story Magazine, Inc.

Douglas, Lloyd C.: THE ROBE. Houghton Mifflin Company. Copyright 1942 by Lloyd C. Douglas.

Fisher, Dorothy Canfield: By permission of the author. THE HILLSBORO SHEPHERD, 1912. The Ridgway Co. HILLSBORO PEOPLE, 1915, Henry Holt & Co.

Foley, Martha: From *Story* Magazine, 1933. By permission of the author.

Gibran, Kahlil: Reprinted from JESUS, THE SON OF MAN by Kahlil Gibran, by permission of Alfred A. Knopf, Inc.

Hemingway, Ernest: THE FIFTH COLUMN AND THE FIRST FORTY-NINE STORIES. By permission of the author and Charles Scribner's Sons.

Huxley, Aldous: GREY EMINENCE. Harper and Brothers. Copyright 1941 by Aldous Leonard Huxley.

James, William: VARIETIES OF RELIGIOUS EXPERIENCE. By permission of Longmans, Green and Company.

Kafka, Franz: THE GREAT WALL OF CHINA. Copyright 1933. Martin Secker, Ltd. Secker, Warburg, Ltd.

Komroff, Manuel: From the *Saturday Evening Post.* By permission of the author.

Lagerlöf, Selma: MODERN SWEDISH SHORT STORIES. 1934. Jonathan Cape, Ltd.

Laidlaw, Clara: First printed in *Atlantic Monthly.* By permission of the author.

Mann, Thomas: Reprinted from STORIES OF THREE DECADES by Thomas Mann, by permission of Alfred A. Knopf, Inc. Copyright 1930, 1931, 1934, 1935 by Alfred A. Knopf, Inc.

Paul, Louis: THIS IS MY BROTHER. Crown Publishers. Copyright 1943 by Crown Publishers.

Peretz, Isaac Loeb: BONTSHE THE SILENT. Stanley Paul & Co., Ltd.

Pirandello, Luigi: BETTER THINK TWICE ABOUT IT. E. P. Dutton & Co., Inc.

Post, Mary Brinker: From *Story* Magazine, June 1936. By permission of the author and Marion Saunders. Copyright 1936 by Story Magazine, Inc.

Rilke, Rainer Maria: STORIES OF GOD. Copyright 1932 by W. W. Norton & Company, Inc.

Saint-Exupéry, Antoine de: FLIGHT TO ARRAS. Copyright 1942 by Reynal and Hitchcock.

Saroyan, William: THE HUMAN COMEDY by William Saroyan. Copyright 1943 by Harcourt, Brace and Company, Inc.

Shaw, Irwin: From *Story* Magazine, January 1939. By permission of the author and Leland Hayward, Inc. Copyright 1939 by Story Magazine, Inc.

Southgate, Hallie: By permission of the author and McIntosh and Otis, Inc.

Strindberg, August: MODERN SWEDISH SHORT STORIES. 1934. Jonathan Cape, Ltd.

Thoreau, Henry David: WALDEN.

Tolstoy, Leo: MASTER AND MAN AND OTHER PARABLES AND TALES. E. P. Dutton & Co., Inc.

Toomer, Jean: ANTHOLOGY OF AMERICAN NEGRO LITERATURE. Edited by
V. F. Calverton. Modern Library. Random House, Inc. Copyright 1929 by
Modern Library.

Undset, Sigrid: Reprinted from KRISTIN LAVRANSDATTER. By permission of
Alfred A. Knopf, Inc. Copyright 1923, 1925, 1927 by Alfred A. Knopf, Inc.

Van Paassen, Pierre: THAT DAY ALONE. Copyright 1941 by The Dial Press,
Inc.

Vatsek, Joan: From *Story* Magazine, January-February 1943. By permission
of the author and Jacques Chambrun, Inc. Copyright 1943 by Story Magazine,
Inc.

Webb, Mary: ARMOUR WHEREIN HE TRUSTED. Copyright 1929 by E. P.
Dutton & Co., Inc.

Welty, Eudora: THE WIDE NET. Harcourt, Brace & Co. Copyright 1943 by
Eudora Welty.

Werfel, Franz: TWILIGHT OF A WORLD. Copyright 1937 by The Viking Press.

Wolfe, Thomas: THE HILLS BEYOND. Harper and Brothers. A note on Thomas
Wolfe by Edward C. Aswell. Copyright 1935, 1936, 1937, 1939, 1941 by
Maxwell Perkins as Executor.

Woods, Glennyth M.: First printed in *The Catholic World*. By permission of
the author.

Yohannan, Nellie Mar: From *Story* Magazine, April, 1937. By permission
of the author. Copyright 1937 by Story Magazine, Inc.

Zukerman, William: From *The Menorah Journal*. By permission of the
author.